RIDE THE PINK HORSE

and two other

GREAT MYSTERIES

RIDE THE
PINK HORSE

and two other
GREAT MYSTERIES

Dorothy B. Hughes

NELSON DOUBLEDAY, INC.
Garden City, New York

Contents

RIDE THE PINK HORSE

and two other

GREAT MYSTERIES

RIDE THE
PINK HORSE

Again, *for my sister,* Calla

I

Zozobra

1

HE CAME IN ON THE FIVE O'CLOCK BUS. HE WAS WELL TO THE back and he didn't hurry. He remained seated there, his eyes alone moving while the other passengers churned front. His eyes moving and without seeming to move, through the windows on the right where he was seated, across the aisle through the lefthand windows. He saw no one he knew, no one who even looked as if he came from the city.

A hick town. He didn't like hick towns. He uncramped his legs, slid out into the aisle soon enough to seem to be one of the surge without being of it. Only someone who was aware, as he was, would know he was alone, separate. The hayseeds he'd traveled with out of Kansas City across the plains into mountain land, didn't know. The yokels sagging on the concrete loading slab in back of this dump station didn't know. It was habit that shoved his right hand into his coat pocket as he stepped off the bus. Not nervousness. He had no nerves; caution yes, but no nerves.

There was no one he knew. He went around the bus to the rear where an officious bastard in a khaki-drab coverall was pulling baggage out of the compartment, dumping it on the concrete. The sheep stood like sheep waiting.

He didn't. He walked over to the heap and yanked out his old valise. The officious bastard started sputtering. The bastard was a greaser, a spic; he needed his face shoved in. Sailor pulled his claim check out of his left-hand pocket, shoved it into the bastard's overall pocket. This wasn't the time or place to push in a guy's face. He didn't want to land in the hoosegow, hick towns were sometimes tough. Particularly on strangers. Besides he didn't want his approach telegraphed. He was to be a surprise, a little surprise package for the Sen.

His mouth twitched as he walked away. Time enough to take care of officious bastards after he'd taken care of the Sen. His mouth wasn't twitching as he moved heavy-heeled into the grimy bus station.

His valise was too heavy. It pulled down his left hand and shoulder. His right hand, habitual, was in his right pocket. There wasn't need for it.

The small station was littered with papers, smelling of people who didn't wash. But there weren't many people, only a few on the dirty benches. On one bench, two Indian women. They had broad flat faces, and their hair was cut like on Dutch dolls, banged to their polished black eyes, squared just above their ear lobes. The women billowed fat under calico, blue and nigger-pink and green, a different color for every skirt and petticoat. One squaw had over her head a purple shawl bordered in bright pink flowers. The other's shawl was orange and green like a Halloween pumpkin. The women looked cheap and sweaty but they wore a mint of jewelry, silver earrings and heavy chains of silver and turquoise, a lot of chains and massive bracelets, lots of big silver and turquoise bracelets on their broad brown wrists. They looked like something out of a circus but he didn't snicker. Something about them kept him from wanting to snicker. They were the first Indians he'd ever seen.

On another bench there was a woman all in rusty black from her shawl to her shoes, the kind of shoes nuns wear. She was as fat as the Indians but she was a spic. There was a little runt of a spic guy with her, in overalls and a shabby dark gray jacket, a greasy hat pulled down over his ears. A mess of little girls was with them, lined up on the bench in their cheap patent-leather slippers and cheap straw hats, their starched clean print dresses. They were all spics but they might have been Indians as well. He knew all the black silent eyes watched him as he hardheeled to the desk.

He asked, "Where's a hotel?"

The fellow behind the desk was any fellow behind a desk in a bus station. He saw too many people to care about any, tired, harassed even in this hick dump. "Inca on the corner. Cabeza de Vaca around the corner."

Sailor nodded, his nod meant thanks. He was chary of words.

The fellow said, "You won't get a room."

He jerked his head around. Suspicious. "Why not?"

"Fiesta," the fellow said. Then he was busy with the phone ring-ing and the sheep starting in through the rear doors.

Sailor slid on outside. He didn't want gab with the ticket agent anyway. He'd find a room. The Inca was a dump. One of those corner hotels with a lobby the size of a dime, a big green fern taking up most the space. Good enough till he found the Sen, after that he'd be moving to a real hotel.

No rooms. He accepted it because the old man behind the desk wasn't insulting. He was an old gentleman; he regretted it but there were no rooms.

From the corner you could see the sign *Cabeza de Vaca Hotel*. It hung over the sidewalk, a big sign, and Sailor cut across the narrow street and started towards it. This was a big hotel, an old one. There was a porch, with armchairs, most of them filled with cackling old men in faded brown panamas. As he passed they looked at him as if he were a stranger. But without interest, only porch curiosity.

The lobby was big and cool and shabby old. Dark. Not a bad place to hole up while he was doing business with the Sen.

The fellow behind the desk was immaculate in gabardine, an ex-pensive handwoven tie. The kind of a handsome clerk you'd expect at The Stevens, not in a shabby old hotel in a hick town. There were no rooms.

The hotel was big enough to hold everyone who'd be coming to a hick town the end of summer.

He got a little tough. "What's the idea?"

The clerk gave a surprise titter. "It's Fiesta."

"What's Fiesta?"

The clerk tittered again. "Fiesta—" he began. He picked up a pink handbill from the desk. ". . . tells you about it."

He took the sheet only because it was pushed into his hand. Took it and thrust it in his left-hand pocket. The clerk wasn't laughing now. He was arranging his tie. "You won't find any rooms during Fiesta—" he began but his voice trickled away in the direction of a pretty girl with hair that curled like a baby's.

Sailor went out again to the sidewalk. The bag was heavier than before. He was hot in the late sunset afternoon; he was sticky and bus-soiled, crumpled. He didn't believe there were no rooms to be had. If he were shined up, he could get a room quick enough in the

Cabeza de Vaca. He ought to punch that fancy clerk right in the nose. But how was he going to get clean without a room?

He lugged the bag back to the corner and followed the street past The Inca towards town. There'd be other hotels. Or a motor court. He turned right at the top of the street, turned to the tinkling sound of music and people. Turned with a city-dweller's instinct toward the heart of town.

A half block, past J. C. Penney's, a grocery store, a drug store and he stood on the village square. He stopped there, against the glass front of the drug store and he set down his valise.

This was what the clerk had been talking about. This was Fiesta. Overhead were strings of colored lights. In the center of the square was a small green park, trees and benches and a bandstand draped in red-and-orange bunting. A low cement wall ran around the park with entrances at each corner. Entrances hung with grotesque papier maché standards. In the street that circled the park were thatched booths, smelling of food, the acrid smell of chile; stacked with cases of pop, decorated with gimcracks, cheap canes topped with celluloid dolls wiggling feathers, and cheap sticks with flimsy yellow birds floating from them, balloons on brittle wooden sticks. This was Fiesta: a run-down carnival.

He picked up his valise again, he'd seen a hotel sign halfway up the street. This one shouldn't turn him down. It was next door to a pool hall. There were no armchairs rocking on a porch, no ferns in the lobby. The bulky clerk was in shirtsleeves. A pinball machine jerked and clattered, almost drowning out his words.

No rooms.

Sailor jutted out his chin. "What's the matter? Don't I look like I got the price of a room? Listen here—" He was reaching for his roll but he didn't.

The bulky guy said, "This is Fiesta. You didn't expect to blow in and get a room during Fiesta, did you? Even us, we got reservations months ahead for Fiesta."

"What's this Fiesta stuff?"

"You mean you came to town right now without knowing it was Fiesta?" The big guy didn't snicker, he just looked as if he were seeing a sight. "Every year for two hundred and thirty-four years there's been a Fiesta here. Account of—"

"Skip it," he said. He would read about it off the pink handbill in his spare time. He didn't care about Fiesta, he was here on business;

the sooner it was over the better. "Where am I going to sleep to-night?"

The guy shook his head. "You better go on to Albuquerque. There's nothing in town." He saw by Sailor's scowl that was no good. "If you got a reason you got to be here, I don't know. You might try the Chamber of Commerce. Maybe they got a private room listed." Doubt plucked at his heavy chin.

The Chamber of Commerce. And some wise guy wanting to know who you were and where from and what you doing in our dump. He wasn't having any. He reached for the valise and then he tipped his hat over to the other side of his head. "How about me leaving the bag here for a little? Maybe I can clean up my business and go on to Albuquerque." He gave it the pronunciation he'd heard on the bus, Albukirk. He knew his business would take longer than that but if he could get rid of the weight he was tugging, he could look around for a place to stay.

The big guy said, "Sure." Friendly enough. "I won't be responsible for it but you can leave it." He wasn't interested. "Put it behind the counter. I'm on duty till nine. You'll be back before nine?"

"Sure." He pushed the bag around behind the counter. The lock was good. The guy wasn't curious anyway. "Sure," he said and he went outside into the pale pink dusk.

He stood there for a moment getting his bearings. This side the square shops. The left side more shops, nothing fancy, nothing like Michigan Boulevard, more like Clark Street. Except for the corner, a fancy shoe store all glass. Right side of the square was the good side, ticket office, a white bank, better shops. And across was a long low, dun-colored building set back from a covered walk. Took up the whole block. It might be a hotel, no sign, but worth looking into.

That was all of the town. The four sides and in the center the park, the village green, all gaudied up and tinkling music. Not many people walking around, a few.

He turned and strode on up the street to the corner. Across, cat-a-corner, was a real hotel, a big one. Not that it looked like one; it was a dun-colored, plastered mass, 'dobe, the wise guys on the bus called it, with terraces and walls, like an old Spanish hacienda. He knew it was the hotel; he'd remembered La Fonda from the signboards coming in, La Fonda, the Harvey House. He stepped across the narrow street, passing the hotel's corner shop slowly. Rich stuff in the windows. Mex and Spanish and Indian. He knew without anyone telling

him that the dark hideous wooden statue, the tarnished silver beads
flung across the base, were loot, out of some old palace.

He walked more slowly. La Fonda was class; from the outside he
knew that. He wasn't class. He was soiled and smelly, he looked like
he'd just come off a four-day bus trip. His money was as good as anybody's. He might pretend he'd motored across the country, mention
his Cad just casually.

He didn't turn in at the arch. He started to but there were two
babes coming down the walk, two babes that had just been washed
and ironed in white linen. They didn't have anything more on their
minds than lying around getting that golden glow on their skin. He
didn't want to pass them; he didn't want to watch them look down
their noses at this bum. He walked on, passing the garden wall, a
high wall to keep out the muck but let them hear the gashing laughter, the tinkling ice of the elect behind the wall. On past drab brick,
the barren, gravel playground of a parochial school. End of the
block. A cathedral across. Gray-brown stone and squat towers. A cathedral blocking the way.

He turned on his heel and walked back, past the school, the garden wall, into the hotel. He didn't give a damn whom he passed or
who looked up or down their noses. This was a hotel.

It didn't look like a hotel; it was more like a Spanish hacienda inside than it was out. Cool, dark and rich, a high, timbered ceiling,
soft leather couches and chairs. There were oil paintings on the
walls, Indian and Spanish. French doors opened to a patio, a splash
of pale light with gaudy umbrellas, bright swings carelessly placed
around a tiled fountain. The fountain banked with red geraniums.

This was where the Sen would be staying. This was for rich blood,
for the sleek and the clean, for the names on the society page, the
boxes at the opera, the clubhouse at the track. Not for him.

He was truculent because he was ashamed to ask for a room here.
The clerk was just somebody in a dark suit and thin hair. Courteous
but firm. There were no rooms. This was Fiesta. Everything had
been reserved months ago.

He took another look around the lobby, not a big lobby like the
Palmer House, you could lose this one in one corner of the Palmer
House, but it seemed spacious. It wasn't noisy but it was gay, there
was movement, and from the bar the usual bar racket. He could use
a cold beer but as his tongue thirsted he turned on his heel and
walked out of the hotel. Walked hurriedly away.

He didn't want to bump into the Sen yet. The Sen looking at him

as if he were dirt. He'd pick his own meeting place, nothing accidental. After he was cleaned up, bathed and pressed.

He went out and crossed to the ticket-office corner. There was still
the big building across the square. He walked towards it past the little white bank and the shops but when he crossed to the building he
saw what it was, a museum. It came like a door slammed in his face
and he was angered. There had to be a place to stay in this dump.
Against the walls of the old museum was a frieze of Indians, a frieze
a block long. They sat there on the wide walk, women and children
and suckling babies, all in calico and shawls and black, bobbed hair,
the women's bulbous breasts and worn brown wrists jeweled with silver and turquoise. Spread before them on the walks were their wares,
bows and arrows and painted drums, beaded doodads, clay birds and
vases and ash trays. Behind them, safe from pawing souvenir collec-
tors and curio hagglers were the good things: heavy woven rugs,
strands of turquoise, massive silver belts. He'd known it all along: Fiesta was any cheap carnival. Having Indians hawking the junk didn't
make it any different.

And then he realized. They weren't hawking the stuff; they were
as silent as if they didn't know he was standing there. But they
knew. Their black eyes, even the kids' black eyes slanted like Chinks,
were watching him. Not with curiosity, not even with particular interest. They looked at him as if he were some kind of a specimen
they hadn't seen before. There was no expression on their brown
faces. It gave him a queer feeling, as if he, not the Indians, were
something strange.

He stood there, helpless anger knotting his nerves. Monotonously
cursing the Sen, the dirty, double-crossing, lying, whoring Senator
Willis Douglass. It was the Sen's fault he was in this God-forsaken
town and no place to rest his feet. He hadn't wanted to come here.
He'd wanted it less and less as the bus traveled further across the
wasteland; miles of nothing, just land, empty land. Land that didn't
get anywhere except into more land, and always against the sky the
unmoving barrier of mountains. It was like moving into a trap, a
trap you couldn't ever get out of. Because no matter how you tried,
no matter how far you traveled, you'd always be stopped by the rigid
mountains. He didn't like it at all when they moved into this town,
his destination. Because this was the center of the trap; it was a long
way back to civilization in any direction. The only thing to do was
get out quick.

As he stood there he heard again the tinkling music. He turned as if he wanted to find where it came from, as if that were important. As if he hadn't been routed by the guard of silent Indians. A small merry-go-round was in the corner of the park, motionless at this hour. Two spics were sitting there, playing a violin and a guitar. Playing for themselves; there were no customers. For all its gala disarray the park was deserted.

He stepped off the curb without direction, crossed the narrow street and entered the little park. He walked to the merry-go-round, not intending to, but because there was life there and the absence of life on the streets and in the holiday square was suddenly a little fearful. He didn't intend to speak to the spics but there he was leaning against the enclosure.

"Not much business," he said. He saw the third man as he spoke, a big brigand, a Pancho Villa, fat and shapeless and dirty, but his brown face was curiously peaceful. He was leaning against the weathered, dark-red pickets of the enclosure. His overalls were worn and faded, held up by dirty knotted string; his blue shirt smelled of sweat and his yellowed teeth of garlic, his hat was battered beyond shape. But his face was peaceful, even happy.

The fat man said happily in his spic accent, "It is because they burn Zozobra."

The tinkling music kept on in the background. An old man squeaking a violin, so old his fingers were warped, so old his face was without meaning, a small man shriveled into age. The man at the guitar was thin to gauntness, greasy black hair falling over his eyes, his empty black eyes.

"What's Zozobra?" Sailor asked.

"You do not know what is Zozobra?" The brigand wasn't patronizing, he was surprised. He hitched up the dirty string. "It is Old Man Gloom." He chuckled deep in his fat belly. "We must burn Zozobra, Old Man Gloom, before the Fiesta commence. When Old Man Gloom he is dead, we have no more troubles. We laugh and dance and make merry. Then there is La Fiesta."

The man at the guitar began to sing in a flat, nasal voice. The fat man chuckled, "See? Ignacio sings to you how Zozobra must die."

Sailor lit a cigarette, scratching the match hard on his heel. "So Old Man Zose is dead and there's no business, Pancho?"

Pancho Villa hitched up his pants. His sigh was light as a leaf falling. "There is too much business. Tio Vivo grows old. Tomorrow, the next day, too much business for poor old Tio Vivo. He is happy to rest a little while."

Tio Vivo was the brigand's little merry-go-round. A hand-cranked merry-go-round, gondolas alternating with fierce white and pink and brown wooden horses. The big paw rested tenderly on the neck of one pink horse. The brown eyes were soulful with love of his battered old carousel.

"Tio Vivo grows old and I grow old too. We are happy to rest this little moment in the Plaza while everybody he goes to burn Zozobra."

He saw then the direction Pancho's eyes pointed. He saw the twos and threes hurrying away from the Plaza. Everyone goes to burn Zozobra. Everyone. If that was the thing to do, that was where the Sen would be. It might be possible after all to see him tonight, under cover of the celebration, to get it over with and out of this dump.

He said, "Thanks, Pancho. I guess I better get on my way if I want to see Old Man Zose kick the bucket."

The fat man laughed and laughed. As if Sailor had pulled a good one. He said, "Yes, you had better hurry." and he laughed some more, hitching himself comfortably against the palings. "Hurry, hurry," he laughed because he didn't have to hurry. Because he was comfortable here by his old Tio Vivo, with the violin and guitar stroking the deepening twilight. Because he had learned long ago that Zozobra could burn without his moving from his comfort.

Sailor flicked away his cigarette stub. He would follow the late stragglers and find his way to Zozobra. To Zozobra and the Sen.

It was as he turned that he saw McIntyre. And for the moment the works thumping inside of him were frozen.

The man was leaning against the pale wall of the little bank. A tall, thin man with a horsey face. A quiet man who didn't belong here. Who didn't belong against the wall of a hick bank with a red ribbon tied around his pants and on his head a flat black hat with little colored bobbles hanging from the brim. If Sailor hadn't frozen for the moment he'd have doubled up laughing. But he was frozen, the hand that had flicked the cigarette was frozen in mid-air.

Softly from behind him, softly and in sympathy he heard Pancho. "Trouble?"

The works started ticking again that fast. "No," he said shortly. His mouth twisted into a grin that the big greaser couldn't see. "No trouble at all," he said.

He walked on out of the Plaza then, sure of himself. Trouble wasn't waiting for him. McIntyre hadn't followed him here. Mac had been here first. There wasn't another bus in until midnight; he knew the schedule. There wasn't a train into Lamy until morning. The trains didn't come to this town. Mac hadn't just driven in from Chicago. He'd been here long enough to buy a silly Spanish hat and a red sash. To know about Fiesta. He wasn't after Sailor; he was after the Sen.

The grimace held on Sailor's face as he walked up the darkening street the hurrying stragglers had taken. Past a library, a vacant lot, past houses. He wasn't the only one who'd caught up with the Sen. McIntyre was here. Tonight the villagers were burning up their troubles. But the Sen wasn't burning his. They'd caught up with him at last.

2

HE'D WALKED TWO BLOCKS BEFORE HE GOT A SENSE OF DIRECTION. There was a swarthy policeman on duty here, diverting cars. There were more people hurrying up the hill. He walked past the cop without even an under-the-eye glance. When he'd passed the big pink building he could see the lights beyond and across. Across on the other road a million pinpoints of light, headlights trying to move forward. Ahead the lights of pageantry. The stragglers were walking faster now; they weren't laughing and talking; they saved even that energy to spur them on before the show began. There was a current of excitement transmitted to him in their rapid silence, a current that lengthened his own stride. He pushed on with them until he came to the footbridge that led into the dark arena.

But he stopped there on the outskirts. He hadn't expected anything like this. He hadn't thought a hick town had this many people. The football field was packed with them, a shifting electric mass of people, like State Street on the day of a big parade. The day Roosevelt was there. He couldn't find the Sen in this haystack. He'd have been better off to have stayed with Pancho and Tio Vivo. Better to be hunting a room.

He could have turned around and beat it back to the Plaza but he didn't. He did what the others were doing, threading forward for a better position in the crowd. And he saw Zozobra.

A giant grotesquerie there ahead on the terrace, a gray specter at least forty feet tall with a misshapen head, hollow eyes, pointed flapping ears, shapeless flapping mouth. A giant puppet with giant clawlike hands, palsied hands lifting and falling. Out of the flapping mouth a sepulcher voice was threatening, scolding. Little threats, yet mouthed by him they were as purest obscenity. *It's going to rain. It's going to rain and spoil your fun.* . . .

Zozobra. Made of papier maché and dirty sheets, yet a fantastic awfulness of reality was about him. He was unclean. He was the personification of evil.

For the moment the personification held Sailor motionless. Then the spell passed and he could see the figures behind the effigy. He could recognize the under-rasp of the loudspeaker that made words for the giant to speak. About him Sailor could hear scraps of conversation. *Shus outdid himself this year . . . the best Zozobra yet . . . isn't Sloan wonderful . . . wouldn't be Zozobra without his voice* . . . The evil was manmade; it wasn't real.

Scraps of conversation but nothing about the Sen. Voices but not the Sen's voice. He threaded further forward and was halted by the quiver of excitement from the crowd. White sheeted mounds were creeping down the far stone steps to posture and scrape before the obscene specter. A lean devil dancer bounded forward in frenzied ritual. A quiver went through the mass as the sheeted figures stooped and laid fire on the dry fagots piled before the evil god. The figures scuttled. Only the danger remained on the steps before the giant, now ranting hysterically before the onlicking flames. The words became hideous groans. The danger leaped free of the consuming fire. The mob cheered as the crimson tongues caught the skirts of Zozobra, lapping higher and higher.

Sailor turned his eyes away. Noise was staccato, skyrockets flaring into the sky, fire crackers exploding as the flames ate away the body of evil. He'd had enough. He'd wasted enough time with this charade. He was here to find the Sen. He began edging through the crowd.

But wherever he turned he found himself looking up again at the terrace where that hideous groaning face floated above the fire and smoke and noise, above the crowd's lust for destruction of evil. In destroying evil, even puppet evil, these merrymakers were turned evil. He saw their faces, dark and light, rich and poor, great and small, old and young. Fire-shadowed, their eyes glittered with the appetite to destroy. He saw and he was suddenly frightened. He wanted to get away.

He couldn't get away. Even as Zozobra couldn't get away. He was hemmed in by the crowd. By the unmoving crowd waiting for the final consummation, holding their cheers until the ghost face alone floated in the flame and smoke. And a band somewhere in the darkness struck up a lusty dirge.

The crowd broke then, laughing, talking too loud, as if for a moment they too realized the bestiality they'd conjured in themselves. As if they would forget. Children squeaked and skipped, here and there a baby in arms cried. People were moving and their feet kicked dust to add to the fumes of smoke. Across on the far road the traffic jam squawked horns and on this side of the field the police held back the people to let pass the cars with badges. The big shots' cars.

He knew then he'd been a fool to think the Sen would be on foot, would be part of a motley crew. One of those cars would be carrying the Sen out of the dirt and confusion. He'd be back in La Fonda with a fancy drink and a fancy woman before the plodders were halfway down the hill.

Sailor pushed with the crowd out of the dark field. He hadn't noticed before how many were in fancy dress, Spanish and Mexican and Indian. All dressed up for the Fiesta. He understood now why McIntyre was wearing a Spanish hat and sash. In his dark city suit and hat, Sailor stuck out like an Indian would on the Gold Coast. He ought to get himself some fancy duds if he didn't want to be conspicuous. Even here, stumbling over the dark stubble, people were giving him the curious eye.

And suddenly he saw the Sen. He was so close he could have touched him. Only the Sen was behind the glass-and-steel protection of an official car and the cops were holding back Sailor with the other peasants to let the tin gods roll by. It was the Sen all right. You couldn't miss that weasel face, the long snout, the sleepy-looking eyes, the thin brown hair receding from the forehead. You couldn't miss him even if he was dressed up in a Spanish black velvet jacket with a red bow under his sloping chin. The car rolled by too fast for Sailor to see who else was in it. He saw only the Sen and he wasn't uneasy any more. His hunch was right. The Sen was here, not hiding out but playing it big, thinking he was safe. Like as not still wearing the mourning band on his sleeve. Sailor spat in the dust after the big black limousine.

When he reached the pavement he cut through the people hurrying down the hill. It might be he could reach the hotel as quickly as the Sen. The cars weren't making much headway. Even those of the elect, allowed to travel on this side of the field, had to creep down the street. There was a traffic tangle at the corner of the pink building. He might beat the Sen to La Fonda, be waiting for him when he came into the fancy lobby. Be waiting with his hand in his right-hand pocket where it was now. Not looking for trouble, just a few words with the Sen. No action, just words, but the comfort of a hand on cold steel. When you came up against the Sen you needed what comfort you could find.

He was delayed on the corner while the cops let a line of cars pass. He looked into each one as it crept by, not seeming to look, standing there with the other sheep waiting by order of the law. The Sen wasn't in any of these cars. Sailor was restless waiting and he watched his chance to break through the line for the opposite side-walk. The cop yelled something as he broke but Sailor didn't pay any attention. He was safe on the other side with another endless stream of people. No spic cop was going to keep him standing on a corner all night. He had business.

The Plaza was alive now. It was wriggling with people, and the street that surrounded it, blocked from traffic, was filled with people. He could hear the tinkling music of Tio Vivo before he reached the Old Museum. He didn't enter the Plaza, he walked big along the bank side of the street not even remembering McIntyre until he had reached the bank. Mac wasn't there any longer. Mac had business here too.

It wouldn't be so bad if McIntyre too were waiting for the Sen in La Fonda lobby. Give the Sen a scare. He'd be easier to talk to scared. Not that Sailor would talk before a Chicago copper, but it wouldn't hurt to have the Sen think he might. Sailor had been striding along feeling good but at the bank he was stopped.

Stopped by an unmoving mass of people jamming to the corner, jamming the walks and the streets, packed like cattle here in the open street. Sailor shoved off into the street behind the crowd where he could crane his neck up and see what they were looking at. Zozobra was dead. His ghost couldn't have beat the crowd down-town.

He looked up just as music blared through the loudspeaker, just as the crowd sighed and sucked its breath and whistled, just as the floodlights were flung on the high terraces of the hotel. He saw it all as a kaleidoscope, the lights, the Spanish orchestra in the corner abutment, the pretty boy leader with the lavender powder on his face. He saw the throne and the dark girl in crimson velvet robes ascending it, the old duck in knee britches and plumes placing the crown of gold on her head. The crowd cheered and the Spanish princesses in white satin preened before the throne. There wasn't a chance of eeling through to the hotel. These weren't separate people; they were a solidified mass. Only darkness on the terraced roof would give them fluidity again.

Sailor stubbed on across to the one familiar spot in this alien night. Knee britches was blaring through the microphone. He spoke in Spanish and the crowd cheered. When he finished he spoke again in English, spic English, and the crowd again cheered. "Viva las Fiestas," he cried and the crowd echoed, "Viva las Fiestas," he cried and the crowd echoed, "Viva las Fiestas." Anything went with these peasants; Old Man Gloom was dead, bring on the Fiesta.

A woman was singing in Spanish, her voice, distorted by the mike, deafened the night. Sailor leaned against the tired fence palings of the merry-go-round. The musicians were standing at the far end, peering up into the sky. Only Pancho Villa was where he was before, big and motionless, one hand on the neck of the pink wooden horse.

He had a wide smile for Sailor. "You see Zozobra burn, no? Zozobra is dead. Viva las Fiestas!" It was as if he were host and anxious that Sailor should enjoy the carnival.

"Sure." Sailor took out his pack of cigarettes. This time he passed it to Pancho. He scratched the match on the peeling, dark-red paint. "Sure he died, but where's the customers?"

Pancho laughed deep. His hand stroked the pink horse. Smoke trickled out of his nose and his big mouth. "This time it is the Queen. The show on the roof for the Queen. After it is over, Tio Vivo and I must work." The sigh came out of his belly but he brightened. "Tonight not so much work. It is late and the muchachos must go home to bed. Tomorrow, ah—" The sigh was long.

Music again blasted the speaker and the sound of dancing, heels tapping, castanets clicking. Sailor dug his elbow between the palings. "This is a spic town. Why'd the Sen pick a spic town?" He didn't know he'd spoken aloud until the brigand answered.

"Spic?" He said it "speec" like a spic. "Spic? I do not know that spic."

Spic. Hunkey. Mick. Kike. Wop. Greaser. Sailor felt for translation. "Mex," he said.

Pancho was solemn. Big and sweaty and shapeless, he was dignity. "No," he said. "This is not a Mex town. This is an American town."

"Then why does everybody talk—" He halted at the word. He supplied, "Spanish?"

Pancho was no longer offended. "It is Spanish-American. The Fiesta, it is Spanish. It tells of my people who come so long ago and conquer the Indian. So long ago." His sigh wasn't unhappy now. It was the leaf falling. "Before the Gringo soldiers, the English-speaking, come and conquer the Spanish. Now we are all one, the Spanish and the Indian and the Gringo." His yellow teeth smiled. "If I were Ignacio I would make a song about it. We are all one in the Fiesta." He shook his head. "I do not like spic. We are not Mexican, Mister. Mexican is south, below the border. I have been to Mexico," he boasted.

A gourd rattle and a chorus of harsh voices broke over the mike. Pancho's eyes leaped with love. "The Mariachi! Ah . . ." He started lumbering to the far end of the enclosure. "The Mariachi are Mexican," floated over his shoulder. "From Guadalajara of Jalisco."

Sailor circled the paddock to where he could crane up to the roof. The Mariachi were singing, strumming and beating their crude wooden guitars. "Guadalajara . . ." they sang. The shouting proud song of the homeland. They wore enormous straw sombreros and white peasant suits with red sashes, woven rugs over their shoulders. Their faces were carved of wood, brown, wrinkled, impassive. The faces of cut-throats, but they carried guitars not machetes; they made fierce music not war. This was Fiesta. The solid mass went wild but the Mariachi showed no emotion. They sang again, a wild, cruel song, baring their teeth, pounding with their knuckles on the gourd-like guitars, sweeping the catgut strings with maniacal speed.

Fiesta. The time of celebration, of release from gloom, from the specter of evil. But under celebration was evil; the feast was rooted in blood, in the Spanish conquering of the Indian. It was a memory of death and destruction. Now we are one, Pancho said. A memory of peace but before peace death and destruction. Indian, Spaniard, Gringo; the outsider, the paler face. One in Fiesta. The truce of Fiesta. Why had the Sen come to this strange foreign place? Did he think he'd be safe in a Spanish— American town? Did he think the native truce was for him too?

Sailor's mouth twisted. This dump might seem out of the world but the busses came in regular from Chicago. It wasn't that far from Chicago.

And again he saw the Sen. Not standing down in the street crick-

ing his neck; not the Sen. He was up on the second roof, where the
pretty young Queen sat; trust the Sen. All dressed up in his tight
black velvet pants and velvet monkey jacket, the red bow flopping
under his chin. He was too far away for Sailor to see his face; he was
too far up. There wasn't a guy so far up he couldn't be pulled down.
The Spanish pulled the Indians down and that's why there was the
Fiesta. Then the Gringos pulled down the Spanish and that's why
the Spanish were spics cranking up an old merry-go-round, smelling
of dirty sweat. While the Sen sat on a roof leching at a phoney
Queen.

A woman in white was dancing on the highest roof, white doves
fluttering from her hands. Around her girls in white were releasing
white doves, the birds winging up against the blue-black sky. The orchestra got more excited and the crowd oohed and aahed. Someone
was singing Spanish into the mike. It looked as if the thing was
about to break up.

Sailor didn't want to be trampled by the sheep. He crossed the
Plaza to the Old Museum, boosted himself up on the ledge. He
wasn't afraid of the Indians' eyes now. He wasn't the lone stranger.
After the mass turned into people again, he'd find his way to La
Fonda. The Sen wouldn't run away. He didn't know Sailor was here.

He pushed his hat on the back of his head, lit a cigarette and
watched the Plaza fill with moving people. Smoke smudged from the
chimney pots in the thatched roofs, and the acrid stench of chile became more acrid. His stomach remembered that he hadn't eaten
since noon. A dry sandwich, a cup of coffee somewhere along the
line. He'd eat later. What he thirsted for was a cold bottle of beer.
Ice cold. Time enough for that after he met up with the Sen. He
could wait.

Through the tree leaves and the colored lights and the moving
people he saw across the Plaza a patch of the hotel where he'd
dumped his bag. He'd forgotten it. Past nine now. He wasn't worried
about the bag. He wasn't even worried about a place to sleep. He'd
bunk with the Sen if the big shot couldn't find a room alone for
him. He could pick up the bag later, or let the Sen pick it up.

About time to move. He dropped down from the ledge to the
street, almost colliding with two giggling girls. The littlest one said
"Hello." She was thin as a child and painted like a whore. He went
past her, past other girls and women and children and men, not seeing them. He went past Tio Vivo, whirling now, children clinging to
the wooden horses, the thin music trying to be gay.

He rolled down the street past the thatched booths to the intersection, crossed over to La Fonda. The roof show was over but the walk in front of the hotel was jammed with people. He shoved through them into the lobby. It looked like The Sherman when the Democrats were meeting in convention. Only the Democrats didn't wear fancy costumes. Finding the Sen was still a needle in the haystack, even if it had narrowed to one particular haystack. He fought his way across the lobby to the Cantina but he couldn't push inside. There were fifty or more ahead of him trying to push their way into the tightly packed cocktail bar. He'd have to wait.

He turned away and started back across the lobby. But he stopped. The switchboard, the single house phone, brought the first right idea he'd had tonight. The place to catch the Sen was in his room. He might not be there now but the desk would furnish the number. He hitched his shoulders and began a casual walk forward as if the desk clerks were conscious of him and of his purpose.

The quiet voice spoke behind him. "Hello, Sailor."

He didn't turn. He halted in his tracks. Then slowly he swiveled. "Hello, Mac," he said.

McIntyre still wore the silly black hat with the bobbles, the red sash winding his white pants. The bobbles were red and green and yellow. "Come for Fiesta?" he asked.

Sailor said, "Sure," hearty as if he meant it.

The Sen couldn't have hired McIntyre to protect him. It couldn't be that. Mac wasn't the Sen's man. He'd gone in when the reform commissioner was appointed. He'd been against the Sen for too many years to have gone over to his side. "You here for Fiesta?" Sailor asked.

"Yeah," McIntyre said.

"Kinda interesting, isn't it?" Two guys from Chicago talking it over in a foreign town. "See Zozobra burn?"

"Yeah, I saw it," McIntyre said.

Close-mouthed, McIntyre. Tight-mouthed and gimlet-eyed, his eyes going through what you said into what you were thinking. Sailor stirred. The silly hat struck him again. He laughed. "Have to pick up a costume, I guess. Only got in this afternoon." He wanted to ask and he did. "You been here long?"

"A week," McIntyre said.

Sailor kept satisfaction out of his face. "Well, be seeing you," he said. His foot was out to move away but McIntyre spoke again.

"Where you staying, Sailor?"

It was a casual question but he was afraid of it. It caught him flat and he answered the truth. "I haven't got a room yet. Kind of hard to find one during Fiesta." He wouldn't put it past Mac to have him jugged as a vag. If it suited his purpose. He laughed quick. "If I'm out of luck, I got a friend here who'll put me up."

"Yeah," McIntyre said. Not "Yeah?" but "Yeah."

He knew the cop was thinking of the Sen and he ought to have been thinking of the Sen too but the funny thing was, he hadn't been. He'd been thinking of the merry-go-round man, of fat, dirty Pancho Villa. If he was out of luck, Pancho would take care of him.

This time he broadened his smile. "Be seeing you, Mac," he said and this time he walked away. Walked away while McIntyre was saying, "Take care of yourself, Sailor." Saying it like he might need to walk carefully. McIntyre didn't know what he knew. McIntyre didn't know Sailor had the Sen where he wanted him.

He walked out of the hotel, not stopping at the desk. Because he'd had a quick one, a real one in the dome. McIntyre was trailing the Sen and the farther Sailor stayed away publicly, the safer he'd be. Mac knew a lot of things. He might know that Sailor was one of the Sen's boys. Was, meaning, had been. But again, he might not know it. Tomorrow was time enough to get the Sen's room number. The Sen wouldn't be running away. Not before he knew Sailor was looking for him.

Sailor went out again into the cool of night. After the fumes of perfume and liquor and body stench in the lobby, the night was a cool drink. He still hadn't had that cold bottle of beer. He still wanted it though the edge was off want after the stink of liquored breaths in the hotel. He didn't care to be caught in another trap like that one. If he could have beer here on the Plaza it would have a taste.

He stopped at one of the thatched booths and asked. The wizened woman could barely speak English. Her head was bound in a blue turban and there were chile stains on her white apron. "No beer," she said. Her smile was toothless. "Pop." He didn't want pop but the cold moisture clinging to the bottles made his dry throat ache. He bought a coke and he drank it standing there, everyone around him speaking in foreign tongue, Spanish-speaking. He felt suddenly lonesome, he who was always separate and never lonesome. He felt uprooted, he who had no roots but the Chicago streets; a stranger in an alien place. He finished the pop and walked on. His throat wasn't dry but he still had a beer thirst. Pancho could tell him where to cure it. His faith in Pancho was childlike. But even as he mocked the faith, it became the stronger.

He swung down into the park and over to Tio Vivo. He couldn't get near. It was ten o'clock but the kids were still lined up knee deep, pushing against the red palings. The music strummed with a thin brightness, Tio Vivo spun about, young not old, around and around. Over the heads of the kids he could see the brigand, sweat running from his broad brown face, his muscles bulging as he wound the crank that sent the horses galloping over their circled course.

Later he'd see Pancho. About a beer and a room. He lit a cigarette and strolled on, out of the Plaza, back to the ledge under the portal of the Old Museum. It was occupied now; in one corner a thin mother with a weary, hopeless face held a sleeping child across her lap. Two brown-skinned punks with loose lips took up the rest of the ledge, swinging their legs over the edge, boasting in spic of their intended prowess during La Fiesta.

3

HE LEANED AGAINST THE WALL WATCHING THE MOVEMENT OF THE Plaza, the dark leaves turning under the strand of lights, the Spanish musicians sawing their strings in the lighted bandstand, the shrill of laughter and the thin whine of tired children, the cries of the vendors. Over it all he could hear, or thought he could hear, the tinkling music and the whir of Tio Vivo.

In the streets the costumed, giggling girls walked clockwise and the slack-mouthed boys counter-clockwise. They spat insult and their eyes invited as they passed. Until the game was worn dull and they stopped together to regroup boy and girl, girl and boy.

"Hello." He hadn't realized that he too was a part of the Fiesta night until she spoke.

It was the same kid he'd almost bumped into earlier. She was just as immature as he'd thought on first glance, her breasts barely formed, her legs and arms thin, child-voiced, wise-eyed. Her small face and mouth were painted, her hair was a black fuzz. But she wore a red rose in her hair, her red flowered skirt was full and gay, her thin white blouse was embroidered bright. She was La Fiesta. She was pretty in a pert, child way; he wanted none of her. None of any woman until this business was done. Then he could have one worth having, a sleek one, washed and ironed and perfumed, one he'd find in La Fonda, not on the streets. He said "Hello" and looked away, waiting for her to move on, wanting her to move on.

But she didn't move. She stood there in front of him, looking up at him out of her bold black eyes, laughing up at him. "What's your name?" she asked.

He said, "Sailor."

She giggled and the girl with her giggled. The girl with her had the red rose and the flowered skirt and the thin blouse, the frizz of black hair and the bold black eyes but she wasn't so young. She had a big nose and big witless mouth smeared with lipstick. Her breasts sagged under the blouse. When she giggled, he looked at her with revulsion. "That's a funny one," she said.

"Is it?" he asked coldly and he looked back at the pretty one, the kid.

She said, "Sailor. That's a funny name, Sailor."

The homely girl said, "My brother, he was a sailor in the war. That is where you get the name Sailor, no?"

"No," he said, and he didn't smile. "I got it because I had trouble with the whole damn Great Lakes navy." He hadn't thought for a long time where the name came from.

"My brother he was in the Army," the kid said. "Were you a soldier, Sailor?" She giggled when she said it that way and her friend giggled with her.

He said, "I wasn't in the war. I had flat feet." It was a lie. The Sen had kept him out of the war. He wanted to get away from the girls but they had him backed against the wall. They saw him shift and they stopped laughing.

"I am Rosita," the kid said. "This is my friend, Irene."

"Pleased to meetcha," Irene said.

Rosita was craning around for something. She found it because she beckoned with her thin hand. "This is my cousin, Pila."

He hadn't seen the third girl until that moment. With the introduction, Rosita diminished her again to the background. There was no reason for him to look in Pila's direction, she hadn't moved, she hadn't spoken. But he looked because he would look anywhere for escape from the scrawny kid and her companion. He looked into Pila's eyes, black fathomless eyes; he saw the stone inscrutability of her brown face. She was square and strong, her face was square, her strong black hair lank about her face. The skirt she wore was bedraggled and worn, her blouse faded, the flower in her hair a joke.

She was young, young as the kid, and she was old, old as this old country.

He was frightened of her, the same fright he had felt earlier when twilight was deepening over the little Plaza and the absence of life under the lights and banners a thing unreal. She was unreal, alien; yet she belonged and he was the alien. She, not the kid, was Fiesta; something deep and strong and old under the tawdry trapping, under the gimcracks. Something he didn't understand because he was a stranger.

He knew a frantic urge to bolt, not only from her but from the skinny kid and the homely girl friend. He was saved by the homely one, by Irene. Tired of his disinterest, her protruding black eyes were watching the walkers and she cried out, "Look, there is Eleuterio!"

She pulled at Rosita's arm, moving as she spoke. Rosita called over her shoulder, "Goodbye, Sailor." He looked again at Pila, fearing she wouldn't leave, but she turned without speaking and tagged after them. He took off his hat and wiped his forehead.

Behind him there was a snicker and he turned on the two gangling youths sitting up on the ledge. He didn't have to say anything, the face he gave them was enough. It usually was enough for punks. He was reassured by their scuttling eyes; the withdrawal of their scorn.

He walked away. The merry-go-round was still turning although the circle of children was thinner. He could breathe Pancho's sweat this far away. Pancho could find him a room but it would be stained with sweat. It would stink of sweat and chile and stale garlic breaths. He didn't live like that; he hadn't come here to live like that.

He stepped up on the curb out of the way of the street crowd, walked slowly towards the La Fonda cross section. The Sen had to take care of him. Or else. McIntyre ought to be gone by now. Sailor was going to see the Sen tonight and the Sen could buy the beers.

He walked hard, swaggering his decision, but at the white bank building he stopped and fell back into the shadow. There was a group rounding the corner of the ticket office, a group of swells. They were laughing; they were too gay, satin-and-silk-and-velvet gay, champagne gay; they were a slumming party, leaving their rich fastness momentarily to smell the unwashed part of Fiesta. The Sen was with them.

Sailor stood there, flat in the shadows. He hadn't planned meeting the Sen bulwarked by blooded friends. In all his plans he'd seen only himself and the Sen, alone, face to face. Nothing like this. Anger swelled in him. A big fair fellow in black velvet cavorted by, his arms around a hard-faced bitch in white lace and a small baby-faced blonde in a coral shawl. The bitch screamed, "Hubert, you're divine!" and the baby face snuggled closer. She had a thin chain of diamonds about her throat and she stunk of whisky.

Sailor didn't see the next couple, he saw the Sen approaching and out of anger he stepped out and confronted him. "Hello, Sen," he said.

The look on the Sen's face was worth waiting for. The protuberance of nose, the sleepy dark eyes, the thin lips and brush mustache—he'd watched them in his dreams react just this way. The moment of total disbelief, the realization and the blank masking of all reaction, the groping for customary patronizing sureness. It was all there just as he'd seen it. He'd surprised the Sen.

The weasel face was coming back to life. The Sen hadn't spoken to him and he didn't now. He spoke to the girl with him. "Go on with the others. I'll catch up in a minute."

Sailor hadn't noticed the girl. He looked at her as the Sen spoke to her. Looked at her and was sickened. For her. He'd never been face to face before with clean beauty. She was young and fair, silvery blonde, and her eyes were blue and clean as sky. She was taller than the Sen, half a head taller, but she had to lift her face to look at Sailor.

When she looked at him he blurred his eyes so that he saw only the starched white ruching of her headdress, the starched white flare of her skirt. She didn't look at him as if he were a bum, her eyes were uncurious, casual.

He knew who she was. Iris Towers. Daughter of the railroad-and-hotel-and-bank Towers. Society page. He didn't know why she'd be with the Sen. He didn't know she was the reason, the why of all; he refused to admit she was that.

"Go on," the Sen said. His voice was rich and tender. The Sen should have been big and handsome for his voice. He was undersized and mean; his voice was a lie. "I won't be a minute."

She smiled. "All right, Willis." She smiled at Sailor too before she ran ahead, calling, "Wait, Hubert, Ellie! Wait for me."

The Sen and Sailor watched her until she caught the group at the corner. When Sailor stopped looking after her, the Sen was watching him out of his narrow eyes. His eyes weren't crafty at this moment; they were dull with rage. "What are you doing here?" he demanded.

Sailor said, "Maybe I came for Fiesta." He wasn't afraid of the Sen or the Sen's rage because the tickets were in his hands. There was no reason to be afraid of the Sen. The big shot wasn't on top any more. He said it jauntily, "Maybe I came for Fiesta."

The Sen wasn't amused. "What do you want?" he asked.

Sailor dropped the antics. "You know what I want," he said.

"What do you want?" the Sen repeated.

His voice was as tight as the Sen's. "I want my dough."

The Sen took a breath. "I paid you off," he said. Said it as if he didn't know it was a dirty lie.

"You paid me five C's," Sailor said. "There's another grand due. You offered fifteen hundred for the job."

The Sen wet his thin lips. "I said five hundred," he began, "and I'd take care there wasn't any trouble. There hasn't been any trouble."

"Not yet." Sailor smiled. He waited a minute. "But you'd better come across with my dough. There could be." He stood there, planted on both feet, his left hand out, waiting. His right hand was in his right-hand pocket where it belonged.

The Sen's heavy black brows twitched. His black mustache twitched too. His eyes were nervous, not because of Sailor, the Sen still thought he was in the driver's seat where Sailor was concerned. He was nervous because the girl was fading from sight. The silvery blonde girl was going away with the fair young fellow and the other big young fellows, the way she ought to.

The Sen hung out his hand, the short nervous gesture of the platform, of the private office. "I can't talk now," he said querulously, "I'm with a party."

"A thousand bucks," Sailor repeated. He was smiling, he was laughing.

Anger bounced up in the Sen. Nothing deep, nothing to tighten the hand on the gun. Just a spurt of mad. "I don't carry that kind of money on me." He implied Sailor should know that. "See me tomorrow."

He was ready to pass but Sailor stood in his way. "Where?" he asked. "When?"

"At the hotel. Tomorrow morning." He brushed by but Sailor's voice caught him before he could run.

"McIntyre's here," Sailor said.

The Sen jerked to a stop. When he looked up at Sailor again the fear had gone out of him. The crafty look had come under his eyelids and under his brush mustache. "McIntyre's here," he repeated unpleasantly.

Sailor gave him his moment. Gave it to him in full. Then he spoke. "He's been here a week," he said. "I only got in today."

He let it lay right there. It was good to watch the snake of fear coiling again in the Sen. The Sen got it all right, same as Sailor had got it earlier. McIntyre wasn't following Sailor.

Words were working in the Sen's mouth but he didn't say any more. He scurried away on his bandy legs. Sailor watched him away. He was playing in better luck than he'd hoped. Mac here. The Sen torn up between trouble and a silver blonde. The Sen couldn't put all his weasel brain on the ball with a blonde taking up most the room. The blonde was important to the Sen. So important he'd crawl over the body of a dead woman to get to her?

Revulsion filled his mouth. Iris Towers was too clean to lie in a bloody bed. What would she want with the Sen anyway? What would any decent woman want with the Sen? He had dough; that explained the tramps. Dough and a big name. But Iris Towers had more and better of both than Senator Willis Douglass. Ex-Senator Douglass. Maybe she felt sorry for him, the tragic death of his wife. Easy to see what the Sen wanted with her. He'd married one rich woman but she got old; he was rid of her. He could have a gorgeous blonde now. But he hadn't paid off.

Sailor's hand tightened in his pocket. The Sen would pay off, pay in full. He'd pay off tomorrow, before McIntyre moved in. McIntyre was waiting for something or he'd have moved before. McIntyre would like to know what Sailor knew. If the Sen tried to welch . . .

He heard his own heels thudding above the tinkle of Fiesta. He was by the ledge of the museum again and anger was knots in his belly. Anger at the dirty, cheap, welching Sen. Playing it big, fine clothes, fine car, fine hotels, society blondes. Screwing the price down on a job and then skipping out without paying off. Thinking he could get by with running out on a deal. If Sailor hadn't read the society page, emulating the Sen himself, he wouldn't have known where to collect.

One little note in the gabby society column. "The popular young Senator, Willis Douglass, is vacationing in . . ." Popular with whom? Not with the guys who did his dirty work. Young was a laugh, a belly laugh. The Sen wouldn't see fifty again if he did have a barber who browned up the gray in his hair and beard. Gabby had only one thing accurate. Where to find the Sen. And Sailor had caught up with the Sen. Because once he'd thought the Sen was big potatoes, once he'd had an idea of being like the Sen, and reading the society page was a part of it.

A thousand bucks. What was owed him. She'd had an insurance policy that paid off fifty times that. If he'd known that beforehand he'd have stuck to the two thousand asking price. Or a percentage deal. The Sen wasn't taking any of the risks; he should pay.

A thousand bucks was small change to the Sen. He'd spend more than that on this Fiesta jaunt, putting up at La Fonda, buying champagne, making a play for Iris Towers. Dressing himself in a black velvet monkey suit. You can bet the Sen didn't ride across country in a stinking bus. A drawing room on the Superchief was his style.

The knots tightened and envy gnawed raggedly at his guts. All he asked was his due, a thousand bucks. A thousand berries to take across the border to Mexico. A man could live like a prince in Mexico with a grand. Zigler said so.

He'd set up a little safe business of his own in Mexico, making book or peddling liquor, quick and easy money, big money. He'd get himself a silver blonde with clean eyes. Marry her. Maybe she'd have dough too, money met money and bred money. All he wanted was his just pay and he'd be over the border. Not that he wasn't safe; the Sen had fixed it so he was perfectly safe. That part of the deal was on the level. He hadn't trusted the Sen on that; he'd seen to it with Zigler himself.

He wasn't going to be put off any longer. The Sen would pay up tomorrow. He'd pay up or— His head turning, Sailor's eyes met the black stone eyes of Pila. Sweat broke under his arm pits. He didn't know how long she'd been standing there beside him watching him; he didn't even know if he'd been muttering out loud. The fear that sweated him wasn't anything you could put a name on; it was formless, something old and deep. He'd had it once before and the memory of that occasion recurred now, recurred so sharply he could smell the cold washed corridors of the Art Institute. He'd been second-year High and for some reason the teacher had taken the class of mugs to the Institute.

There'd been the granite head of a woman in one corridor. He'd looked at it, it hadn't affected him at all in that first look, just a hunk of stone, a square hunk of stone with lips and eyes chiseled on it. The teacher had herded them by and he'd scuffed along. What returned him to that stone head, he didn't know to this day. But he'd looked backward and he'd returned. As if he were seeing a picture he could see himself, a skinny kid in a limp blue shirt and shabby gray pants standing there staring at an ugly hunk of stone. Until he was as cold as the stone head, he'd stood there. Until one of the guys was sent to drag him back to the class.

He'd known fear, real fear, for the first time in his life as he'd stood there. He'd thought he'd known it before. Fear of the old man's drunken strap, fear of the old woman's whining complaints, fear of the cop and the clap and the red eyes of the rats that came out of the wall at night. Fear of death and hell. Those were real fears but nothing like the naked fear that paralyzed him before the stone woman. Because with the other things he was himself, he could fight back, he had identity. Before her, his identity was lost, lost in the formless terrors older than time.

He had to say something, say anything fast to take that stone look from Pila's face. He said, "Where are your friends?" His voice came out like an old husk.

"They have gone to the Federal Building."

When she spoke he heard again the shrill, accented voices of Rosita and Irene. Heard them in other painted girls flouncing, giggling by. Pila's accent was heavier but it was a part of her, it was the speech of this land. Her voice was sweet, gentle, almost a sing-song. He knew for the first time that the stone woman was Indian. He knew Pila was Indian.

He said roughly, avoiding her face, "Why didn't you go with them?"

"My father he would beat me."

He looked quickly again at her but there was no emotion, nothing but black eyes in a square brown face. He said, "What for? What's wrong with the Federal Building?"

"They lay with the boys."

Again he avoided her face, her terrible eyes that saw everything and saw nothing. She didn't move. He could see her scuffed black oxfords, cheap shoes, under the bedraggled hem of the limp flowered skirt. He realized now that she was very young.

"How old are you?" he asked.

She said, "Fourteen." She stood there unmoving, her black eyes unmoving on his face. He couldn't tell her to go away and leave him alone. He could but the words wouldn't speak. She had fastened to him as if he were the one familiar thing in this waning scene. He, the stranger. He said, "Come on, I'll buy you a pop."

She didn't say anything. She followed him, walking behind him, to the thatched stand. The old crone was washing up the dishes. "A pop," he said.

He rang the dime on the counter while the old woman uncapped the bottle. She handed it to him. He pushed it to Pila. She didn't ask why he wasn't drinking, she lifted the bottle and tipped it up. She took it from her mouth, rested a minute, tipped it again. Behind the booth, within the park, the merry-go-round spun tiredly; the music was faint. There were a half dozen children still riding this late, dark boys in faded overalls, a girl of about fourteen with eyes crossed together. Pila sucked from the bottle.

He said, "You're Indian."

She lowered the bottle. "I am Indian, yes. San Idlefonso."

"What are you doing here?"

"I came for the Fiesta."

"Did you want to come?"

She laughed at that, her whole face laughed at him. It was startling because he didn't know she could laugh, that she was human. Some of the rigidness left his spine.

"I want nothing so much as to come," she said. "Always I want to come to Fiesta."

He saw it out of her eyes for the moment, the brightness, the music and dancing, the good smell of red chile, and the chill of pink pop, the twirling merry-go-round, the laughter and the happiness, flowered skirts to cover old black shoes. He said, "Come on, I'll give you a ride on the merry-go-round."

She set down the bottle. She was reluctant. "Tio Vivo is for children. Only for the children. Rosie would not be caught dead riding on—"

He said harshly, "She'd be better off caught dead there than where she is. Who's Rosie anyway?"

"She is my cousin. My uncle and her aunt are man and wife. I am sleeping at Rosita's house for the Fiesta." She seemed to think it was an honor.

He was angry without knowing the reason for it. "I suppose she dressed you up in those clothes?"

"Yes. This last year was Rosie's costume. She has loaned it to me this year." She was pleased, proud as punch of the dragging, faded skirt; of the blouse where the reds and purples and greens had run together in the wash. "I have not before had the Fiesta costume."

Remembering the Indian women, he said, "I should think you'd like your own costume better than this." His gesture was back towards the Indian frieze.

Pila understood. She spoke with something of scorn, something of pride. "I do not wear Indian clothes. I go to the Indian School."

They had reached the red palings and words were silent. Her eyes were following the turning horses. The eyes of a child; his eyes looking at a shiny new bike behind Field's window, a bike for kids whose folks could buy them bikes at Field's. He said, "Well, do you want to ride?"

She began to say, "Yes," then she said, "I am too big." She didn't say it with any emotion, she accepted it.

He shook his head out of that troubled anger. "The boss is a friend of mine. He'll let you on if I say so." He studied her face. "Haven't you ever ridden on a merry-go-round?"

She said, "No."

"Is this your first time at Fiesta?"

Again she said, "No. When I was little I came with my family." Her head turned to the Old Museum and back to him.

"But you never had a ride?"

"No."

The horses were moving, slowly, slowly moving, they swayed and were still. The girl with the crossed eyes slid from the green pony and stubbed awkwardly out of the enclosure. The dirty little boys set up a Spanish jabber. Pancho stood, arms akimbo, talking back at them. "Vaya!" he shouted. "Vaya."

Pila said without disappointment, "It is too late."

"He's a friend of mine," Sailor repeated.

He waited until the boys were shooed away, threatening, scolding, swearing in spic. Kids like he was once, street kids, nothing to go home to. Pancho saw him standing there as he banged the gate. He lumbered over. The night air had dried the sweat of his shirt. He wiped his fat arm across his forehead. "You think I have no customers?" he winked.

"Yeah," Sailor said. "You got a customer now." He pushed Pila forward.

Pancho shook his head. "Tonight it is too late. Mañana. Tomorrow."

"Tomorrow is too late," Sailor said. "Rosita will be around again tomorrow." Pancho didn't know what he was talking about. But he knew the dollar that Sailor pulled out of his pocket.

"I am old and tired," he began. "Tio Vivo is tired. Mañana—"

"One ride," Sailor said.

Pancho shrugged. He took the dollar sadly, opened the gate.

"A full ride," Sailor warned. Pila walked to the horses, put out her hand to one, to another. He saw beyond her the old withered man encasing his fiddle. He dug for another dollar. "With music. Gay music." Sailor called to Pila. "Ride the pink one."

He felt like a dope after saying it. What difference did it make to him what wooden horse an Indian kid rode? But the pink horse was the red bike in Field's, the pink horse was the colored lights and the tink of music and the sweet, cold soda pop.

The music cavorted. Pancho's muscles bulged at the spindlass. Pila sat astride the pink horse, and Tio Vivo began its breath-taking whirl. Sailor leaned on the pickets. He didn't know why giving her a ride had been important. Whether he'd wanted to play the big shot. Whether it was the kid and the bright new bike, the bum with his nose pressed against the window looking at the clean silver blonde beyond reach. Whether it was placating an old and nameless terror. Pila wasn't stone now; she was a little girl, her stiff dark hair blowing behind her like the mane of the pink wooden horse.

4

He'd never be rid of her now. She stood before him and she said, "Thank you." As if he were a great white god.

Pancho came up behind her. "It was a good ride, no?"

"Yeah," Sailor said. She didn't say anything. Her black eyes were fathomless on Sailor. He tried to be jaunty. "Come around tomorrow and I'll buy you another ride. And another pink pop." He settled his hat and he strode off, to get away, not that he had any place to go.

He'd been too intent on springing the surprise of McIntyre on the Sen to remember he hadn't a place to lay his head. All of his anger flared up again, refreshed, and with it the added fuel of remembering the Sen trotting off after Iris Towers, leaving him with an Indian girl in a tart's hand-me-downs. He found himself in front of La Fonda and he strode inside bumping past the couples on their way out. If his money could buy a merry-go-round ride for an Indian, it was just as good for a beer at La Fonda.

There was still noise in the lobby and the patio, a scattering of couples, none of them sober. He walked over to the cocktail room. It was closed, the door locked. He hadn't paid any attention to the time. He saw now it was past midnight. A dark youth in a blue smock was wet-mopping the floor. The revelers in the patio sang mournfully off key.

The clerk at the desk was a woman now, a woman with yellowed white hair and a dyspeptic mouth over her receding chin. He could ask the Sen's room but she'd want to know why. She was the kind who'd call the hotel dick if he told her where to head in. He didn't want any trouble. Not tonight. He was tired, so tired his head was turning around and around like Tio Vivo. He wanted a cold beer.

He was out of the hotel on the darkened street before he faced the truth. He could have called the Sen's room, and with the number in his head, made his way there later. The way he'd planned it before he ran into McIntyre. What had stopped him this time was a girl with clean blue eyes. He was afraid she might be on the same floor with the Sen; he knew the scene the Sen would stage if he returned and found Sailor on his doorstep. He didn't care what the Sen said to him alone, the things were now he could give it back with change. But he was ashamed to have her witness it, to have her eyes see him as a bum. A dame he'd never seen but once in his life, a dame that was as far away from his touch as the dim star way up there almost out of sight—he didn't want to be a bum in her eyes.

He walked straight on down the street, past the hotel where his bag was stached. His eyes slid through the plate-glass window. There was another guy behind the desk, a tough-looking bouncer. He wasn't the kind who'd take to bums sleeping in the lobby. For that matter there weren't any lobby chairs that he could see. Nothing but pinball machines. He walked on by. He turned and crossed at a drug store and walked on the far side of the Plaza. Dark shops, deserted walk. In the Plaza there were still stragglers. Sitting on the benches and on the circular low stone wall around a memorial slab. On the corner was a deserted garage and he cat-a-cornered across to the museum side again. But he didn't turn under the portal of the Indians. Up this street, halfway up, he'd seen a neon sign, red and orange wiggles, spelling it out, Keen's Bar. It wasn't closed. He could hear the raucous noise this far away, the sardonic blare of a juke box, the muffled roar of men mixing with liquor, the shrill screams of women mixing with men and liquor.

He didn't hesitate. He walked straight towards the sign. A dump. A dive. There was where he belonged. Not with the swells in their snotty hotel. He wasn't that good yet. Not on the street with spics and squaws. He wasn't that bad off. He opened the screen door of Keen's and went in.

The pack around the bar was yelling over the juke. The air was fog blue with smoke. Every table jammed, the square of dance floor jammed. Everybody drinking, everybody screaming, the only silence a scowling spic waiter, scuttling through the narrow space between tables, a tray on his uplifted paw. There wasn't a chance for a beer here.

Black rage shook him. He hadn't a place to sleep, he hadn't had food, he couldn't even get a beer in this goddamn stinking lousy town. He was ready to turn and walk out when he saw wedged at a table against the wall, McIntyre. In the same silly hat, the red sash. Mac hadn't seen him yet. Mac was watching the dance floor. Sailor knew then that the Sen was here. The Sen and Iris Towers. He took his stance in the room.

The waiter had pushed under elbows to the bar. By some trick he was coming out again balancing his loaded tray. Part of the load was a bottle of Pabst, a cold bottle, the drops of moisture still beading it.

Sailor stuck out his hand and lifted off the bottle. The ape began to sputter out of his warped mouth. Sailor said, "Stow it." He clinked a half dollar on the tray. "Crawl under and get another." He put the bottle to his mouth and his eyes warned the ape what he could do if he didn't like it. The burning ice was heaven in his throat, down his gullet, into his hollow stomach.

He walked off, the malevolent black eyes following him. He took another swig and bumped through the narrow space towards McIntyre. He was himself again. The noise, the smoke, the dirty glare was all part of the usual to him. Even McIntyre, alone, watching, waiting was part of it. He felt good. McIntyre wasn't waiting for him. He shoved on until he reached the wall. Mac looked up at him. Not surprised to see him.

He said, "Hello, Mac. Enjoying yourself?"

Mac was alone at the table which might have been a table and might have been an ash stand with a wooden top put on it to take care of the Fiesta trade. Sailor reached out and swung an empty chair around to the table. Whoever it belonged to could fight it out later. "Mind if I sit down?" he asked and he sat down.

McIntyre had an almost empty glass in front of him.

"How about a drink?" Sailor asked. "Looks like you need a refresher." He took another long drink of the beer, his hands rolling the cool bottle as if it were a woman's body. "If we can get that ape over here."

McIntyre said, "I'll get him." He came near to a smile. "He thinks I'm a cop."

They could smell a cop, those in the half world where a cop meant trouble. You couldn't fool them; they could smell.

Sailor laughed loud. "That's a good one." He drink again. "That's a real one. I was just thinking the same thing myself." He stopped laughing. He was soft spoken. "You wouldn't be here on business, would you?"

His head tilted the way McIntyre's did. He saw them across on the other side of the dance floor. The Sen; the big guy called Hubert; Ellie, whichever she was, the lace bitch or the baby-face blonde; the two big young guys and Iris Towers. An angel strayed into hell. Part of it but still clean, still aloof from it. Clean and white-starched. Even through the fog he could see the Sen's red nose, red eyes, the way the Sen got from drink. The Sen wasn't having a good time. He was brooding over his glass of Scotch. He had plenty to brood about.

McIntyre was talking. "You wouldn't know anything about my business, would you?"

Sailor kept his eyes on the Sen. He laughed some more. "I wouldn't know if it's business or if you came for the Fiesta."

McIntyre said, "Quite a Chicago contingent here for Fiesta. There's Senator Douglass over there."

"Yeah. I saw him. And Iris Towers."

McIntyre sounded a little surprised. Or he would have sounded surprised if McIntyre could. "You know Iris Towers?"

Sailor laughed out loud. "I know who she is." He tilted up the bottle, drained it. "You don't think a mug like me would know Iris Towers, do you?" He jarred the bottle down on the table. He felt good and cool and warm all at once. His eyes felt bright. He said, "Can you get that ape to bring us a drink?"

McIntyre turned his head barwise. He lifted a finger. The waiter came over swinging his gorilla arms. When he saw Sailor at the table the hate was fresh in his eyes. Sailor said, "I'm buying, Mac, what'll it be?" If the spic ape had a knife under his dirty apron, it was good to be on first-name terms with Chicago Homicide. Sailor wasn't looking for trouble with the locals.

McIntyre said, "The same. Bourbon and water."

"Same for me. Pabst Blue Ribbon."

McIntyre was eyeing the Sen's table again. "Know the rest of the party?"

"Uh-uh."

"That's Hubert Amity," McIntyre pointed out. "Amity Engines. Mrs. Amity's the one in the lace mantilla." The hard-faced bitch. Old man Amity had been one of the Sen's heaviest backers when the Sen was in Washington. A guy with a face like a hatchet. Nothing like son Hubert.

McIntyre went on, "Kemper Prague is the one in the sombrero. The one about to slide under the table." Kemper Prague. Millionaire playboy of the North Shore. Plenty of dirty scandal tainting him. Always hushed up. McIntyre said, "Don't know the others. Must be local talent."

Sailor said and his voice was hard, "I'd be willing to bet they don't have to work for a living." Oh, the Sen had done all right for himself since he left off selling soap and had gone into politics. There'd been his wife's money to get him started. She'd been older than he, ten years at least, but there wasn't any age on her money. He'd come a long way from the little frame house on the South side. Graft and his wife's money, all his now, he'd done well by himself. Only not well enough. Now he was going into the millionaire class. Nothing but the best for the Sen. But he'd welch out of a thousand-dollar debt if he could. He couldn't.

"Wouldn't take that one," McIntyre said. "I wonder what the Senator's after now." He was idly curious.

Sailor could tell him. McIntyre ought to be able to see it himself, he could see her there. Couldn't McIntyre see her, the white rose, the pale white star?

"Maybe it's the governorship."

Sailor hooted his amazement. "What would he want to be governor for? He's been senator."

"Being governor of the sovereign state of Illinois isn't a bad job." McIntyre was mild. "Not only does it carry prestige, it could be remunerative."

The waiter was sliding in with the tray. He'd brought the beer. He glared at Sailor. "Sev'ty-seex sants," he mouthed. Sailor peeled a dollar, threw it on the tray. "Keep the change," he waved. The ape gave him hate instead of thanks. But the beer was cold. He trickled it into his mouth tenderly. He wiped the corner of his mouth with his knuckle as he set down the bottle.

"I don't think he needs dough that bad," Sailor said. He was thinking of that insurance policy. Fifty grand. Besides the estate.

"Nobody ever has enough," McIntyre said dryly.

The beer was good but his head was getting a little light. He knew it was time to make a move. He had better sense than to talk to a copper when he was drinking. He wasn't a drinking guy, never had been. That was one reason he'd stayed in the Sen's inner circle. The Sen could trust him not to get woozy and muff things. Strictly a one-bottle-of-beer guy. Two bottles wasn't too much, only he hadn't had anything to eat today. Coffee and a cinnamon roll for breakfast, dry sandwich and coffee for lunch. He'd finish the beer and go. He took another long drink. It was good, good.

"I don't think he'll ever be governor," McIntyre mused.

The Sen was getting up on the floor now. She was getting up too. He was going to dance with her. He was putting his arm around her clean white waist. Sailor clenched the bottle with hard knuckles. He spat through his teeth, "Son of a bitch."

McIntyre heard him. He'd said it under his breath and the juke was blaring the Woody Herman "Apple Honey" and men were bellowing at each other and glasses were clanking and women were squealing and chairs were bumping but McIntyre heard him say it. McIntyre turned his steady colorless eyes on Sailor.

Sailor said, "He'll be governor if he wants it." He laughed just as if he'd not said son of a bitch and McIntyre hadn't heard him.

The homicide detective studied him mildly for a moment then repeated, "I don't think he'll ever be governor." He turned back to the dance floor.

Sailor didn't know what McIntyre was trying to say. He didn't know because that was the way McIntyre was. He never said anything out straight like dumb flatfeet. He let you guess. He could be trying to say the Sen would never be governor because he was going to fry. Fry for the murder of his wife.

Sailor finished the beer. The Sen was still hopping around, his arm clamped around white Iris. Sailor said thickly, "I haven't eaten all day. I'm going to go get something to eat."

"You can order here," McIntyre said.

Sailor pushed away from the table. "I'm going where I can taste it. Be seeing you, Mac."

McIntyre nodded. "Take care of yourself."

He wasn't drunk, he wasn't even tight but his head was light. He bumped through the aperture. Bumped into one drunk shoving out from the table. The drunk was in fancy pants like the Sen's. The drunk threatened, "Watch where you're going."

Sailor said, "Button your lip." He didn't stop to button it for the drunk, he pushed on out of the dump into the night. He pumped the stale air out of his lungs, pumped in the night freshness. The night was sweet and chill, there was a faint smoke smell in it, like fresh pine burning. He walked back to the Plaza, to the museum corner. The Plaza was dark and quiet, only the circlet of dim colored lights hung over its darkness. He saw deeper shadows under the shadows of the portal. Mounds, blanket-wrapped, shawl-wrapped. The Indian peddlers were asleep, the stuff they'd had spread out earlier wrapped now in big calico bundles like laundry in a dirty sheet. He might borrow a blanket and sleep with the Indians. He put a filthy word into a vicious whisper. He'd never had to sleep on the ground yet.

There was no place to eat on the Plaza. The Plaza was asleep, dark, quiet, asleep. The thatched booths were asleep and the smokestacks which had trickled thin smoke. The shops squaring the Plaza were dark, asleep. The cheap hotel was only a dim light. He crossed into the park and took the path to the right. He hadn't investigated the street that led down away from the square. There could be another hotel. With no rooms. Fiesta, you know. There must be, somewhere, an all-night eating joint. Even hick towns must have some place for night workers to feed their faces. He turned sharp where a street came up to meet this one. He'd walked up it earlier today. He hadn't noticed the restaurant down on the corner, across from The Inca. He hadn't been thinking about food then.

A lighted sign hung out over the sidewalk. He didn't read the big red letters. He read the little blue ones. "Kansas City Steaks." As he read, he saw a couple of men go up to the door and walk in.

It didn't take him sixty seconds to reach the corner. The cafe was open all right. There were plenty of people sitting around the counter, people in booths. Sailor went in.

He found a place at the counter between a guy in shirtsleeves and a doll in a cheap silk dress. The doll looked at him out of big eyes when he straddled the stool. He didn't look at her. He fixed his eye on the long tall sandy drink in the chef's cap. Kept it there until the guy came over and asked, "What's yours?"

"Couple of steak sandwiches without garbage, side order French fries, bottle of milk."

The guy said, "Rare?"

"And thick." He pulled a cigarette from his pocket and lit it. The doll said in a flat nasal Kansas twang, "What's happened to the pie, Gus?" She said it like she thought she was something cute but she wasn't. She had a face like a rubber doll, round and empty, and a Kansas twang in her nose. She didn't know that her eyes were predatory; she thought they were big baby-blue eyes and that nobody could see what kind of a spirit she had.

Gus said, good-natured, "We're baking it. Keep your shirt on, Janie."

He dumped a glass of water in front of Sailor and a handful of tin to eat with. You could fish your own paper napkin out of the container.

The girl said to the girl beside her, "The service here is getting terrible." She said it to the other girl but she kept the corner of her eye on Sailor. When she started to crawl in his lap, he'd slap her down. Until then he'd ignore her. Though she could probably find him a bed. Trouble was what went with it.

He hunched her out of sight with his shoulder. The guy on the other side of him was shoveling in ham and drinking coffee. He wasn't with anyone; he was like Sailor, all he wanted was food. Sailor said, "You don't know where I could get a room?"

"Naw." He didn't stop eating. "No rooms during Fiesta." He wasn't interested in gab and Sailor didn't bother him again.

You couldn't outrun Fiesta even in a hashery. Across the circular counter were costumes, costumes in some of the booths. Youngsters mostly, blondes and red heads and brunettes with gawky looking guys. Kids with good appetites, with nothing on their minds but having fun; Zozobra is dead, long live Fiesta. When he was the size of the punk with the ears, directly across, McIntyre had already run him in once for stealing cars. Mac was just a flattie then. They'd both come up in the world quite a ways.

He'd always liked Mac. Mac didn't lecture; he said take it or leave it. If you steal cars, you'll do time. What Mac didn't know was that the boys behind the car barns had a better angle: If you don't get caught stealing cars, you won't have to do time. He hadn't seen much of Mac since he moved north. A hello now and then, when you weren't expecting it. Mac hadn't tried to move in. Mac was honest, you could say that for him. He wasn't looking out for a cut. He believed what he told you. You hurt somebody and you're going to get hurt yourself. He was an honest copper, in his mind and heart as well as in his job. That was why the reform commissioner had named him head of Homicide. Now he was out working again.

It had to be something big to put Mac on the street. Something like nabbing ex-Senator Douglass for murder. That silly hat he was wearing might fool some of the yokels but not anyone who'd ever seen Mac at work. Who had ever noticed Mac's quiet slate eyes.

Gus slapped down the thick crockery platter, two open steak sandwiches oozing pink juice on the toast, another platter with French fries. "Coffee?"

"Bottle of milk." His mouth was full already. The potato was too hot. He crunched it, keeping his tongue out of the way.

"Yeah, I remember." Gus opened an ice chest, pulled out the milk.

"Make it two," Sailor said. He didn't wait to cut the sandwich. He bit in big and chewed. He'd known he was hungry but not this hungry. The milk was even better than the beer had been. He finished half a glass while he was still chewing.

He didn't recognize the man with the full greasy mouth, the red-rimmed eyes, the dirty collar line at first. Not until the mouth opened to push in a hunk of bread and meat. He was looking in a mirror. The man was he, dirty, crumpled, his unkempt hair straggling from under his hat down on his forehead, beard shadowed on his chin. He had to find a place to clean up before seeing the Sen tomorrow. He could sleep on a park bench but he must shave, shower, change to fresh linen. He chewed in ugly impotent rage at what the Sen had done to him this day. He ought to be made to pay for the indignities. Five thousand wouldn't be enough to make up for it.

The screen door flopped open and he heard the laughter of an entering group. He was afraid to look, under his eyes he could see the costumes. They passed the opposite side of the counter and he pushed his hat forward over his eyes. After they had passed he looked after them. It wasn't the Sen's party. It was just another group of stay-up-late Fiesta revelers.

He ate faster then. He didn't want to be caught in the glaring light of the hash house by the Sen's crowd. His stomach was bloated when he finished and the cigarette tasted good again, not like an old dry weed. He picked up his check, paid at the cashier's wicket and dived outside banging the screen after him. But the Sen and his party weren't standing there ready to enter. There was no one on the walk.

From the corner the lights of the Cabeza de Vaca up the street sneered at him. Across, the lights of the little Inca ignored him. Damn them and damn their neon. He'd find him a room better than in those dumps.

He rounded the corner and retraced his way up the slight hill. He turned left and continued down the street. There must be some place with room for him. Book stores, jewelry stores, shoe stores, furniture stores. He walked on in the darkness, the shops growing meaner, the way more dark. Nothing across, a blatant movie house dark, he could pitch a tent in the lobby if he had a tent. Murky bars with muted sounds and sounds not muted, acrid smell of cheap liquor stenching your nostrils. Only a couple of blocks and the street ended. Nothing beyond. Dark little houses, country, vacant fields. Beyond that, mountains. No hotels, no room signs, not even a whore house. Nothing more in this direction and he turned back. He stood for a moment lighting another cigarette, trying to know out of his head what to do, where to go.

And standing there the unease came upon him again. The unease of an alien land, of darkness and silence, of strange tongues and a stranger people, of unfamiliar smells, even the cool-of-night smell unfamiliar. What sucked into his pores for that moment was panic although he could not have put a name to it. The panic of loneness; of himself the stranger although he was himself unchanged, the creeping loss of identity. It sucked into his pores and it oozed out again, clammy in the chill of night. He was shivering as he stood there and he moved sharply, towards the Plaza, towards identity. He heard the pad of walking feet as he moved and he slung his head over his shoulder quick, his right hand hard and quick in his pocket. No one walked behind him. Yet when he moved again, he heard again the soft padding. He had a momentary stab of something like fright, remembering the black hatred in the eyes of the mug waiter. Then he realized. There was no one abroad but himself. It was himself he heard. His short laugh was an ugly, out-loud sound in the dark and the night. He walked on, striking his heels viciously into the broken sidewalk. He wasn't afraid. He wasn't afraid of the spic waiter or of any man who walked. He had never known man fear since the old man had been buried, his strap fastening his pants around his obese middle.

He walked back up the dark street, one block, the second, and he cut slantwise across to the murky bar by the barber shop. Not because he wanted a drink. Because he saw the cadaverous frame of Ignacio, the guitar player, through the smoky open doorway. Because he would find Pancho, and Pancho would find a place where he might rest.

This wasn't a dump like Keen's Bar, this was a dive. A two-by-four saloon with a dirty bar and no fixings. Not even a juke. This was where men, poor men, went to get drunk when the whip of poverty fell too hard for endurance. This was the kind of saloon the old man had hung around whenever he had the price of cheap rotgut. Where the old man had spent the dimes that the old lady brought home for bread. When the old man couldn't stand up on his feet, he'd stumble home and beat the hell out of the kids because there wasn't any bread to give them.

The old man lay in a pauper's grave where he belonged. The old lady lay beside him; it wasn't her fault that she wore out scrubbing floors for bread and left the kids on the street. Some day he'd dig her up; have a white headstone put over her old bones. The girls were drabs, the boys worked for a living. Some living clerks, day laborers. All but him. That hadn't been good enough for him. He'd known what he wanted, money, enough money to go North Shore. No small change. No more stir. Safe jobs. Big pay. He was useful to the Sen because he didn't drink and he looked good in the clothes the Sen bought him. He was a good-looking kid and the Sen liked the men around him to look North Shore. He had good shoulders from boxing; he was quick and tough; he'd done the Sen's dirty work since he was a punk of seventeen and never let the Sen down. The dirty stinking Sen.

A nice white headstone. Maybe with an angel praying on top it. Here lies. He didn't know when the old lady was born or where. Died: Chicago slums, 1936. Rest in peace. The only peace she'd ever known.

He was inside the red murk of the bar and the stench turned his stomach. Rotgut. And marijuana. But he had to find Ignacio, find out where Pancho slept. He went along the bar, craning his head into men's faces, dark, ugly faces, sotted with cheap liquor, babbling in their strange tongues. He went along smelling their dirty pants and dirty shirts, their dried sweat and dung and foul breaths. Until he found Ignacio.

He demanded, "Where's Pancho?"

Ignacio looked at him as if he'd never seen Sailor before. Blank, black eyes, sad drunken eyes in his half-starved face. He said something in Spanish. "Quien es Pancho?"

The language barrier was stifling. More stifling than the foul smell of the dive. "Pancho," Sailor shouted. He remembered then, Pancho Villa was the name he had given the fat man; he didn't know the man's real name. He said, "Your boss. The fat guy. The guy who runs the merry-go-round." He found the Spanish. "Tio Vivo."

The cadaver continued to look at him out of sad, blank eyes.

But he'd been talking too loud and the others at this end of the bar were listening, watching. Suspicious of Sailor's city suit and hat, matted as it was; suspicious of his nose and his eyes and his English-speaking tongue. Suspicious and wary, waiting for Sailor to edge across the line, waiting with knives for him to start something. His fists knotted as the squat man behind Ignacio stumped forward. But the man didn't lash at him, he grinned from behind his snag teeth.

"He say who ees Pancho," the man said, grinning like a monkey. His accent was thick as the red smoke. "He no spic the Englees. He no understand what you say. I taal him." He tapped his wilted blue shirt.

"Listen, you—"

"I am Pablo Gonzalez'" the man said. "I speak the Englees. He no speak the Englees. I taal him."

"Tell him I want to know where Pancho is." He scowled quickly. "His name isn't Pancho. He's the big guy. The boss of the merry-go-round. Tio Vivo."

Pablo Gonzalez rattled Spanish at the blank eyes. Sailor waited, hopeful, hopeless. The thin guy was shaking his thin head.

"For Christ's sake, he works for the guy—"

Pablo interrupted patiently. "He does not know where ees Don José Patrico Santiago Morales y Cortez—" his grin was more monkey—"that you call Pancho."

That ended it. He flipped a quarter at the monkey face. "Buy yourself five drinks," he growled. He got out of the dive fast.

Ignacio was lying. Or the monkey face didn't spic the Englees any better than the guitarist. The barrier of language was even more frustrating. If he could talk to Ignatz he'd find out where the long name was. Pancho had a name like a duke, not like a guy playing the carnivals.

He couldn't talk Spanish and that left him where he'd been before, on the street. Walking up the narrow street, pounding the pavement of a hick town. Standing on a street corner in a dark strange town, with colored lights festooned above his head and grotesque paper masks leering at him.

There was nothing to do about it now but camp on the Sen's doorstep. Give the old biddy at the desk a tall tale and get to the Sen. Scorn in the clean blue eyes of Iris Towers wasn't as important as getting between the sheets. He walked on, past the dark shops, past the dim lighted pane of the hotel where his bag was parked, on to the corner. But he didn't cross to the hulk of hotel. He stayed his steps. Stayed them to a voice in the night. A voice in song.

Through the trees he saw the gentle rocking of a gondola of Tio Vivo. The song came from there, a ragged minor song, lifted into the night. He turned his back on the hotel and he walked towards the little merry-go-round.

Sailor remained in shadow until the song was done. "Adios," the singer sang. "Adios, mi amigo." The sweet voice trailed into silence. But the silence was not the silence of the dark street with the mean shops. The leaves in the trees were rustling and the gondola creaking and the echoes of the sad song were in the ears. Pancho gurgled a bottle to his mouth. He lay sprawled in a gondola, his girth swinging it gently. His hat was on his knees and his bare feet were propped on the seat across. He lowered the bottle, smacked his lips, corked it and laid it in his hat. He saw Sailor then.

"Ai yai!" he cried. "Mi amigo!" His face dented with smiles. His arms flopped open, warm and wide. "Mi amigo! Where have you gone to? Come have a drink."

Sailor unlatched the gate and entered the enclosure. "I don't want a drink," he said. "I want a bed."

"I will share with you my bed," Pancho vowed. "But first we will have a drink." He held up the unlabeled bottle, peered through the glass and beamed. "We will have a drink and another drink. And I will sing for you." He pulled the cork with his teeth, held out the bottle.

Sailor said, "No, thanks. All I want is some sleep." The fat man could sing him all the lullabies he wanted if he'd just show him a bed.

"But no!" Pancho's mouth dropped. His whole face drooped. "You are my friend, no? You are my friend and you will not drink with me?" He looked as if he were going to cry. He'd killed half the pint already. Even without the evidence you'd know that; he was too ready to laugh, to cry, to sing, to vow friendship.

Sailor took the bottle. You couldn't argue with a drunk. He wiped the mouth with the palm of his hand, tipped and drank. Only friendship kept him from sputtering as he set the bottle away. The stuff burned like lye; it tasted like pepper, black pepper. He pushed the bottle back to Pancho.

"Ahh!" The fat man nuzzled it. "It is good, no? Tonight we drink tequila. Not pulque. Not sotol. Tequila. Because it is Fiesta." He drank, corked the bottle and replaced it in his hat. He moved his bare feet. "Be seated, my friend. You think business is not good with me? But tonight it is tequila. That is good, no?"

Sailor slid into the gondola beside the bare feet. He'd like to take off his own shoes. They were hot and heavy after this day. "That's swell, Pancho," he said. The gondola was set in motion as he sat in it. It stirred with the dark, glittering leaves over the square, and the ponies stirred gently as if in sleep. Sailor pushed back his hat and the night was cool on his forehead.

"Zozobra is dead," Pancho said. "Viv' las Fiestas!" He uncorked the bottle and passed it in one swoop. "We will have a drink, no, because business it is good?"

"No more," Sailor said. He stymied the sad face. "Promised my mother when I was a kid. One drink, no more. My old man was a drunk."

Pancho shrugged. "Sometimes it is good for a man to be drunk." He tipped the bottle. There couldn't be more than one drink left after this swig. One more and he'd herd the fat man to that bed. Pancho smacked his lips. He began to sing dolefully, "Adios, adios, mi amigo . . ." His eyes swiveled sly. "Where is the Indian girl?" he asked.

"I left her here," Sailor said. "With you."

"She was most unhappy you leave her," Pancho said.

"I had business."

"Always you think of business." Pancho was sad. Only for a moment. His mouth twinkled. "But it is good business for me you think of business. Hola! I drink tequila."

"You find me a bed and I'll buy you another bottle tomorrow night," Sailor promised.

"With you I will share my bed." Pancho repeated the vow. "I will share my serape. You are my friend. But first another drink." He tipped the bottle but the bottle smile didn't come over his face. "Aaah," he grunted. He tossed the bottle into the shadows that flickered under a tree.

"I'll buy you another tomorrow," Sailor told him again. "Let's go to bed now." He stirred the gondola.

"One moment," Pancho stayed him. "First we drink together."

His big hand brought forth in triumph from his hip another pint of the colorless liquid. He grinned as his teeth pulled the cork. He proffered the bottle.

Sailor said, "Remember? My promise."

"It is true," Pancho sighed. "I too have given my promise. Many times." The twinkle bobbed back to his lips. "But this is Fiesta. To-night we will drink."

Sailor took the bottle. He wasn't a drinking man and this Spanish white mule wasn't a drink fit for man or mule. It was like fire in your gullet. Nevertheless he drank. It didn't matter. Nothing mattered further tonight. If he couldn't sleep, he would drink. There was no reason for him to be alert. He drank, choked, and passed the bottle over to Pancho.

"Bueno!" Pancho applauded. "That is good, no?" He gurgled it, repeated his ritual of recorking the bottle, standing it in his greasy hat. "The little Indian girl . . ." he began slyly.

"Her friends had ditched her." Sailor put his foot on that idea. "I didn't know what to do with her. She was trailing me around. So I gave her a pop and a ride on your merry-go-round. She'd never rid-den on one."

"No," Pancho said. His eyes roved across the width of the Plaza to the museum portal where the Indians slept silently. "No." It might only have occurred to him now. "The Indian children they do not ride Tio Vivo."

"Don't have the price?" Sailor asked blackly.

"Maybe no, maybe yes," Pancho shrugged. He passed the bottle. Sailor took it and drank. "The Indians they are funny peoples. They are proud, the Indians. Maybe they do not wish their little ones to be bumped about by the Mexicans and the Gringos. Maybe they do not wish them to be screamed at, 'Get out of here, you dirty In-dians.' The Indians are funny. They stay to themselves." He took a philosophic swig. "The Spanish people say that they are proud peo-ples. Maybe one time, yes. Maybe they come on their horses, a proud peoples, with gold on their saddles. It is said this is true. That is why there is the Fiesta. Because the proud Spanish conquered the Indian. Don Diego de Vargas in his coat of mail and riding in his fine leather saddle on his fine proud horse. That is what they say."

Sailor remembered vague history. "I guess it's in the books," he said. The gondola stirred gently and the dark glittering leaves were a-rustle in the night.

"It is not good to be a conqueror, I think," Pancho said. "The

Spanish were a proud peoples when they conquered but they are no longer proud. The Gringos came after and conquered the Spanish. Not by the sword. With business." His lip drooped and he winked at Sailor. "Business it is. Land and hides and wool and the buying and selling of money. That I do not understand. The buying and selling of money. But the Gringo sonnama beetches, they understand it." He took a big happy breath. "They are funny peoples, the Gringos, no? Maybe once they were proud peoples but I do not think so." His nose wrinkled. "No, I do not think so. Proud peoples do not root like pigs for fifty cents, two bits, a dollar, do they? Proud peoples are too proud."

"What about those proud Spanish people of yours?" Sailor asked. He didn't wait for invitation; he reached out and took the bottle from the hat. "Weren't they money grubbers too? Didn't you just say they were rooting for the almighty dollar too?"

"No, no," Pancho denied. "They were not looking for two bits fifty cents. They look for gold—*mucho oro*—the seven golden cities of Cibola. Do you think once there was the seven golden cities?"

"Could be," Sailor said. If going after big dough instead of little made you proud, he'd be pretty proud himself tomorrow. He wasn't listening very hard. The cradle was rocking and the leaves were rocking and there was a quietness in him, a peace in the gentle rocking darkness.

"Maybe so, maybe not," Pancho sighed. "The Spanish was a proud peoples then. But they was not good peoples. They was greedy and selfish and cruel peoples. They do not come with peace in their hearts and love. Love for the sky and the earth and the peoples of this land. They come to steal." His eyes glittered like the dark leaves over the Plaza. "Something happen to them. The land do not like them. They are cruel to its peoples. I am an Indian."

"I thought you were," Sailor murmured. Like Pila. There was a sameness in the big man and the stone girl; he didn't know what it was but he recognized it as there.

"My grandmother was an Apache," Pancho said. "I am Spanish also. The Spanish they are good peoples now. Because they are humble peoples. It is good for them to be humble as it is good for the Indian peoples to be proud. It is the way this land would have it be."

The way Pancho talked about this country you'd think it was some heathen god that must be obeyed. That you had to sacrifice to. Not just a lot of wasteland stretching on and on until the mountains stopped it. Until the mountains uprose, a barrier against the sky.

"What about the white folks?" Sailor asked.

"The Gringos, pah!" Pancho scorned. "They are not of this land. They do not bring nothing to this land. All they want is to take away the two bits fifty cents. Never are they of this land."

The aliens. The ones without existence.

Pancho said comfortably. "I am an Indian and I am Spanish. My grandfather was a Spanish don. That is why I am called Don José Patricio Santiago Morales y Cortez. It is the name of my grandfather. My grandmother was his slave."

"Lincoln freed the slaves," Sailor said. He said it like he was reading from a book, a history book in grade school and outside the window the smoke and grime and cold of a Chicago winter rattled skeleton claws. He went to school because it was warm in school. He'd rather have hung around the pool hall, it was warm there too, but the truant snoops were always busting into the pool hall looking for kids. And the fat guy who ran the pool hall didn't want any trouble with the officers. He peddled reefers under the table and he couldn't afford to get mixed up with the truant officers. He'd push the kids right into the snoops' hands. The kids were afraid to snitch on him about the reefers because they'd seen him kill a man once. Picked the guy up and broke his back like you'd break a stick. He was so fat you wouldn't think he could move so quick or be so strong. He didn't get sent up for breaking the guy's back. Everybody in the place, even the kids, swore it was self defense. The guy was doped and had pulled a knife on the fat guy. Besides the coppers probably knew about the reefers anyhow. Anybody could smell them that walked by. You didn't have to go inside. The same sick smell like in the dive where Sailor'd found Ignatz tonight. The coppers probably got their cut. If he hadn't gone to school to keep warm, kept going even to high school, the Sen wouldn't have picked him out of the bums in the corner pool hall. The Sen wouldn't have sent him to college, yeah, the University of Chicago, for a year and a half. He'd had a good education. He wasn't any bum.

Pancho was shrugging. "Who is this Mr. Lincoln? The Spanish peoples do not know of him. The Indian do not know he has free them. They are poor slaves. After while the Gringos come and say Mr. Lincoln free the slaves. You do not be slaves. You go home now. And you Mexican sonnama beetches you work for us now." He smiled. "You know why you are my friend, Señor Sailor?"

"Haven't any idea," Sailor yawned.

"Because I am an Indian," Pancho said. "And you are good to a little Indian girl. You do not say to her come to my bed and I will give you a ride on old Tio Vivo."

He didn't say, "I haven't got a bed." He said, "For God's sake, she's only fourteen."

"Does it matter?" Pancho shrugged. "She is older I think at fourteen than the pale lily Gringos are at twice fourteen. But you are a good man. You buy her pop and a fine fast ride on Tio Vivo with music playing. On the pink horse." He smile was open, warm. "You do this for her only that she may have pleasure. Not to steal nothing from her. You are my friend." He broke into song again. "Mi amigo, mi amigo, mi amigo, amo te mucho . . ."

"That's fine," Sailor said. He was awake again. The bottle was almost empty. He left enough for one last drink for Pancho. "Let's go to bed, ok?"

"You are also my friend," Pancho said with a sly squint, "because you do not say, 'You goddamn Mexican, give this girl a ride or I—' with your hand on the gun in your pocket."

Sailor's hand went quick to his right-hand pocket. The gun was still there, safe. But how had Pancho known it was there? Did McIntyre know? He didn't want any trouble.

Pancho was effusive. "No, no. You are a good man. You pay much money for the favor. For the little Indian Pila to ride on the pink horse. You make rich presents to poor Pancho and to poor Ignacio and poor old Onofre Gutierrez. You make everyone happy for the Fiesta."

"Zozobra is dead," Sailor quoted ironically. "Viva las Fiestas." He laughed out loud. The laugh startled the quivering black night. Nobody had ever called him a good man. Nobody had any reason ever to call him good.

"Thus you are my friend, my primo. I too am a good man. A proud man and a good man."

The old brigand had probably killed a dozen men in his day. Broken their backs like he was breaking sticks.

"Unless you are good you cannot be proud," Pancho said. He lifted the farewell drink, squinted at its meagerness. If he had another pint hidden in the elephant hide of his jeans, he, Sailor, would pop the old devil. "You cannot be proud if you are afraid, hiding in the corners. You cannot be proud if you are bowing this way and that way to the Gringo sonnama beetches. You cannot be proud and be scheming to steal two bits fifty cents. No, no. Only the Indians are proud peoples."

"Sure," Sailor said. "Let's go."

"Because they do not care for nothing. Only this their country. They do not care about the Gringos or even the poor Mexicanos. These peoples do not belong to their country. They do not care because they know these peoples will go away. Sometime."

"A long time," Sailor said, seeing the little shops, the dumps and the dives. It wasn't easy to get rid of the stuff that brought in the two beets feefty sants.

"They can wait," Pancho said patiently. "The Indians are a proud peoples. They can wait. In time . . ."

One thousand years. Two thousand. In time. Maybe it was the way to do things, not to worry about the now, to wait for time to take care of things. What if the measure of time was one thousand, two thousand years? In time everything was all right. If you were an Indian.

Maybe that was the terror the stone Indian generated. In time, you were nothing. Therefore you were nothing. He'd had enough of Pancho's tequila philosophy. Enough of thinking.

"Drink up," he said. "I got to get some sleep. Got business to take care of tomorrow."

Pancho squinted at the small remaining drink. "You promised your sainted mother." He filled his mouth with the tequila, rinsed it from cheek to cheek, savoring it.

Sailor swung his feet over the edge, jumped out lightly.

"Now we will sleep, yes." Pancho sighed. He scratched his belly, wriggled his dirty toes, and put the greasy hat on his head, pulling it down over his ears. He grunted and groaned as he lumbered out of the gondola, stood swaying on the earth. He clapped Sailor on the shoulder. "We will sleep side by side because we are friends. Only the good friends have good talk as we have had this night. Good talk and a bottle to share. Not sotol, tequila! To warm the heart and the belly."

His big hand, his swaying bulk nudged Sailor towards the center pole of the merry-go-round. "You are my friend," he chanted. He took his hand away, bent swaying over a pile of dirty rags by the pole. He didn't fall, he lurched perilously but it was with a dancer's grace he swooped up one of the rags, stood straight again. "For you my serape," he said. He held up the dirty rag with moist-eyed affection. A long piece of wool, woven of colored stripes that were ravaged by dirt and night into only light and dark. Tenderly he held it to Sailor. "For you, mi amigo. Wrap it about you and you will be warm this night."

Sailor took it. Awkwardly. Reluctant. There was nothing else he could do. Not without hurting the old goat's feelings. He'd hurt plenty of people in his life, sure; but he didn't want to hurt this poor old goat. He took the serape but he didn't wrap it around him. He said, "I'm warm enough. I got a coat, see? You take it. You need it."

"No, no." Pancho shook his head. With the movement he wobbled on his big bare feet. "By your friendship I am kept warm." He stepped aside. "Wrap it about you and lie here."

Sailor broke in. "Here? On the ground?" His fist closed on the dirty serape. "You mean you sleep here?"

"But yes," Pancho said. He scowled. "Could I sleep closed into walls, in the bed where many have sleeped, many have died? No, no, no! I sleep where I may breathe, Señor Sailor. Tonight you will sleep with me, no? Where you may breathe and dream good dreams."

For Christ's sake. He didn't curse aloud. For a bed on the ground he'd spent hours listening to a conglomeration of broken English and Spanish, for this he'd drunk tequila, for this he'd endured an old peon's ideas of the world he lived in. To lie on the ground. Like an Indian. While the Sen lay in La Fonda, on clean sheets, in a seven-dollar-a-day bed.

"You did not think I have a room?" Pancho asked anxiously. "You did not think I would trust my little ponies to the thieves in the night?"

He'd never slept on the ground in his life. He'd been poor, he'd been slum poor, but he'd never slept without a roof over his head. He was burned up but when his eyes met Pancho's saddened eyes, he lied. He didn't know why he lied. Maybe the tequila had made him dopey. He said, "This suits me," and watched the happiness seep back into the brown brigand face. "Suits me fine."

Pancho used his toes to push forward a hunk of gunny sack. "That is good, Here is the pillow for your head. Wrap the serape about you so." He pantomimed. "You will sleep well, my friend."

Sailor wrapped it about him so. He got down awkwardly as a camel on the earth. He didn't take off his hat when he lay on the gunny sack. Bad enough to be wrapped in this flea-bitten rag. No telling what was on the sacking.

"You are comfortable, no?" Pancho asked.

No, he said in his brain and aloud, "I'm fine."

Pancho knelt like a graceful elephant beside him. He made prayer.

Spanish prayer. God be with us. The saints preserve and bless us. He stretched himself out on the earth, his arms beneath his head. "It is good to sleep beneath the stars. Goodnight, my friend," he said. He closed his eyes and he was asleep. Asleep and snoring.

Under the stars. The crazy old coot. They were under the canopy of the merry-go-round. Not a star in sight. Ignacio and Onofre were in a room. Pila was in a room. The girls who earlier lay on the Federal Building lawn were in their rooms. The baby face who'd given him the eye in the restaurant was in a room. McIntyre had a room and the gorilla waiter had a room and the Sen had a seven-dollar-a-day room in the best hotel in town. Everyone sleeping in a room, in a bed, except the Indians who didn't care because two thousand years from now there wouldn't be any rooms or any beds or any Gringos or Mexicans to sleep in them. Everyone but the crazy Indians and a crazy old fool who was half and half, Indian and Spanish, and the wise guy from Chicago who thought he was finding a bed by sticking with him.

The ground was hard and Pancho's snores were lusty. The serape scratched and bit. And Sailor's rage against the Sen bit harder, like an aching tooth, scratched like hair cloth. The Sen would pay. He'd pay for all the indignities but he'd pay heavy for making Sailor sleep on the hard ground. Like an Indian. Like a crazy halfbreed spic brigand. Like a dog.

The leaves of the tall trees in the park rustled like rain. Afar there were snatches of laughter and aftermath of deeper silences. The wind was a small cool sound through the shadowed Plaza. Pancho snored. A dog bayed at the loneliness of night; a chorus answered with sharp-toothed barking; silence closed again over night. The silence from the museum portal was deeper than the dark there. No one living could be in that dark, that silence. Maybe that was the secret in stone; the Indians were not living; they were spirits from a long forgotten day, walking the earth, waiting. Waiting in knowledge that they alone would not pass, the excretions of the white man would pass away and they would remain.

The loneness, the lack of identity that had terrified him twice tonight, once in remembering the past through Pila's face, later in that moment of dark and silence on the hooded, unfamiliar street, stabbed again. He rose up, but slowly he sank down again on to the ground. Pancho was there beside him. The wooden ponies were quivering gently. The Plaza was unchanged.

Sleep came into him because he was too tired to allow discomfort to put it to rout. Even the tremble of an unknown fear, the anger at his present humiliation, could not banish it. He closed his eyes, the tightness went out of him. He drifted between the hard earth and the cradle of oblivion. He was drifting into blissful oblivion when through his closed eyes the gray-white face of Zozobra floated above him. The dead eyes burned, the hideous mouth croaked. *I am evil. I am the spirit of this alien land. Go away. Go away before all good becomes evil. All is evil. Go away. It's going to rain. I'm going to spoil your fun. . . .*

He knew he was asleep but he couldn't wake up. He couldn't get away from the obscene floating face. Fire billowed higher, higher, but even fire couldn't destroy the evil thing. He knew he was asleep and then—he was asleep.

II

Procession

1

HE WAKED TO THE CLANGOR OF CHURCH BELLS. BRIGHT AND STRONG AS sunshine they rang in the chill of early morning air. Pancho was rolling on one elbow. His sleep-sanded eyes blinked happily at Sailor.

"It is morning," Pancho announced. He lumbered to his feet, hitching his jeans up over his fat hips. He yawned and stretched and shook off sleep as a dog shaking off water. "A good morning, my friend. Señor Sailor. The little birds are singing songs in the tree tops—"

Sailor glinted at his watch. Not quite six o'clock. They had talked, Pancho had talked, to past three. He muttered, "Church bells," and closed his eyes. He heard the birds as he eyes closed; they weren't singing, they were setting up an infernal twittering din. Clang clang twitter twitter tweet. He pulled the serape up under his chin and grasped for sleep.

When he waked again the church bells were still ringing. Loud and strong but his watch said eight and now the sun lay in bright patches on the green Plaza. Sailor sat up, flung aside the dirty serape, dug under his coat and scratched his shoulders.

Pancho said, "You sleep well, my friend?" He was sitting on Igna-cio's camp stool, chewing a doughnut. Sugar frosted his lips.

"Not exactly The Stevens," Sailor grinned back. The big man didn't know what he was talking about. "But I feel pretty good." He stretched and yawned, breaking off when the two girls crossing the Plaza gave him the eye and giggled to each other. They were all dressed up in cheap silk dresses, pink and turquoise-blue silk. They teetered on high-heeled white sandals and they had dabs of white straw on their black hair. Their mouths were painted. Peasants off to early morning Mass.

Eight o'clock, kid's Mass. The bells would be ringing and the old lady would nag: *Hurry, hurry, hurry. That's the first bell. You haven't your shoes laced yet your neck washed yet your coat buttoned yet . . . you'll be late for Mass. Hurry, hurry, hurry.*

The old man would be shaving, he shaved on Sundays, his face the color of raw beef. How he could stand on his feet after Saturday night's binge was a marvel to the kids. It slowed them up on Sundays. He honed the razor on the thick strap and scraped the gray pig-bristles off his face. Sounded like sandpaper scraping against itself. *Hurry, hurry, hurry. That's the last bell. Do you have your prayer book your rosary your penny your handkerchief . . . you'll be late to Mass. Hurry hurry hurry.*

The kids stumbling on ahead, clumping shoes shined blackly, faces shined raw with yellow soap. The old lady in her Sunday black, mincing fast behind them in her Sunday shoes, high laced black shoes with pointed toes pinching her feet. She'd take off the shoes when she got home from church, put on the old felt slippers, one pompom gone, the color they'd once had turned dirt gray in the soot and grime of a Chicago tenement. The old man striding along a little in front of her in his black serge, too tight about the middle; the good suit he'd bought years ago when he worked at the yards and was an upstanding young fellow. Too many years ago for the kids to remember. The old man swaggering along like he was the Lord High God of the Universe they were going to the slum church to pray to, not the old souse who stole the money the old lady brought home for bread, brought home in the wan weary dawn hour after scrubbing marble floors all night. *Hurry, hurry, hurry . . .*

The church was only around the corner and they made it as the last bell was an echo, marching down the aisle together, the old man and the old lady and the kids, the eight kids. Eight kids and not enough bread for one. Kneeling together, praying together, marching out again into the cold gloomy Chicago Sunday. The hot sweating Chicago Sunday.

"It's a fine family you have there, Mr. . . . ."

The old man puffing himself up and accepting the compliments on the church steps and the old lady smirking timidly and fingering her worn black gloves. She blacked them with shoe blacking on Saturday nights. The kids standing like clodhoppers with their welts itching under their sawtoothed winter underwear, under their sweaty summer floursacks.

The priest in his stained cassock looking like a pale, pious, near-sighted saint. Saints didn't belong in a slum church; there ought to have been a fighting priest like an avenging angel with a fiery sword. To whack the old man down. To strike the old man and his sancti-monious Sunday smile dead on the church steps.

The pale, near-sighted saint priest and the waxen saintly nuns preaching and teaching about the Lord Jesus and the kids trying to sit still on their blistered backsides and their stomachs crying for want of bread. If you didn't sit still you had to stay in after school unless the nun with the wart was your teacher and then you just got a whack on the head with a ruler. Maybe she knew about the blis-tered backsides and the welts on the kids' backs, maybe that's why she whacked the ruler on the kids' heads. Maybe she'd been a slum kid before she was a nun. Maybe she whacked them to keep from weeping over them. Slum kids didn't want weeps over them.

But none of that was the reason he quit the parochial school, quit on his own and the truant officer picked him up after four days and took him to the old man and the old man's eyes were like red rat eyes when he took off his belt and slowly moved forward. That was the time he used the knife on the old man. The old man half-killed him and he didn't kill the old man though he wanted to. He cut up the old man and they sent him to reform school as a criminal kid. They didn't do anything to the old man but patch him up.

Reform school was better than home. Three meals a day and you didn't get beaten for no reason. You learned how to steal cars and you smoked cigarettes if you didn't get caught. That was the first time he went to reform school. It wasn't the last time. The last time he didn't stay long. They let him out when the old man died. The old lady cried like a baby, like the old man had been good to her. She wore a mourning veil over her face. It hid her crying and the shiner the old man had given her before he dropped dead. The other kids went to the funeral but he didn't. He went to the pool hall and one day he met the Sen.

The clangorous bells rang out and he scratched himself and watched the stragglers hurrying across the Plaza and up the sun bright street. *Hurry Hurry Hurry.* He didn't have to hurry. The last time he'd been in church was when the old lady died. Cancer, the doc said. The doc should have said she'd just worn out. On her knees scrubbing marble floors all week, on her knees in church on Sundays.

That was why he'd run off from the parochial school. Because he wouldn't get down on his knees every morning, noon, and afternoon and thank God for his blessings. Thank God for the vicious rats in the walls and an obscene old man who beat the hell out of his kids. Thank God for his mother killing herself trying to feed eight kids. Thank God for not enough to eat, for dirt, for shivering winter, for stifling summer, for bad teeth, for pains in the belly, for never enough to eat. Maybe if he was an Indian it would have been all right. He'd have known in time it didn't matter. Poverty, cruelty, injustice were excretions; time would take care of them. You could sit up there on a cloud pillow twanging a harp and laugh like hell in two thousand years. Or stop stoking a fiery pit long enough for a snicker. Screwball philosophy. But old Pancho meant well. He was friendly as a puppy, holding out his sack of stale doughnuts, urging, "Go on. Have something to eat."

"No, thanks," he said. He took off his hat, pushed back his dark hair, settled the hat again. He shook the kinks out of his legs. "I got to be about my business."

"You slept well, no?" Pancho was anxious, chewing the rubbery doughnut.

"Slept fine," sailor said. "Feel like a new man." Funny thing was he did feel pretty good. Awake and alive and the air, hot and crisp both, pumping into his lungs.

"That is good," Pancho beamed. "You will be back?"

"Sure. Be seeing you." He turned and walked out of the Plaza towards the hotel where his bag better be safe. He was himself again. A night on the ground hadn't changed that. He was himself and all he needed was to get cleaned up, have a cup of coffee, and he'd be ready to face the Sen.

There were, this early, old women in the little thatched booths, building the fires, opening locked cases, setting out the sucker bait, the flimsy yellow birds on their sticks, the canes and the balloons, the black hats with the red and yellow and green bobbles. McIntyre wasn't a bad guy; he'd bought his hat off a booth on the Plaza. He wasn't like the Sen, hiring a dressmaker to fix him up in satins and velvets like a Spanish grandee, price no object, and trying to rat out on a business deal.

Sailor strode across the street, climbed up the high curb to the sidewalk. He went in the hotel. The big shirt-sleeved guy was back behind the desk, looking glum, too much Fiesta. He eyed Sailor. "You didn't pick up your bag."

Sailor leaned his elbows on the counter. "Couldn't find a room," he said. "Had to sit up all night. You couldn't fix me up today, could you?"

"Naw," he growled. But he wasn't mean, he was hopeless. "I got 'em sleeping in shifts now. You know anybody'll give you a shift, it's okay by me."

"Don't know a soul in town," Sailor said cheerfully. "Aren't any of them moving out today?"

"Naw. Nobody's going to budge till Fiesta's over."

"You mean it goes on?" He hadn't read that pink piece of paper crumpled in his pocket. He'd taken it for granted Fiesta was like the Fourth of July or Memorial Day or something.

"Today and tomorrow," the clerk said bitterly.

Sailor echoed the bitterness for the moment. Then he remembered. He'd get his business done and move on. To Albuquerque, El Paso, across the border. He didn't have to stick around here. "Listen," he began. "Look at me. I been in the Plaza all night. I got to see a guy on business this morning. A big shot. I can't go looking like this. I haven't had my clothes off for four days. I stink."

The guy's face agreed gloomily.

"All I want is a shower and a shave." He dug into his pocket. Took out a five. You couldn't offer a hardbitten Gringo a one. You wouldn't get any place if you did. This guy wasn't mi amigo; he was clerk-bouncer in a cheap hotel. "You've got a room here. Just let me go wash up in your room. That's all."

The guy eyed the fiver with the right look. "I don't know," he began. "I sleep on shift with the night guy."

Sailor covered the bill in his fingers, began to inch it off the counter.

"He's out having breakfast now," the guy said hurriedly. "If he gets back, I could keep him down here a while." He stood up. "You make it snappy," he ordered. "I'll keep him down here." So he wouldn't have to split. He pushed Sailor's bag out from under the counter. "Come on." He didn't offer to lug it. Sailor picked it up; the locks hadn't been tampered with.

He followed the guy up the steep uncarpeted stairs to the floor above. The guy took a key out of his pocket and unlocked a door just off the head of the stairs. A dinky room with an unmade single bed, men's neckties on the oak bureau, a couple of chairs with clothes

flung on them. Nothing fancy but a room and it looked good. Sailor
set down his bag easy on the dusty carpet. Not that he cared about
stirring up the ancient dust; he didn't want the bag's weight to
sound.

The guy held out his hand for the five.

"Sure," Sailor said easy. He started to hand it over but he waited.
"Look at this suit." He eyed it himself in the mirror. It looked as if
he'd slept in it for a week, in a sticky bus seat, on the ground with
leaves and grass and dirt rolling in it. "I can't talk business with a
big shot looking like this." He reached in his pocket and took out a
one, handed both to the clerk. "You can get it pressed for me."

"It's Sunday," the guy said. But he shoved both bills in his pocket.

"Sure, but this is a hotel." Sailor eeled out of the coat jacket. He
carried it to the bureau and emptied the left-hand pocket, a
crumpled pink slip of paper, the Fiesta program; a mashed pack of
Philip Morris, two cigarettes left; a paper folder of matches, Raton
hotel. He slid the gun into his right hand while he fussed with the
left-hand pocket. And he kept talking fast. "Hotels got tailors who'll
press suits on a Sunday. Wish I could get it cleaned, maybe he can
spot it a little." He slid the gun out and under the pink paper and he
didn't think the guy saw. He faced him again quick, his shoulders
hiding what was cluttering the bureau, unhooked his belt and unbuttoned his pants. "You can send somebody out with it. It won't take
long. A guy's got to make a good impression when he's talking over a
business deal." He emptied the pants pockets, wadding the handkerchief around the bills so the guy couldn't see the roll. Not that it was
anything to bug the eyes out. Around seventy bucks wasn't any for-
tune. But this buzzard looked as if he'd roll you for a ten spot. Or
even a fiver.

The guy said, "I'll have to keep Alfie downstairs longer."

"Not much longer. Shouldn't take long to press a suit. Sponge and
press." He went over and hung the dark suit on the guy's big fore-
arm. "You're picking up some change the management won't have
to know about." He winked. "Or Alfie?"

"Okay," the guy said.

Sailor stood there on the ugly, dust-drenched rug, his hat on his
head, his shirt tails hanging over his blue silk jockey shorts. Until the
guy closed the door. He stood there until he heard the big feet slapping down the stairs. Then he moved fast. Turned the key in the
lock and left it there. He took off his hat and sailed it at the bureau. It lit. "Jesus," he breathed. A locked door, a shower, a can. All

his own. Until the suit came back. He was playing in luck. He stripped off his dirty shirt and dirty shorts, wadded them together, took off his shoes and socks. To get clean again, to scrub. No wonder he'd been thinking about the old man and the old lady and him a kid. He hadn't been this dirty since he was a kid.

He didn't stop to open his suitcase. He stopped only long enough to grab his gun and he headed for the bath. He parked the gun on the back of the can and he got under the shower, turned it on full force. It hit him like rain in the middle of Chicago summer. Like rain from Heaven. He just stood there for a while soaking it up, the way a tree soaked up the rain.

Butch and Alfie were obliging. They'd left a big cake of pine soap on the wash basin. A bottle of Fitch in the medicine cabinet. He soaped and shampooed and soaped again. He washed away all the stench of the bus and Pancho's serape and lying on the ground like a dog. He stepped out clean. He could have stayed another hour. If he'd been sure Butch hadn't noticed the gun and might get tough if he didn't hurry it up.

He borrowed the best razor, shaved. Borrowed the face lotion and the hair tonic. The stuff must be Alfie's, the day man wasn't any sweet-smelling guy. He carried the gun with him as he whistled back to the bureau. He was clean in the mirror; he looked good. He even washed his pocket comb before combing his short curly black hair.

He whistled as he unlocked the suitcase, threw back the lid. Clean socks, clean underwear, clean shirts. If he'd had any sense he'd have carried an extra suit along. But he'd been counting on a quick finish to the deal and he'd be in Mexico, having linens tailor made. He'd have brought an extra anyway if there'd been room. A suit wasn't as important as the baby. It gleamed dully in the bottom of the suitcase. The sweetest tommy-gun a fellow ever owned. A little present from the Sen two years ago. His baby. He'd never used it; he was too important in the organization to handle artillery. That was for the mugs. But he wanted one and the Sen gave him what he wanted then. It might come in pretty handy now when he started in business for himself in Mexico. A tommy was handy on the Sen's business in Chicago. He rubbed his hand over the stock and he grimaced. At himself. He was like a kid with a toy. But it was a sweet baby.

He picked out pale green silk shorts, dark green hounds' tooth socks; a white shirt and a foulard tie of the same green patterned in gray. He was a neat dresser; he'd learned from the Sen. Nothing loud; that was mug stuff. He could look as good as the Sen any day; better, he was young and not a bad-looking guy; the Sen was a little squirt with a weasel face. If Iris Towers bumped into him today she wouldn't look down her nose.

He put on his shorts, his socks and his shoes, polishing the shoes with his dirty laundry. He wadded the laundry in a corner of the suitcase. He was getting ready to lock up when there was a rap on the door.

He froze. Called, "Whozit?"

"Your suit, it is ready."

It wasn't the day clerk; it was an accent. Count on Butch to send it up by a boy, another tip. And he'd take a cut. He said, "Okay," and he slapped down the lid of the suitcase. He took a quarter from his small change on the bureau, pushed the automatic under a handkerchief, went over and opened the door.

The kid was little and brown. He held the suit by the hanger. The suit looked swell.

"Thanks," Sailor said. He gave the kid the quarter, shoved the door shut in his face. He locked it. It was worth a quarter to finish dressing without the big clerk standing around watching.

He looked swell when he was dressed. Looked and felt swell. He filled his pockets again, the gun in his right pocket resting easy there. It was a small automatic; it looked like a toy but it wasn't any toy. It worked. He lit a cigarette, took a long drag, borrowed Alfie's brush for his hat. A good hat shaped itself up again with brushing. Even if you'd been sleeping in it. This was a good one. Fifteen bucks from the same place the Sen bought his hats.

He locked the suitcase, looked around. Everything the way it had been. Nothing of his left behind. The pink program. He folded it and stuck it in his pocket. Maybe he'd have a chance to read it yet, find out what was going on.

He dragged the suitcase down the stairs to the desk. The big fellow was alone there, glomming. Sailor rang the key on the counter. "Thanks," he said. "Sure was a life saver."

There was some respect in the guy now seeing Sailor the way he looked usually, the way he looked in Chicago. The guy said, "That's all right. Want to leave the grip again?"

"No, I'm taking it up to La Fonda." Sailor said it casual, just to see more respect in the guy's piggy eyes.

"Let me have a couple of packs of Philip Morris." While the guy was getting them out he asked, "Have any trouble with Alfie?" It

wouldn't be smart to play it too big here; he might need to ask another favor some day. He might have to come back to this town
some day.

The guy put the Philip Morrises on the counter and made change
from the half dollar. "I sent him out on an errand," he said. "I got
tired of listening to how his wife used to treat him. Before he
skipped out. If she was that bad, I don't see why he stuck it twenty-
two years. You ought to hear him. Twenty-two years in a doghouse
like he tells it."

Sailor said, "Thanks, Butch. Be seeing you." He hoisted the suitcase and went out on the sidewalk. The Plaza was still quiet enough.
Fiesta didn't get started particularly early. It was only a half block
and across to La Fonda; a good thing no more. The bag wasn't any
lighter than it had been yesterday.

He was almost to the corner when the bells rang out again.
Louder now, stronger now, and against their clangor he heard the
tinkle of guitar and scrape of violin. He saw them up by the cathedral, the crowds on the church terrace; the people lining the streets.
People on the streets as far down as La Fonda. As he reached the
corner a brass band blared in a marching hymn. Band and tinkling
and the cymbal crash of church bells, all sounding together in Sunday morning triumph. He crossed quickly and set down his bag as
the parade rounded the corner. It wasn't much of a parade but he
stood on the curb gawking like the rest of the peasants. First the
brass band, then maybe a dozen people, men and women, all dressed
in dark velvet, wine and purple and black velvet with woven gold
chains around their necks. Behind them the queen in her white lace
with a crimson velvet cape around her shoulders and the gold crown
on her head. The princesses in crimson velvet walked behind, all
pretty, dark girls. At the tail end came the court musicians, guitars
and violins.

It was like a picture of Queen Isabella's court when Columbus was
asking for her jewels. Like a court of old Spain, here in a little village
street in the bright hot sunshine, lords and ladies and the royal retinue marching up a little village street to the mass of brown gray cathedral on the terrace.

The bells rang out and the band played and the court moved in
slow regal dignity up the short block. Sailor goggled after them like
everyone else, even moving up the street a way the better to gawk.
The court stopped at the intersection and from around the corner
came another procession. An archbishop in his crimson and white

and gold, brown-robed friars following. The bells pealed louder as the archbishop's procession ascended the stone steps, passed slowly up the walk and through the open doors of the cathedral. The royal retinue followed. And the people closed in behind them, poured into the church. The bells stopped and there was a great void of silence in the street. Until the street watchers who weren't going to High Mass broke the void with their little sounds of talk and laugh and movement.

Sailor turned and went in the hotel. He carried his suitcase over to the check room by the closed bar. There was a pretty girl there, black-eyed, black-haired, small-boned. She had a red flower in her hair, a red and green skirt sparkling with sequins, a sheer blouse heavily embroidered in red and green and blue flowers. She smiled, she had a fresh morning look to her.

"Mind if I check this a while?" Sailor asked.

She said, "Certainly," and passed him a numbered check and another smile. Not a come-on smile, a nice clean one.

He smiled back. "It's pretty heavy. Too heavy for you. I'll set it in."

She opened the counter gate and he put down the bag in the farthest corner where it would be out of the way. Where no one would be kicking it around wondering what made it so heavy. He said, "Thanks."

He walked over to the desk, his arms swinging free, sure of himself, swaggering a little. The old hag with the yellowed white hair was gone. The man behind the desk was just a part of the equipment, like in the Palmer House or Stevens. A gent you wouldn't know if you met him on the street five minutes later.

Sailor asked quickly, "Senator Douglass? Willis Douglass?"

The clerk knew without looking. He gave the room number. Sailor turned around and picked up the house phone, letting the clerk see him pick it up, hear him ask the room number. The switchboard girl wouldn't have needed earphones to get the number; she was sitting on the other side of the desk, only a square pillar between them. If this had been a big hotel with more than one house phone and them around a corner, out of sight, he wouldn't have to go through this hocus-pocus. Heaven help the small-town peasants. Everything was made tough for them, inconvenient. You couldn't have any secrets in a village.

He could hear the ringing and he had a moment's shock that maybe the Sen wouldn't be in at nine-thirty on a Sunday morning.

Maybe he'd be dressed up in his velvet panties marching to bells and band into the cathedral for more Fiesta. The Sen in the cathedral was a laugh. Sailor held his left hand tight around the instrument; his right hand, automatic, digging his right-hand pocket. It was another shock after the ringing when the Sen snarled, "Hello."

Sailor cupped his hand over the instrument, spoke silkily through it. "We are sending up a package, Senator Douglass."

He hung up without waiting to hear the Sen start cursing. He would imagine well enough the way the Sen would talk to a hotel clerk who dared wake the ex-senator of Illinois to bring up a package. The smile on Sailor's lips felt good as he cut down the left-hand portal. The portal separated the dining rooms from the patio. There were a couple of people sitting in the patio this early. He wouldn't mind sitting out there himself in a bright-covered swing. At a table under a striped umbrella with a cold beer bubbling. Later. Right now a little business. The smile twisted. He wouldn't waste time standing in the corridor pounding on a door; the Sen would be up and waiting. The good old Sen!

He didn't know the whereabouts of the elevators, he only knew they weren't in sight in the front lobby so they must be somewhere at the rear. There had to be at least one elevator or the Sen wouldn't have a room on the fourth floor. The Sen wouldn't be climbing any four flights to a room if there were a flock of Fiestas going on.

He turned right where the portal angled into a wider one. Big couches and chairs here and a fireplace big enough to roast a sheep. This one has glass doors opening out to the patio too, and more big potted bushes in the corners. He didn't see any elevators and he walked on to where the right portal met this one. There was a blue-smocked boy with a dark stupid face cleaning the ash trays on a table.

"Where's the elevators, Bub?" Sailor asked.

The boy looked more stupid than ever pointing a brown finger. He didn't say anything.

Sailor followed the finger direction. He wasn't sure the boob knew what he was after; maybe he thought Sailor was inquiring about the can. This didn't look like elevators, it looked like a Spanish palace, dark beams and big rich chairs and on a dark polished table a brass bowl filled with little chrysanthemums. He looked in the open doorway of an immense sunken room, rich and somber, grand piano, red velvet chairs, a fireplace. Opposite the door tiled steps and a wrought-iron balustrade led upwards. He was wondering whether this was up when he saw the check girl leaning against the wall beyond.

"Hey there," he began and then he saw it wasn't the check girl. Another dark-haired, dark-eyed kid; another glittering Spanish costume. He went up to her. "I'm looking for the elevators," he said and in saying he reached that turning and saw the elevator, just one.

She didn't say anything. She giggled soundlessly and stepped into the carved cage. He followed her. "Four," he said. If there was trouble he'd sure played it dumb. She'd remember him. The city guy who was bungling around looking for elevators early on Fiesta Sunday. But there wasn't going to be trouble. His hand rammed his right pocket and stayed there.

The girl let him out on four and he waited for her to close the cage and start down before he moved. A carved and painted sign arrowed him in the right direction. His hand was easy in his pocket but it was there all right when he knocked at the door.

It was opened and the lecture started, "I cannot understand why —" and then the Sen took in who it was. "It's you," he said.

Sailor had his foot in the door. He grinned, "Sure, it's me." He pushed in past the Sen and left the Sen to close the door. The Sen was a sight, a scrawny turkey wrapped in a black-and-maroon satin striped bathrobe, too good-looking a robe for an old guy. His face sleep-soiled, his thin hair dripping, his mustache towsled.

"You asked me to come, didn't you?" Sailor crossed the room insolently, knocked a magazine and a newspaper off to the floor and sat down in the best bright yellow chair. The Sen said nothing.

"Not bad." Sailor gave the room the eye slowly. It was a big room with twin beds, one of them made up neat with a yellow bedspread tufted in black. The other one was crumpled like the Sen. "I don't have a room," Sailor said. He eyed the good bed with meaning.

The Sen got it. Got it and was needled. He was in good shape to talk business, good shape for Sailor. When the Sen was cold and collected, he was dangerous. He was hot enough now, too hot to talk.

"Couldn't get a room for love nor money," Sailor said. He leaned back in the chair and pulled out the fresh pack of Philip Morris. He took his hand out of his right pocket long enough to open the pack and put a cigarette in his mouth. He was safe enough. The Sen wasn't packing a gun in his striped bathrobe. Nothing but fists in those satin pockets. "Too bad I didn't know you had an extra bed," Sailor said, lighting the cigarette. "I'd have moved in." He blew the match out with a swirl of smoke. "Guess I won't be needing a room here tonight. I'll be on my way."

The Sen had got words together by now. "What's the idea of waking me up at this hour?" he demanded. He tried to be cold and haughty about it but it didn't wash. He was too mad to do a good job.

Sailor opened his eyes wide, like an innocent guy. "You told me to see you this morning," he said. "Didn't you?" he asked when the Sen said nothing.

"I didn't tell you to wake me up at the crack of dawn," the Sen said out of thin lips. "I expected you to wait until a civilized hour." He started over to Sailor and the right hand tightened in the right-hand pocket. Not too tight, just ready in case. "Give me a cigarette," the Sen said.

"Sure." Sailor passed the pack, kept his hand out to get it back. Wouldn't be the first time the Sen forgot to return a fresh pack of cigarettes. When he was young and wide-eyed and thought the Sen was really the sharpest guy that ever strayed off the North Shore reservation, he'd thought that was class. A guy that couldn't be bothered with such trifles. Yeah, that's what he'd thought. He hadn't known how chinchy the Sen was then.

He kept his right hand firm and his eyes steady on the Sen until he got the deck back. He let the Sen find his own matches. The Sen lit up, his hand shaky, and took a lungful. Then the Sen asked him, cold now but the jitters were under it. "Just what do you want?"

Sailor laughed. The Sen wasn't doing so well when he couldn't think of anything better than that. Sailor could afford to laugh at him. He laughed, "You know what I want, Sen. I told you last night what I wanted." He drew in slow and easy on his cigarette. "My dough," he said not laughing.

"You got paid off," the Sen said.

"I got the down payment." Sailor dragged on the smoke, taking his time. "I got five hundred. The price was fifteen hundred. Remember?"

The Sen said through his teeth, "A thousand dollars. It's a holdup." He scowled and paced. Sailor waited until the Sen stopped wearing out the rug, stepped across the room and looked down his long snout. "If I give you a check for the thousand, will you get out of town today?"

Sailor leaned back comfortable. He was easy as if he was rocking in Tio Vivo's gondola. He said, "No." He waited until the Sen bristled like a porcupine, waited until the Sen opened his mouth, then he spoke before the Sen could. He sounded good-natured. "The price has gone up."

He'd struck sparks with that. He'd known he would. He felt like a million dollars when the Sen's mouth dropped open. "Are you crazy?"

"Not me." Sailor's lips twisted. "Maybe I was once but not any more." He punched it. "I want five grand."

"You won't get it," the Sen snapped.

"I think I will," Sailor said. He squeezed out the butt in the sombrero ash tray. He looked the Sen over carefully and he repeated with quiet emphasis, "Yes, I think I will."

The Sen didn't say anything. There were too many words in his mouth and he didn't know which to use first. He was too livid to think fast and straight, maybe he had too many things on his mind or too many memories. He couldn't lay the words out precise and nasty the way he'd have done if he were in the driver's seat.

Sailor continued punching. "I'll get it. And it won't be a check. It'll be cash. Five thousand cash." He looked under his eyes at the Sen. "Seen McIntyre yet?"

The Sen's lips were bloodless, like the lips of a toothless old man. "It's blackmail," he said. There was a spark came into his eye, a nasty spark. "There's laws against blackmail."

"There's laws against murder," Sailor said evenly.

The Sen had the shakes putting out his cigarette, sitting down on the edge of the unmade bed. "What does McIntyre want? What's he doing here?"

Sailor watched him for a minute before he answered. "I don't know," he said. "I haven't talked to him"—the added word was a hot rivet—"yet."

"You were with him at Keen's Bar last night."

He hadn't known the Sen had seen him and McIntyre there. The Sen had been way across the murky red room, the Sen had been with a classy party and the silver-gold girl, the Sen had been drinking too much. But the Sen hadn't been too far gone to spot Sailor with McIntyre.

Sailor said, "Yeah, we had a drink together."

The Sen's mouth curled. "I didn't know you and McIntyre were such friends."

"Sure." Sailor lit another cigarette. The match he struck on his heel made a sharp crack in the silence. "Sure. Known him since I was a kid. One of my oldest friends."

The Sen's adder tongue spit out, licked his dry lips. "What did he have to offer?"

"Nothing," Sailor said. "Nothing at all."

The Sen was forced to press it. Because he didn't know what McIntyre knew or hunched, because he didn't know what Sailor had told the copper. He wasn't really scared as yet because he didn't know what Sailor knew. He didn't have the faintest idea what Sailor knew. Sailor was saving it, hoarding it up for the final punch. The knockout.

But the Sen was uneasy; seeing McIntyre and Sailor together was enough to make him uneasy. He'd have been uneasy enough seeing them together in Chicago. Here in this foreign town it was like whisperings among strangers. The Sen asked, "What did he have to say?" When Sailor didn't answer, the Sen insisted. His voice cracked like dry plaster. "What did he talk about?"

Sailor didn't want to mention her. She didn't belong in this dirty business. But he had the Sen on the skids and he'd use everything to keep him sliding down. "He was telling me about the people in your party," he began. He forced the name out. "About Iris Towers."

The Sen's face went purple. Almost purple. "What right does he have gabbing about her?" He was hoarse with rage.

"Coppers are funny," Sailor said. He sounded like he thought there was a laugh in it. "They think they got a right to be nosy about anybody." He threw it away. "Especially McIntyre."

The thin lips began to weave, to spew whey-like obscenities about the copper. When they stopped for breath, Sailor agreed, "Sure." He yawned. "But you can't argue with the guy in the driver's seat."

That stopped the Sen. It was his own statement, the one he used to hold the boys in line. You can't argue with the guy in the driver's seat. Not if you want to live.

"It's politics," the Sen said. He began to dance up and down the rug again, his skinny hairy legs sticking out one end of his satin bathrobe, his scrawny neck and weasel face out of the other end. "It's nothing but dirty politics. Because I supported Lennie." He took one of his own cigarettes off the bed table. That calculating look was in his eyes. "I'd like to find out just why McIntyre is here. Who sent him."

Sailor knew what the Sen meant. He'd like Sailor to find out. Another job. All work and try to get your pay out of the chiseling Sen.

Sailor smiled. "I got a pretty good idea why he's here."

The Sen took it up quick. "Why?" His suspicions of Sailor and McIntyre drinking together were sticking out all over him.

Sailor said slowly, soberly, "I think he's looking for the man who murdered your wife."

The color went out of the Sen. It oozed away until he was grayer than the grayness on the old lady's face when she used to come home in the gray tired morning. He came out of it quick enough but the color didn't return, not for a long time. He said, "Jerky Spizzoni killed her."

Sailor's heart was pounding. The Sen couldn't know it, on the face of things he was calm and cool as a cucumber. "Jerky's gun killed her," he smiled.

"What are you trying to do?" The Sen's lips lifted nastily. "You know what happened. You testified—"

Sailor broke in, "It looked good on paper."

The Sen's voice faded out. "What do you mean?"

"There was a little hitch," Sailor said. He went at it just as calmly as if there weren't trumpets blowing inside him. He wished Ziggy were here to see the Sen. He wished he'd let Ziggy come along. Only he couldn't. Because even Ziggy didn't know what he knew. He must have had an idea even then that this was going to turn into something good. For him. Hidden down under layers of subconscious it must have been there waiting for something to knock it loose. Something like having to sleep on the ground in a one-horse foreign town.

Ziggy was going to get a boot out of this scene when they met up in Mexico. Ziggy always got a boot out of Sailor's imitations of the Sen; this one would top them all. It would be even better if the Sen hadn't put in his upper bridge to open the door for the package. Well, he could play the scene as if the Sen didn't have his top teeth in. It would be funnier that way.

"There was a little hitch," he said. "Oh, the boys sprang Jerky that night. Just like you fixed it. And Jerky got it in the back later that night. Just like you fixed it." His lips were thin as the Sen's. "Sure, I know Jerky wasn't worth anything to us any more. He'd gone stir-crazy all right. He'd have sold us out for nose drops."

"What went wrong?" the Sen asked through his teeth.

"You couldn't guess," Sailor said good-naturedly.

"I have no intention of guessing," the Sen gritted. "What—went —wrong?"

"Engine trouble," Sailor said.

The Sen was speechless with fury.

"Happened right after they got away. They were starting back to

Chi with Jerky and—engine trouble. Lucky thing though. There was a farmhouse pretty near. So the fellows didn't have to stand out in the rain—remember how it was raining that night?—while they fixed the car. The farmer let them run it in the barn—"

"Why didn't they phone in?"

"The yokel didn't have a phone."

"They could have—"

Sailor interrupted again. "It looked swell on paper. But there were a couple of hours' delay. Too bad you didn't know. In those hours, you called the cops about Mrs. Douglass being killed."

The Sen stood very still. "Why didn't I know about this?"

"The fellows were afraid to tell you." Sailor mock sighed. "They were afraid you might get mad at them."

"Why didn't you or Ziggy tell me?"

"I'm telling you," Sailor said.

He was actually shaking, his skinny little legs couldn't hold still. "Why wait till now? Why didn't I know before I left Chicago? If I'd known—"

"You skipped out too fast," Sailor said reprovingly. "And you didn't leave a forwarding address. Ziggy thought you were in Canada fishing."

"You found me." He was ice cold.

"Yeah," Sailor said. "I found you."

He got dancing mad again. Wiggling back and forth on the rug. "How did you know where I was?"

Sailor laughed. "That's a funny thing. I read it in the *Trib*."

The Sen didn't believe him.

"I did," Sailor nodded confirmation. "On the society page. That society reporter must have somebody out here that feeds her the news." He quoted, "*The popular young Senator Willis Douglass . . .*" He shut up without being told. Laughing soundlessly.

The Sen was thinking. Thinking hard. "Does Mac know about this—hitch?"

"May be," Sailor said. "Ziggy and I didn't know about it ourselves till last week," he admitted. "The boys didn't intend to mention it. But the yokel saw a picture of Jerky in some horror mag and came to town." He snickered. "He was going to tell the guys about the crook who'd been in their car."

"You mean he went to the boys, not the police?"

Sailor grinned. "Humpty was sharp that night at the barn. Told the old boy if he ever came to Chi to drop by his hash house and he'd give him a free spread. Saved himself a tip that way." He sobered. "Good thing he's close with his dough. The yokel was set to go to the cops but Humpty stalled him. Then he and Lew came running to Ziggy."

"What's Ziggy doing about it?" the Sen asked quick.

"Nothing." He smiled at the Sen's open mouth. "He told the fellows to give the yokel a yarn about their finding out and helping the coppers land Jerky. He gave them enough dough to show the guy the town with trimmings. Wear him out and send him home." The Sen's mouth hadn't closed. Sailor said coldly, "Ziggy warned the fellows not to let anything happen to the yokel. He didn't want the case blown wide open by another—accident. He told them to take as good care of the guy as if he were a two-year-old kid." He let the Sen soak that in before finishing up. "Ziggy's blown town."

All the Sen said was, "Ziggy's smart." The phone couldn't have had neater timing. It rang just as the Sen was getting back a little confidence. He picked it up and his, "Hello," was normal.

It was the girl. The silvery Iris Towers. The Sen's voice went into its act, the rich sweet tones rang in it. "Yes, this is Willis. Yes, I was awake." He sat down on the edge of the bed and hunched his back to Sailor. "I'm sorry you waited. I've been delayed on a little business matter. . . . No, I won't be much longer. I'll meet you in the Placita in twenty minutes." His voice was intimate. "Order me a Daiquiri and save my special chair. . . . Goodbye." He hung up and took a moment to compose his face before turning back to Sailor. He started in just as if there'd been no interruption; and as if he hadn't been craven most of the past hour and a half. He even kept his organ pipes turned on for Sailor. He said, "I don't blame you for wanting to get over the border until this blows over. I take it you're heading for Mexico?" He nodded his head briskly not waiting for an answer. "I'll get the thousand for you. I don't know how, exactly, since you refuse my check. You know I don't carry that kind of money on me. The banks aren't open on Sunday. If you can wait until tomorrow—"

"The banks aren't open on Labor Day," Sailor said. Then shut up, giving the Sen all the rope he wanted.

"That's right, tomorrow is Labor Day," the Sen recalled. "Well, I'll get the thousand for you some way. Come back this afternoon, about five, and I'll have it for you. I have to dress now. I haven't had breakfast."

"Neither have I," Sailor said. He didn't budge. He sat there looking over at the Sen. He said, "I told you the price had gone up. It's five thousand now."

The Sen scowled. "You won't get it." His mouth snapped. "You'd better take the thousand and get over the border while you can. You're in no position to dicker."

Sailor spoke softly. "Yes, I am."

The Sen looked at him, trying to read what he meant, sure that it wasn't what the Sen alone knew; wondering if Sailor had sold out to McIntyre, sure that he wouldn't dare; boring into Sailor's impassive face and getting no answer. He rattled Sailor's words in his brain and couldn't get an answer without asking for it. "Now what?" he demanded.

Sailor said, "I didn't kill your wife."

It was the moment he'd been moving up to and the moment was worth the feints and thrusts of delay. The Sen stood frozen where he was. He looked really old, shriveled and old. He was in that moment one with the aged violinist of Tio Vivo. There was only a mechanical shell left.

Sailor said, "I shot at her, yes, but I didn't kill her. Somebody else did it." His voice was quiet but distinct. "Somebody was coming. I had to get out fast."

The Sen whispered when he could, "No one will believe you." He shook his head hollowly. "No one would ever believe you."

"Maybe not," Sailor said. "But I can blast things wide open if I talk. And I'm in the clear, I can talk. Whether anyone believes me or not." He stood up and his hand was so tight on his gun, the fingers ached. He had to get out of here. At this moment the Sen would kill him if he could. Kill him with his own hands, not hire a torpedo.

He walked to the door, keeping the Sen covered with his eye and his pocket. The Sen knew what was in his pocket. At the door he said, "I'll see you at five o'clock." He wouldn't come back here again. Not with the Sen having time to plan. He grimaced, "In the Placita. Have the five grand ready for me by then. I don't care how you get it. Bring me the five grand at five and there won't be any trouble."

He opened the door and swung out, closed it, all in one move. As if the Sen were reaching for a gun, not standing there numb and shriveled and old. As he made his way to the elevators, his hand was still cramped until it ached in his right-hand pocket.

2

HE BUMPED INTO McINTYRE WHEN HE TURNED INTO THE SOUTH END OF the portal. The end where the big fireplace was. He hadn't noticed before but there were Indian figures blasted on the fireplace. In the same sand color as that head he'd seen in the Chicago Museum when he was a kid. He didn't give them more than a quick glimpse because he didn't want to be reminded of that experience. He had too much on his mind without that.

He didn't know exactly why he'd turned there into the portal instead of walking straight ahead, following the side portal to the front door and out of the hotel. Maybe he'd had some idea of sitting down on one of the comfortable leather couches and getting hold of himself. He didn't know why he should have the shakes. Things had gone his way. It had hit him only after he'd sprung the big news, only when he'd known he had to get out of that room, fast, before it was too late. It had been the way the Sen had taken it, like something dead, like a zombie. He'd never seen the Sen like that before. It gave him the creeps.

The mixed-up part was that he knew why the Sen had been hit that way. It was the girl, the lovely clean girl waiting for him in the Placita. The Sen wouldn't have been scared to point of death otherwise. He'd have been the old Sen, crafty and wicked and smart. The mixed-up part was that he didn't want the Sen beaten like that; he wanted the old Sen, the one he'd been waiting to kick in the teeth for months, maybe longer. He didn't want to kick the teeth out of a zombie. All he wanted to do now was run, get out of town quick, not even wait for his dough. Maybe that's why he was heading for the couches, to try to put the Sen back together again the way he ought to be, to forget the wizened old man he'd left upstairs.

Because the Sen would put himself back together again. Sailor knew that as well as he knew his own name. And it was up to him to be ready to met the real Sen, not to carry around the image he had right now in his head.

He was making for the couch when McIntyre spoke to him. McIntyre was sitting on that couch. He said, "Hello, Sailor."

He had to put on an act quick. He had to smile as if the smile weren't cutting his mouth, pull his cramped fingers out of his right-hand pocket and hope McIntyre wouldn't see that they had no circulation left in them. McIntyre who saw everything. He said, "Hello, Mac."

"Been having breakfast with the senator?" McIntyre asked.

Sailor laughed. "Haven't had breakfast yet. Not even a cup of coffee." McIntyre thought he and the Sen were having business together. McIntyre was right but he was wrong. He thought Sailor was here because the Sen had sent for him. It wasn't hard to know what McIntyre was guessing, seeing Sailor coming from the elevators.

He didn't want any trouble from the copper. His alibi was okay and McIntyre knew it was okay. But he didn't want Mac trumping up something to send him back to Chicago. He wanted Mac friendly like he'd been up to now. He might have to spill to Mac yet. He said, "Why don't you come have breakfast with me? In the Placita."

"Make it lunch," McIntyre said, standing up and joining him.

It was too quick. McIntyre wanted something. Might be he was getting ready to move in. Might be the Wisconsin yokel had gone to the police after the fellows poured him on the train. But it was done now. He and McIntyre were walking up the portal. Maybe McIntyre knew where the Placita was. Sailor didn't, he only knew that if he'd see the Sen with the girl again, his fight might come back to him. Rage made a man fighting. He couldn't collect off the Sen unless he wore bare knuckles.

McIntyre walked like he knew where he was going. Ambling but direct. Sailor cut his stride to match. McIntyre was still wearing the silly black hat and the red scarf around his middle. But he didn't look silly. He looked more like McIntyre than ever.

Sailor asked, "Where you staying? Here?" He didn't like walking in silence with a cop.

"Yes," McIntyre said. "Here."

"Pretty swell rooms."

"Not the one I have." He smiled on that.

"How'd you rate a room here during Fiesta?" The tension was going out of him just by walking with McIntyre. Mac was an easy guy to be with.

"Reservation," McIntyre said.

He was a liar. He hadn't made any reservation in advance. He'd come after he'd found out the Sen was here. But the head of Chicago's Homicide would rate a room. Somebody in Chi would see

the Harveys and the Harveys would send word to the Harvey House.
Put up McIntyre. Same way the Sen would rate a room.

McIntyre walked to the doorway of the bar, La Cantina.

"Want an ice-cold Daiquiri?" Sailor grinned.

"Little early in the day for me," McIntyre said. He went on in the
bar though and Sailor went along. "You drinking these days, Sailor?"

"Not me," Sailor said. "A bottle of beer's my speed." He wondered if McIntyre had been watching him last night. That was one
of the dangers with Mac; you never knew when a shadow wasn't a
shadow, when it might be a man in the shadow.

McIntyre walked through the bar. They couldn't have had a drink
if they'd been drinking men; the bar was shuttered with a scene
painted in bright Spanish colors. McIntyre said, "Sunday." He was
still leading and they turned into the Placita, the walled Spanish garden. It was set with white tables and the waitresses were in costume,
flowered skirts, flower-trimmed blouses. This was Fiesta from the
right side of the tracks. On a bench built around an old shade tree
there were Spanish velvet men, girls in shimmering Mexican skirts
wearing flowers in their hair. There was Iris Towers, her pale hair
wreathed in golden roses, her white skirt painted in golden wreaths.
He saw her and the church bells began to chime over the peaceful
garden. The chimes grew to a paean of triumph, the band brassed
into proud sound, guitars and violins plinked merrily. All because his
eyes beheld a fair blonde girl under a tree in an old Spanish garden,
and she was fair, not what he'd been afraid of after this morning.
And the rage was eating him again. And the rage was good but he
mustn't let McIntyre know.

The bells and the music were real; the sound of them came louder
as the parade passed outside the high wall. This time he was on the
right side of the wall where the brightest laughter lay. The Placita
began to fill after the music faded, and the laughter and noise were
more gay. He and McIntyre had a table in the corner by the far wall
where they could watch the entrance, where they could see who sat
at each table. McIntyre had chosen it.

They ordered and they were silent, sitting in white wrought-iron
chairs side by side where both could watch. They were both waiting
for the same man. He came, immaculate in white shirt and white
flannels, a bright sash wound about his waist. He was fresh and
shaven, his hair combed, his mustache brushed. He was neat and he
looked like himself unless you noticed the deeper pockets under his
narrow eyes.

Sailor didn't want to talk about the Sen now. He asked, "Ever drink any tequila, Mac?"

It caught McIntyre's attention but not his eyes. Like Sailor's they watched the Sen make an undeviating path to the tree, to Iris Towers and the velvet men and glittering women with her. They watched the welcome of the Sen, the Sen's suave explanation and regret.

McIntyre said, "Never have.

"I tried it last night," Sailor kept on talking as if McIntyre were interested. "Couldn't say no. Funny old duck that runs the merry-go-round insisted. I'm his mi amigo for some reason."

The Sen and his party were seated at the largest table with the Sen making sure that Iris was beside him. The table was near the one McIntyre had chosen, almost too near. Maybe Mac had known it was reserved for the Sen.

McIntyre said, "It's because you gave some Indian girl a ride on Tio Vivo."

Sailor was shot with cold. Mac was keeping an eye on him. Him as well as the Sen. Only Mac couldn't be after him. Mac was here first. Sailor gave a laugh, a short one. "Checking up on me?"

McIntyre spoke mildly. "I just don't want to see you get in any trouble. I don't want anything to happen to the senator."

He'd been checking to see if Sailor was trying to buy a local torpedo to rub out the Sen. That was a good one on Mac. Pancho, the philosophical old brigand, the man of peace. He really laughed at that. His laughter caught the Sen's ears and the head turned quickly, the mean eyes saw Sailor and McIntyre, turned quickly back to his party. Maybe his hand shook a little as he put a light to Iris Towers' cigarette. Maybe his malevolence solidified.

Sailor said, "You don't think I'm looking for trouble, Mac? I'm here for Fiesta like the rest of you."

McIntyre turned his look on Sailor at last. "You aren't here about Jerky Spizzoni?"

McIntyre knew. Sailor was cautious now, cold and cautious. He wasn't ready to talk. He'd play straight if the Sen played it straight. "What about Jerky?"

"He didn't kill Eleanor Douglass."

Sailor acted surprise. He was careful not to overact. "Who did?"

If McIntyre pointed the accusing finger at him he'd have to spill. Mac didn't. It might mean the same but it was the McIntyre way. It didn't require denials. He said only, "I thought you might know who."

"Me?" Sailor was mildly indignant. "You know damn well I was with Leonard Ziegler all that night in the Sen's office going over the tax books." He and Ziggy had alibied each other for that night and the alibi was sound. No one but they and the Sen knew the way out of the building without passing the elevator guy. Through the warehouse on the other street. Or did McIntyre know?

"That's right," McIntyre said. "You're Senator Douglass' confidential secretary, aren't you?"

"Yeah." I was. Until I found out what a lying, chiseling weasel the Sen was. Then I quit. Fired myself. "I didn't even know Mrs. Douglass was dead till you guys showed up that night looking for Jerky."

"Yes, we found Jerk's gun by the body. With his fingerprints on it. Too bad we never got to talk to Jerk."

"Ever find out who bumped Jerk off?"

The waitress brought them their jellied consommé at last. "Coffee right away," Sailor asked. He smiled up at her as if there weren't anything on his mind. "Got to have breakfast before lunch."

She was tall and pert and blonde. She said, "Right away," and swished her flowered skirts at him.

McIntyre began to eat. "Never did. Plenty who might have."

"Yeah," Sailor said. "He double-crossed every gang in Chi." Including the Sen's. But you didn't call the Sen's a gang. They were employees of the Sen. Because the Sen was mixed up with so many enterprises, not rackets. You didn't call the mugs, guys; they were fellows. If you fellows will do this, or that— The mugs ate it up; they liked being fed their pap with a silver spoon.

"But he didn't kill the senator's wife," McIntyre said. "She was dead before he got to town that night."

He couldn't ask how McIntyre knew. How'd you know that? He acted surprised a little more. "You don't mean it!"

"Yes," McIntyre said. "Senator Douglass telephoned the office at ten o'clock. He'd just reached home and found his wife dead. It looked as if she'd surprised a burglar. It looked as if Jerky was the burglar. His gun and his fingerprints on it. It even occurred to us that he might have planned to kill the senator. You know it was the senator's testimony that sent Jerky up."

"Yeah, I know. And Jerky got himself bumped off that night." The blonde poured coffee from a round glass pitcher. "Thanks,"

Sailor said. He put two spoons of sugar in his cup, stirred it, and drank. Then he started on his consommé. Iris Towers was telling her table something. Her hands were a delicate gesture and her clear blue eyes were like the sun on a blue lake. The Sen laughed just as if there were laughter left in him. When he put his hand on her arm Sailor's eyes snarled again to his soup. "What makes you think Jerky didn't do it?"

"At ten o'clock that night Jerky was just leaving a farmhouse in Wisconsin. He'd been there from quarter of nine on."

Sailor whistled low. The blonde thought he was whistling at her and she came over and filled his coffee cup. He said, "Thanks, doll." He put some more sugar in, stirred it and drank. He said, "Where'd you get that dope? Somebody rat?"

"Strangely enough, no. Mr. Yost, the farmer, talked around to his neighbors and the sheriff heard about it. Sheriff sent him down to Chicago to see me. Nice honest man, Mr. Yost. But slow. If he'd talked sooner about the three men whose car broke down by his farm the night of March twelfth—"

"You found out who sprung Jerky that night?"

"Mr. Yost identified one of them. Johann Humperdink was one of them. The other was probably Lew Barrows. They've both skipped." He was quietly certain. "But they'll turn up again. Or we'll turn them up again."

Humpty and Lew had got away in time.

"You know Humperdink and Barrows, Sailor?"

He finished the jelly soup. "Sure I know them. You know where I come from. I know everybody in the old ward. I've eaten at Humpty's hash house plenty. But they aren't friends of mine if that's what you're asking, Mac." He winked at the blonde as she took the soup dishes. Only because he didn't feel like winking. The Sen wasn't paying much attention to the big blonde guy telling some long-winded tale to his table. Iris Towers had her eyes breathless but the Sen was wondering what Sailor and McIntyre were talking so much about. The Sen ought to be sitting in. Sailor would have felt better to have him here. The Sen could turn things off better than Sailor ever could. The only reason Sailor wasn't walking out on Mac, telling him to go roll his hoop, was because he'd watched the Sen in action. He'd learned some things.

Sailor said, "I'm surprised Humpty was in on anything like that. I always thought he was an honest hasher. Of course Lew had a little trouble in the past. He was in Sleagle's gang once." He was supposed to know things like that. Not because he'd had a little trouble in the past himself. Because he was the Sen's secretary and was supposed to know the guys who delivered the votes in the old ward.

"I was kind of surprised myself about Humpty," McIntyre said.

That was good. That meant McIntyre didn't know too much about the Sen's organization. "You sure it was Humpty?"

The blonde brought a big smile with the salad for Sailor. He could date her up tonight if he were looking for a blonde.

"Positive identification there. Even if he hadn't skipped to clinch it. 'Gone on a vacation,' " he quoted.

"Maybe he did." The salad dressing was right. Sailor knew about dressings because he'd eaten with the Sen in good restaurants. On the Boulevard. In the swank hotels. The Sen and Ziggy were particular about salad dressings.

"He didn't leave a forwarding address. He entertained Mr. Yost a couple of weeks ago, showed him the town. When Yost saw Jerky's picture in an old true-detective magazine at the barber shop, he took a trip to Chicago just to tell Humperdink the kind of guy that had been in his car that night. Yost didn't know Jerky was dead. He'd liked Humpty, thought he was a nice homey sort of fellow. Wanted to warn him before Jerky did him in, or out, of his store teeth."

"Funny the way things happen." Maybe Ziggy'd been wrong letting the yokel go. Maybe it was better this way. If Yost had disappeared in the city, that country sheriff might have caused trouble and none of them would have got away. As it was nobody was in a jam. Only the Sen. McIntyre was watching the Sen, feeding scrambled eggs mechanically into his mouth while he watched the Sen.

"It is funny. It's what makes police business interesting." McIntyre buttered bread. "You never know what will turn up next." He didn't take his eyes off the Sen. "Humperdink told Yost he'd found out who Jerky was the next day. In the newspapers. His story was he'd picked up Jerky hitchhiking."

"Maybe he did," Sailor said.

"Maybe he did," McIntyre agreed. "Maybe Humpty is on a vacation." He wiped his mouth with the big orange square of napkin. "But Jerky didn't kill Mrs. Douglass."

"I guess you're right there," Sailor nodded.

"Somebody did."

That's what McIntyre intended to find out. Who did. That's why he was here. He must have something more than hunch to be here wearing a red sash and a toy Spanish hat. Something more than a fifty-thousand-dollar insurance policy.

"I'd like to meet Senator Douglass," McIntyre said.

"You mean you haven't met him?" Sailor wasn't pretending surprise.

"Not for a long time." McIntyre smiled, a true smile. "They don't send us department roughnecks to interview someone like the senator. The commissioner handled him when Mrs. Douglass died."

The flowered skirts brought a painted menu. "Dessert, sir?"

He wanted dessert but he wanted more to get away. Before McIntyre asked the wrong questions, the right ones. He waited for the cop to answer. McIntyre deliberated. The Sen's party was still at their table and Mac said, "I'll have some peach pie and more coffee."

"Make mine a chocolate sundae." He might as well eat. He couldn't tell Mac he had important business to be about. Mac knew he didn't have a thing to do but walk the streets.

The Sen said something to Iris Towers and she slanted her eyes up at him and the smile on her mouth was the way you wanted a woman to smile at you. The way you didn't want a woman to smile at a murderer; not a young, beautiful, untouched woman.

Sailor said harshly, "I'll introduce you."

"I thought you might." McIntyre was matter of fact.

"I'm meeting him here, in the Placita here, at quarter after five. You turn up and I'll introduce you." Fifteen minutes was all he needed alone with the Sen. If the Sen didn't come through it wouldn't be bad to have McIntyre show up.

"I'll be here," McIntyre said.

The blonde brought the desserts, wrote out the check and put it in the center of the table. Sailor took it up.

McIntyre said, "Better let me have it. I've an expense account."

"Not today." He could afford to buy Mac a lunch. Mac was helping him to get on easy street. Someday when he had a hotel of his own like this down in Mexico, he'd invite Mac down. Everything on the house. Mac wasn't a bad guy. He wondered if Humpty and Lew were in Mexico. He didn't want to go on with the old set-up. He wanted to be strictly on his own. No cuts. Though Lew was about the best trigger man in the business.

McIntyre said, "Got a room for tonight?"

He didn't want that question. Mac mustn't get a hunch that Sailor was leaving tonight.

He said, "Yeah, I'm okay for tonight."

McIntyre finished his pie. He said, "Funny the senator didn't have a room for his secretary last night. It's almost as if he wasn't expecting you."

Sailor put a fiver on the check. Then he had to wait for change. Wait and try to think up answers for McIntyre. The cop was closing in. If he said the Sen wasn't expecting him it was like telling Mac he'd come running to bring the Sen the news about Jerky. If he said the Sen was expecting him, there would have been a reservation for him unless he and the Sen were split. That would mean the Sen expected him to bring trouble.

He laughed it off, repeated the old gag. "I didn't come on business. I came for Fiesta." He lit a cigarette, drew on it, passed the pack to McIntyre who shook his head. "I didn't know you had to make reservations in a one-horse town. I wasn't as smart as you."

The Sen and his party were still at the big table when he and McIntyre went out. They passed so close behind him you could see the hairs on the back of the Sen's neck prickle. The Sen was scared. He should be.

They left the Placita, walked through the empty bar into the lobby. Sailor said, "See you at five-fifteen, Mac." He didn't want to carry the cop with him all afternoon doing nothing. He left McIntyre standing there and walked out of the hotel like he had some place important to be in five minutes. When he got outside he slowed down. It wasn't two o'clock. He had more than three hours to kill. And nowhere to go.

The sun was baking hot on the little street. He walked slowly across to the Plaza. Into Fiesta.

The street that fenced in the square was littered with papers and the remains of food and horse dung and children dragging bright costume skirts. There were kids riding burros and other kids tagging after for their turn. There were two ragged boys in jeans selling rides on a big roan horse. Enough kids waiting on the curb to keep the horse busy till day after tomorrow. The merry-go-round was whirling full speed, the tinkling music lost in the clattering mass of kids pressing against the palings, shouting to be next. Over the heads of the crowd he could see Pancho's muscles bulging, his back aching, sweat bathing him as he endlessly turned the windlass. The counters of the little thatched booths were all jammed. On the bandstand a Mexican band blared through big metal loudspeakers. It wasn't all kids jamming the square, old and young, babies squalling in arms, white beards spitting tobacco on the walks; old women, middling women, younger women gabbing Spanish at each other; gangling youths and painted girls eyeing each other, exchanging provocative insults, working up to night and the lawn of the Federal Building.

There wasn't a place to sit down. Every inch of curb, the concrete wall around the small memorial shaft, even the corner steps that led into the square were packed tight with people. You had to step over them to get back into the street. Sailor stepped over a woman with a baby sucking at her breast, to get out of the stifling square into the street again. To escape the trap of Fiesta. He escaped and he looked back at the box.

At Fiesta. At the crowded little park, hung with faded banners and grotesque masks and colored electric-light bulbs strung on wires. Smelling of chile and pop and dung and cheap perfume and sweat and diapers; chaotic with music and laughter and screams and insults and jabber and crying kids. For this Zozobra had burned. So these people could believe that this tawdry make-believe was good. He slanted through the jostling, careless street strollers and reached the opposite curb, stepped over more people to stand under the portal of the museum. This too was crowded, too crowded to fight through. The costumed and the city visitors, uncostumed—he'd been here long enough to spot the stranger—were blocking sidewalk traffic, bending over the Indian wares spread on the walk.

The Indians alone were not a part of the maelstrom. They sat against the wall, their bright calicos billowing about them, their black eyes inscrutable, ironic. They sat in silence, not speaking unless spoken to, not offering their goods, selling if asked, their brown hands exchanging goods for money with amusement if not scorn. Because they knew this to be make-believe; because in time these strange people did not exist. Pila was once a child sitting here with almond black eyes, inscrutable as her elders and as aloof. Sailor couldn't push through the crowd, he managed to twist back to the curb, to step over the heads of the curb squatters into the street.

He couldn't spend three hours fighting this Fiesta saturated mob. He couldn't spend three hours on his feet. The sun and heat and the lunch he'd put away combined to hit him with the full weight of his weariness. He wanted only to lie down and sleep.

He knew it was hopeless but it was something to do. There was always a chance. He made the rounds again of the hotels. It was to no avail as he'd known it would be. There were no rooms. There wasn't even a vacant chair in a lobby or on the Cabeza de Vaca porch. The only thing the round trip availed him was, for a brief spell, to get him out of the stench of Fiesta. But he returned to it. With a hopeless kind of fatality, because there was no place else to go, because all directions led to the Plaza.

The streets were whirling louder, faster; on the bandstand a fat black-haired singer blasted the microphones and the crowds screamed, "Hola! Hola!" as if it were good. A running child with remnants of pink ice cream glued on his dirty face bumped into Sailor's legs, wiped his sticky hands there. Sailor snarled, "Get out of my way." A balloon popped behind him and the kid who held the denuded stick squalled.

He had to get out of this. His feet burned and his eyes ached and his nose stunk. If he could reach Pancho, the brigand would know somewhere he could rest. He'd know a cool quiet bar that opened its back door on Sunday. A bar with cold beads on the beer bottles and without any Spanish music. He rammed through the revelers until he was on the outskirts of the solid phalanx surrounding Tio Vivo. Twice as many as before. He was stopped there. Kids were unyielding in mass. Or too fluid. If he advanced past one child, six more cut in front of him, jabbing elbows and knees in him, wiping the dirt of their hands and feet on his neat dark suit. The kids were like ants. They multiplied as he stood there. They were terrifying; he knew if he should be knocked over in their rush, they would swarm over him, devour him without knowing or caring what they did. Pancho was as far away from him here as if he were marooned on the Wrigley Tower.

He turned away, more frightened than angry. If he didn't find a place to rest, he wouldn't be fit to face the Sen at five. And without warning his eyes came against the eyes of Pila. He had the same shock he'd had last night when he first looked upon her. The same remembrance of terror, of a head of stone which reduced him to non-existence. His first quick reaction was to turn away, not to recognize her. But he could not. She was there. She existed. He was the one without existence, the dream figure wandering in this dreadful nightmare.

She was there, in the same bedraggled flowered skirt, the same blouse in which the embroidery had run in savage purple and red streaks. Her black hair hung straight down her back and the red flower was falling to her temple. She stood motionless. She didn't speak to him. But her eyes, black and empty and wise, were on his face as the blind stone eyes once had been.

He said roughly, "Hello."

She said, "Hello." Her mouth had been painted like the mouths of Rosita and Irene but she's smeared it somehow, pop or hot dog or chile, not man; it stained her face as the embroidery stained her blouse.

He said, "Want another ride on the merry-go-round?"

"No," she said. She didn't offer any explanation but the flicker of her glance at the churning, pushing children was Indian. It was the look in the eyes of the fat calico women sitting silently against the museum wall, aloof, disdainful of the vulgarians who pushed by.

Pila didn't say any more and he started past her, wanting to get away, away from the nightmare and the recurring figure in the dream of this girl woman, of stone made flesh. And then he laughed, laughed harshly at himself for letting a hick carnival get him down. Him, a Chicago mug, getting nerves because a dumb Indian girl didn't know how to talk slick. She wasn't a spook, she was a gift from Heaven.

He went over to her and he grabbed her arm. "You've got a room, haven't you?" he demanded.

She looked up at him blankly.

"You've got a place to sleep, haven't you? A bed?"

She said, "Yes."

He tightened his hold on her arm. "We're going there now," he told her. He began walking her through the crowd, not caring who he bumped or shoved. "How far is it?"

She said, "About a mile."

"We'll take a cab." He pushed her out of the Plaza and Fiesta, to-wards the frame shack where the pink neon sign had flashed taxi last night.

They were in luck. An old black sedan, dented, scaling, loose-jointed, was pulling up in front. Sailor knew it was a taxi because the word was stenciled on the door. "Come on," he said.

She wasn't pulling back but he could feel the reluctance pressing through her arm. He repeated, "Come on," and she spoke then. "I cannot take you to this house."

It was he who was stopped cold. Before they reached the cab. He didn't know how much he'd counted on that hour in bed until her refusal sharpened his want. "You can't, can't you?" His demand was ugly. "Why not?"

She stood unmoving where he had released her. Like a sack of flour; like something hewed from stone. She wasn't moved by his anger, neither troubled nor embarrassed nor curious. She repeated without any inflection, "I cannot take you to this house."

"Why not?" he demanded again. "What's the matter with 'thees house'? Don't you think I'm good enough—" He began to laugh then. He thought what she'd probably been thinking since he'd grabbed her in the Plaza.

He laughed, "For God's sake, Pila. I don't want you. I just want a place to sleep for a little while." She was as safe with him as she'd be behind the convent wall. He didn't knock up fourteen-year-old kids. He didn't want her; he wanted her bed.

He stopped laughing because of the look on her face, the older-than-time look. It wasn't the look of a floozie like Rosie and yet he knew that if he'd wanted her he could have had her. As easy as he could give her a pop or a ride on Tio Vivo. He was no more important to her than that.

He wouldn't have her on a bet. Because he was uneasy, he blustered, "You don't need to worry about your old man knocking you around."

She said, "My father is at the pueblo."

He didn't know what a pueblo was or where but he knew from the way she said it that her old man wasn't around town. She didn't have to worry about him turning up. It wasn't that bothering her. Not understanding made him mad. He demanded, "Then what's eating you? Let's go."

She parroted, "I cannot take you to this house."

He was really mad by now. He was good enough to buy soda pop for her but he wasn't good enough to take home. He might not look like any prize package at this moment but he was still good enough to go to an Indian shack. He said, "Okay. If that's the way it is. Skip it." He swung away from her up the street, not having any direction in his head, only to get away from a snotty Indian kid who didn't think he was good enough to take home. He pounded on the broken bricks of the sidewalk, ignoring the presence on the walk of Fiesta.

He walked on, away from the Plaza, anywhere to get away from the gilded muck, from people who thought they were happy because they were all dressed up in ribbons and bobbles, eating hot dogs and chile, drinking pop, listening to plinking music. The smoke of Zozobra's pyre had blurred their eyes; they believed their cry "Old Man Gloom is dead" meant just that, that a word could be fact by the act of being spoken.

He was halfway up the street when she brushed his shoulder. He hadn't known she was following; it came as a surprise, a dirty surprise. He was savage, "What do you want now?"

She said, "I will go with you."

He didn't stop walking. He said, "Scram. I don't want you." He hit his heels harder on the walk, as if he were thumping her. It didn't send her away. He felt the brush of her brown arm against his sleeve. "Beat it," he said.

He might have been talking at the stone woman in the cold corridor of the Art Museum; not to a kid, old and young, on a dirty village street in a sun hot foreign town.

He stopped on the corner and faced her. "Go on," he said, "beat it."

It had been a mistake to look at her. Because looking at her he saw her eyes, her expressionless black eyes. He'd been afraid she might be about to turn on the weeps the way he'd talked to her. He hadn't expected her to look just the same, so terribly unchanged, as if he weren't there. She said, "I will go with you."

He could have threatened her maybe and got rid of her. But he didn't. All of a sudden it didn't matter whether she came along or went away. It had no more importance than that; no more importance than his existence had to an Indian.

He crossed the street and walked on past the filling station, past the big house walled to the eaves, knowing she walked with him, not knowing why, not caring. He cut across beyond the big house, across to the sound of music over by the big building set in an ironfenced park, the Federal Building. He hadn't meant to go there. But when he reached the walk encircling the park he turned in at the iron gate, set ajar, into quiet greenness. The music somehow went with the quietness. It wasn't good. It was nasal and plaintive, four adolescent boys lying there on the grass, singing in harmony, "Adios, mi amigo, adios . . ." It might have been the song, the song Pancho had sung, which made it sound good in the hot afternoon with the grass smelling sweet and cool under the big trees.

He walked across the graveled paths, away from the music, to a spot alone where the singing was a fainter quiver. He flung himself down on the spired grass. He didn't look at Pila; he knew she was beside him. The sun sprayed through the tree leaves; heat cooled by greenness to a good warmth. He took off his hat and put it over his eyes.

Pila said, "I would not take you to this house. You would not be welcome."

"Sure," he said. "Sure." He'd got it a long time ago. She didn't have to draw a picture. He didn't give a damn now. He was comfortable, a lot more comfortable than he'd be in a flea-bitten adobe dump.

"You would not be welcome because I bring you to this house. Because you come with an Indian to this house."

He shifted the hat, enough so that his eyes could see her although she could not look under the brim shadow at him. "What they got against Indians?" he demanded. "They're Indians, aren't they? Your uncle and aunt?"

"My uncle, yes. He marry with a Spanish woman—Español—my aunt she is a Spanish woman. She, her people, do not think the Indians are so good as the Spanish people. If I take you to this house they will say you are a friend of a dirty Indian."

"To hell with them," he said. Zozobra was dead and everybody was down on the Plaza acting like they were all friends, Spanish and Indian and Mexican and Gringos. But the real Indians were sitting under the portal of the museum and the rich Gringo sonnama beeches were safe behind the garden walls of La Fonda and the Mexicans were remembering they'd once been the conquerors of this land and there wasn't any brotherhood between them even if it was Fiesta. It didn't mean anything to him; he was an outsider who'd wandered into this foreign land; all he had to do was finish his business and get out. He wasn't losing any sleep over Pila and her folks.

He pulled his hat down over his eyes. "How come you're staying with them?"

"It is very good of them to let me stay with them for the Fiesta."

He couldn't tell if she was sarcastic or not, her voice didn't have any inflection. Nor her face. He didn't bother to look.

"I must cause them no trouble. It is good of them to let me stay there." She was repeating what someone had told her. "I have not been so lucky before. I must not bother Rosie."

Drowsiness was green all around him, green and grass-smelling and sun-warm. Her light voice and the singing of the lazy boys all blurred together.

There was no period between waking and sleeping. He slept. Nor was there a period between sleeping and waking. He woke. He pushed away his hat. Pila was still sitting there, cross-legged beside him. She might not have moved in the interval.

The sun had moved. It slanted low over the lawn. He yawned,

"What time is it?" He looked at his watch. Four-thirty. The gun was hard in his pocket.

He had slept and he was revived. She had watched over him while he slept. He sat up, punched his battered hat in shape. "Thanks. I needed that." He could finish the job now.

He stood up and stretched. A dash of water in the face, comb his hair and he was ready for the Sen. Maybe not as spruce as he'd be on Michigan Boulevard but his hand was just as steady. He said, "Come on." They walked out of the park.

Pila said, "You slept so long you missed the parade."

"What parade?"

"The De Vargas parade. It is a big parade. I could hear the horses and the music."

He scowled, "Why didn't you go to it?"

"You were asleep," she stated.

"What the hell—" he began.

She said, "I did not want you to be alone while you sleep."

He shook his head. "Did you think something might happen to me?" She didn't know he carried a gun. "I can take care of myself any time."

Her voice was soft. "When I am in a strange house I do not like to be alone while I sleep."

He shut up. Feeling a little queer inside. Because she'd said it, said he was a stranger, said he wasn't he in this strange house. That he couldn't take care of himself in this alien world. He needed a guardian, even if it was just an Indian kid.

They could see the Plaza from the street they took, hear the muted music, the human sounds over it. They scuffed through litter, walking the last block in silence. When they reached the museum he stopped her.

"You can't go with me now," he said. "I got business." He felt good. Because he'd been wrong thinking she was hostile to the stranger; she was his friend. "Meet me later at Tio Vivo and I'll buy you a flock of rides." He felt better than he had since he boarded the bus in Chicago. "If the deal comes off I'll buy you anything you want. What do you want more than anything else in the world?"

She said solemnly, "A permanent wave."

He was still laughing as he swung away from her, cutting across the Plaza, to the hotel, and to the Sen.

3

IT WASN'T MORE THAN A FEW MINUTES PAST FIVE WHEN HE CAME UP
from the men's room. He'd washed up, brushed himself off as best
he could. He didn't look as if he'd been sleeping in the park. The
patio was filled but quietly; a few, not many persons milled in the
lobby. He started towards the Cantina. Started and didn't dare turn
aside when McIntyre rose up to meet him. Mac hadn't any business
being here yet. It wasn't time for his appointment.

McIntyre said, "Hello. You're early."

"A little." It hadn't occurred to him that Mac would be here waiting. He didn't know what to say to the cop. He couldn't tell him to
beat it until his own private confab with the Sen was done. He had
to carry Mac with him. Not knowing if the Sen would join him if he
saw the cop there. Not knowing how he'd get rid of Mac for the necessary moments alone.

"Going in now or wait for him here?" McIntyre asked.

"Might as well go in," Sailor said. He laughed a short one.
"Maybe he's still in there."

McIntyre followed Sailor this time. He said, "He isn't. He and his
party left about two o'clock."

McIntyre was watching close. Watching the Sen as close as he was
watching Sailor.

Sailor asked wryly, "You been counting noses in the lobby all afternoon?" But he wanted to know.

McIntyre said, "No. I took a nap."

Were McIntyre's eyes knowing? He couldn't tell. Did McIntyre
know he'd been sleeping up on the Federal lawn?

He asked ironically, "You haven't been doing Fiesta?"

McIntyre chose the table again. Not in line of the entrance this
time. Around in back of the tree where the Sen would have to look
for them. And finding them couldn't act as if he hadn't seen them.
McIntyre was smart as hell. He even chose the chair he wanted, putting Sailor's back to the entrance, placing himself where he could
glimpse anyone coming in. But the branches of the tree hid his face.

"I caught a bit of the parade," McIntyre said, "but I decided to
skip the Chocolate. Not that it didn't sound peaceful but the fashion show with it—" he shook his head. "I didn't think a guy like me

would be any asset." He smiled. "Mrs. McIntyre will be mad at me for missing it."

He'd never thought of McIntyre having a Mrs. McIntyre. He'd never thought of McIntyre having any life but on the Chicago streets. Like a dog. Smelling out trouble, trotting after trouble, digging up old bones of trouble. Until the commissioner boosted him to a desk and a leather chair. Where he could rest his nose and his feet, send other cops out to follow trouble.

Sailor said, "I didn't know you were married."

"Eighteen years," Mac said. "Have one girl in college this year."

The waitress who came to the table wasn't pretty or young; her mouth wore tired lines and she didn't care that they weren't ready to order. She left the table and stood with another waitress by the open-air fireplace. The pert blonde wasn't around.

Sailor said, "Sure you don't want something?"

"I'd take a drink. This Sunday law is a hindrance. To a working man."

"I could use a beer." Then he grinned. "Thought you were here for the show."

"That's right," was all McIntyre said. "What did you do this afternoon?"

"Took a nap," Sailor said like Mac had said.

McIntyre didn't ask any questions. As if he knew where. But he didn't know if he too had been sleeping. Sailor didn't want Mac to know. He didn't want to have to explain that he hadn't been laying with an Indian girl; that she had tagged after him, that was all.

There were a few parties in the Placita, drinking parties. None of the Sen's crowd. The parties had brought their own bottles; the men pulled them out from under the tables like in prohibition days. The waitresses brought set-ups. The Sunday law evidently didn't cover drinking, only selling of drinks.

Sailor said, "I wonder if he went to the Chocolate." He could see the Sen's greedy eyes watching dressed-up girls trot by. No. The Sen would be watching Iris Towers. No one else. But his eyes would still be greedy.

"No. He went to Tesuque to a private affair."

It surprised him again, that McIntyre was keeping that close tabs on the Sen.

"The Van der Kirks' ranch," McIntyre said. "They came over during the war and stayed. Not poor refugees. Diamonds."

Not poor if the Sen were there. The Sen didn't visit the poor. He used them. For his dirty work.

"Will he get back in time?" Sailor wondered aloud before he realized it was out loud.

"I think he will," McIntyre said. "I think he'll be anxious for you to tell him what I was talking about at lunch."

Sailor pulled in his belt. "I can't talk to him with you sitting here."

"I'll tell him myself," McIntyre said without inflection.

If he could only bust open McIntyre's head, see what was inside it. If he could only lay out those little squares, like lottery tickets, each one labeled with a name and a thought and a plan. Was his name on the winning ticket, the losing ticket; or was it the Sen's? He couldn't ask McIntyre; he could only sit tight and wait. And make talk.

"How many kids you got?"

"Two girls and a boy." Talk suited McIntyre. He too had to wait.

McIntyre would live in a suburb, Evanston probably. A nice house, maybe white pickets, maybe a green hedge. A green lawn and trees and flowers; Mac cutting the grass on a summer Sunday, shoveling snow off the walks on a winter morning. Mrs. McIntyre in a tiled kitchen fixing him and the kids good dinners.

"Patsy, the oldest, she's the one in college. University of Chicago. Molly, she's the pretty one, still in High. She wants to be a criminologist." He smiled at memory. "Ted's only twelve. Eagle Scout this year. Scouting's a good thing for boys."

"So is being born in the right part of town," Sailor said.

McIntyre said quietly, "I was born four blocks from where you were, Sailor."

He hadn't known that. Long as he'd known Mac, he hadn't known he came from the old ward. His mouth twisted. "How did you get out?"

"Not any easy way." His eye was on Sailor.

"You think I came out easy?"

Mac didn't answer that. He said, "I joined the force when I was twenty-one. That was twenty years ago, twenty years last spring." He kept his eye on Sailor. "It isn't easy pounding pavements summer and winter. Lots of work, little pay in those days." His mouth tightened. "What I grew up with down there, from the time I was a kid, made me want to make the world better, not worse."

Sailor said belligerently, "Your old lady didn't scrub floors, I bet. I'll bet your old man wasn't a drunken sot."

"My mother worked in a laundry. My father in the yards. No, he wasn't a drunk, Sailor." His eye was steady. "I've wondered often why with what you went through, you didn't grow up feeling like I did. Wanting to make things better, not worse."

"I've made them better for me," Sailor bristled.

McIntyre didn't say anything. He just looked until Sailor moved his eyes, pulled out his cigarettes. Sailor said to the cigarettes, "I don't owe the world nothing. It never did anything for me."

McIntyre said, "I've heard a lot of you say that. It's always seemed to me you were blaming the world for something missing in you."

"What are you trying to say?" Sailor scowled.

"The world doesn't care much what happens to us. Least that's the way I've always figured. Like this table." He flattened his hand on the painted metal. "It doesn't care if you bump your shin on it. It doesn't even know you're around. That's the world. The way I see it." He lifted his hand and looked at the palm as if the paint had smeared it. He had a broad hand but his fingers were thin. "It's up to you what you are. Good or bad. You get the choice. You can do anything you want to with yourself. You can use the world"—again he touched the table—"or you can break your toes on it. The world doesn't care. It's up to you." He smiled faintly. "Seems I tried to tell you that a long time ago, Sailor."

Sailor said out of his scowl, "Maybe you think I chose to be starved and beaten when I was a kid."

McIntyre's eyes saddened. Briefly. "I guess kids can't choose. Not while they're kids." Then he looked straight into Sailor. "But when you're old enough for choice, it's up to you. The right way or the wrong way. Good or bad."

"You think I chose wrong." Sailor was casual, drawing on his cigarette. "You think I shouldn't have let the Sen help me out? Send me to college. The U of Chicago like your kid. You think maybe I ought to have pounded the pavements like you instead of letting a good guy help me out." The Sen had been a good guy once. Sailor wouldn't be where he was today if the Sen hadn't given him a lift.

McIntyre said, "There's a lot of old stories, might be true, about a man selling his soul to the Devil."

Sailor jerked back his head and laughed. A good long laugh as if it were funny. Mac just sat there. And it wasn't funny. The Devil could look like the Sen. The Devil didn't have to have red horns and a forked tail and a red union suit; he could have a big snout and a brush mustache and wear the best clothes in Chicago. The Sen was a devil. If Mac knew half what Ziggy and Sailor knew, he wasn't just shooting off his mouth, Sailor said, as if it were still funny, "As long as you're preaching, Mac, what about God? He's supposed to take care of us, isn't He? That's what they used to tell me at school. God'll take care of you."

Mac said, "I don't know." He spoke slowly, like he was thinking it out. "Maybe it's like it says in Scripture. You can choose between God and the Devil. Good or bad. Right or wrong. It's written that way, more than once in The Book. I'm no preacher, Sailor. You know me better than that. But I see a lot of the wrong way. Makes a man think. The only way I can see it is that maybe God doesn't want those that choose the Devil. The Devil's own they used to call them. Maybe He withholds His hand, waits for them to turn to Him. To decide to go right, not wrong." He added it so quietly he might have still been thinking. "Want to tell me where the senator was the night she was killed?"

It was like something not real, sitting there in the quiet walled garden with the sun slanting through the crooked branches of the old green trees. Something in a book, Mac talking about God and the Devil and right and wrong. With a funny hat on his head. Not preaching but talking like a preacher only straight, a man to a man, not set up high in a pulpit talking to too many people and most of them not listening. Most of them having a Sunday-morning snooze. Then Mac said it and he was a copper again. A smart copper, catching you off guard. Only when he said it his face put on its mask suddenly and Sailor looked where he was looking. The Sen was there. The Devil in a white shirt and white pants and a red sash. And a vicious look that went from his eyes so quickly you wouldn't believe it had been there.

The Sen was looking for Sailor and he was caught by the eyes of Sailor and Mac before he could act as if he were looking for someone else.

He tried not to be caught. He nodded as if he were greeting an acquaintance. Sailor spoke fast, knowing he had to grab onto the Sen before he faded out for another night. Even knowing how the Sen would be when they were alone, he spoke. "Hello. Thought you weren't coming," he said.

That was when the viciousness fleeted through these narrow dark eyes.

McIntyre took it over fast. He said, "I hope you don't mind my intruding, Senator. I asked your secretary if he'd give me an introduction to you."

The Sen was caught. He stood there while Sailor said, "This is Chief McIntyre, Senator Douglass. From Chicago too." As if the Sen didn't know.

The Sen sat down then, as if he were brittle, as if he might break if he sat down in the white metal chair. But his tongue was smooth the way it could be. "I've heard a lot about you, Chief. Seems strange we'd travel across the country to meet, doesn't it?" His smile was right.

"Yes," McIntyre said.

"I'd offer you a drink but the bar's closed. As you know, doubtless." He took his cigarette case and passed it. McIntyre took one. Sailor didn't. He wasn't offered. "You here on business, Chief?"

"Partly," McIntyre said. He accepted a light from the white-gold lighter. The lighter that never sputtered, that always made a good pointed flame.

The Sen touched it to his own smoke. He acted surprised. "A little far from your bailiwick, isn't it? It must be important for the Chief of the Bureau to handle it."

"It is important," McIntyre said. "It's about the death of your wife."

The Sen didn't show any surprise. He just looked properly solemn. Solemn and a small bit touched with grief. He didn't say anything. He could act; he was good at acting. But when he was acting, he wasn't safe. He was too sure of himself, on top. Sailor didn't like it. He kept his eyes under his lids on the Sen. He could keep them there because the Sen wasn't paying any attention to him. This was between the Sen and McIntyre. The Sen finally put surprise and curiosity into a question. "Really?"

"Yes," McIntyre said.

"But—" The Sen touched ash to the tray. McIntyre didn't help. The Sen had to go on with it. "I thought you did a splendid job in solving her tragic end so quickly."

"We thought so too," McIntyre said. "But Jerky Spizzoni didn't kill her."

The Sen looked properly shocked. He could have said a lot of different things then but he didn't. He was smart. He waited.

"That's why I'm working," McIntyre said. "I'm looking for the man who killed her."

The Sen took that and mulled it. He said, "It's hard to believe. The commissioner was sure—"

"New evidence," McIntyre cut in. "Spizzoni didn't get to town that night until after she was killed."

"The gun— The fingerprints—" The Sen acted innocent as hell. He fumbled as an innocent man would.

"Somebody had Jerky's gun. With his fingerprints still on it. It was smart," McIntyre admitted.

He didn't know how smart it was. Ziggy had taken care of that. Visiting day. Ziggy had told the Jerk somebody wanted to buy his gat; to put a price on it.

Jerky had handled that gun every day before he was sent up. When he was shipped, the Sen had made sure the gat was tucked away in a clean handkerchief, that no one else touched it. Maybe the Sen had known then. Maybe that was why Jerky had been sold out.

"Have you any leads?" the Sen asked.

Mac took his time. "I wouldn't exactly say we had," he admitted. "I thought maybe you could help us out. Maybe you knew something that might give us a lead."

The Sen shook his head. "I wish I could." He put out the cigarette, half-smoked. "As I told the commissioner that night, I knew of no one who wished harm to my wife. She had no enemies. She wasn't a woman who could ever make an enemy." His eyes looked moist. When his voice made music that way, he could turn on the waterworks. "I appreciate your coming so far to tell me of this, McIntyre. I'd like to go over it with you more thoroughly." His wristwatch was bold and expensive, a platter of gold that looked like platinum. "Right now I must dress for an engagement. Perhaps after Fiesta, or are you leaving before then?"

"I'm staying for Fiesta," McIntyre said. "Might as well as long as I'm here."

They were both getting up and Sailor got up too. He followed them out of the Placita, through the dim bar into the lobby. He didn't know what they were saying, he tagged like a mongrel. In the lobby they were bowing goodbye. The Sen said, "Sailor will give you any information you need about that night. He knows the details. We've been over them often. In fact I don't doubt he knows more than I about the death." That was the undercut. There might have been others. "You'll excuse me now."

He wasn't getting away with this run-out, not if McIntyre's whole bureau were standing with fixed attention. The dough was to be ready now. He wasn't going to get away with not paying off.

Sailor said, "I'll go up with you while you dress." The lips pulled back over the Sen's teeth but Sailor continued, "There's some stuff to go over." And his hand was cold and hard in his right pocket. He wasn't afraid. The Sen wouldn't dare pull anything in the room right now; not with Mac knowing the two were going up there.

The Sen said brusquely, "It can wait till later."

"This is new stuff," Sailor said. That did it. Because the Sen didn't know what Mac might have let out at lunch. He couldn't take a chance. "You'll excuse us then?" he asked McIntyre.

"Yes," McIntyre said. "I'll see you later."

The Sen's skinny legs were ill-tempered. They pecked the portal flagstones. Sailor swung easily at heel. Neither spoke until they reached the elevator, had to wait for the descent of the cage.

The Sen said, "What else did he have to say?"

Sailor didn't answer because the elevator was down and some swells in blue-white hair and a lot of glitter were coming out. They had a speaking acquaintance with the Sen and he put on the platform manner automatically. He could always do it. Give him an audience and it didn't matter what was knocking him out, he performed. As soon as he was in the elevator, behind the little elevator girl's back, he put it away. But he didn't repeat the question, not until they were on the fourth and outside his room. Not until he had put in the key and was pushing open the door. "What else did McIntyre have to say?"

Sailor stood behind him while the Sen picked up the two telephone message slips off the rug, read them before folding them tight in his palm. Sailor walked when the Sen did. The Sen went over by the telephone table. Sailor took the good chair, settled in it, his hat on his head, his hand comfortable in his pocket.

"He was wondering about the insurance."

The Sen forgot the telephone. His black eyebrows were a tight angle. "What about it?" he demanded.

"Nothing," Sailor said. "Just wondering. Maybe he'd like to know how long you had that policy on her. That fifty grand."

The Sen sat down slowly. On the edge of the bed. "So that's it," he said. He read the messages again. One he slid in his pocket, the other he held in his hand. As if it were warm and living, a warm white body.

"I don't know," Sailor said. "I don't know what the angle is. All I know is he's looking for the guy who killed your wife."

The Sen's eyes were mean little slits. "He doesn't have to look far."

"No, he doesn't." Sailor kept his look steady on the Sen. Steady and with meaning.

The Sen shifted his shoulders. "You'd better get off to Mexico. Right away. I can let you have five hundred now. I'll send you the other five hundred when the banks open—"

Sailor laughed at him. Laughed hard and harsh. "It's five grand, Sen," he said. "Not five C's." He was suddenly mad. He'd had enough waiting. "Don't you have it yet?"

"No, I don't." The Sen got mad too. He was like the old Sen when things didn't suit him. "The banks are closed. I can't pick five thousand dollars out of thin air. Or even one thousand. You'd better take the five hundred now and get out of here. Before Mac finds out you're the one he's looking for."

Sailor's mouth was easy. The words came out of it easy. "I didn't kill your wife."

He liked the way the Sen's mouth opened. Like a fish. He liked the fury that stiffened the fancy white shirt. He even liked hearing the Sen's voice grate across the space between them. "You tried that one last night. If you didn't kill her, who did?"

Most of all he liked his own soft answer. "You did."

The Sen wasn't shriveled with fear yet. Because he didn't know yet what Sailor knew, how much he knew. He thought it was an accusation, no more. He thought he could afford to pull his lips up in a sneer. "You won't get anywhere accusing me."

Sailor said, "I think I might. If I told Mac the whole story." He lit a cigarette, let smoke snort out of his nostrils. "Jerky wasn't the only one whose plans hitched that night."

The Sen didn't know of knowledge yet. But he burned. "You mean you had car trouble too? You were late?" He didn't believe it. He was refusing to believe it.

"Uh-uh," Sailor said. "She was." He let the Sen have it now, have it both barrels. Now was the time. "I got there the time you told me. Storm and all. I did it just like you said, pulled things around to make it look like a loot. And I had the lights out when the taxi drove up outside. Just like you planned it."

He was remembering it as he spoke. Not with any emotion, like something he'd seen in a picture show sometime. Kind of a dull picture. The Sen's library there at the front of the house, books and couches and a desk. French doors opening out to a little yard. He'd come in the French doors like the Sen told him, they were easy to open. His hands gloved. Good grey suede gloves, soft, expensive. He'd pulled out papers from the desk, opened the wall safe. Like he was Jerky looking for blackmail and maybe a haul of easy dough.

"I had Jerky's gun all ready to let go when she came in. Only she didn't get there the time you counted on. I guess she couldn't get a taxi for a while account of the storm. She came in just like you said she would, front door, with the key she hooked. Only she hadn't hooked a key; it was hers. She wasn't Jerky's dame. She was Mrs. Douglass."

The Sen's mouth was so thin, the brush mustache hid it. He opened it only a slit to speak. "And so you killed her by mistake. But I protected you. I knew you never would have shot her if you'd known. It was an accident, a bitter accident."

"That's what I thought, then," Sailor said. Carefully he lit another cigarette from the stub of the first, not moving his tight right hand from his pocket. "There was a big slash of lightning right after I fired and I saw I'd made a mistake. An awful mistake." He pulled in a lungful of smoke remembering the dread moment. The tall gray-haired woman, the horrified surprise on her face as she fell. "I didn't know what to do." Letting out the smoke fogged the small mean figure sitting there on the bed, sitting like a mummy not a man.

"I didn't know what you'd do. I started over to her, to see if I could do anything for her—" The remembered moment was stark again. "I heard a car come in the drive. I dropped the gun. And I got out quick."

The Sen said again angrily, "I took care of you. I didn't mention you to the police. What's the point of all this?"

"The timing was wrong. You got home too soon. That was your car. I was outside the window."

The Sen's rigidity was electric.

"She wasn't dead. She was pushing up, trying to get up. You picked up the gun and let her have it. You had your gloves on."

The Sen began to curse him, to curse and revile him with obscene eyes, a toneless throat. But the Sen didn't move. He knew he was covered by Sailor's right-hand pocket.

Sailor waited until he was quiet. "I'm no killer," he said. "I never killed anyone only in self defense. You knew you couldn't hire me to kill your wife. You needed a triggerman. But you didn't dare put one of those fellows on anything that important. I believed your bull about getting rid of Maudie Spizzoni before she landed us all in the Federal pen. I thought about it like it was self defense. She wasn't any good to anybody. Even so I wasn't a killer. I didn't want even to kill Maudie cold like that. I wouldn't have done it only for the chance to do something on my own. Only for the dough." If Mac hadn't talked like a preacher . . . "All right, so it was wrong. I shouldn't have said I'd do it. But I didn't know it was your wife you wanted killed." His teeth were bare. "And I didn't kill her!" He caught hold of himself. "All I want is five grand and you won't ever see me again. Mac won't ever find out what you and I know."

The Sen snarled, "It would be your word against mine."

"Mac's not looking for me," Sailor said. "He's looking for the guy who killed your wife. The guy that got fifty grand for killing her." He said harshly, "Five grand isn't much."

The Sen didn't know what to say. There wasn't anything he could say, he was caught. The way all the fellows hoped and knew he'd be caught some day. But none of them ever thought Sailor would be the one to catch him. Sailor never thought so.

"After all I've done for you." He'd turned on the music in his pipes. "Taking you out of the gutter. Educating you like you were my own—" The phone spoiled his art. Interrupting as it had earlier today. It rang short, then long. The Sen looked at it the same way Sailor was looking at it, as if it had no business sounding. As if its intrusion were insolent.

The Sen reached out a withered hand. He said, "Hello," and was silent. Sailor knew who was calling. The hopelessness that came over the Sen was the hopelessness of the damned. Even her voice couldn't help him at this moment. He listened silent. When he spoke his voice was dry, old. He said, "I'm sorry. I'll be down right away. I'm sorry, Iris." There was no caress in the name. He replaced the phone.

Sailor said, "Well."

The Sen moved unsteadily. Standing up from the bed, standing there as if he were a blind man in an unfamiliar room. Sailor's hand gripped tight in his pocket. But the Sen only began to unbutton his shirt. He said, "You've got to give me more time."

Sailor was silent.

"I promised my friends to go with them to the Procession. I have to dress and shave." He might have been talking to himself, telling himself what was on his mind. "Dress and shave." His eyes wavered across to Sailor. "You've got to give me more time." He was querulous as a child. "The banks are closed. Tomorrow is a bank holiday. Labor Day. I can't do anything until Tuesday."

Sailor stretched up from the chair. He was as sure and cold as steel was cold before a hand hotted it. "You got friends," he slurred. "You're a big shot. You're Senator Douglass." His voice cracked like a whip. "I'll give you till midnight."

"I can't—" The Sen was going to whine.

Sailor cut him off. "Midnight. By Tio Vivo"—he translated—"the merry-go-round." Pancho for bodyguard in case the Sen came out of his trance. "I don't want Mac in on this any more than you do."

He walked sharp to the door while the Sen was pulling off his shirt. While his claws were caught in satin cuffs.

"I won't go to Mac unless you want me to." Sailor gave the Sen a sudden grin as his left hand turned the knob.

The Sen's lips moved. He forced the word through them. "Guttersnipe!" It was more evil than the obscenities had been.

4

HE WOULD HAVE SAT DOWN IN THE LOBBY. ON A COMFORTABLE BROWN leather couch. Only he saw a Spanish hat with bobbles there. It wasn't Mac but he remembered Mac. He walked out of the hotel. He didn't want Mac around him tonight. While he was watching the Sen. The Sen wasn't going to run out on him this night. The Sen wasn't going to get by with any monkey business.

He took his stand outside the display windows, next to the entrance arch. There were painted tin platters in the windows, kids' chairs with red and blue roses daubed on them, a hideous wooden saint holding out a bleeding wooden hand, a couple of fat yellow painted pigs. A hodge-podge for the La Fonda rich guys to take back to civilization, to remind them of the Fiesta visit in a foreign country.

He could stand there; no one cared. There were people standing all over the streets, leaning against shop windows, tired of making merry, tired of the music and the dance and the gimcracks, tired of a three-day Feast before the second day was done. Tired, just tired. In the feet and the eyes and the guts, leaning like warm wax against the windows and walls. The Plaza spun on in its tawdry tinsel cage. But it was tired too, the children's voices on the merry-go-round were

muted, the violin and guitar were faint music, even the leaves on the
tall trees were still. Everything was quieted in the weary twilight. He
could stand there as long as he wanted waiting for the Sen. With no
one paying attention, no one knowing him, no one caring that the
man in the rumpled suit with the hat pulled over his eyes was holding a gun in his pocket.

Before the bells began to ring, he saw the shawled women moving
towards the cathedral. He saw the gray stone mass of the cathedral
overshadowing the little street, the purple clouds piling behind its
squat towers, the black-shawled women and the children dangling
from their hands, the church yard filling with men and women and
children, quiet and dim as ghosts. Sunday night. Vespers and benediction. The old lady used to slip off and go to vespers when things
weren't too tough at home. The old man never went. By Sunday
night he was sitting around in his dirty stocking feet, bloated with
beer or red-eyed with whisky. The kids wouldn't go to vespers, all the
kids in the neighborhood went to the movies on Sunday evenings.
But the old lady wanted to go, and she'd come home looking rested,
almost as peaceful as she did years later when she was dead.

When the bells began to ring the cathedral doors opened like a
kid playing church-and-steeple with his hands. Standing there Sailor
could see into the lighted nave, see all the way to the altar with its
burning candles. He didn't know vespers were part of Fiesta, not
until the Sen came hurrying towards the church. He almost missed
the Sen in the depth of twilight and him watching the shadows gathering on the church terrace. He might have if she hadn't been beside
him.

He followed the pale white froth of her skirts. Even as he followed
he didn't believe they were heading for the church. Catching the
Sen in church would be like catching the Devil in a prayer book.

He almost didn't keep on when they walked up the steps towards
the open doors. He hadn't been inside a church since the old lady
died and he didn't want to go in one again. A lot of pious talk, a lot
of praying, a lot of that turn-the-other-cheek, love-your-enemies stuff.
Nothing about how to get out of a Chicago slum into the Gold
Coast. He'd learned that in a pool hall. The church had never done
anything for him.

But he followed. He wasn't going to lose sight of the Sen. The Sen
didn't know Sailor was trailing, there were too many in the church
yard besides him. The Sen went on in as if he weren't something to
be exorcised with holy water. Sailor let some of the crowd go first.

When he got inside, his eyes found the white mist, the silver-gold hair, down in front with the wine velvets and gold chains. The black velvet beside her was still the Sen.

Sailor slid into a back pew where he could watch them. The cathedral was big and tall and wide, dim even with its lights. It looked old and sanctified. It wasn't packed but it was pretty well filled. A lot of fancy costumes, yet it wasn't all Fiesta. There were the mourning women in their black dresses and black shawls. There were men in old jeans and blue work shirts; and old men in their Sunday bests, their netted brown faces peaceful under their white heads. There were brown children kneeling rigidly, like wooden images.

He didn't pay any attention to anything but the white-and-silver girl down in front. She belonged here; she was something holy, like one of the altar candles, like an angel. He didn't pay attention to the altar. There were priests up there chanting the litany; their white-and-gold benediction vestments draped over the red velvet chairs. There was a choir of seminarians singing. Singing the responses. Their faces were foreign like the town; brown Mexican faces, somber, and their voices, unaccompanied, were like a heaven choir. He didn't care about that. He hadn't come here to pray; he'd come with a gun to keep his eye on a rat. He wasn't going to be sucked in by holiness. He kept his mind and his backbone rigid when the golden censers swung the musk-scented smoke, when the organ and choir blazoned together the O *Salutaris Hostia*. He got on his knees only because everyone else did, because he didn't want to be conspicuous. Even the Sen was on his knees down there in front.

He didn't know why the dim perfumed cathedral didn't belch the Sen out of its holy portals. But looking down the long aisle to the lighted altar, up to the high vaulted roof, he did know. The church was like the stone of its walls, like the stone of the woman. It was too strong, too fast, too great to be aware of a small crawling thing like the Sen. The Sen was dwarfed to unimportance, he was without identity here.

God on the high altar could strike the Sen down in his mockery of prayer. God wouldn't. God had infinite patience. He had infinite mercy. He had infinite justice as well. The finality of Justice. Someday the Sen would pay.

The choir's voices lifted in the *Laudate* and everyone rose. It was over. Sailor was ready to get out quick, to take his stand near the door, shadowed, to watch the Sen and the girl leave. But a monk in brown robes was speaking from the altar. Something about the formation, Sociedad this, Sociedad that. The ushers were passing candles. The Sociedads were lifting painted satin banners on golden poles. The church bells began to ring out above the organ. Outside a band faltered into a hymn.

Sailor slid over to the side pew. A pillar protected him from the eyes of those moving up the aisle. The old men and the little children. The rich and the poor. The alien and the native, the magnificent and the black shawls. The monks and the choir and the Sociedads, a slow-moving, silent procession to the open cathedral doors, out again into the night. Candles flickered like fireflies from all the vasty corners of the cathedral. When the Sen and the girl passed, Sailor moved up the side aisle fast. But he couldn't follow. He had to wait to press into the line; balked, impatient, he had to wait. By the time he reached the open doors he had lost the Sen, lost him completely in this, the Procession to the Cross of the Martyrs. The town had been blacked out, no neons, no shop fronts, candle flame alone, flickering from the hands of those who walked to the cross. Down the long street rounding the Plaza, he could see only the twin lines of moving light in the unaccustomed depth of dark. The silence was deep as the dark; silence deeper than the choir chant, the somber hymn of the band, the tinkle and strum of the tamed Mariachis breaking their hymn against the brass, the shuffle of feet. No voices.

Sailor fell in with the right-hand line, his lighted candle in his left hand, his right hand where it belonged. He didn't know when his candle had come to light. As in a dream he remembered a Spanish voice speaking while he had been blocked in the side aisle. Beyond that no memory.

He maneuvered forward in the line because he knew how, because he'd trailed men before and in Chicago crowds. Snaked forward until he saw the white girl again, in the left-hand line, forward. The width of street separating, and the dark. The Sen was behind her.

The slow procession wound the Plaza when even the garland-colored bulbs that crowned Fiesta were dark. Around the square, turning up the wide lightless street where last night the cacophony of Keen's Bar had smeared the night. Those doors too were dark, shuttered. Up the street, past small wood fires burning at the intersection, to circle a park and its dark massive building. The Federal Building park where the girls and their chosen had lain last night. Deserted now. Another narrow street lit by small fires and candle flame, a bridge ahead, across it the pinpricks of light winding up a hill, clusters of candlelight atop the hill. Against the sky, a wide white cross. The sky was blue black as the night, the stars were distant, flickering like the candle flames. Across the band of naked horizon a zigzag of lightning ran through far violet clouds. And a wind came up as out of the lightning, wavering the candles.

Sailor couldn't see the Sen as he toiled up the hill but he could see the misty white skirts. He kept his eye on the skirts. The Sen's velvet was blacked out in the night. He wouldn't lose the Sen if he watched Iris Towers.

He hadn't known there would be such a crowd until he too reached the top of the hill. This wasn't just for church people; this was Fiesta and everybody of Fiesta was there. He'd lost the skirt and he had to push through massed humanity before he found its whiteness again. There was a brown monk standing up in front of the cross talking through the loudspeaker. Talking of an ancient vow. The vow Don Diego de Vargas Zapata Lujan Ponce de Leon had made when he reconquered the ancient pueblo of Sante Fe. The old unforgotten vow.

Sailor didn't care about old vows, about old Spanish and Indian wars; he'd lost the girl in the shifting of the dark, candle-pricked mass. He edged quickly towards where he'd last seen white and again the veil of it fluttered behind a blurred wall of man shapes. As he shifted to keep the white in his view, someone's elbow caught him under the shoulder bone. He growled, "Watch where you're going," but his words were broken by a sword of lightning cutting the sky. In the flash he saw the face of the girl in white. It wasn't Iris Towers.

Impotent rage filled his mouth and with it the pain thrust. A shaft of pain under his shoulder. With the pain the lightning of fear. He dropped his lighted candle as if it burned. His hand went slowly under his coat, touched the pain and returned to sight. The hand was wet with blood. He'd been knifed. He swiveled slowly, ready to kill, his trigger finger itching to kill. Behind him were the brown listening faces of grave men and women, their eyes lifted to the monk at the white cross. They hadn't seen who'd jostled past in the crush. You didn't turn around and catch a knifer wiping blood from a blade. Only a dope would expect that.

Only a dope would seek in the quiet brown faces a face with secret triumph on it, with the laughter of hate distorting it. Would, with the pain thrumming now, stalk the silent circle of faces for a face. Sailor's hand gripped the gun and the force opened the slant wound. He felt the flesh pull apart, felt the slow trickle of blood. Whoever

had cut him, behind him in shadow stood the Sen. This was the
Sen's answer to Sailor's demand. He should have expected it. He
should have known the Sen wouldn't wait to bring out his killers
from Chicago; he'd use the local thugs. Every town had its killers;
the Sen knew how to find them. The Sen knew all the root paths of
evil.

He had to get away from here, before someone noticed. Before
someone got officious and stuck him in a hick hospital, before the
police got nosey. He swung his eyes again to the white skirts; it was
still the wrong girl. The Sen and Iris Towers were lost in candlelight
and darkness and a sermon at the cross.

He made his way warily out of the crowd, alert to danger in back
of him, at his side. If the lightning hadn't cleaved when it did, rocking him forward in the shock of the wrong white skirts, the knife
thrust would have been deep and true. It wasn't meant as warning;
the Sen didn't give warning. Death in the back; a gun for Jerky, a
knife for Sailor.

If the lightning hadn't cleaved when it did, he would have killed
Eleanor Douglass. The Sen's own hand had had to kill. Because of
rage in the heavens. The Sen wasn't going to get a chance to take
care of this failure. Sailor was clear of the crowd now and he
scrambled down the stubble of the hill, no longer a target, hidden by
the hill. He wasn't bleeding much; not enough to be weakened. All
he needed was a patch and he'd be ready to meet the Sen. That was
the only thing he wanted, to meet the Sen face to face.

At the foot of the hill he looked back upward. Nothing stirred but
candles in the wind and the mockery of white skirts. He walked on
over the bridge, down the dark street where the bonfires flickered
into reddened ash. The sky was lit again with lightning and in the
distance thunder threatened. The monk's voice, distorted by microphone, followed him.

He walked on, not too fast, not wanting movement to harry the
pain. Around the dark circle of the Federal park, shying at the few
couples he met. The heavy trees held in their boughs the glitter of
candles from the hill but were lost as he went on, lost with the echo
of the metallic voice.

Shadow and silence rested heavily on the Plaza. Under the portal
were the mounds of Indian women, their cigarettes reddening the
dark, fading, glowing. He didn't know who might be hidden among
them. He cut swiftly across the square and headed towards Tio Vivo.

Only then did he realize this was the haven he sought. Pancho would fix him up.

The square was as deserted as if the ghostly hand of Zozobra had smote it. But the way was small and he was outside the faded red palings. The locked fence. He cursed then. The unease he'd experienced the night before on the dark unfamiliar street ran in his veins. That quickly it came, the feeling of one lost, alone in an alien deserted world. He cursed it away, shaking the padlocked fence, fearing to climb over its height lest the gap under his shoulder widen.

Lightning flickered again in the hidden sky, and with the thunder rumble, the deeper thunder. He wasn't alone; under the canopy Pancho snored.

He called out, his voice too loud in the silence. "Hey, Pancho. Pancho!" He didn't expect to wake the sleeping hulk; he was afraid to shout too fully, afraid of the shadowy silence. But the snore choked in Pancho's throat and the man rose up, alert as an animal stirred from sleep. "Who is it? Who calls Pancho?"

"It's me. Sailor. Let me in."

Pancho groaned up from the earth, scratched his belly and his lank black hair as he plodded to the fence. "It is Sailor. Waking a poor old man from his little rest. *Pancho! Pancho!* Waking a man from his slumbers, por que?" He unfastened the gate, grumbling as if he meant it, his face a caricature of sleep, his eyes awake, lively.

"I need some help." Sailor walked through the gate, waiting within for Pancho to fasten it.

"Que pase? You have another muchacha for whom I must wear out this old arm?" He had turned again to Sailor and the jest went out of his mouth. Out of his merry eyes. "Por que?" he repeated but it was question to be answered now.

Sailor asked, "You know any doctors? One that doesn't ask foolish questions?"

"Doctors. For what is a doctor?"

"Somebody scratched me."

Pancho's eyes were pinpoints. "The police?"

"They aren't in this. They aren't going to be. What about a doc?" He was impatient. The pain was slitting him.

"The police are not looking for you?"

"For God's sake, no," Sailor snarled. "They don't know anything happened. Somebody stuck a knife in my back while I was up there watching the show—"

Pancho had interrupted lazily, almost happily. "It was a knife."

"What'd you think scratched me, a pin?"

The big belly joggled. "You are so funny, my friend, the Sailor. A pin?" He went off into fat giggling anew and the jut of pain under Sailor's shoulder twisted. The black eyes slit soberly at the rage gnarling Sailor's lips.

"Perhaps I think the gun in your pocket met with a friend, no?" He was reassuring. "The police will not bother about a knife. Certainly no. A gun, yes. A knife, it is nothing."

Sailor gritted the words. "What about the doc?" The old brigand would stand here gabbing until the Plaza filled up again, until there were eyes to notice a wound in a dark coat. He'd stand blatting until it was time for him to crank up the merry-go-round. And Sailor biting on pain, pushed around by a bunch of kids, bleeding away the strength he needed to take care of the Sen. He put it all into the question, "What about the doc?"

Pancho hitched up his pants. "You come with me. I will take care of you, my friend. You need not be disturbed." He unlocked the padlock, carefully locked it again after them. "We will be back before the sermon it is over. The little abuelita will make you good like new." Thunder cracked his words. He shuffled his feet a little faster. "Yes, we will be back soon enough unless it should rain." He eyed the sky. "A little rain and the sermon it will end more quickly." He shrugged. "But no one will ride Tio Vivo in the rain. I do not think." He smiled complacence. "Besides it does not rain in Fiesta. Not often. Zozobra is dead. It will not rain."

Sailor walked beside him. He didn't give a damn about rain or sermons, all he wanted was someone to fix him up, fix him enough that he could meet the Sen tonight. His lips pulled back from his teeth. Maybe the Sen thought he was dead by now. Maybe the Sen meant to be awfully surprised when he showed up at midnight and no Sailor met him. He could see the Sen looking for Mac in the hotel lobby, wondering to Mac what had happened to Sailor. Snickering that Sailor was probably lying with a girl and had forgotten to show up. It was Sen who'd get the surprise. Sailor would be there.

He hadn't attended the way Pancho was leading. Any more than he'd been listening to what Pancho was saying. The streets away from the Plaza were dark; Sailor recognized nothing until Pancho said, "This is where we go." Familiarity was shock. For they stood on the dark alien street where he had strayed the night before. Returning here now was the fearsomeness of a bad dream. A dream of wandering in a labyrinth, of being unable to escape from the murky maze, of returning over and again to this unknown yet terrifyingly known place. Pancho's big hand was on the closed wall. He said, "Come. This way, my friend."

He did not see the rejection on Sailor's face. The dark masked all but shape. Pancho opened a gate in the wall, bent down and squeezed through. Sailor moved after him. If this was the trap, and it was a trap, he could not refuse to enter. The whole town was a trap. He'd been trapped from the moment he stepped off the bus at the dirty station. Trapped by the unknown, by a foreign town and foreign tongues and the ways of alien men. Trapped by the evil these people had burned and the ash had entered into their flesh. That evil the Sen had seen and known and used. In Chicago he wouldn't have had a knife in his back; he would have been alert to Sen treachery. Now he was following a brigand into a box from which there was no escape. Only by shooting it out. The Sen would be waiting inside. There was no way to surprise the Sen; Pancho's bulk crunched loud across the sandy courtyard towards the small lamp shine at the rear. No way to walk quietly after Pancho, only to grip the pain and the ready gun. Pancho knocked at the low door, stooped to enter. Sailor, his temples wet, followed.

The Sen wasn't there. It must have been part of the bad dream to expect the Sen in this dump. He must be running a fever. Pancho was his friend, mi amigo; the Sen couldn't buy Pancho away from him. He must have been nuts.

Pancho saw his face. He was gentler. "You are afraid? Do not be afraid. A knife it is nothing. I have many times been scratched with the knife. It is nothing. Nada!"

Sailor said, "I'm not afraid." He couldn't explain why he wasn't afraid now. He couldn't tell Pancho he'd been nuts. He looked at the room. A low room, rigidly clean, rigidly barren. An oil lamp on a bare wood table, bare wooden chairs; a bench of plaster, part of the wall. There was a small fire, piñon scented, in the little fireplace. A gaunt crucifix above it. The woman on the low stool before the fire was older than time. Shriveled, scant hair more colorless than white, her brown scalp shining bald through it—she sat there without words, without life, even in her eyes. Her gums mouthed a cigarette, as brown, as withered, as lifeless as her face, as her needle-thin arms. Pancho crooned over her. In Spanish; Sailor heard nothing but the repeated abuelita; the pantomimic cuchara, cuchara mas grande. He could catch the drift of it; Pancho was describing a great knife battle. But he wished Pancho would stop performing and get the old lady to fetch the doctor. He hurt.

Pancho turned back to Sailor. "It is all right," he beamed. "The little abuelita will take care of you. Let us now see the scratch."

Sailor stepped back. "Wait a minute." Suspicion webbed his face. "Where's the doc? I want a doctor."

Pancho's whole body grieved. "For why you want a doctor? I bring you to the little abuelita. She will take care of you. Because I ask it. Because you are my friend."

He didn't want a witch woman mumbo-jumboing over him. He wasn't a spic; he wanted a doctor. He wanted to be fixed up.

Pancho's grief quivered his lip. "You do not wish the abuelita to help you? She knows better how to take care of the knife cut than any gringo doctor could ever learn to know." His eyebrow cocked slyly. "Besides the gringo doctors might tell the police."

The pain was cutting hard. Something had to stop it quick. Pancho was probably right; the old witch would know all about knifings. She hadn't moved; she hadn't even appeared to understand what Pancho had said to her. Sailor reluctantly let Pancho help him slide off the coat. He unbuttoned his shirt; it was Pancho's hand that eased it away from the wound. Pancho turned him to the fire where the old lady could see the damage. If she was conscious. If she was anything but a grass-stuffed dummy, set before the fire to dry.

Pancho gave a rumble of joy. "It is nothing! Like I say, nada."

The croak was the old woman. "Nada." It must be her dirty spike of finger probing the pain. Sailor cursed between his teeth.

Pancho danced about to face him. "A scratch. A pin. You were right, my friend. Nada!" He beetled his brows into Sailor's face. "You do not worry now about the abuelita? Look!" He ripped off his dirty shirt. His big finger jabbed the scars on the grimy sofa cushion of his chest. He turned his back, feeling for the welts. "This one," he jabbed. "And this one, how deep! But always the abuelita fix me up good like new."

The finger had stopped, only the fire heat licked at the sore. Sailor hadn't heard her leave the room; he didn't know she was gone until she returned with no more sound than a ghost. She carried a dirty wadded handkerchief. He watched her spread it on the table, watched her old twig of a finger pry into the stuff there, brown and withered old weeds like herself. Herbs! A knife in his back wasn't enough. He had to come to an old herb woman to get it fixed.

Pancho scoffed. "You are not afraid. You are a man." Thunder quavered across his voice and the lightning flickered like firelight across the room.

"No, I'm not afraid," Sailor denied. But the jumps in his stomach shook his muscles. He wasn't afraid of anything where a gun was good. But a gun wasn't any use now; you couldn't turn a gun on the germs of a witch woman and her seed bags and her spittle. You could only stand and take it, take the leap of pain, take her grunts and Pancho's encouraging, "Now it is good. Muy bueno. You will lie down and sleep, tomorrow you will not know there was an arroyo under your shoulder."

"Sleep where?" he scoffed. Pancho was helping him on with his shirt.

Pancho rubbed his big nose. He scrubbed at it and as if the thought sneezed out, he cried, "But where? Here with the abuelita. Always she has a room."

Sailor stopped him. "Thanks. But I can't go to bed. I'm seeing a guy later. Business deal. Give me a hand."

Pancho eased the coat on him. "It would be better you sleep—" He shut his mouth at Sailor's decision. "Okay," he said cheerfully. "You do not have to sleep. A bottle of tequila—that is as good as sleep." He directed. "Give me a dollar for the old woman."

Cheap enough. One dollar for a first-class infection. But the pain already was easing. He handed over a rumpled dollar to Pancho. He stood at the door while the two of them gibbered Spanish, Pancho's loud and bright, the old woman's a mutter. He waited, watching the lightning run with the wind across the barren patio. Waited until Pancho said, "We must go. We are now late."

He followed to the street, the dark, silent, known and unknown street. Walking into the whirlpool of wind towards gimcrack music and flowered lights. He asked, "What about the tequila?" as they breasted the bar of Un Peso. A burning drink would put the bone back into his spine.

Pancho slapped his pocket. "Why you think I need the dollar?" he gurgled. "The little abuelita has the worthless son. He brings from Mexico the best tequila."

"You mean you didn't pay her for fixing me up?"

"For that, it is nada," Pancho shrugged. "Who would not help a poor traveler who has been hurt?" His lips pursed. "Quien sabe? It might have been the worthless son who sharpened the knife."

"What for? Why would a guy I've never laid eyes on want to knife me?"

Pancho said gently, "Why you carry a gun?" He didn't want an answer. They were entering the Plaza, the Plaza with lights again garlanding it, with music strumming the whirling pink and green and purple horses; with the wind gyrating the smoke from the chimney pots of the little chile booths. He remembered how long since he'd eaten but he didn't want food. He didn't feel up to food. The couples, the men and women and children and sleeping babies over tired shoulders were seeping into the Plaza. The prize package which had held vespers and procession and sermon at the cross was consumed. They were buying another box of crackerjack now. Fiesta Sunday evening on the Plaza. In the bandstand the Conquistadores in their shapeless old-fashioned uniforms blared out of tune into the loudspeakers. The lights above the bandstand blazoned the faces circling it, the faces as still and remote as they had been in church or on the hill. In the distance was thunder.

Pancho said, "We are a little late. It does not matter. Ignacio can make Tio Vivo lively enough. Not so good as me. But good enough till I get there."

He lumbered over the paths; Sailor let the big man break trail. Outside the palings, Pancho pushed through the children to the fence. "Vaya, vaya, chiquitos! Out of my way, you little scrubs." His big hand lay on the gate.

Sailor touched his arm. "Mind if I sit inside for a little? To get my breath?"

Pancho's head thrust around, quick and anxious. "It cut deeper than we think?" He scowled. "You come inside, yes. You must rest. You should have this night a bed."

"I'm okay," Sailor grunted. "I can't go to bed until I get my business finished."

He went inside with Pancho. The string-bean Ignacio wound the crank while the old man made thin music on his old fiddle. Pancho spouted Spanish at both as his great hands took over the windlass. Ignacio plucked quickly at his guitar. The music quickened. Pancho sweated and heaved and Tio Vivo became Uncle Lively anew.

There was no place to sit but on the ground, on the bunch of dirty blankets that was Pancho's bed. Sailor let himself down before he fell down, he was lightheaded as if he'd just got out of a hospital bed. The earth was good and solid to feel. He lit a cigarette and leaned on his good elbow. Then he lay back, his head crooked on his good arm. Above and around him Fiesta spun and sang and made laughter. He knew he was drifting away from it, knew and didn't care. It wasn't his Fiesta. These hicks thought it was something special. They should have seen the Chicago World's Fair. That was a show. He was thinking about the World's Fair when sudden panic came upon him and he fought to hold to this small tinkling square. He wondered in his panic if he were dying, if he were drifting out of this unknown into a vaster unknown. But he couldn't hold on; whatever purpose the witch woman had in her withered skull, it was stronger than he. The fog of blackness closed Fiesta away.

5

HE MIGHT HAVE BEEN CONSCIOUS THE ENTIRE TIME HE LAY UNDER THE blackness. He heard the sound of Fiesta the entire time or thought he heard. And he thought he heard roar of thunder and splash of sheeted rain; he thought Zozobra's evil ghost had returned to spoil the fun.

All of this was in the dream, if it were dream, and he a mite floundering through the storm, trying to push through the blackness to the tinkle of music and shimmer of flower-like lights which grew beyond. When he fought most furiously he found he could open his eyes and he was lying where he had lain, on Pancho's dirty blankets. The merry-go-round was motionless, save for the sway of one gondola, the one where Pancho sprawled contemplating his own bare toes.

Sailor sat up, brought his wrist quick to his eyes, remembering as he moved that he should move warily. But there was no sudden pain, no pain at all but a vague smarting under his shoulder blade. The herbs weren't half bad. And it wasn't yet midnight, only a bit after eleven. He stretched up to his feet, picked up his hat from the earth, dusted it and set it on his head.

"Hola!" Pancho said. "You feel better, my friend?"

"Feel fine." He swung over to the gondola, leaned on it. "Business over early?"

"For me. The little ones must get some sleep. Tio Vivo does not stay open late like the saloons and the movie pictures." He removed his feet for Sailor to sit down. "Besides there was a little shower."

He hadn't dreamed. The wetness of rain smell was in the night. Sailor said, "I'm hungry. I don't know when I've eaten." Besides there was nothing to do in this dump to kill time waiting on the Sen but eat and sleep.

The bandstand was dark and only a drift of people was left wandering under the heavy wet leaves of the tall trees. In the street, there in front of the museum, a group was singing. "Ai, Yai Yai Yai," they sang, and they danced while they sang, a country dance, lively as Tio Vivo. Their laughter scrawled across the quiet Plaza. Behind them, against the museum wall, was the dark frieze of the Indian women and children, scornful in their immobility. *Ai, Yai Yai Yai* . . .

"How about a little food, Pancho?" There was time before the Sen.

"I think yes," Pancho said happily. He stuffed his feet into the dust-colored shoes, let the frayed laces dangle. "We will go to Celestino's booth. His wife, she makes the most fine chile on the Plaza."

Sailor had meant food, a steak and French fries, maybe a piece of cherry pie to top it. He didn't say anything. Maybe he was too tired to walk farther than the nearest thatched booth. As if Pancho held to his hand, he followed the brigand. Pancho was smarter than he. They could keep an eye on the merry-go-round, could see any stranger who approached it.

They sat on a wooden bench, sat in a welter of smells, garlic and onion and chile and cheese, coffee, fried beans and garlic and chile. Pancho bellowed flowery compliments at the woman behind the counter by the hot coal stove. She was big and billowing, black-eyed, black hair bound with a kerchief, a white apron, specked with chile red, over the billows. Sailor knew Pancho was being flowery from the toss of her head and the flirt of her black eyes. She wasn't young, her breasts were big with suckling, her arms were soft and brown but muscled like a man's. And her eyes were bright as a girl's. She was giving Pancho good as he gave her. He turned good nature to Sailor. "For me and you, my friend, Juana has fix the finest of enchiladas. And frijoles with the best chile."

"And coffee," Sailor said.

"And coffee. Fresh tortillas she will make for me, and for you because you are my friend. I tell her we do not want the slop she feeds the touristas. We are hungry men." He drummed his fists happily, sang in echo, "Ai yai yai yai . . ."

Sailor said, "You get around, Pancho."

The big man giggled. "I have known Juana since we were little fellows. And that Celestino, that no good. Drinking sotol with Ignacio when he should be washing the dishes for his good esposa. He is my primo, is Celestino. Primo—how you say—my cousin."

"You get around," Sailor repeated.

Pancho growled content. The woman's hand slapped the thin, round, white-and-blue tortillas. She sang, "Hoopa, hoopa, hoopa—" Her bare hand flipped over the tortillas on the hot range.

"Maybe you can find out who knifed me."

Pancho's face was round and innocent as a baby's. And as sad. "I should know that?"

"No," Sailor denied. "Im sure you don't know anything about it." He insinuated, "But maybe talking around the way you do, you'd hear who did it."

Pancho shook his head. "It is better you do not know. All this killings, they do no one good."

"I'm not going to hurt him," Sailor protested. He spoke slow truth. "I just want to ask him one question. Just one." Pancho's eyes were curious. "Who paid him."

"Don't you know that?" Pancho asked with disbelief.

"Yeah, I know." His hand dropped to his pocket, to the reassurance of steel. "I know but I want the guy to tell me. I want to hear him say it."

The woman set the bowls before them, red as fire, hotter than the flames of hell. The first mouthful scorched Sailor's throat, steamed his eyes.

"Take it easy," Pancho warned. "With the tortilla, so!" He folded a spoon of muddy blue, shoveled up chile and beans, opened his mouth. His face glowed happily. He had a spic throat for spic food.

Sailor stuffed white tortilla into his burning mouth, swallowed coffee. He took it easy after, hungry as he was, hungry enough to eat a horse, a raw one. But not hungry enough to burn up his mouth and throat and stomach with food tasting like lye. This wasn't chile and beans on Randolph Street. He took it easy and the devil food became good to eat. Enchiladas, with cheese and raw onions smothering the egg; tamales, the corn husks steaming; the bleached white kernels of posole. Pancho slathered everything with the chile gravy; Sailor went warily and the heat of food began to warm him, to fill the hollow curves of his insides. Pancho shoveled gluttonously into his mouth and the big woman leaned her big arms on the counter and smiled on the big dirty man.

When he was gorged, Sailor lit a cigarette, drew deep and good, shoved the pack at Pancho. "How about it?" he asked.

Pancho said, "Muchas gracias." He offered the pack to the woman before helping himself. She said, "Muchas gracias," and her smile was crimson velvet.

Pancho smiled back at the black-eyed woman. Pancho was in a familiar place with the comfort of a woman who spoke his own sweet tongue, his belly distended with the foods of his desire; the sweet sad singing, faint across the wet-leaved night, turned into lullaby by his own peace. Sailor dwindled into a loneness more intense than his dream; he was the wayfarer, the stray, the lost. He flipped away the butt, gathering his loneliness into a hard ball of anger. He stood, dragging bills from his pockets. He flung them on the counter. "Let's go," he said. He'd been knifed, he had the hand behind the killer to meet within the hour, but Pancho could dally with an old dame and ignore his needs.

Pancho, with a final burst of Spanish, a flowery doff of his battered old hat, lumbered after him. The brigand wiped the palm of his hand across his mouth. "It was good, muy bueno, no?" He unlocked the gate enclosing Tio Vivo, made for the gondola. He settled there, an elephant of a man, rubbed off his shoes and belched garlic.

Sailor leaned against the pole. He couldn't sit down; his nerves were too quick. He stood with his back protected, in an angle where he could watch the corner of La Fonda from where the Sen would come. If he came. He'd come because he thought Sailor was cut down.

There was a shape crossing cat-a-corner from the hotel. Sailor's eyes pried into the night. But it wasn't the Sen. It was a bigger man and he turned and passed the botica on the corner. Sailor's hand relaxed.

Pancho sighed. "When first I see you, you are alone and a stranger. I welcome you, the way it is the Spanish people welcome a stranger. My house is poor but I make you welcome. My house is your house. I give you my friendship. Perhaps you too will give the friendship." He sighed again. "Why did you come to Fiesta with a gun in your pocket?"

"I didn't come to your lousy Fiesta," Sailor flung at him.

Pancho's eyes were sad, "Ai yai," he keened.

Sailor grimaced but his mouth tasted bitter. "Maybe I got a gun so I'll stay alive. Maybe you might figure it that way. Sort of looks like I was right, doesn't it?"

It was past midnight. The Sen ought to be coming. But the street was dark. Even the hotel corner was deserted. The Sen wasn't coming. The Sen thought he'd taken care of Sailor; he didn't have to come. He thought no one would know there was to be a meeting at the Plaza tonight.

"Ai yai." Pancho grieved. "You are too young to die."

"That's what I think," he swaggered. "That's why I keep a gun handy." He'd have to go after the Sen again. With a handy gun. This time he'd get the dough. Even if he had to rough up the Sen, he'd get it. Time to leave this dump while he was still healthy. Healthy enough to leave. He tilted his hat.

Pancho came out of his sorrow. "Where do you go, Sailor?"

"Business."

"It is late." The old guy was scared for him. "Better to wait until tomorrow. Mañana. We will drink tequila and then we will sleep. We are tired. Tomorrow the business."

"I'm not tired. I feel fine. You drink the tequila." He'd never felt better. Now was the time. When the Sen wasn't expecting him. "See you later."

"You will come back?"

"Sure. I'll bring you a present." He'd give Pancho a fin, maybe a C note when he got the dough. For caring what happened to him. For fixing him up tonight. He'd give it to him just to see the guy's brown eyes get as big as moons. "Don't wait up," he laughed. "I may be late."

Under his breath Pancho said, "Vaya con Dios, Sailor."

The hotel lobby was quiet, quiet as a hotel lobby in a hick town that had never heard of a Fiesta. The night clerk didn't even look up from his ledger. The blue-smocked kid mopping the tiled floor looked but he didn't care. The news-and-cigar stand was shuttered with a steel fence. Sailor passed it, walking down the dim right-hand portal towards the elevator. At the far end of the portal someone stirred on the dark couch.

Sailor's hand caught the gun tighter, pointed it through his pocket. The voice of McIntyre came from the darkness, the ordinary voice of McIntyre. "I'd almost given you up."

His hand dropped the pocket into place before McIntyre could notice. "What's the idea?" he asked.

"I've been waiting for you a long time." Mac's voice was a little tired. "I'd almost given up. Thought maybe you weren't coming." He stepped quietly as a shadow to Sailor's side. "Ready to talk yet?"

Sailor made something like a laugh. "I might. A little later." He nodded his head towards the elevator sign.

Mac took his hand off Sailor's arm. "I wouldn't go up," he said.

When a cop like McIntyre said he wouldn't do something, said it like that, it was better to agree. To pretend to agree. Not to snarl: what the hell is it to you? The way he wanted to snarl it. He'd waited too long for the Sen to see it his way; he was ready for the showdown and McIntyre had no business sticking his snoopy nose into it.

Sailor set his jaw. "Why wouldn't you?"

Mac was casual. "I'm interested in keeping you on your feet."

"For a witness?"

"Could be."

He couldn't bolt to the elevator. He couldn't knock Mac out and get away with it. He had to stand there with frustration tying him in knots. Until he could get rid of Mac.

McIntyre said, "After tonight, I should think you'd like to talk."

"What about tonight?" he demanded.

"Sort of a close shave, wasn't it? If it had been a gun, someone who could shoot straight . . ."

He hadn't seen Mac. Not in the church or the procession or at the Cross of the Martyrs. He hadn't seen anyone; only white skirts and the brown mass of faces. He hadn't had his eyes open. He demanded, "How do you know about it?"

Mac said, "I'm interested in keeping you alive, Sailor. You and the senator both." He ran his eye down Sailor's coat to the right-hand pocket.

"Who stuck me?"

Mac shook his head. "The local police have him. For being drunk. A kid with a record. He isn't important." He touched Sailor's arm. "Come on up to my room. I've got a bottle. We can talk it over where it's comfortable."

He had better sense than that. Letting Mac feed him booze, loosen his tongue. But it was a way to get rid of Mac. Go up for a drink, then say goodnight. Get to the Sen.

He said, "I don't drink."

Mac said, "I do. And I need one."

He went along. Not back to the elevator. To the front staircase, up a long flight, down a long dim corridor. This was a hotel room, just a hotel room, nothing grand and Spanish like the Sen's.

Mac said, "Found a room yet?" He flung his hand towards one of the twin beds. "Get comfortable. Take off your shoes. Maybe you'd like to bunk here tonight. Be more comfortable than lying on the ground."

He scowled. Mac even knew that, knew he'd slept wrapped in Pancho's dirty serape. He ignored the bed for the stiff armchair. Fat chance he'd sleep with a dick. Talk and drink until you were tired enough to say anything, to spill. He wasn't going to spill until he got his hands on the money. If he didn't get the money, he'd talk. He lit a cigarette and threw the match on the rug.

Mac poured himself a slug. "Want to change your mind? Should think you'd need one after tonight."

"No, thanks. Strictly beer."

Mac said, "I prefer rye." He carried his tumbler to the bathroom, filled it with water. He came back and he wanted the chair. He wanted Sailor on the bed relaxed and himself in the chair. Sailor had outsmarted him there. Mac sat on the foot of the near bed holding his glass. "I prefer Irish, matter of fact. They didn't have any downstairs." He switched off the conversation. "Why does the senator want to rub you out?"

Sailor was flip. "Maybe he doesn't like me any more." This wasn't going to be hard. Mac was too tired to keep it up long. His eyes were wrinkled; when he took off the silly hat and hung it on the bed post, his head sagged.

"Why didn't he rub you out in Chicago where it would have been easy?"

"Maybe he liked me then."

Mac took a swallow of the drink. "What are you holding out for, Sailor? You'd be safer if you told me about it. Didn't you discover that tonight?"

Sailor looked at the smoke coming out of his mouth. "You're trying to tell me dead men can't talk?" He shook his head. "I've known that a long time, Mac. That's why I'm staying alive. I like to talk. When I got something to say."

Mac rubbed the sag of his forehead. "I might be wrong." He sounded a little surprised at the idea. "Maybe it's you who doesn't want the Sen to talk."

Sailor's eyes slit. He'd better go carefully. Mac was smart; Mac was used to making guys talk. He didn't need a rubber hose to do it. Not Mac.

Sailor said, "You could find out easy enough. Why don't you just up and ask him?"

Mac didn't say anything. He looked down into his glass as if it were a wishing well, not a bathroom tumbler half-full of rye and lukewarm water.

Sailor drew up his lower lip. "He's too big a guy isn't he? You got to pick on somebody more of your own size, don't you? You can't ask questions of a big shot like the Sen."

"I can ask them when I'm ready," Mac said. He took a drink out of his finger-smudged grail and then he lifted his eyes to Sailor. "You could help me get ready a lot quicker."

Sailor let out a laugh. "You mean me work with the cops?"

Mac ignored him. "What I can't understand is why you're still holding out. Unless you're expecting a bigger cut."

Sailor held his breath. Mac knew too much. He had to be guessing but he guessed too much. His breath oozed out regretfully. "Now, Mac," he said. "You wouldn't expect me to rat on the Sen. After all he's done for me."

Mac's quiet eyes just looked him over. From his hat with the twigs and dirt on it, down his crumpled suit to his dusty shoes. Sailor's knuckles were tight. Mac wouldn't have looked at him that way in Chi. Sailor was the best-dressed, best-looking guy in the Sen's outfit. Mac knew it. Mac had no right looking at him as if he were a bum. As if the Sen had made a bum out of him. Mac knew this was temporary. Mac was trying to needle him. He held on to the palms of his hands and he laughed. "He's been like a father to me. He's been my best friend since I was a punk."

"Loyalty is the last thing I'd expect from you, Sailor. I knew you had ambition and a kind of pride." He shook his head. "If you'd used them right—" There was a lot of gray through Mac's hair. His hair wasn't as thick as it was when he'd first picked Sailor up for stealing cars. "But I didn't expect loyalty. The others have run out. Or been run out. I don't know why you're sticking."

He didn't know and Sailor covered his small triumphant smile. He didn't know how much Sailor had on the Sen. That's why he had Sailor up here, trying to find that out. Sailor said, like he was still the wide-eyed goofball he once had been, "He's been good to me. He took me uptown."

"There's just as much bad uptown as downtown. I guess you know that. Maybe there's more. It's just hidden better."

"You ought to know, Mac," Sailor said. He tipped his chair and pitched the cigarette butt out the window. "You're always digging for trouble. He let the chair down. "You look all in. I'd better run along."

Mac yawned. "The Sen's gone to bed. I wouldn't bother him." He yawned again. "We had a long talk tonight. He's tired out."

Sailor didn't quiver a muscle.

"He won't run out. Iris Towers isn't leaving for another week."

Her name didn't belong in Mac's mouth with the Sen's name. She was a white angel. Mac should know that if he was so smart.

"He doesn't feel so good tonight. Better wait till tomorrow." Mac was serious.

Sailor cocked his shoulders. "Maybe he'd like me to cheer him up."

Mac looked up into Sailor's eyes. Sailor wouldn't look away because Mac's eyes weren't saying anything. They were colorless as water. Colorless as Mac's voice. "He'd like me to believe you killed his wife."

Rage was red in Sailor's brain. He began to curse and then he broke off because he wasn't sure. This could be Mac's trap. To make him talk. To make him spill. His tongue was thick. "I didn't—"

Mac interrupted, "I'd hate anything to happen tonight to make me not believe that. Better wait till tomorrow."

6

HE DIDN'T HAVE TO LEAVE THE HOTEL. WHEN HE GOT TO THE FOOT OF the stairs he could turn to the right. He could go to the Sen's room. He could squeeze the dough out of that skinny neck. He could knock it out of that weasel snout. He didn't have to use a gun.

The lying, double-crossing, skunking Sen. How did he expect to make that stick? Sailor's alibi was set. Set by the Sen himself and the Sen's brain man, Zigler. How did the Sen expect to break it down without giving himself away?

The Sen could do it. He could make up a yarn that would sound as true as if it were true. That was the kind of brain the Sen had, twisting lies around it and making them true on his oily tongue. Mac wouldn't believe that crap. Mac was too smart. Mac knew the Sen had done it himself. Mac could know if Sailor would talk. He ought to march right back up the staircase now and tell Mac the whole story, just like it happened. Mac would take care of him if he'd talk. And Mac would know who was telling the truth. Mac was too smart to believe the Sen's lies.

If he would talk. He could put the Sen where he ought to be. In the hot seat. Where he couldn't ever get at Iris Towers. If he'd talk. He was going to talk. He was going to tell Mac the whole thing, just what happened that night. It wouldn't put him on a spot; he'd be state's witness. The only witness. He and the Sen and the dead woman. No one else knew.

He'd talk just as soon as he got the money. He wasn't going to give up that kind of money. He needed it; it belonged to him; he was going to have it. What was owed and what he deserved above it. Five thousand dollars. The most he'd ever had at one time. Peanuts. He should have asked ten. The dough wouldn't do the Sen any good where he was going.

As soon as he got the money, he'd walk right back to McIntyre and spill. The Sen had crossed him; he deserved nothing better than the cross in return. He deserved a lot more than that. And he'd get it.

Sailor was at the foot of the stairs and he itched to turn right. Only trouble was if he did, and he and the Sen had it out, he was mad enough to do something dangerous. That's what Mac was warning him about. He mustn't kill the Sen, even in self defense. He mustn't do anything to make Mac believe he was a killer. Cool off first, see the Sen tomorrow early, hard and sure of himself. He turned left, out of the hotel.

Out on the street. The night cold closed around him. Cold enough for frost on the earth. And he had nowhere to go. No place to lay his head. But on the earth. He shoved his hands in his pockets and hunched his shoulders. There should be a warm room, a soft enough bed. He shouldn't have to sleep in the dirt another night.

He didn't have to. He could have a room at the old witch's. He could have one of Mac's beds. He could even yet go wake up the Sen and sleep with his elegance. He was returning to Pancho out of choice. Better an old blanket under the cold sky with the warmth of Pancho's heart thrown in. With the safeness of a friend. He set out to the corner. In the deserted silence of the night his steps were loud, too loud. It was as if he were the only person left alive in an empty world, as if his clangor were disturbing the sleeping dead. He scudded across to the Plaza, wove through shadows to the red palings. Pancho's face peered over, little anxious lines netting his brown eyes. His smile rubbed them out.

"You are back. I hear you coming."

Sailor went in through the gate. "Did you think I wouldn't be?" he grinned. He went first, bunching his shoulders against the knife cold while Pancho wound the chain over the lock.

Pancho sighed, "I do not know. Who knows when a man goes if he will return? The good God has brought you back." He didn't lumber over to the gondola. He went to where the blankets were spread out. The serape, the best blanket were folded for Sailor. Pancho wrapped himself in the tattered one and lay himself upon the earth.

Sailor said. "I brought myself back. What were you worried about?" He wrapped himself in the serape, lay down beside the brigand. "I don't need that other blanket. You take it."

"It is for you, mi amigo." Pancho pulled it over Sailor, as if he were a little kid who'd kicked off the covers. "My fat, it keeps me warm," he gurgled.

Sailor lit two cigarettes, handed one over. "Did you think somebody was going to take another crack at me?"

Pancho sighed deep in his fat belly. "I do not know but I am afraid when you leave tonight. It is not good to go looking for a man when there is anger like was in you then." He sighed to his toes. "But the good God has taken care of you. When you leave me I say a small prayer that you will return unharmed." His voice smiled in the darkness. "And you return safe to me."

Sailor watched the thin blue swirl of smoke rise from his mouth. It was good to rest with the heavy woolen robes warming him, and the cigarette good under the cold stars. He mocked gently, "I wouldn't expect you to go in for the holy stuff, Pancho. Not with all those knife scars you carry around."

Pancho said, "When I was young, sometimes there is a little trouble. Not bad trouble because the good God, He takes care of me. Should I not now say gracias to Him that He takes care of me?"

"I don't know." Sailor let the smoke slowly out of his mouth. "I stopped praying a long time ago."

"But one does not stop praying," Pancho stated.

"I stopped. It wasn't getting me anything. It didn't get my old lady anything and she was always praying. Nothing but work and more work and death. I don't know what she was praying for but it didn't get her anything."

"Maybe she pray for you," Pancho said slyly. "That the good God take care of you."

Maybe she had at that. It would have been like her. Even to pray for the old man. She wouldn't have prayed for herself. She never asked anything for herself. What had it got her? What it got anyone who didn't look out for himself first.

"Now that she is gone to Heaven," Pancho said comfortably, "maybe you better start praying the good God take care of you."

Sailor laughed. "I'll stick to my rod, thanks. I know what'll take care of me."

Pancho sighed down deep. "Then I will pray for you."

Sailor laughed louder. It was funny. Everybody preaching at him. A cop and an old brigand. If the Sen started preaching, he'd bust a gut laughing. He snickered, "I sure never sized you up as a Holy Joe, Pancho."

"Holy Joe, I do not think I know this," Pancho said in dignity. That meant he was offended.

Sailor said quickly, "I don't mean anything. You're a good guy, Pancho. You're my amigo."

"I am not so good," Pancho was comfortable again. "But it is good to be good. Maybe it does not fill the belly or warm the heart but it is good. It feels good." He crunched on the earth turning his bulk over. "A man wishes to die in his bed, I think. Even if he has no bed, no more than a serape under the stars. It is more comfortable that way." He propped his chin on his big fist. "It is in the Good Book, I think, if you live by the sword, that is the way you will die. It is not good to live by the gun, I think, Sailor."

"It is if someone is gunning for you," Sailor said flatly.

"But why? What have you done someone should wish to kill you? A young man like you?"

Sailor said out of his thought, "I haven't done anything. Nothing but want things better than they were. I only wanted what others had—I didn't want to be poor like my folks, like everyone around me. I wanted things better than that."

"What is for you, will come to you." Pancho's sigh shimmered like the dark leaves overhead. "The way of the poor it is hard. It is better not to be poor. If you must be poor, it is better to thank God for it. Better than the gun in the pocket, I think."

"Maybe no one ever kicked you in the teeth."

"Ho, ho, ho," Pancho laughed. Like that: Ho, ho, ho. "I have not been kicked around? A poor native not kicked around?"

"What do you do about it?"

"When I was young," Pancho said solemnly, "with the hot blood, you understand, there are the knife scars which you have seen. But now I grow old. I am at peace with everyone."

"Even with the guys that kick you around?"

"Even with the gringo sonnama beetches," Pancho said cheerfully. "When I am young I do not understand how it is a man may love his enemies. But now I know better. I think they are poor peoples like I am. The gringo sonnama beetches don't know no better. Poor peoples."

The Sen wasn't any poor peoples. He was a stinking rich bastard who would welch out of a two-bit deal. Loving him was like loving the Devil. Even the Good Book didn't tell you to love the Devil. Sailor said, "You're a good man, Pancho. You've been good to me. When this deal of mine comes off, I'm going to pay you back."

Pancho said, "With the Spanish peoples, there is no pay between friends. If this deal does not come off, my house is your house. I am your friend."

Pancho was a good guy. He meant it. He'd take Sailor home with him and they'd hoe the bean plot or whatever you did with beans. No thanks. He wasn't going to be trapped in this wilderness; the deal was coming off.

Sailor said, "Don't worry. The deal is coming off. Tomorrow." He yawned. "And I'll buy you the biggest case of tequila in town."

Pancho's voice was beaming. "That is good, Sailor. Tequila too is good for a man's soul, I think."

III

Baile

1

On the third day there was shouting and squealing and whinneying and barking, laughing and crying and squealing and singing. Sound heralded the morning. The morning of the Fiesta children. When Sailor pushed open his eyes the children were seething in the Plaza. Children with painted cheeks and flower-decked hair, in glittering red-and-green skirts and long full Indian calico skirts, in velvet trousers and cheesecloth britches, children playing Navajo and Mestizo and Spanish señora, Mexican peon and Mexican charro and Spanish caballero; children everywhere laughing and crying and shrilling their voices into the sun.

Children in the streets striding horses and burros, children leading dogs and cars and ducks and lambs and tiny sisters, a child with a parrot perched on his shoulder, a child dragging a little red wagon in which rode one goldfish in a bowl. Children swarming over the walks and the curbs, climbing into the bandstand, running and pushing and swirling like dervishes. Only the red fence kept Sailor safe from them. The kids pressed against the palings, shouting, demanding Tio Vivo.

Old Onofre sat like a slab of wood on his campstool, his fiddle across his knees. Sat there as if he didn't know the horde was threatening the gates. Ignacio smoked a twisted brown cigarette, his guitar at his feet. His face didn't like kids anymore than Sailor did. Pancho wasn't around.

Sailor flung off the blanket, shook himself out of the serape and pushed to his feet. The hard floor of the earthen bed left him, after two nights of it, full of kinks. His shoulder hurt. He settled his hat, pulled down his coat jacket. Wrinkled, dirty, unshaven, his tongue sour with last night's garlic, stoned by the jeers in the mouths of the ragged Mex kids outside the gate. Without being able to translate their tongue. He muttered, "Shut up, you little bastards." He didn't need them to tell him he'd have to clean up before he could see anyone today. He'd have to have a clean shirt, clean linen. His suitcase was where he'd left it, in the check room at La Fonda. He was ashamed to go for it, ashamed to walk into the hotel looking like a derelict.

He put a cigarette in his mouth, lit it. It tasted dead. There was no use asking Ignatz or the old man about Pancho; they wouldn't know even if they could speak his language. He brushed off the dust from his trousers and stalked to the gate. If any of the kids gave him a dirty look he'd slap them down so fast they wouldn't ever forget it.

His approach quieted them. In a fearful way. Their eyes, the battery of their unmoving eyes, lay on him as if they'd never seen a Gringo before. Flat black eyes, hundreds of them watched his hand unfasten the gate. Their silence heightened the whirl of noise in the streets outside the Plaza. Their silence was more menacing than any words they could have flung. He walked through the gate, banging it after him, fastening it. He got away from the kids quick; they let him pass. As soon as he had passed, their gibberish rattled again. He walked on fast. Kids weren't hypocrites. When the copper showed up they were like statues, hostile-eyed, withheld breaths. The older folks cranked up smiles or words, but not the kids. The old folks pretended that Fiesta made all a oneness in the land, Indian, Mexican, Gringo. The kids didn't hide their knowledge of the enemy among them. They were too smart.

The raw sunlight hit his eyes as he left the green shade of the Plaza, left the squawking kids parading their pets, pushing and yelling and slamming their sticky hands against your only suit. Yesterday dozens; today hundreds of them. He didn't know where to go next. He must pick up his suitcase. The thought of lugging it winced his shoulder. And after he picked it up what would he do with it? No Turkish baths in this two-bit-fifty-cent town. He walked down the street, passing the hotel where he'd bummed a bath and shave yesterday. The same shirt sleeves were leaning on the cigar counter. He didn't think it would work again, the guy had a snarl for a face this morning. Maybe he didn't like kids either.

It wasn't a good idea to try it again anyway. The guy might start wondering how the slick-looking fellow of yesterday morning had changed back into such a bum. He might wonder out loud. Sailor walked on and turned in at a cafe. Coffee would help him out.

It was a glossy place outside but inside it wasn't more than any hashery. He sat at the counter, ordered. The food wasn't good when it came, it was strictly hashery, but he ate it, drank a second cup of coffee. He felt better. He didn't look any better. The mirror over the cigarette machine showed him that. He fed in coins for Philip Morris, lighted up and went out on the street. The smoke didn't taste so bad after the coffee.

He could go to Mac. But he couldn't take his suitcase up to Mac's room. Mac would find a way to have a look in it. Mac wouldn't like the baby inside it. He'd get wondering. He'd get chilled up. Besides he didn't want to talk to Mac. He was mad enough to spill. He'd better stay out of Mac's reach until he had his gab with the Sen.

The Sen's last chance. He was a boob to give the Sen a chance after last night. He was a boob, yes, but he needed that dough. His roll had sunk and there wasn't anyone in Chicago to send him more. Ziggy in Mexico. Humpty and Lew, God alone knew where. The Sen right here. The Sen had to pay up. It wasn't a question of what was due any longer; not the way it had been. It was getting to be a matter of need.

He walked aimless, on down the street, past a men's store, a little one; past a five-and-ten, drug store, grocery store, Penney's, end of the block. He could buy a change of clothes; razor, tooth brush and stuff. But after he bought them, he had no place to use them. He turned around and walked back up the street, back to the squealing Plaza. Tio Vivo was spinning. On the circular bandstand a brass band had moved in; a little kid with a reedy voice and a cowboy hat sang into the mike. Kids were still swarming everywhere.

He walked to the corner, ducking the ones coming out of the corner drug store dripping ice cream cones and greasy popcorn. He crossed over to La Fonda, only because there weren't kids there. He wouldn't go in; he wouldn't dare go in looking like this. If the Sen saw him now he wouldn't pay up a thin dime. Not without real trouble. He cursed the big hotel, cursed every room in its terraced bulk. All those rooms and baths, and he couldn't borrow one long enough to look like a human being. Long enough to get the scum off his teeth. He walked on by, muttering his helpless anger.

He felt the hand on his arm and his own right hand jammed his pocket before he looked down. It was a kid. A dirty little kid, a pipe-stem kid in colorless jeans and a torn shirt. He'd got away from the Plaza of kids and one came tagging him.

"Get the hell out of here," Sailor said. He bumped off the thin brown hand.

The kid said, "Don José he wants to see you." The kid's black eyes were too big for his face.

"Who the hell is Don José? What does he want with me?"

"Don José he wants to see you," the kid parroted in his spic accent.

He was ready to tell the kid to tell Don José where to head in but it came to him in time. Don José was Pancho Villa; Don José was his friend. Maybe Don José had miracled a bathroom with a shower.

He made sure. There could be another Don José; somebody the Sen had dug up who could thrust a knife straight. "Where is he?"

The kid rattled. Don José was at Tio Vivo and the kid was going to get a free ride for running after Don José's friend if he caught up with Sailor. . . . Sailor tossed a dime. "Have one on me," he grunted.

"Gracias, Señor! Gracias." You'd think he'd thrown the kid a grand. The thin dirty face flashed a quick smile before the kid's bare brown feet cut out across to the Plaza.

Sailor cut across too. So he wouldn't have to pass La Fonda again. There were clean people coming out of it. He knew Pancho hadn't uncovered a bathroom. By his smell he knew Pancho didn't bother about soap and water and a scrub brush for his teeth. But something must be up. Pancho wouldn't have sent for him if something wasn't up.

He had to wade through the anthill of kids to get to Pancho. Even then he wouldn't have made it to the fence without stepping on a mess of them if Ignatz hadn't noticed him and signaled Pancho. It must have been a signal. At least after the flip of greasy black hair, Pancho's eyes searched over the heads and his warm anxious smile found Sailor.

Sailor had to stand there until Pancho finished winding up Tio Vivo. Like he was some kid's old man. He looked around for Pila but she wasn't there. Too early for the older gang.

As the merry-go-round began its unwinding, Pancho lumbered over to the palings. "Vaya, vaya ustedes!" he yelled at the kids. And something about mi amigo. He must have told the kids to let Sailor through. They weren't willing but he could nudge his way forward.

"What's up?"

Pancho wiped away his face sweat with the sleeve of his shirt. "It is the abuelita. She wants you should come to her."

"What for?" He was suspicious. A payoff. Or the cops. Asking questions. Questions he wasn't going to answer.

"It is to fix—how you say—the shoulder."

"My shoulder's okay."

Pancho shook his head. "You must go, my friend. You do not wish poison to set in. You must go to her."

It felt all right. A little stiff but nothing sore about it. He didn't want her poking and pushing around it again. Yet he didn't know what she'd done to it. The weeds and herbs might have to be changed or there'd be infection. He couldn't know, he'd never gone to a witch doctor. The Sen had the best doc in town for Sailor, not even a political one, the time Sailor had cut his arm. On a broken windshield.

He asked, "You'll go along?"

"How can I go?" Pancho rolled his eyeballs and his hands. He didn't have to explain. Right now the kids were like savages, ready to break down the barricade if Tio Vivo didn't hurry up and spin again.

"I don't know where she lives," Sailor told him. He was ready to give up the whole idea, glad to give it up. He wouldn't die of blood poisoning this soon; he could see her later when Pancho was through working; when he'd tended to his business.

"Lorenzo will show you the way. Lorenzo!"

It was the same kid, the same dirty little bag of bones. Pancho rattled Spanish at the kid, threats and promises. The kid rattled back just as fast.

Sailor said, "Come on. I'll give you another dime." Get it over with. Maybe afterwards he could borrow the abuelita's bathroom and get himself cleaned up. Maybe there'd be a razor around he could borrow too. He pushed away from the fence, through the kids. Lorenzo tagged after him.

After they were clear of the Plaza he asked, "You Pancho's kid? Don José?"

"Oh, no!" Lorenzo said. And after a moment, "Don José he is my uncle." He was proud of it. Don José was the most wonderful man in the Fiesta of Children. The man who owned Tio Vivo. He was more important than the Sen had ever been.

"You know where you're taking me?"

"Si." The word came long drawn from his lips. "The abuelita," he explained, "she is my grandmother. Abuelita is grandmother. In Inglis-speaking."

Sailor's eyes opened. "Pancho's mother?" The small dried up twig, mother to big fat Pancho? "Pancho. Don José."

"Oh, no!" The kid was amused.

"But he's your uncle?"

"Si." Again the "e" sound dragged out. Again the kid was proud.

He didn't care about Pancho's family relations. He'd just been making conversation, to keep from walking in silence. Because he didn't want to go back to the old crone but must go. It was so ordered.

They went on down the narrow street. He recognized the house though he hadn't before seen it by daylight. Flush on the street, the blank wall of the gate closed. The kid stopped at the gate. "You geemme a dime now, Meester?"

His hand was out, his eyes scooting back up the street to where Fiesta flourished.

"You take me to her house," Sailor said. "That's the bargain."

The kid didn't want to waste the time. But Sailor didn't want to cross the alien courtyard alone, stand alone outside the door. The kid pushed open the gate and Sailor followed, ducking under the frame. Ducking in time to keep from cracking his head, remembering how Pancho had bent down to go through the gate last night.

The kid ran across the barren sandy patch of the courtyard to the door. Sailor crunched after him, regular steps, just as if he didn't feel funny about coming here. He wasn't scared the way he'd been last night; he just didn't like coming. He didn't belong in this kind of a setup. He was a city guy, used to the best after he met up with the Sen. He'd have the best again, too; splitting with the Sen was going to make things better not worse. He was going to get that wad and do better on his own. Mexico City was just as swell as Chicago. Better, Ziggy said. It wasn't grimy or too cold or too hot and there were flowers blooming everywhere. It was going to be like a wonderful dream only it would be real.

"You geemme a dime now, Meester?"

He said, "Sure." He'd like to keep the kid along until he was safe out of here but he didn't have the heart. He'd been just as hungry-looking and dirty himself once when a dime looked big as a grand. He dug in his pocket. "Sure," he said. "Here's a quarter. Keep the change."

"Gracias, Meester!" The kid bowed. The quarter made his eyes bigger than ever in his ragged little face. He stuck it in his jeans and skipped. Sailor knocked on the abuelita's door.

There was some kind of sound from inside that might have meant come in; he went in. The old woman was by the cold fireplace but she wasn't alone. On the wall bench were two other dames. One as old as the abuelita, older, her black shawl pulled over her thin white hair, her hands clutched on her cane. It wasn't a real cane, it was the dead twisted branch of a tree. She bent over it, her lips mumbling without sound. The other woman was younger, there was a familiar look to her but she didn't look like anything. Her face was dull, only her dark eyes had any living quality. She wore rusty black, like the old woman, the shawl pushed back over her dark hair. Her breasts were big with milk, her hands work knotted as his mother's had been. He knew then what was familiar in her; she was the hopeless face and sagging shoulders and defeated flesh of all poor women everywhere. He wanted to bolt. Even in this small way he did not want to be pushed back into the pit of the past. The pit he believed he had escaped forever.

The abuelita said something. It was in her own tongue and the thongs of helplessness wound tighter about him. The woman from whom he had turned his eyes said in her heavy accent, "She say take off your coat."

He looked at the abuelita. Her claws pantomimed it. He turned an almost frantic look towards the old crone and the work woman. They had not moved. They weren't going to move. They had come to see the show. Or they'd come to gossip by the cold hearth and this was all a part of the everyday at the abuelita's.

He took off his coat, began unbuttoning his shirt. Unbuttoned it slowly, feeling naked, ashamed. He hadn't known shame since he was a kid, a cowed kid taught shame by his mother's old-fashioned scruples. In the Sen's world nobody thought anything about taking off his shirt before strangers. The Sen did half his business while he was dressing.

Sailor didn't try to track down his queasiness; shaming the shame, he pulled off his shirt and stood there as if he were naked, not merely half-naked. Fear had returned to him, atavistic fear; he was helpless before three witches. It was this which had delayed his hand; before their incantations he needed all the protective barriers of civilization, even a dirty shirt. He knew now the root of his hesitancy in coming to this house; a fear of the primitive, root fear of the alien and the strange which had been threaded through these three

days. He was a city man. The city didn't have to be Chi. He'd been
in Detroit and Minneapolis and Kansas City, once to Philadelphia;
he was at home in any of them. He wasn't a foreigner on city streets.
But this place wasn't civilized. Behind the strangeness, lay the primitive; this land was too close to an ancient past. He would not be
caught in its caves; he would get away before he was buried, before
the stone woman turned him to stone.

He swaggered, "Okay, Grammaw, how does it look?" He was
shivering as he had last night, unable to control the shakes, even before she laid her lifeless fingers on the place of the knife.

He smelled of the earth and Pancho's serape and unwashed sweat,
his breath smelled of stale garlic. He was unclean and he knew himself to be. Yet he had to stand there naked in his filth while she wadded and mumbled and pried and smelled him. While the other
witches watched with obscene eyes.

He took it she was satisfied by the mumbling, by the little shakes
of her head. He took it she was finished with him when she began
tucking the little packets of twigs back into her dirty handkerchief.

"Got a place I can wash up?" he asked.

She didn't know a word he said but the younger woman did. "You
wish to wash?"

"Yeah." He gathered up his shirt and coat. She led him into the
kitchen, a big old-fashioned kitchen with a coal stove warming it.
The table and chairs were old and ugly; green-and-red-and-yellow
plaid oilcloth was tacked on the table top. She poured water from a
tea kettle into a tin basin, cooled it from the tap, set it on the table.
She put a broken cake of Ivory beside it. Then she went away.

No bathroom. Outhouse in back, you could see it from the kitchen
windows. Some way to live. Even if you were a bunch of old
witches. This one was back with a clean towel for him. He said,
"Thanks. Gracias." They'd have him turning into a spic if he stayed
around much longer.

She sat down on a wooden chair and he saw she'd brought needle
and dark thread. She was mending the tear in his coat. He didn't
have the nerve to do a sponge bath before her. Just his hands, but he
washed them as if they were embedded with grime. Kept washing
them, hoping she'd get out and let him splash his face. She didn't.
He dried his hands, took up his shirt.

She said in a heavy accent, "If you wait a minute, I will mend
your shirt."

He gave his head a shake. "Thanks. Haven't time." He wanted to get away fast. From his mother mending his broken clothes. He hadn't worn patches since he left home. He wasn't going back to patches. He'd throw these clothes away. Tomorrow. He was awkward with the shirt, the new dressing burning his shoulder; she came over to him and helped him.

He said again, "Thanks. Gracias," even as he withdrew from her. She helped him with the coat. Her hands were work-veined like those of slum women.

He could get out now. Almost as dirty as when he came, and his shoulder jumping when it hadn't hurt before. He strode into the front room, handed a dollar to the abuelita. She'd probably have to split with her big fat nephew who'd brought him here when he'd wanted a doc and no questions asked. He'd be out of this town by night, with his dough. Pick up a plane in Albuquerque and be in Mexico City tomorrow. Get him a real doc there. Get him a new suit. Tomorrow night he and Ziggy would be sitting in the best hotel ordering champagne. Toasting the Sen, the late, unlamented Sen.

2

IT WAS PAST TEN-THIRTY. HE COULDN'T WASTE ANY MORE TIME. HE didn't want the Sen to skip out on him. The Sen had seen him without a shave before. The La Fonda swells could turn up their noses; they wouldn't when he had that five grand in his pocket. The Sen didn't have any choice after last night; he knew he had to pay up or Sailor would hand the noose to Mac. He knew Sailor wouldn't be taking any more of the stall. What the Sen didn't know was that choice had been eliminated; he was going to pay and swing both.

The Plaza was strumming, music on the bandstand, music on twirling Tio Vivo, strolling musicians on the paths. Chimney pots smoking, costumes glittering, voices lifted in laughter and singing. Sailor didn't enter the square. He walked on up the street, crossed to La Fonda. He paid no attention to those coming out or those entering with him. He walked right on in. The lobby was seething this early, like a convention, a convention of fancy-dressed actors. There was a lot of noise coming from the bar. In the patio the sun and the fountain, the geraniums and the striped awnings of the swings and umbrella tables were like something on a stage.

Sailor didn't waste time, he made for the house phone, called the

Sen's number. He could hear the ringing, over and again, no answer. He clapped down the phone. The Sen didn't get up early; not unless he was running out. Maybe he'd told them not to put through any calls. Sailor strode to the elevator, rode up to four. His knock on the door was the only sound in the empty corridor; he tightened the hand in his right-hand pocket while his pounding shattered silence. But there was no answer from within.

He went back to the elevator, put his finger on the buzzer and left it there. The Sen was probably in the Placita having his morning cocktail and coffee. Dressed up clean and white, using his voice tenderly on Iris Towers' clean whiteness, fooling her with soap and water and a razor and his rotten sweet voice.

The pretty little elevator girl didn't say anything when Sailor got in. Didn't give him hell for hanging on the buzzer, the way a Chi yahoo would have done. And get his teeth broken for it. The elevator slid down in silence. He left it in the same silence, walked up the portal, seeing no one. He couldn't go out in the Placita after the Sen, not until he was clean. He turned downstairs to the barber shop. It looked swank as the hotel but there were only two operators and both chairs filled. He walked through the room, out to the street and across to a shop that looked like any barber shop. He didn't have to wait; the customers of this one weren't steaming out hangovers, they were dancing in the streets.

"Shave and shine," Sailor said.

The fat, bald barber wasn't gabby. Maybe he wanted to close up and get out into the streets too. The job didn't take long. Sailor looked a lot better already.

The biggest men's store was closed, Labor Day; but the little one further on down was open. He bought a blue shirt, a pair of socks and shorts. He started back to La Fonda but he changed his mind on that. Somebody might get officious; all Sailor needed right now was a bastard to get officious. There'd be trouble. He didn't want trouble; he was saving that for the Sen.

He went to the bus station, changed in the can, wrapped his dirty laundry and checked it in a locker. He looked okay. He looked swell. He could sit in La Fonda all day if he wanted to. Sit there until he caught up with the Sen. He went back to the hotel. It was noon now. He pushed into the Cantina. The Sen wasn't there. Hundreds of costumes were cramming the cocktail room but no Sen. He edged and shoved through to the Placita. The head waitress was crisp as her white dress. But polite. She said, "I haven't a table right now."

He could tell that. He said, "I'm just looking for a friend.
Thanks." He counted faces. And he saw hers. Delicate, fine, her
silver-gold hair tracing the shape of her face. There were white
flowers in her hair; her dress was white peasant stuff, the blouse cut
low off her golden shoulders. The mucker, Kemper Prague, was pressing against her shoulder but he couldn't touch her. She was clean as
sunshine; the other women looked as if they'd been soaked in rum
all night, their eyes haggard, but she was clean. The men looked like
hangovers, young men, not an old weasel among them.

Sailor moved his eyes clockwise across the tables, counter clockwise back again to hers. The Sen wasn't there; he wasn't in the
Placita. Sailor could have walked over to her table, it was only a few
paces. He looked a lot better than the guys she was sitting with. She
wasn't a princess or an angel from heaven; she was Iris Towers, a
Chicago girl. The same as any other Chicago girl only her father was
a big millionaire. He could walk right over and ask it courteously like
he'd learned from the Sen. "Do you know where I could find Senator Douglass?" She'd be polite too because she was brought up that
way. She'd tell him where the Sen was. She'd know. He stood there
and her head moved and he was looking into her eyes, her clear blue
eyes. She looked at him. But there was no recognition; only that a
man was standing there looking at her. He turned on his heel and
left.

He didn't care whom he elbowed getting out of the Cantina. He
saw no one, only the fact that the Sen still wasn't there. There was
the jingle of sleigh bells, the thud of drums, as he stepped into the
lobby. And a crowd blocking further exit, a solid half circle moving
in to where four Indians stood, Indian men, painted, feathered, looking like Indians should, like Indians in a book. Two were naked but
for the bells on their wrists and ankles, the beaded breech clouts, the
gaudy circles of parrot feathers decorating the clouts before and
behind. Their braids wound with ribbons, a few feathers in their
hair. The other two men wore bright shirts and blue jeans, moccasins
on their feet, silver and turquoise beads and belts. One thudded an
enormous tapering drum, almost waist high, hung with feathers. The
second began to chant as Sailor moved into the circle, and the naked
Indians were dancing. Pawing and thudding the floor, bells ringing,
feathers shimmering, naked muscles tight under lean brown flesh.
The dance ended as sharply as it began; the singer was silenced, the
dancers circled bell-like, quietly; the drum was a muffled roll.

It began again with the high-pitched call. With hoops now, a dozen or more thin willowy hoops in the dancers' hands. Wilder than before, shivering their bodies through the hoops, bent double through the smallest circles, their feet beating incessant with the drums, the bells jeering. The Sen ought to be here. The Sen liked to go back to Chicago and tell about the fancy things he'd seen.

Sailor's eyes quickened about the massed circle. Across was McIntyre. Mac's eyes were watching the Indian dancers, not scanning the crowd for the Sen or for Sailor. That meant Mac knew where they both were. That meant Sailor could find out about the Sen.

Another dance. A warrior dance, the dancers lunging at each other, without warning letting out startling whoops. It made him jumpy. Then it was over, the dancers jingling away on soft feet, the drum beating away into silence. The crowd broke, speaking silly things to exorcise the spell.

Sailor started around the outskirts, to come on Mac by accident. His step faltered. He picked up his stride again; he didn't want to think about that. About the Indian faces with no expression; even when they war-whooped, no expression. Like the Indians in the street and under the museum portal. Under the brown stone faces, this violence. Under the silent wastes of this land, their land, what violence? The fear, the unknown fear was rising in Sailor but he set his steps hard, pushed it down. And Mac wasn't around.

Sailor went down the right-hand portal, crossed the lounge, looked in the New Mexican room and the dining room. No Sen. No Mac. He could wait. He didn't have anything else to do. More comfortable here than walking the dirty streets. He was in luck for once. Somebody moved off a leather chair right in the middle of the lobby, across from the desk. Nobody could come in the side door or front door, nobody could leave the bar or go to the desk without him seeing. He'd like to try the house phone again; it was over there, the Sen might be on the other end of it. But the Sen's room had been too empty and he didn't want to have to stand up all afternoon for nothing.

He lit a cigarette, nice hammered-copper ash tray at hand. If he only had a beer, he'd be more comfortable than he'd been since he blew in. He rested, comfortable, in the chair. Only his eyes moving, watching left and right, not seeming to watch. He didn't need to keep his right hand where it usually was. There wouldn't be any punk stalking him in the center of La Fonda lobby.

"Looking for the senator?"

He lifted his eyes easy. "Hello, Mac. How's Fiesta?"

Somebody got up from the couch next to his chair, as if they'd been holding the place for Mac. Mac sat down.

"Viva las Fiestas," Mac said. Even he was turning Spanish like his hat and sash.

"Sure," Sailor said. He wasn't going to be in a hurry to talk about the Sen. Mac wasn't apt to get too far from the subject. "When you going back?"

"Maybe tomorrow," Mac said. He wasn't gabby this afternoon. He was taking things just as easy as Sailor. "When you going back?"

"I don't know," Sailor said offhand. It sounded too much as if he were waiting for orders from the Sen, and he added, "I haven't made up my mind yet."

"You're going back?" Mac didn't have any expression on his face.

"To Chi?" Sailor shouldn't have sounded amazed, even to his own ears. But he was. The idea of Mac thinking he wouldn't be going back to Chicago. He couldn't wait to get back. Back where you knew what to expect, back where there were lights and buildings and shows and people—and life! He woke up. He wasn't going back. He was going to Mexico. His laugh wasn't good. "What made you ask that?"

Mac was calm as ever. "I thought maybe you weren't counting on going back."

"I can't wait to get back." State Street, Michigan Boulevard, North Shore, The Stevens, the Palmer House, the Lake, the cold wet wind off the Lake. Field's and the Athletic Club and the Trib Tower and Ziggy's office right about next door. Ziggy's office was closed up. For good. Sailor wasn't staying in this dump anyway. He was going down to Mexico City and it was a city, a swell city. Ziggy knew; he'd been there. Sailor didn't say it again, not out loud; there was only the echo in his ear: I can't wait to get back.

There were other places as good as Chicago. Plenty of them. He took a deep drag off the cigarette. "I thought you'd be waiting for the Sen."

Mac said, "I think he'll be leaving tomorrow."

He wasn't sure the way Mac said it, whether Mac had found out all he wanted and was taking the Sen back with him or whether the Sen was running out and he was just tagging along. The Sen wasn't going to wait for Iris Towers, or he'd changed her plans. The Sen didn't like Mac's breath warming his neck. He didn't know Mac would be plodding behind him waiting for the break. The Sen's time was running short. Sailor was the break. The Sen would settle today or Sailor would give Mac what he wanted.

He asked it casual. "Where is the Sen today? You seen him?"

"He's sick," Mac said.

Mac was trying to catch Sailor off guard. That's what he was doing sitting here, popping out with stuff you weren't expecting, with that dead-pan face of his.

Sailor didn't even move his little finger. He just laughed. "What's the matter with him? Too big a night?"

"I don't think that's it. Not all of it." Mac threw another fast one. "How's your shoulder?"

"Fine." The Sen wasn't in his room. Unless he was holed up there not answering the phone, not answering the door. Unless he was that sick. He wouldn't be that sick with Iris Towers likely to be outside the door, on the other end of the phone. "It was only a scratch," Sailor said. "Some guy must have make a mistake."

"Yeah, it was probably a mistake," Mac droned.

He could be meaning the guy was a poor judge of distance. He didn't know about Sailor ducking just at the right time. That was one thing even Mac couldn't know. When lightning would flash. "What's the matter with the Sen?" He brought it back.

"I don't know. Just not feeling too good, according to Amity. You ready to talk yet, Sailor?"

"What about?" He was just as noncommittal as Mac. He'd play it Mac's way. But he knew where the Sen was. Mac had told him that much. Not that Mac knew he'd been giving out. Sailor should have thought of it before; it was one of the Sen's favorite dodges. Holing up in another guy's room when he didn't want anybody to know where he was. When he'd come in from Washington unexpected to do a little business. Holing up in Sailor's apartment.

The Sen might be in Amity's. He might be in Iris Towers' room, lying on her bed sick because he was worried, because things hadn't gone his way for once. Because Sailor had roughed his game.

"Where were you the night of Mrs. Douglass' death?"

A quick pitch but the same old question. Sailor was gentle. "Why, Mac," he said. "You know where I was. I was down at Ziggy's working on the books. We worked there till your boys came in to tell us about the tragedy. We never left the place."

"You never left the place."

"You know we didn't, Mac."

"I'm not asking about Zigler," Mac said. "I'm asking about you."

"For God's sake, Mac. You know every step I took that night. You sat in on the testimony."

"You never left the place," Mac repeated.

His own lips were as tight. "I never left the place," he lied with emphasis. It was kind of funny swearing to a lie now and maybe by evening telling Mac the truth. Mac wouldn't think it funny; he was used to it. Mac would know it was all in the game. "You're not trying to pin that rap on me, Mac?"

Mac said, "I don't pin raps, Sailor. I'm after Mrs. Douglass' killer."

"You're not after me."

"Maybe not."

"You're not." He'd talk this much. "If you were you wouldn't have been here ahead of me. You'd have been trailing." He explained Mac's own moves to him. As if Mac didn't know what he was doing. "You didn't get here first because you knew I was heading this way. I didn't know it myself until the day I took the bus."

Mac didn't answer him. Not straight. "What happened between you and the Sen?" He wanted the answer to that one. Something different in the way of asking.

"What do you mean?" Sailor sounded as innocent as he wanted to sound. Let Mac take the lead here. Until later when he spilled the whole business. But as he spoke they came out of the Cantina, Kemper Prague and the lovely Iris Towers. They gave Mac his question.

"It wouldn't be his new friends?"

They didn't come across the lobby. They went out of sight into the left-hand portal. Going up to see the poor sick Sen. The hidden Sen. Take him a drink. Or an aspirin. Or a satin white hand for his aching head.

Sailor was short. "No." He couldn't say that he and the Sen were the same as ever with the Sen accusing him to Mac last night. That was too raw. That was why he'd spill everything to Mac once he collected. He had to collect first or Mac might take the Sen away before Sailor had his chance.

Mac said mildly, "I didn't know. See you later, Sailor," and he was gone. No excuses, just gone, down the right-hand portal. To ride up in the elevator with them. To find out where the senator was holed. Beating Sailor to it. And the Sen's new friends, his rich society friends wouldn't even notice the quiet man in the funny Spanish hat and sash. Any of the old organization would. Not one of the old organization who wouldn't spot a cop on sight.

He was too restless to sit there longer. The Sen wasn't going to come out, not until he thought he was safe. Mac would find out where and Sailor could get it out of Mac later. He could, if he had to, make a deal with Mac. Promise the story if he could have fifteen minutes with the Sen alone first. That was all he needed. He could cut it down to ten.

He might as well eat lunch. Not here where they'd soak you; he'd go back to the Kansas City steak house. Eat his kind of food. Fool around a little, have a cold beer later, get back to the hotel around cocktail time. If he couldn't get to the Sen by that time, make the deal with Mac. One thing sure; he had to get out of town tonight. If he didn't, Mac might see to it that Sailor turned back to Chicago tomorrow. He'd have to say he was returning with them tomorrow and pull a sneak tonight. After he'd told Mac the truth.

The momentum of music and color and motion, of sound and smell had increased on the Plaza. Fiesta was revolving to climax, as if by moving faster and faster the end might be delayed. As if accentuation of its gayety might delay the return to tomorrow's dull everyday.

Sailor walked in the street, it was simpler than being pushed off the high curb by the sidewalk crowds. Past the corner of Tio Vivo, Pancho sweating at his toil; Ignatz and Onofre plinking and plunking mechanically. Past the thatched booths, past the chile and the pop and the cardboard canaries swinging on their willowy rods. Past the balloon man. Stepping aside for the burro carts and the horses with their costumed riders, past the corner where strolling musicians sang to little clusters of listeners.

"Hello, Sailor."

She giggled when she said it, giggled and blocked his way. It was Rosie, with the paint on her mouth and cheeks, the invitation in her black eyes and in the twist of her immature body. She was arm-linked with a different girl today, a girl lush as the flaming roses in her hair, a girl with rippling black hair and swelling breasts and wide hips. A girl with a dirty neck and a gum-chewing mouth and wide beautiful eyes.

"Looking for Pila?" Rosie giggled.

He said, "No," and started by them.

"I bet Pila she is looking for you," Rosie said.

He'd push her out of the way, the little slut, if she didn't move.

Her and the exquisite slattern with her. He made another attempt to pass.

"I bet she is looking for you to say goodbye," Rosie giggled.

He stopped. "Is Pila going somewhere?"

"Yes, she is going." She evidently couldn't talk without the silly giggle.

"Where?"

"She is going home," Rosie said. "Her father he has come to take her home. Back to San Ildefonso. They are Indians." Her giggle went up and down again like the shrill of a flute.

"I know it," he said brusquely. "When is she going?" He owed her a pop or another ride or a permanent wave. He'd promised her.

Rosie shrugged. "I don't know when," she singsonged in her accent. "Maybe tonight." He'd been interested; she hadn't expected it. She'd thought he would laugh at Pila too. He wanted to knock the frizz off her head, knock the paint off her mouth.

The slattern put her slow black eyes into him. "Muy macho," she slurred.

Rosie remembered her then and perked up. "This is my friend, Jesusita. 'Sita, this is Sailor I was telling you about."

Jesusita said, "Hallo." With the same look.

If he was going to be here, time on his hands, he might stick around with these two. He might give the slattern a knowing eye. She'd be worth a trip to the Federal Building. But he was getting out. He didn't need to fool around with slovenly dames; he'd have his pick in Mexico City.

He said, "Tell Pila I want to see her before she goes," and he moved quick, past them, out of the Fiesta square, covering the quarter block and turning the corner to the steak house. He didn't look back. He didn't know if Rosie had any intention of passing on the message. Nor if Pila could get away from her old man for the last afternoon of Fiesta on the Plaza.

He walked on fast to the restaurant. It wasn't crowded this time of day. If Pila was staying over till tonight he could treat her to the permanent wave. With the Sen's money. He'd have it tonight. He had forty dollars left and a pocketful of change. Not much. Not enough to take care of Pancho and Pila like he wanted to. Enough for now. He'd been saving money, sleeping and eating and doctoring with the natives. If anyone had told him before he left Chi that he was going to move in with a spic carnival operator and play Lord Bountiful to an Indian kid during Fiesta, he'd have told them how nutty they were. If anyone had told him he was going to take in a Fiesta he wouldn't have known what they were talking about. Travel was sure broadening, he didn't think. That was just another of the Sen's crummy ideas. Maybe it was broadening if you had your dead wife's fifty grand to splurge with.

He paid the check, stuck a toothpick in his mouth. Outside he threw away the toothpick. The Sen had taught him better. He walked back up the street, taking his time. That was all he had to do now, waste time. Until five o'clock. It wasn't quite three.

3

THE CLOUDS HAD PILED UP OVER THE CATHEDRAL, NOT STORM CLOUDS, big white ones, soft and thick as marshmallows. The sun was hot, the sky a burning blue. If he had a room, he'd go take a nap. When he got to Mexico City he'd get the best room in the best hotel and sleep for a week. He'd lay in the bathtub for another week.

He didn't want to go back to the Plaza but there wasn't any place else to go. Unless he went to La Fonda and sat in the lobby. And talked to Mac. He'd never run into Pila in La Fonda lobby. He wanted to tell the kid goodbye. He wondered how much her permanent wave would cost. It wasn't her fault the Sen had ratted again last night. She'd look like hell with a permanent wave.

He wandered up the street, automatically ducking the kids, his ears filled with cacophony of noise, music and jabber and singing and laughing and crying, all kinds of noise mixed up into one big Fiesta noise. He wandered on up to the corner where Fiesta was most noisy, where Pancho made Tio Vivo gallop a lively course. Pancho was a funny guy. He didn't have anything to be happy about but he was always happy. He didn't care about getting any place. He didn't care where he slept or what he hung on his back or what he put in his stomach.

A funny guy. Sailor wondered what Ziggy would make of Pancho. Ziggy studied guys, figured them out. Sailor went around in back of the merry-go-round, leaned against the fence. The kids weren't on this side. They crowded in by the gate. He could watch Pancho without Pancho knowing it. Watch the big muscles swelling under the sweaty shirt. He couldn't figure Pancho out. Working like a ditch-digger for nickels. Not for nickels, to make a bunch of kids happy.

Maybe that's why Pancho was happy, because he was making other people happy. Even making an amigo out of a stranger. A funny guy.

While he was leaning there, he saw Pila. She was on the other side, in back of the kids, watching Tio Vivo. He didn't know her at first. She wasn't in the costume; she was wearing a plain blue dress, the kind kids wore in orphanages, white collar on it, big buttons down the front of it. Her hair hung in braids; she looked like the little kid she was. He went around to her as quick as he could push the mob of kids aside, came up behind her.

"I'll buy you a ride on the pink horse," he said.

She turned slowly. "No. My father he is waiting for me. To take me home."

"I'll buy you a pop. A pink pop." He took her arm. "You can take it with you, drink it on the way home." He pushed her through the crowd, out of the park to the pop stand. He rang down the dime for the bottle.

Pila said, "Rosie, she say you want to see me."

He put the pop bottle in her hand. "Yeah. About that permanent."

Her eyes didn't leave his face. The eyes of the kid in front of the bike window. Not hopeless, simply without hope.

"How much would it cost you?"

"For three dollars, Rosie she can get a permanent."

Things were cheaper in the sticks. The dames the Sen knew paid twenty bucks in Chicago. He grinned, "It's a deal. He took the bills from his pocket, peeled a five, added another.

She looked at the money in his hand but she didn't touch it.

"Go on, take it," he said. "I promised you, didn't I?"

"It does not cost this much."

He put the bills in her small brown hand. "After you get it, you'll need a new dress, won't you?" He looked down at the orphan shoes on her feet. "And some shoes."

"My father—"

"You don't have to tell your old man, do you?"

She crumpled the bills into her pocket, pushed her hand down on them. "Thank you." She didn't grin and jump around like Lorenzo. If somebody had handed Sailor the red bike out of Field's window, he wouldn't have jumped around. He'd have stood there looking up, saying, "Thank you," like he hadn't any other words in his heart.

She said, "I must go to my father."

"Sure." He swung along beside her.

She was clutching the pop bottle to her blue dress.

"I don't know what you want a permanent for," he said. Making conversation. Just wondering.

She looked at him. Like he was the Sen. "Then I can come into town and go to work. Like Rosie. Rosie gets five dollars a week cleaning houses. I can clean better than Rosie, I learn at the Indian school. At nights Rosie goes to the picture show and to dances—"

The bright lights of the big hick town. A permanent and a new dress and working out like Rosie. Meeting the boys after dark. Next year the old man wouldn't count. Laying with the boys on the Federal Building lawn. Like Rosie.

"Listen," he said. He grabbed her arm and she almost dropped the pink pop but she caught it, clutched it more tightly. "Listen," he said. "Don't you do it. You stay where you are. Stay at the pueblo. Get yourself fixed up if you have to but you stay there. With your own people. Find you a guy there, a good guy. One your old man likes. You don't belong here, Pila. You're too good to be like Rosie." He didn't know what he was talking about. Old Mother Sailor. He didn't know why he was afraid, why he was warning her off. She'd do what she wanted to. But he could try.

"Don't forget what I'm telling you. Stay where you belong." He was trying to tell her. "Fiesta only lasts three days. After that Zozobra isn't dead any more." Maybe she'd get it. Maybe she'd think about it. He didn't say any more. They were at the end of the museum portal and she turned to him.

"Goodbye."

He wasn't to go any further with her. He got it. He watched her cross the street, watched her walk down to a pickup truck in front of the Art Museum. She climbed in the back of it. There were already a bunch of kids in it and a couple of women with calico shawls over their heads. One of the two men against the side of the truck must be her father. The two looked like all the men around here, old jeans, old shirts, battered hats. Lean brown faces. They both climbed in the front of the truck. Sailor stood watching while the truck backed out, shook and clanked on its way. She didn't wave goodbye; she didn't know he was there watching. She was drinking the pink pop.

He'd tried. He didn't know now why he'd given her ten bucks. Ten from forty left thirty. Not much money to go on. Maybe he thought she'd be his lucky piece. Maybe he was paying off the look in her eyes, the look that scared him. Because it knew too much, it knew what had happened and was to happen; the look that denied him existence because in time, Indian time, he was without existence. He'd paid off; it wasn't his fault if it backfired. If she turned into a Rosie by next Fiesta. He'd warned her. The rest was up to her.

And if someone had warned him to stick to the straight and narrow when he was fourteen? Someone had. Mac had. Sailor shook away thought. Maybe she'd be better off if she did leave the dump where she lived and the old man beating her and came to the bright lights of town. There was nothing wrong with trying to better yourself. It had worked for him. But then he hadn't been an innocent kid. Ignorant but not innocent. He wasn't either one now. The Sen had taken care of that.

The clouds were a blazing white in the bright blue sky. The Plaza was bedraggled as the flowered skirts trailing in the dust. On the bandstand an orchestra of Spanish kids was squeaking out of tune. The curbs were solid with women and babies and old men getting off their feet. You'd think they didn't have a home to go to. He strolled over to Tio Vivo, knocked the kids out of the way to reach the palings. He felt good for no reason; he'd feel better to get out of the hot dirty square into a place where you could know the feel of a cold bottle of beer. Only he didn't want to be alone. Or with Mac.

He yelled over the fence, "Hey, Pancho."

Pancho heard him. He gave the crank a couple of more turns and left it to unwind. He wiped his face with a blue bandanna as he came over to the fence.

"How about a beer?"

"Un tragito," Pancho sighed and swallowed his spittle. "I would like a beer, yes. Muy bueno."

"Come on. I'm buying."

Pancho shook his head. "But now I cannot go." He gestured to the horde of waiting children. "Come back in a little while, Sailorman. Six o'clock when it is supper time and not so many are here. Ignacio will do well enough when there are not so many."

"Okay." He had to say okay. Pancho was already shuffling back to his labor.

Well, he could get himself a bottle. Nothing wrong with that. He could go sit in the Placita behind the protecting wall. Under a tree. Only he'd run into Mac and it was better not to see Mac. He could go to Keen's. It was a tossup between Mac and the ape; a tossup between luxury and a smoky, smelly bar. He moved on to La Fonda.

He could handle Mac. And the Sen might be recovered, might be cooling his fever with beer in the Placita.

The lobby was still like a convention; the Cantina like the El at rush hour. He pushed through them just the same. The Placita wasn't much better but it was quieter. And it didn't smell. In front of the open fireplace, there was a guitarist and a singer that were in tune. There wasn't a table, not just then. There were a half a dozen fancy costumes waiting for a table. He didn't wait. He cut across to where a party was about to leave and when they left he sat down. The crowd at the entrance didn't like it but he didn't mind. The pert blonde was waiting tables again in his corner. When she flipped her starched skirt past him he said, "How's for a big bottle of beer?"

She nodded. She had too many tables to serve and she'd be a long time coming back with the beer. He didn't care. He was comfortable. The Sen wasn't around nor any of his party. The people out here were having fun without thinking they had to make a lot of racket like the hicks in the bar. Sailor shoved back his hat. He could sit here till five o'clock if he wanted to. The blonde finally brought the beer. She poured half of it into a glass. Pouring it right, slowly, handling the head.

He said, "On your next trip in from Gary how about another?" He thought she was eying the empty chairs and he said, "I'm expecting friends."

She said, "I'll be glad when Fiesta is over. This place is a madhouse."

"Yeah." She wasn't as pert as yesterday; there were tired smudges under her eyes. "Why don't you have one with me?"

Her eyes flirted. "I wish I could. But I won't be through till nine."

She wanted him to make a date. She wasn't bold but she was invitational. He pretended regret. "I'm leaving before then."

"You're not staying for the Baile?" She was stalling for a little rest. Resting her feet and her nerves.

"What's that?"

"The big dance. And there'll be street dancing on the Plaza."

He shook his head. "Can't do it. Got to get my business wound up and be on my way."

She laughed. "If you're here on business, you're the only one here on business." She flipped her starched skirt. "I'll bring you the beer when I can."

"Make it two."

He hadn't seen Mac. The copper was sitting there at the table; the waitress had blocked him from sight until she moved away.

"Don't mind if I join you, Sailor?"

"No," he said heartily. As if he didn't mind. "They're pretty busy. You'll probably have to wait for the beer."

"I can wait," Mac said. That was McIntyre. He could wait. For a beer or a man or a story he was after. "How did you rate a table, Sailor?"

"Hijacked it." He lifted a glass. "You don't mind?"

"Go ahead." Mac lit a cigarette, laid the pack on the table. "Sailor?"

"Have my own, thanks." He set down the glass. Good beer. He lit up, left his pack on the table. Mac wasn't the Sen; he wouldn't snitch them. "You see the Sen?"

"No."

"Find out where he is?"

"Yes."

"Where?"

"You can't get to him, Sailor. Doctor's orders. He's to see no one. That's why his room is changed."

If Mac would tell him where, he'd see him. No doctor would keep him out. "What's wrong with him?"

"Nervous exhaustion."

Sailor's laugh was a vulgar noise. "That's a new name for it."

Mac smiled, a faint smile. Then he didn't smile. "You were at the senator's the night Mrs. Douglass was killed."

"Uh-uh." He poured some more beer in the glass. Steady and smooth, watching the amber bubbles lift into foam white as snow-white clouds.

"Fingerprints don't lie."

He drank comfortably. "I was there a lot. But not that night."

"You weren't there a lot," Mac denied quietly.

The blonde brought two more bottles and his change. "Thanks, doll," Sailor said. He left a quarter, put another bill on the tray for the bottles.

Mac was pouring from his bottle. "The senator didn't take his business associates to his home."

"I was his confidential secretary," Sailor pointed out.

"You hadn't been there that week. The panes were washed on Tuesday. Your prints are on the French doors."

He'd worn gloves. Mac wanted him to say he'd worn gloves. He didn't let McIntyre have any idea he'd like to slug him, pulling something like this on him. He brazened, "So you got a witness who'll perjure himself."

Mac said, "When the time comes, I have some good witnesses."

"What have you been waiting for?" Sailor demanded. "If you got all these swell witnesses, if you think you can break my alibi, what have you been waiting for?" He'd let his anger come up and he shouldn't have. He took a quick drink to cool him.

Mac was calm as a mill pond. "Sure, I could have picked you up. In Chicago weeks ago. I didn't want to, Sailor. I wanted to get the man who killed her." Sailor relaxed. "You know who killed her. So do I."

Sailor didn't say a word.

"But until you tell me, I can't get him." Mac spoke mildly, "A confidential secretary knows a lot about what goes on."

"He doesn't spill."

Mac said, "After he's quit?"

"You think I've quit?"

"The senator says that you killed her."

He saw red again, at the dirty, lying Sen. But he clamped his mouth.

"What do you say?"

"I say I didn't. I didn't. You can take me in but you'll never prove I did it. I didn't."

Mac said, "How about another beer?"

Sailor's hand touched the second bottle. "I'm all right. You have another." He looked around for the blonde but he didn't see her. He saw another one. She was over in the corner and her shining head was bent to a good-looking blonde guy and his head was bent to hers. It wasn't the Prague mucker. Their shoulders were touching. Under the table maybe their knees were touching. More than their knees. Because in their look was longing. They weren't smiling at each other; they weren't happy.

He could give McIntyre the story right now. Then he could walk over and say to Iris Towers and the young fellow, "It's okay now. The Sen's out of it." He didn't. He said to Mac, "I've got to see the Sen. Give me ten minutes alone with the Sen and I'll talk."

Mac should have perked up. But he didn't. He didn't look any happier than Iris Towers.

"It's a deal," Sailor insisted.

Mac said, "I'd rather you didn't see him."

"Why not?" He'd offered Mac a good proposition; Mac ought to accept it, not start making trouble. Mac needed him; he should play ball.

"I don't think it's safe." Mac looked straight at Sailor. The Spanish hat wasn't funny right now; it was a policeman's hat.

"I'm not worried," Sailor boasted. "I can take care of myself."

"I'm not worried about that," Mac stated. "You can take care of yourself against someone else. You know how. Can you take care of yourself against yourself?"

He got it. He wasn't dumb. Mac didn't trust him not to use the gun.

Mac said, "I don't want anything to happen to Senator Douglass. I told you that before. Moreover I don't want anything to happen to you." He took a long drink of beer. "Why I should care about that, I don't know, Sailor," he said in that quiet way of his. As if he were wondering about it for the first time. "All these years, every time I've tried to give you a hand, to steer you right, I might as well have hollered down a well. I don't know why I've thought you were worth saving. Why I still think so."

The sun had gone down, there was already a faint evening chill in the Placita. Beyond the wall, echoing from the Plaza, was singing, wild gay singing, ". . . alla en el Rancho Grande, alla donde vivia . . ." The voices whooped. The Placita was filling with lavender light. Iris Towers and the young man were nearer each other. The tinkle and strum of Tio Vivo was a faint shimmering sound. And somewhere there was monotone of a muffled drum.

"Perhaps because I could have been you. If the wrong person had got hold of me when I was a kid. If the Devil had tempted me, I might not have been any stronger than you were."

Mac was going preachy again.

"You're free of him now, Sailor. You're still young; that part's over. You mustn't make a mistake now."

"I'm not going to hurt him," Sailor smiled.

"You don't know," Mac said. "It could happen. You don't want to take a chance."

He wasn't going to kill the Sen. All he was going to do was get the dough that was due him. He didn't have to kill the Sen; Mac and the State of Illinois would take care of that for him. He laughed. "You got me wrong, Mac. I wouldn't cheat you out of the Sen. I'm not gunning for him." He shoved his hand in his right-hand pocket. All of a sudden he wanted to explain to Mac. If Mac could have been him, he could have been Mac. They'd always been mixed up together, one on one side, one on the other, like one man split in half. Maybe it was explaining to himself.

"Listen Mac," he said. "You don't have to worry about me. I never used a gun in my life except when I had to, to protect myself." Except once. And that hadn't come off. It didn't count. "Against guys you'd have shot it out with yourself. I never killed anyone. It's the mugs that handle that line." He was too good for mug stuff. He was uptown, a confidential secretary. Mac ought to know that.

Mac still didn't trust him. "How do you know what you'll do with a gun in your pocket? Sometimes the wrong person gets in the way. A gun's a bad thing to have handy, Sailor. I don't like guns. I haven't packed one since I quit pounding pavements."

That was all right for Mac. Guns didn't worry Sailor. He spoke with confidence. "This is for protection, that's all."

Mac said, "I can give you better protection. If you'll tell me about that night, I'll see you're protected."

But Mac couldn't give him five grand, even one grand. Mac didn't have it. Mac was a good enough guy for a cop but he wasn't smart about money. He was an honest copper. He'd never be swanking it in Mexico City dressed up in a white Palm Beach suit, ordering champagne cocktails for a girl like Iris Towers. He wasn't that smart.

And Mac wasn't going to fix it up for Sailor to see the Sen. He was on his own about that. The lavender light was deepening. "I got a date," he recalled suddenly.

Mac was tensed, ready to stick with him.

He laughed. "Not with the Sen. With a friend of mine. For beer."

Mac relaxed. "Think it over, Sailor. I'll be right here."

"Okay." He'd already got it thought over. He was seeing the Sen if he had to go to Iris Towers to work it. McIntyre, no one, could stop him.

4

THE TWILIGHT WAS HUNG WITH EARLY STARS AND THE FLOWERED lights. Sailor cut across to the whirl of Tio Vivo. He was late. He peered over the fence palings. Ignacio was turning the crank. Old Onofre fiddled. Neither one had the heart of Pancho; Tio Vivo was spiritless and the music was tin. Sailor shouted over the hubbub of Fiesta, "Where's Pancho? Hey, where's Pancho?"

Ignacio heard him. He shrugged, "Quien sabe?"

Well, he could catch up with Pancho later. He walked away but before he reached the curb he bumped square into the big fellow. There was a smear of chile on the dirty chin, the smell of garlic would knock you down.

Pancho beamed, "Ah there, Sailor? Where you been?" His hands patted Sailor's shoulders tenderly.

"I got held up. Business," Sailor said. "Listen, we'll have that tragito a little later." He stepped out of the embrace and his hand pulled a bill from his pocket. It was a ten. It didn't matter; he'd be fixed up in a little while now. "Tequila, how about it?"

Pancho's brown eyes took a happy squint at the bill. "Hokay," he said.

A farewell party with his good angel, Pancho. Some angel. A dirty old spic who cranked a merry-go-round. "Hokay," Sailor echoed.

He felt good swinging out of the Plaza, stepping over the curb, into the street. Not paying any attention to the villagers. They weren't so bad; they didn't have much fun. No wonder this tinsel Fiesta looked good to them. Nobody could have much fun living in this one-horse town. He'd be out tomorrow. It wouldn't be Chicago but Mexico City would be even better. Sure it would; no more dirt and cold and sweat; no more jumping when the Sen lifted his little finger. Like Mac said, he'd be starting a new life. He could have it any way he wanted it. He was going to have it good with the Sen's stake.

He returned to the hotel. He tried the Sen's room first. No luck there. The old bitch with the yellow-gray hair was at the desk. He asked her polite, "Will you give me the number of Senator Douglass' room?" She gave it to him like it hurt her.

"He isn't in that room now," Sailor explained. "I just called."

She was snippy, "Well, I don't know where he is."

Somebody ought to push her nose into her face. She ought to learn some manners from the spics. From the Indians. She probably came from some small town in Kansas, so small she thought this was a metropolis. Thought this hotel was the Palmer House.

"Give me Iris Towers' room," he demanded.

She gave it to him with another dirty look. He'd come back here someday and have the biggest suite in the place and he'd get her fired. He rang the room.

A man's voice answered. "Hello."

It wasn't the Sen. It was a young voice. A little drunk.

Sailor said, "I'm trying to reach Senator Douglass. Could you tell me where I could find him?" He talked like he was a rich playboy himself. Casual and a little bored.

"I'm sorry," the fellow said. "I don't know where he is."

Sailor caught him before he hung up. "May I speak to Miss Towers, please?"

The fellow was reluctant. He said, "Well—" And then she was on the phone. Her voice was husky and far away. Sort of breathless. Like she'd been interrupted.

Sailor said, "Do you know where I could reach Senator Douglass?"

"No, I'm sorry. Who is calling?"

He gave a phoney name. The Sen was hiding out in her room. He knew that as he turned away from the phone. She wouldn't have taken a drunk to her room if it was her room. She wasn't that kind. She and the Sen had traded rooms. But he was stalled again. He couldn't have his talk with the Sen with Iris Towers present.

She wouldn't stay there all evening nursing the Sen. She wasn't in love with the Sen. He'd hypnotized her some way, like he'd hypnotized others. But you didn't stay that way. You caught on after a while. You found out the Sen was cold as steel, you found out he was using you. Even a lug like Sailor caught on after a while. She'd be going to dress pretty soon. To dress for dinner and the big Baile. Going with a young fellow. Because the Sen was sick. All Sailor had to do was wait. Wait till she and the young fellow came downstairs. Then he'd go upstairs. Easy as that.

He strolled out of the crowd, to the back portal. There wasn't a place to sit down. The Mexican orchestra in their satins and velvets were playing the dressed-up crowd into the New Mexican room. A crimson velvet rope held off the crowd, like it was the Pump Room. If it was the Pump Room Sailor could go up to the rope and there'd be a reservation. He was one of the Sen's fellows.

The patio outside was filled too. The fountain splashed and the swings creaked lazily. The bar boys' white coats were luminous under the blue floodlight, the geraniums were dark and scented. Laughter spilled over the fountain, the laughter of those who were young and protected by the best families and beautiful homes with green lawns, who were born right. Who didn't have business here, nothing to do but dance out the Fiesta.

He stood there leaning against the door between the patio and the portal. He wasn't surprised that Mac joined him.

Mac said, "How about dinner?"

"Too early."

"I have a table in the dining room," Mac said. He went on along. But he left hunger behind him.

Sailor didn't have to stand here and wait. He could take an hour off to eat. Kill time, eat and sleep. Get off his feet. No other way to get off them during Fiesta. It would take her that long to get dressed. The New Mexican room had a better smell than a greasy joint. He could get away from Mac easy enough later.

He didn't think about it any more. He followed the way Mac had gone. It wasn't the New Mexican room; it was the main dining room. Another rope, another crowd, but he edged through it. "Mr. McIntyre's table."

He hoped Mac had done something about letting the tall girl on the door know a friend might be along. Mac had. He looked up amused when she brought Sailor to the table.

"Not too early now?"

Sailor took it. "Time sure passes quick during Fiesta." Just as if time hadn't been dragging her heels these days.

Mac held the menu. "Have a cocktail? Forgot, you don't drink." He caught the eye of a nice looking Spanish-American fellow in a dark business suit. "Could I get a martini?"

"I think so." The fellow smiled. He didn't have any accent. "And you, sir?"

Sailor nodded. "I'll celebrate with you, Mac. Make it two." The fellow made him feel at home. Two city-looking fellows in a roomful of gaudy costumes. Even the waitresses in costume. The fellow was polite too, not like the old hag at the desk. She could use a dose of Spanish blood.

"Going to the Baile?" Sailor asked Mac.

"I don't think so. Are you?"

Mac would keep close guard on the Sen tonight. Sailor smiled inside. It wouldn't be close enough. Mac didn't know what room the Sen was in.

"I might," Sailor told him. Just as if he had a girl somewhere that he was going to take care of. A lovely silver girl, not an Indian kid, or a skinny little slut with frizzy hair, or a slattern with sultry eyes and a dirty neck.

The nice looking Spanish-American in the business suit was directing a dumb kid in shapeless whites to their table. The kid had an Indian face. He handled the martini tray as if he were certain he was going to spill it. But he made it, set the cocktails down. Just slopping them a little.

Mac lifted his glass. "Viva las Fiestas!"

"Viva las Fiestas," Sailor echoed.

The martini was cold and dry and right. When he got to Mexico City he'd start having a cocktail before dinner. It gave you a feeling of luxury to be sipping a cocktail in a gay dining room. He'd laid off liquor long enough for the Sen's business.

He could do as he damn pleased from now on. He'd be his own boss tomorrow. Mañana.

He said, "They got you doing it, too."

"Doing what?" Mac was writing the order.

"Talking Spanish. Viva las Fiestas. Mañana. Mi amigo. Who'd have thought we'd ever be talking Spanish together?"

Mac handed the order blank to the small dark girl. Her skirts rustled away, "Funny world," Mac said.

Sailor kept on talking. He didn't want Mac to get back to the case. And he didn't want Mac to start preaching. He wanted to enjoy this hour.

"Yeah, it's funny. When I got in here I thought they were all just a bunch of dirty spics. I didn't have any use for any of them. But you take Pancho now."

"Who's Pancho?"

"The guy that runs Tio Vivo." He thought Mac knew about Pancho. Then he saw that Mac did, only he didn't know him by that name. "I call him Pancho. Pancho Villa. He's got a long Spanish name. Don José de something or other. Says he's a descendant of a conquistador way back when Fiesta got started. He looks more like Pancho Villa to me."

Mac smiled, "He does."

"Well, you take Pancho. He's dirty all right. I bet he doesn't take a bath once a year. Probably never owned a tooth brush in his life. But he's muy macho. He'd do anything for you if you're his amigo—" He broke off. "There I go again thinking Spanish." He took another sip. "Not because he wants something out of you but because he wants to do something for you. That's the kind of guy Pancho is."

Mac nodded.

"Maybe they're not all kind of simple that way. But they don't shove you around. They give you a smile. Even if you don't talk their language they don't shove you around. The way we shove them around when they come up to our town."

"I know," Mac said. "I've thought sort of along that line myself. We're the strangers and they don't treat us as strangers. They're tolerant. Only they're more than tolerant. Like you say, they're friendly. They give you a smile not scorn."

Sailor was thinking of Pancho. And he was talking too much, it could be the martini. "They're poor. It isn't good to be poor," Sailor quoted Pancho. "But if you have to be, it's better to be out in this country, I guess. Where nothing matters much."

He was somewhat startled at hearing the words come out of his mouth. If he had to stay here, this alien land would get him, just like it got everyone. He'd be a mañana man himself; he wouldn't have any more ambition than Pancho. He'd start believing like Pancho, ambition and pride got you nothing, only to be conquered by two-bit-fifty-cent gringos. Better to forget grandeur and glory, to sing and dance and work a little, un tragito on Saturday nights, go to Mass on Sunday mornings. Better to be happy in your little life than to be important. You could hold on to your pride because it was all you had left; you wouldn't know it was only a word you'd learned long ago.

This was what the Indians had done to the intruder, this was how they would diminish him to non-existence. The Indians and the land were one, strong, changeless, unconquerable.

The frozen terror he had known as a kid before a piece of sculpture was a chill in him now. For that inanimate hunk of woman had known then that his world, squalid and miserable as it was, was not the rock he thought it was. She had known the rock would disintegrate, that in time there'd be the Sen, and the Sen would run out on him and he'd be driven into this alien land. She hadn't warned, she hadn't pitied or gloated; she'd known. He out of all the kids in the Art Museum that day would be trapped in a land where she knew he did not exist.

He was getting screwy. Why did he keep thinking trap? Why had he thought trap ever since he came here? A piece of land couldn't trap a man. Even if it spread on and on like eternity all over the earth until the mountains stopped it. He wasn't trapped. He was getting out.

He didn't know what McIntyre had been talking about. He heard only what the copper was saying now.

"It's good for us to see how other people live. We get awfully narrow in our own little lives. We get thinking we're so all-fired important that nobody else counts. We forget that everyone counts, that everybody on this earth counts just as much as we do."

Sailor said, "Yeah. You're right, Mac." He grinned. "Just the same, good as these people are, I'm thankful I don't have to live here. Give me Chicago, U.S.A." He began to eat.

Mac said, "This is the U.S.A."

"This wouldn't be the U.S.A. in a million years. No matter what flag they fly." Mac didn't know the secret. "It's a foreign land. We don't belong here." Mac didn't have to worry about the secret. He was going back to Chicago. He hadn't been exiled by the evil of a nasty old man. Sailor wasn't going to be exiled either. He'd get out of here and set up business in Mexico but once he was a big shot with plenty of dough to oil the wheels, he would go back to Chicago. His hands were plenty clean. He'd keep them clean. He wasn't going to use the gun on the Sen. He could collect without that.

This was the way a man ought to eat. Service. No hurry. Clean people around you. This was the way he was going to live from now on. Free. Not just on sufferance as a gentleman with the Sen paying the bills. Nobody was going to look down a nose at him any more.

They both lit up. Comfortable. Waiting for their ice cream. Lulled.

"How long has the senator known Iris Towers?"

Mac knew when you were lulled. He was never off his single track even when he pretended to be. He was trying to add up two and two; trying to make the murder the getting rid of an old wife to make room for a young one. As if there were need for any more motive than a fifty-grand insurance policy. Mac didn't need to add it up to five; four was good enough.

Sailor said, "I didn't know he knew her. Until he took this trip."

"She's a pretty girl."

She was lovely as a dream; she was the only lovely thing in this strange dream.

"The Sen tell you he was going to marry the Towers girl?"

Sailor snapped it short. "He didn't tell me a thing. He never mentioned her to me." He didn't want to talk about this. Maybe Mac was trying to needle him. Maybe Mac knew how he felt about this girl being mixed up with the Sen. "It's always been strictly business between me and the Sen." He didn't know how to get off the subject. "Ever since he hired me that day down at the pool hall. Remember the old pool hall, Mac? I was pretty good at pool till I moved up with the Sen." He was moving away nicely. He grinned. "Then I learned bridge and gin."

Mac wasn't moving so fast. "You took care of the business records."

"That was Zigler's job." Mac was probably going to impound the records. If he hadn't already. They wouldn't be pretty. Real estate covered too much in the Sen's books.

"You could probably explain them pretty well. A confidential secretary."

The ice cream arrived. And the coffee.

Sailor tried the coffee first. "What you after, Mac? A political stink?"

"I'm after the murderer of Senator Douglass' wife," Mac said calmly.

"But you don't mind if you break the organization wide open." It was his turn to heckle. "The Sen shouldn't have opposed you in the elections."

"The Sen offered me his support. Through an emissary. I turned it down." Mac lifted an eyebrow. "You knew that?"

He hadn't known. The Sen didn't talk about his failures. All he'd known, all the gang had known, was that the organization was out to beat Mac's bunch. And they hadn't. Because the Sen's mind even then was on Iris Towers?

"I don't like men who corrupt and destroy. I don't like crooks who get rich off the poor. I just don't like them. The senator offered me a job when I was a young cop, Sailor. I turned it down." His mouth was set. "Ask me why, Sailor? I'll tell you without asking. I'd just fished one of his confidential secretaries out of the lake. After that he picked fellows like you. Those who already had a record. Those who could stomach it."

"Why did he act like he didn't know you today?"

"Maybe he's forgotten. Maybe he prefers not to know me. I've stayed out of his way. But I knew that long ago that he wouldn't let anything stand in his way. What were you doing at his house that night?"

Sailor said stubbornly, "Let me see him and I'll tell you."

Mac picked up the check. Sailor reached out his hand. "It's on me."

"Not tonight. I invited you."

It would help; he was low enough after his handouts. He'd buy Mac a better dinner in Mexico City. He said, "I won't argue. My turn next." He could excuse himself now but he'd be polite, wait with Mac for the change.

Mac put a bill on the tray. His face was solemn. "You're still determined to take the chance?"

"There's no chance, Mac," Sailor insisted. "Only I got to see him before I talk. I owe him that much."

"You don't owe him a damn thing, Sailor."

He didn't. Nothing good. But he owed the Sen plenty for these three days of bunking on the ground. Plenty for that slit under his shoulder. Plenty for making him wait for his just pay.

He urged, "Let me see him." As if Mac could. As if Mac had the Sen shut up incommunicado. No Zigler to bust him loose with a habeas corpus.

Mac said flatly, "He doesn't want to see you."

"He tell you that?"

Mac smiled, "Let's stop the dodging, Sailor. Give me a name, the name of a murderer, and I'll get you to Senator Douglass quick. If you can't see it any other way, take it your usual way. The way that'll pay you off."

But not in greenbacks. They left the dining room, wading through the crowd still hungering against the velvet rope. Sailor knew how to get away. "Let me think it over. You'll be around?"

"I'll be around."

5

HE WENT OUT OF THE HOTEL, INTO THE COLD NIGHT WARMED BY THE excitement of Fiesta. He turned his back on it, walked away up the brief street. The dark bulk of the cathedral loomed there, implacable as Judgment Day. It didn't bother him any. A long time till Judgment Day. He turned past it and circled the block. There could be a back door to the hotel.

If there was he didn't see it. Walls and then the balconies of La Fonda tiering up to the high flat roof. He could climb to a balcony but it wasn't a good idea. Not if someone were inside the room he tackled, someone who'd start yelling for a cop. He went on up the street passing under the canopy of the side door, and again he was smack against Fiesta.

You couldn't escape it tonight. He walked right into it, through it, drenched with it to the opposite street, to the museum. The Indians were no longer under the portal; their absence was somehow more frightening than the black, silent, watching eyes had been. The Indians knew these days must end. They had never believed in the dream. They had never been of it.

He boosted himself up to the ledge as soon as there was space and he sat there, marking time until nine o'clock. Just sitting and watching Fiesta dance by, listening to the musicians overplaying each other from the bandstand and the platform down below where the Mariachi sang and the scrape of Tio Vivo and the strolling guitarists. It would be too bad if a fellow's life wasn't any more than a merry-go-round, somebody cranking you up to whirl around in style, then letting you peter out into where you started from. That might have been the way it would be for him if he hadn't got what he did on the Sen. Because the Sen was ending the organization; the Sen wasn't carrying it with him into the world of Iris Towers and her wealth and influence. If Sailor hadn't waited around that night, he'd be whistling for his supper. The way Humpty and Lew would be if they ever went back to Chi. Luck had been on his side and he was keeping it there. He'd be just as careful of the Sen as Mac would be. He wanted to deliver the Sen in a neat package to Mac as bad as Mac wanted him delivered. To pay the Sen not only for what he'd done but for what he would have done if he could have married Iris Towers.

He waited until nine and then he started back to the hotel. By now she'd be gone for sure, she and the rest of the Sen's party. Off to dinner and the Baile. The only thing was to avoid Mac. He'd figure it out earlier. At the side door. He didn't even have to enter the lobby.

Through the side door, pass the entrance to the Indian shop on the left; on the right, pass the steps leading down to the barber shop. Then the small flight of steps leading up to a corridor, Woman's Rest Room, Beauty Shop, hotel rooms. The corridor ran parallel to the right-hand portal, you came out of it down another small flight of steps and you were by the elevator. You never went into the crowd in the lobby. It was that easy.

The elevator was deserted as usual. "Four," Sailor said. The fourth-floor corridor was as deserted, a ghost walk. No sounds from any of the closed doors. Past the Sen's closed door, past three more closed doors and this was the number of Iris Towers' room. The room she'd originally had.

There wasn't a sound inside. Empty of sound as the corridor where Sailor stood. He knocked, knocked again, kept knocking. The silence within deepened, the echoes of his left-hand knuckles on the door wavered in the emptiness. He couldn't shout in to the Sen; he mustn't attract attention. It could be someone was in a neighboring room. The overhead transom was dark, the Sen could be asleep. He could be lying there in the dark, scarcely breathing, knowing who was outside.

There was only one thing to do now. Go inside. The key was on his ring, the key that opened locked doors. A little present from the Sen, when the Sen needed him to open some stubborn doors. There was no risk in using it. If Iris Towers or any of the others were in there, they'd have answered his knocking.

The door opened noiselessly. He moved with its opening to stand in protective darkness against the wall. His foot kicked the door shut. The gun was in his hand. Its dull metallic gleam would show up even in the lightless room. That much light came from the night outside the windows.

He said, "All right, Sen. It's me." His words dropped into emptiness. Not even a rustle answered him, not the beat of a pulse.

His eyes were beginning to see in the dark. They saw the beds, smooth covers pulled over them. They saw the empty chairs, the empty corners of the room.

He walked swiftly to the bathroom, kicked open the door as he snapped the light. There was no one there. The door of the clothes closet was shut. Before he walked over, pulled it open, he knew what he would find. A closet full of woman's clothes.

He began to curse the Sen under his breath. He didn't bother to turn out the bath light. He left the room. He didn't even remember the gun open in his hand until he'd used the key on the Sen's own door. He didn't put it out of sight; he slid in, cursing the Sen, cursing the Sen in the room that had once been the Sen's, that was empty now, not even a cigarette butt remained of the Sen.

The Sen had skipped. Mac had kept Sailor entertained with dinner and fine talk while the Sen got away. Sailor shoved the gun in his pocket before leaving the room. He kept his hand on it. Mac had let the Sen go. Knowing he could pick him up, maybe a guy already waiting, to meet the Chief at the La Salle street station. Playing it smart; keeping the Sen safe, keeping him out of Sailor's way. Figuring Sailor would talk any time now. Sailor would think the Sen had run out on him and he'd be mad enough to talk. Mac didn't know about the five grand. Mac thought he was waiting for a payoff; he didn't know how big the stakes were.

He'd go down and see Mac. He'd tell off Mac. But he wouldn't talk. Not until he went back to Chicago and faced the Sen. Even that could be what Mac was after, get both of them back to Chi. Back to where Mac was boss. You never knew when you were playing Mac's game. And how was Sailor going to get back to Chi? He hadn't twenty bucks left. He'd have to let Mac buy the tickets. Travel with Mac, not under arrest, no. Just with a copper bodyguard.

He wasn't alone in the elevator. But he didn't see the faces with whom he rode downstairs. They were paper dolls someone had cut out and pasted there. They smelled like booze and they made a lot of noise. He left the elevator first and he started with angry determination towards the lobby. He had to stop a minute at the opening to the portal. Another bunch of noisy drunks were blocking the way. He wanted to flail through them and their silly faces but he waited. Waited and got the break.

The group of the elevator had moved in behind him. And a girl whined. "Why don't we get Senator Douglass before we go? I want Willie to go with us."

A man said, "I told you he's already gone to the Baile. He and Iris left an hour ago."

"Iris!" the girl cackled.

Sailor didn't turn around. He had no idea who they were. He said, "Thanks," under his breath.

He got out of the crowd and strode on to the lobby. It was a whirlpool of color and smell and sound. But he didn't see the black hat with the bobbles. He took the time to look. He didn't want to be followed now. He turned to leave the hotel by the side door when he realized he didn't know where to go. There wouldn't be a chance to pick up a cab quick, not on the last night of Fiesta. He stopped at the newsstand. "Where's this Baile?"

The girl behind the counter didn't smile but she looked him over as if she might if she wanted to. "It's at the Armory."

"Where's that?"

"Out College. The street that runs into the back of the hotel."

"Is it far?"

"No," she said.

He bought a pack of cigarettes from her and left the hotel. Out the side entrance, down the street away from Fiesta into the darkness of College Street. A convent on one side, a filling station on the other. His hands dug into his pockets, right hand closed over ugly steel, left hand cramped in his left-hand pocket. He didn't know what his left hand was shredding until he looked. Pink paper. The handbill the fancy clerk had given him. To tell him about Fiesta. If he'd read it, he'd have known the Sen wouldn't miss the Baile. The Baile that was the golden crown of Fiesta.

On up the street, up the hill. Little stores; dark houses, nobody staying home on the last night of Fiesta; another brick school with the cross over it. He walked on. An occasional car roared by. At the intersection a street lamp cast a little puddle of light. On. Nights were cold here, the stars were sharp and cold above the trees.

The narrow street twisted, the street lamps were small and spaced too far apart. Had he known how far the Armory was, he'd have waited for a cab. A rattletrap that passed for a cab in this dump. He walked on. He was alone on the long street, alone on the long, dark, strange street. The houses he passed were dark, soundless. He was alone as before in his bad dream. But he wasn't lost. He knew where he was going. To meet the Sen. To the final meeting with the Sen.

The long street ended on top of a hill. It became a road there, a two-branched road. He didn't know which was the way he should take. Under the white moon both led to empty space, to cold endless wastes of desert, blocked by the finality of mountains against the white-starred sky. He stood there and a car passed, behind it a few paces, another car. They veered to the right and he chose.

It was the right choice. A little further on and he could hear music and the jangle of laughter. The Armory didn't look like an armory. It was another fancy Spanish 'dobe building, pale in the moonlight. There were figures clumped outside, passing the bottle, twining together in the night. Figures gathered at the lighted doorway, peering into the ballroom. Slackmouthed, gangly boys with their dark Mex faces. No costumes on them, no dough to go inside to the Spanish Baile. They could look but they couldn't touch. It was too long ago they'd been the conquerors; they were the conquered now. The Indians were better off; they didn't want to look.

He went up to the door. The stale hot breath of the big room pushed into his face. It was so crowded you couldn't see anyone inside, only the kaleidoscope of moving color under the muted lights. He'd never spot the Sen in this mob. That was why the Sen thought it was safe to sneak out to the Baile. He didn't think Sailor could find him.

Sailor stepped inside. He wasn't going to shell out dough to talk to the Sen. He didn't have to argue it. There wasn't anyone on the door. Too late for that. Midnight already. He began a slow circle around the outside of the floor. Looking for a little man with a big snout and thin hair, a little man in black velvet pants and a black velvet jacket to cover his black soul. Looking for the white skirts and silvery-gold hair of an ivory girl who shouldn't be let come within miles of the rotten Sen.

Moving his feet snail-like, his eyes not moving, his hand not stirring, sure in his pocket. Watching the dancers swaying to the rattle of maracas, the scratch of gourds, the sultry frenzy of Latin music; watching the shape of bodies melting to oneness, breaking apart only to melt again. Listening for a voice in the muted thunder of too many voices.

When he saw her, he went rigid. As if he weren't ready for the meeting. Or as if he'd come to act, not talk. She turned in the dance and she was with the Sen. Sailor was all right then. The muscles in his stomach weren't clutching; they were tight. As if he and they were alone in the vast packed room, he cut across the floor, by instinct alone avoiding the dancers who flowed like tide about him. He would have lost them, one couple among so many, but his eyes never left her once they had found her. He would have lost them but the coldness of his anger was a lead wire stretching between him and them. When he came to them he knew what had solidified his anger so that it was no longer anger, but the ice of rage. She wasn't white and beautiful; tonight she was what she was, her skirts dyed scarlet, her eyes blurred by her half-closed lids. He should have known before, the way she'd been with the rich muckers, the way she'd even looked at him once. He hadn't known until he saw her tonight; she was the slattern, Jesusita, with a million dollars. It was the slattern's slow eyes smiling into his now. It was her harlot's mouth that saw him and thought him good. She hadn't been clean for a long time. She was the rottenest part of this dream. The Sen turning, saw him too.

Sailor said, "Do you want to come outside or do you want it here?"

The Sen's tongue flickered over his pale lips. His eyes drooped to Sailor's rigid right-hand pocket, scuttled quickly up to Sailor's face. To Sailor's stone face.

"I'll come outside."

The Sen was a shell, about to break apart. He thought Sailor had come to rub him out. It was a good idea. Let him think so. The scar-

let girl swayed against his arm. "Willis, where are you going?" But
her eyes were on Sailor. And her mouth.

The Sen said, "I'll be back in a minute." He didn't believe that.
He was a yellow-bellied coward, his voice was dust and ashes.

"But, Willis—"

"I won't be a minute, Iris. I'm sorry." He couldn't explain. He had
no words to explain to her.

Sailor said harshly, "I don't have all night."

The Sen's eyes flicked the right-hand pocket again. "Find Kemper.
I'll be back right away."

He left her standing there, alone in the crowd. Annoyed at his
leaving her, or annoyed at Sailor because he was leaving her, but she
wouldn't be alone or annoyed long. Her scarlet body would be cleaving to another man while the music languored and thudded, while
the Sen paid off in the cold night. Paid what he owed.

Sailor said, "Just walk on out that door." His hand in his pocket
touched the Sen's side. Guided him to the side door opposite. Past
the couples screaming there, swaying hot bodies there. Guided him
across the dark stubble, around to the rear of the building. Where it
was quiet. Where they were alone.

The Sen quivered his nose towards the ballroom.

Sailor's mouth twisted. "Don't worry about her. All she wants is a
man. Any man."

The Sen didn't say anything.

Sailor went on harshly, "I don't know what she wants with you.
Maybe she thinks she's going to sit in the governor's mansion.
Maybe that's what she's looking for. Or is she out for a cheap
thrill?" Hate poisoned his words. "The wife of the condemned man
looked so beautiful in black—"

The Sen's voice jumped hysterically. "Shut up."

Sailor smiled. He didn't feel like smiling. It hurt him in the pit of
his stomach. "What's the matter? You getting cold feet?" He ought
to shoot the Sen down, the dirty, sniveling, yellow-bellied Sen.
Shooting was too good for him. Shooting was easy. Let Mac put him
in the chair where he'd suffer. Let Mac send him to hell. The smile
on Sailor's mouth was cold as the cold moon, fixed as the cold,
white, faraway stars.

The Sen's voice was a thin whine. He tried to make it rich and full
but it didn't come out that way. "Let's talk it over, Sailor. After all
you've been to me. Like my own son. After all I've done for you
. . ." He was like one of those shoddy yellow canaries quivering on a

cheap stick. It was funny. Sailor began to laugh. He stuck out his chin and he laughed and laughed at the funny little canary that once he'd thought was the most important guy in the world.

When he finished laughing he said again, "What's the matter, Sen?" He could kill the canary easy; there wasn't anyone around out here. They were as alone as if they'd invented this alien wasteland for their final meeting, invented it that they might be utterly alone for their goodbye. He didn't want to kill; he just wanted his money. His honest pay. He said it. "I'm not going to rub you out. I just want my dough. That's all."

He watched the Sen stop shaking, watched the blood fill up the wizened face, watched the shame in the coward turn to vengeful rage. His own hand tightened on the gun in his pocket. Because he knew the Sen's anger. Too well to trust him.

But the Sen didn't start at him. The Sen stood quietly and his eyelids drooped. The brush covered the shape of his mouth. He said flatly, "You've sung. You're waiting for Mac."

Sailor's lips set hard. "I've never sung yet," he said. "You know it. What Mac knows isn't from me. He's guessing." He spat the lie. Only at the moment it wasn't a lie. "Give me what's coming to me and you can handle Mac your own way. I'm getting out tonight. Have you got it?"

The narrow eyes shifted to look into Sailor's. "I've got it," the Sen said in his sweet voice. "Yes, I've got it." He smiled, smiled at him as if Sailor were his white-haired boy again, as if it were the way it was when he'd first moved Sailor uptown.

He reached into his inner coat pocket, where his flat wallet would have been if he'd been wearing a coat, not a velvet monkey jacket. Reached in and Sailor stood there like a dolt waiting for it, waiting for the hand to come out holding a gun, shooting a gun.

Only the Sen wasn't good at it. He'd never been his own gunman. Sailor was good. He could shoot before the Sen did, could watch the Sen's gun explode towards the stars, too far away to know or care; watch the Sen crumple down on the dark stubble of the earth. "God damn you." Sailor sobbed it through his clenched teeth. "God damn you." He was standing over the Sen and he could have emptied his gun into the shadow on the cold earth. He was ready to shoot and shoot again. But he heard the crazy scream in the lighted doorway, heard the babble and he ran.

Ducking around the back of the building, running low to the ground in and out of the lanes of parked cars. His belly sobbing, the breath sucking from his teeth. *God damn him, God damn him, God* . . . He stumbled on; he didn't know where he was going. Only he was getting away. Before they got him. For killing the Sen.

He hadn't meant to kill him. It was self defense. Anybody would know it was self defense. Only nobody would believe him, because the Sen was the Sen, had been the Sen, and Sailor was a mug from down behind the car barns who did the Sen's dirty work. Until the Sen sold him out.

There wasn't anyone behind him. *Hurry, hurry, hurry* . . . He was alone cutting through back yards, around silent sleeping houses. There was no sound of a siren screaming through the night silence. Maybe it hadn't been a scream in the doorway; maybe it was just some bitchy dame with a whisky breath, laughing. Maybe the guns hadn't sounded loud inside where the music was thumping. He swerved away from the houses to the empty street. Not the main highway street; instinctively he'd avoided that one.

Somebody would stumble across the Sen before the dance was done. Mac would be around somewhere; Mac would know whose gun had killed him. If he could hop a late bus, get to Albuquerque quick, get on board a plane to Mexico, he'd be safe. If he could do it quick enough. Before somebody found out what that thing was on the dirty ground by the Armory.

He hadn't enough money for a plane ticket. He hadn't twenty-five dollars left in his pocket. Sickness was a dirty lump in his stomach. He'd been so sure he'd collect. Been so sure the Sen would fork over to save his neck. If he could get to Pancho, borrow back the ten, borrow a little extra, enough to get to Mexico. Ziggy would have something lined up by now. He'd send Pancho back double the loan; he'd send it back right away. *Hurry, hurry, hurry* . . . He had to see Pancho and get away quick. That was no siren; the Sen was still playing his big scene all alone.

He didn't know where he was but he was headed right, the reflection of colored lights lit the sky over the buildings ahead, the quickness of music strummed the night. Under the music he heard the thud of the Indian drum, relentless as heartbeat, as the following footsteps of a smart cop.

He saw the Kansas City steak house, and he crossed, slanted up the hill, turned to the Plaza. As he turned the night was shattered with noise; this was the climax, this was the final glittering twirl of the Fiesta merry-go-round.

6

THE SQUARE OF STREETS WAS DENSE WITH DANCERS, WITH SONG, WITH confusion of color and costume and the earth smells that would be forever in his nostrils. With the warmth of life. On the hill the outsiders played at Fiesta with their fancy Baile but Fiesta was here. In the brown faces and the white faces, the young and the old; capering together, forgetting defeat and despair, and the weariness of the long, heavy days which were to come before the feast time would come again. This was Fiesta. The last moments of the beautiful and the gay and the good; when evil, the destroyer, had been himself destroyed by flame. This was the richness of life for those who could destroy evil; who could for three days create a world without hatred and greed and prejudice, without malice and cruelty and rain to spoil the fun. It was not three days in which to remember that evil would after three days rise again; for the days of Fiesta there was no evil in this Fiesta world.

And so they danced and sang in the streets under the colored garlands of light, under the wreathed white smoke of the thatched booths. And the Mariachi shouted their fierce nostalgic songs of the homeland from one corner of the Plaza, and the lugubrious band of the Conquistadores blared their brassy dissonance from another. And the strolling musicians sang with the singers under the dark glittering trees and the children who should have been in bed ran laughing up and down the paths. And the white-haired old nodded their heads to the laughter and the song. And all clutched tightly in their hands the last moments of the Fiesta, as tightly as if they didn't have to let it go, as if tomorrow would never find its way into the dream.

There was cover in this swirling crowd. Sailor fled into it, safe for the moment, making his way to where Tio Vivo spun and tinkled in the far corner. To where Pancho would be, his friend, his amigo, Pancho.

Tio Vivo was motionless and dark. In the whole shimmering Plaza, Tio Vivo alone was still. Not even a small wind stirred the pink and brown and purple horses. Not a big, sweaty, bare-toed brigand rocked the gondola. Pancho wasn't there. No one was there.

In sudden panic, Sailor darted from the dark loneliness out again into the street, into the street crowd. It didn't matter who he was, it didn't matter that he was alien, or what he had done. He could not do wrong in Fiesta because there was no wrong existent. His hands were caught, he was swept into the dance, the girl beside him might have been Rosie, might have been the slut, might have been the abuelita. Or Juana or the woman with his mother's heavy shoulders. Whoever it was, she was honest, not a harlot masquerading in angel white, smirching the ancient and holy Feast. Sailor danced and he sang with the crowd, "Hola, hola!"; spinning around like a merry-go-round horse, "Ai, yai yai yai." He danced and his eye watched for Pancho and his eye watched for Mac. His ears listened for the scream of the siren—and he heard the thud of the drum.

He hadn't imagined the drum. It was right there in the Plaza. A big Indian was thumping it. The dancers were falling in beside him, arms linked, following his slow side shuffling step around the square. All the dancers were joning in the circle. Without knowing, Sailor knew this was the end. Without raising his eyes to see the bandsmen putting away their instruments, without seeing the Mariachi becoming silent shadows in the night. He knew the finality. And panic was gray dust in his throat.

Pancho? Where was Pancho? His friend. His guardian angel. His feet shuffled in the endless linked circle edging to drum thud around the Plaza. Watching the couples fade out of the circle, and he couldn't stop them, neither he nor they could hold back the end of Fiesta; watching the bonfire on the corner flicker lower. He could run but where? Pila was gone. Pancho was gone. Everyone gone. Everyone but Mac.

The circle was thinning, when it reached the corner again, it was small. It broke in front of the museum. Fiesta didn't end in fireworks, it faded away. His hands clenched to keep from reaching out to someone, anyone for help. Before all were gone and the Plaza empty, empty but for him alone there.

Desperately he looked towards Tio Vivo, as if by will he could force it to swing and tinkle. He breathed again. Pancho was there.

He ran across the street into the park, running until he was stopped short by the palings. It wasn't Pancho. It was a fat man but it wasn't Pancho. Not one of four men was Pancho. Dark faces, battered hats, worn jeans but not Pancho. Not even Onofre or Ignacio. The four men were taking down the merry-go-round. They knew how; they knew where to lay the pink horse, the brown, where the fence should be stacked.

Sailor said, "Where's Pancho?"

They didn't pay any attention to him. He might not have been there.

"Where's Pancho?" He wanted to yell it into their deaf ears, into their blank faces. "Where's Pancho?" But he mustn't raise his voice. The Plaza was too silent. Fiesta was over, the only sound was the sound of men working, and faintly, far away up on the hill, the plaint, "Adios, mi amigo . . ."

He grabbed the skinny fellow who passed with an armload of red palings.

"Where's Pancho?" he demanded. Blank eyes looked into his.

Sailor said in angry desperation, "Don't any of you know what I'm talking about? The guy who owns the merry-go-round? Pancho, Don José? The big fellow. My friend. Mi amigo. Where is he?"

They didn't know. They jabbered Spanish at each other. They gestured, they were vehement. Then they turned empty faces to Sailor. They shrugged. "You no se."

The horses looked like dead things lying on the ground. Pancho would return any minute now, return to put his big brown paw on the neck of the pink horse, to reassure the little horse that tomorrow he would gallop again.

Sailor's head darted at a shadow coming across the La Fonda corner. His breathing was noiseless but heavy. His hand gripped his pocket. It wasn't Mac. *Hurry, hurry* . . . He ought to be running, not standing here. The Sen should have been found by now. But maybe the swells on the hill hadn't stopped dancing to look for the Sen. Pancho would come. Pancho must come.

The four men were leaving. He stood in their path. "Where are you going? Where's Pancho? Where's Pancho?"

They shook their heads. They babbled, "Yo no se," but they didn't stop moving. They were shadows disappearing into the deeper shadow of the Plaza. Going away, gone, leaving him here alone. Alone.

He started to plunge after them. The voice halted him. The quiet voice from behind him, in the black soundless shadows behind him.

"Going somewhere, Sailor?"

He didn't move. He stood like a tree while Mac came up beside him.

"I wouldn't," Mac said.

He might have meant Sailor's finger pressing the trigger of the gun in his pocket. He might have meant not to run. Whatever he meant, Sailor's hand came out of his pocket limply.

"You couldn't get away," Mac said.

Mac was always so sure and so right. Mac could be wrong but he was right. There had been no escape from this, from the very beginning no escape. From the day in the pool hall. Sailor couldn't get away.

Sailor said slowly, "I didn't mean to kill him. He was going to kill me. It was self defense."

Mac offered a cigarette to Sailor. Sailor took it; he struck the match for both. Mac sat down on a stack of red palings. Mac, so sure of himself, so sure Sailor wouldn't shoot or bolt. He said, "I know."

Sailor didn't believe him. But Mac's face was plain as truth was plain. He had been there, unseen, silent as a shadow. He had watched it happen.

There was a bitterness on Mac's tongue. "I didn't want you to kill him. I tried to tell you." The bitterness was iron. "I wanted him to stand trial. I wanted him to pay." He looked up at Sailor. "It's too late for our talk now."

Sailor sat down beside Mac. He began to curse the Sen, out of the rage and self pity eating him.

Mac said, sort of wondering, "And you stuck with him despite that. Knowing what he was like."

"No," Sailor said. "I was through. I was getting out. You know I was getting out, Mac."

"Why didn't you get out? What were you waiting for?" And then Mac remembered without being told. "The payoff."

"He owed it to me," Sailor said stubbornly. He'd never collect a dime. He'd be working for Ziggy. Doing the dirty work for Ziggy just like he'd worked for the Sen. Or working for a mug in Chicago, not a gentleman like the Sen. If a smart mouthpiece got him out of this. It wouldn't be Ziggy. Ziggy had got away; he wouldn't come back. Some mug would get him a mouthpiece then he'd be sold down the river to the mug. He wanted to cry.

A guy up from the Chicago streets didn't cry. He'd get out of this. "It was self defense," he said. "You know it was, Mac." Mac was his only witness. Mac would have to testify for him.

"Yes, it was self defense," Mac agreed. "It won't always be self defense, Sailor. There'll be a time when it won't be self defense."

"If I get out of this," Sailor vowed.

"You won't change." He shook his head. The bobbles danced on his black Spanish hat. His voice didn't dance.

"I can go straight," Sailor insisted. "I was going straight."

"You don't want to go straight. You turned your back on the right way a long time ago. You chose the wrong way, the easy way. You can't do wrong and not pay for it." He was matter of fact. "Sure, you could turn around and go back, but it's a long way back and the going would be tough. Twice as tough as it would have been if you'd taken the right turn a long time ago. Too tough for you. You couldn't take it."

Sailor set his chin. "I've taken plenty. I'm not soft. I could take it."

The silence was heavy. "You don't know how tough it would be. You don't know how tough it is to be good." Mac put his cigarette on the ground. Carefully he stepped on the color of fire. "I could be wrong," he said. "I could be wrong all around. Maybe you didn't go bad because that's the way you are inside. Maybe you want to be good. Maybe you just never knew how. I've always wanted to help you, Sailor. I've tried. Because but for the grace of God, there go I." He stood up. "I'll try it again. If that's the way you want it. If you don't, God help you. If you don't, you can't get away from what's coming to you." His eyes were sad on Sailor's face. "You can't get away."

That was the end of Mac's sermon. He was the cop again. "You can have one of my beds tonight. Tomorrow we'll start back. I've fixed it with the locals. I had a warrant for Senator Douglass' arrest. They think you were helping me out."

Sailor got to his feet, slowly, listening to words, words that were like dream words, like in a bad dream.

"It won't go hard on you. He pulled the gun first. If it weren't for your record . . ." His voice was kind. "When you get out, I'll be there. If you want my help, I'll be there."

If the organization were working he'd get off quick. But there wasn't an organization any more. There wasn't a Sen. He was alone.

He'd get off easy. Maybe four or five years. And after he came out of the rotten pen, Mac would find him a job, maybe paying twenty-five bucks a week. He'd brush his teeth and go to church on Sundays and report to Mac once a week and say thank you Mac for helping me be a sucker.

He could do it if he wanted to. He wasn't soft; he could do it. He didn't want to. It wasn't good enough for him.

Beyond the mountains was freedom. So near, just beyond the horizon line. He could hitch a ride, heist a car if he had to, be over the border by morning. With the gun it would be easy. He could make it. Once over the border they'd have a hard time getting him back. He could call Ziggy from Juarez to write him dough. Ziggy needed him as bad as he needed Ziggy. They would make a sweet thing out of a partnership in Mexico; Ziggy, the brain; Sailor, the trigger man. If he had to, he'd be a trigger man. They'd be big shots in no time, white Palm Beach suits and the best hotel suites and the dames hanging around their necks. That was better than stir or grubbing in a factory all your life. Mac was nuts.

The wind blew cold across the dark Plaza.

"Come on," Mac said. He yawned. "Bed's going to feel good tonight."

Sailor said, "No."

Mac's eyes jumped to his face. Cop eyes that quick, colorless, hard as flint. Sailor's hand tightened on his gun.

"Listen, Sailor—" He started to move in.

Sailor said, "No."

He shot McIntyre.

And he ran. Fled down the street, away from the sound that had shattered the dark of the night, the silence of the deserted Plaza. There were no echoing shots; Mac didn't carry a gun. He hadn't wanted to do it. Mac was a good man. But Mac was a copper.

Sailor was weeping as he ran, weeping for Mac. No sound stirred behind him, there was no sound in the night but his running steps, his tears. Somewhere in the silence Pancho prayed for him, not knowing he prayed for the damned. Or Pancho slept with tequila sweet on his lips. Pancho who would have helped him. Who could not help him now. It was too late.

He ran on, into open country this quickly; plunging into the wastes of endless land and sky, stretching forever, for eternity, to the far-off barrier of the mountains. The night was cold, colder than before. All he had to do was keep moving, keep moving on and on until he reached the mountains. On the other side was freedom. Escape from this dread dream.

You can't get away. It couldn't be Mac he heard pitying, Mac was dead. You can't get away.

Blindly he stumbled on.

IN A
LONELY PLACE

"It's in a lonesome place you do have to
be talking with someone, and looking
for someone, in the evening of the day."

F. M. Synge

For
CHARLOTTE

I

1

IT WAS GOOD STANDING THERE ON THE PROMONTORY OVERLOOKING THE evening sea, the fog lifting itself like gauzy veils to touch his face. There was something in it akin to flying; the sense of being lifted high above crawling earth, of being a part of the wildness of air. Something, too, of being closed within an unknown and strange world of mist and cloud and wind. He'd liked flying at night; he'd missed it after the war had crashed to a finish and dribbled to an end. It wasn't the same flying a little private crate. He'd tried it; it was like returning to the stone ax after precision tools. He had found nothing yet to take the place of flying wild.

It wasn't often he could capture any part of that feeling of power and exhilaration and freedom that came with loneness in the sky. There was a touch of it here, looking down at the ocean rolling endlessly in from the horizon; high above the beach road with its crawling traffic, its dotting of lights. The outline of beach houses zigzagged against the sky but did not obscure the pale waste of sand, the dark restless waters beyond.

He didn't know why he hadn't come out here before. It wasn't far. He didn't even know why he'd come tonight. When he got on the bus, he had no destination. Just the restlessness. And the bus brought him here.

He put out his hand to the mossy fog as if he would capture it, but his hand went through the gauze and he smiled. That too was good, his hand was a plane passing through a cloud. The sea air was good to smell, the darkness was soft closed around him. He swooped his hand again through the restless fog.

He did not like it when on the street behind him a sudden bus spattered his peace with its ugly sound and smell and light. He was sharply angry at the intrusion. His head darted around to vent his scowl. As if the lumbering box had life as well as motion and would shrink from his displeasure. But as his head turned, he saw the girl. She was just stepping off the bus. She couldn't see him because he was no more than a figure in the fog and dark; she couldn't know he was drawing her on his mind as on a piece of paper.

She was small, dark haired, with a rounded face. She was more than pretty, she was nice looking, a nice girl. Sketched in browns, the brown hair, brown suit, brown pumps and bag, even a small brown felt hat. He started thinking about her as she was stepping off the bus; she wasn't going to a party, the tailored suit, sensible shoes. She must be coming from work; that meant she descended from the Brentwood bus at this lonely corner every night at—he glanced at the luminous dial of his watch—seven-twenty. Possibly she had worked late tonight, but that could be checked easily. More probably she was employed at a studio, close at six, an hour to get home.

While he was thinking of her, the bus had rumbled away and she was crossing the slant intersection, coming directly toward him. Not to him; she didn't know he was there in the high foggy dark. He saw her face again as she passed under the yellow fog light, saw that she didn't like the darkness and fog and loneness. She started down the California Incline; he could hear her heels striking hard on the warped pavement as if the sound brought her some reassurance.

He didn't follow her at once. Actually, he didn't intend to follow her. It was entirely without volition that he found himself moving down the slant, winding walk. He didn't walk hard, as she did, nor did he walk fast. Yet she heard him coming behind her. He knew she heard him for her heel struck an extra beat, as if she had half stumbled, and her steps went faster. He didn't walk faster, he continued to saunter but he lengthened his stride, smiling slightly. She was afraid.

He could have caught up to her with ease but he didn't. It was too soon. Better to hold back until he had passed the humped midsection of the walk, then to close in. She'd give a little scream, perhaps only a gasp, when he came up beside her. And he would say softly, "Hello." Only "Hello," but she would be more afraid.

She had just passed over the mid hump, she was on the final stretch of downgrade. Walking fast. But as he reached that section, a car turned at the corner below, throwing its blatant light up on her, on him. Again anger plucked at his face; his steps slowed. The car speeded up the Incline, passed him, but the damage was done, the darkness had broken. As if it were a parade, the stream of cars followed the first car, scratching their light over the path and the road and the high earthen Palisades across. The girl was safe; he could feel the relaxation in her footsteps. Anger beat him like a drum.

When he reached the corner, she was already crossing the street, a brown figure under the yellow fog light marking the intersection. He watched her cross, reach the opposite pavement and disappear behind the dark gate of one of the three houses huddled together there. He could have followed but the houses were lighted, someone was waiting for her in the home light. He would have no excuse to follow to her door.

As he stood there, a pale blue bus slid up to the corner; a middle-aged woman got out. He boarded it. He didn't care where it was going; it would carry him away from the fog light. There were only a few passengers, all women, drab women. The driver was an angular, farm-looking man; he spun his change box with a ratcheting noise and looked into the night. The fare was a nickel.

Within the lighted box they slid past the dark cliffs. Across the width of the road were the massive beach houses and clubs, shutting away the sea. Fog stalked silently past the windows. The bus made no stops until it reached the end of that particular section of road where it turned an abrupt corner. He got out when it stopped. Obviously it was leaving the sea now, turning up into the dark canyon. He stepped out and he walked the short block to a little business section. He didn't know why until he reached that corner, looked up the street. There were several eating places, hamburger stands; there was a small drugstore and there was a bar. He wanted a drink.

It was a nice bar, from the ship's prow that jutted upon the sidewalk to the dim ship's interior. It was a man's bar, although there was a dark-haired, squawk-voiced woman in it. She was with two men and they were noisy. He didn't like them. But he liked the old man with the white chin whiskers behind the bar. The man had the quiet competent air of a sea captain.

He ordered straight rye but when the old man set it in front of him, he didn't want it. He drank it neat but he didn't want it. He hadn't needed a drink; he'd relaxed on the bus. He wasn't angry with anyone anymore. Not even with the three noisy sons of bitches up front at the bar.

The ship's bells behind the bar rang out the hour, eight bells. Eight o'clock. There was no place he wanted to go, nothing he wanted to do. He didn't care about the little brown girl anymore. He ordered another straight rye. He didn't drink it when it came, he left it there in front of him, not even wanting to drink it.

He could go across to the beach, sit in the sand, and smell the fog and sea. It would be quiet and dark there. The sea had appeared again just before the bus turned; there was open beach across. But he didn't move. He was comfortable where he was. He lit a cigarette and idly turned the jigger of rye upon the polished wood of the bar. Turned it without spilling a drop.

His ear caught the word spoken by the harsh-voiced woman. He wasn't listening to her but the word spun and he thought the word was "Brub." He remembered then that Brub lived out this way. He hadn't seen Brub for almost two years; he'd spoken to him only once, months ago when he arrived on the coast. He'd promised to let Brub know when he was settled, but he hadn't.

Brub lived in Santa Monica Canyon. He left his drink on the bar and went quickly to the phone booth in the corner. The book was tattered but it was a Santa Monica book and there was the name, Brub Nicolai. He found a nickel and clanged it in the slot, asked the number.

A woman answered; he held on while she called Brub. Then Brub's voice, a little curious, "Hello."

He was excited just hearing the voice. There wasn't anyone like Brub, those years in England wouldn't have been real without Brub. He was gay as a boy, calling, "Hello there, Brub," wanting Brub to guess or to sense who it was. But Brub didn't know. He was puzzled; he asked, "Who's calling?"

Excitement titivated him. "Who do you think's calling?" he demanded. And he cried, "It's Dix. Dix Steele."

It was a good moment. It was the way he'd known it would be, Brub taking a gulp, then shouting, "Dix!" Where you been hiding out? Thought you'd gone back East."

"No," he said. He was warm and comfortable in Brub's pleasure. "I've been sort of busy. You know how it is. Always something here. Something there."

"Yeah, I know." Brub asked, "Where are you now? What are you doing?"

"I'm sitting in a bar," he said and heard Brub's answering crow. They'd spent most of their free time sitting in bars; they'd needed it in those days. Brub didn't know Dix no longer depended on liquor; he had a lot of things to tell Brub. Big Brother Brub. "It's down by the ocean, has a ship's prow by the door——"

Brub had cut in. "You're practically here! We only live on Mesa Road, couple of blocks from there. Can you come up?"

"I'm practically there." He hung up, checked the street number in the phone book, returned to the bar and swallowed the rye. This time it tasted good.

He was out on the street before he realized that he didn't have his car. He'd been walking up the street this afternoon and he'd climbed on a Wilshire-Santa Monica bus and he was in Santa Monica. He hadn't thought of Brub for months and a scarecrow dame in a bar said what sounded like "Brub." She hadn't said it at all; she'd been calling the scarecrow guy with her "Bud," but he'd thought of Brub. Now he was going to see him.

Because it was meant to be, a taxi was held just then by the red light. At first he didn't recognize it as a cab; it was a dark, battered car with a young guy, hatless, driving it. It was empty. He read the lettering on it: "Santa Monica Cab Co.," even as the lights turned, and he ran out into the lonely street calling, "Hey, Taxi."

Because it was meant to be, the driver stopped, waited for him. "Do you know where Mesa Road is?" His hand was on the door.

"You want to go there?"

"I sure do." He climbed in, still in his happiness. "Five-twenty."

The driver turned and drove back the way he'd come, a few blocks up the hill, a left turn and a steeper hill. The fog lay a deep and dirty white in the canyon, the windshield wiper pushed away the moisture. "This is Nicolai's," the driver said.

He was pleasantly surprised that the driver knew where he was going. It was a good omen; it meant Brub wouldn't have changed. Brub still knew everyone, everyone knew him. He watched the driver's fog lights circle, turn, and head down the hill. It was unconscious, the waiting and watching; in his thoughts was only the look of the amber swinging across the pillow of fog.

There was a gate to open; and the mailbox was white beside it. Lettered in black with B. Nicolai, 520 Mesa Road. He embraced the name. The house was high above the flowered terrace, but there was a light of welcome, amber as a fog light, in the front window. He climbed the winding flagstone steps to the door. He waited a second before he touched the brass knocker, again without consciousness, only a savoring of the moment before the event. He had no sooner touched it than the door was flung wide and Brub was there.

Brub hadn't changed. The same short-cut, dark, curly hair, the same square face with the grin on the mouth and in the shining black eyes. The same square shoulders and the look of the sea on him; he rolled like a sailor when he walked. Or like a fighter. A good fighter. That was Brub.

He was looking up at Dix and his hand was a warm grip on Dix's hand. "Hello, you old son of a sea cook," he said. "What do you mean by not calling us before now? Let me see you."

He knew exactly what Brub saw, as if Brub were a mirror he was standing before. A young fellow, just an average young fellow. Tanned, medium light hair with a little curl, medium tall and enough weight for height. Eyes, hazel; nose and mouth right for the face, a good-looking face but nothing to remember, nothing to set it apart from the usual. Good gabardine suit, he'd paid plenty to have it made, open-necked tan sports shirt. Maybe the face was sharpened at the moment by excitement and happiness, the excitement and happiness of seeing an old and favored friend. Ordinarily it wasn't one to remember.

"Let me look at you," he echoed. Brub was half a head shorter and he looked down at Brub, as Brub looked up at him. They made the survey silently, both satisfied with what they saw, both breaking silence together. "You haven't changed a bit."

"Come on in." Brub took his arm and ushered him out of the dim, pleasant hallway into the lighted living room. He broke step as they crossed the comfortable lamp-lighted room. Things weren't the same. There was a girl there, a girl who had a right to be there.

He saw her as he would always see her, a slender girl in a simple beige dress, curled in a large wing chair by the white fireplace. The chair was a gaudy piece patterned in greens and purples, like tropical flowers, with a scrawl of cerise breaking the pattern. Her hair was the color of palest gold, a silvery gold, and she wore it pulled away from her face into a curl at the back of her neck. She had a fine face, nothing pretty-pretty about it, a strong face with high cheek bones and a straight nose. Her eyes were beautiful, sea blue, slanted like wings; and her mouth was a beautiful curve. Yet she wasn't beautiful; you wouldn't look at her in a room of pretty women, in a bar or night spot. You wouldn't notice her; she'd be too quiet; she was a lady and she wouldn't want to be noticed.

She was at home here; she was mistress of the house and she was beautiful in her context. Before either spoke, he knew she was Brub's wife. The way she was smiling as the two of them entered, the way her smile strengthened as Brub spoke. "This is Dix, Sylvia. Dickson Steele."

She put out her hand and finished the sentence, "—of whom I've heard you speak constantly. Hello, Dix."

Dix stepped forward to match her smile, to take her hand. Except for the first moment, he hadn't shown anything. Even that wouldn't have been noticed. "Hello, Sylvia," he said. She was tall standing, as tall as Brub. He held her hand while he turned to Brub, a prideful, smiling Brub. "Why didn't you tell me you were married?" he demanded. "Why hide this beautiful creature under the blanket of your indifference?"

Sylvia withdrew her hand and Brub laughed. "You sound just like the Dix I've heard about," she retorted. She had a nice voice, shining as her pale hair. "Beer with us or whiskey as a stubborn individualist?"

He said, "Much to Brub's surprise, I'll take beer."

It was so comfortable. The room was a good one, only the chair was gaudy, the couch was like green grass and another couch the yellow of sunlight. There was pale matting on the polished floor; there was a big green chair and heavy white drapes across the Venetian blinds. Good prints, O'Keeffe and Rivera. The bar was of light wood —convenient and unobtrusive in the corner. There must have been an ice chest, the beer was so cold.

Sylvia uncapped his bottle, poured half into a tall frosted glass and put it on an end table beside him. She brought Brub a bottle, poured a glass for herself. Her hands were lovely, slim and quiet and accurate; she moved quietly and with the same accuracy. She was probably a wonderful woman to bed with; no waste motion, quietness.

When he knew what he was thinking, he repeated, "Why didn't you tell me you were married?"

"Tell you!" Brub roared. "You called me up seven months ago, last February, the eighth to be exact, told me you'd just got in and would let me know soon as you were located. That's the last I've heard of you. You checked out of the Ambassador three days later and you didn't leave a forwarding address. How could I tell you anything?"

He smiled, his eyes lowered to his beer. "Keeping tabs on me, Brub?"

"Trying to locate you, you crazy lug," Brub said happily.

"Like the old days," Dix said. "Brub took care of me like a big brother, Sylvia."

"You needed a caretaker."

He switched back. "How long have you been married?"

"Two years this spring," Sylvia told him.

"One week and three days after I got home," Brub said. "It took her that long to get a beauty shop appointment."

"Which she didn't need," Dix smiled.

Sylvia smiled to him. "It took him that long to raise the money for a license. Talk of drunken sailors! He spent every cent on flowers and presents and forgot all about the price of the wedding."

Comfortable room and talk and beer. Two men. And a lovely woman.

Brub said, "Why do you think I fought the war? To get back to Sylvia."

"And why did you fight the war, Mr. Steele?" Sylvia's smile wasn't demure; she made it that way.

"For weekend passes to London," Brub suggested.

He stepped on Brub's words answering her thoughtfully. He wanted to make an impression on her. "I've wondered about it frequently, Sylvia. Why did I or anyone else fight the war? Because we had to isn't good enough. I didn't have to when I enlisted. I think it was because it was the thing to do. And the Air Corps was the thing to do. All of us in college were nuts about flying. I was a sophomore at Princeton when things were starting. I didn't want to be left out of any excitement."

"Brub was at Berkeley," she remembered. "You're right, it was the thing to do."

They were steered to safe channels, to serious discussion. Brub opened another beer for the men.

Brub said, "It was the thing to do or that was the rationalization. We're a casual generation, Dix, we don't want anyone to know we bleed if we're pricked. But self-defense is one of the few prime instincts left. Despite the cover-up, it was self-defense. And we knew it."

Dix agreed, lazily. You could agree or disagree in this house. No one got his back up whatever was said. There was no anger here, no cause for anger. Even with a woman. Perhaps because of the woman. She was gentle.

He heard Sylvia's amused voice as from afar, as through a film of gray mist. "Brub's always looking for the hidden motive power. That's because he's a policeman."

He came sharply into focus. The word had been a cold spear deliberately thrust into his brain. He heard his voice speak the cold, hard word. "Policeman?" But they didn't notice anything. They thought him surprised, as he was, more than surprised, startled and shocked. They were accustomed to that reaction. For they weren't jesting; they were speaking the truth. Brub with an apologetic grin; his wife with pride under her laughter.

"He really is," she was saying.

And Brub was saying, "Not a policeman now, darling, a detective."

They'd played the scene often; it was in their ease. He was the one who needed prompting, needed a cue for the next speech. He repeated, "Policeman," with disbelief, but the first numbing shock had passed. He was prepared to be correctly amused.

Brub said, "Detective. I don't know why. Everyone wants to know why and I don't know."

"He hasn't found the underlying motive yet," Sylvia said.

Brub shrugged. "I know that one well enough. Anything to keep from working. That's the motto of the Nicolais. Graven on their crest."

"A big healthy man reclining," Sylvia added.

They were like a radio team, exchanging patter with seemingly effortless ease.

"My old man was a land baron, never did a lick of work. But land baroneering is outmoded, so I couldn't do that. The girls all married money." He fixed Sylvia with his eye. "I don't know why I didn't think of that. Raoul, my oldest brother, is an investment broker. That's what it says on his gold-lettered office door. Investment broker."

"Brub," Sylvia warned, but she smiled.

"Up and to the office by ten," Brub proclaimed. "Maybe a bit after. Open the mail. To the club for two quick games of squash. Shower, shave, trim and lunch. Leisurely, of course. A quiet nap after, a bit of bridge—and the day's over. Very wearing."

Brub took a swallow of beer. "Then there's Tom—he plays golf. A lawyer on the side. He only takes cases dealing with the ravages of pterodactyls to the tidelands. The pterodactyls having little time for ravaging the tidelands, he has plenty of time for golf." He drank again. "I'm a detective."

Dix had listened, with his face a half smile, but he kept his eyes on his beer glass. His mouth was sharp with questions, they were like tacks pricking his tongue. Brub had finished and was waiting for him to speak. He said easily, "So you took the easy job. No investments or law for you. Sherlock Nicolai. And were you right?"

"No, damn it," Brub wailed. "I work."

"You know Brub," Sylvia sighed. "Whatever he does, he does with both hands. He's full fathoms deep in detecting."

Dix laughed, setting down his beer glass. It was time to go. Time to put space between himself and the Nicolais. "Brub should have taken up my racket." To their questioning eyebrows, he elucidated, "Like ninety-three and one-half percent of the ex-armed forces, I'm writing a book."

"Another author," Sylvia mused.

"Unlike ninety-two and one-half percent I'm not writing a book on the war. Or even my autobiography. Just trying to do a novel." A wonderful racket; neither of them knew what a smart choice he'd made. Not haphazardly, no. Coldly, with sane reasoning. He stretched like a dog, preliminary to rising. "That's why you haven't seen me before. When you're trying to write, there isn't time to run around. I stick pretty close to the old machine." He smiled frankly at Brub. "My uncle is giving me a year to see what I can do. So I work." He was on his feet. He had meant to ask the use of the phone, to call a cab, but Brub wouldn't allow it; he'd insist on taking him to the busline; he'd want to know where Dix was living. Dix didn't mind a walk. He'd find his own way to town.

He said, "And I'd better be getting back on the job."

They demurred but they didn't mind. They were young and they were one, and Brub had to get up in the morning. He slipped the question in sideways. "After all, Brub has to have his rest to detect for the glory of Santa Monica, doesn't he?"

"Santa Monica! I'm on the L.A. force," Brub boasted mildly.

He'd wanted to know; he knew. The L.A. force.

"Then you do need sleep. Plenty of work in L.A., no?"

Brub's face lost its humor, became a little tired. "Plenty," he agreed.

Dix smiled, a small smile. Brub wouldn't know why; Brub had been his big brother but he hadn't known everything there was to know. Some things a man kept secret. It was amusing to keep some things secret.

"I'll be seeing you," he said easily. His hand opened the door. But he didn't get away.

"Wait," Brub said. "We don't have your number."

He had to give it. He did without seeming reluctant. Brub would have noticed reluctance. Brub or the clear-eyed woman behind him, watching him quietly. He gave his telephone number and he repeated his good-night. Then he was alone, feeling his way off the porch and down the path into darkness and the moist opaque fog.

2

HE WALKED INTO THE NIGHT NOT KNOWING THE WAY, NOT CARING. He'd moved more than once during his seven months in California. He could move again. It wasn't easy to find quarters, the right ones for him. He liked the place he had now; he'd been lucky about it. A fellow he'd known years ago in college. Years, eons ago. He hadn't cared for Mel Terriss then; he'd cared even less for him on running into him that night last July. Terriss was going to pouches; under his chin and eyes, in his belly. He had alcoholic eyes and they were smearing the blonde with Dix. He didn't get an introduction. But he blatted waiting for it and Dix had found the flat he'd been waiting for. He was sick and tired of the second-rate hotel off Westlake Park. It smelled. Terriss was telling everyone about being off to Rio for a year, a fat job to go with his fat head.

He could move again but he was damned if he would. He liked Beverly Hills; a pleasant neighborhood. A safe neighborhood. It was possible he could change his phone number, Terriss' number. Get an unlisted one. He'd considered that before now. But Terriss' number was as good as being unlisted. There was no Dix Steele in the book.

Automatically he walked out of the small canyon, down to the beach road. He crossed to the oceanside; he could hear the crash of waves beyond the dark sands. He considered walking back along the waterfront but sand walking was difficult and he was all at once tired. He turned in the direction of the Incline. There was no bus, no taxi, and no car stopped for him. He walked on, in the street most of the way because there was no sidewalk, keeping close to the building because in the fog he was no more than a moving blur. He was damned if he'd move or even bother to change his number. He didn't have to see Brub and his woman again. He'd proffered his excuse before it was needed. He was writing a book; he had no time for evenings like this, gab and beer.

He walked on, quiet as the fog. It had been pleasant. It was the first pleasant evening he'd had in so long. So terribly long. He tried to remember how long. Those early days in England when he and Brub knew each other so well.

He hardened his jaw and he trudged on toward the yellow ring of fog light on the pavement ahead. He watched the light, watched it come closer as he moved silently toward it. He shut out thought, clamping it between his set teeth. It wasn't until he reached the light that he saw the Incline looming slantingly across. And realized that the house into which the brown girl had disappeared lay just beyond. He stopped there, in the shadow of the clubhouse. The club's parking lot, wire fenced, empty of cars, lay between him and the huddle of houses. The pounding of the sea recurred in changeless rhythm and he could smell the salt far beyond the wire fence.

He had to walk up to the three houses; that was where the white lanes of the crosswalk lay on the highway. He smiled a little as he started forward. He was halfway past the fenced lot when the hideous noise of an oil truck, ignoring the stop sign, thundered past. A second one speeded after the first, blasting the quietness with thumping wheels, clanging chains. Spewing greasy smoke into the fog. He stood there trembling in anger until they passed. He was still trembling when he reached the huddle of houses, and when he saw what he saw his anger mounted. There was no way to show beyond which brown gate the brown girl had vanished. The gates of the first and second houses stood side by side. Abruptly he crossed the street and started up the Incline. He had been so certain she had entered the center house. And now he didn't know. He'd have to watch again.

He was to the midsection, to the hump of the walk, before he was calmed again. He stopped there and looked out over the stone railing. There was a small replica of the Palisades on this other side of the railing. And here, just over the rail, was a broken place in the wild shrubbery, even the pressure of a footpath down the cliff. A place where a man could wait at night. He smiled and was easy again.

He walked on up the Incline, undisturbed when a car heading downward splashed light on him. He wouldn't move from Terriss' flat. He was satisfied there. There was something amusing about Brub Nicolai being able to lay hands on him whenever he wished. Amusing and more exciting than anything that had happened in a long time. The hunter and the hunted arm in arm. The hunt sweetened by danger. At the top of the Incline he looked back down at the houses and the sand and the sea. But they were all helpless now, lost in the fog.

He went on, not knowing how he would get back to Beverly, not caring. He was surprised crossing to Wilshire to see the lights of a bus approaching. He waited for it. It was the Wilshire-L.A. bus. After he boarded it, he saw by his watch that it was still early, a little past eleven o'clock. There were only two passengers, working men in working clothes. Dix sat in the front seat, his face turned to the window. Away from the dull lights of the interior. Others boarded the bus as it rumbled along Wilshire through Santa Monica, into Westwood. He didn't turn his head to look at the others but he could see their reflections in the window pane. There was no one worth looking at.

The fog thinned as the bus left Westwood and hurried through the dark lane framed by the woodland golf course. At Beverly you could see street corners again, as through a gray mesh. You could see the shop windows and the people on the streets. Only there were no people, the little city was as deserted as a small town. Dix kept his face pressed to the window.

At Camden Drive he saw her. A girl, an unknown girl, standing alone, waiting alone there, by the bench which meant a crosstown bus would eventually come along. At night buses didn't run often. Dix pulled the buzzer cord but he was too late for Camden. He got off at the next stop, two blocks away. He didn't mind much. He crossed the boulevard and he was smiling with his lips as he started back. His stride was long; his steps were quiet.

3

THE PHONE WAS A JANGLE TEARING SLEEP FROM A MAN'S FACE. IT WAS the scream of bus brakes, the clanging chain of an ugly oil truck on a beach road, the whine of a spiraling bomb. Dix opened his cramped eyes. He didn't know how long the phone had been ringing. It stopped when his eyes opened but as soon as he'd closed them again the fretful noise began anew. This time he didn't open his eyes. With his outstretched hand he knocked the phone from its cradle, ending the sound. He buried his head in the pillow, grasped at waning sleep. He didn't want to talk to anyone this early. He didn't care who was on the other end of the phone. No one important. No one important had his number.

His eyes reopened. He'd forgotten Brub Nicolai. He'd given Brub his phone number last night. For a solitary moment the coldness of fear gripped his entrails. As quickly the moment passed. He was without fear. But sleep had gone. He turned his head to look at the bedside clock. It wasn't so early. Eleven thirty-five. He'd had almost eight hours' sleep.

He needed eight hours more. God knows he needed it. He'd fallen into bed in complete exhaustion. It took more than eight hours to refuel a body exhausted. But his curiosity could not let him return to sleep now. He shoved away the covers, and pulled on his bathrobe. He didn't bother with his slippers. He walked barefoot through the living room to the front door, opened it and brought in the morning *Times* from his doorstep. His hands were eager but he closed the door before opening the paper.

There was nothing unusual on the front page. The ways of civilization, international and national strife, wars and strikes, political propagandizing. Nothing he was expecting on the second page. That meant there'd be nothing. He thrust the paper under his arm. There'd been no reason to leave his bed. But now that he was up, he wanted coffee. He padded to the kitchen. Terriss had good stuff; he plugged in the electric percolator and opened the kitchen door to bring in the cream. The apartment was a corner one, easy for a man to keep to himself and to hold his affairs his own. No snoopy neighbors here. Most of them were connected with the studios; Terriss had told him that, told him with Terriss' fathead pride. They kept themselves private, too.

While he waited for the coffee he began to read the paper. He drank three cups, finishing his reading. He left the spread paper and the coffee cup on the kitchen table. There was maid service; he made it a point to be out during that period. The maid was a shapeless sack with heavy feet. She came to this apartment between two and three in the afternoon. He didn't know the maid's name; he wouldn't have recognized her on the street.

He returned to the bedroom. There wouldn't be time for a good sleep before she came plodding in. If he were asleep, she wouldn't do the bedroom and he didn't like an unmade bed. He sat down on the edge of it, noticed the phone and replaced it in the cradle. He just sat there for minutes, not thinking, not seeing. Then he got up and went into the bathroom. His face in the mirror was the usual face, drawn from sleep, his hair rumpled. He'd feel better after a shower and a shave. He was taking his razor from the case when the phone rang.

He wasn't going to answer it and then the quickening of curiosity stirred him. He took his time returning to it. Again he sat down on the rumpled bed. His hesitation before lifting the phone was so minute, his hand didn't realize it. He said, "Hello."

"Dix?"

It was a woman's voice, a woman querying, "Dix?"

He took a breath. Only one woman could be calling. Sylvia Nicolai. He forced life into his voice. "Speaking. Sylvia?" He'd surprised her.

"How do you know?"

"Recognized your voice," he said amusedly. She would believe him.

"Where have you been? I've been trying all morning to reach you."

He didn't like having to account. Nor did she care; it was conversational gambit. Because he didn't like it, he lied. "I've been right here. Working. Phone didn't ring."

She said, "Phones," then went on in her cool, lovely voice, "Brub and I wondered if you'd like to join us for dinner at the club tonight?"

He didn't know what to say. He didn't know whether he wanted to be with them or not tonight. He was tired, too tired for decision. It was always easy to lie, so easy. He asked, "Could I ring you back, Sylvia? I've a tiresome date tonight, business. If I can get free of it, I'd much rather join you." The charm was in his voice, he turned it on. But she didn't match it. She was businesslike, as if she were Brub's secretary, not his wife. As if she preferred his refusal. "Yes, do call back. If you can't make it, we'll try it another time."

He echoed her good-bye and set back the phone. She didn't want him along tonight. It was Brub's idea and she'd said, "If you want him, Brub," because she was in love with Brub, the newness hadn't been rubbed off their marriage. He wouldn't go. He wouldn't intrude on their oneness. They had happiness and happiness was so rare in this day of the present. More rare than precious things, jewels and myrrh. Once he'd had happiness but for so brief a time; happiness was made of quicksilver, it ran out of your hand like quicksilver. There was the heat of tears suddenly in his eyes and he shook his head angrily. He would not think about it, he would never think of that again. It was long ago, in an ancient past. To hell with happiness. More important was excitement and power and the hot stir of lust. Those made you forget. They made happiness a pink marshmallow.

He stood up again, rubbing his untidy hair. He wouldn't go out with the Nicolais to their lace-panty club. He'd go out alone. The lone wolf. There was a savage delight in being a lone wolf. It wasn't happiness. It was the reverse of the coin, as hate was the reverse of love. Only a thin press of metal between the sides of a coin. He was a lone wolf; he didn't have to account to anyone nor did he intend to. Sylvia Nicolai wanting to know where he was this morning. It was none of her damn business. This morning she didn't care, but get mixed up with the Nicolais and she would care. Women were snoopy. He hated women. Brub would be snoopy too; he was a detective.

Yet the game would be heightened if he teamed up with a detective. Dix went into the bathroom, plugged in the razor and began to shave. Hating the noise, the grinding buzz of noise. He could have used a safety razor but there were mornings when his hands had the shakes. He didn't know when those mornings would occur. Better the buzz than to have people noticing the cuts on your cheeks and chin. His hands were steady as iron this morning.

He finished shaving as quickly as possible, scrubbed his teeth and sloshed mouthwash. He was feeling better. Under the shower he felt considerably better. It might be definitely amusing to be with the Nicolais tonight. It might be that Sylvia was the one who wanted him along, that her play of indifference was a cover-up. He was clinically aware of his appeal to women. He'd seen their eyes sharpen as they looked at him. Sylvia's hadn't, true, but she was smart. She wouldn't let it happen with Brub there. He'd like to see Sylvia again.

He thought of her as he stood scrubbing himself with the towel. The long lines of her, the silvery look and sound of her. He'd like to know a woman of her caliber. Brub was lucky. He flung the towel on the floor. Brub was born lucky. For an instant he stiffened, as if a cold hand had touched his spine.

His laugh shot from his throat. He was lucky too; he was more than lucky, he was smart. He strode out of the bathroom. It was close to two; he'd have to hump it to get out before the ugly beldam of the brooms showed up.

He put on a blue sports shirt, blue slacks, comfortable loafers. No jacket. From the open windows he knew the day was a sultry one.

September was summer in California. He transferred his wallet and keys and other stuff from the gabardines, opened his closet and gathered up the other suits and odd trousers needing a cleaner's attention. He'd beaten the maid; he was ready to leave. The phone started to ring as he reached the front door. He ignored it and left the apartment.

The garages were in back of the court. His was almost a half block away. Just another of the advantages of Terriss' quarters. No insomniacs sitting up in bed checking you in and out. The garages fronted on an alley; a vacant lot across. He unlocked the one housing Terriss' car. A nice car Terriss had left for his use. He'd have preferred something flashier, a convertible or open brougham, but there was an advantage in a black coupé. All black coupés looked alike at night. He drove away.

He dropped the bundle of clothes at the cleaner's on Olympic, then drove leisurely up Beverly Drive, parking near the delicatessen. He was hungry. He bought an early edition of the *News* at the corner and he read it while he ate two smoked turkey sandwiches and drank a bottle of beer. The delicatessen was fairly crowded even this late. It was a popular place and a pleasant one. Noise was a blur here, like in a club.

There was nothing in the paper. After checking the headlines, he read the comics, the café columnists and Kirby, Weinstock, and Pearson, loitering with his beer. He looked over the movie ads, sometimes he went to a movie in the afternoons. It was too late today. He had to phone Sylvia Nicolai.

He walked down to the Owl after eating and bought a carton of Philip Morris. It was after three then. The beldam would be out of his apartment, he could return, call Sylvia, and catch a nap before joining the Nicolais at their club. The afternoon heat and the beer had made him sleepy again. Or he could get the letter written to Uncle Fergus. Damned old fool expected a letter once a week. It had been two weeks since Dix had written him. He wouldn't put it past Uncle Fergus to stop sending checks if he didn't get his damn letter from Dix pretty soon. He'd say he'd been sick. Maybe he could jack up the income for medical expenses. Something needing treatment, something acquired overseas. A back or a kidney. Not anything that would jerk the strings, drag him back East.

He got in his car, backed out, and drove a little too fast around the block. Uncle Fergus didn't have to be so dirty cheap; he didn't have another living relative. Two hundred and fifty a month was pennies. Medical treatment was a good idea, he should have thought of it before. He could get three hundred for sure, maybe three fifty. He'd write a whale of a letter. He was the boy who could do it. He knew Uncle Fergus like the palm of his hand. He felt all hopped up returning to the apartment.

He flung the Philip Morris on the divan, got out the portable and opened it on the desk. He rolled in the paper and started, "Dear Uncle Fergus," before he remembered the phone call to Sylvia. He left the desk and went to the bedroom. Before dialing—Terriss had extended service of course, Terriss had everything easy—he lit a cigarette.

Sylvia answered the phone. Her hello was natural. When he said, "Sylvia? It's Dix," her voice became a bit more formal. She was conscious of him all right. She was fighting that consciousness. He'd played the game so often of breaking down that withdrawal but never with this variation, the wife of his best friend. It stimulated him.

He asked, "Do you still want me tonight?"

She was conscious of his phrasing because there was a minute hesitancy before she counter-asked, "You mean you can join us for dinner?"

"If I'm still invited."

"Yes, indeed." She acted pleased. "Can you make it about seven? That will give us time for a drink before we go to the club."

"I'll be there."

He was pleased that he had decided to go. He lay back on the bed to finish his cigarette. He was still lying there leisurely when the phone sounded. He was surprised, more so when it was Sylvia again. Her voice wasn't standoffish now. "Dix? I forgot to say, don't dress. We're informal at the beach."

"Thanks," he said. "You eased my mind. My dinner coat is out at the seams. It shrank while I was away flying."

"Brub's, too. They fed you gentlemen altogether too well," she laughed.

They had some easy conversation before ringing off. He didn't want to return to the damn typewriter. He was comfortable here on his spine; he wasn't sleepy now, just restful. It was just such delaying tactics that had let two weeks go by without writing the old skinflint. He pushed himself up and returned to the machine. Today, there was incentive. He needed money for medical treatments.

Inspiration returned to him at the typewriter. He wrote a peach of a letter; it was just right, not too much nor too little. He didn't ask for money. He was certain his back would be all right without the treatments the doctor ordered. Stuff like that. He reread the letter twice before putting it in the envelope. He decided to go and mail it now. It was a little after five. Before sealing the envelope, he drew the letter out and read it again. Yes, it was all right. He sealed it quickly, put on an airmail stamp, and left the apartment.

He was walking fast. That was why he didn't see the girl until he almost collided with her at the arched street entrance of the patio. It shocked him that he hadn't noticed her, that he hadn't been aware. He stepped back quickly. "I beg your pardon," he said. It wasn't a formality as he said it; shock made each word apology for a grave error.

The girl didn't move for a moment. She stood in his way and looked him over slowly, from crown to toe. The way a man looked over a woman, not the reverse. Her eyes were slanted, her lashes curved long and golden dark. She had red-gold hair, flaming hair, flung back from her amber face, falling to her shoulders. Her mouth was too heavy with lipstick, a copper-red mouth, a sultry mouth painted to call attention to its promise. She was dressed severely, a rigid tailored suit, but it accentuated the lift of her breasts, the curl of her hips. She wasn't beautiful, her face was too narrow for beauty, but she was dynamite. He stood like a dolt, gawking at her.

After she'd finished looking him over, she gave him a small insolent smile. As if he were a dolt, not Dix Steele. "Granted," she said and she walked past him into the patio.

He didn't move. He stood and watched her, his mouth still open. She walked like a model, swaying her small buttocks. She had exquisite legs. She knew he was watching her and she didn't care. She expected it. She took her time, skirting the small sky-blue oblong of the pool which lay in the center of the patio. She started up the stairway to the balcony of the second-floor apartments.

He swung out the archway fast. He wouldn't let her reach the balcony, look over the balustrade and see him standing there. He'd find out about her some other way, if she lived here, or whom she visited. He'd left his car down the block a bit, by the curb. Although he'd intended driving to the Beverly post office to mail the letter, he didn't. He half ran across the street to the corner mailbox, clanged in the letter and ran back to the court. He was too late. She was already out of sight.

He went back into his own apartment, sauntered in as if he

weren't damning luck. If he'd bumped into her on his return from the box, he could have bungled at his doorway for the key, discovered which apartment she entered. He walked inside, slamming the door after him. It had been years since he'd seen a girl who could set him jumping. The redhead was it. He went out to the kitchen and although he didn't want a drink, he poured a double jigger of rye and drank it neat. The slug calmed him but he wandered back into the front room, wanting an excuse to slip out into the patio, to look up at the second floor balcony.

The excuse came as he wished for it. He heard, just short of the doorstep, the thud of the flung newspaper. He moved quick as a cat. But as soon as he picked up the paper, unfolding it, he forgot why he'd hurried outdoors. He saw only the headline: *Strangler Strikes Again.*

II

1

It was quarter past seven when Dix pulled up in front of
Nicolai's gate. There was no woolly fog tonight, only a thin mistiness
lay in the canyon. It was like gauze across the windshield. He could
see the flagstoned steps clearly, even the geranium border framing
them. The windows of the house were golden with light; the porch
light was also on to welcome him.

He was again pleased that he had decided to come. He had
dressed for deliberate effect, an eastern friend of the Nicolais, well
off, the right background, even to ex-Air Corps. Gray flannel suit; an
expensive tie, patterned in navy, maroon, and white; a white shirt;
well-polished brown shoes, English shoes. He settled his tie before
climbing to the porch. He didn't hesitate before ringing the bell and
there was no hesitation in the opening door.

Sylvia was standing in the doorway. She had on her coat, a soft
blue coat, and her bag, a white envelope, was under her arm. "Hello,
Dix," she said. "I'll be right with you."

She didn't ask him in; the screen door was between them and she
didn't push it open. She left him standing there on the lighted porch
while she turned back into the hall and switched off some overhead
lights. There was dim light still glowing in hall and living room
when she came outside.

"We're meeting Brub at the club," she said in her high clear voice
as she started down the steps. "He called and asked me to bring you
there for drinks. He couldn't make it home."

He followed her. He had to raise his voice to speak to her, she was
that far ahead of him. She was accustomed to the steps; he must
watch them. "Brub pretty busy?"

"Yes," she said but she didn't continue on that. "Do you want to take your car or mine? It isn't far, only a few blocks."

She wasn't talking particularly fast yet there was a breathlessness to it, as if she didn't want any silence between them, as if she were too conscious of him. She stood there by his car, tall and cool and lovely, but not quiet as she was last night.

He smiled at her; he put no intimacy into the smile. "We might as well take mine, it's here. You can direct me."

"All right," she agreed.

He helped her in and went around, took his place at the wheel. She'd rolled the window down on her side, and she rested her arm on the frame. She remained there in the far corner as she gave directions. "Just down to the beach road, turn left, the club's on the ocean side."

It didn't take five minutes to get there, no time for the furthering of acquaintance. She talked of club friends, names he didn't know. There was no silence on the short ride. On direction, he drove through the pillared gateway into the parking court. She let herself out of the car, not waiting for him to help her.

The clubhouse wasn't large. There was a young feel to it, like an officer's club, the couples in the entrance hall, in the lounge beyond, were the kind you'd expect the Nicolais to know. A pattern you found all over the country, decent, attractive young people. The norm. They didn't look dull to Dix tonight. He was warmed by their safeness.

Sylvia said, "I'll drop my coat." She smiled at him, an open, friendly smile. "Be right back, Dix."

She wasn't long. She looked lovely, her dress was cream color, an expensively simple dress. He had pride entering the lounge with her.

"Brub doesn't seem to have shown up yet. Unless he's beaten us to the bar." She nodded to several couples as they crossed the room. There were more couples in the nautical bar but Brub wasn't there. "I'll substitute for Brub and buy you a drink while we wait," she said.

"I approve the substitution. But I'll buy the drink," he told her.

She moved away from him to a table. "You can't. Not at the club. This is Brub's party."

She introduced him to all who stopped by their table. The question of the passersby was inevitably the same: "Where's Brub?" It didn't occur to any of them that she had any interest in Dix.

Her answer was always the same. "He'll be along soon." And her introduction never varied. ". . . Dix Steele. Brub's best friend in England." Only once did she show any disturbance. She said quietly, "I wonder what's keeping him."

At eight the bar was emptied of all but those whose goal was alcoholism. Her nervousness lay near the surface now. She pushed away from the table. "We might as well go to dinner. I'm sure he'll be here any moment."

He deliberately broke through the commonplaces then. "Don't apologize, Sylvia. I'm not missing Brub." His voice smiled at her. "I'm enjoying you—quite as much as I would Brub."

She laughed. And she said with a small moue, "I'm missing him. I haven't seen him since morning."

He mock sighed. "Still on your honeymoon."

"Definitely."

But he'd broken through, only a wedge perhaps, yet enough for a starter.

He waited until they were at the dinner table before he asked the question casually. "Is he on a big case?"

She looked at him. Her eyes were anxious. Then she looked away. "I don't know," she admitted. "He didn't say. Only he'd been delayed."

She hadn't seen the evening paper. He could have told her but he didn't. Let Brub tell her. What she feared.

He saw Brub at that moment crossing the room. Brub looked worn, he put on a smile in answer to greetings as he passed the various tables, but it was a thin smile, it slipped away as quickly as it came.

Sylvia saw him almost as soon as Dix did. Anxiety sharpened her face. They were tacitly silent until Brub reached the table. He bent and kissed Sylvia. "Sorry I'm so late, darling." He didn't smile at them; he didn't need to pretend with his wife and best friend. He put out his hand to Dix, "Glad you could join us," then he sat down, dog-tiredness in every muscle. His suit was dog-tired too and his linen showed the wilt of the day. His dark hair was crumpled. "I didn't have time to change." He smiled at Sylvia. "You can pretend I'm your chauffeur."

The waiter, a young colored man, whiter of skin than the beach-brown guests, was unobtrusive at the table.

Brub looked up. "Hello, Malcolm. Do you suppose you could get me a double Scotch from the bar before you start my dinner? I've just come from work and I need it."

"I'm sure I can, Mr. Nicolai," Malcolm smiled. He went away.

Sylvia's hand covered Brub's on the table. "Hard day, darling?" She'd started casual but she couldn't keep it up. Something about the set of Brub's mouth released her fear in a little gust. "It wasn't another——"

Brub's mouth was tight; his voice deliberately matter of fact. "Yes, another one."

"Brub!" She whispered it.

He began to light a cigarette, the flame wavered slightly. Dix watched the two with the proper attentiveness, and the proper curiosity. When neither spoke, he let his curiosity become audible. "What's it all about?"

"Another woman killed. . . . The same way."

Sylvia's hands were clenched.

Malcolm brought the drink.

"Thanks," Brub said and saw Dix. "I'm sorry, chum. How about you?"

"The same," he grinned. He didn't want it for himself; an extra for Brub. To relax Brub. He began on his shrimp cocktail. "Are you assigned to the case?"

"Everyone in the department is on it," Brub said. He drank again and he grimaced. "No, it's not my case, Dix. They don't put juniors on big stuff." He turned to Sylvia. "The commissioner called in the whole department. We've been with him since five, since I called you. Even hizzoner the mayor sat in." His mouth tightened. "We've got to stop it."

"Yes," Sylvia said. Her eyes were frightened, the color under her tan was gone. It was as if she had personal fright, as if the horror were close to her.

Dix said, "Someone important who was killed?" Malcolm set down the highball. "Thanks."

"No." Brub was halfway through his drink. "It's never anyone important." Again he realized he was talking to someone, not thinking aloud. "I forgot. You wouldn't know about it. Being a visitor." He could speak about it calmly; it seemed to relax him as much as a highball would. "The first one was about six months ago. March, to be exact."

"March sixteenth," Sylvia said. "The night before the St. Patrick party."

"We didn't know it was only the first then. It was a girl down on Skid Row. She was a nice enough kid for the life she lived, I guess.

Danced in a bump-and-grind house down there. We found her in an alley. Strangled." He picked up his glass, emptied it. "No clues. Nothing. We wrote that one off as the neighborhood even though we didn't get any leads. You usually can on Skid Row. The next one was in April." His hand reached for his empty glass.

Dix shoved his across. "Take mine. The shrimps are too good to dilute. Try them, Sylvia."

"Yes, don't wait for me," Brub said.

Sylvia picked up her fork but she didn't do anything with it. Just held it loosely, her eyes on Brub's face.

He took a drink before continuing. "In April. We found her in Westlake Park. There wasn't any reason for it. She was a nice normal girl, young, attractive. She'd been to a movie with a couple of girl friends. She lived in the Wilshire district, blocks from the park. No clues. She'd been killed the same way." He looked at Dix angrily. "There wasn't any reason for her to be killed. There's been no reason for any of them." Again he drank.

"There've been others?"

"Last night was the sixth," Brub said heavily. "One a month. Since March."

"Except last month," Sylvia said quickly. "There was none in August."

Brub continued, "No motive. No connection between any of them. Never the same neighborhood."

"Last night's——" Sylvia's voice was hushed, as if she dreaded the question.

Brub said, "A new neighborhood. Beverly Glen Canyon—up where it's country. She wasn't found until late this morning. She was lying in the brush at the side of the road." Anger clanged in his voice again. "It's like hunting a needle in a haystack. Los Angeles is too big—too sprawling. You can't patrol every street every night, all night. He's safe. A maniac walking the streets, looking just as normal as you or me, more normal probably."

"You'll get him," Sylvia said, pushing conviction into her wish.

"We'll get him." Brub believed it. "But how many women will be murdered first?" He tipped up the glass.

"You'd better eat, dear," Sylvia said. She forced herself to start eating.

"Yeah." Brub began spearing the shrimp, eating hurriedly, not tasting the food. "Take this girl last night. A nice girl like the others —except perhaps the first was a different cut. This one was a stenographer. Worked downtown. Lived in Hollywood. She'd been playing bridge with friends in Beverly. On South Camden. Just four girls. They played once a week, rotating the meeting place. They always quit early. None of them wanted to be out late, alone that way. Last night they stopped around eleven. The three left together, walked up to Wilshire together. The other two lived downtown farther. They took the Wilshire bus. Mildred was taking the Hollywoodland bus. Her name was Mildred Atkinson. She was still waiting when the girls' bus came along. She waved good-bye to them. No one saw her after that."

Sylvia had stopped eating. "It's horrible," she said.

"Yes, it's horrible," Brub agreed. "There's no reason for the pattern. If we could just get at what's behind it."

Dix put on a thoughtful frown. "Have you no leads at all?"

"Not much," Brub said. "There are no clues, there never are; no fingerprints or footprints, God, how we'd like just one fingerprint!" He returned to monotone. "We've double checked all the known sex offenders."

"It's a sex crime?" Dix interrupted.

Brub nodded. "That's part of it."

Sylvia's shiver was slight.

He continued, "We know one thing, of course. He works from a car."

Malcolm brought the chowder.

"How do you know that?" Dix asked.

"He has to. Take last night, for instance. The place is inaccessible without a car."

Dix scowled. "Can't you check tire prints?"

"We can't check every car in L.A.," Brub said helplessly. "It's the same as footprints. We can't check every pair of shoes in L.A."

"I understand that," Dix nodded. "Excellent chowder." But they'd have the tire tracks in plaster. If you could get them off concrete.

"We have an excellent chef at the club," Sylvia said. She had no appetite. Her soup was barely tasted when Malcolm brought the abalone steaks.

Dix began on his with relish. "What you know, then, is that there is a man and he has a car——"

"Yes. In the fourth case, he was seen."

Dix's eyebrows lifted. He held his fork in midair. "You mean you have a description?"

Brub sighed. "The fourth girl was seen leaving a movie with a man. As for description, hell!" He gestured. "The guy who noticed them, a tailor waiting for a streetcar, was half a block away. All he knew was the man was kind of young and sort of tall and normal looking. Only one head and no fangs!"

Dix smiled slightly. "Maybe he saw two other people."

"He saw them all right. But he was so busy looking at the girl's red suit, he didn't notice the man."

"No one else has ever seen him?"

"If they have, they've taken a vow of silence. You'd think he——"

Sylvia broke in, "Brub, let's talk about something else. Please, Brub. We asked Dix to a party, not a postmortem."

"Okay, sweetheart." He patted her hand. "I'm sorry. Sorry, Dix. How about another drink? Malcolm!"

Dix smiled. "I'll have another with you." He hid his annoyance. Just like a woman, interfering, imposing her whims on the party.

"Who's here tonight?" Brub edged his chair to look around. He lifted his hand to the group at the next table. "Hi, there."

Dix lit a cigarette and also surveyed the room. Nice people, healthy and wealthy. Normal as you and me. Normal as Sylvia when she didn't have the megrims. But you didn't know what was beneath beach-tanned faces and simple expensive clothes. You didn't ever know about thoughts. They were easily hidden. You didn't have to give away what you were thinking. No one exchanging pleasantries now with Brub would know that the man's mind was raw with murder. No one watching Sylvia replacing her lip rouge, smiling over the mirror of her bleached wooden compact, would know that fear was raveling her nerves. Even he, permitted as friend to know that there was fear in her veins, didn't know whether the fear was for Brub's safety or her own. Or an atavistic fear of reasonless death.

The color under her sunbrown had returned as she did the little normal things of lipstick, cigarette. He could make it recede so easily, a word, or one more question on the subject. He could make her heart stop beating as easily. With a simple statement. His lips smiled. And his eyes again turned to the room. Away from temptation.

It was then that he saw her, the little brown girl. It almost shocked him for a moment. She didn't belong here; she belonged out in the dark. She wasn't a brown girl tonight, save for her healthy beach color. She was in starchy white, an evening dress, cut low on her brown back, flaring to her white sandals. She had a young, laugh-

ing face, short brown curly hair. She was at the table directly across
the floor. He should have seen her earlier. He had, he realized, but
only the brown back and white pique dress. She'd shifted her chair
as Brub had, bringing her face to the room.

He took a long draw on his cigarette before he asked, deliberately
casual, "Who's the girl over there?"

Brub turned back to their table. "Which one?"

Sylvia followed Dix's gesture.

"Over there. In white."

Brub peered. "Oh, that one. I've seen her—who is she, Sylvia?"

Sylvia had placed the girl. "Betsy Banning. You know, Brub. The
Bannings bought the Henry house up the beach." Sylvia said to Dix,
"I've met her but I don't really know her." She smiled. "Or I'd intro-
duce you."

Dix laughed. "Don't start matchmaking. I'm happy. She looked
familiar, that was all. Is she in pictures?"

"No," Sylvia answered. "She's at the university, I believe." She
smiled. "She doesn't need the pictures; the Bannings are Texas oil,
floating in it. Otis Banning, her father, is the bald one. They say he
has seven millions in a little black box. No doubt an exaggeration."

Brub said, "Sylvia ought to be the detective in the family. She
knows everything about everybody."

"Otis and I share the same dentist, darling."

"She's a cute kid." Brub was again looking across at the girl.

"You're married now," Dix reminded him.

"To me," Sylvia added sweetly. "I may not be a cute kid but I'm
nice."

They exchanged that happy intimate look. Then Brub turned his
eyes again to the Banning girl. "You're right though. She does look
familiar." He was scenting her, the way a detective would, narrowed
eyes, his brows pulled slightly together, his nose keen.

"Come on home," Dix laughed.

Brub's head snapped to Dix quickly. His dark eyes were lighted.
"That's it! You know who she looks like? Brucie!"

The name was spoken before he could warn Brub not to speak it.
He'd known in that split second of Brub's remembering, in the second before the name. It was said and for the moment he could see
nothing, only the red blur before his eyes and the dread roaring of
sound in his ears. He didn't know his knuckles were white knobs
gripping the table, his cigarette mashed between his fingers. The mo-

ment passed and he was in control of himself again. He let the cigarette brush to the floor. In another moment he could speak.

Sylvia spoke first. "And who is Brucie, darling?"

"A girl we knew in England. She was a Red Cross worker when we
were stationed near Dover. Scotch—that's where the Bruce, Brucie,
came from. Cute as a button."

Brub had noticed nothing. But he wasn't sure about Sylvia.
Behind her civilized attention, her humor, her casualness, he wasn't
certain. Something was there behind the curtain of her eyes, something in the way she looked at Dix, a look behind the look. She
might have been watching him at that wrong moment.

Dix said, "She was, all of that." His voice wasn't thick; it was as
casual as Sylvia's.

"Wonder what ever happened to her? She was sure a cute kid.
You kind of went for her, didn't you, Dix?"

Dix laughed, a normal laugh. "You kind of liked her yourself,
didn't you?"

"Brub!" Sylvia's eyes opened, wide surprise. She was pretending.
She was too levelheaded, too secure to care.

"You bet I liked her. I guess every man in the platoon sort of liked
Brucie. But you needn't worry, honey. No one had a chance with old
lady-killer Steele present."

Dix was very careful lighting his cigarette. Because Sylvia was
watching him. With the look behind the look.

"You ever hear from her, Dix?"

He shook his head. He was surprised at how easy it was to talk.
"No, Brub, I never did."

"Out of sight, out of mind. That's the great Steele. Don't ever fall
for a guy like that, Sylvia." Brub began on his neglected ice cream.

"No, darling," Sylvia murmured. She wasn't looking at him, yet
Dix had a feeling she was seeing him. And probing him with her
mind.

"If I had a girl like Sylvia," he began, and he realized there was
some honesty in the play, "I wouldn't have looked at anyone else. I
wouldn't have been like you, ogling all those U.S.O. legs."

"I'm learning things." Sylvia nodded a severe head. "Go on, Dix,
tell me more."

He invented lazily but his mind wasn't there. It was remembering
Brucie and the ache in him was the ache of a wound torn open. His
face covered his mind, as his voice covered the pain crying from his

throat. "Remember the redhead contortionist?" and he remembered the redhead in the patio this afternoon. With a woman like that, he might be able to forget. Nothing else brought forgetfulness, only for a brief time. Another section of his mind moved as the brown girl stood up from her table with her young crew-cut escort. The look of Brucie, not the face, the swagger of her shoulders, the echo of laughter. Perhaps married to seven million dollars you could forget. You could have fast cars, fast boats, a good plane to climb up there into the vastness of eternity. Brub and Sylvia were happy. Marriage could be happy.

He realized there was music when the brown girl and her partner began to dance. He should ask Sylvia to dance. But he didn't want to. He wanted to get out of here, to go home. He couldn't leave abruptly, not two nights in a row. However, he didn't think the Nicolais would stay much longer; off guard their faces returned to somberness. He could nudge them. He said abruptly, "You're tired, Brub."

Brub nodded. "Yeah. But I've got to go back to work."

"No, Brub," Sylvia cried.

"I shouldn't have left when I did."

"You're worn out now. You can't, darling. It's an hour's drive downtown——"

He interrupted, "I don't have to go downtown, Sylvia. To the Beverly Hills station is all. That isn't fifteen minutes. Why don't you keep Dix——"

Sylvia shook her head.

Dix said, "I ought to get back to work myself. So don't be polite."

Sylvia said, "I couldn't stay. You understand."

He gave her an appreciative smile. "I understand."

"It's been a punk evening for you, Dix," Brub was apologetic. "We'll make it up to you."

They almost hurried from the dining room into the lounge. As if, once it had been admitted, all three could make up with haste for the spent time. Sylvia said, "I'll get my coat." She hesitated, "You are on the case, Brub?"

He admitted ruefully, "Just a little bit, honey."

She didn't say anything, simply turned and went to the cloakroom. Brub watched her go.

"Why is she afraid?" Dix asked.

Brub started. "Wha——" He realized Dix's question. "I guess it's pretty much my fault. Ever since this thing started, I've been afraid for her. She's lived in the canyon all her life. She never had any fear, wandered all over it, any time of day. But the canyon at night, the way the fogs come in—it's a place for *him*." His face was again angry, helplessly angry. "I've scared her. She's alone so much. I never know what hours I have to keep. We have good neighbors, a couple of our best friends are right across the road. But you know our street. It's dark and lonely and the way our house is set up there——" He broke off. "I'm the one who's scared; I've infected her. And I can't help it. I can't pretend. Until we've caught him——"

Sylvia was coming into the hall. She looked herself again, tall and lovely and unruffled, her gilt hair smooth, her movements unhurried.

Brub said under his breath, "If we could only find the way of the pattern——" He didn't finish because she was there, and the three were moving out of the club into the sea-fresh darkness. The swish of the breakers was liquid against the night.

"I could take Sylvia——" Dix began.

"No, I'll run her home, get her settled. Unless you'd like to sit with her until I——"

"Dix has to work," Sylvia said. "And I'm tired." She put out her hand. "Another time we'll do better, Dix."

"We certainly will," Brub vowed.

He watched Brub wheel the car out of the drive. In a hurry, hurry to get back to the Beverly Hills police station. He would take Sylvia into the house, make sure there was no shadowy stranger lurking. They would cling together for a moment, fear in both of them. The woman fearing to have her man sniffing the spoor of a murderer, fearing lest he catch up with evil. Fearing less for herself; only the unease she must feel, infected by Brub's fear for her. Brub fearing for her because she was a woman, because she was his woman, and women were being stalked in the night. Fearing, he would yet leave her, and quickly, because he was a hunter and this was a big hunt. For wild game.

Dix circled back to his car, Terriss' car. The plain black coupé. He warmed the engine. It was a good car and he kept it functioning smoothly. He released the brake. Fifteen minutes at the outside and Brub would be gone. He could go there then; she'd let him in. Brub's friend. He could have an excuse, Brub could have infected him too with the fear. She'd be glad to see him. He could coax her into driving up to Malibu. For a drink. For fresh air. She wouldn't be afraid—at first.

He slid the car to the gates. Left lay the canyon. Left lay Malibu.

Right was the California Incline. Right was Wilshire, the road back to town. She was Brub's wife. Brub was his friend. Brub, the hunter.

He was very tired. He hadn't had much sleep last night. He turned to the right.

2

THE MORNING PAPER HAD COLUMNS ON THE CASE. HAVING BEEN scooped by the afternoon papers on the original story, this sheet at least was making up its loss by intensive research. It had pictures of the girl, Mildred, of her family, of the apartment house where she'd played bridge, of the lonely spot in Beverly Glen Canyon where her body was found.

Her name was Mildred Atkinson and she had led a very stupid life. Grade school, high school—Hollywood High but she was no beauty queen—business college and a job in an insurance office. She was twenty-six years old and she was a good girl, her parents sobbed. She played bridge with girl friends and she once taught a Sunday school class. She didn't have any particular gentleman friend, she went out with several. Not often, you could bet. The only exciting thing that had ever happened to her was to be raped and murdered. Even then she'd only been subbing for someone else.

The sleuths had found that she and the man had had a cup of coffee about midnight in a nearby drive-in. The couple had been served inside, not in a car. She'd been standing there alone, waiting for a bus. Her girl friends had waved good-bye to her. The man had seen her standing there alone, a little nervous. He'd said, "Buses don't run often at night," as if he too were waiting. She hadn't wanted to talk; she'd been brought up not to talk to strange men. "Mildred was a good girl," her parents sobbed. "She'd never let a man pick her up," her girl friends chorused, but they wondered how much they hadn't known about Mildred. "Not unless she knew him." The cops were scouring the town now, talking to every man Mildred had known. They'd be thorough; they'd check every man who'd passed through that insurance office. Believing they had a lead at last on a man apparently as normal as you or I, who tracked the women at night. The lead editorial called him Jack the Ripper and demanded more and better police protection. The editorial—it was a non-administration paper—sneered at politics and got in some snide cracks about the mayor.

She didn't want to talk but he was a decent-looking young fellow waiting for a bus and the mist grew cold on the lonely corner. When he knew she was ripe for the suggestion, he mentioned coffee at the drive-in up at the corner of Linden Drive. The pert car-hop remembered Mildred when she saw the picture in the paper. She'd been carrying out a tray when they entered. Remembered possibly because by then Mildred was pleased at having coffee with a good-looking young fellow. She preened a little.

The car-hop told the other girls, "That's her"; the boss heard the gabble and he called the Beverly Hills police. The car-hop couldn't describe the man, sort of tall, nice looking, in a tan suit. She was sure he couldn't be the strangler; he wasn't that kind of a man at all. She would always be sure that what happened to Mildred happened after she left her drive-in escort.

He read every line of every story in the morning paper. He felt good today after last night's sleep. It was a wonderful summer day. He stretched out in bed lazily and he thought about the redhead. She would be poison but it wouldn't hurt to think about her. He couldn't get mixed up with a woman, with a damn snooping dame. But God, she'd be worth knowing. It had been so long a time since he'd had a woman to hold to. He hadn't wanted one.

He didn't want one now; it was a hangover from seeing Sylvia and Brub looking at each other. Maybe the crazy thought that had flickered in his mind about the little brown girl and her seven million dollars. It would be a good day to lie on the beach at Santa Monica. In front of Betsy Banning's house at the foot of the California Incline. He might even find out which house was Banning's.

He stretched off the bed. If he were going to sun on the beach, it might be smart to call Brub. Brub shouldn't be working on Sunday. He should be beaching. Talking about the case. New developments. He smiled. It was neat to have a source of information on a case.

A quick shot of thought jabbed him. The tires. They were good tires, no patches, no distinguishing marks. Only somewhere in the back of his mind, he remembered that all tires had distinguishing marks, like fingerprints. Could they get a cast of tire marks, like fingerprints. Could they get a cast of tire marks from dry concrete? He doubted it. As he had doubted it last night. But he should make sure.

Certain gambles were legitimate. Like appearing in a lighted place with Mildred. Gambling on the muddled memory of waitresses and countermen who served hundreds of average-looking men and women every day, every night. Risks were spice. Stunt flying. As long as you used them like spice, sparingly; like stunts, planning them with precision, carrying them out boldly.

He fingered his lip. He could grow a mustache. No reason why he should. He didn't like lip brushes. He looked like a thousand other men. He'd never been in that drive-in before. He never intended to go in it again. Risks he took; mistakes he didn't make.

It would be better to call up the Nicolais. He could find out where the Bannings lived easily enough. If he was going to marry the girl he'd have to find out where she lived. Too bad she wasn't a pal of Sylvia's. That would make it easy. He lifted the phone, dialed the Santa Monica number. There was no answer, only metallic ringing. Too late; they'd probably already gone to the beach. It was past one o'clock.

He wasn't too disappointed. He dressed leisurely, tan gabardine slacks, a white T-shirt. He left the house by the front door. On the balcony were open doors, musical radios, laughter. If she lived in Virginibus Arms—he was certain she did; she hadn't walked like a visitor—he'd run into her again. Plenty of time. Mel Terriss wouldn't be back for a long time.

He walked around the block to the garage, opened the noiseless doors. Before taking out the car he circled it, kicking the tires. They were in good shape, not worn, good solid tires. He didn't need new ones; there was no reason to go to that expense. Brub had said it: the police couldn't check every set of tires in L.A.

He backed out and swung over to Wilshire, turned west. The road to the beach. About three million other drivers had the same idea on this blue sky, golden warm day in late September. He took the San Vicente cutoff, as he turned noting the eucalyptus grove with one small corner of his mind. Not exactly secluded, yet late enough . . . At Fourth Street in Santa Monica he turned right again, descending into the canyon. The sign pointed this as an alternate road to the beach. He was prospecting. This descent would be pretty well deserted at night. But no underbrush except fenced. He dropped into the canyon and found Mesa Road. He didn't expect to find the Nicolais at home, but it was worth a try.

It was well worth it; the door was open, through the screen he could see into the hallway. He pushed the bell, pleased with himself, relaxed, comfortable. It was Sylvia who answered and she was surprised to see him. By her startled look, you'd think he was someone unexpectedly returned from Limbo.

"Hello," he said easily. "Anyone home?"

"Dix—" She unhooked the screen, pushing it open. "I didn't recognize you at first. The sun behind you." She had an open white beach robe over brief white shorts and a white cleft brassiere. Her skin was deep tan and her gilt hair was loose about her shoulders. Without the cool poise she seemed much younger. She was flustered. "Excuse the way I look." Her feet were bare and dappled with sand. "We've just come up from the beach and Brub beat me to the shower. I didn't expect you. Some friends were coming over——"

He cut her off, "I'm a friend, too."

She colored. "Of course, you are. I mean old friends." She sighed. "I'm making it worse. Go on in and get comfortable. Help yourself to a drink. I'll tell Brub." She went quickly, too quickly.

Maybe his open admiration embarrassed her. He didn't understand Sylvia. She was too many women. He settled himself on the living-room couch. Friends coming in. He wouldn't stay on. He'd have a dinner date.

Brub wasn't long. His face lighted when he saw Dix, it had been heavy at the doorway. "Where's that drink? Sylvia said you were mixing them."

"What am I, the bartender?" Dix lunged off the couch. "Name it."

"No," Brub waved him down. "I'll do it. I'm handy."

He felt too good to bother with a drink. "I don't care. Whatever you're having."

"Then you'll settle for Scotch and splash," Brub said from behind the bar. "That's the only English I learned in the service. We'll have it with ice, though." He filled the glasses. "What you been doing all day?"

"Working," Dix answered. "Tried to reach you earlier. I wanted to play hookey on the beach." He took the glass. "Thanks. I thought you were probably on the job."

Brub frowned a little. "I worked this morning." He pushed away the frown. "Spent the afternoon on the beach."

Dix tasted his highball. "How's the case coming?" He had just the right casual curiosity in his voice. It pleased him.

The frown returned to Brub's forehead. "It's not. Right where it was."

Dix's foot edged the paper on the floor. "But you found someone who saw her with the man."

"Yeah." Brub's voice was flat. "Maybe if he'd walk in again, that car-hop would remember him." He was disgusted. "She's looked through the files of every known offender and she can't even describe the guy anymore. She thinks he was this and maybe he was that. She doesn't even know the color of his eyes."

"That's too bad." Dix was gravely sympathetic. "No one else noticed the couple?"

"If they did, they've got stage fright. No one else has volunteered any information. And it was a crowded time at the drive-in. The after-movie crowd. Somebody else must have seen them."

"Yeah," Dix said. "Though you can see people without noticing them." He enlarged on it as if he'd never thought of it before. "How many times in a restaurant do you notice people around you? You don't pay any attention to them when they come or when they go. At least I don't."

"That's it," Brub agreed. He went on, "There's one thing we do know."

Dix lifted his eyes with renewed interest.

"We know he was in Beverly Hills on Friday night." Brub was sardonic. "But whether he was in the neighborhood for an evening's pleasure"—he bit his lip—"or whether he lives there, we don't know. He can't live all over Southern California. He's probably never operated in his own neighborhood; he'd be too cagey for that."

Sylvia came in on the end of his sentence. "Brub, you're not talking about the case again. I can't take it." She was as different from the girl who'd opened the screen door as from the frightened woman of last night. She looked glowing, slim as a birch, in pale gray slacks, a brilliant green sweater. Her damp hair was braided on top of her head. "That's all I've heard this afternoon. Everyone on the beach hounding Brub for details. Do I get a drink, darling?"

"You do. Same as us?" Brub went to the bar again.

"Please, darling." Sylvia dumped ashtrays with zeal. "Why people are so damn morbid," she returned to the subject with emphasis. She'd set up a hearty defense mechanism to battle her fears.

Dix remonstrated. "I don't know that it's exactly morbidity. Isn't it rather self-importance?" He grinned. "It isn't everyone who can get a firsthand account from the detective in the case."

Brub said, "Yeah, Junior G-Man tells all. He don't know nothing but he gotta say something." He swizzled the soda.

Dix smiled into his drink. "I'm different. I have a personal interest in the case." He let his eyes lift lazily as he spoke. Sylvia had frozen where she stood, her eyes alone moving, her eyes slewing swiftly to his face as if he'd suddenly revealed himself as the strangler. Brub went on swizzling.

"You see, I'm writing a detective novel," Dix added.

Sylvia moved then, setting down the ashtray she held. It made a small clack on the glass-topped end table.

Brub brought her the highball. "Here you are, skipper." He sat down, hanging his feet over the arm of the green chair.

"So that's what you're writing. Who you stealing from, Chandler or Hammett or Gardner?"

"Little of each," Dix agreed. "With a touch of Queen and Carr."

"It should be a bestseller if you could combine all those," Sylvia said. She sat opposite Brub.

"Can't miss," Dix admitted. "But for God's sake don't tell Uncle Fergus what I'm doing. He thinks I'm writing literature."

"I don't know Uncle Fergus," Sylvia murmured.

"You wouldn't like him. He's vehemently conservative. He hasn't relaxed since Hoover left Washington," he added cheerfully. "He won't mind what I've written when the royalties roll in. He won't read it anyway." She'd tried to stymie his questioning; he'd fixed that. He said, "Now you take that business about tire tracks that Brub mentioned last night. Instead of beating my brains out at the library, all I have to do is ask him. It's a good touch for a story. Makes you sound like an expert." He lifted his glass. "Do they really make plaster casts of tracks, Brub?"

"They try," Brub said gloomily. "But it takes cooperation. For good ones you need skid marks or mud or virgin territory. No chance this time. There weren't more than several hundred tracks superimposed on that particular stretch. Not worth lifting them."

"But you lifted them, didn't you?" Dix wondered. "The thoroughness of the police——"

"Sure," Brub grunted. "Thorough as hell. Maybe next time——" He broke off. Sylvia had gone tense. "There musn't be a next time," he said heatedly. "Only now——"

Dix said seriously, "Let's skip it, Brub. With you working on it, feeling the way you do, you'll get him." Sylvia's eyes were grateful. "I'll take a refill and I'll tell you about the redhead at my apartment. You still like redheads?"

Sylvia's gratefulness was gay. "He'd better not."

"Who is she?" Brub played up, taking Dix's glass and his own. But it was an effort, he was pulling himself by his bootstraps.

"Well, I haven't met her yet," Dix laughed. "But I'm working on it." He knew better than to be talking about a woman publicly; he knew he shouldn't even think about her. "As soon as I find which apartment is hers, I'm going to get a job reading the light meter or delivering laundry. She's the sweetest built job I've seen in Hollywood."

"You better have me look her over before you make any commitments," Brub said. "Don't forget that blonde in London. Whew!"

"How was I to know her husband was a brass hat? With brass knuckles." He wanted the second drink less than the first but it tasted good.

"You'd better let me look her over," Sylvia suggested. "I don't trust Brub's taste. He just looks at the envelope. Now I'm a psychologist. I find out what's inside."

"You're both invited. As soon as I read the meter."

"That shouldn't take you long," Brub railed. "Unless you're getting old." He squinted his eyes. "You don't show much wear."

Voices clacked on the porch.

"That'll be Maude and Cary," Sylvia said. She called, "Come on in."

They were about what Dix had expected. A cute, babbling brunette, big eyed, hips too wide for her salmon slacks. A nice, empty-looking guy in gabardine slacks and a sports shirt. The Jepsons. Maude liked Dix. She baby-eyed him while she headed for the couch. He'd finish the drink and get out.

She said, "You're the ace, aren't you? I've heard all about you." There was a Texas drawl in her voice. She put a cigarette in her mouth and waited for him to light it. She smelled of perfume and liquor. "Make mine weak, Brub. We had one before leaving." She turned back to Dix. "You were in England with Brub." She babbled at Dix until Brub put the drink in her hand. She started on Brub then; it was inevitable what she would say.

"Have you caught that man yet, Brub? I tell you I'm so scared I don't know what to do. I won't let Cary leave me alone for a minute. I tell him——."

She ought to be scared. It would be a pleasure to throttle her.

"Anything new?" Cary put in.

"No," Brub said.

Sylvia said firmly, "We're not going to talk about it tonight."

Maude ignored her. "Why can't the police catch him?" She was highly indignant. "Nobody's safe with him running around loose." She whispered in sepulchral tones, "The strangler." She shivered closer to Dix. She was having a swell time.

Sylvia took a preparatory breath but Maude raced on, "How are we supposed to know who he is? He could be anybody. I tell Cary maybe he's our grocery man or the bus driver or those dreadful beach athletes. We don't know. Even the police don't know. You'd think they could find out."

Sylvia said desperately, "For God's sake, Maude. Don't you think they're trying?"

"I don't know." Maude tossed her head. "Maybe it's one of their own men. Well, it could be," she insisted to the rejection on the faces of the others. "How do we know? It's simply silly to think that this nice-looking fellow she had coffee with is the one. How did he get her into Beverly Glen Canyon?" she demanded. "Did they walk?"

Cary grunted, "He had a car, of course, Maude."

"Ah." She pounced on it. "But he didn't have a car. They went into the drive-in for coffee." She cocked her triumph at all of them. Her husband looked tired of it all but a thin layer of fear came over Sylvia's doubt.

Brub was scowling. He said, "That's just one of the things we're trying to find out, Maude. He must have had a car."

"I don't get it," Dix admitted.

"Our effete Easterner." Brub seized the diversion. "Dix is from New Jersey," he explained and turned to Dix again. "No one goes into a drive-in for a cup of coffee. Not if he has a car to sit outside in."

"But I've seen people in the drive-ins," Dix argued.

"Kids without a car. Or folks who've walked to the neighborhood movie. Or someone who's after a full meal, something he doesn't want to balance on a tray. But not for a shake or a cup of coffee. That's the point of a drive-in. You don't have to get out of your car."

"If you don't have a car, then you have to sit inside." Maude wagged her head. "He couldn't have had a car. Because," she took a deep breath, "because if he was the strangler and had a car, he never would have taken her inside where people could identify him. That man didn't have a car. But the one who killed her did have a car or she wouldn't have been found up Beverly Glen." Her triumph skittered joyfully. "There has to be another man with a car."

Dix narrowed his eyes, as if with the others he was pondering her conviction.

Sylvia broke the pause. "You think, then, that there was a second man, an accomplice." She looked quickly at Brub.

Brub shook his head. "He works alone." There was certainty in him.

Dix didn't jump on the statement. He asked simply, "How do you know that?"

"His kind of killer always works alone. He can't risk an accomplice."

Cary said, "He's insane, of course."

Dix turned his glass in his hand. Cary Jepson was a clod. He wouldn't be married to a stupid little talking machine if he had any spirit. The obvious reach of his imagination was, "He's insane, of course." It would never occur to him that any reason other than insanity could make a man a killer. That's what all the dolts around town would be parroting: *he's insane, of course, he's insane, of course*. It took imagination to think of a man, sane as you or I, who killed. He hid against his highball glass the smile forming on his lips.

Brub was explaining, "—but doubtless he's a loony only in that respect. Otherwise he's probably an everyday citizen. Going about his business like any of us. Looking normal, acting normal until that urge comes on him."

"About once a month," Maude said goggle-eyed and then she screamed, "Oh."

Dix moved slightly away to look down at her. There was nothing wrong, she was just acting up. Sylvia didn't like it. Sylvia's face was granite. Dix didn't like it either; he was getting out of here.

Brub said, "Just don't be out alone at night, Maude, and you needn't worry." He added almost to himself, "We'll get him. He'll make a mistake yet." His mouth was grim.

"Suppose he doesn't," Maude wailed. She savored it, "Suppose it goes on and on——"

"Maude!" her husband complained wearily. "She keeps raving like that——"

Sylvia said definitely, "She isn't going to rave here. That's all, Maude. It's a truce—no more talk about crime tonight." She put on a bright smile. "Where will we eat? Ted's for steak? Carl's for shrimp? Jack's for chowder?"

He could leave now. Dix glanced at his watch and stood upright fast. "Why didn't someone tell me? I've a dinner date in Hollywood at seven. I've got to beat it."

Maude pushed out her spoiled underlip. "Break it."

"With a redhead?" Brub grinned.

Dix grinned back. "Not yet. I'll keep you informed. Thanks, Sylvia. Ring me, Brub. We'll have lunch." He nodded good-bye to the Jepsons, not saying it was a pleasure to meet them; it hadn't been.

He took a deep breath outside to expel the odor of Maude from his lungs. He'd like to meet her on a dark corner. It would be a service to humanity.

He drove along the beach road to the Incline, casually glancing toward the three houses there. The traffic was still fairly heavy, in Wilshire it became irritating, at Sepulveda's intersection it was a slow-moving mass. Enough to make anyone's nerves short. He turned left at Westwood Boulevard, cutting sharp, just missing a right-turning car. He saw the motorcycle cop as the brakes of the other car screamed. But the cop didn't come after him.

He drove slowly up through the university gates and onto Sunset. Only one stop sign, at Beverly Glen. Sunset seemed deserted after Wilshire, he picked up speed. The light was against him at the intersection. He glanced casually at the Bel-Air gates; the road north jogged here, dividing into Bel-Air Road and, just beyond, Beverly Glen.

His hands tightened on the wheel. Cops again. Not on cycles; in a prowl car. Parked there watching cars. He slid with the change to Go, not gathering speed until he had rounded the corner of the twisting woodland Sunset stretch. The rearview mirror showed no car following. His hands relaxed and he wanted to laugh. Out loud, noisy.

The cops were as unimaginative as that Jepson. Could they actually believe the killer would return to the scene of the crime? He did laugh and loud. He could see them sitting there all day, waiting for a loony to drive up the canyon. Fools.

He cut south at Rodeo, swinging back to Wilshire. He had nothing to do with himself and tonight he didn't want to be alone. The routine dullness of his nights, eat alone, go to a movie, go home—or, skip the movie, go home and read, write a little sometimes. The end, the same. Take some dope to sleep. Unless he could sleep of exhaustion. That wasn't often.

A man couldn't live alone; he needed friends. He needed a

woman, a real woman. Like Brub and Sylvia. Like that stupid Cary and that stupid Maude. Better than being alone.

It wasn't often it hit him hard. It was a balmy night at early dusk with the look of lamps through open windows and the sound of music from radios in the lighted rooms. He'd eschewed human relationship for something stronger, something a hell of a lot better.

The car had followed its lead to the apartment; he hadn't intended to come back here yet. He parked at the curb; he'd have to go out to eat. Later.

He didn't have to give up normal living; that had been his one mistake. Brub and Sylvia proved it. He could be with them and be himself and not give away any secrets. His nerves were steady, his eyes level. It was time to gather friends again. Someone besides Brub and Sylvia. He couldn't be constantly at their home. They might start wondering. Sometimes Sylvia's eyes were disturbing, they were so wise. As if she could see under the covering of a man. Ridiculous, of course. You didn't ever have to give yourself away. Not if you were smart.

His spirits had jutted back up to a normal level. It wasn't often he got the dumps. His life was good, a slick apartment, a solid car; income without working for it, not half enough, but he could get by. Freedom, plenty of freedom. Nobody telling him what to do, nobody snooping.

He pulled the keys from the ignition and walked, tinkling them, the few paces to the court entrance. It was amusing to enter boldly, announcing his entrance with the metallic percussion. He didn't let into actual consciousness the thought that the redhead might be on her balcony.

The first time he'd seen the patio, he hadn't believed it. He hadn't been long enough in Southern California to believe it. It wasn't real; it was a stage set, a stagy stage set. In the center was the oblong blue pool. By day the pool was sky blue, it was tiled in that color, the water in it had to look that blue. By night it was moonlight blue. Two blue spotlights, one at either end of the balcony, made certain of that.

Dix had never seen anyone swimming in the pool by day or night. He'd never seen anyone lounging in the bright, striped gliders or around the gaudy umbrella tables. The idea was good, the semi-tropical flowers spotted in the corners of the square prettied it up still more, the high oleander hedge was protection from street eyes, but nobody used the patio. The people in the Spanish bungalows boxing the court on three sides, and those upstairs off the Spanish-Colonial balcony, weren't clubby. Dix hadn't laid eyes on a couple of them in the weeks he'd been here.

He was thinking about the artificial moonlight in the artificial patio when behind him the blare of a horn jabbed. Jangle of voices scraped across his nerves. Anger shook him; for a moment he was tempted to turn out of the court and raise hell. Instead he tightened his fists and walked to his door, the first bungalow on the left. He was only at the door when he heard the heels clicking across the flagstone patio. Before he turned he was certain whom he would see.

She hadn't noticed him standing there by his door, she was hurrying. In the blue light her hair and her slacks and jacket were all blue, different depths of blue.

What he did was out of impulse, without thought. Thought would have rejected the idea. With long strides he quietly circled the pool. He was at the stairs almost as quickly as she. She was only on the third step when he spoke to her.

"I beg your pardon."

She wasn't startled although she hadn't known he was there. She stood arrested in motion of ascent, her head turning without any haste until she could look back down at him. When she saw it was a man, the glint of dare touched her mouth, her eyes.

"Did you drop something?" he continued. He held one hand cupped before him.

She looked down at herself, at her purse, touched her blown hair. "Did I?" she puzzled.

Quickly, impudently, he thrust both hands in his pockets. He looked up boldly at her. "I don't know. I was hoping so."

Her eyes narrowed over him slowly, in the way they had last night. She liked the look of him. Her eyes lengthened and she began to smile. "Why?" she countered.

"I just lost my dinner date. I thought maybe you'd lost yours, too."

She stopped smiling and she froze up just a little, not much. His eyes didn't waver; they held on to hers until she smiled again. "Sorry."

"I'm your neighbor. One A." His head gestured. He didn't want her to think he was a stranger, trying for a pickup.

"Sorry," she repeated and she moved up to the fourth step. "My dinner date will be here at any minute and I'm not dressed. I'm rushing."

"I'm sorry too," Dix said. He said it warmly, with all the charm he could summon, and only a touch of arrogance for diversion.

She broke in, "If I ever lose a dinner date, I'll let you know." She ran up the stair lightly, not looking back at him.

He shrugged. He hadn't expected success, therefore he wasn't disappointed. He'd made the preliminary maneuver, the question now was of time. He was stimulated by merely talking with her; she was a lure, even with that ghostly blue light coating her face. He moved back to his own quarters. Hearing again the tap of her heels, he swung suddenly and looked up to the balcony. She was just entering her apartment, the darkened one, the third. He continued, content, to his bungalow. He'd made headway. He knew now where to find her.

3

HE DIDN'T HAVE TO HURRY. AS A MATTER OF FACT, HE NEEDN'T LEAVE the apartment. There were tins of food, crackers, some cheese and fruit, cold meat in the ice box. He could get comfortable, cheese and beer were good enough for any man on the evening of a scorcher day. But he didn't want to get comfortable; he wanted something lively. Something amusing and stimulating and male.

He switched on the radio, found music, and fetched himself a cold beer from the kitchen. He was sprawled on the couch, half listening to the program, half thinking about the things he'd like to do tonight. If he had the money and the woman.

The slow beer was half gone when his front doorbell sounded. It startled him momentarily; his front bell was never rung. Slowly he got to his feet. He didn't delay moving to answer it. But he didn't hurry. He walked with caution.

The breath he took before setting his hand to the knob wasn't deliberate. Not until he flung open the door and heard the breath expelled did he realize he'd been holding it.

On the doorstep was the redhead. She said, "I've just lost a dinner date."

He tried not to sound too foolishly pleased. "Come in. Maybe you'll find him here."

"I hope not," she said dryly. She moved past him into the living room. She was eyeing it. It didn't look so good, the Sunday papers crushed on the couch, spilling over the floor. The limp sofa cushions. The ashtrays dirty, the beer bottle standing on the rug. Yet even in disarray it was class. The gray-green walls might have been indigenous to Virginibus Arms but the furniture was handpicked by Terriss. All modern bleached wood and glass and chrome, upholstery in yellow and crimson and gray. Terriss had boasted of his decorating taste. It wasn't personal taste, it was money; with Terriss' money you were steered to taste. You couldn't go wrong.

Dix said, "Tillie doesn't come on Sundays."

"You should see my place." She slid down in the wing chair as if she belonged there. She was still wearing the slacks; the outfit wasn't shades of moonlight blue but pale yellow, the pullover deeper yellow; the jacket, loose over her shoulders, was white. And her hair wasn't red, it was burnt sienna with a shimmer of gold dusting it. She'd done over her hair and her face but she hadn't taken time to change.

Dix held out the cigarette box to her. "What do you mean, you hope not?"

She put the cigarette in her mouth, lifted her face, waited for the light. From the thin gold lighter, Mel's lighter. "Because I told him I had a lousy headache and was going to bed." She blew the plume of smoke directly up at Dix. "And that I was disconnecting the phone."

He laughed. She was bold as her rust-red mouth and her slanted eyes, sharp as her painted tapering nails. She was what he'd needed. She was what he wanted. "Drink?"

"No. I want dinner. I had enough cocktails before I came home." She moved her body in the chair. "Maybe that's why I'm here." Her eyes studied the room.

"Mind if I finish my beer?"

"Not at all."

He returned to the couch and picked up the bottle. He didn't bother to pick up the newspaper. The way the first section had fallen revealed half of Mildred's whey face. He rested his foot on the paper.

The redhead turned her eyes suddenly back to him. "This is Mel Terriss' apartment." It wasn't a question.

"Yes. He's in South America. He turned it over to me while he's away."

"Who are you?" she demanded.

He smiled slightly. "I'm Dix Steele." In turn demanded, "Who are you?"

She wasn't accustomed to being given her own treatment. She didn't know whether she liked it. She tossed back her autumn hair and waited, her eyes watching him. And then accepted his equality. "Laurel Gray."

He inclined his head. "How d'y'do?" Exaggerated politeness. He switched to impudence. "Married?"

She bridled. Retort was on her tongue but she withheld it, her eyes going over him again in that slow slant fashion. There was no wedding ring on her finger, there was a lump of twisted gold, channelled with rubies and diamonds. A glittering bauble, the kind that cost fat money, the kind you looked at in jewelers' windows on Beverly Drive. You looked through the thick plate glass of the windows and wondered about those jeweled hunks. Wondered how a man could get his hands on the kind of dough it took to touch.

Somebody had put it on her finger. But there wasn't a wedding ring beside it.

She answered coolly, "It's none of your business, son, but since you asked, not now." She lifted her chin and he knew what she was about to say. He didn't want it said, he fended it away quickly.

"You were a friend of Mel Terriss?" The ring might have come from Terriss.

"Not much." She stubbed her cigarette into the ashtray. "Dropped in on a couple of his parties." She eyed him. "You a friend of Mel's?"

She was like all women, curious about your private life. He laughed at her; she'd find out only as much as he wished. "An old friend," he laughed. "Pre-war. Princeton." Princeton meant money and social position to her, calculation came that quickly under her skin. She was greedy and callous and a bitch, but she was fire and a man needed fire. "I'm from New York," he threw in carelessly. It sounded better than New Jersey.

"So you looked up old friend Mel when you came to the coast," her voice mocked.

"What do you think?" He saw the way her leg curved and lengthened into thigh. "Terriss isn't the kind of guy you look up. He's the kind you run into." She had put another cigarette into her mouth. He crossed to light it. Her perfume was of flesh as he bent over her, and her eyes were wide and bold. It was too soon. He snapped shut the lighter, but he stood over her for a moment longer, smelling her. "You won't change your mind about a drink?"

"It's food I want." She didn't want food, she wanted what he wanted.

"You'll get it," he told her. But not yet. He was comfortable. He didn't want to start out again. He wanted to sit here opposite her, feeling for knowledge of her in his mind. He knew her; he had known her on that first evening when he'd bumped into her. But it was satisfying to corroborate the knowledge. He said, "First, I'm going to have a drink."

She gave in. "Make it two."

He smiled to himself as he went to the kitchen. He'd thought she would change her mind. A couple of drinks and they'd get acquainted faster. When he returned to the living room with the drinks, she was still curved in the chair. As if she hadn't stirred but was waiting for him to infuse movement into her.

She had moved. The paper his foot had trodden was by her chair. She took the glass from him and she said, "I see where the strangler's been at it again." She wasn't very interested; it was conversation, nothing more. "Someday maybe those dopes will learn not to pick up strange men."

"You've picked me up."

She'd taken a long swallow of the highball. As he spoke, she lifted her eyebrows. "You picked me up, Princeton." She purred, "Besides, you're no stranger." She knew it too, the instinct of one for the other. "Mel's liquor is good as ever."

He said, "Yes, he left a good cellar for me." He went on, "I ran into him in a bar."

"And you had an old home week."

"He was potted and trying to make my girl." His eyes spoke meaning beyond the words he slurred. "A blonde."

"That you'd picked up somewhere," she retorted.

He lied, "Friend of mine from home. She was just here for a week. Not Mel's type." He drank. He couldn't remember the girl or her name. "Did you ever try to get rid of Mel when he was soused?"

"When wasn't he?"

"Well," he shrugged, "I promised to lunch with him next day. I lunched with him. I was trying to find an apartment. He was going to Rio on this new job. So—"

"Wait a minute," she called out. "Not Mel. Not a job in Rio."

"That's what he told me," Dix said. That's what Mel had said. He could have gone on a job. Some alcoholics tried to make a new start.

She was laughing to herself. "So you moved in."

"Yes, I moved in." He wasn't irritated. She didn't mean he was a charity case; she wouldn't be here drinking with him if she didn't think he had the stuff to spend. She probably thought he was another stinking rich loafer like Mel Terriss. He was casual. "I needed a quiet place for my work."

She was still laughing within her. "What do you do? Invent bombs?"

"I'm a writer." He didn't let her put the question. It was time again for her to answer questions. "I suppose you're in pictures?"

"Not often. I don't like getting up mornings." She knew all the tricks, to speak in commonplace phrases, to say more than words could say. He wondered who was keeping her. He could see the guy, fat paunched, fat jowled, balding. Too old, too ugly to get it without paying for it. Paying plenty. A guy with nothing on his side but money. A bad idea slapped him. Could Terriss have been the guy? He didn't fit the picture of Old Moneybags. But if you revised the picture. A younger fellow, dopey with drink, his looks ravaged by the booze, a dullard always, even before alcohol narcotized what he had for a brain. And that stinking ego. He could just hear Terriss boasting about his girl, wearing her in public the way she wore that hunk of a ring; making himself believe he didn't have to buy it, he was just treating the gal right.

It couldn't have been Terriss. Terriss would have bragged about her. At least he'd have mentioned her. It wasn't Terriss. But doubts were worms crawling in his mind. She could twist a man about those taloned fingers, a man like Terriss. She could have excuses to keep her name out of it. Her career. A jealous ex. A divorce not quite complete.

She hadn't been talking. She'd been having her drink, eyeing him. Nor had his thought run across his face. It was trained to remain expressionless.

He finished his drink. "I don't like mornings either," he said. "That's why I'm a writer."

"Trying to break into pictures?"

He laughed at her. "I write books, lady. When I try to break into screen work, it will be because I need the money." He'd said the right thing, some of the speculation about him went out of her that quickly. There was an imperceptible relaxing of her muscular tension. He watched her over the edge of his glass as he tilted it, finished his drink. "Another?"

"Not now—"

He broke in, "I know, you're hungry. Wait'll I get a jacket and we'll be on our way." He didn't take a minute, catching up the heavy tweed jacket, a fuzzy, wiry tweed, rich brown, rich stuff. He slipped into the coat—he had about twenty dollars, enough for a Sunday-night dinner. Not a dress-up dinner, not in slacks.

She had retouched her lips, combed out her hair, resettled the white coat over the yellow sweater. She looked as fresh as if she'd just tubbed. She turned from the mirror as he reentered, the mirror near the desk. Her bag was on the desk. Good thing he'd mailed Uncle Fergus' letter. She was the kind who wouldn't care how she got her information on a man.

"Ready?"

She nodded and she walked toward the door. He came up behind her. In time to open the door. She looked up at him. "Do you have Mel's address in Rio?" The question was sudden. Why the hell couldn't she forget Mel Terriss?

"I'll give it to you when we get back," he told her. He opened the door. They went together into the night.

He touched her then for the first time, his hand against her elbow, escorting her into the blue courtyard.

He asked, "How would you like to drive up to Malibu?"

III

1

SHE WASN'T AFRAID. SHE RESTED HERSELF CARELESSLY AGAINST THE seat of the car, her left knee half-turned toward his thigh. In the rounding of a corner she would touch him. She knew it; she curled herself deliberately in this fashion. It was one of her tricks. Yet, even knowing it was a trick, he was stimulated, waiting for that pressure.

This was the beginning of something good, so good that he was enjoying its immediacy without thought, without plan. She was beside him, that was enough. He had needed her for so long a time. He had always needed her.

It was a dream. A dream he had not dared dream, a woman like this. A tawny-haired woman; a high-breasted, smooth-hipped, scented woman; a wise woman. He didn't want to go to Malibu, he wanted to swing the car around, return to the apartment. He could wait. It was better to wait. She knew that.

The traffic lanes were quieter at this early evening hour. He followed Wilshire to the eucalyptus grove of San Vicente. The spice of eucalyptus scented the darkness. San Vicente was a dark street, he hadn't noticed before. And the smell of the sea came in to meet them long before they reached the hill that dropped into the canyon, long before they reached the sound of the sea.

She was quiet on the drive. He was grateful for her quietness. He wondered if she were feeling for knowledge of him in her quietness or if she was only tired. She didn't speak until he turned into the canyon.

She remarked then, "You know the back roads."

"You recognize them," he smiled.

The touch of her knee on his thigh was more deliberate. She tossed back her hair. "I've driven along them often enough," she said in that slow, husky way which gave words meaning. She laughed. "I've friends in Malibu."

"The particular friend?"

"Which one?" she countered.

"Isn't there a particular one?" Curiosity nagged him. He wanted to know about her. But he couldn't ask questions, not open questions. She was like him; she'd lie.

"There usually is," she said. They had reached the ocean road, turn right to Malibu. "Where will we eat?"

"Any place you say. You know Malibu."

"I don't want to go to Malibu."

He turned his head, puzzled at her abruptness. Afraid for the moment that this was to be the end of it, that she would put him off as she had the other man. Afraid that he'd said the wrong thing or done the wrong thing although he didn't know where he'd gone wrong. But she was still relaxed. She said, "I'm too hungry to drive that far. Let's stop at Carl's."

Anything that she said. The neon sign of Carl's slatted over the road ahead. He remembered the Nicolais and their friends had mentioned a Carl's or Joe's or Sam's. He wouldn't want to run into them. He wanted Laurel alone, unshared. Not touched by the anger and terror which entangled the Nicolais. He didn't ever want her touched by ugly things.

Yet he had no reason to reject Carl's. No reason to instill controversy in what had been between them, quiet, uncluttered. If Carl's had been the Nicolais' dinner choice, they would be gone by now. It had been more than two hours since he left them; they were planning to eat at that time. A car was pulling out from the front of the restaurant. Instinct made him avoid the lights. He drew up on the road at the side of the building, parked there.

She said, "I'll slide through." He stood there watching her come to him, taking her hand, touching her waist as he helped her from the car. The sea was a surge and a hush in the darkness across the road. She stood close to him for a moment, too close, before he removed his hand. She said, "You don't mind stopping here? The shrimp's good."

She led him around to the steps and they went up into the dining room. There were few in it, his quick look saw that he knew no one. Nor did she. Her look was quick as his own.

It was a spacious room, warm with light, circled with windows overlooking the dark sea. They sat facing each other and it was good.

To be with a woman. To be opposite her, to have his fill of her face, the shape of it, the texture of it, the bone structure beneath the amber flesh. The set of her eyes and the shape of her mouth . . . her fire-tipped mouth.

"You think you'll know me the next time you see me?"

He returned to her actuality. He laughed but his words weren't made of laughter. "I knew you before I ever saw you."

Her eyes widened.

"And you knew me."

She let her lashes fall. They curved along as a child's, russet against her cheeks. She said, "You're pretty sure of yourself, aren't you, Dix?"

"Never before."

Her eyes opened full again and laughter echoed through her. "Oh, brother!" she breathed.

He didn't answer her, only with the look in his eyes. He hadn't been surefooted with her before. He was now. He knew how to play it. She was brittle only on the surface. Underneath she too was seeking. Exhilaration heightened him. He knew then the rightness of this; she was for him.

The waitress came to the table before he could further it. He said, "You order, Laurel. I'll double it. Drink first?" He was irritated by the interruption. The waitress was a little chit, too much hair and flat face.

"No drinks." Laurel ordered for both, competently, without fuss. "Bring the coffee now, will you?"

The waitress went away but she was back too quickly. She poured the coffee. This time she'd be away longer.

Laurel said, "If you don't want your coffee now, I'll drink both, Princeton."

"You're out of luck." She knew what a man wanted, coffee, now, not later. He lighted her cigarette, realizing her as he leaned across the table. She was real, not a begging dream in his loneness. She was a woman.

She settled herself in comfort. "How long have you been living at Mel's place?" She was deliberately veering from intimacy. It didn't matter; postponement added zest.

He tried to remember. "About two months—six weeks, I guess."

"Funny I haven't run into you."

"Yes." Yet it wasn't. He'd used the back door, shortcut to the garage. He hadn't been in the blue patio half a dozen times. "I thought you were a visitor when I bumped into you last night. Have you been away?"

"No."

"Guess our hours didn't coincide. They will now."

"They might," she admitted.

"They will," she said with certainty.

Again she veered. "When did Mel leave?"

He figured it in his mind. "August. Around about the first. Before I moved in."

The waitress divided them again. She wasn't too long about it, and she was agreeable despite her flat face. The shrimp looked good and she poured more coffee without request.

He waited only until she was out of hearing. "Why the interest in Mel? I thought you'd only been in his place a couple of times." It wasn't jealousy but she'd think there was a twinge of it in him. She was thinking it now, maybe that was why she kept harping on Mel. Just another trick, not actual curiosity. "You weren't carrying the torch there?"

"Good Lord, Princeton!" That ended that. She needn't try that trick again.

He smiled slightly. "I was beginning to think he might have been the jeweler." His forefinger touched the mass of gold and ruby.

Her lip curled. "Mel was more careful of his money than that. Liquor was the only thing he could bear to spend it on." Her eyes touched the ring. "My ex."

He lifted his eyebrows. "It's a nice piece."

She said suddenly, "Don't ever marry money. It isn't worth it." She began to eat as if her hunger had reawakened.

"I've always thought it might be a good racket." He added, "For a woman."

"There's nothing wrong with the money. It's what goes with it." Her face was stony. "Bastards."

"Exes?"

"Rich men. And women. They believe the earth was created for them. They don't have to think or feel—all they have to do is buy it. God, how I hate them!" She shook her head. "Shut up, Laurel."

He smiled patiently. "I don't believe that's true of all of them." As if he were a rich guy himself, one of the dirty bastards himself.

She said, "I can smell them a mile off. They're all alike."

"They aren't all like Mel—or your ex."

She went on eating. As if she hadn't heard him. And he had to know. If Mel had been in on the rent. He seized it. "After all they pay the rent. And the jeweler."

"They don't pay mine," she said savagely. Then she smiled. "I said shut up, Laurel. But I'm surprised Mel went off without saying good-bye. He was always in my hair."

"I'm surprised he didn't take you with him," Dix said.

She grimaced. "I told you I'd learned my lesson. Don't marry money."

No one was paying her rent. She was on her own; the ex, the rich one, must have settled up. She'd see to that; she and a battery of expensive lawyers. He said lightly, "It's the man who pays and pays. It couldn't have been so bad. You can sleep mornings and not have to worry about the roof over your head."

She said, "Yes," and the hardness came about her mouth. "As long as I don't marry again."

He understood her bitterness, but, understanding, he was disturbed. There could be someone she wanted, the way he was going to want her. She wouldn't have the hatred of the ex if there wasn't a reason; she had his money to live on and was free of him. Dix couldn't go on asking questions; he'd asked too many now. He was prying and she'd know it when the anger went out of her. He smiled at her again. "I'm glad that's the way it is," he said.

"Why?" She flashed at him.

"Because I wouldn't have found you in time—if it hadn't been that way."

Because she was desired, she softened. Giving him the look and the dare. She said, "Why, Princeton!"

"Or am I in time?"

She smiled, the inscrutable smile of a woman who knew the ways of a woman. She didn't answer him. There could be someone else. But at the moment, here with her, he was sure of his own prowess. Because he knew this was intended; that he and she should meet and in meeting become enmeshed. It was to be; it was.

They were the last guests to leave the restaurant. Again in the dark, sea-scented night, he was filled with power and excitement and rhythm. But tonight it was good. Because he was with her.

He didn't want to turn back to the city. He wanted to go on with her into this darkness, with the sound of water echoing the beat of his heart. He wanted to keep her with him always in this oneness of the two. He wanted to lift her with him into the vastness of the night sky. He said, "Shall we drive on up to Malibu?"

But he didn't want to drive, he didn't want to be occupied with the mechanics of a car. He was relieved when she refused.

"Let's keep away from Malibu."

He turned back, but driving without plan, he found the place where he could silence the car. An open stretch overlooking the dark beach and the sea. He said, "Do you mind? I just want to smell the salt."

Her eyebrows quirked. She'd thought he was parking the way a kid parked with his girl. She liked it that he hadn't meant it for that. She said suddenly, "Let's go down where we can really smell it."

The wind caught at them as they left the car and descended to the beach. The wind and the deep sand pushed at them but they struggled on, down to the water's edge. Waves were frost on the dark churning waters. Stars pricked through the curved sky. The rhythm pulsed, the crash and the slurring swish repeated endlessly, the smell of the sea was sharp. Spindrift salted their lips.

He had taken her hand as they walked to the water, he held it now, and she didn't withdraw it from his. She said, "I haven't done this for a long, long time." Her voice wasn't brittle; she wasn't playing a game with him. She was alone here, with him but alone. The wind swirled her hair across her face until he could see only the slant of her forehead and her cheek. Happiness rose like a spire within him. He hadn't expected ever to know happiness again. His voice stirred, "Laurel—"

She turned her head, slowly, as if surprised that he was there. The wind blew her hair like mist across her face. She lifted her face and for the first time, there in the light of the sea and the stars, he knew the color of her eyes. The color of dusk and mist rising from the sea, with the amber of stars flecking them.

"Laurel," he said, and she came to him the way he had known from the beginning it must be. "Laurel," he cried, as if the word were the act. And there became a silence around them, a silence more vast than the thunderous ecstasy of the hungry sea.

2

To sleep, perchance to dream and dreaming wake. . . . To sleep and to wake. To sleep in peace, without the red evil of dreaming. To wake without need to struggle through fog to reach the sunlight. To find sleep good and waking more good. It was the ringing phone that woke him. He reached for it and he felt her stir beside him.

He spoke into it quietly, not wishing to wake her. Yet he willed her to wake, to open her eyes as he had opened his, into the full sunshine. "Hello."

"Dix? Did I interrupt your work?"

It was Brub Nicolai. For the instant there was a waning of the sun, as if a cold hand had pushed against it. Dix softened his voice to answer. "Not at all."

Brub didn't sound depressed today; it could have been the old Brub speaking. "Who was that redhead I seen you with last night? Was that the redhead?"

He couldn't answer quickly. It was impossible for Brub to have seen him last night with Laurel. Unless Brub were having him followed. That was more impossible. That would be incredible. He asked, "What are you talking about?"

"The redhead, Dickson. Not the blonde you were meeting in Hollywood. The redhead. Was that—"

Dix said, "Hm, a Peeping Tom. Where were you hiding, Tom?"

Brub laughed. As if he hadn't a care in the world. "You didn't see us. We were pulling out of Carl's when you went in. It was Sylvia spotted you. I spotted the redhead."

The car he had avoided by parking at the side of the building. There were always eyes. A little tailor on his way home from a movie. A waitress in a drive-in. A butcher-boy on a bicycle. A room clerk with a wet pointed nose. A detective's wife who was alert, too alert. Whose eyes saw too much.

There were always eyes but they didn't see. He had proved it. His hand relaxed on the phone. "You would. And what did the little woman say to that?"

"I couldn't repeat such language." There was an imperceptible change in Brub's voice. Back to business. "How about lunch with me? You bring the redhead."

He could hear the stir of her breath. She was awake but she was silent. "She's tied up." He wouldn't put her and Brub together. She belonged in a different compartment from the Nicolais.

"Then you're not, I take it. How about lunch?"

He could refuse. But he didn't want to. Even to be with her. Because the game with Brub was important; it had to be played. There was renewed zest to the game in having Brub make the approach today.

"Sure," he agreed. "What time and where?" He noted the clock. It was past eleven.

"Noon? I'm at the Beverly Hills station."

His pulses leaped. The game was growing better. To walk into the police station, to be the guest of Homicide for lunch. But he didn't want to hurry. He wanted to watch her rise from sleep, to see her woman ways, the clothing of her, the combing of her hair. He asked, "Can you make it one or do you punch a time clock?"

"One's okay. Meet me here?"

"I'll be there, Brub." He replaced the phone and turned to look on her. She was beautiful, she was younger than he'd thought her on first meeting; she was beautiful in the morning after sleep. Her hair was cobweb on the pillow, her dusky amber-flecked eyes were wide. She didn't smile up at him, she looked at him with that long wondering look.

She said, "Who's first in the shower?"

He put his fingers to her cheek. He wanted to tell her how beautiful she was. He wanted to tell her all that she was to him, all that she must be. He said, "The one who doesn't fix the coffee."

She stirred, lazy as a cat. "I don't cook."

"Then you do the scrubbing, lady. And don't take all day."

"You have a lunch date," she mocked.

"Business."

"It sounded like it."

He didn't dare touch her, not if he were to make it to Brub. He slid away his fingers, slowly, with reluctance. Yet there was a pleasure in the reluctance, in the renunciation. This moment would come again and he would not let it pass. Postponing it would make it the sweeter.

"Go on," she urged. "Make the coffee."

She didn't believe that he meant to leave. He surprised her when he rose obediently, wrapped his bathrobe about him. He wanted to surprise her; he wanted her interest. She knew men so well although she was too young to know so well. Only by whetting her interest would she remain with him long enough to become entangled with him. Because she was spoiled and wise and suspicious.

He put on the coffee in the kitchen and then he went to the front door. The paper had hit the doorstep today, he didn't have to step outside for it. It was habit that unfolded it and looked at the front page. He didn't really care what was on it. The story wasn't there; it was on the second page, the police quizzing friends of the dead Mildred, the police admitting this early that there were no leads. He read the story scantily. He could hear the downpour of the shower. There was no mail in the slot. Too soon to hear from Uncle Fergus. The old buzzard had better come through. He'd need money to take Laurel where she should be taken. To expensive places where she could be displayed as she should be.

He flung down the paper, went back to the bedroom, impatient to see her again. She was still in the bathroom but the shower was turned off. He called, "How do you take your coffee?" Touching the soft yellow of her sweater there on the chair. Wanting to look on her, to smell her freshness.

She opened the door. She was wrapped in a borrowed white terry bathrobe, it was a cocoon enfolding her. Her face was shining and her damp hair was massed on top of her head. She came to the quick take of his breath, came to him and he held her. "Oh, God," he said. Deliberately he set her away. "I've got a business luncheon in one hour. How do you want your coffee?"

Her eyes slanted. "Sweet and black."

He hurried as she sat down at the dressing table, hurried to return to her. She was still there when he brought the coffee, she was combing out her hair, her fiery gold hair. He put the coffee down for her and he carried his own across the room.

"You'd better shower, Dix. You don't want to be late for that business appointment."

"It is business. Someday I'll tell you all about it." He drank his coffee, watching the way she swirled her hair below her shoulders. Watching the way she painted her lips, brushed her lashes. As if she belonged here. Jealousy flecked him. She knew her way around. Had she been here before? He couldn't bear it if Mel Terriss had touched her. Yet he knew she had been touched by other men; there was no innocence in her.

Abruptly he left her, long enough to shower. He couldn't stay with her, not with the anger rising in him. It washed away in the shower. Mel Terriss wasn't here. She couldn't have had anything to do with Terriss. She wouldn't ever have been that hard up. He opened the door when he'd finished showering, fearing that she might have slipped away from him. But she was there, almost in the doorway. "I brought you more coffee," she said.

"Thanks, baby. Mind the noise of a razor?"

"I can take it." She was dressed now. She sat on the edge of the tub with her coffee, watching him shave. As if she couldn't bear to leave him. As if it was the same with her as with him. The burring didn't annoy with her there. He could talk through it, gaily. "I knew you'd be busy. That's why I said okay."

"And if I weren't?"

"Aren't you?"

"I have a voice lesson at two," she admitted.

"What time will you be home?"

"Why?" she mocked.

He didn't bother to answer, only with his eyes. He finished shaving, cleaned the razor. "Busy tonight?"

"Why?" she repeated.

"I might be free," he said.

"Call me."

"I'll camp on your doorstep."

She frowned slightly, ever so slightly. He might have imagined it. Only she said, "I'll come here." And she curved her lips. "If I'm free."

She didn't want him to come to her place. It could be the ex, yet how could it be? It could be she was tied up with someone else. She could have lied. There might be a Mr. Big in the background. The man she'd lied to last night.

He said definitely, "If you aren't here, I'll be on your doorstep."

She followed him into the bedroom again, lounged on the edge of the bed while he dressed. Gray slacks, a blue shirt—he wouldn't need a coat, warmth filled the room. From the back of the chair he took the tweed jacket he'd worn last night. He'd forgotten to hang it.

She said, "That looks like Mel's jacket. He was a good dresser."

He turned with it in his hands. She hadn't meant anything, it was just a remark. He admitted, "It's Mel's." Casually but boldly. "In Rio it's summer. Mel was going to buy all the best Palm Beach. He left his old stuff here, told me to help myself." He explained it, continuing into the closet, the closet filled with Mel's expensive clothes. "My own things shrank when I was in the service. And thanks to the shortages, I arrived here practically destitute."

She said, "I'm surprised anything of Mel's would fit you."

He closed the closet door. "His backlog before he developed that paunch. He was skinny enough at Nassau."

He transferred his billfold and car keys.

She said, "He even left you his car. You must have done him a favor once. I never thought he'd give away an old toothpick."

He smiled. "He's making up for all of it on the sublease. But I did do him several favors."

"At Nassau," she mimicked.

"Yeah. I used to speak to him." He took her arm, steered her to the door. "Is your phone still disconnected?"

"Why?"

"Because I'll start calling you the minute I'm back here."

"I'll call you when I get back."

They were at the front door and she turned to him, into his arms. Her mouth was like her hair, flame. This time she broke from him. "You have a business date," she reminded.

"Yeah." He took his handkerchief, wiped his lips. "Somebody might be in that empty patio."

She laughed. "The nice part about departing at noon, Dix, is that no one knows what time you arrived."

They left together and he heard her footsteps passing the pool to her staircase. He knew he was behaving like a love-smitten sophomore but he waited by the entrance until she was on her balcony, until she lifted her hand to him in good-bye.

He'd left his car standing in the street. There hadn't been time last night to put it away. He was pleased it was there, that he didn't have to go through the back alley to get it out. He felt too good to do more than step into it and swing away on its power. He was even on time for the appointment with Brub.

He drove up Beverly Drive, turning over to the city hall. It looked more like a university hall than headquarters for the police, a white-winged building with a center tower. It was set in green grass, bordered with shrubs and flowers. There was nothing about it that said police save that the huge bronze lamps on either side of the door burned green. He climbed the stone steps and entered the door.

The corridor inside was clean and businesslike. A sign directed to the police quarters. He went up to the desk, it might have been the desk in any office. If it hadn't been for the dark blue uniform of the man just leaving, it would be hard to believe this was the Beverly Hills police station. The pleasant young man behind the desk wore a brown plaid sports coat and tan slacks.

Dix said, "Brub Nicolai?" He didn't know a title. "Detective Nicolai. He's expecting me."

He followed the young man's directions up the hall, entered another businesslike room. Brub was sitting in a chair. There were a couple of other men present, a little older than Brub, in plain business suits. They didn't look any different than ordinary men. They were L. A. Homicide.

Brub's face brightened when he saw Dix. "You made it."

"I'm seven minutes early."

"And I'm hungry." Brub turned to the other men, the tall, lean one and the smaller, heavier-set one. "See you later." He didn't introduce Dix. But they were Homicide. It was in the way their eyes looked at a man, even a friend of one of their own. Memorizing him. Brub said, "Come on, Dix. Before I start eating the leg of a chair."

Dix said, "Sawdust will give you a bay window if you aren't careful."

They walked down the corridor, out into the sunshine. "My car's here."

Brub said, "Might as well walk. We can't park much nearer. Where do you usually eat?"

"If you're hungry and don't want to stand in line, we'll go to my favorite delicatessen. Or the Ice House."

They walked together the few blocks. The sun was warm and the air smelled good. It was like a small town, the unhurried workers of the village greeting each other in the noon, standing on the corners talking in the good-smelling sunshine. He chose the Ice House, it was the nearer, just around the corner on Beverly. Man-food in it. He was surprised that he too had an appetite. Good sleep meant good appetite.

He grinned across the table at Brub. "For a moment this morning you startled me. I thought you were clairvoyant."

"About your redhead?" Brub whistled. "That's a piece of goods. How did you arrange to meet her?"

He could talk of her to Brub. And like a love-smitten swain he wanted to talk of her. "It's time the Virginibus Arms had a good-neighbor policy."

"Virginibus Arms? Not bad," Brub said.

He realized then that Brub hadn't known his address until now. He'd given his phone number, not his address.

"Yeah, I was lucky. Sublease. From Mel Terriss." Brub didn't know Mel. "Fellow I went to school with at Princeton. Ran into him out here just when he was leaving on a job."

"Damn lucky," Brub said. "And the redhead went with it?"

He grinned again, like a silly ass. "Wish I'd known it sooner."

"Is she in pictures?"

"She's done a little." He knew so little about her. "She's studying."

Brub wasn't prying; this was the old Brub. Brub and Dix. The Two Musketeers. A part of each other's lives.

"Laurel," he said, and saying the name his heart quickened. "Laurel Gray."

"Bring her out some night. Sylvia would like to meet her."

"Sylvia, my eye. You don't think I'd expose Laurel to your wolfish charms, do you?"

"I'm married, son. I'm safe."

"Maybe. What about that little gal yesterday? Wasn't she cooing at you?"

Brub said, "Maude would coo at a pair of stilts. Cary's sort of a sixth cousin of Sylvia. That's why we get together. Maude thought you were wonderful, hero."

"Did she ever stop talking?"

"No, she never stops. Although after she saw you with Redhead, she subdued a bit."

It was good to know that it didn't matter how many saw him with Laurel. That he could appear with her everywhere, show her everywhere; there was no danger in it. Only he wouldn't take her to Nicolai's. Not to face Sylvia's cool appraisal. Sylvia would look at her through Sylvia's own standards, through long-handled eyeglasses.

"She was certainly hipped on your case," Dix said. It was time to steer the conversation. "How's it coming?"

"Dead end."

"You mean you're closing the books?"

"We don't ever close the books, Dix." Brub's face was serious. "After the newspapers and the Maudes and all the rest of them forget it, our books are open. That's the way it is."

"That's the way it has to be," Dix agreed as seriously.

"There've been tough cases before now. Maybe ten, twelve years the department has had to work on them. In the end we find the answer."

"Not always," Dix said.

"Not always," Brub admitted. "But more often than you'd think. Sometimes the cases are still unsolved on paper but we have the answer. Sometimes it's waiting for the next move."

"The criminal doesn't escape," Dix smiled wryly.

Brub said, "I won't say that. Although I honestly don't think he ever does escape. He has to live with himself. He's caught there in that lonely place. And when he sees he can't get away——" Brub shrugged. "Maybe suicide, or the nut house—I don't know. But I don't think there's any escape."

"What about Jack the Ripper?"

"What about him? A body fished out of the river, an accident case. A new inmate of an asylum. Nobody knows. One thing you can know, he didn't suddenly stop his career. He was stopped."

Dix argued, "Maybe he did stop. Maybe he'd had enough."

"He couldn't stop," Brub denied. "He was a murderer."

Dix lifted his eyebrows. "You mean a murderer is a murderer? As a dectective is a detective? A waiter is a waiter?"

"No. Those are selected professions. A detective or a waiter can change to another field. I mean a murderer is a murderer as . . . an actor is an actor. He can stop acting professionally but he's still an actor. He acts. Or an artist. If he never picks up another brush, he will still see and think and react as an artist."

"I believe," Dix said slowly, "you could get some arguments on that."

"Plenty," Brub agreed cheerfully. "But that's the way I see it." He attacked his pie.

Dix put sugar in his coffee. Black and sweet. And hot. He smiled, thinking of her. "What about this new Ripper? You think he's a nut?"

"Sure," Brub agreed.

The quick agreement rankled. Brub should be brighter than that. "He's been pretty smart for a nut, hasn't he? No clues."

"That doesn't mean anything," Brub said. "The insane are much more clever about their business, and more careful, too, than the sane. That's part of the mania. It makes them difficult to catch up with. But they give themselves away."

"They do? How?"

"When is more important. But plenty of ways. Repetition of the pattern." Brub finished off the pipe and lit a cigarette. "The pattern is clear enough with the strangler. It's the motive that's hard to fix on."

"Does an insane man need a motive? Does he have one?" He lit a cigarette.

"Within the mania, yes."

Dix said offside, "This is fascinating to me, Brub. You say you have the pattern. Doesn't that in a way incorporate the motive?"

"In a way, yes. But you take this case. The pattern has emerged.

Not too clearly but in a fuzzy way, yes. It's a girl alone. At night. She doesn't know the man. At least we're reasonably sure of that. This last girl, as far as we can find out, couldn't possibly have known the man. And there's no slight connection between the girls. All right then: it's a pickup. A girl waiting for a bus, or walking home. He comes along in a car and she accepts a ride."

"I thought you were figuring he didn't have a car. What were you talking about?"—he appeared to try to remember—"Going into a drive-in to eat——"

Brub broke in. "He had to have a car. Not in every case but definitely in the last one." His eyes looked seriously into Dix's. "My own theory is that he doesn't make the approach from the car. Because girls are wary about getting into a car with strangers. The danger of that has been too well publicized. I think he makes the approach on foot and after he has the lamb lulled, he mentions he's on his way to get his car. Take this last one. She's waiting for a bus. He's waiting on the same corner. Buses don't run often that time of night. They get talking. He invites her to have a cup of coffee. It was a foggy night, pretty chilly. By the time they've had coffee, he mentions his car isn't far away and he'll give her a lift."

Dix set down his coffee cup carefully. "That's how you're figuring it," he nodded his head. "It sounds reasonable." He looked at Brub again. "Do your colleagues agree?"

"They think I may be on the right track."

"And the motive?"

"That's anybody's guess." Brub scowled. "Maybe he doesn't like women. Maybe some girl did him dirt and he's getting even with all of them."

Dix said, "That sounds absurd." He laughed, "It wouldn't hold water in my book."

"You're forgetting. It's mania; not sanity. Now you or I, if we wanted to strike back at a girl, we'd get us another one. Show the other gal what she'd lost. But a mind off the trolley doesn't figure that way."

"Any other motives?" Dix laughed.

"Religious mania, perhaps. There've always been plenty of that kind of nut out here. But it all comes back to one focal point, the man is a killer, he has to kill. As an actor has to act."

"And he can't stop?" Dix murmured.

"He can't stop," Brub said flatly. He glanced at his watch. "I've got to go up Beverly Glen. Want to come along?"

Dix's eyebrows questioned.

"To the scene of the crime," Brub explained. "Would you like to have a look at it? It'll tell you more than I can in words of what we're working against."

His pulse leaped at the idea of it. To the scene of the crime. For book material. He said, "Yeah, I think I will." He glanced at his own watch. Two-twenty. "I can take another hour from work. Particularly since I can charge it up to research."

Brub picked up the checks. At Dix's demurring, he said, "This is on me. In the line of business."

The cold touch at the base of his spine was imaginary. He laughed. "You mean detectives have a swindle sheet? Authors aren't so lucky."

"I'll put it down, 'Conferring with an expert.'" He queried, "All mystery authors claim to be crime experts, don't they?"

"I'll dedicate the book to the dick who bought me a lunch."

He and Brub emerged into the sunshine of Beverly Drive. The lunch hour was done; the workers had returned to their offices. Women shoppers were beginning to stroll the street, they clustered at the shop windows. They held little children by the hand. They chattered as they went about their aimless female business. There wasn't a brilliant redhead in sight.

The news vendor on the corner talked the races with a passing customer. His folded papers, the early edition of the *News*, lay stacked on the sidewalk beside a cigar box holding coins. Dix's eyes fell to the papers but he didn't buy one. There wouldn't be any fresh news anyway. He was with the source of news.

They returned to the city hall. "Shall we take your car or mine?" Brub asked.

The cold hand touched him quickly again. How would he know? Brub couldn't be suspicious of him. There wasn't a shred of reason for thinking it. Brub included Dix with himself, "normal as you and I." Yet how could he be sure? Brub had once known him so well. That was long ago. No one could read him now. Not even Laurel.

Did Brub want him to take his car back up the Beverly Glen Canyon? Was this luncheon arranged? Were the two ordinary men, who were L. A. Homicide, waiting for Brub to report back to them? He had hesitated long enough in answering, too long. It couldn't matter which car. There couldn't be eyes waiting to identify a black coupé, a coupé like a thousand others. It couldn't be tire marks they were after; they were unable to get marks off a clean, paved road. Brub had said so. Had intimated so. Too many cars had passed that way.

He pretended to come to. "Did you say something? Sorry."

Brub grinned. "Thinking about the redhead? I said, Whose car shall we take? Yours or mine?"

"It doesn't matter," he answered promptly. But he knew as he answered that he preferred to take his own. He'd been a panty-waist to have considered anything but that. That was what quickened his mind, that was what put zest into the game. To take the dare. "Might as well use mine."

Brub said, "Okay," but he stopped at the doors to the building. "I'll go in and see if Lochner wants to ride up with us. You don't mind another passenger?"

"Not at all." He followed Brub. To watch faces, to see if there were interchange of expression.

Only one of the Homicide men was left. He was talking to a couple of motorcycle cops in uniform. Talking about the local baseball club. Brub said, "Want to go up Beverly Glen, Loch?" He made the introductions then. "Jack Lochner—my friend, Dix Steele."

Lochner was the tall, thin man. His clothes were a little too big for him, as if he'd lost weight worrying. His face was lined. He looked like just an ordinary man, not too successful. He didn't give Brub any special glance. He didn't examine Dix now as he had earlier; he shook hands and said, "Nice to know you, Mr. Steele." His voice was tired.

Brub said, "Dix is a mystery writer, Loch. He wants to go along. You don't mind?"

"Not at all." Lochner tried to smile but he wasn't a man used to smiling. Just used to worry. "Nothing to see. I don't know why we're going back. Except Brub wants to. And the Beverly Hills bunch seems to think he's on the right track."

Dix raised one eyebrow. "So do you have some ideas?"

Brub's laugh was embarrassed. "Don't you start riding me, too. All I've got is a feeling."

"Psychic," Lochner droned.

"No," Brub denied fast. "But I can't help feeling we're on the right track here in Beverly." He explained to Dix, "The Beverly bunch sort of feels the same way. That's why we're hanging around here. Beverly has its own force, you know, separate from L.A., but they're doing everything they can to help us."

"And they know how to help," Loch said. "A smart bunch."

They left the building together. Dix said, "We're taking my car." He steered them to it. He wasn't going in a police car. Only a man off his trolley would consider riding around in a police car with Homicide. Homicide with psychic hunches.

"Do you know the way?" Lochner asked.

"I know where Beverly Glen is. You can direct me from there." With the dare taken, his mind was sharp, cold and clear, sharp as a winter wind back East. They could direct. Not a muscle would twitch to indicate he knew the place. He began laughing to himself. Actually he didn't know the place. He didn't even have to worry about making the unwary move.

"Go over to Sunset," Brub directed. "Turn right on Beverly Glen."

"That much I know." He swung the car easily toward Sunset, enjoying the power of the motor, the smoothness of the drive. A good car. He held it back. You shouldn't speed up with cops in your car. "There were a couple of cops guarding the portals when I went by Sunday. On my way home after I left your place, Brub." Were they there to look him over? He was getting slap-happy. The cops couldn't have picked him out of all the drivers passing that intersection Sunday afternoon. Just him, one man. His fingers tightened on the wheel. Did the police know more than they had told? Had there been someone else in the canyon on Friday night? He went on talking. "What were they doing? Waiting for the killer to return to the scene of the crime?"

"They were checking traffic," Lochner said in his disinterested voice. "I never knew a killer yet who went back. Make it easy for us if they did. We wouldn't have to beat our brains out all over town."

"All we'd have had to do was post a couple of the boys and wait," Brub enlarged. "They could play checkers until he came along—easy."

"How would you know him from the sightseers?" Dix joined the game.

"That is an angle." Brub looked at Lochner.

The older man said, "He'd be the one who was too normal."

"No fangs? No drooling?" Dix laughed.

"Of course, he wouldn't know the cops were watching," Brub said.

They'd reached Beverly Glen and Dix turned right. "You can direct me now."

"Just keep on going," Brub said. "We'll tell you when."

It was a pretty little road to start, rather like a New England lane with the leaves turning and beginning to fall from the trees. He had no tension, perhaps a slight fear that he might recognize the place, muscular reaction might be transferred from him to Brub seated close beside him. He relaxed. He said, "This reminds me of home. Autumn in New York, or Connecticut, or Massachusetts."

"I'm from the East myself," Lochner said. "I've been away twenty years."

It wasn't pretty for long. A few estates and it became a road of shacks, little places such as men built in the mountains before the rich discovered their privacy and ousted them. And then the shacks were left behind and the road became a curving pass through the canyon to some valley beyond.

It would be lonely up here at night; there were deep culverts, heavy brush, on the side of the road. It was lonely up here and now they passed no cars. It was as if they had entered into a forbidden valley, a valley guarded by the police. Keeping the sightseers away. Only the hunters and the hunted allowed to enter. The walls of the canyon laid shadows over the road. There was a chill in the air, the sun was far away.

He drove on, waiting for them to give the word to stop. They weren't talking, either of them; they were on the case now, a case that had them angry and bitter and worried. He kept quiet, it wasn't the time for a conversation piece. He realized his fingers were tightened on the wheel and again he relaxed them. He didn't know if the detectives would shout a sudden stop command or if they'd give warning or just how it would be done. He kept the speed down to twenty and he watched the road ahead, not the culverts with leaves like brown droppings in them. He didn't recognize any of the road. That was the good part of it.

It was Lochner who said, "Here we are. Just pull up along here, Mr. Steele, if you will."

The stretch of the road was no different from the others. There was nothing marking it as the place where a girl had been found.

The detectives got out, and he got out on the other side of the car. He walked beside them across the road. "He came this far, and then he turned around," Brub said. "Or he may have been on his way back to town."

"This is where you found her?" Dix wasn't nervous. He was an author in search of material, a man along just for the ride.

Brub had stepped up into the rustling brown leaves. He said, "It's a little heavier here. He could have known that. He could have figured she wouldn't be found for a long time, with the leaves falling on her, covering her."

Brub was scuffing through the rustle, as if he expected to find something under the sound. A clue. An inspiration. "Every day there'd be more leaves. Not many people look off at the side of the road when they're driving. Not unless there's something scenic there. Nothing scenic about this thicket."

Lochner stood with his hands in his pockets, with the worry lines in his tired face. Stood beside Dix.

Dix could ask questions, he was supposed to ask questions. He said, "How was it she was found so quickly, then?"

"Luck," Brub said. He stood in the ditch, leaves to his ankles. "The milkman had a flat right at this point."

Lochner said, "He picked this place on purpose."

"The milkman?" Dix looked incredulous.

"The killer. Take a look at it. The way the road curves here—he can see any lights coming from behind, two loops below. And he can look up to the top of the hill, see the lights of a car approaching him when it makes the first of those two curves. He can sit with her in the car, looking like a spooner, until the other car goes by." His eyes squinted up the road and back down again. "Not much chance of traffic here in the middle of the night. He was pretty safe." His voice had no inflection. "He does it. He opens the door of the car and rolls her out and he's away. No chance of being caught at it. Strangling's the easiest way. And the safest."

Brub had stooped and brushed aside the leaves.

Dix moved closer to the edge of the thicket, looked up at him. "Find something?" he asked with the proper cheerful curiosity.

Lochner monotoned, "The experts have been over every inch with a microscope. He won't find anything. Only he wanted to come back up so I said I'd come along." He put a cigarette in his mouth, his hands about the match. "The only place we'll find anything is in his car."

A wind had come up, a small sharp wind. Lochner wouldn't have cupped the match if it hadn't. It wasn't imaginary. Dix said, with the proper regret, "And you've not been able to get a description of the car yet?"

"Not yet," Lochner said. In that tired way, but there was a tang underneath the inflection. Not yet, but they would. Because they never closed the books. Because a murderer had to murder. Dix wanted to laugh. They knew so little, with all their science and intuition; they were babes in toyland.

"When you do, you mean you might find a hairpin or a lipstick or something?"

Brub did laugh. There in the brush it sounded hollow. "Good Lord, Dix. You're old hat. Girls don't wear hairpins. You ought to know that."

"Dust," Lochner said.

"Dust?" He was puzzled now.

Brub climbed down from the thicket, one big step down. He began brushing the crumpled leaves from his trouser legs.

"That's dust," Lochner said. He turned back to the car. "We've got dust from the drive-in. We've got the dust from her clothes and her shoes. There'll be some of that same dust in his car."

Dix held the mask over his face. He shook his head, his expression one of awe and admiration. "And even if it's ten or twelve years, the dust will be the same?"

"Some of it will," Lochner said.

They all got back in the car. Dix started the engine. He asked, "Is there a better place to turn than here?" They were supposed to know. The police cars had been all over this territory. They'd drawn circles around it and carried laboratory technicians into it. They'd done everything but dig it up and carry it to headquarters.

"Go on a bit," Burb said. "There's a side road a little farther on."

Dix ran the car up the hill. He saw the side road and he turned in. The side road wasn't paved. If there were any suspicion, this could be a trap, to check on his tires. Behind the brush there could be the two cops, playing checkers, watching. Cops with plaster, ready to make casts. But they were wrong. He hadn't turned here before. There was a better place farther on. He maneuvered the car, headed back toward town.

He could be talkative now. He was supposed to be impressed and curious. He said, "Did you find anything, Brub?"

Brub shook his head. "No. I didn't expect to. It's just—I get closer to him when I do what he did. What he might have done. I've got a picture of him but it's—it's clouded over. It's like seeing a man in the fog. The kind of a fog that hangs in our canyon."

Dix said cheerfully, "The kind you had when I was out at your place Friday night."

"Yeah," Brub said.

Lochner said, "He's from the East."

Dix's nerves were in strict control. Not one nerve end twitched. Rather was he stimulated by the sharp and cold blade of danger. He

said, "That's a bit of information you've kept to yourself, isn't it?
Did the waitress recognize an Eastern accent?"

"It isn't information," Brub answered. "He talked just like anybody else. No accent. No particular quality of voice. That's Loch's
reconstruction."

Lochner repeated, "He's from the East. I know that." He was deliberate. "He's a mugger."

"What's a mugger?" Dix asked quickly.

"Certain gangs used to operated in New York," Brub explained.
He illustrated on himself with his right arm. "One man would get
the victim so, the others would rob him. Until they found out it
could be a one-man job. You don't need more than two fingers to
strangle a man. Or woman."

"He's a mugger," Lochner repeated. "He doesn't use his fingers.
There're no finger marks. He uses his arm. He's from the East."

Dix said, "As a fellow Easterner, Mr. Lochner, you might admit
that a Westerner could have learned the trick."

Lochner repeated, "I've seen the way they did it in New York. He
knows how. The same way."

They came out of the shadowed canyon, out into the sunshine,
into the city again. But the sun had faded. There were clouds gray-
ing the blueness of sky. And the winding road from Sunset to
Beverly was heavy with shadows of the late afternoon. It was almost
four o'clock when they reached the city hall.

Dix pulled up and Lochner got out. He intoned, "Thanks for the
lift, Mr. Steele."

Dix said, "Thank you for letting me go along." He shook his head.
"It's pretty gruesome though. I don't think I'd go for police work."

Lochner walked away to the hall. Brub leaned against the car
door. He was frowning. "It isn't pleasant," he said. "It's damned unpleasant. But it's there, you can't just close your eyes and pretend it
isn't. There are killers and they've got to be caught, they've got to be
stopped. I don't like killing. I saw too much of it, same as you did. I
hated it then, the callous way we'd sit around and map out our plans
to kill people. People who didn't want to die anymore than we
wanted to die. And we'd come back afterward and talk it over, check
over how many we'd got that night. As if we'd been killing ants, not
men." His eyes were intense. "I hate killers. I want the world to be a
good place, a safe place. For me and my wife and my friends, and my
kids when I have them. I guess that's why I'm a policeman. To help
make one little corner of the world a safer place."

Dix said, "That's like you, Brub." He meant it. It didn't matter how unpleasant a job was, Brub would take it on if in the end it meant the righting of something wrong.

Brub pushed back his hat. He laughed, a short laugh. "Junior G-man rides his white horse. I suppose in a couple of years I'll be as stale as Loch. But right now it's personal. It was apology for his emotion. He said, "Hang around till I check in and I'll buy you a drink."

"Sorry." Dix put his hands on the wheel. "I'm late now. We'll do it again. And thanks for a valuable afternoon, Brub."

"Okay, fellow. See you soon." Brub's hand lifted and he rolled off, like a sailor on the sea. Like a policeman tracking an unknown foe.

IV

1

HE RANG LAUREL AS SOON AS HE REACHED THE APARTMENT. BEFORE HE fixed a drink, before even lighting a cigarette. There was no answer to the call. He rang her every fifteen minutes after that, and at six, when the dusk was moving across the open windows, and when there was still no answer to his call, he stepped out into the courtyard where he could look up at her apartment. But there were no lights in it.

His toe stubbed the evening paper as he returned to his apartment. He'd forgotten it. His impatience to reach her had made him forget the news. He lighted the lamps in the living room when he reentered. He'd had two drinks and he didn't want another. He wanted her. He took the paper with him back into the bedroom where he could lounge on the bed, where the phone was close to hand. He turned on the bed light and he looked through the paper until he found the story. It was on an inside page tonight. There was nothing new. The police were still working on the case. That was true. They had valuable leads. That was a lot of eyewash. He read the sports page and the comics and he rang her again. And again to no avail.

He was beginning to be upset. If she hadn't intended to come home this evening, she could have told him. She'd said she was going for a singing lesson. No singing lesson lasted until this time of night. She knew he was expecting her. She could have called him if she'd been delayed. He tried to look at it reasonably. Honestly tried. She had a lot of friends, of course she did. A girl with her body and hair and strange, lovely face would have more friends than she could handle. He was a newcomer, a nobody in her life. After all, she hadn't met him until yesterday. She couldn't be expected to drop everyone else and devote herself to him alone. She didn't know yet how it was going to be between them. She didn't know it was to be just these two. Two that were one. Until she understood as he did, he couldn't be disturbed that she had other obligations. But she could have told him. She needn't have left him here hanging on the phone, afraid to go out lest it should ring. Lying around here without food, smoking too much, reading every line of the damn dull newspaper, waiting for the phone to ring. Wearing out his finger dialing.

The door buzzer sounded with an insolent suddenness while he was still lying there, trying to down his anger, trying to see it reasonably. He jumped off the bed, and he almost ran to answer. He was angry, yes; he'd tell her plenty, but the heat of it was already dissipated in the eagerness to see her. In the joy of rushing to behold her. He opened the door, and his hand tightened over the knob as he held it wide. Sylvia Nicolai was on the threshold.

"Am I interrupting anything, Dix?" She stood there, tall and slim, at ease, her hands thrust into the deep pockets of her cashmere burberry, her gilt hair pulled smoothly away from her slender face.

He couldn't believe it because it wasn't she he expected. It was as if the fire of Laurel had faded, had become polite and cool and lady wise. He recovered himself quickly. He was hearty. "Come in, Sylvia."

"You're quite sure I'm not interrupting you?" She hesitated on the doorstep, looking beyond him into the room as if she expected Laurel there. He knew then, whatever the explanation would be, why Sylvia had come. To get a good look at Laurel.

"Not a bit. I'm not doing a darn thing. Sitting around thinking about dinner and too lazy to start out. I suppose you've eaten?"

She came in, still slightly hesitant. She looked at the room the way a woman looked at a room, sizing it up, and approving this one. She loosed her coat with her hands in the pockets, remained standing there on her high-heeled pumps, politely, but easily. Like a family friend. Like Brub's wife, who wouldn't want to be an intrusion into a man's privacy. "Oh, yes," she said. "We ate early. We were just starting to Beverly to see a movie when Brub got a call." A slight cloud fleeted over her eyes.

"Not another one?" he asked somberly.

"Oh, no." She shook her head hard. As if she couldn't bear to consider that. "Lochner wanted to see him, that was all." She put a smile on her wide, pleasant mouth. "So Brub suggested I run in here and let you amuse me until he could get back. He said it wouldn't take long."

Fleetingly he wondered if it had been Brub's suggestion or if it had been Sylvia's. She had withdrawn from him previously, she didn't now. She was forwarding herself, her smile at him wasn't reluctant as it had been. It was free. He would have been interested day before yesterday. Now he only feigned it. "I'm delighted, Sylvia. Let me have your coat." She allowed him to help her. She had on a brown sweater and a slim checkered skirt in browns. She was made long and lovely, like a birch tree. Laurel was made lush and warm, like a woman.

She sat down on the couch. "You have a nice place."

"Yes, it is. I was lucky to get it. You'll at least have a drink, won't you?"

"I'll have a Coke. If you have one?"

"I'll join you." He passed her a cigarette, lit it, and left her to get the Cokes. He wondered what Lochner wanted with Brub, important enough to interrupt his evening. He'd find out, for Brub would come here from Lochner. He'd want to talk about it. It was a break. If only they'd be out of here before Laurel returned.

He brought in the Cokes. "Did Brub tell you he and Lochner let me go along today with them?"

"Yes. Thanks." She took the Coke. "How did you like Loch?"

"He seemed bored with it all. Is that his cover-up for being the best bloodhound on the force?"

She said, "He has a wonderful record." Her mouth widened. "As a bloodhound, as you say. He's head of Homicide."

His eyes opened. "He's the head man?" He smiled. "I would never have guessed it."

"That's what Brub says. He seems so different. I've never met him."

"He's worth meeting." Dix relaxed comfortably in the armchair. Head of Homicide. That worried old boy. "A character." He felt easy. "I still can't get used to Brub being a policeman."

"It's funny," Sylvia said seriously. "He always wanted to be one. I suppose lots of little boys did when you and Brub were little boys. Nowadays they want to be jet-propelled pilots, from what I can gather. But Brub never gave up wanting it. And when he asked me if I'd mind, I said I'd be delighted."

"So you're responsible for it," he said with mock solemnity.

"No," she laughed. "But he asked me and I said I'd be delighted and I meant it. Anything he wanted, I'd be delighted. It isn't much of a life. Like a doctor, twenty-four hours a day. And you never know when the phone will ring."

"Like tonight."

"Yes." There hadn't been that underlying fear in her until now. It was just a twinge; she'd recovered from the terror that had closed over her Saturday night and yesterday. She could put it away tonight. She could lose it in a bright change of subject. "We saw you last night."

"So Brub told me."

She was the reason for her visit now. She was eager. "Who was she? The one you were telling us about?"

"Same one. She lives in this house."

"How did you meet her?" She was asking for romance.

He said, "I picked her up."

She made a little face at him.

"As I told Brub, it's the Virginibus Arms' good-neighbor policy," he said. "And high time there was one. It's bad as New York here. There you see your neighbors but don't speak; here you don't even see them."

"You saw her."

"And I picked her up," he said impudently.

"What's her name?"

"Laurel Gray."

"Is she in the movies? She's gorgeous enough to be, from what I saw of her."

"She's done some movies." Again he was struck by how little he knew of her. "She doesn't care much about it. Too early in the mornings for her." He said it with deliberate meaning; she understood.

She said after a moment, "Will you bring her out some evening? We'd like to meet her."

"We'll fix up a date." It was so easy to say, and so easy to avoid doing it. He was feeling better all the time. It had been right that Laurel was delayed. It was in order that she wouldn't have to be inspected by Sylvia. Sylvia wouldn't like Laurel; they weren't cut out of the same goods. Even as he was sure of the rightness, the telephone rang. He excused himself and went to answer, certain it wouldn't be she. It was time for Brub to check back in.

He was so certain it wouldn't be she that he left the bedroom door open. And it was Laurel.

She said, "What are you doing, Dix?"

"Where have you been?" Irritation gnatted him again. She stayed out until—after nine o'clock now by the clock. And she turned up asking lightly what he was doing!

"At dinner."

"I thought you were having dinner with me."

"Really? I must have forgotten."

Anger threatened him.

"Why don't you come up?" she asked.

He couldn't. Not now. He said, "I can't."

"Why not?"

"I have company." His anger lurched at Sylvia then for being here, at Brub for sending her here.

There was a sharpness came into her voice. "Who's the girl?"

"What girl?"

"The one on your couch, sweetheart."

She'd seen Sylvia. She must have come to the door and she'd seen Sylvia and gone away. That explained the insolence in her voice. She was annoyed about it. And again the anger went out of him in the upwelling of emotion; she didn't like his having another woman here.

He couldn't talk openly; the bedroom was too close to the living room. The door open. And Sylvia sitting there silently, listening. Trying not to listen because she was a lady but being unable to miss what he was saying.

"An old friend," he said.

"Business, I presume?" She was sharp.

"As a matter of fact, it is," he agreed.

"In that case, I'll come down."

"No!" He didn't want her to come here. Not until Sylvia and Brub had gone. She must understand. But he couldn't speak out. He spoke as quietly as possible into the mouthpiece. "I'll come up as soon as I'm free."

"What's the matter with my coming down?" she demanded. "Don't you think I'm good enough for your friends?"

He wondered if she'd been drinking. Belligerence wasn't like her, she was slow and sultry and she didn't give a damn for him or anyone. That was in her last night. And tonight, brushing him off for

something better or more amusing. Now she was deliberately posses-
sive. There was a reason and he didn't know the reason. He wanted
to shake the hell out of her. She must have known he couldn't talk
openly.

"Well?" she demanded.

He said, "I'm busy. I'll see you as soon as I can."

She hung up; the crack smote his eardrum. He was infuriated; he
wanted to hang up on her but he hadn't. She'd done it. He went
back into the living room scowling, forgetting that he shouldn't
scowl, that he wasn't alone.

Sylvia was apologetic. "I am intruding."

"No." He said it flatly. Without explanation. "No." He meant it,
he had no objection now to her presence. All anger was transferred
to Laurel. The ear she had smote stung sharply. When he saw Sylvia
studying his anger, he smiled at her. The smile was hard to come, it
pained when it cracked the hard mold of his face. He said, "As a
matter of fact, I'm delighted you dropped in, Sylvia. It gives me a
feeling of belonging. I think it calls for a celebration—or perhaps a
plaque: On this night at this spot Dickson Steele was no more the
stranger from the East. After long months, he was at home." He was
talking idly, to get that look, that seeking look out of Sylvia's eyes.
He wasn't doing half bad.

Most of it was gone when she said, "You've been lonely?"

"I expected it." She wasn't trying so hard now. Pity had expelled
calculation. He didn't want the pity and he spoke lightly. "It takes
time in a new place. I knew that before I came."

"You could have called on us sooner." It was all gone now, the
look and the search.

"Now, would you?" he demanded. "You know how it is. There's
always the knowledge that you're making a forced entry into the
other fellow's life. Sometimes friendship survives it. More often it
only spoils a good memory."

"It's worth trying," she said. "How else can—"

The doorbell rang. Brub, and it hadn't taken long. The business
with Loch couldn't have been too important. He went to the door
talking, breaking in on Sylvia's words. Wanting Brub to see how ordinary this had been. "Sometimes the dissent isn't mutual, Sylvia.
The fellow who closes the door feels a hell of a lot worse than the
eager beaver. I wouldn't want to be—"

Laurel stood there. Because she had been angry, because she had
hung up on him in anger, he was so amazed that his words didn't

dissipate; they became an utter void. He didn't realize he was scowling at her until she mirrored it ludicrously. "And what did the big bad wolf say then to Little Red Riding Hood, darling?" Deliberately she stepped past him and went into the room while he stood there scowling and empty-mouthed.

They were together, Sylvia and Laurel. Each had come for that reason, to look upon the other. He didn't know exactly why it mattered to either of them. He wasn't a sweepstake. Sylvia didn't care at all; Laurel cared little enough. They were eyeing each other in the faint patronizing manner of all women to women, no matter the stake, when he turned into the living room.

He'd had a slight apprehension over the phone that Laurel might have been drinking. She hadn't been. Her scent was perfumed, not alcoholic; she had never looked more glowing. She was in white, all white but for her radiant hair, and painted mouth and eyes. Before her Sylvia was colorless and yet before Sylvia, Laurel was too richly colored. Between them was the gulf of a circumstance of birth and a pattern of living.

He said, "Sylvia, this is Laurel." And to Laurel, "This is Sylvia. My friend, Brub Nicolai's, wife."

They acknowledged the introduction in monotone, in the same manner of social courtesy, but it did not diminish the gulf. There was nothing could diminish the gulf.

He said, "Let me take your coat, Laurel. Drink?"

"No, thanks. I've just had dinner." Her eyes were strange amber flowers. She opened them full on him. "I've been trying to call you for hours. Where have you been?"

She was a dirty liar. She was trying to tell Sylvia it hadn't been she on the phone getting the brush-off. He looked at Sylvia and his mouth quirked. She wasn't fooling Sylvia. You didn't fool Sylvia. She burrowed under words, under the way of a face and a smile for the actuality. He was suddenly cold. For he knew, was certain of the fact, that Sylvia had been burrowing beneath his surface that night he had come out of the fog into her existence. Irritation heated him. She had no business trying to find an under-self in him; she should have taken him as he was taken, an average young fellow, pleasant company; beyond that, her husband's old friend. It couldn't have been Brub who set her on him. There could have been no suspicion when he came to Brub's house that night. Nor was there; yet Sylvia had searched his face and the way he spoke—and she hadn't liked him.

He knew it with cold clarity, he'd sensed it from the first moment of meeting, she didn't like him. He didn't like her either with her damn prying mind. Her bitching, high-toned mind. Brub was all right; she wasn't going to spoil Brub with Dix. She wasn't going to be allowed.

He said to Laurel, "I've been right here since five o'clock." He lit her cigarette. "Maybe you had the wrong number."

"Maybe I did." She took her eyes from him and laid them again on Sylvia. She didn't think anymore of Sylvia than Sylvia of her. She was more open about it, that was the way of her, the way that couldn't be helped. Yet she had a fear of Sylvia that had no echo in Brub's wife. She was harder than Sylvia could ever be but she wasn't fine steel; she could be broken. She said to Sylvia and the smear of insolence was under the surface, "Where's your husband?" She let it rest until Sylvia was ready to answer and then she didn't wait for the answer. "I've wanted to meet him. I've heard so much about him."

A dirty little liar. He'd not told her much or little of Brub. Brub's name hadn't been spoken between them.

Sylvia said, "He'll be along. He had some business and I decided Dix would be more amusing than business." She gave him a woman smile. Not for him, for Laurel because she scorned Laurel.

"And Dix wasn't," Dix said, waiting for her disavowal.

She was provocative as Laurel would have been. "I don't know," she said.

"Is your husband on the Mildred Atkinson thing?" Laurel asked abruptly.

He hadn't thought she knew who Brub Nicolai was but she had known. And she'd brought up from the shadows that which Sylvia and Dix had been pretending didn't exist there. She didn't care; all she was attempting was destruction of their mood. Succeeding better than she could know.

"Yes, he's working on it." Sylvia didn't like the mention of the case. That quickly the tightness was in her fingers, the set of her lips. She didn't dissemble well.

"Gorgon told me he was," Laurel nodded. She didn't explain Gorgon nor did Sylvia. But Sylvia knew the name; she admitted knowledge by accepting Gorgon as casually as he was offered. Laurel went on, "He was talking about it tonight. He says Brub Nicolai's the smartest young dick in the department."

He felt Sylvia cringe at Laurel's use of the word dick for detective. He didn't see it; he saw nothing. His mind was knotted too tightly, so tightly the room was a blur. He steadied himself against the table.

It was good that Sylvia was there; that he was not alone with Laurel. She had been out with someone named Gorgon while Dix waited here for her. The desperate need to be alone with Laurel, to force truth from her, began hammering against his temples until he wanted to cry out from the pain of it. He had to stand there, holding himself by the pressure of his palms on the table, while the two made conversation about Brub, Brub who should be here and take his wife away.

He had to stand braced there listening to Laurel quote Gorgon to Sylvia, all of Gorgon's damn omniscience about Brub Nicolai's growing prowess as a detective.

He couldn't have endured it much longer. The door buzzer reprieved him. He left the two women without excusing himself. They didn't know he was there. It was Brub at last; the Brub of these days, a frown between his eyebrows, a distant look on his face until he saw Dix and smiled.

"Hello. Sylvia still here?"

"Yeah. We've been gabbing. Come on in." He let Brub precede him into the living room. He didn't want to hear any more about Gorgon. He didn't have to. By the time he rounded into the room, Sylvia was making introductions.

"Brub, this is Laurel Gray. My husband, Mr. Nicolai."

Laurel's eyes took stock of Brub in the same way they had taken stock of Dix on first meeting. Thoroughly, boldly, despite Sylvia's presence. It might be Laurel knew no better, it might be unconscious. The only way she knew to look at a man. Sylvia watched, but she wasn't disturbed. Not about Laurel. Only when Brub had acknowledged the introduction and turned to his wife did the waver of fear come to her.

Her voice was controlled but the fear cooled it. "Everything . . . all right, darling?"

He nodded, his smile reassured her. But it wasn't real, it came and went. As brief as a flicker of light in the darkness.

Dix said heartily, "How about a drink, Brub?"

"Thanks." The response was automatic, without thought, for with thought Brub shook his head. "But not tonight." As if that had been what he meant to say in the first place. "I'm too tired. Ready, Sylvia?"

"Yes." She spoke brightly as if unaware of Brub's depression.

Dix didn't attempt to delay them. He knew Brub had information on the case to impart; he knew Brub would talk if he remained for a drink. The case wasn't important to Dix at the moment; he wanted one thing only, to be alone with Laurel.

He only said, "Sorry," putting real feeling into it, as real as if it were honest. "You better take it easy a few days, you do look tired. Can't you fence him in, Sylvia?"

"I wish I could." But she too was acting, her thoughts were on Brub only.

She and Laurel said the false and polite things required. Brub nodded; he was in a hurry to be gone. His arm held Sylvia's closely.

"I'll give you a ring," Dix promised. He held the door ajar until they had crossed the patio, until they walked under the arch to the street. He closed it then, definitely. One stride carried him to the entrance of the living room.

Laurel coiled in the chair, her eyes smoldering, her mouth insolent, ready to strike.

He struck first. "Who is Gorgon?"

She didn't answer. "What's the idea of that woman here?" she demanded.

He repeated, "Who is Gorgon?"

"Giving me the runaround, telling me not to come down here. Business!" Her voice spat.

He only repeated, "Who is Gorgon?" He began to move toward her then. There was no sound of him crossing the room.

There was no sound but her voice berating, "You can't play me that way. There isn't any man I'll take that from. God knows, I won't take it from you."

He was standing over her. "Who is Gorgon?" The knots in his head were tightening. He couldn't stand the tightness. His hands reached down, clamped on her shoulders and he pulled her out of the chair. "Who——"

She spoke with cold nastiness. "If you don't take your hands off me, you won't be any good to any woman anymore." Through her shoulders, he felt the shift of her weight and he released her, stepped away quickly. She had meant the words. The knots loosened as quickly, the shock of her intent was as ice flung in his face. With the diminishing of pain, he was weakened, his forehead was wet. He drew his sleeve across it, across the dampness of his eyes.

He heard her say, "I'm getting to hell out of here."

He couldn't have stopped her, weakened as he was. His voice was husky. "Don't go."

He didn't even look at her. He didn't know why she didn't leave;

curiosity, perhaps. It couldn't have been pity, she wasn't a woman to have pity on a man.

He was surprised at the sound of her voice; it wasn't hating now, it shrugged. "I think we both need a drink."

He heard her go to the kitchen and he flung himself face down on the couch, his fingers gripped tight into his palms. He had wanted to kill her.

When he heard the sound of her returning, he turned. She was standing over him and she held out the glass. "Thanks, Laurel."

She went back to the chair, sat down, and drank.

He took a swallow from his glass, another. She'd mixed it strong.

"Feel better?" she asked.

"Yes. I needed this."

"Shall we start all over?"

His eyes went quickly to her. She meant it. He was ashamed of his anger; it hadn't been he; some stranger had performed that way. But the stranger was himself.

"Let's do."

"You want to know who Gorgon is. He's my lawyer."

He was more ashamed. He didn't say anything.

"I ran into him when I was leaving the studio. He wanted to talk some business. It was nearly six." Her eyes hardened. "I figured it wouldn't hurt him to buy me a meal." She looked away. "I couldn't call you, Dix. I didn't want him—snooping."

It was all explained. Warmth filled him, good and tender warmth. She'd wanted to be with him, to run back to him. Wanted it as much as he. He hadn't been wrong; they were meant to coexist. He was ready to rush to her when she hardened again. "What about her?"

He laughed. "It's as dull as yours. Brub dropped her off while he went on business. I didn't want her here."

Her words barbed. "Then why did you try to keep me away? Didn't you think I was good enough to meet her?"

"Good God, Laurel!" He was exasperated, the more so because she wasn't up to Sylvia's par. Yet she soared above Sylvia.

"Didn't you?" she demanded.

He wasn't going to get angry again. He wouldn't let her make him angry. "Listen," he said, "I didn't want you let in on something that would bore the tar out of you. That's point one. Two, I was sore at you for not showing up."

"You expected me?"

"You know damn well I expected you. We were going to have dinner together——"

"Three?"

She was pleased, there was an upcurve of her rich, the mockery was again in her golden eyes.

"Three, I wanted you alone, for myself, all alone, not cluttered up with a lot of dumb people." His voice wasn't steady, nor was he as he pushed up to his feet. Yet he could move and he went to her, pulling her again out of the chair. His hands were strong this time, not cruel.

She said, "Wait a minute, Dix." Her palms pushed against his shoulders, her body twisted but he didn't let her go. His mouth closed over hers and he held her until she quieted. He held her for a long time.

When he released her, there was laughter in him where there had been pain. Exultant laughter. He said, "That's the way it is, Laurel. That's the way it has to be. You—and me."

She was as beautiful as if set aflame. Her eyes slanted up at him, even her eyes were aflame. She pushed back her chair. "I guess you're right," she said. She rubbed at her arm. "But don't try the rough stuff again. I won't take it."

"I'm sorry." He was, and for a moment he tightened. He was more than sorry, he was afraid. He might have hurt her. He might have lost her. With her he must remember, he must never take a chance of losing her. If it had happened—he shook his head and a tremble went over him.

She said anxiously, "What's the matter?"

He didn't answer, he took her into his arms and held her. Held her without explanation until he was quieted again.

2

IT WAS MORNING AND THE SUN LAY BRIGHT BLUE AGAINST THE OPEN window. And it lay mildly gold where her hair had flamed on the white pillow, where again her head would rest. The room was swirling with sun and he rested there content in brightness. It was good to wake to sun, to warmth, and remembrance of warmth and bright beauty. It was good to know she would return after her little errands and business appointments and lessons were done, would return eagerly to his eagerness. For him there were the hours of day to pass, but they would trickle through his hands as quietly, as simply as sand. The sun and the day would pass; there would come night. And the night would flame with a radiance surpassing the sun.

The day passed and there was the night and another day and another night and another. Until he did not know the count of the hours or of the days. Or of the nights. They were one unto the other, a circle whirling evenly, effortlessly, endlessly. He knew beauty and the intensity of a dream and he was meshed in a womb he called happiness. He did not think: This must come to an end in time. A circle had no beginning or end; it existed. He did not allow thought to enter the hours that he waited for her, laved in memory of her presence. He seldom left the apartment these days. In the outside world there was time; in time, there was impatience. Better to remain within the dream. Even the broom-and-mop harridan could little disturb the dream.

He did not say: This will not endure forever. He did not face the awakening. There was the morning when the fleet of clouds passed over the sun but he did not accept the augury. He did not admit to mind the chill that came through the windows of an afternoon even as he closed the windows. He did not admit the scrim of gray shutting away the stars on that night.

He knew, but he did not admit. It might have been a week, it might have been a day or two, or perhaps there was no time. But the restlessness was coming into her. She could not be content too long to be bound within the confines of this dream. It might have been the way her shoulders moved to a dance orchestra over the radio. It might have been the small frown as they sat again for dinner in the living room. It could have been her evasion of his questions about her hours of that particular day. Or the way in which she stood at the doorway, looking out into the night.

He had known from the beginning she was meant to be displayed. She could not be hidden away long in the cave of his dream. Yet he could not admit. She had to be the one to speak.

She telephoned him. Late, five o'clock or later. She said, "Dix, I can't meet you for dinner tonight. . . . It's business."

He knew a little more about her now, not much, a little. She didn't talk of herself, no more than he did. There had been slight need of words within the cave. But he knew she was studying and waiting for the big chance. Her sights were high; others had been discovered by the magical screen. She intended to be. Talent wasn't of the same import as knowing the right guardians of the portal. The philosopher's stone was contacts.

He couldn't let her know his disappointment. They hadn't played it that way. They hadn't been soft lovers; they'd been aware of worldly needs. He wouldn't have dared let her know his adolescent urgency. He said, "Sorry," as if it didn't matter. "See you later?"

He could sense her hesitation.

"If I'm not too late. There's a party after." There was definite hesitation now, if slight. "I'm to sing."

He knew better but he demanded, "No matter how late, come. Wake me up."

She didn't say yes or no; she said nothing in a rush of words. After she had rung off, it began. Slowly at first. Like fog wisping into his mind. Only a small doubt. He could, at first, brush it away. But it moved in thicker; tightening around the coils of his brain, blotting out reason.

She was with another man. Someone with money to spend on her, big money. Uncle Fergus! Dix almost ran to the desk. He hadn't looked at mail during these days, once or twice maybe riffled for a Princeton postmark, not finding it, finding nothing but bills for Mel Terriss. Then he had forgotten mail, forgotten the dunning bills, forgotten everything in her. He pawed through the neat stack of envelopes and he found it, the letter from Uncle Fergus. There was a check inside, he glanced at the figures, two hundred and fifty dollars. He pushed open the brief typewritten letter. It said,

"DEAR DICKSON,

"If you have a bad back and are not just inventing same to get out of work, I suggest you apply to the Veterans' Hospital for treatment. As for my sending you additional funds, the idea is as stupid as yours usually . . ."

He crumpled the letter into a tight, angry ball and hurled it across the room. He didn't even finish reading it, he knew too well the pious platitudes about work and pay, he'd heard them all his life. When other fellows had cars and clothes and free spending, he had platitudes. It wasn't that the old skinflint didn't have it. There was plenty of money for stocks and bonds, real estate. Everything salted away for an old man's idea about being a solid citizen. You'd think Uncle Fergus would have recognized the need for the things that made living worth living. He'd been a poor clod, son of a dirt farmer. He'd never had anything either, starting to work in a Princeton hardware store when he was fourteen (how well Dickson knew every step

of Uncle Fergus' meager life; he could recite it like a nursery rhyme),
studying nights to get himself into the university. Dickson could see
him, one of these poor boobs, peasants, owning one dark, ill-fitting
suit and a pair of heavy-soled shoes, clumping to class, study, and
work, and nobody knew he was in Princeton but the other peasants.
Not even coming out of it cum laude, the needed touch for a big
success story. Nothing, just grubbing through, worrying along to
graduation; getting nothing but a diploma and a fixed belief that to
be a Princeton man was like being a senator or maybe Jehovah.

Dix hadn't wanted to be a Princeton man. Not that kind. If it
could have been right, if he could have been one of the fellows he
saw around town, driving a fast car, careless about expensive clothes
and money and girls, club fellows, he'd have grabbed it. He might as
well have wanted to be senator or the Jehovah, he was Fergus
Steele's nephew, and he worked in the hardware store after hours all
through high school. Either he worked or he had nothing to spend.
That was Uncle Fergus' hand-embroidered, gold-framed motto: No
work, no money.

A fellow had to have money, you couldn't get a girl without
money in your pockets. A girl didn't notice your looks or your sharp
personality, not unless you could take her to the movies or the Saturday night dance. And feed her after the show.

Dix hadn't learned then how to get money without working for it.
Except maybe filching a dime or a quarter from the cash register
now and again. Lying about it. Once he took five dollars; he needed
it, too. You couldn't take a girl to the junior Prom without sending
her flowers. Uncle Fergus fired a delivery boy for that one.

Dix knew damn well he'd go through hell at the university. He
did. He suffered, God how he suffered, that first year. He'd have
quit, he'd have flunked out quick but the alternative was far worse;
being packed off like a piece of cattle to a farm Uncle Fergus owned
in western Pennsylvania. Either he had to be a gentleman, according
to Uncle Fergus' standards, or he could revert to the peasantry. Dix
was smart enough to know he couldn't get a job, stand on his own
feet. He didn't want to work that hard. He took the first year, working in the hardware store after school, afraid to look anyone in the
eye, afraid he'd see the sneers openly, or the pity.

It was along in the spring that he started getting wise. Latching on
to boys with money, rich stinkers who hadn't any better place in the
university scheme than Dix himself. They were really stinkers; Mel
Terriss was a good example of the breed. But they had money. They

were good for a tip if you knew a place to get a bottle of booze after hours, or took their cars to be serviced, or picked up their cleaning. They were good for a cash loan in return for a hard luck story. You could wear their clothes, smoke their cigarettes, drink their liquor. As long as you toadied, you had a pretty good life. It notched them up higher if they could sneer at a boob of a townsman who had less than they. He took the sneers with the tips and the second year wasn't so bad.

The second year he found Mel Terriss, who hadn't even made the stinkers' set. He got Mel into the circle and he saw that Mel repaid him. It was easy sailing for Dix after that, with Mel's clothes and Mel's car and the babes thinking Dix was the rich guy and Mel the stooge. Dix had the looks and the air; he had everything Mel needed. Mel was kept soothed by Dix bringing him the women that Dix couldn't be bothered with. And by booze. Mel was headed straight for alcoholism even then, a kid in college. The booze made him believe he was what he alone thought he was, not a stinker. Only it made him a worse stinker, of course. End of the term, Dix was Mel's only friend. That suited Dix. It looked like two good years ahead if he could keep Mel in college; so far he'd showed Mel how to manage it with Mel's money, paying grubs to tutor Mel through. He and Mel hated each other's guts, but each without the other was lost. They stuck together.

That was the summer when the young men knew war was fact. The only question was when it would be acknowledged. And that summer Dix enlisted in the Air Corps. All the top men of the campus were enlisting.

The war years were the first happy years he'd ever known. You didn't have to kowtow to the stinking rich, you were all equal in pay; and before long you were the rich guy. Because you didn't give a damn and you were the best Goddamned pilot in the company with promotion coming fast. You wore swell tailored uniforms, high polish on your shoes. You didn't need a car, you had something better, sleek powerful planes. You were the Mister, you were what you'd always wanted to be, class. You could have any woman you wanted in Africa or India or England or Australia or the United States, or any place in the world. The world was yours.

That life was so real that there wasn't any other life. Even when the war was over there was no realization of another life. Not until he stood again in the small, dark living room of his uncle's home. It came as a shock, return to Uncle Fergus; he hadn't really known it wasn't going to be always the way it had been in the war years. He had mistaken interlude for life span.

Uncle Fergus had done well for himself, too, during the war years. He'd invented some kind of nail or screw or tool and manufactured it. But getting richer hadn't made a change in the old man. He lived the way he always had lived, in the same uncomfortable house, with the same slovenly old housekeeper, the same badly cooked meals, and bad lighting. The only difference was more stocks and bonds and real estate. It was a bathos of patriotism that Uncle Fergus consented to Dix's year in California to write a book. Oh, Dix had had to do some fast talk. The old skinflint thought he was living with friends who could help him, who would keep him in line. He explained the frequent change of address as difficulties in getting office space. Once the offer was made, Uncle Fergus regretted his generosity; that was obvious. But it was too late, Dix didn't let him withdraw.

In excess of anger Dix took the measly check now and tore it into little pieces, tore it and retore it and scattered it all over Mel's rug. The usual check, the pittance on which to exist another month. Go to a Veterans' Hospital. Beg, you're a veteran, aren't you?

He sat there at the desk, holding his hot head with his steeled fingers. Seeing through his fingers the stack of bills addressed to Mel Terriss. It was rotten luck running into Mel that night. Why couldn't he have met Mel during the war years, when he could have sneered down at him the way he'd wanted to all his life? But Mel had been hiding out in some factory; even the Army hadn't wanted Mel. When they met, the war was long over and Mel was a rich stinker again.

Dix had tried not to speak to Mel in the bar that night, he'd avoided the recognition, forgetting you couldn't avoid an ass like Mel. Mel had to weave over and poke his fat, stupid face across the table. Dix could see what was churning in Mel's mind as he looked at the blonde. Ready to start over the same old way, let Dix do the dirty work, procure the girls in exchange for tips. Well, it hadn't worked that way; he'd stopped bootlicking six years ago. And maybe it wasn't so bad running into Mel. Dix had the apartment and the car and the clothes; the charge accounts wouldn't hold out forever but they were still good enough. That was the sort of money Mel had. And Mel was in Rio, good old Mel!

Without Mel, there would have been no Laurel. His brain cooling, the hunger for Laurel began gnawing again. Maybe she had

had a chance to sing at some big event; she wouldn't turn it down, he knew that, even if she hungered for him as he for her. She was like him that way, she was after big time. The only difference was she wasn't looking for money; she wanted a spotlight.

Hatred of Uncle Fergus surged anew. Unless Dix could help Laurel get that spotlight, he'd be sloughed. As soon as the new wore off him. As soon as she found out he was broke. He couldn't lose her, she was the only thing he had, the only right thing he'd had since he took off his uniform. In shame he got down on his hands and knees and began gathering up the tiny pieces of the check. He had to have this much money; it wouldn't last long but it would prolong things for another week, maybe by that time he could raise more. There must be ways to get gravy out here; there were sure to be, only he hadn't been looking for them. He hadn't needed to, the two-fifty did well enough before he met Laurel. Delicately he picked up each small piece, being careful not to crumple them. And then came the fear that Laurel would return suddenly, find him in this ridiculous position. He began to work faster, nervously. When he had retrieved all the scraps, his hands were wet and shaking. He had to wipe the palms on his shirt before he dared piece the check together. He was careful despite his shaking fingers, putting each small piece in its proper place. It had to be a piece of value, the "Fergu" of the signature. Frantically he searched for it, crawling on the floor like a baby, trembling with the fear that she or someone would come before it was found.

He spied it finally, under the desk chair. He had the check again! He didn't know if a bank would accept it, whether it would be necessary to write again to Uncle Fergus with some excuse about its destruction. The maid mixing it with advertising folders, tearing it up. Uncle Fergus wouldn't believe his story. He'd stop payment on the first check and then wait to make sure it hadn't been cashed before he sent a second. It would be a month at least before Uncle Fergus would return the check to Dix, a month with not more than a ten spot in his pocket.

Worrying about what could happen, a sickness came over him, so real that he felt weak as a cat. He could scarcely make it to the couch. He flopped there, his eyes closed, his fingers tight in his palms. He couldn't lose Laurel. He wouldn't lose her. No matter what he did. He could go to work. There must be plenty of jobs. Laurel knew a lot of rich people; maybe he could give her a story about needing to get into something. Not for money. For research. Or Brub. Brub might get him on the police force.

He could smile at that; and he then felt better. Only what would Laurel be doing while Dix was on call twenty-four hours a day? She wouldn't be sitting at home; she wasn't a Sylvia.

He couldn't go to work; there were other ways of getting money. If only Laurel would introduce him to some of her friends; the easiest way to get money was through those who had money. He knew how to do it that way. Why was Laurel keeping him hidden? Anger was rising; he mustn't get angry now. He couldn't take another spasm. He went to the bar and he poured a heavy slug of the stuff; he didn't want it but it settled his stomach.

If he knew where Laurel was, he'd go to her now. If she cared anything about him she'd have wanted him there tonight to hear her sing. He didn't believe she was singing. She had another man; whenever she got a chance to be with that man, she didn't care whom she knocked down.

He couldn't remain here all evening thinking these thoughts, suffering these agonies. He'd go nuts. He had to get out, go where he could breathe. Go hide himself in the night.

He caught his breath. He didn't care. It was too soon. The police were still on the alert. And there was Laurel. He didn't dare do anything that might spoil what he had with Laurel. But he couldn't stay here. He had to get away from thinking his thoughts.

He went to the bedroom, seized the telephone. He didn't know how many times Brub had called during these days, these weeks. Dix had abruptly turned down all advances. But he'd left the door open. When the surge of work was over, he'd call Brub. He didn't notice the time until after he'd dialed; he was relieved to see that it wasn't late at all, not quite nine o'clock.

It was Sylvia who answered. She sounded not only surprised to hear from him but almost as if she'd never before heard his voice. He asked for Brub. "Is he home? Thought I might run out for a little if he isn't busy."

By that time she seemed to know him again. She was cordial. "Do come out. We've been wondering when you'd get your nose out of that book."

"Sure you don't mind?"

"We welcome you," she said quickly. "And I do mean it. Brub was so bored just sitting around with me, he's gone next door to borrow a rake or a deck of cards or something."

"He isn't at home?"

"He will be before you get here," she said with certainty. "Come along."

He felt better right away, he felt himself again. Sure of himself, happy, easy. He'd stayed in too closely with Laurel; that wasn't good for a man. Maybe she'd felt it too. Maybe that was why she'd taken this job tonight. But she couldn't have felt too shut in, she'd been out every day on lessons or beauty appointments or some excuse.

He didn't bother to change his clothes. He grabbed the nearest jacket, putting it on as he returned to the living room. He had to delay there. The torn check was on the desk. He wouldn't want Laurel to see it. He scooped the pieces into an envelope, sealed it to make certain he wouldn't lose any precious bit, and stuck it in his jacket pocket. He looked down at the stack of bills addressed to Mel, wondering if Laurel had noticed them, and if she had, why she hadn't said anything. Someone had stacked them in that neat pile, not he. It could have been the slattern, but it could have been Laurel. It probably had been Laurel; he could see her hands now arranging the paper and the magazines on the table. Idly, deliberately. She could have done the same to the mail while he was dressing or putting on the coffee. Idly, but she would have noticed. Noticed and wondered. He swept the mail into the drawer, banging it shut. He wasn't going to think in circles; he was going to Brub's and forget.

3

HE LEFT THE APARTMENT BY THE BACK DOOR. IT GAVE HIM A GOOD feeling as soon as he stepped into the night; he was doing something familiar. The night, too, was good; there were no stars, only hazy darkness. He went softly through the alley to the garage. The sound of the door opening couldn't carry back to the apartments. The hinges were well oiled.

The car looked good. He hadn't had it out for days, and it felt good to be at the wheel. He didn't have to back out quietly, he let it purr; he was going to visit his friend, his friend the policeman.

By the time he reached the Nicolais' there was no anger, no tension left in him. He whistled his way up the walk. Brub opened the door and things were good again, the way they'd been that first night. Brub in sneakers and a pair of pants as wrinkled as his own.

Holding out his hand saying, "You're a sight for sore eyes. What's the idea of the brush-off, Genius?"

It was all good until they came into the living room together, as they had on that first night. And as on the first night, Sylvia was there. Filling the room, for all her quietness. Fading out the bright colors for all the monotone of her silver-gray slack suit, her pale gold hair, her pale, serious face. There was no welcome in her eyes for him, she was looking at him as at a stranger. In an instant she smiled, but the smile was a pale thing and in her eyes there was no smile. He felt himself an intruder and he was angry; if she hadn't wanted him to come here tonight she could have said so, she could have said Brub was out and let it go at that. But she'd urged him to come; she'd even called Brub home for his coming.

When she spoke, it was better. "Finished that book?" she asked as if they'd been together daily. "I'm dying to read it." Yet in the midst of her words, she chilled again. And recovered, giving him a wider smile. "How about a beer?"

"Let me," Dix said, but she was already up from the chair, crying, "I'm the official beer-getter around here. You sit down." She wasn't smooth and polished in her motions tonight; there was nervousness as she went to the bar. Maybe she and Brub had had a scrap; maybe that was why he'd gone to the neighbors, and why she'd urged Dix to come, to get them past the awkward stage. At any rate there was no difference in Brub, good old Brub, reclining himself on the couch and saying, "I was afraid you'd skipped back East, Dix."

"Just work," he answered. He sounded like anyone who worked, regretful of the time it took, almost apologetic.

"Finished?"

"God, no!" He laughed easily. "But the heat was off so I decided a break was in order." Sylvia set the glass and bottle at hand on the end of the table. Dix took the opposite side of the couch, pushing Brub's sneakers aside. He smiled up at Sylvia. "That's why I barged in on you. Hope I'm not in the way."

"Not at all! I told you we were bored, didn't I?" She looked down at Brub. "Beer, darling?"

"Might as well."

But there wasn't the smilingness between them as on that first night, not the ease and two-is-one perfection. Something was wrong. Dix didn't care about their troubles. He'd needed a quiet evening like this, with beer and Brub gabbing about his boat. Brub was a kid about boats. Dix didn't want to talk; he wanted only to be lulled by this kind of aimless conversation.

There was no mention of the case; there was no case until Dix mentioned it. Until he said, "How's the case coming?"

Under his eyes he watched Sylvia, waited for her reaction. He was disappointed. There wasn't a reaction tonight. She was too quiet, too colorless to be more quiet or of less color. There was no change in her at all.

"Nothing new," Brub answered. "It's stymied. Same as the others. No clues, no fresh evidence, no hints."

Brub wasn't lying to him, Brub was disgusted but he wasn't discouraged as he had been before. The life had gone out of the case. It wasn't closed because the police didn't close the books, but it was as good as closed. Brub even switched the subject. "Remember Ad Tyne, Dix?"

He didn't.

Brub insisted, "Sure you do. Adam Tyne. The flight commander from Bath. Nice quiet fellow. We saw a lot of him that spring of forty-three. The blond one."

He searched for memory but he didn't find Adam Tyne. There'd been a lot of good fellows, Adam Tyne could have been any of them. Not that it was important. Brub was continuing, "Had a letter from him the first of the week. I wrote him when I got back but hadn't heard a thing. He's married, settled down. Wish I had the letter here, darn it, but I left it at the office." Brub's voice changed, became grave. The transition was so sudden that there was no time to attune to the change before the words were spoken. "He had a sad piece of news. Brucie is dead."

Brucie is dead. The words quivered in the vacuum of quietness. *Brucie is dead.* They resounded thunderously in the silence. *Brucie is dead.*

When he could, he began to echo them as he should with proper shock, with the right incredulity. "Brucie is——" He couldn't finish above a whisper. His voice broke, "—dead." The tears were rolling down his cheeks; he covered his face, tried to withhold the sobs that were clawing him. *Brucie is dead.* The words had never been spoken before. He had not known what would happen when they were spoken.

He heard from a far-off place Sylvia's little, hurt cry, "Dix!" He heard Brub's embarrassed apology, "Dix, I didn't know——"

He couldn't answer them. He couldn't stop crying. It was a long time before he could stop; it seemed eternity within the confines of the shocked silence. He lifted his head when he could and said huskily, "I'm sorry." It released Sylvia and Brub. They didn't know the agony raking his heart.

He said simply, "She meant everything in the world to me." *Brucie*, his soul wept; *Brucie*. He took out his handkerchief and blew his nose. Sylvia's eyes were large as moons, pale moons, sad. "We didn't know," she whispered.

"No," he shook his head. "I guess no one knew. It was all over." He put his handkerchief away. He could talk all right now; they didn't know anything he was thinking. "How did she die? Buzz bombs."

Brub said, "She was murdered."

He could show shock because he was shocked. He had never expected to hear it said. It was so long ago. He echoed, "Murdered."

Brub nodded. His face looked as if it hurt.

Dix had to ask. Painfully as it should be asked by a man who'd loved her. "How did it—what happened—who did it?"

Brub said, "The police have never found out." He blew his nose again. "Better not talk about it, Dix."

His jaw was firm. "I want to know." His eyes promised that he could take it.

"She was down for a weekend at a small beach place. Her husband was coming to join her. At least that's what she told the landlady." Brub told it with starts and stops; he didn't want to tell it. Dix was forcing him to tell it. "Her husband didn't come. Or if he did, no one saw him. She went out Saturday evening alone; she didn't come back. She wasn't found for several weeks. In a rocky cove—she'd been strangled."

Dix couldn't speak. He could only look at Brub out of unseeing eyes.

"It was some time before she was identified. She hadn't signed the register under her own name." Brub said almost apologetically, "I wouldn't have dreamed she was that kind of girl. She was always gay —but she was so—so nice—you know, like a girl from home."

"She wasn't that kind," Dix choked. "She wasn't."

Sylvia wanted to say something but she didn't. She just sat there like a ghost with her sad, luminous eyes on Dix. He knew he had to get out, before he broke down again. He didn't know how to leave.

"They never found any trace of the husband. It must have happened just after our outfit left England. That's why we didn't know why we never heard about it." And he said what was true. "There'd been so much killing, one more wasn't news."

Brucie had died but no one cared, only he. All of them had lost so many, dear as brothers, as their own selves, they had learned not to talk about death. Even in the heart's inmost core where each dwelled alone, they did not admit death.

Dix said unsteadily, "I'd better go." He tried to smile at them. "Sorry."

They tried to stop him. They wanted him to stay and forget in their sympathy and their understanding, in their love for him at this moment. He couldn't stay. He had to get out, to be alone in his lonely place. To remember and to forget. He brushed aside their urging the way you brushed away smoke; knowing it would recur but you could again brush it away. He went into the night while they stood close to each other in the doorway. Together. Never alone.

He drove away not knowing where he was going or why. Only to get away. He did not know how far he drove or how long. There was no thinking in his mind; there was only sound, the swish of the dark wet water over the cold sand, colder than Brucie; the water was the voice of a girl, a voice hushed by fear, repeating over and over, *no . . . no . . . no. . . .* Fear wasn't a jagged split of light cleaving you; fear wasn't a cold fist in your entrails; fear wasn't something you could face and demolish with your arrogance. Fear was the fog, creeping about you, winding its tendrils about you, seeping into your pores and flesh and bone. Fear was a girl whispering a word over and again, a small word you refused to hear although the whisper was a scream in your ears, a dreadful scream you could never forget. You heard it over and again and the fog was a ripe red veil you could not tear away from your eyes. Brucie was dead. Brucie whom he had loved, who was his only love.

She had loved him! If there hadn't been a marriage, one of those secret war marriages. Only she couldn't see it was unimportant; she loved Dix but she loved that unknown husband too. She didn't know the unknown one would die so soon. Somewhere over Germany. So many died. She was all mixed up; she wasn't bad. She was good! He didn't know until she died how good she was. She hadn't done anything wrong; it wasn't wrong to love. When you were filled with love, overflowing with love, you had to give love. If it weren't for that boy who was to die over Germany. If Dix had only known. The swish of the waves whispering *if . . . if . . . if . . .* And Brucie dead. Little Brucie.

How long, how far he drove, he didn't know. With his fingers clenching the wheel and the waves crashing in his ears. He didn't once stop the car. He drove until emotional exhaustion left him empty as a gourd. Until no tears, no rage, no pity had meaning for him. At some point he turned the car to home. He had no memory of the act until he reached the garage, rolled the car into it. He was so tired he walked like one drugged, dragging his leaden body through the dark alley to the dark apartment. He went in through the kitchen, pushing one heavy foot after the other. It wasn't until he entered the bedroom and saw her that he remembered the existence of Laurel. Until he remembered with agonized relief that he was no longer alone.

She must have heard him coming for she'd turned on the bedside lamp and she was standing by the bed holding the yellow chiffon of her negligee tightly about her. Even in his exhaustion he realized the fear on her face. It was gone before the realization.

"I didn't know it was you," she said, then her voice sharpened. "Where have you been all night?"

He was too weary to answer questions, to ask them. He stumbled to her, she couldn't back away more than a step, the table halted her. He put his arms around her and he held her, holding her warmth and the life that flowed beneath her flesh. He held her and he said, "Help me. I'm tired—so tired."

4

IT WAS AFTERNOON BEFORE HE AWOKE. THERE WAS NO SUN ON THE windows, outside was grayness, the sky was watered gray silk.

He wasn't rested, he was very heavy, tired, although his sleep had been dreamless. He took a cigarette from his pack on the bed table, lighted it. He wondered where Laurel was. Without her last night, or this morning, he wouldn't have dared sleep, fearing the dream. She had known; she hadn't asked questions after that first one. She had given comfort, helping him undress, laying back the covers, laying herself and her warmth beside him, within his arms.

He ought to get up, not lie here in the comfort of bed. Shower, shave, dress before she returned. She'd come back as soon as she'd finished her business. She wouldn't call, she'd come, she knew he needed her. She had cared for him last night. Laying back the covers . . .

She hadn't been in bed! She'd just come in; she, too, had been out all night.

He didn't lose his temper. He lay there calmly, considering it. Weighing it the way a judge would, quite calmly and objectively, almost coldly. She hadn't been in long enough to lay back the covers. That was all there was to it. It was no reason for anger. She would explain where she had been and the why of it; she might lie about it but she would explain. He would know if she were lying. He would have no difficulty in nailing the lie.

She'd been afraid of him when he came in last night. Because she had a guilty conscience? Not necessarily. He was still being calm about it. She had feared because she hadn't known it was he, his dragging steps were those of a stranger. It was fear of the unknown; not fear of him.

Her conscience hadn't been guilty. Because she'd demanded explanation of him, where he had been. She had a legitimate reason for her lateness, she'd come directly to him to explain. And he hadn't been there. Yet she'd forgiven him. She'd asked no further questions; she had taken him to comfort.

It was well after four when he stopped thinking, arose and dressed. He hurried then, to shower and shave. He dressed in the suit he liked best; he didn't wear it often. It was distinctive, a British wool, gray with a faint overplaid of lighter gray, a touch of dim red. It fitted him as well as had his dress uniforms; he'd had it made up for himself at Mel's tailors, when Mel first went to Rio leaving his credit at its peak.

When he was dressed, he went into the living room. It was neat, everything in place; the sloven must have been here while he slept. The kitchen, too, was spotless. He decided to mix martinis, Laurel liked them. This was a celebration night. They'd do it big; go out to dinner at some place swell, maybe Ciro's. He didn't have dinner clothes; he'd never bothered to have Mel's altered. He must see to that; he and Laurel were going to put on a campaign although she didn't know it yet. He could help her as much as she could help him. A good-looking fellow who knew how to get what he wanted was what she needed. He'd get the spotlight for her and be satisfied to pick up the gold pieces that slid off the outer rim.

He mixed the cocktails, sampled one and found its coldness good. Only one. He hadn't eaten and he didn't want to spoil the evening by starting too soon. He brought in the evening paper from the door-step, smiling to think how once the news had been more important to him than anything else. He smoked a cigarette, being careful to drop the ashes neatly into the tray, being careful to keep the chair in its place, the creases in his best suit. One cigarette and a careless reading of the paper; almost seven o'clock and she hadn't come, hadn't called.

She couldn't be going to stay away again. She wouldn't stay away without letting him know. For fifteen more minutes he riffled through the paper, reading with his eyes alone, wondering, anger beginning to take shape within his mind. Yet the words in his mind reiterated, she wouldn't, she couldn't.

Against his will, on stiff legs he stalked to the door, flung it open and stepped out into the dim blue courtyard. He was afraid to look up to the balcony, the muscles of his eyes moved stiffly as his bones. He let out his breath in a slow, strangely relieved sigh. Her apartment was dark.

He returned to his, and he heard the phone ringing as he stepped into the hallway. He ran to answer, bumping against the doorway, wondering if it had been ringing long, fearing this, too, might be laid on him, missing her call.

He shouted his "Hello," and heard the answering "Hello" with irritation. A man's voice, Brub's voice. Brub saying a jumble of words, sorry to call so late, just got in, going to the club for dinner, could Dix make it?

He had no wish to make it. To sit in their goody-goody club through a wasted evening, with Sylvia staring at him and Brub trying to act if he hadn't been made different by being chained to a woman. Even as Dix was making excuses, he heard the front door, and he revised his excuses quickly. He was a quick thinker, changing, "I'm afraid not, Brub," to "I'll tell you what, if I can I'll meet you there. You go on ahead. I have to find out what Laurel has up her sleeve." As if he, too, were chained. Quick thinking. If he could take Laurel to the club, as Brub's guest, he'd give her a big night and he wouldn't have to borrow the money from her to pay for it. Dix ended the conversation fast; his nerves jumping with the reasonless fear that she would leave before he could see her.

As he was hurrying to her, he wondered why she hadn't come to the bedroom. Wondering, his steps slowed and he stopped in the doorway, a reasonless and terrifying fear chilling him. There might come a day when he would face strangers, quiet, businesslike strangers.

He called out, questioning, "Laurel?"

"Who were you expecting?"

It was Laurel and he went in happily despite the quarrel underlying her voice. She was stretched out on the couch, her arms behind her head. She'd evidently just returned from whatever her afternoon business was; she was wearing a pin-checked sorrel suit; she'd unfastened the jacket; the narrow skirt was wrinkled above her long tapering legs. Her slant amber eyes were hostile on him. Her lip curled. "Going some place?"

He didn't want to quarrel; he looked at her and was immediately filled with realization of his love for her. He loved her more than he had ever loved before. More than Brucie. For the first time he could think of Brucie while he thought of another woman. And he knew he loved this other woman.

"Sure," he smiled. But he didn't go to her. "How about a cocktail?" Get her in a good humor first; he didn't want to be pushed away. "I mixed martinis."

"Who with?"

For a moment he didn't get it. When he did, his smile was wide. She was jealous! She thought he had another woman. He wanted to laugh.

"With you, Baby. Who else?" He did laugh then. "I'll get the mixings."

He felt good, he whistled as he went to the icebox for the shaker. He caught up two glasses. She hadn't moved and her eyes were no less hostile. "You haven't dressed up for me before," she said.

"We're going places tonight, Baby," he told her. He poured carefully, the dry, dewy liquid. It even smelled good.

"Where? To a drive-in?"

His hand was steady. Only one drop spilled. She couldn't mean anything. She was trying to start a fight because she was jealous. Because he'd never taken her out and she thought he took other women out. He turned slowly, holding her glass.

"No drive-ins." Carefully he handed the glass to her.

His eyes beheld her beauty but he didn't touch her. "You aren't the drive-in type," he smiled down on her body.

She tasted the drink. "What type am I?" she asked sullenly. "The kind you wouldn't be caught dead with in a public place?"

He wouldn't quarrel. He'd keep his good nature. He went back to the chair with his drink. He smiled over the glass, "Definitely the bedroom type. Beautiful. Haven't you enjoyed the honeymoon."

"So it's over?"

He had her where he'd wanted her all along. With him holding the reins. He'd been afraid before that she'd leave him; he'd been jumping through her hoops. It was good to be top man. "You weren't tired of it?"

She didn't answer; she demanded, "Where were you last night?"

He could have played it along but he didn't. He didn't want to prolong her anger. "At Nicolai's," he said. Last night seemed years away. Brucie was dead but it didn't matter any longer. Laurel was his love. "Drink up, Baby, we've got to hurry. They're expecting us."

Deliberately she set her glass on the floor. "Who's expecting us?"

"Nicolais. We're to meet them at their beach club for dinner."

Her dark eyes were cold jewels. "So she's the one. That stiff-necked horse."

"Oh, Laurel!" he sighed. "What on earth are you getting at?"

She put down the words one after the other, like thuds on a drum. "You aren't the kind of man to stay out all night alone."

"Listen, Laurel." He was patient, even long-suffering. "Brub Nicolai was my best friend in the A.A.F. He's my best friend out here. His wife is his wife and I'm no more interested in her than I am in the dame who sells me cigarettes at the drugstore or the old cow that manages these apartments and right now I couldn't tell you what they look like. I went out to see the Nicolais last night only because you weren't here. They've asked us to have dinner with them tonight at their club. Now will you drink up that cocktail and get dressed so we can get to the club before it's too late?"

She picked up her glass and drained it slowly, set it back on the rug. "I'm not going," she said.

"But, Laurel——" She ought to be beaten like a rug. "Why not?"

"Because I don't like stinking rich bastards and their stinking rich clubs."

"Laurel!" He was still patient; he clutched his patience. "They're not stinking rich bastards. They live in a little house and their club is just a little informal club."

She snorted, "I know the Nicolais."

"Certainly, Laurel, the Nicolai family——"

"Rich society bastards."

"Will you listen to me?" He raised his voice. "Just because the family had money, doesn't mean Brub has it. He doesn't. He just has his salary, his salary as a cop, that's all. God knows that can't be much. He and Sylvia don't have as much money as you have." He added quickly, "Or as I have."

"So you've got money?" Her mouth was a sneer. "Did your check come in?"

"My check did come in," he said, holding his anger. "As a matter of fact, I got dressed thinking you'd be in early and we could celebrate tonight. Ciro's or any place you wanted. Then Brub called and I thought you might prefer that. We can go to Ciro's anytime."

She yawned, insolently stretching her mouth wide. "I'm not going any place tonight," she said. "I'm going to eat something and go to bed. I'm tired."

He held in the words only for a moment. When he spoke they came out cold, quiet. "I guess you are. After your night out."

She hadn't known that he knew it. She turned her head. "What do you mean?"

"You didn't beat me home last night by very long, did you? Not even time to warm the bed."

Sullenness settled over her face like a hood. "It's none of your business," she said evenly.

He didn't speak. At that moment he couldn't trust himself to speak. He couldn't trust himself to look at her, at her insolent length, her stubborn mouth. It was his business. She was his woman; she belonged to him. He waited for her to say more but only silence roiled about them. He knew better than to turn his eyes in her direction; when he did, he was walking toward her and he could feel the pain of his steeled fingers. There was no sound of his measured steps on the carpet. He was standing there over her before he knew. And his voice was one from far away, from out of the fog. "Laurel," it said. "Don't say that, Laurel."

Her smooth, cold eyes didn't water. Yet something like a flicker of light or scrap of cloud went into them and out of them. So quickly you could not say it was there, because that quickly it was not there. Something that might have become fear. And he turned away his head. He had almost become angry; she was trying to make him angry but he wouldn't let it happen. He was stronger than she. He stooped over and picked up her cocktail glass. His voice was closer in now. "How about another?"

"Might as well," she grudged.

He walked carefully to the table, poured the cocktail for her, carried it back to her.

"Thanks," she said. Not graciously. As sullen as before, the same sullen insolence in her eyes.

He smiled down at her. The bad moment was over and he could smile. "How about it, Baby? Think that one will put you back on your feet? It might be fun to drive out to the beach club——"

"It would stink." Deliberately she yawned. "If you can't be happy without your precious Nicolais, go on. I'm not going."

He drew a deep breath and forced a smile. She was acting like a two-year-old, you had to treat her like one. Ignore the tantrums. "Not without you. I'm taking you to dinner. If you feel that way, I'll phone Brub we can't make it." He started to the bedroom. "Shall I call Ciro's and reserve a table for"—he glanced at his watch—"ten o'clock?"

"Save your money," she yawned. "You can take me to a drive-in tonight." She was still yawning.

He stopped short. Slowly he turned to look at her. "I won't take you to a drive-in." He stated it flatly.

She flared, "Why not? What's the matter with a drive-in?"

"Nothing," he admitted readily. "But you're tired. You need a good dinner tonight. Not drive-in stuff."

"What's the matter with drive-in stuff? I eat at Simon's all the time, up on Wilshire."

It couldn't be deliberate. It was still part of the tantrum. He spoke slowly, carefully. "We're not going to eat there tonight."

She turned on the couch, lifted herself to one elbow. "What's the matter?" she demanded. "Are you afraid someone might see you there?"

She didn't mean a thing. She meant his bigshot friends, his rich friends like Mel. Someone might see him and think he was broke.

As if he had put the name in her mouth, she said, "You don't have to be afraid. Even Mel used to eat there when he was rocky."

He breathed easily. "I'm not rocky. I got a check today." She could get someone to cash it for him, or she could loan him enough for tonight. He built it. "Look, I got all dressed up to go places and do things. Come on, let's celebrate. We don't have to go to Ciro's. We'll go any place you say—the Kings, Tropics——"

She broke in again, "You look. I'm tired. I'm pooped. I don't want to get dressed up and go places. All I want is to go up to the drive-in——"

"We're not going up to the drive-in!" He didn't mean to shout. It came out in spite of himself. He closed his throat and he kept his lips together in a tight line. His hands had begun to shake; quickly he thrust them into his coat pockets.

She was looking at him out of her lozenge eyes, slyly looking at him, pleased that she'd made him lose his temper. "Okay," she said finally. "We'll go to the beach club."

He didn't believe what she'd said. His mouth fell open as if he were a character in a cartoon strip.

She said, "I changed my mind. We'll join the Nicolais." She got off the couch. She stretched like an animal, one of the big cats, a young golden puma. She came over to him there in the doorway. "Call and see if we're too late while I go and change." She stood there beside him but she didn't touch him. And he didn't touch her. There wasn't time. Not if they were to make it to the beach club. And he didn't want to go; unpredictably he had changed. Because she had? Because he wondered why she had. After she'd been so insistent about the drive-in.

He watched her walk away to the front door. She said, "Go on, call. I won't be long." And she went out.

He wanted to cry her back, to rush after her and bring her back here. They didn't have to go out. It was better for them to be alone, together. He had a feeling of desolation as she closed the door, as if she were gone forever. Although he knew she'd only run up to her own apartment to change, although he knew she would return, it was as if never again would she return to him.

He even took a step after her but he reversed at once and went to the bedroom phone. He should have gone upstairs with her; he could have called from her phone. At least he should have tried to go with her. He'd never been in her apartment. He couldn't see what difference it would make; she came to his, but she insisted that the woman manager was a snoop. The old bag would throw them out if she thought anything went on between them. And the old bag's own apartment was at the right of the stairs; she knew everyone who went up and down those stairs, Laurel said. Mel's apartment was safer, isolated from prying eyes.

This wasn't the night to take issue with Laurel over any of her notions. He'd coddled her into a fairly decent humor, try to keep her there.

He looked up the beach club, dialed, waited while someone went to find Brub. He hoped it was too late, that the Nicolais had long ago gone home to bed. But it was only nine o'clock and Brub's voice denied his hope.

"What happened to you?" Brub asked.

"Laurel was delayed. Are we too late?" He hoped they were too late but he couldn't deliberately try to call it off. Because he'd won the scrap with Laurel; he couldn't pull out of it now.

Brub said, "No. It's buffet tonight. We're serving until ten. Can you make it by then?"

"We'll be there right off."

"I'll try to hide out a couple of plates. Hurry up."

He hung up; they were committed now. He lit a cigarette and went back to the living room. There was still half a martini in the shaker. He drank it; it wasn't very good.

There was no reason to stand around here waiting. The old bag couldn't get her morals up if a man went to his girl's doorway to fetch her. Yet he didn't go. He started twice but he didn't go. He didn't want another fight precipitated.

He was pushing out his second cigarette when she returned. He hadn't seen this dress before; it was some knit stuff, dull amber like her flesh, and it clung like flesh. It was cut low, sleeveless, and the short coat about her shoulders was cornflower blue. He whispered, "You're wonderful."

He went to her but she sidestepped. "Later, Dix. There's no time to make up all over again. Let's go."

They were outside in the court before he remembered that his car was in the garage. "Do you want to wait here until I get it? Or shall we take yours?"

"I put mine up."

She went with him; he didn't want it, through the alley, the block to the far garage. But she was stubborn and again there was the fear that she would vanish if she weren't at his fingertips. She didn't say a word until they reached the garage, until he was opening the noiseless door. Then she said, "No one at the snoopery would ever hear what time you got home."

He laughed it off. "It's rather a jaunt."

She didn't go into the dark garage with him; she waited until he'd backed out before she got in the car. He headed to Wilshire. He said, "I'm surprised Mel would walk that far."

"He never put the car up. When's he coming back?"

"Who? Mel?"

"Yes."

"I don't know." He headed west on Wilshire. There was a faint haze in the night, the approaching headlights had a misty look. A few coming in from the beach showed golden fog lights.

"Don't you hear from him?"

"Good God, no." He laughed at the idea. "Can you imagine Mel writing me?"

"He might like to know how his apartment's getting along. And his car."

She was being deliberately nasty again. He said, "The rent I'm paying him, he should worry."

"You never gave me his address."

"I don't have it," he said. Why did she have to get on Mel?

"You told me you'd give it to me." Why had he mentioned Mel tonight?

"When I got it. He said he'd send it but he never has."

"Is that why you're holding his mail?"

She had snooped. His jaw was tight. He snapped, "That's why." She had snooped so she knew what kind of mail was coming for Mel. He said, "Maybe he doesn't want his bills, maybe that's why he doesn't send his address. I still don't know why you want his address."

"You don't know why," she slurred. Then her voice edged. "I'll tell you why. Because he went off owing me seven hundred dollars, that's why."

Dix was honestly amazed. "Mel owed you seven hundred dollars!"

"Yes. And I'd like to collect."

"Was Mel broke?" He couldn't believe it.

"He was always broke at the end of the quarter. Before his check came. This is the first time he didn't pay up as soon as it came."

They were in Santa Monica, and the haze was a little heavier. Not too much. The fronds of the palms in the parkway on the Palisades were dark against the mist-gray sky. The fog smelled of sea.

"Mel was a heel but he paid his debts."

Again she could be meaning something, but her face, as the car rolled through the orange fog light on Ocean Avenue, meant nothing.

"It's probably the Rio mails," Dix dismissed it. He pushed the car right on the avenue, and down the California Incline to the beach road. The car rolled down the dark, lonely Incline. No one was walking there tonight. He said briskly, "I hope Brub saved us a lot of food. I'm hungry." He reached over and put his hand on her thigh. "I'm glad you decided to come, Baby."

She hadn't thawed. She said, "I just came for the ride. But maybe I can entertain your best friend while you muse with his fancy wife."

He withdrew his hand. He said from his heart, "I don't want anyone but you, Baby."

She was silent. Even her face said nothing.

V

1

THE CLUB DOORS OPENED AS IF THEY HAD BEEN SEEN APPROACHING.
They hadn't been, it was dark in the mist-hung forecourt and they
had been silent as they left the car. The opening of the door, too,
was quiet and some trick of silence held sound within the clubhouse
for the moment before the girl appeared.

It was trick again that she appeared alone and within the veilings
of mist assumed another's form and face.

He choked, "Brucie," yet beneath his breath the word was aloud.

He knew at once, even before speaking the word, that this was no
apparition of Brucie. The word was no more than reflex. This was
the little brown girl, the Banning girl, and she was not alone. Two
young fellows followed her. They didn't notice Laurel and Dix
standing in the mist and the night; the trio cut across to a car on the
opposite side of the court, laughing together.

He knew that Laurel had heard the name even before she spoke.
"Who's Brucie?"

"A girl—I used to know." He walked away quickly from the words
and the memory. Into the lighted club, the clear, unmisted light of
the living. He didn't know or care that Laurel followed him. Yet he
was grateful to find her there. He was all right again in the light, he
smiled at her. "Come on, let's find Brub fast. I'm starving."

Brub lifted a greeting hand from a table by the far windows of the
dining room. Dix took Laurel's arm. "There they are." Laurel hadn't
softened any; there was a sulkiness in the arm he touched. She'd get
over the mood; put some food into her and she'd cheer up. She
hadn't come along just to stage a scene; that hadn't been the purpose of her reversal of mood. Yet he looked at her with a touch of
apprehension as they reached the table. He was reassured; Laurel was

civilized. She had on the same company-polite smile that Sylvia was wearing.

She didn't revert until after dinner and leisurely coffee. Until he asked her to dance. Even then he was the only one who could know. "You've forgotten your manners, Dix," she said, so sweetly, so lady-like. "A guest dances first with his hostess."

It was mild enough and he played up. "If Sylvia will do me the honor."

"He's a wonderful dancer," Laurel cooed.

She didn't know; she'd never danced with him. But as long as she didn't act up any more than this, he was satisfied.

Sylvia's long and lovely lines fitted well against him just as he'd known they would the first time he saw her. He was stirred by the touch of her, almost exulted by it. If she were not Brub's wife, if he were to be alone with her—the fact that she consciously withheld herself from intimacy was knowledge that she, too, was aware of body. They danced well and easily, whatever awareness lay beneath the mind and perceptions.

He knew the absurdity of his reaction; he had a woman, a far richer woman than this. He had no need of Sylvia, and yet there was need, the sensual need of pitting his mind against the mind of another. Until this moment he had not realized his itch for the chase, deprivation had made him jumpy these last days. Even in this incident which could not be furthered, he had begun to soar. He was breathing as a man could breathe when he was lifted into the vastness of sky, when he knew himself to be a unit of power, completely in himself, powerful in himself.

Sylvia said, "Laurel is very lovely, Dix."

Her commonplace words brought him thudding to earth. Brought him to annoying consciousness of the noisy room, the disturbing shuffle of dancers' feet, the coils and scraps of conversation, the metallic music of the phonograph. He said, "Yes," although for the moment he hardly knew to what he was assenting. His inner ear echoed her statement and he said with more enthusiasm, "Yes, isn't she? Something special." He turned Sylvia in order that he too might look upon Laurel, he had not ever seen her in dance motion. She should be something special.

She was not dancing. She was sitting with Brub at the table, their heads together, their words intent. He didn't understand, he knew that Brub had risen to dance with Laurel as Sylvia and Dix left the table. But they hadn't danced; they had remained together to talk;

they were talking as if they had waited a long time for this moment. "You've known Laurel before!" he said quickly. He didn't mean it to sound suspicious but he spoke too quickly.

Sylvia's answer was unperturbed. "We've met her. When she was married to Henry St. Andrews. I didn't realize it when you introduced me at your apartment. Not until she mentioned Gorgon. We met her at Gorgon's."

"Who is Gorgon?"

"He's a lawyer." She wasn't as easy now. She was making up words. "A friend of Henry St. Andrews. And Raoul Nicolai, Brub's oldest brother. We don't know them well, we don't travel in that crowd. Can't afford it."

He remembered it now. Gorgon had had opinions on the case. Laurel had quoted Gorgon's opinions. And he remembered he'd seen the name, it must be the same name. Thomas Gorgonzola. Criminal lawyer. A name to conjure with in L.A. courts, a name that meant a feature to the newspapers. He smiled; not Sylvia, not anyone would know the meaning of that smile. Laurel's friend, the great criminal lawyer.

"What is St. Andrews like?" he asked curiously.

"I didn't like him," Sylvia answered. She wasn't hesitant any longer; she was on even keel. "One of those spoiled young men, too much money, mamma's darling, an ego inflated by too much attention and absolutely no discipline all of his life."

"Heavy drinker?" St. Andrews sounded like Mel. Laurel hated the first; it was a cinch she hadn't had any doings with Mel.

"That goes without saying. Liquor is such a nice substitute for facing adult life. I understand Laurel took quite a beating."

"Yes," he agreed. "She doesn't say much, but I gathered that."

"She wasn't good enough for the sacrosanct St. Andrews. And anyone with a functioning mind is an insult to their irrationality. You know, before I met Brub I was afraid he'd be that kind. The Nicolais and the St. Andrews—all that clan."

"Aren't you?" He was a little surprised.

She laughed. "What you said! My grandfather was delivering babies, and not getting paid for it, while the clans were grabbing everything that might turn into silver dollars. No, I'm just a poor girl, Dix. And fortunately Brub's a throwback to when the Nicolais worked for a living."

The music ended. He would have liked to continue the talk, to ask more about Gorgon. But she started to the table and he followed.

The dark head of Brub and the glowing head of Laurel separated as they approached. He put Sylvia in her chair. "Thank you," he said with mock formality. "It was indeed a pleasure." He sat down beside her. "Now that my manners have been made, let me tell you it really was a pleasure." There was a drink in front of him and he sampled it. "What's the matter, Brub? Laurel step on your new shoes?"

Laurel said, "I was tired. I didn't want to dance." She hadn't lost her hostility although her words seemed simple statement of fact. Her eyes were watching him with the same intensity as earlier. He ignored it. He said pleasantly, "I'm sorry. I wanted to dance with you. Couldn't you take one little spin?"

"I'm too tired," she said. She wasn't sorry. She had no intention of dancing with him, of giving in to him.

It didn't matter. He could handle her later. He could handle anyone. He was Dix Steele, there was power in him.

"Who is Brucie?"

He was shocked that she would ask, and she would deliberately instigate a quarrel before Brub and Sylvia. He'd even forgotten the episode in the doorway; she too should have forgotten it until later tonight when they were alone, where he could explain it in private. His eyes went quickly to her but she wasn't asking the question of him, and he realized she'd tricked it in a small, curious voice, asked it to all.

Brub could have answered her, Sylvia could have, but both were silent. Brub was looking into his drink, turning it in his worried hand. Sylvia was shocked as Dix, her eyes were wide on him. It was up to him to answer. He said quietly, "She was a girl I knew a long time ago. That Brub and I knew. In England." He was furious but he was quiet. He'd told her that much outside, she shouldn't have nuzzled the name, kept it alive in her consciousness. He completed her knowledge. "She's dead."

He opened his eyes on her as he spoke and he saw the shock come into hers. He wanted to shock her. He wouldn't have said it otherwise, not bluntly, not out like that. He didn't know if there was fear in her as well as shock; you couldn't tell; it was hard to tell what lay behind gem-smooth, gem-hard, amber eyes.

"Dead," she repeated, as if she didn't believe him. "But she was——'"

He smiled, "That girl wasn't Brucie." He explained to Sylvia, to Brub who had looked up at him again. "As we were coming in tonight, we saw that girl, the one who was here that other evening.

You knew her name, Sylvia, and she reminded you of Brucie, remember, Brub?"

Sylvia said, "The Banning girl."

"Yes." His voice wasn't quite steady remembering that moment in the mystery of the night and fog. "She looked so much like Brucie tonight, it——" He smiled ruefully. "It was rather startling."

He was pleased now that Laurel had brought up the name when she did. Brub and Sylvia were corroboration of the fact that there was no Brucie in his life; Laurel might have doubted him if he'd explained it away in private. He was pleased, too, that the name had remained with her, that it had given her jealousy. He was still important to her. She had thought he was shaken because he'd run into a girl out of his past.

Again he asked her to dance and this time she didn't refuse. He held her closely, he said to her hair, "You didn't think there was anyone else for me, did you, Baby?"

"I don't know what I thought," she said. "How does anyone ever know what they really think?" She was defensive but she was weary, it was in the strands of her voice.

He said, "Let's go home."

"All right," she agreed.

He didn't wait for the music to end; he danced her to the table and saw Sylvia and Brub move apart, in the same fashion that Laurel and Brub had earlier. He didn't wonder at the repetition; only briefly did it occur to him that Brub must be in one of his confidential moods. And that Brub, too, must be tired tonight, otherwise he'd be cutting capers on the dance floor.

2

IT DIDN'T OCCUR TO DIX TO WONDER WHY BRUB WAS TIRED. NOT UNTIL he and Laurel had ridden in the silence of her weariness almost to the apartment. He'd been thinking of Laurel, watching her as she rested there in the corner of the seat, her eyes closed, her lips parted as if she slept. He'd been thinking of her beauty and her fire, and tonight, her lack of fire. Thinking without thoughts, conscious of her and of the fact that this many mist-dulled streets must be covered before he could put the car at the curb, until he and Laurel could be alone.

He didn't consciously bring Brub to memory. It was one of those minnows of thought, darting through the unruffled pond of his thinking. But why should Brub be beaten? The case was closed, insofar as work activity was concerned. In the files of unfinished business there was an entry; girl murdered, murderer unknown. There were plenty of like entries, another wouldn't mean that a young fellow playing cop should have all the high spirits knocked out of him. Plenty of reasons why Brub could have been tired, he could have thrown one the night before, he could have sat up reading all night; he and Sylvia could have continued their dissension, if there had been one, far into the dawn. Or they could have pitied Dix far into the dawn. Because of Brucie.

And that had been only last night, the revelation of Brucie's death. Dix should have been the one holding his head in his hands. But he knew how to get away from trouble, from grief and from fear. He knew better than to indwell with it. He was smart.

He said aloud, "I don't know why everyone should be so tuckered tonight, I'm not."

She wasn't asleep. She didn't open her eyes but she said, "Why should you be? You slept all day."

It wasn't much farther home. And he waited to answer, waited until they could be alone. It wasn't worthwhile to whittle off little edges of disagreement; you must get at the roots. As soon as he found out what was in back of her hostility, he would uproot it. They'd have it out tonight, before she slept.

He said, "We're here."

He held the door and she slid under the wheel to get out of the car. She might have slept on the way home, her eyes were half closed yet. She walked ahead of him under the arch into the blue-lighted patio, dulled in tonight's mist. She must have been half asleep for she didn't turn to Mel's apartment, she was starting back to the steps when he caught her arm, asking softly, "Where you going, Baby?" He turned her, holding her arm, "You're walking in your sleep."

She stood there quietly while he opened the door, but she waited to enter, waited until he touched her again and explained, "We're home, honey. Wake up."

He had left the lamp burning in the living room. He shut out the blue mist and turned to the welcome of the light. It was good to be home. With her. "Go get undressed and I'll fix you a drink."

"I don't want a drink," she said. A little shiver twisted her shoulders.

"Something hot," he said. "Milk? Coffee?"

"Coffee," she said. "I'd like coffee. Hot, black coffee."

"Coming up!" He filled the electric percolator in the kitchen, he'd make it in the bedroom. With her. He fixed the tray and hurried back to her.

She hadn't started to undress. She was sitting on the edge of the bed, just sitting there looking into the monotone of the rug.

He plugged in the percolator. "Be ready in a minute. Why don't you get undressed while it's perking? I'll serve you in bed, solid comfort."

She didn't make any move, not even to take off her coat. She just looked up at him. Not saying anything, not even with her eyes. Not even hostility now in her eyes.

He came over to her and he sat down beside her on the bed. "Look," he said gently. "Get it off your chest. What's bothering you?"

She shook her head and her hair fell across her cheek. As if mist were bright as sun, it obscured her face.

"It isn't fair not to tell me, Laurel," he continued. "You don't give me a chance. How can I explain if you don't let me know what's the trouble?"

Her sigh was audible. She started to say, "What's the good——" but he stopped her, turning her to face him.

"You're the most important thing in the world to me, Laurel. No matter what it is, I want to get it right with you." He didn't mean to say much, he meant to keep it light, but he couldn't when he had touched her, when he was looking into her face. "I couldn't bear to lose you, Laurel. I couldn't take it."

She studied his face while she released her shoulders gently from his hands. She could see in him truth of what he had said. Her voice was very tired. "All right, Dix," she said. "Let's talk about it. Let's start at the beginning. Where were you last night?"

That was easy. "But I told you. At Nicolai's."

"Where were you after you left Nicolai's?"

She'd been checking up on him. He got up from the bed and began to walk the room. She was Laurel, but she was a woman and she was snooping on him. His laugh was short. "So you didn't believe me. You checked with Brub. That's what you two were talking about."

"That was part of it," she admitted.

"What did Brub tell you?"

"You needn't be annoyed. I didn't ask him outright. I simply found out you'd been there early and left early."

"You didn't believe me," he accused.

"I didn't believe you'd come from Nicolai's at four in the morning in the shape you were in," she said flatly.

The coffee was beginning to bubble. It was a small sound, a bubble forming, breaking, a small, annoying sound. He shut it out of his ears. He wouldn't let it start roaring. He didn't have to listen to sounds any longer; he had Laurel. He had her voice and her presence to shut away sound. He could explain to her and he didn't mind explaining. He didn't mind anything that would keep Laurel near to him.

"How much did Brub tell you?" he asked. "Did he tell you the news he gave me last night?" If Brub had, she wouldn't be asking these questions. She'd be avoiding the subject as did Brub and Sylvia. He was pleased Brub had kept silent; it was better that he tell Laurel himself; it was another tie to her. "No, I didn't come right home from Nicolai's. I couldn't. You see, Brub had just told me that Brucie was dead."

Her eyes widened. With a kind of terror of disbelief.

"I couldn't see anyone. I was too shocked. I drove. Just drove. I don't know where, up the beach, I guess. I remember hearing the water." The shush of the water, the hush of a girl's voice. His own voice was uneven. "That's why I came home—the way I did."

She said, "No." In disbelief. In pity. And then she said, "Brucie must have meant a lot to you."

"She did."

"More than anyone."

He came to her swiftly, knelt before her, taking her hands. "That was true until I met you, Laurel. But there's never been anyone like you. Not ever." His hands tightened over hers. "Marry me, Laurel. Will you? We're meant for each other, you know it. You knew it the first time we looked at each other just the way I knew it. Will you, Laurel?"

She had released her hands. And the weariness on her face wasn't because she was tired, it was because she was sad. She shook her head. "It's no good, Dix. If I married you, I wouldn't have a dime."

"But I——" He didn't get a chance to build a dream.

She looked at him out of seeing eyes. "You don't have a dime ei-

ther, Dix. Don't bother to lie. I know you. Yes, I knew you the first
time I looked at you just like you knew me. Because we're just alike.
We're out to get it, and we don't care how we get it."

He had left her, he was walking around again, listening to what
she had to say, hating what she knew, hating that there wasn't truth
with which to demolish it. Because he couldn't lie to her now. She
knew too much.

"I thought I could get it marrying St. Andrews. All the money in
the world and a position where I could look down my nose at the
small-town big shots that looked down their noses at me when I was
a kid. I didn't know how hard it was. I couldn't take it. The St.
Andrews weren't a bit different from the Buckmeisters back in Ne-
braska, they just had more money and bigger noses. So I got out. But
I'm still after what I want. And I'll get it. I'll get it on their money,
and don't think that doesn't burn them. And when I get there I'll be
so high I won't even know they're down there under my nose."
There was an excitement in her as well as hate. She was getting
there. That was all the business she'd been attending to while he
slept; she knew she was getting there. When she did, she'd carry him
along. But he couldn't risk waiting; when she did, there might be
someone else. He walked around trying to figure what he could do. If
he had Uncle Fergus' money, he could have her right now. They'd
go to the top together. If there were some way to get the money
that was his, that was going to be his. He heard her voice again.

"—I don't know how you got rid of Mel so you could take over
here. I don't even care. But I know you're living on borrowed time. I
know Mel will come back from wherever he is——"

"He's in Rio."

"Rio or taking the cure again, I don't know."

"He's in Rio," he insisted.

"Maybe he finally went. He'd been talking about Rio ever since I
met him three years ago, and before that. The big job he was going
to take over in Rio. Next week. Next month. Maybe you got him to
take it, I don't know. Anyway you fell into the apartment and the
clothes he didn't want and his car. How you wangled it, I don't
know; he wouldn't give his best friend the cork out of a bottle. But
he's going to come back and take them all again and then what are
you going to do? Move in on somebody else? You can't carry a wife
with you living that way. Get a job? You don't want a job. And you
couldn't get one that would pay enough to keep me in war paint.
I'm expensive, Dix."

He was choked up. "My uncle——"

"What uncle?"

"My uncle, back in Princeton. You're wrong about that, I've got an uncle and he's got the chips."

"You haven't got them," she said cruelly. "Don't try to tell me he's cutting you in. I know guys in the chips. They don't keep a girl cooped up in an apartment, they're out spending."

In the silence, the roar of the coffee percolator blurred his ears. He saw her as she walked over to the table, he was grateful when she shut out the sound. She drew two cups, handed one to him.

"Let's face it, Dix. It's been swell but——"

Panic made his voice too loud. "You're not calling quits?"

She spoke quickly, stammering a little. "No, no. I didn't mean that. But it can't be for keeps, Dix. You know that as well as I. I'm not saying that if you had half the money that stinker of an ex had, I wouldn't marry you. I want to marry you." She finished her coffee and drew another cup.

Automatically, he said, "Don't drink too much of that. You won't be able to sleep."

"I don't expect to sleep very well." There was sadness in her voice again.

She moved to the dressing-table bench as he went to the end table. He put sugar and cream in his coffee. He stirred it, the spoon whorled the liquid, churned it as a storm churns the sea. He put away the spoon and he drank some of the coffee. He said, "You're not telling me everything, Laurel. You're keeping something back. You're through with me."

"No, no, I'm not," she protested quickly. He ought to tell her to stop saying that—no, no, no.

She went on haltingly, "There's only one thing. If I land what I'm after, it'll mean leaving town."

He waited until he could speak quietly. "What kind of a job is it?"

"It's a show. Musical. They're casting it here on the coast. I've got a good chance." Life returned to her eyes. "It means Broadway— after that, the pictures. Starring, not a peasant in the background."

"Broadway." He could go back East, he could get things fixed up with Uncle Fergus! Everything was going to be all right. He was sick of California anyhow. "Broadway," he repeated and he smiled. "Baby, that's wonderful. Wonderful."

A childish surprise came into her face at his reaction. He finished his coffee, set down the cup. He walked with excitement. "That's terrific, Laurel. Why didn't you tell me? I've got to go back home in a couple of months anyway. You're right about my uncle. The old skinflint has hardly given me enough to eat on, that's why I've been pinching the pennies. And if it weren't for Mel letting me use this place, I'd have been in a furnished room somewhere, I'd never have had a chance to lay eyes on you. Good old Mel."

He was burned up with the radiant promise of the future. Even if he couldn't fix things with Uncle Fergus, by that time she'd have so much money she wouldn't need the St. Andrews' income, she wouldn't need Dix's income. She'd move him in and he'd get a chance to pick off the outer leaves of dough. The rightness of it all laid a sanctity on it. And he could embellish a bit now, because of the rightness it would ring true. "We'll be hitting the east coast about the same time. You're wrong about my not wanting a job, I'm used to working. I was raised on work." He laughed. "You don't know my Uncle Fergus! The only reason I've been laying off a year was to get a chance at writing a book. Now I'll go back and take on the job he wants to give me, and it'll pay for more than your war paint. He's got a factory that turns out stocks and bonds. He wants me to handle the advertising. That means New York, Baby," he grinned, "and I think by the time your run is over with we'll be doing some California advertising. I'll be around, Laurel!" She laid down her cup just in time. He caught her tightly in his arms. "Laurel," he was laughing, he was half-crying, "Laurel, I knew we were meant to be. Forever. For always."

She didn't say anything. She couldn't say anything. She was trembling within the cup of his arms.

3

HIS SLEEP WAS RESTLESS. EVEN WITH HER BESIDE HIM, DREAMS DROVE him fretfully to the surface of the night. Too often. She, too, was restless. For he heard her stirring each time he half-awakened, heard her breath of wakefulness, not sleep. The dreams were shapes in the mist, he could not remember them when he awoke at last from the final stretch of deep if uneasy sleep.

He hadn't slept long enough. She was gone, as she was always gone when he awoke these days. There was no sun in which to remember her. The morning was a dirty gray rag. He felt cramped within the misshapen room. The dregged coffee cups were there, one on the dressing table, one by the tray.

He had to get out of here. He showered, hating the sound of the rushing water; shaved, hating the buzz of the razor. He dressed quickly, not caring what he put on. He had no plan, only to get out of this room, to get away from the unremembered shape of his dreams.

He didn't take the car. In order to breathe, in order to put motion into the staleness of his body. He didn't know why he should feel this way; everything had been all right, everything was going to be all right. Laurel had made it right. There'd be a few weeks of separation while she was on the road but that was unimportant. A separation would whet the emotions of both. Absence was a heady spice.

He felt better by the time he'd walked as far as Wilshire, and he continued up Beverly Drive to his favorite delicatessen. He turned in there, he was suddenly hungry. He was a little ahead of the noon crowd, he ordered salami and swiss on rye and a lot of coffee. It was when he was paying for it, breaking his last ten, that he realized he must do something about the torn check. The envelope was in his pocket, he had automatically transferred it with the rest of his stuff when he dressed.

He was pretty sure he'd need help to cash it. He'd only been in the bank twice in Beverly; no one knew him well enough to accept a mutilated check. The deal called for Brub's help, a Nicolai and a cop ought to throw a little weight.

He finished eating, left the delicatessen, and went into the nearest drugstore. He called Santa Monica first but there was no answer. It was a guess but he called the Beverly Hills station. It wasn't Brub's bailiwick but at least they could steer him to the right number.

The cop who answered said Detective Nicolai wasn't there. Dix hadn't expected Brub to be there. He said, "I know. I just want to find out what number to call to get in touch with him." He thought the cop was stupid but the cop was thinking the same thing of him; it finally cleared up, Brub was in Beverly but he'd gone out to lunch. The cop didn't know where.

Dix was irritated when he left the booth. It shouldn't have taken that long to find out that Brub was in the neighborhood. He didn't want to go sit in the police station to wait; he wasn't in the mood for that kind of amusement today. He hadn't anything to do. He could probably run into Brub if he made the rounds of the nearby eating spots. It would be better to run into him instead of seeking him out. Make it casual.

He was lucky. He found Brub in the second place, the one he called the Ice House. Always a carved cake of ice in the window. Dix said surprised, "Well, look who's here!" Before he saw the other man, the lean-visaged Lochner. Before he wondered why the two were together again in Beverly Hills.

Brub was surprised to see Dix. "Where'd you come from?"

"A guy gets hungry." He spoke to Lochner, "How d'you do, Captain Lochner."

Brub moved over in the booth and Dix sat by him. It was an invitation to join them. He had to eat again but he didn't care, he ordered a chicken sandwich and a bottle of beer. It was a good omen, running into Brub as he'd wanted, not having to seek him out. It made him feel more cheerful. "More trouble in Beverly?" he asked.

"No," Brub shook his head, took a big bite of spaghetti, blurring his words. "Same old case."

"You're still working on that?" He was surprised.

"We don't give up," Lochner said in his flat voice.

He really was surprised. "It's still important enough that the head of Homicide is giving special attention to it?"

Lochner said, "We aren't going to let it happen again."

"Then you honestly believe it stems from this neighborhood."

Lochner shrugged. "It's the last clue we have."

"Seems rather hopeless," Dix said kindly.

Brub's words were audible again. "We pick up a little every time we check."

Dix didn't show any disturbance. He was as calm as an innocent bystander. "But where do you check? How?"

"We've been talking to the help again. At the drive-in where he stopped with her that night."

He was more calm. When there was anything to face he could play up to it. "Any luck?"

There wasn't. He could tell by Brub's expression. Lochner said, "There may be. Nicolai's got a good idea there." The chief left it for Brub to tell.

Brub said, "I don't know that it will amount to anything. But in these neighborhood spots, a lot of the same faces recur pretty regularly. Down at Doc Law's, for instance, in the canyon, you get to know people just seeing them over and again. I got to thinking about it. There must have been some of the regulars around that night when he took Mildred in for coffee." He let out a gust of breath. "God, the nerve of him! Walking in there, facing all those lights and gambling no one would remember what he looked like."

"Like you and me," Dix dared, "an ordinary man."

Brub nodded slowly. "Yeah. An ordinary man. With the nerve of a jet pilot." He took another bite of spaghetti fast and talked through it. "My idea, whatever good it is, is to have the help ask questions of the regulars when they come in. Were they at the drive-in the night of the murder, and did they notice the couple?"

"Not bad," Dix said, as if he were thinking about it. "And I suppose you're hoping this fellow is a repeater, too."

"Yeah. That would be a break." Brub was exasperated quickly. "What a break, but no chance. Except for his nerve."

"You mean he might have the nerve to walk in again."

"Yeah."

"And you think the help would spot him in that case."

"I'm sure they would. At least I think they would. They're keyed up to remember. The little girl, Gene, her name is, is sure she'd know him if he came in again. She says she'd know him if she ever saw him. Only she can't describe him."

"The trouble with people in these cases," Lochner droned, "is that they're not articulate."

"What about the tailor?" Dix asked.

"What tailor?" Brub frowned.

"The one you told me about. The one that saw this fellow and that earlier girl come out of the movie in Hollywood." He'd nearly said the Paramount. He took a swallow of his beer. "Are you working on him too?"

Brub shook his head. "He wasn't close enough to them to be any good at identification. The guy could go in and be measured for a suit and he wouldn't know."

"He might," Dix smiled. "Mightn't he? A tailor might be expected to recognize the shoulders or the body length, don't you think?"

Lochner hummed and Brub thought that the tailor might. Dix had given them an idea. And welcome to it. Brub was thinking out loud again, "Walking right into that battery of lights. What a nerve!"

Dix said, "Maybe he didn't intend to do anything to her. Maybe it wasn't so much nerve but no intention."

"We've considered that," Brub said thoughtfully. "But it doesn't fit the pattern. He picked them up to kill them. It wasn't ever without intention."

"According to your reconstruction."

Brub's smile was a little abashed. "I don't think I'm far off base. He's first of all a killer, that we know. He kills because he's a killer." He tallied on. "He's a gambler. He's reckless, I mean he'll take chances, like that drive-in, or taking the other girl to the movies. But he's not so reckless that he doesn't realize his chances; it's the recklessness we had at the sticks during the war, we took chances but we were sure, God willing, that we'd pull out of them."

"He's an ex-serviceman," Lochner supplied.

Dix raised his eyebrows. When Lochner didn't explain, he said, "That's something new."

"Ten to one," Lochner said. "He's the right age, good healthy specimen, average. The average were in the service."

"He's a nice-looking fellow, nice clothes," Brub said. "We know that from our inarticulate observers. He's well off, he has a car. He has a pleasant approach, we know that, too, or these girls wouldn't have let him pick them up. Except maybe that first one."

"What was a fellow like you reconstruct doing on Skid Row?"

"That's one of the things we don't know," Brub admitted.

"Maybe he was slumming," Lochner said.

"Maybe he knew he was off on a kill," Brub was feeling it out, "maybe he didn't want to do it. Maybe he thought it wouldn't matter so much if he picked a girl that didn't matter."

"And after the first time, he didn't care?" Dix asked soberly.

"It wasn't the first time," Lochner said with authority.

Dix's eyes slewed to him, letting his surprise show through.

"It was too professional," Lochner explained. He picked up his check. "I'm going back to the station and go over these Bruce reports again. Coming?"

Bruce reports. Bruce wasn't an uncommon name. There must be a hundred thousand Bruces in the United States. Hundreds in L.A. Dix didn't show any reaction to the name. He went right on eating the sandwich. They could have been examining him, putting out this information to get reaction from him. There was no reason for them to have any suspicion of him. There was nothing at all that made him open to suspicion. Absolutely nothing.

"I'll be along shortly," Brub said. "Soon as I finish eating." He'd ordered apple pie and coffee, the girl was bringing them now.

Dix waited until Lochner was at the door. "Smart guy," he said.

"The best." Brub was testing the pie.

Dix got away from the subject, on to a natural one. "You and Laurel hit it up pretty chummy last night, didn't you?"

Brub didn't grin it off. He said seriously, "I like her."

"I didn't realize you and Sylvia had known her before."

"Just met. Never had a chance to talk to her until last night."

"You did pretty well last night. Looked like a serious confab." He was fishing. But he could fish openly; Laurel was his girl. He didn't catch anything.

Brub said, "I have my serious moments."

Dix said, "Won't do you any good. Looks like Laurel and I aren't going to be around much longer."

Brub wiped his mouth. His eyes were opened in surprise.

"Didn't she tell you about the show she's going into? And it's about time for me to head back to New York."

"You're going back East?" Brub was surprised. He added with mock rue, "Just when I thought we had you sold on California." He took another bite. "What's the trouble? Mel Terriss coming home?"

Laurel had talked to Brub about Mel Terriss. Brub wouldn't have had the name so glibly if she hadn't. Harping on Mel. Wondering aloud to Brub if Mel was in Rio? He bit his anger between his teeth. "I haven't heard from Mel. No telling about him. I've got to go back and get refinanced." He remembered the check. "By the way, Brub, wonder if you could help me out?" He was quick. "This isn't a touch, pal. I tore up my check, got the envelope mixed in with a bunch of ads. I'm too stony to wait for Uncle Fergus to send another, and the old boy wouldn't wire money if I were selling pencils. Would you want to vouch for me at the bank here?"

"Sure. I don't know the rules but it's worth a try." Brub picked up both tabs. Dix took them out of his hand. "I'm not that stony. My turn."

The gray day settled over them as they emerged. It was depressing; no matter how good you'd been feeling, to step into this dirty wash was depressing.

The bank was only across the street. He'd borrowed trouble about the check. There was none. Brub's identity was good. The bank manager was pleasant, saying, "I don't know why anyone should be penalized for making a mistake. As long as you have all the parts." You could tell by his manner he considered Dix an honest young fellow, a friend of the Nicolais was certain to be all that.

He felt better with the two-fifty in his billfold. The day even looked brighter. He said, "Thanks, Brub. Thanks a million." He was ready to go. He'd buy a present for Laurel, he'd never given her anything. He couldn't splurge, not on these peanuts, but he could buy her something, if only one orchid. He'd drape her in orchids someday.

It was Brub who was making the delay. Brub who blurted it out, "These reports."

He knew what was coming. He felt the gray close in on him again but he showed only polite courtesy.

"Would you want to look them over? They're the reports on Brucie." Brub was rattling. He was embarrassed. Expecting Dix to break down? Or ashamed that he was suspecting a friend, a friend he had no reason to suspect? A shocked, grave look was the right one from Dix.

"I was talking to Lochner about her. I couldn't help talking about her, I was knocked off my pins when I heard the news. He cabled for a report of the case from the London police." Brub was speaking more slowly now. Because Dix hadn't burst into sobs? Because he was warning Dix? "He thought it might help us out. That maybe Brucie was one of a series, like our series. It's farfetched, but this killer might have been an American, England was full of G.I.'s at that time. Maybe even a California man."

He asked only one question. "Was she one of a series?"

Brub's face was torn. "They don't know. There was a series but it didn't start right after Brucie. A couple of months—and then it began. The same pattern. A strangler."

"He was never caught?"

"No, he was never caught." Brub hesitated. "After six months it stopped. As suddenly as it had begun. Maybe he was shipped back home."

"And did it start then, over on this side?" It was a good question. Brub slurred it. "N-no."

No series, no pattern. Isolated cases. They hadn't caught up with the isolated cases. On the east coast. Or had they? Was Brub keeping quiet because it might sound too pointed? Why should Brub suspect him?

He knew he'd better get away. He was beginning to grow angry. Brub had no business suspecting him. Yet he didn't believe that was any part of it. Only a part of his own depression. He said, "I don't think I could take the reports, Brub. You understand?"

"Yes, Dix." Brub's face showed sympathy. "See you soon."

He watched Brub's stocky figure roll away in the crowd. He shook his head, regretfully. Poor guy. Going around in circles trying to find an invisible man. Brub must be desperate if he were suspecting his best friend. Dix felt better. He rambled down Beverly Drive, shopping the windows as if he were one of the chattering females obstructing the walks. At Leonard's he took a chance, turned in. The moment he'd decided to chance it, he felt right. The whole trouble with these past weeks was playing it safe; that was what love did to you, love and being stony; and the result, the megrims.

He walked in and he put it over smooth. Too bad he couldn't get a suit out of it but he did well enough. Several jackets, navy flannel, white tweed, gabardine in tan, pinks was what it was called a couple of years ago; shirts, ties, a nice haul all wrapped up to be shipped to Rio. Dix Steele signing for it, he'd established that fact when he first moved into Mel's. Dix Steele taking care of Mel's affairs while Mel was in Rio. Maybe the credit was strained a bit but he brushed that off, first of the month, check coming any day now. And Mel wanting some of Leonard's good stuff, Rio togs didn't suit him. A dust of flattery and man-to-man and gab, and he'd mail the box himself as he was on his way to the post office. His car was just around the corner.

He wished for the car as he lugged the heavy box down the street. He'd get the address label ripped off as soon as he got home, before Laurel snooped around and saw it. She might try writing Mel at Avenida de Perez, nice-sounding street. Letters could go astray. However, she might be anxious enough to cable. Not so good. Besides he'd said he hadn't known Mel's address.

He shifted the box. He should have had it delivered. But he wanted the navy flannel jacket for tonight, wanted to show her that the check was bigger than she thought it was. He shifted it again as he passed the Beverly Theatre. And he stopped. It was only four o'clock. Laurel didn't ever return until six, nearer seven. There was a special showing of some big picture, hence there was a continuous run. He hadn't seen a picture in weeks. He went in.

It was after six when he came out. The street lamps were lighted in the early, hazy dark. He was a damn fool for walking, not bringing the car. There was no crosstown bus line that serviced his neighborhood. He had to walk it, carrying the awkward box. No taxis in sight.

It wasn't far but his arms ached when he reached the dark apartment. Automatically he looked to the balcony, her apartment, too, was dark. He went in and lighted his. He wondered if she'd tried to call, to tell him she'd be late. Not tonight. After the wrangle of last night, she'd get home tonight. She'd go places with him. He took another shower, leaving the door open to listen for the phone.

He dressed elegantly, the gray flannels, the navy coat. He looked like a million dollars. And felt like it. Although it was past seven and she still hadn't phoned. He was certain that she was coming, otherwise he'd have heard from her before now.

He went out and mixed himself a tall, comfortable highball. He stretched comfortably in the chair, took up the evening paper. Tonight he wasn't going to get annoyed waiting for her, he felt good.

She didn't come at all.

4

Discomfort wakened him. He'd fallen asleep in the chair, his legs were cramped, his neck was rigid. He turned off the lamp and the windows became gray. He didn't care what time it was, he didn't think about time. There was no reason to go again into the court, to gaze up at her apartment. He wouldn't know if she were there or not. She hadn't been there at four. Her lights wouldn't be on now if she had slunk back like the alley cat she was.

She could wait. He was too foggy now to knock her awake and demand explanation. Even if foggy, he was smart. No one in the Virginibus Arms was going to remember him at Laurel Gray's door.

He flung himself fully dressed on the bed. If he could sleep without taking anything, he would. He didn't want to be put out, he must be alert for the ringing of the telephone.

His sleep was sodden although much too brief. The gray of daylight was still pasty on the panes. He felt dirty and sick. The new flannel jacket was a sweaty mass. He peeled it off and hurled it to the floor. The best gray slacks were crumpled like a concertina. He pulled off the heavy brogues that leaded his feet. They were good shoes; he'd bought them in England. When he had money and position. When the best was none too good for Colonel Steele. He rubbed his fist hard across his upper lip. No tears. He hadn't the strength for tears.

He pulled off the slacks, left them where they fell. A shower would revive him, at least enough to put him on his feet for a few hours, until she came home.

He stayed under the gentle shower for a long time. The water was soothing, even the sound of it was soothing. He'd always, all of his life, loved the sound of breaking water. Nothing that had happened had changed that. The crawling of water over sand, the hush of a word *no . . . no . . . no . . .* not even that had changed his love of the power of the sea.

He put off shaving. His hands were trembling when he picked up the razor, he knew what the rasp of it would do to his nerves. Undo the good of the water. Yet he must shave. A man didn't look like just any ordinary man unless he were clean-shaven.

It was almost six o'clock before he was dressed. In the protective coloring of tan gabardines, a white sports shirt. Too late to take the discarded clothes to the cleaners. He wadded them into a bundle and pushed them in the closet. It hurt him to see the navy blue flannel jacket, the good-looking, high-style jacket, dumped there. He rubbed his lip again. He'd wear it yet, he'd wear it to the best places in town, the places where that kind of a jacket ought to be worn. He was through living in a hole; he was going places and doing things. Big places and big things.

He lit a cigarette and took a deep drag. His head felt light as mist. No wonder, he hadn't eaten since noon the day before, a couple of sandwiches then. He wasn't hungry. His mouth tasted stale as the smoke of the cigarette. He didn't want to go out into Mel's kitchen, eat the old stuff that had been in the refrigerator for days. If only she would come.

There was no reason to believe that she wouldn't come. Something she couldn't foresee had happened last night. Maybe a job out of town. He hadn't returned to the apartment until almost seven. She must have called him all afternoon, then had to leave without getting word to him. There was no way she could leave a message. No possible way.

She'd return any minute now. She'd explain as she had the other time—and what had her explanation been? He'd explained to her, but had she ever explained to him? She'd said it was none of his business. She'd talked about the big show she might land. But she hadn't said where she was all night.

She'd meant to. And he'd meant to question her after he explained himself. But the conversation had channeled; they'd never returned to the subject. It didn't mean that she hadn't a simple and reasonable explanation, as she had the night when she'd been caught by her lawyer.

She'd come in pretty soon now. She'd be full of news about the show. There wouldn't be any wrangle tonight; they'd talk it all over, make plans for New York. God, it would be good to be back in New York again! Where no one knew you; where there weren't Nicolais parking on your doorstep. Brub was a great guy—the old Brub. But marriage changed a man. Being a cop changed a man.

The phone hadn't rung all day. It wasn't going to ring now, not while he stood here in the bedroom looking at it. There wasn't any girl worth getting upset over. They were all alike, cheats, liars, whores. Even the pious ones were only waiting for a chance to cheat and lie and whore. He'd proved it, he'd proved it over and over again. There wasn't a decent one among them. There'd only been one decent one and she was dead. Brucie was dead.

Laurel couldn't disappoint him. He'd known what she was the first time he'd looked at her. Known he couldn't trust her, known she was a bitchy dame, cruel as her eyes and her taloned nails. Cruel as her cat body and her sullen tongue. Known he couldn't hurt her and she couldn't hurt him. Because neither of them gave a damn about anyone or anything except their own skins.

He was neither surprised nor disappointed that she hadn't turned up. He'd expected it. He wasn't going to fight with her when she came back; he was going to take her out and show her the town. Whatever she was, she was his. She was what he wanted.

He wouldn't sit around any longer, yenning at the phone. He turned on his heel, half-expecting its ring to summon him back, and he went into the kitchen. The bread was dry, the cheese hard, but he put together a sandwich. His throat closed to the tasteless stuff; he was hungry, he needed a well-cooked dinner, something good to eat, served in style. He threw away most of the sandwich; he couldn't stomach it.

It was after seven, way after, and she hadn't come, hadn't called. He wouldn't wait around any longer. He was hungry. He strode through the living room and out the front door into the blue court-yard. There were no lights in her desolate apartment; she wasn't there, she hadn't been there.

Slowly he went back into his apartment. At the door he sprinted; he thought he heard the phone, but the ringing was only in his mind, the apartment was quiet as dust. She wasn't coming. She hadn't come last night and she wasn't coming tonight. Only a fool, only a mawkish loon would hang around waiting for her to come.

This time he did quit the apartment, definitely, defiantly. Without leaving a note behind. The car was in the garage, he hadn't had it out for two days, time it was moving again. The garage doors opened in smooth silence. He backed out the car, left the motor running while he closed the doors after him. Just in case he didn't get back until late. Just in case his garage neighbors, not one of whom he'd laid eyes on, were the kind who'd wonder what a fellow was doing out so late.

He drove over to Wilshire, not knowing where he'd eat. The Savoy, on up to Rodeo, Romanoff's, the Tropics. He was after good food but he didn't want to waste a lot of money on it. Not until Laurel went with him to those spots. There was always the Derby or Sheetz—not for tonight. Neither could fill the hollow within him.

He passed Judson's, and the brilliant lights of the drive-in, Simon's drive-in, glittered ahead. He thought only for a moment, a brilliant gash of thought that splintered his indecision. Quickly he slewed the car into the parking space.

It was a dare, a magnificent dare. He and he alone of those outside the case knew the police were watching Simon's, knew the help was alert for the face of an average young fellow. It was the kind of dare he needed, to return here openly, to take the chance. Knowing they were watching for a man of a certain height, of a certain look under the garish lights of the circular counter. They weren't looking for a fellow in a black coupé, shadowed in the twilight of a car. The same fellow and they couldn't know.

Simon's was always busy; even at this early hour cars were circled close in to the car hops' pavement. There were a couple of holes and he pulled in boldly, cut his lights and waited for the hop. A middle-aged couple, a bleached blonde and a balding man, were in the car on his right. Two young fellows in the car on his left. He was certain neither was of the police. It would have amused him to smell cop. He was never more certain of himself than when he attacked. Cringing in corners alone was fearful. He was through with that stuff.

The girl who came with a menu and bright "Good evening" was young and pretty, as young as sixteen. Pert nose, blue eyes, long light brown hair under her ugly brown cap.

He smiled at her. "Hello," he said as if he'd been here often, as if he were one of the regulars. "I'm sure hungry tonight," he told her before she went to service another car. He wanted to be noticed, wanted her to remember him as something usual.

Dust. Lochner and his dust. Dix would have plenty of Simon's

Drive-in dust in his car. He lived in the neighborhood; he could eat
here often. Even the rich Mel Terriss ate here. Even Laurel Gray.

He wondered what name was on the identification card the girl
had left on the outside of the windshield. He wasn't foolish enough
to investigate. But he hoped it was Gene, the girl who'd recognized
Mildred from her picture in the paper. He wasn't the same fellow.

She returned with her pad and he ordered steak, french fries,
tomato-and-avocado salad, coffee. Cars pushed in and out on the lot.
The late diners left and the first show crowd moved in. Constant
motion, comings and goings, the countermen too busy to look up,
the girl hops too busy running from car to counter to car to know
whom they served. He was as safe as in a church.

The food was okay. He flicked the lights, ordered a chocolate
shake for dessert. He wasn't in any hurry. He'd give any and all of
them a chance to look him over. He wished the police were here to
look him over. But he didn't go into the lighted building. He liked a
chance but he was too smart for a risk.

No one paid any attention to him. When he drove out of the lot,
no car followed. As soon as he was away from the lights, depression
settled on him again. His hands itched to turn the wheel back toward the apartment. She might be there by now, waiting for him.
He set the car forward. Let her wait. He'd waited enough for her.

He didn't consciously plan to drive out Wilshire to the sea. But
the car was set on its course and the road led to the dark, wet horizon. The fog blew in at Fourteenth Street and he should have
turned back then. He didn't. He went on, through the opaque cloud,
until he had passed into the yellow spray that, following into a pool,
marked the Ocean Avenue intersection.

He knew then what he was going to do. He swung left and pulled
in at the curb by the Palisades park. Out of the fog-light glow, all
things became an indistinguishable blur in the night. He left the car.
The fog was cool and sweet as he drifted through it. Into the park,
the benches, the trees assuming shape as he neared them. He walked
to the stone balustrade. He could hear the boom of the breakers far
below, he could smell the sea in the fog. There was no visibility, save
for the yellow pools of fog light on the road below, and the
suggested skyline of the beach houses. There was a soft fog-hung silence, broken only by the thump of the water and the far-off cry of
the fog horn.

He drifted through the park on quiet feet, looking for the shape of
a living thing, of a woman. But he was alone, the living were

huddled behind closed doors, warming their fears of the night in the reassurance of lighted lamps. He came to the corner that jutted out over the cliffs, to the corner which was the beginning of the California Incline. He stood there quietly for a long time, waiting, remembering the night he had stood in the same place almost a month ago. The night he had pretended his hand was a plane swooping through the fog; the night he had seen the little brown girl. He waited without allowing himself to know why. He kept his hands dug into his pockets, and he leaned over the edge of the balustrade, his back to the avenue. But no bus came to shatter the silence and the fog. There were not even cars abroad, not at this particular time and place.

He tired pretending after a time and he began to walk, down the Incline, past the mid hump, pausing there to examine the beaten brush where, in the sunshine of the day, kids took the short cut down the hill to the beach. It wasn't a good cave, too small and shallow; it offered too little protection from the lights of cars traveling up or down on the Incline. Less protection from the beach road below. There were better places, places of seclusion, of quietness. He thought of the spiny trees in the eucalyptus grove, of the winding road that dipped down into the canyon.

And he walked on, down the Incline to the pool of fog light at the intersection. He didn't hesitate, crossing the deserted road to where the three houses huddled together in the night. He passed them slowly, as if reluctant to accept the closed gates, barring the intruders of the night. He went on to the open lot through which, in sunlight, the beach crowds passed over the broad sands to the sea beyond. He knew where he was going. He sludged through the sand until he stood in front of the third of the huddling houses. It was a tall peaked house, standing dark in the thick fog. He knew this was not the one, the brown girl had entered one of the two gates that stood side by side, the first or the second house.

He scraped through the damp sand to the center house, two stories, both pouring broad bands of light into the fog. There was warmth and gaiety within; through the downstairs window he could see young people gathered around the piano, their singing mocking the forces abroad on this cruel night. She was there, protected by happiness and song and the good. He was separated from her only by a sand yard and a dark fence, by a lighted window and by her protectors.

He stood there until he was trembling with pity and rage. Then he fled, but his flight was slow as flight in a dream, impeded by the deep sand and the blurring hands of the fog. He fled from the goodness of that home, and his hatred for Laurel throttled his brain. If she had come back to him, he would not be shut out, an outcast in a strange, cold world. He would have been safe in the bright warmth of her. He plowed on up the beach, to where there was no light, where the empty beach clubs loomed in the dark. Groping on, his feet chained in the sand, he stumbled and fell to one knee. He didn't get up again, instead he slumped down there on the slope of a dune, and he buried his head in his arms.

He was there for a long time. Lost in a world of swirling fog and crashing wave, a world empty of all but these things and his grief and the keening of the fog horn far at sea. Lost in a lonely place. And the red knots tightened in his brain.

He was there for a long time but there was no time in this sad, empty shell of the night. He was there for so long that he was startled when he heard something running; almost frightened when the small dark shape hurtled upon him. He realized quickly that it was a dog, a friendly terrier. He said, "Hello, fellow," and the dog nosed his hand. He wanted to cry. He said again, "Hello, fellow."

And then he heard footsteps coming over the sand, and he no longer wanted comfort of tears. Excitement charged him; where there was a dog there was a master . . . or a mistress. His hand slowly stroked the dog's curly head. "Nice fellow," he said.

The dog was nuzzling him when the girl came out of the fog. Dix looked up at her and he said, "Hello." She wasn't afraid. She said carelessly, "Hello."

He smiled. She didn't know that behind that smile lay his hatred of Laurel, hatred of Brub and Sylvia, of Mel Terriss, of old Fergus Steele, of everyone in the living world, of everyone but Brucie. And Brucie was dead.

VI

1

She hadn't returned. All night again she had been away. The apartment was empty and cold. He put out the lights before the gray fog of night became the gray fog of morning.

He did not dare sleep. Not until he had covered the mistake. The first mistake he had made. The mistake of sand. For sand was an evil and penetrating thing, no matter how much of it you brushed away, particles adhered as if cemented, particles leered where there had been none a moment before. If dust divulged a story, sand screamed its secrets.

It hadn't mattered before. When he could walk away from it, when he need answer to no one. Now uncertainty riddled him. Not knowing how much was in his mind alone, how much was real. It had been a mistake to look up Brub Nicolai, to embrace friendship. If he had remained lone, he wouldn't have had to worry about sand. It was good he was leaving for New York soon. He'd had enough of this neighborhood. He was getting nervous. It was nothing but nerves. Yet he'd take no chance on sand fouling him up.

He didn't smoke much while he waited. He was too physically exhausted even for that. He could have slept easily, slept long and deep, yet it was not hard to remain awake. His mind was alert. He knew exactly what he had to do and how he would do it. It was only necessary for morning to break. And for no one to come here until after what must be done, was done. He did not even want to see Laurel until he was again safe.

Safe! He was safe! He had no fear, no anxiety. He had never permitted fear to engage him. His annoyance at the occurrence of the word safe in his mind reawakened him and he saw it was morning.

He stretched his arms and his body in the first pale gray of light. He felt as if he'd been cramped in a foxhole all night.

He scrubbed his face and hands again, scrubbed his teeth. His suit looked as if he'd lain all night on the sand. That was all right too. He took off the trousers now, put on bathing trunks, and pulled his trousers back over them. The trunks weren't new, he'd bought them when he first came to California. He'd expected to spend quite a bit of the past summer on the beach. But he hadn't had a car and he couldn't take being packed into an ill-smelling bus or clanging street-car. His swimming had been done at the community pools in the various neighborhoods where he'd lived. He hadn't had a chance to enjoy the city until Mel's car became available for use.

It angered him that he'd wasted so much time, hanging around public swimming pools and cheap eating houses and neighborhood movies. If he'd known how to get started sooner, he'd be established by now, living high, clubbing with the right people, the people who had money and leisure. There was always room for a good fellow in those circles. For a moment he half-wished for Mel.

The day was lightening and it looked as if the break for which he'd dared not hope was coming his way. It looked as if the fog was clearing.

He fixed coffee at eight, drank two cups black. He was edgy now. No one ever came to the apartment in the morning, yet the very fact that he was up and about at this hour could draw a passerby. There was yet one more thing he must do before leaving. He was reluctant, not afraid, merely reluctant to bring in the morning paper. Yet for his plan, it must be done.

He didn't get a break on that. The delinquent who delivered the paper hadn't left it on the doorstep. From the living-room window he could see it, not even on the porch but on the walk beyond. He waited at the window until a man he had never seen before hurried out of the patio. An oaf on his way to work, just a little late.

It was the wrong hour for Dix to be up, the hour when the members of Virginibus Arms set out to their jobs. Twice again he started to the door and each time he was forced to wait until a clos-ing door and retreating footsteps were silenced. He finally opened his door a small wedge and watched from behind it. He could go put on his bathrobe, it would bolster his story of working all night, but he didn't want to waste the time. He was in a nervous frenzy to get away, to do what must be done before it was too late. And there was within him still the fear of Laurel returning. He could not face a scene with her this morning. He hadn't time.

He chose his moment to duck out for the paper. He didn't hurry the act. He made it a matter of everyday business, something a man did without deliberation. He was lucky; he saw no one. But he didn't know how many were watching behind their living-room windows, wondering what the young fellow in Mel Terriss' apartment was doing up so early. Well, he had the answer to that one too. He'd worked all night. Finished his book! That angle hadn't occurred to him before; it was a good one. He'd worked all night, finished his book. He'd been exhausted but too keyed up to sleep. He'd decided to go out to the beach, it wasn't too good a day but it looked as if it might clear and there was nothing more relaxing than lying in the sand, listening to the roll of the water. So he'd packed up the manuscript, mailed it on his way, and gone to the beach.

For Christ's sake, for whom was he plotting this minute alibi? He wasn't going to be questioned. He was nuts to think he had to account for his time, as if he were a reform-school kid on parole or a hen-pecked husband. He didn't have to do a damn thing but climb into bed, take a couple of pills and get the dreamless sleep he needed. Who cared what he'd done all night and today? Who in hell cared why he'd done it?

The answer was no one and he certainly wasn't boob enough to proffer an alibi to Brub. He wasn't reaching for trouble; there was only one reason for going to the beach, to put a day, today, on the sand which was in the car and imbedded in his shoes and tucked in unseen crevices of his suit. It wasn't that he had nerves; it was because he was smart, because he didn't miss bets.

He had been standing in the middle of the living room, holding the folded paper in his hands. One thing more to do and he did it. He opened the paper and looked at the front page.

Relief bathed him, relief flowed gently, excitingly, over him and through him. There was nothing on the front page of the paper, nothing. There was no way he could know what happened. He was off to the beach.

He flung down the paper on the couch, part of it spilled to the floor. Good. As if he'd been reading it. He started for the kitchen but he hesitated. In case he should run into anyone at the garage, he needed a prop. He pulled out a large manila envelope, gave it bulk with some magazines, sealed it and carried it under his arm. He needed nothing more. The apartment would tell no story to anyone who came in while he was away. Who the hell was going to come in? Not even Laurel hung around anymore.

He didn't need the prop. He saw no one on his way back to the garage. No one showed up while he was taking out the car. He was on his way. Not as early as he'd expected to start out but this was better. He wouldn't have to sit so long on the Goddamned cold beach.

He had to stop at a post office somewhere along the line. Better to avoid the Beverly one, too much danger of running into Brub. The police station was too near the post office in Beverly. There were Westwood and Santa Monica offices. He decided on the latter; he knew where it was located. There was the danger of hearing rumors, but what if he did? It would make no difference now.

He drove from Olympic to Sepulveda, then North to Wilshire, thus avoiding easily the Beverly business district. The road to Santa Monica was a new one by day, even on this dull day with a watery sun trying to break through the overcast. He didn't have to hurry, there was no hurry now, no hurry at all.

He maneuvered the car into the inner lane. There wasn't much traffic at this hour but he was careful. He couldn't afford an accident or a near accident, he couldn't chance attention from a cop. It annoyed him that such an idea should enter his consciousness, and in annoyance he swerved too quickly. It was luck that nothing went wrong on the swerve. Pure luck. But it meant that luck was with him again. He could stop jittering.

He pulled in at the post office. There were people wandering in and out, like extras in a movie. No one who knew him, no one who would notice him. He addressed the envelope in the car. He hesitated over the address, wanting to make sure that this mail fodder would never turn up again. He rejected sending it to himself either at Mel's, to General Delivery, or back to Princeton. If by any outside chance his mail should be checked, it wouldn't be good. Not in his own handwriting; not in disguised handwriting, too many experts; not from a Santa Monica address. He rejected addressing it to Uncle Fergus or to Mel Terriss for the same reasons. He hit on the solution without particular thought and wrote out a name, a fellow who'd died over Italy a long time ago. The name dribbled into his mind, a simple name, Tommy Johns. The address, General Delivery, Chicago, Illinois. No return address; it would end in the dead-letter department, where it wryly belonged.

He took it in to be weighed. The post office was fairly busy, he was third in line at one of the windows. No one knew him, no one noticed him. He paid for the stamps and took the envelope back to a desk as if to write on the return address. The desk he chose had no one at it; he affixed the stamp and mailed the envelope.

Nothing could have been more anonymous than the transaction yet the palms of his hands were wet when he returned to the car. He'd never had nerves like this; he couldn't understand it. Yet looking at it rationally, it could be understood. He'd been under a terrific strain; that, followed by no sleep, would make anyone jumpy. Before he'd always been able to sleep long and heavily; he'd never had to go through stunts like this. He damned the circumstances which necessitated this stunt.

He was careful to avoid the California Incline approach to the beach; he was taking no chances on getting mixed up with a police inquiry. He drove on down Ocean Front and followed the winding canyon way to the beach. He wasn't the only one who had come for a day on the sands. There were a fair dozen cars parked in the enclosure by State Beach. He parked his own car and went down the concrete steps to the sand.

The beach wasn't crowded. There were a couple of fellows and girls, sweaters over their bathing suits, backed against the concrete wall. They were playing cards, a portable radio giving out music. There was a heavyset man and his scrawny wife farther down the sands. A scattering of young men, singly and together, beach athletes. Dix chose a place against the wall on the other side of the lifeguard station. He took off his coat, folded it, laid it on the sand. He took off his trousers, folded them on top of the coat. He kept his shirt on, the off-shore wind was chill under the streaked sky. He took off his socks and shoes, set them aside, and stretched out, his head on his folded suit. The ocean was a hushed sound, the sun was beginning to break through, even faint strips of blue were appearing in the sky. He closed his eyes and he slept.

On waking he was amazed. He had evidently dropped into the pit of sleep as soon as he lay down for he had no memory past that moment. Luck was with him that he hadn't slept too long, it was only a little past three. Discomfort had evidently aroused him for the afternoon had turned chill, the sky was completely grayed again. Dix shook out his clothes and put them on, their wrinkles, their sand were legitimate now. The same was true of his shoes and socks. He could take all these clothes to the cleaners not caring who might snoop. He could go home, have a warm shower, clean things, sleep in a comfortable bed.

First he must make certain that he was remembered. He had planned that last night. He drove the car into the gas station across, said to the dark-haired owner, "Fill her up, will you?" and as if in afterthought, said, "If you don't mind I'll phone while you're filling her." The gas station operator might not remember him, but he could be reminded by the call. He called his own number; when there was no answer, his coins were returned.

The car was ready; Dix drove away. He would have liked to stop at the hamburger stand for food and coffee, particularly coffee. He was chilled from his sleep on the cold sand. But he didn't want to chance running into Sylvia or even Brub; this was their corner. He drove on, winding up through the canyon to San Vicente. There were no eating places on this boulevard, nor were there any drive-ins until he reached Beverly. He had no intention of dropping into Simon's at this odd hour, no intention of forcing his luck. Thinking about food had made him ravenous, yet he could not face going into a restaurant until he'd changed clothes. He wouldn't pass unnoticed at any place in Beverly in his doubly wrinkled suit. By now everyone would be babbling about the latest murder, anything out of line might be suspicious. Anything sandy would be suspicious to the yokels.

He drove on back to the apartment. He didn't want to put the car away; he'd be going out again as soon as he was clean. It was double work putting up the car, yet it meant getting into the apartment without walking openly through the patio. He preferred entering without being observed.

Reviling the need of precautions, he went through the routine. Brake the car in front of the garage, get out of the car, open the garage doors, get in the car, loosen the brake, run the car into the garage, get out of the car, close the garage doors. Doggedly he walked through the alley to the rear door of his apartment. He slowed his walk as he approached. He wasn't unobserved. A yahoo was trimming the hedge just beyond his doors. A little measly Mexican fellow in faded overalls, a battered hat bending his ears, a mustache drooping over his mouth. The shears were bigger than the man. Clip, clip, clip, clip, the shears chopped with Dix's approaching footsteps. The fellow looked up as Dix reached his back door. "'Allo," he said brightly.

Dix didn't say hello, he nodded only, and he went into his apartment. He wouldn't have been surprised to find something wrong, he'd been thrown that much off beat by the unexpected gardener. But the apartment was unchanged. The slattern had been in and cleaned, that was all. The coffeepot and cup were clean, the newspaper in the living room was folded on the table. The ashtrays in the bedroom had been emptied, the bed he hadn't slept in was smoothed. Everything was okay.

He restrained himself from looking out to see if the evening paper had come; he knew it was too early. The paper didn't arrive until past five o'clock. He peeled off his clothes, added them to the bundle on the closet floor and he took a long and hot shower. He shaved without hearing the electricity. He was beginning to feel great. While he dressed, dressed well in a dark tweed, a white sweater under his jacket, he wondered if Laurel would return tonight. Surely she would. She'd been away two nights now. He hoped she would come tonight; he wasn't angry with her. She had a good reason for her absence. He would accept her reason without recriminations. He'd accept anything if she'd just show up, join him for a big feed, come home with him after it.

He decided he might as well wait an hour to see if she'd come. Postponing food had taken the edge off his appetite. He poured a shot of rye, drank it straight. Not that he had need of it, he felt swell. It was a fillip to top his good spirits.

He switched on the radio, earlier in the day he hadn't thought of that news source. He rolled the stations but there was nothing but music and kids' adventure yarns; he was between news reports. He turned off the nervous sounds, he preferred the quietness of the apartment.

It was possible the paper had come early. He needed to know what had happened, not have it sprung on him. He opened the door, stepped out and looked on the porch and walk. No paper. But the Virginibus Arms had suddenly gone in for gardening in a big way. There was another peasant out here in front, doing something to the flower beds. This one was younger, a tall, skinny character, but his face was just as droopy as the little fellow in back. He didn't say hello; he looked at Dix and returned his attention to his spadework.

Dix went back into the living room. If she hadn't shown up by six, he'd go on to dinner. He wouldn't wait around tonight. She definitely must have gone out of town on a job. Probably afraid he'd raise a fuss if she mentioned it in advance. He was pretty sure she'd show up tonight and he wasn't surprised at all when the doorbell rang. It didn't occur to him to wonder why she'd ring instead of walking in until he was opening the door. And in that split second he was amused by it; she was returning humbly, not on her high horse.

Thus he opened the door and faced Brub Nicolai across the threshold.

2

BRUB SAID, "HELLO, DIX." HE WASN'T SMILING; HE WAS STANDING there, a stocky, foreboding figure.

The cold breath of danger whistled into the inmost crannies of Dix's spirit. He answered mechanically, "Hello."

There was then a moment when neither man spoke, when they remained unmoving, looking each into the other's face. A moment when each knew the other for what he was, the hunter and the hunted.

It was broken when they spoke together, Brub asking, "Aren't you going to ask me in?" and Dix crying, "For Pete's sake, what are you standing out there for? Come on in."

They could feign ignorance of each other's identity after that. They could pretend they were two old pals getting together for a drink. Brub rolled in on his stocky legs, dropped down on the couch and sailed his hat toward a chair. "I could use a drink."

"Good idea. What'll it be?"

"Scotch. Soda if it's handy."

"There ought to be some around." He stood the Scotch and rye bottles on the small bar, found a soda and opened it. "I'll get some ice."

Brub's voice followed him to the kitchen. "You aren't the two-fisted grogger you used to be, are you? Imagine having two kinds of liquor at your place."

Dix pulled out the ice tray, pressed up the cubes. "You're not such a souse yourself since you grew up, are you, chum?"

But it was hollow interchange. It died before he had the drinks mixed. He tried again, lifting his own highball. "To our youth," he toasted. "Those careless rapture days seem kind of far away, don't they?"

"Like they were of another world," Brub said gravely.

Again silence moved in on them. In the void, he heard the faint plop of the evening paper flung at his door. He couldn't go for it now. Not until he knew why Brub had come. He could even hear far away, or thought he could, the clip-clip of the gardener's shears.

He couldn't take the emptiness which should be filled with man talk. He asked, "What's the trouble, Brub? You look beat."

"You should ask. I am beat."

"I'm asking." He didn't know a thing. He hadn't seen the paper, hadn't heard a radio. He threw a curve, "Is it Sylvia?"

Brub's eyebrows slanted quickly. "What about Sylvia?"

Dix said apologetically, "I thought the last time I was at your place that maybe you were having a little trouble. There was sort of a strained feeling——"

Brub had started to laugh as Dix spoke. It was a real laugh, a laugh at something funny. When Dix broke off, Brub said, "You couldn't be farther off the beam. Sylvia is—she's Sylvia." He didn't have to say anymore. The whole was in Brub's face and on his tongue and in his heart.

Dix murmured, "That's good." He took another drink from his glass. "What is it then? What's the trouble?"

"You mean you don't know what's happened?"

Dix said with mock exasperation, "I mean I don't know from nothing. I've been out at the beach all day——"

He had only to say "beach" and Brub tightened. He had said it deliberately. He went right on, "I just got in about an hour ago, cleaned up, had a quick one and settled down to wait for Laurel." He glanced at his watch. "I hope she won't be too long tonight. I'm starved."

"You were at the beach all day." Brub said it with wonder, almost with awe.

It was what Dix wanted. He relaxed in his chair, comfortable in his well-being, enjoying his drink. "Yes, I'd worked all night, finished my book," he threw in with modest pride. "I was worn to a pulp but I was too high to sleep so I decided to go out to the beach. Looked as if it might clear—what's happened to the California sunshine? I'm sick of this gray stuff—but it didn't." He took another drink, he wasn't talking too fast or too emphatically. He was rambling like a man enjoying the cocktail hour. No alibi, just discussion of the day. "It did relax me, though, enough that I took a nap out there. Wonderful what the briny will do for a man, even on a day like today. I feel like a million dollars tonight." It was exciting to sit there behind the pleasant mask and watch the suspicion simmer out of the hunter.

Brub exclaimed, "Finished the book! That's great. Going to let Sylvia and me have a look at it?" He was trying to reorient his thinking while he made expected talk.

Dix shook a rueful head. "I've already shipped it East. This morning. I'll send you an autographed copy when and if it's published. I promised you one for your help, didn't I?"

"Help?" Brub tried to remember.

"Sure. About tire tracks, and that day you let me go up the canyon with you. I appreciated that."

Brub remembered. Remembered more. Depression settled heavily on him again.

"Now, what's your trouble?" Dix demanded. "Here, let me fix you another." He took Brub's glass. His own wasn't half empty. He was watching it. With no food and his already high spirits, he didn't need alcohol. He talked while he poured a fairly stiff one. "Tell me what's weighting your strong shoulders." He carried the drink to Brub. "Try this."

"Thanks." Brub looked up at him. "You haven't seen the papers?"

He went back over to the easy chair. "I had a quick look at *The Times* this morning——" He broke off, getting it out of Brub's eyes. "Brub—you don't mean——"

Brub nodded heavily. There wasn't an atom of suspicion left in him. If there ever had been. "Yes. Another one."

Dix let out his breath. He exclaimed softly, in shocked disbelief, "God!"

Brub kept on nodding his head.

"When—where—was it . . . ?" Dix stammered.

"It was," Brub said grimly. "The same thing."

"The strangler," Dix murmured. He waited for Brub to go on with the story. It wasn't a time for questions, only for shocked silence. Brub would talk; he was too tightly crammed with it to keep from talking. He had to have the release of words.

"It was last night," Brub began. He was having a hard time getting started. He wasn't a cop at all, he was a man all choked up, swallowing the tears in his throat. "Last night or sometime early this morning." His voice broke. "It was Betsy Banning. . . ."

Dix let the horror mount in his face. "Bets . . . the little . . . the girl who looked . . . like Brucie . . ." He didn't have to control his voice.

Anger, the hard iron of anger, clanged in Brub. "I'd kill him with my bare hands if I could lay them on him."

Had Brub come to kill? On ungrounded, fathomless suspicion?

Dix waited for him to go on. Brub was steady now, steadied by the iron anger that was holding him rigid. "Wiletta Bohnen and Paul Chaney found her."

Wiletta Bohnen and Paul Chaney were top picture stars, Bohnen was Mrs. Chaney. The publicity on this one would be a feast to the peasants who got their thrills through the newspapers.

"They walk their poodles on the beach every morning at eight o'clock. Walk from their house, it's the old Fairbanks place, up to the pier and back." Brub took a swallow from his glass. "They didn't see her on the way up. They had their dogs on leash and they cut across slantwise several houses to the water. But the dogs were running free on the way back. . . . The dogs found her. Almost in front of the Fairbanks house, just a little above the high-tide mark."

It was hard for Brub to talk. He had to stop and swallow more than once.

Dix made his own voice husky. "That's—that's all you know?"

"We know she went out a little after eleven," Brub said angrily. "She had friends there earlier, college friends of hers . . . the boy she was going to marry. She always took her dog out for a run at night, no matter what time it was. Usually it was earlier. She wasn't afraid —she was like Sylvia, the ocean was always something soft, something good. Her father——" Brub swallowed again. "Her father sometimes worried—especially these last few months—but she wasn't afraid." There were angry tears in Brub's eyes. "And she had her dog."

"The dog—"

Brub said jerkily, without intonation, "We found him. Buried in the sand. Dead . . . strangled."

"Poor fellow," Dix said from his heart.

"One thing," Brub spurted with hard anger, "nothing had happened to her." Then he laughed, a short, grating laugh. "Nothing but death." He said with irony, using that weapon to combat tears, "It's some comfort to her father and the boy—nothing happened to her."

"Was it the same man?" Dix asked dubiously.

"Who else?" Brub demanded belligerently. "It's been just about a month. Every month. Every damn stinking month——" He wiped the back of his hand across his eyes without shame. Then he picked up his glass and drank a third of its contents.

Dix looked at him with sorrow. "God!" he repeated. It was terrific, the most terrific show of all. With Brub here weeping and flailing impotent anger at an unknown, a killer who killed and went quietly away into the night. And Brub would never know.

Dix asked, "No clues?" as if he were certain this defeat, too, followed the pattern.

"On the sand?" Brub snorted. "No, no clues. No buttons, no fingerprints, no cigarette stubs, no match folders, not even a calling card."

Dix rubbed his cheek. It was apology for a foolish question.

"Mind if I use your phone?" Brub asked abruptly.

"Go right ahead. In the bedroom. Can I fix you another——"

"No, I've got to get on downtown to headquarters." Brub left the couch and went into the bedroom. He didn't close the door. He wasn't going in to snoop; a lot of good it would do him to snoop.

Dix was quiet, deliberately listening to the call.

"Sylvia?"

Dix relaxed but he listened.

"I'm calling from Dix Steele's. . . . No, Sylvia! No, I can't come home yet, I have to go down to headquarters. . . . I dropped in on Dix for a drink and a few minutes' rest from . . . Nothing . . . No . . . Absolutely nothing . . . You'll stay there until I come for you? . . . Be sure to wait for me. . . . Good-bye, darling. Good-bye."

Dix didn't pretend he hadn't heard the call. Brub knew that every word was audible in a small apartment. Brub didn't care; he'd left the door open. Dix asked, "Sylvia frightened?"

"I am," Brub said. He walked over and picked up his hat. "She's not staying alone at night until we catch the murderer."

"I don't blame you," Dix agreed. "Can't I give you a quick one before you leave?"

"No, I'd better not." He seemed reluctant to go, to face the blank wall again. There would be ants scurrying around the wall, with plaster casts and fingerprint powder and chemical test tubes, but it wouldn't change the blankness of the wall.

"Come again, Brub." Dix said it with true urgency. "Come anytime. Anything I can do to help you out——"

"Thanks." He put out his hand, clasped Dix's. "Thanks. You've helped me over a rough spot, fellow. And I'm not kidding."

Dix smiled. The inner smile didn't show, the outer one was a little embarrassed. The way a man is embarrassed at any show of emotion from a friend. "The bottles aren't empty. Come back."

"Oke." At the door, Brub hesitated. "Leaving town soon?"

Dix was surprised at the question. As much as if it had been a police warning. He remembered, then, and he laughed easily. "Now that the book's done? Oh, I'll be around a couple of more weeks at least. Maybe longer. Depends on Laurel's plans."

From the doorstep he watched Brub start away. Watched Brub stoop on the walk and a splinter of doubt again chilled him. But Brub turned back to him at once. "Here's your paper," he said.

He didn't want the paper. He didn't want to look at it. The moment it was opened in his hands, there again in the solitude of his living room, he was sickened. He'd never felt this way before. He hadn't felt this way when Brub was talking about it. Actually he hadn't thought then, he'd been too busy playing the required part.

He didn't want to read about the girl and her dog, he didn't want to look at the smile on her clean-looking, vital face. Even with the same morbid curiosity of the peasants tickling him, he didn't want to read about it. He put the paper down with trembling hands.

He hadn't needed a drink for a long time, not the way he needed it now. He'd had enough. Another might be too much, might be the edge to start him on a binge. He didn't dare go on a binge. He didn't dare anything other than complete alertness in all of his senses.

What he needed was dinner, a big, hearty, tasty dinner. Steak and french fries and asparagus and a huge fresh green salad, then a smoke and coffee and something special for dessert, strawberry tart or a fancy pastry and more coffee.

Hunger ached in him. If only Laurel were here. He knew damn well she wasn't coming; he'd known it all along but he'd been kidding himself. Teasing himself with hope. Wherever she was, whatever guy she'd gone off with, she didn't think enough of Dix even to let him know. She'd never cared for him; she'd made him a convenience while Lover Boy was tied up with some kind of ropes. Once Mr. Big was loose, she didn't even say good-bye. The old couplet taunted him . . . *she didn't even say she was leavin'* . . . and he was furious at its popping into his head. The situation wasn't funny. It hurt. It would hurt if he weren't angry.

Well, he wasn't hanging around any longer waiting for Laurel. He was going to eat. He went fast, strode out the back door, down the alley to the garage. It was annoying to have to go through the whole stupid routine again. He shouldn't have put the car up. Tonight he wouldn't. If the police wanted to pry into the dust he'd make it easy for them. The car would be left at the curb.

There was a young fellow peering into the works of a Chevy in the alley. He didn't turn around to look at Dix. Or to say hello. Dix jutted his car out and drove away fast. He didn't bother to close the garage doors. He hesitated at the Derby but he wanted something better tonight. Something as good as the Savoy. He could afford it. He had two hundred and fifty bucks, damn near, and he was hungry.

This was the kind of a place in which to dine. These were the kind of people a man wanted to be part of. People who knew the man who seated you, who spoke to him by name. This was the way he was going to live someday. Nothing but the best. No worry about money. Or about nosy cops.

He ordered a rich meal, and he ate it leisurely, appreciating every well-cheffed bite. He lingered as long as he possibly could, he didn't want to leave this haven. Eventually there was nothing to do but go out again into the thin cold night. The fog had dissipated but there were no stars in the covered sky. And now? Not back to the unutterable loneliness of the apartment. There was always a movie. He drove down Wilshire slowly; he'd seen the Beverly, he parked around the corner from Warner's. He didn't care what the picture was; it was a place to pass time.

There was a double bill. A mild comedy; a tear-jerking problem story. Neither was absorbing, he could scarcely stay awake during the tear-jerker. But the time was passed; it was midnight when he came out of the theater. There was nowhere else to go now, the streets of Beverly were quiet as the streets of a nine o'clock town. Nowhere but back to the apartment.

He dreaded sleep, sleep and dreams. If only she would come back, if only she'd take him and comfort him as she had on that other night. He didn't tell himself a tall tale now, that she might be waiting for him, in all her beauty and warmth. He went into the soda fountain next to the theater. It was closing, but he didn't care. He gathered a handful of magazines from the stand, the only kind of magazines there, movie stuff, crime stuff. Anything to keep his mind serviced until he was forced into sleep.

He didn't put the car up. It didn't matter who saw him coming in. And he wasn't going out again. If he changed his mind and did want to go out again, it was nobody's business.

He came to a sudden stop just inside the patio. It wasn't lone and desolate, a figment of a blue dream. Someone was there. A dull red circlet was burning in the shadows, back by the rear apartments. For a moment he thought it might be Laurel, but in the silence he heard the flat paced steps of a man, an unknown man.

Dix covered his pause, stooping down as if he'd dropped something on the ground. Something small that had fallen without sound. Feeling for it until he found it, perhaps his latchkey or a packet of matches. Without another glance to the red circlet, he went to his own place, entered and shut the door, shut away the menace that might lie in the night. He was breathing heavily.

It was ridiculous to have let the presence of a man affect him simply because there had not before been a man waiting in the shadows. How did he know but that this man had a last cigarette nightly in the patio before turning in? How could he know? He, Dix, always came the back way when he was late. The man might be a musician just home from work, pumping the stale air out of his lungs before bed. Maybe it wasn't a guy who walked nightly, maybe he was locked out tonight and waiting for his wife to get home. Or it could be a guest, somebody's uncle or cousin, who beat the family home. Dix could think up a thousand and one explanations. Any of them good. Any of them stamped with logic. Any except the first one that had hit him, that for some unfathomable reason the man had been put there to find out what time Dix Steele came in. As if anyone would care.

He was all right now. He dropped the magazines on the couch and made for the bar. He'd have a nightcap, a small one before turning in. He was slightly chilled; there was a definite hint of autumn, if only the mildness of California autumn, in the air tonight.

The guy might be, he smiled, a private dick. Somebody's ex might have put him there to see how the lady was behaving. Maybe Dix wasn't the only one wondering where Laurel was keeping herself. There was something funny about the divorce relationship between Laurel and her ex; she was so damn careful to keep men out of her apartment.

He tossed off the drink, gathered up the magazines, and put out the lights in the living room. He needn't worry about the man outside, it wasn't someone interested in—He heard the footsteps then, the flat, muffled footsteps. They were coming this way. Panic squeezed him. Unhurried, inexorable, the footsteps were bringing the man up the portal to Dix's door. Without sound, Dix quickly crossed to the window, flattening himself against the long drape. He could see out; the man could not see Dix even if he stopped and peered into the room.

Dix stood, not breathing, not having breath. Listening, seeing the shadow, the approach of the red dot, the shape of the man himself, a dumpy, shapeless shape topped by a shapeless hat. The man did not pause. He walked past Dix's door and out into the patio, crossed to the opposite portal and started again to the rear.

Dix leaned weakly against the curtain. Within his head his thoughts sounded shrill, falsetto. No one cared what he did. No one cared. No one cared. . . .

He left the window, walked the silent blue-dark room to his bedroom. He didn't put on the lights, he lay on the bed with the darkness broken only by the red dot of his own cigarette. No one cared; Laurel didn't care. She'd gone off without saying good-bye. She'd known, known that night that it was their farewell. He'd almost known it himself—he'd even questioned her. And she'd denied. She'd lied in his face, lied in his arms. . . .

He hated her. She was a cheat and a liar and a whore, and he hated her while tears rolled from his eyes down his cheeks to salt his mouth. No one cared, no one had ever cared. Only Brucie. Brucie who had gone away leaving him alone, alone forever, for all his life.

He ground out the cigarette. It wasn't ended with Laurel. He didn't end things that way. She'd find that out. She'd come back; she had to come back. She wouldn't walk off and leave everything in her apartment, her clothes would be important to her if nothing else was. If no person was. When she came back, he'd be waiting. He'd end it his way, the only way that meant a thing was finished.

3

STARTLED OUT OF SLEEP, HE SNATCHED UP THE PHONE, WITH THE WILD lurch of hope that it was she. The humming of dial tone answered his shout, "Hello." And the long sound of the buzzer brought him fully awake, it was the door, not the phone, which had awakened him.

The door at nine in the morning, with dreams heavy in his mouth and smarting in his eyes. Sometime in the night he had undressed, sometime he had fallen into frightful sleep.

He pushed out of bed. Taking his time. Knowing that nothing of meaning to him could be leaning on the door buzzer at this morning hour. Knowing he did not want to answer the summons. Yet knowing that he must. It might be a wire from her. It might be Brub.

He grumbled, "Keep your shirt on," while he roped the belt of the silken paisley robe about him, slid his feet into the morocco leather scuffs. He plodded into the living room, a man disturbed at his rightful slumbers, making no pretense at a smile as he flung open the front door.

There were two men waiting outside; he had never seen either of them before. One was a portly man in a brown suit, a man with a heavy inexpressive face and spaniel-brown eyes. The other was a young fellow in gray, a neat-looking young fellow with bright gray eyes. The portly man wore a shapeless gray hat with a faded hatband; the young fellow wore a well-shaped brown fedora. It wasn't that each hat belonged to the opposite suit; it was that they wore hats at all. Men didn't wear hats in Beverly Hills. These men were strangers, strangers with a purpose.

The younger said, "We're looking for Mel Terriss."

Dix didn't say anything. He didn't believe what he heard for the moment, it was a shock but it was a dull shock. Whatever he had been expecting, it wasn't this. After a moment he managed to say, "He isn't here."

"This is his place, isn't it?"

"Yes," Dix said. "But he isn't here."

The young fellow looked a little disappointed or maybe he was perplexed. He seemed to be trying to figure it out. He said finally, "Mind if we come in? I'm Harley Springer." He gestured to his partner. "And Joe Yates."

Dix didn't want them in. He didn't want to talk about Mel Terriss at any time, certainly not now before his eyes were open, before his brain was quick. But there was nothing he could do outside of shutting the door on Harley Springer's foot. The young fellow had it in the door.

Dix said, "Yes, come on in. I'm Dix Steele."

"Looks like we got you out of bed," the big Yates commented. He had a snicker in the corner of his mouth.

"You did," Dix agreed. He wasn't going to get angry at this pair. Not until he found out why they'd come to him. And he wondered if Laurel had set them on it. Laurel with her stubborn determination to get Mel's address. He didn't believe Mel owed her any seven hundred. She'd put that in hoping Dix would think it was important enough to give out with the address. Thinking money would tempt him.

He led the way into the living room. A neat living room, he hadn't hung around it last night. "Sit down," he said. There were no cigarettes in his pocket, none on the tables. He had to have a cigarette. A drink would help, too, but he couldn't take a drink at this hour. It wouldn't be a good tale for them to carry back to whoever had sent them. A cigarette was essential.

He said, "Excuse me while I get my cigarettes, will you?" He went quickly into the bedroom, gathered up a pack and his lighter, returned before the men could have had time to walk over to the desk. They were still on the couch, the younger man with his leg crossed one way, the big fellow with his crossed the other. They hadn't moved, only to light cigarettes of their own. He took the chair across from them. He was as much at ease as a man could be, dragged out of bed, entertaining a couple of strangers while he was wrapped in a bathrobe. Entertaining without knowing why. But he smiled at them. "What can I do for you?"

The young one, Harley Springer, took off his hat. As if he should have remembered to do it before. As if he were a cop, someone from the D.A.'s office, not used to taking off his hat when he invaded a man's privacy. He repeated then his first remark, "We're looking for Mel Terriss."

"And he isn't here," Dix smiled.

"Where is he?" Yates flipped.

The young Springer gave Yates a look, a look that meant: Shut up, let me handle this. A look that meant: You're an oaf and this guy's a gent, let a gent handle it.

Dix was actually beginning to feel at ease. He didn't have to worry about being on his toes with Springer and Yates. They weren't that well coordinated; it wasn't like being with Lochner and Brub. He answered Yates as if Yates weren't oafish. "He's in Rio," he told him. "He went down there on some big job. I subleased from him before he left."

The two exchanged a look. Dix waited. Let them explain it. Make them do the talking. He'd changed his mind about these two being cops, more like from a collection agency, trying to get on Mel's trail over those unpaid accounts.

"You're sure he went to Rio?" Springer frowned.

Dix laughed. "Well, I didn't fly him down and get him settled. But he told me he was going there. I took his word for it. I don't know why he should have told me that if it weren't true." He laughed again. It was his turn now. Time for their explanation. He stopped laughing. "Are you friends of his?" he demanded.

"Nah," Yates said.

Springer gave his partner another shut-up look. He said, "We're from Anson, Bergman and Gorgonzola. Lawyers. Our firm handles Mel Terriss' trust."

It was time to walk softly. He didn't know about trusts.

Springer continued, "We haven't heard from Mel Terriss since July." Evidently it was unusual. The way that Springer said it. "He hasn't even been around for his check."

"He didn't communicate with you from Rio?" Dix showed surprise.

"No. We had no idea he'd gone to Rio until recently. Mr. Anson and Mr. Bergman heard something about it."

Or Mr. Gorgonzola. From an alley cat who'd blabbed, who for some reason wanted to get in touch with Mel Terriss. Bad enough to ask her lawyer about him. Her lawyer and Mel's lawyer. There wouldn't be two Gorgonzolas prominent in legal circles.

"It's strange he didn't communicate with Mr. Anson before leaving. Or since. Particularly since it was Mr. Anson who had so often urged him to go there."

Yates said, "Anson thought he might straighten up if he got out of town."

Harley Springer gave a light sigh.

Yates went on doggedly, "Mel's been gassing about getting a job in Rio long as I can remember. Every time he was extra loopy. He never had no intention of going to work."

Springer cut in quickly, "Do you know when he left?"

"He told me I could move in the first of August. He'd be gone before then."

"You don't know by any chance if he went by boat or plane?"

"I don't," Dix smiled slightly. They were going to check passenger lists. "He did say something about going by freighter, a sea voyage to get in trim." He shrugged, widened his smile. "I can't say I believed him. He was too fond of comfort for such rigors." Let them try to check all the freighters that steamed out from the California ports. They'd get nowhere.

He'd had enough of this. He wanted his coffee. He wanted peace. He prodded them, "I'm sorry I can't help you any more than this, gentlemen." He rose. "I didn't know Terriss particularly well. He'd hardly confide his plans to me. I'm a tenant, that's all."

Yates was going to stick his big foot into it again. There was a malicious look in his soulful brown eyes. "The trust pays Mel's rent in advance. To keep him off the street. How'd you arrange to pay him?"

Even Springer's embarrassment didn't quiet the rage in Dix. He smiled wryly as if it were none of Yates' business to so question a gentleman, but being asked, he would reply. "I gave him a check for a year's rent, Mr. Yates. He said he intended to be away at least that long." This time he was polite but firm. "If that is all——"

He waited for them to rise. Springer made apology. "I'm sorry to have had to bother you, Mr. Steele. You understand it's a job—when Mr. Anson——"

"Or Mr. Bergman or Mr. Gorgonzola," Dix smiled wholeheartedly. "I understand." He didn't include Yates in his understanding. He moved the two men to the door, opened it. Yates went on outside. Springer stopped on the doorstep. "Thanks for your help."

"Little enough," Dix said.

Springer had another question. He'd been holding it, now he sprang it. "What about his mail?"

It came too fast for preparation. But Dix could think fast. He could always think fast in a pinch. "I suppose some has been coming," he said as if it had never occurred to him. "I'll ask my secretary ——" He laughed, "She keeps everything so efficiently I wouldn't know where to look. I'll tell you, leave your address and I'll have her forward it." He accepted the card from Springer, said good-bye. Yates was already out in the patio, watching the gardener plow up geraniums.

Dix shut the door with a thud. He crushed the card in his fist. Damn snoops. Why should they or anyone care what had happened to Mel Terriss? Stupid, sodden, alcoholic Mel. The world was better off without Mel Terrisses in it. Why should Laurel care? Unless she were trying to get Dix into trouble.

Let them prove, let them try to prove he didn't have a secretary. He'd go through the bills and the ads. Send the harmless ones, the ones without purchases after July. He shouldn't have used the charge accounts, but it was an easy way to do it. So easy.

It was Mel, fat-headed Mel, who was going to run him out of California. Before he was ready to go. Before Laurel came back. He'd be damned if he would. He'd settle with Laurel before he left. They couldn't hang a man for using a friend's charge accounts. Particularly if the friend had told him to make use of them. No one could prove Mel hadn't told him that.

He wanted a drink more than ever; he was so angry he was rigid. Again he didn't dare. At least not until lunch time. It was legitimate then, not before, unless you were a confirmed alcoholic like your friend, Mel.

He should have asked them about another disappearing client. He should have said, By the by, what's happened to your client, Laurel Gray? She's missing, too, didn't you know? Maybe she'd gone to join Mel.

His face darkened with rage. He flung the crumpled card into the basket. He wasn't going to sit around and be questioned by any lugs who happened by. He'd dress and get out of here. Quick.

But the phone stopped him. The silent phone by his bed. He sat down and he dialed Laurel's number. The sound of ringing went on and on until he hung up. She hadn't sneaked back in. There was an idea nagging at the back of his mind; it had been there last night; it was there again now. It had to be faced. Laurel could have moved out of the Virginibus Arms.

He didn't dare go to the manageress' apartment and ask. The old bag might start thinking up her questions about Mel. He'd had enough of Mel today. He could go up to Laurel's apartment; that he would dare. But it was pointless; she wasn't at home. She'd answer the phone if she were; she'd be afraid not to, afraid it might be a business call. He picked up the phone book, then laid it down. He wouldn't phone the manager from here. Not and chance having the call traced. Go out to a booth, disguise his voice. Not that the manager would know it, but someone might be around who did.

He was thinking as if it were Laurel the lawyer's narks were asking about. As if it were Laurel's life the cops were prying into. He could ask anything he wanted about Laurel. It was perfectly safe. Yet he didn't pick up the phone.

He was just starting to the shower when the doorbell buzzed again. His fists clenched. It couldn't be those two back again. It couldn't be anything important. Yet he must answer. Slowly he returned to the living room.

There was only one man on the doorstep this time. And he didn't look like he'd come from the cops or the lawyers. He was hatless, coatless, an ordinary guy in pants and shirt. "I'm from the telephone company," he stated.

Dix had the door half closed as he spoke, "You have the wrong apartment. There's nothing wrong with my phone."

"Yeah?" The man talked fast before the door was closed. "There's something wrong with the lines running into these apartments. We got orders to check."

"Come in," Dix said wearily. "The phone's in the bedroom." He led the way, pointed it out. "There."

The fellow had a black satchel, like a plumber's satchel. He was going to rasp and ring bells and yell to Joe somewhere on the line. Dix said, "Listen, I'm late. If you don't mind, I'll start getting dressed."

"Sure, go ahead," the man said comfortably. He was already taking the phone apart.

Dix went into the bathroom, closed the door and locked it. With the shower running he didn't have to listen to the racket. When he'd finished bathing and shaving, he opened the door. The man was just repacking wire in his little black bag.

"Find any bugs?" Dix asked.

"Not here. Thanks. Shall I let myself out?"

"Go ahead."

Dix lit a cigarette. Maybe there'd been something wrong with his phone. Maybe Laurel had been trying every night to get in touch. It was fixed now, if that were it. That was no longer an excuse.

He heard the front door close and at the same time he heard the clip-clip of the gardener outside the window. If he didn't get out of here, his head would split. He hadn't noticed the weather, he'd had too much on his mind. It was still gray, but there were splits of blue in it. Clearing. He put on the same tweeds he'd worn last night. He didn't know where he was going but he'd be dressed for no matter what. He knew the first stop, the cleaners. With the sandy gabardines, and the sweaty clothes in which he'd slept two nights ago, two hundred nights ago. He rolled the bundle of clothes under his arm, left by the back door. The goofy, mustached gardener offered his daily bright saying, "'Allo."

Dix acknowledged it with a nod, striding on down the alley to the garage. The garage doors were closed. He swung them open. The car wasn't there. It was a shock. And then he remembered; he hadn't put it up last night. He hadn't even closed the garage. He began to tremble. With sick anger, sick, frustrated anger. He couldn't pass the gardener again. He'd smash the man's stupid face to a pulp if he heard, "'Allo."

He walked out of the alley, all the way around the long block to the walk in front of the apartment. The car was where he'd left it. He got in, threw the clothes on the floor and drove rapidly away. He drove too fast to the cleaners on Olympic. He wasn't picked up. The cops were all out at the beach or hanging around the drive-in. He ought to go up there and eat, see how many he could spot. That would be a laugh. Or out to the beach with the curious.

He dumped the clothes. He'd forgotten he had others here, now he had to drive around with them hung over the seat. He asked for a special on this load, three-day service. In case he left town soon, he wasn't going without that new navy jacket.

He drove on up the boulevard, not knowing where he was going. Not caring. When he saw a corner drugstore he remembered the phone call and drew up at the curb. There wasn't anyone much in the store, a couple of women at the lipsticks, a few young fellows at the soda counter. Dix closed himself in a booth, looked up the Virginibus Arms number. While he was waiting for the call, he took his handkerchief from his pocket. He didn't hang it over the phone, someone might look in and wonder. But he held it to his mouth, his back turned to the folding door. It would muffle his voice just enough.

The manageress' voice was strident to match the strident hennaed head he remembered.

"I understand you have an apartment to rent," he began.

She was annoyed as if he'd asked for a loan. She not only had all the apartments rented but on long lease. She wondered where he ever got such an idea.

He said, "A friend of my wife's understood that Miss Gray's apartment was for rent."

Her voice was suspicious. "Who was that?"

"A friend of my wife," he repeated. "She said that Miss Gray was moving."

"Well, it's the first I've heard of it. She's paid up—who is this?" she suddenly demanded.

He said, "Lawrence. A. B. Lawrence," reading initials penciled on the wall. He had no idea where the Lawrence sprang from. "Thank you." He hung up before she could ask more. He had what he was after, information. And no one to know he'd called.

He came out of the booth, ordered coffee and a toasted cheese sandwich at the counter. It wouldn't be very good from the looks of the place but it was better than nothing. While he was waiting, he took a morning paper from the rack. He hadn't had a chance to bring his in from the doorstep.

The murder was still front-page copy. The police were doing the usual, following every clue. Captain Jack Lochner of the L.A. force was working with the Santa Monica force. Captain Lochner was quoted as believing this was another of the strangler murders.

Dix didn't read all the drivel. The L.A. police were rounding up a maria full of known suspicious characters. The Santa Monica police were rounding up beach bums. There was a lot of questioning going on and no answers. No one had noticed any cars parked along the beach road that night. No one had noticed anything. They never did.

Dix finished his poor breakfast and left. There was more blue in the sky now. The sun was bringing warmth into the day. It was nothing to him. It was an empty day, a day to be passed, before another night would come. Another empty night, and yet another empty day to follow. He ought to leave town at once, not wait for his clothes to be returned by the cleaner, not wait for a woman who would not come again.

He swung the car over to Santa Monica Boulevard, drove into Santa Monica. He intended stopping at the Santa Fe office, to find out about railroad tickets east. He'd have to hold out enough money for return fare. But there was no place to park and in irritation he drove away, cutting across to Wilshire. He had no intention of turning west, yet he did. And he followed the avenue to the Incline, down the Incline to the beach road. It didn't look any different. There were no police lines. There were perhaps more cars than usual parked along the streets. Yet perhaps not. With the day warming, the beach regulars would be out in force. Dix didn't slow the car. He drove on down the road, turned off into the canyon and back to town.

He didn't realize that he was being followed until he was held by the light at the San Vicente eucalyptus grove. Until he remembered that the shabby sedan that drew up beside him had been behind him when he turned to the beach. Digging back, he knew it had been behind him when he left the drugstore; uncertainly, he remembered seeing it before then. His hands were cold against the wheel. It couldn't be.

And he was right, it couldn't be. The two men in the sedan were ordinary, and the car didn't wait for Dix to turn, it headed out ahead of him on the green. It was nerves, induced by the early morning visit of Springer and Yates, by the irritation of the gardeners and the lineman and forgetting where he'd left the car. You couldn't drive many blocks without running into a shabby black sedan with two men in it. Wilshire was full of like cars right now.

He wasn't being followed. Yet he drove back to the apartment. If there'd been anything he wanted to do, he wouldn't have cared how many cars were following him. But he was tired. Too tired to fight traffic for no reason. He would go home and sleep.

The front gardener had at last finished with Dix's side of the patio. He was leaning against a pillar, laying off with a cigarette. If anyone was hanging around, trying to find out what Dix had done with himself this morning, it was obvious. A trip to the cleaners, here was the evidence. A stop at a drugstore and if anyone wanted to know what call he'd made there, he'd have an answer. He'd called to see if Laurel was in. On to Santa Monica to the ticket office but no place to park. The drive down the beach? Simple curiosity. It was legitimate. He wouldn't be the only man in town with curiosity.

He picked up his paper off the walk, let himself into the apartment. He'd forgotten the cleaning woman. She was flicking the dust off the living-room tables as he entered. She was no more pleased to see him than he to see her. She didn't speak, she substituted a surly bob of her head.

He gave her a like bob as he carried his clothes into the bedroom to hang them. Hoping she would have started with the bedroom but she hadn't. It was still in ugly disarray. He left it abruptly, wanting to snarl at her, to ask her why she hadn't done the bed and bath first. Knowing why, because too often he was asleep at this hour.

Even as he stood there, hating her, the hideous siren of the vacuum cleaner whined suddenly in the next room. He rushed to the doorway. "Get out!" he shouted. She didn't turn off the infernal machine, she only glanced up at him dully. "Get out," he screamed. "Take that thing and get out!"

Her eyes bulged at him then, her slack mouth opened. But she didn't speak. She pulled out the cord fast, gathered her dust cloths, and scurried out the kitchen way. He heard the door bang behind her.

He steadied himself for a moment against the wall. He shouldn't have lost his temper. He was left with a slovenly bed, an unkempt bathroom. He held himself rigid until he had stopped shaking.

Slowly he walked into the kitchen and bolted the back door. He knew the front was locked but he returned to it, and made sure. He had to have sleep, undisturbed sleep. Slowly he plodded back to the bedroom, drew the curtains against the sun. He was desperate for sleep.

He tried to pull the bedcovers into some shape but his hands were witless. He did manage to slip out of his jacket and kick off his shoes before flinging himself face down, begging for oblivion.

He lay there, trying to quiet his thoughts, pleading to any gods who might heed to give him rest. And he heard it again, clip-clip, clip-clip. Outside his windows, clip-clip, clip-clip. His breath hissed from between his set teeth. It had begun and it wouldn't stop. It would go on, louder and louder, sharper and sharper. He began to tremble. He wouldn't dare order the man away, he couldn't risk having another employee run to the manageress with tales. He tried to stop up his ears with his tight fists, he sandwiched his head between the pillows, he tried to will his ears to close. But the inexorable rhythm continued, clip-clip, clip-clip.

He began to weep. He couldn't help it, he tried to laugh but tears oozed from his smarting lids. His whole body was shaken. He twisted the covers in his clenched fists. He couldn't stand it. He'd go crazy if he lay here longer.

Shaking, he moved into the living room, dropped weakly on the couch. He thought he could still hear the shears but he couldn't. It was only echo in his brain; it would go away. If he closed his eyes, lay quietly, it would go away. His hand fell on the newspaper; he'd dropped it automatically on the couch when he came in with the cleaning. He didn't want to look at it. He knew what it said. He knew all about it. But he found himself opening the sheet, staring at the black headlines. He'd read the story once, but he found himself reading it again, reading every word, every tired word. Strength returned to him and he crushed the paper, hurled it across the room. He turned over on the cramped couch, turned his back to the room, clamped his eyes as tightly as his teeth. He must find sleep.

Even as he turned, the door buzzer began its sickening rasp. He ignored the first three drones. Lying there rigidly, willing whoever it was to go away. The buzz continued, in longer pressings now, like a drill boring into his tortured head. Whoever it was had no intention of going away. Whoever it was knew that he was within. There was to be no sleep. It didn't matter now. Even the need of it was no longer alive. He got up and padded in his sock feet to the door. He opened it without hesitation. He didn't care who was outside.

Two men. Two men in plain suits and hats and shoes, plain faces to match. Two quiet men. Before either spoke, he knew them for what they were.

4

HE STOOD ASIDE TO LET THE MEN COME IN. HE REFUSED TO KNOW WHY they were here.

One of them said, "Mr. Steele?"

"Yes?"

One of them said, "Captain Lochner sent us to see if you'd mind coming up to the station, Mr. Steele."

He had no defenses. He said, "Certainly not." No matter how pleasantly it was offered, it was a command. "Will you wait while I get my jacket?" He felt naked without his shoes; he was ashamed to mention them.

"Take your time," one of the men said. He was the one who moved over to the desk as Dix left the room. The other moved to the windows.

He put on the tweed jacket, pushed his feet into the brown loafers, brushed his trousers with his hands. They weren't badly wrinkled, not as they would have been had he slept. His hair was tousled. He took time—they'd said, take your time—to brush it. Cigarettes, in his pocket. His lighter—it wasn't his, it was Mel's, narrow, gold, real gold. No initials, no identification. He slipped it into his pocket.

The two plain men turned to meet him. They let him lead the way out of the apartment, walked beside him casually, not one on each side, not clamping his arms. The car at the curb was a plain sedan, not a police car. One of the men said, "Maybe you'd rather follow us in your own car."

Dix caught his breath. He didn't understand; they couldn't be offering him a getaway. He couldn't get away. Not in the fastest car made. He could delay them but he couldn't escape them.

He said, "It doesn't matter."

"You might as well take yours. You know the way?"

"Sure." He didn't get it. And he didn't like it. It wasn't until he was following them up Beverly Drive that he did get it. This wasn't an arrest. How could it be, they had no charge to place against him. They hadn't a thing on him. But this did put his car into their hands where they could get their Goddamned dust. He had to laugh at that. Little good the dust would get them. And if they took casts of the tires while he was in the office, little good that would do them.

The laugh had picked him up. Enough so that he felt himself as he parked across from the station. The two plain men had pulled up just beyond him. Not in the police drive. He joined them to cross the street. He didn't ask what Lochner wanted. He could have now, but it might point up his silence before. Therefore he was silent, going along with them into the flowered grounds, up the stone steps, beyond the door flanked by the great bronze lamps holding green lights.

He showed his ease by knowing the way to the office. He was certain it would be the private office; it was. He was surprised to find that Lochner wasn't alone, to find Brub there with him. Somehow he hadn't expected Brub to be in on this. His hands twitched slightly. Why hadn't Brub come for him instead of sending the two zombies? Nevertheless, he gave Brub a wise smile as he spoke, "Good afternoon, Captain Lochner. You wanted to see me?"

"Yeah. Sit down."

Dix sat down and he calmed down; this wasn't Brub's show. Lochner was the boss. Brub looked like a clerk, sitting there at the table surrounded with papers. Dix didn't see the plain men leave the room; he only realized they had gone when they were gone.

Lochner gave him a chance to settle down. The Homicide chief was as drab as before, as tired of it all. He waited for Dix to light a cigarette before he spoke. "Thought you could help us, Mr. Steele."

Dix lifted his eyebrows. He didn't have to pretend to be puzzled. "I'd be glad to. But how?"

"It's that Bruce case."

His hand didn't twitch. He lifted his cigarette calmly to his lips.

"Nicolai told you something about it."

"Yes." He might have spoken too quickly. He added, "You mean the English case?"

"Yeah. You knew the girl?"

"Yes." He directed a small glance at Brub. "We both knew her. A wonderful girl." Lochner was waiting for him to say something more. Dix didn't fumble. There were several things he could have said. He chose a surprise one. "Are you taking over that case, Captain Lochner?"

"Uh-huh," Lochner said. "But I got to thinking——"

Dix nodded. "Brub told me your idea. It could have been the same man."

"I got a list." Lochner rooted out a paper from under Brub's hands. "These men were friendly with the Bruce girl. All Americans. All in England when it happened. Now I wonder if you'd look it over." He held on to the paper, swinging it in his hand. "Just read it over, see what you can remember about these men. Anything they might have said or done. Anything you can remember, no matter what it is." He pushed the paper at Dix suddenly. "Here."

Dix got up from his chair, walked to the table. He didn't look at the list as he carried it again to his chair. There was a trick in this. Some kind of a trick. He hadn't been called in to look over a list. He took his time studying the names, keeping his expression grave, thoughtful. Time to think. To get ready for questions. When he was ready, he smiled up at Lochner, moved the smile to Brub. "My name's on it," he said.

"Yeah," Lochner nodded.

Brub said, "But you'd been transferred before then, Dix. I told Jack."

"My transfer wasn't completed until after I returned from Scotland," Dix explained, as if surprised that Brub didn't know. "I had a month's leave, accumulated." Brub hadn't known. Brub had been shipped out before the changes.

"You came home after that?" Lochner asked.

"No," Dix answered. Walk softly. "I was sent to Paris and into Germany. On the cleanup. I was overseas another year." Say nothing of the months in London. He'd been proud of the cushy job. Adjutant to the general. Say nothing. Lochner was too snoopy. Dix's war record was none of his business.

"Then you saw something of those men?"

He couldn't deny knowing the names. Brub knew them too. They were, most of them, part of the old gang. Some he'd liked; some he'd have liked to kick in the teeth. For instance, Will Brevet. If Brub weren't sitting here, he could send Lochner looking into Brevet. But with Brub present, he couldn't. Brub knew the louse had tried to grab off Brucie.

Dix shook his head. "I'm sorry but I didn't. I was transferred immediately after my leave. I didn't run into any of these men after I left." Sure he'd run into Brevet in London, he'd even pubbed with him one lonely night. He could lie about that. Lochner wasn't going to track down all these guys.

Whatever the purpose of this summons, it wasn't to look into the whereabouts of a bunch of harmless guys or of Will Brevet. It was funny, in this small world, that Dix hadn't run into any of them after he left London. Not even after he got back to the States. But that was how it turned out, even in the small world.

He walked over and handed the list back to Lochner. He faced the chief squarely. "I don't know a thing against any man on this list. They were all swell guys. There isn't one of them that could have had anything to do with—with what you think." He'd delivered the defense stirringly; he meant what he said. Brub's eyes applauded. "Is there anything else?" Dix asked quietly.

"That's all." Lochner's big forefinger rubbed over the names. "I guess that's all, Mr. Steele." For a moment, his eyes weren't sleepy. "You can't blame a guy for trying," he said.

He took his list then and walked out of the room, through a communicating door. Dix looked at Brub.

Brub tilted back his chair. "I've tried to tell him. He wouldn't take my word for it." He brought the chair forward again. The legs hit hard on the floor. "You can't blame him for trying. Even if the administration weren't riding him, he'd feel the same. It's a personal failure. That these things could be happening while he's the chief."

Dix sat on the edge of the table. "Yes, I can see how he'd feel." He took out another cigarette, lit it, pushed the pack to Brub and held the lighter. Held the lighter right under Brub's nose. "It's hard lines. For you, too."

"We'll get him," Brub said. There was fight in him, no defeat now.

"Keep me posted. I'll want to know how you brought it off. The tec who solved the perfect crimes."

"They aren't perfect," Brub said softly. Then he turned his head fast to look at Dix. "You're going back East soon? Thought you said you'd be around some weeks more—or months."

"I may have to take off sooner than I expect," Dix grimaced. "The beckoning hands of business."

"Don't just disappear," Brub warned. "I want to give you an aloha ball. That'll bring you back."

"I'll make my farewells." He slid off the table. "I won't take up any more of your valuable time now, Brub. Give me a ring and we'll have lunch or dinner in a day or so. How about it?"

"Sure." Brub walked with him to the door. When they reached it, he asked, "How was Scotland?"

He'd forgotten that tangent, it took him a minute to balance the question. He answered, "It was wonderful."

"I didn't know you traveled there."

"Yes." He was thinking about it, not the way it was, the way he'd wanted it to be. "She loved it so. She talked so much about it. It was everything she said." And she was dead, but no one had known. Brub was thinking, and Brucie was then dead but Dix hadn't known.

Dix lifted his shoulders, lifted the memory away. "So long, Brub." He didn't look back; he left Brub remember him as a strong man who could, after a first shock, keep his sorrow in check.

He'd carried the whole thing off well. If Lochner had been playing a hunch, he'd lost his wad. He knew now there was nothing to get out of Dix Steele. There was nothing damning in being in Scotland when Brucie died. There was nothing damning in having been in London afterward. Except that he'd told Brub he knew nothing of what had happened. He might have been expected to know from London. Actually there'd not been a thing in the papers to tie unrelated crimes with the death of Brucie. He'd never seen Brucie's name in print. But he didn't want to go into such explanations, they sounded like alibis. He had no alibis; he needed none.

The car was where he'd left it. If the police had gone after dust, they hadn't taken much. The floor mat was no cleaner than it had been. He felt swell only he was hungry. It was too early for dinner, not more than a bit after four. A big delicatessen sandwich and a bottle of beer wouldn't spoil his dinner. Not after the starvation wages he'd been on today.

He was lucky, finding a parking place directly in front of the delicatessen. He was always lucky. He ought to kick himself for the megrims he'd had these last couple of days. Something must be wrong with his liver. Or perhaps he was coming down with a cold. From that nap on the beach. Actually he knew what was wrong. It was having Laurel walk out on him. If she'd been around he wouldn't have had a case of nerves.

He ordered salami and swiss on rye with his beer. Someone had discarded an afternoon paper in the next booth. He reached out for it, folded it back to its regular paging, first page first. The story was still on first. The police had given up questioning the fiancé and the college friends and the father; they were satisfied none of them knew any more about the Banning case than did the police themselves.

The police were taking fingerprints now. That was a lot of eyewash. Sand didn't take fingerprints.

Lochner was probably having the force develop fingerprints off that piece of paper right now. Because Lochner would be thorough. Or maybe he'd had them lifted off the steering wheel, you could get dandies off a steering wheel. Only trouble was he had nothing to match them up with. A beachful of sand.

Dix enjoyed the sandwich. The beer tasted fine. So good that he considered another but he didn't want to hang around here. The phone might be ringing at the apartment. Laurel might be waiting there. He bought a couple of bottles to take out and he hurried away. His luck had turned, and that meant Laurel was coming home.

He was turning left off the drive when he caught sight of the car. The same shabby black sedan with the same two average men in it. He was certain it was the same. He slowed his speed, eased his car around the block. He drove the entire block and the car didn't show up behind him. Rage flushed him. It was reasonless to imagine such things now. He'd come through the interview with banners flying, he'd had a good snack, all the indications were that luck had caught up with him. He couldn't revert, even for an imagined moment, to the weaknesses of these last days. He wouldn't let it happen.

As he was crossing the intersection, he saw the car again. It hadn't followed him around the block. It had come the other way to meet him. It followed him to the apartment. It was almost as if the men didn't care if he knew they were following. As if they wanted him to know.

When he parked in front of the apartment the other car plodded past. He didn't get a good enough look at the men to recognize them again. They didn't have faces to be remembered: they were background men, familiar only in their own setting, in the front seat of an old sedan.

Slowly he entered the patio, thinking, trying to understand. He'd passed Lochner's examination; he was sure of it. Why should he still be followed? He hit on an explanation, the men didn't know it as yet, Lochner hadn't had time to call them off. He took a deep breath of relief. Luck hadn't defaulted, she was still along with him.

Automatically he raised his eyes to the balcony. He stopped short, his eyes widening in disbelief. The door to Laurel's apartment was ajar. He didn't think about who might be watching, he didn't care. Laurel had returned.

He covered the patio quickly, ran up the stairs, reached the door in seven-league strides. He was about to tap but he let his hand fall. He'd walk in on her, surprise her. He still carried the sack of beer. They would celebrate.

Softly he entered the small foyer, moved through the arch into her living room. It was better than Mel's living room; she'd had an even better decorator. It was as exciting as Laurel herself, silver-gray and gold and touches of bronze; in this room Laurel would glow, it had been fitted to display her as a Reingold window displayed a precious jewel. The room was empty. But the apartment wasn't empty; he could hear the water running in the bath. She'd come home! She was getting bathed and then she'd dress and they'd have a swell evening. He was so excited that he couldn't have called out to her if he'd wanted. But he wanted to surprise her. He set the beer down on the couch, carefully, so that the bottles wouldn't click. And he started softly toward the bedroom door.

He passed the piano, a magnificent baby grand of a strange bronze-looking wood. The piano had caught his eye before. It was meant to. He must have noticed the photograph, but he hadn't seen it. He'd taken it for granted a picture of Laurel or of someone in her family. It wasn't. He saw it now. A too handsome, patent-leather-haired gigolo, smiling his too pretty smile, holding the inevitable cigarette wisping smoke. It was a theatrical photo and it was inscribed in bold and banal theatrical style. "To the only one, the wonderful one, Laurel. With all the love of Jess."

Dix was turned into stone. He knew he had been turned into stone, he was fully conscious of it. The heaviness, the coldness, the roughness of stone. He was perfectly normal otherwise. He could think more clearly than ever. This photograph wasn't something old, someone discarded. It still held the place of honor. Nor was it something new. Not that new. The look of the ink wasn't that new.

He was surprised that stone could have movement. Movement that was noiseless. He entered the bedroom, her bedroom, as lush, as feral as she. From the dressing table, that face smirked at him. From the bed table that face leered. From the chest of drawers, whichever way her eyes would lift on waking, she could see only that face. As if the man were a god, her household god. And she'd cheated on him! She'd cheated even on her god.

The sound of running water had ceased in the bathroom. There were only little sounds, the gathering up of towels, the closing of a medicine cabinet. He stood there waiting.

VII

When the door opened he was as silent as stone, only his eyes had movement. The door opened and the cleaning woman came out. She took one look at him. Her face twisted, her voice was shrill. "What you doing here? Don't you look at me like that! Don't you yell at me!" She lifted the bath brush, threatened him.

He spoke with quiet dignity, "I thought Miss Gray had returned." He turned and stalked out, leaving her standing there brandishing the brush. He stalked out of the apartment. But he picked up the beer as he passed the couch. He wouldn't leave it for the vicious old harridan.

He didn't relax until he was within his own apartment. The hag would go running to the manageress. Sniveling about a man yelling at her, about a man following her to Miss Gray's apartment. A certain man. The one in Mr. Terriss' apartment. He wouldn't deny he'd spoken to her sharply. Not yelled at her, a gentleman didn't yell at a charwoman. He'd spoken to her courteously, asked her not to use the vacuum cleaner this day. That was perfectly reasonable. He wasn't the only man who couldn't stand that infernal din. As for his following her to Miss Gray's apartment, that was absurd. He'd gone upstairs to see if Miss Gray had returned from her trip. He would deny, of course, that he'd entered the bedroom. He had been in the living room when the char appeared and started berating him. His word was certainly better than that of a desiccated old hag.

He put the beer on ice. He didn't want it now. He was cold, too cold. He poured a shot of rye. To warm him, for no other reason. He didn't taste it when it went down his throat.

There had been another man all along, a man she loved, the way Dix loved her. Perhaps the way in which her husband had loved her. There had always been this other man. She couldn't marry him, Henry St. Andrews had fixed that. It explained her bitterness against St. Andrews. She couldn't marry Jess because he didn't have enough money to give her what she wanted. She didn't love even Jess enough to give up the luxury she'd learned with the rich man.

Why had she played Dix? Why had she given him what she had, where had Jess been then? Dix rocked his head between his tight palms. Why? She alone could tell him; if there'd been a lovers' quarrel, if Jess had been on tour, if she and Jess had decided to split up and do better for themselves. But it hadn't worked. She'd gone back to her love, her little tin god.

And after she got into it with Dix, she'd been afraid to tell him. Because she knew him too well. Because she knew that he wasn't a man to give up what was his. She had been his; brief as it was in that time, she had belonged to him. She'd even cared for him. He knew it, he wasn't fooling himself on that angle. That was the hardest part of it to face. She had cared for him. The way in which Brucie had. But he'd been second best. He'd been good enough only if the number one was out of the way.

He sat there while the early twilight dimmed the room. Sat there and hurt and bled until he was again cold and tough and unyielding as stone. Until even the hot blade of anger gave him no warmth.

He sat there trying to understand. So many things. Why he had been born to live under the rules of Uncle Fergus. Why he couldn't have had what Terriss had, what St. Andrews and the Nicolais had without raising a finger. Why Sylvia had distrusted him. From the first moment he'd walked into their house, he'd known she raised a barricade against him. Why? Why had she been suspicious of him, without any faint reason to arouse her suspicion?

Brub had said it once; Sylvia looks underneath people. Yet how could she see what was beneath the façade? Brub had not been suspicious; even now Brub didn't trust his suspicion. Yet Brub listened to Sylvia and passed it on to Lochner in line of duty. How could they suspect him? He could open the pages of his life to them; they would find nothing there. Why, why should they suspect?

There were no slips, no mistakes. There had never been. There would never be. He had no fear, no reason to fear. They could not hold him. He would go back East. He'd get the trunk off tomorrow by express. He'd go by plane. He'd tell Brub good-bye. Good-bye Brub, good-bye Sylvia. Thanks for the buggy ride.

He could find a room, not too far away, a room to hole up in for just a few days. Once he was gone, Laurel would come back to her apartment. He'd be in the shadows watching. He'd take care of Laurel before he actually left town. He would take care of Laurel.

The room was dark now, he sat there in the heavy darkness. His fingers ached, clenched in his hands. His head was banded with iron. He'd been hounded all of his life by idiot fate. He'd had to smash it in the face ever to get anything good. He wasn't licked. He could still smash, walk over the broken pieces, come up bigger than ever. Bigger and smarter and tougher than anyone. He was going to get what he wanted. He was going to have money and he knew where he was going to get it. Once he had his hands on the money, there'd be no more second best for him. He'd be the top man wherever he wanted to go. No one would put him in second place again.

While he sat there he heard the steps in the patio. He swung around quickly and looked out. It wasn't Laurel. It was some man coming in from the office, briefcase in hand. The man entered one of the apartments across the court.

Tonight Dix would watch. Tonight she might come. Because he'd been cleared by the police; he'd even cleared himself with the lawyers she'd set on him. Because no one need be afraid of him tonight.

He watched. A man and woman went out, dressed to the teeth. A couple of fellows went out talking about their dates. Another man and a petulant woman who railed at him for being late. It was Saturday night. Everybody going out, putting on the dog, Saturday night out.

He watched the mist begin to fall over the blue light of the patio. To fall and to hang there, listlessly, silently. He waited there in his dark room, behind the dark window. Waited and watched.

His anger didn't diminish. Not even when the hopelessness of his vigil filled him as mist had filled the patio. Even then the spire of his anger was hot and sharp. Yet so heavily did the hopelessness hang on him that the sound of a woman's footsteps wasn't communicated to his anger until she was within the patio. High pointed heels. Slacks, a careless coat over the shoulders, the color washed out by the blue mist. A scarf to mask her flaming hair. He moved swiftly, moved before recognition was telegraph to his anger. He was out the door, softly through the shadows.

He came up behind her just as she reached the steps. "So you decided to come back," he said quietly.

He had startled her, she swung around in quick terror. It wasn't Laurel. He looked into the face of Sylvia Nicolai. "What are you doing here?" he asked. And he saw that he was not mistaken, this was the very coat that Laurel had worn so often. It had the feel of her coat.

Sylvia shrank away from his touch. She didn't answer him. Fear alone spoke from her wide blue eyes.

"Where's Laurel?" He demanded again, still softly but more sharply, "Where's Laurel? What have you done with her?"

Sylvia was caught there, backed against the step. She wanted to move away from him but she couldn't; she was trapped. She found her voice. "Laurel's all right," she said gently.

"Where is she?" He caught her shoulders. His hands tightened over them. He held her eyes. "*Where is she?*"

"She——" Her voice failed. And then swiftly she moved. She twisted, catching him off guard, breaking through. Leaving the coat in his hands.

He turned. She hadn't run away. She hadn't sense enough to run away. She was standing there, only a slight distance from him, there by the blue pool. Her breath was coming in little gusts. She spoke clearly, "She isn't coming back, Dix. She's safe. She's going to stay safe."

He unclenched his hands and the coat fell. It lay there on the ground, slumped there. He said, "You've poisoned her against me. You've always hated me. From the beginning you hated me." He took one step toward her.

She backed from him. "No, Dix. I've never hated you. I don't hate you, even now."

"From that first night, from the beginning——" He was about to step toward her but she was ready for him. He didn't move. He wouldn't warn her when he moved again.

"From the beginning I knew there was something wrong with you. From the first night you walked into our living room and looked at me, I knew there was something wrong. Something terribly wrong."

He denied it. "You didn't know. You couldn't know." Neither had to fill in; both knew they spoke of the same terror. He jeered,

"You were jealous. Because you wanted all of Brub. You didn't even want a friend to have a part of him."

She didn't get angry. She shook her head, a little sadly.

"But that wasn't enough. You had to take Laurel from me, too. Because you hated me so."

She spoke now. Without emotion. "Laurel came to Brub. Because she was afraid. Afraid of the way you looked at her. That night she asked you to take her to the drive-in."

He gripped his hands. "And you lied to her."

Sylvia ignored him. "It wasn't the first time she'd been afraid. But it was beginning to grow. Every time she spoke of Mel——"

"Damn Mel!" he cut in.

"What happened to Mel?" Her voice lifted. "Where is he? Without his car—and his clothes—without the cigarette lighter Laurel gave him, the cigarette lighter he wouldn't let out of his hands?"

He watched her, watched her in her little moment of triumph.

"What happened to Brucie?" she went on, softly now. "What happened to the girl who drank coffee in the drive-in with you? What happened to the girl in Westlake Park, to the girl who let you take her to the Paramount, to the girl on Spring Street——"

He broke in again. It didn't sound like his voice when he whispered, "I'm going to kill you." He leaped as he spoke. He didn't telegraph the movement and he was on her, his hands on her throat before she knew. It was his hands that failed him. Because they were shaking, because before he could strengthen them enough, she was screaming and screaming. By the time he'd throttled the scream, the men were running to close in on him. One from the patio entrance, one from the shadows beyond the steps, one from the shadows behind him, He didn't release his grip, not until he saw who it was running full toward him. Brub. And Brub's face was the face of a killer.

It was Sylvia who saved Dix. Because she whirled and went into Brub's arms, clung to him, keeping him from killing. She wasn't hysterical. What she cried was bell clear. "It worked," she cried in her husky voice. "It worked!"

They took him into his own apartment. Into Mel's apartment. Brub and Sylvia, although they didn't want Sylvia to come. They wanted to protect her from the ugliness they expected. Brub and Sylvia and Captain Lochner who had come from the shadows. The shapeless man with the cigarette who had come from other shadows.

And the two cops who had driven him to the Beverly station earlier today. They'd come from somewhere.

They turned on the lights and they sat him down on his own couch. They stood around him like vultures, looking down on him, looking down their noses at him. All but Sylvia. They stood between him and the chair where Sylvia was huddled.

Lochner said, "I'm arresting you on suspicion of the murder of Mel Terriss."

He laughed. He said, "Mel's in Rio."

Lochner went on, "And suspicion of the murder of Mildred Atkinson."

He laughed again.

"And suspicion of the murder of Elizabeth Banning."

They didn't have anything on him. Not a thing.

"And the attempted murder of Sylvia Nicolai."

He hadn't hurt Sylvia. He'd lost his temper over her vicious taunts but he hadn't done anything to her. A good lawyer would take care of that one.

"Have you anything to say?"

He looked straight at Lochner. "Yes. I think you're crazy."

The shapeless man said, "The girls were safe in August. You killed Mel Terriss in August, didn't you?"

It was Brub who began talking to him as if he were a human being. "It's no use, Dix. We have Mildred Atkinson's fingerprints in your car. There's only one way they could get there."

Brub was lying, trying to trap him. They hadn't had time to take all the fingerprints out of that car while they talked with him today. They had time to take them while the car stood in the garage or at the curb, while a gardener guarded each door of the apartment by day, while men in the shadows watched the doors at night.

"We have the dust——"

He'd covered the dust. His lawyer would make a monkey of the dust expert.

"—lint from the Atkinson girl's coat——"

His eyes lifted too quickly to Brub's impassive face.

"—hairs from the Bannings' Kerry Blue on the suit you took to the cleaners this morning——"

You couldn't think of everything. When you were rushed. When your luck had run out.

For one moment the old Brub broke through the deadly, grim-visaged cop. The old Brub cried out in agony, "For God's sake, why did you do it, Dix?"

He sat there very quietly, trying not to hear, not to speak, not to feel. But tears rose in his throat, matted his eyes, he could not withhold them longer.

He wept, "I killed Brucie."

THE DAVIDIAN
REPORT

For my son,
Anthony Allen Hughes,
with my thanks for his help
in preparing this story

THE GIRL HAD BOARDED THE PLANE AT KANSAS CITY. SHE WASN'T A GIRL he would have noticed particularly on the street or in a crowded room. He wouldn't have given any special attention to her in an empty room, or on this plane, if she hadn't taken the seat beside him. There were other unoccupied places—no window seats, it was true, but plenty on the aisle. All right, she had to sit beside someone and she'd selected him. Maybe he looked harmless. Actually she'd not given the impression that she'd seen him at all. It was rather that she'd decided to select the third row left up front.

She was medium size and yellow-haired, her dark green suit was a tweed import; her felt hat was shaped like a riding hat, the kind society girls affect to appear country; and her suede pumps were the exact color of the darker weft of the tweed. Her purse was large, of good black leather, well rubbed; she protected it against her in the seat. It was big enough to be a formidable barrier between her and a seatmate. She kept her hands gloved, yellow crochet gloves, and she used a five-cent yellow pencil on her book of crossword puzzles. It was a long time since he'd seen anyone as devoted to a crossword puzzle as was this girl.

Her face was shadowed in the miniscule overhead shaft of light invented for plane travel, but he had photographed it with his memory on initial appearance. A small chiseled face, a cold little face, but that might have been put on like her horn-rim glasses to preserve her privacy while traveling. The cross-word puzzle book could have been for the same purpose.

He knew the detail of each other face on the plane as well as hers. Not only the passengers remaining, but also those who had left the plane at Kansas City and at Albuquerque, including the thin-faced man, jockey size, who had been his seatmate preceding the girl. Most of them were, by his figuring, safe. The dubious ones he went over in his mind until he would recall a scrap of elbow, a hunch of shoulder, an ear tip, no matter how or where he met it again. Despite the most careful planning, it was never possible to say that the Feds didn't know about a job. They were like the wind, invisible, but able to penetrate the impenetrable room.

It was one reason for his insistence on playing a lone hand. Only because he'd had good luck in carrying through a couple of his initial errands did he get anywhere with the insistence, and because his friends had managed to mess up one of his simplest jobs with their nursemaids. He couldn't be certain that they hadn't set someone to follow him, despite the hell he'd raised the last time that was pulled on him. He could never be certain they weren't having him watched. The bossman was an old woman about a man on a man ad infinitum. No imagination, no scope. But he was the bossman.

He wasn't sure of the young soldier, crumpled asleep in the right aisle rear seat. In front of the pretty, competent hostess, a safe one, with her bright painted-on smile. What was a gawky boy with not so young eyes, wearing a government issue, ill-fitting uniform, doing on board the Constellation from New York? He looked as if he should be thumbing a truck on the highway. And there was the beefy character with the brown hat pulled over his hatchet eyes. Midsection right. Another, Albuquerque on, a withy man, who kept turning discreet attention to the tweed girl.

And the front section right, New York these, a team with bulging briefcases resting against their ankles. The one by the window was a small sandy man in horn-rims. The aisle one was a big fellow, his features handsome in a big vivid face, his well-cut dark hair carrying just the right flair of gray for current glamour. His gray suit was of rich material and rich tailoring. He had a rich voice to match. He could be a big-shot lawyer, the kind you were able to retain for a basic fee of ten thousand per annum. His hands were big and square and clean as the rest of him; he smoked an indefatigable cigarette.

Steve Wintress didn't know why he was particularly uneasy about this one. Maybe the man was too much the sure-of-himself success guy. Maybe because the fellow had tried to strike up a conversation at the Albuquerque break. Not that this should have appeared suspicious. After flying together across the continent, after excusing themselves at the previous stop for trying to be the first off into the smell of fresh air after cold, stale altitude, it wasn't out of line to speak a friendly word. But if the guy was looking for conversation, why didn't he talk to Junior next to him? They'd scarcely exchanged a sentence during the flight.

There was something wrong with the picture, although as yet Steve hadn't figured it. The man couldn't be on his side, he was too assured for that, too lacking in furtivity. Yet he could scarcely be a Federal and for near the same reasons; the Feds went in for quietness, anonymity. To be sure, there was no telling what either side had dreamed up to make sure of this deal. The Davidian report was too important not to take bold steps to win.

The plane was losing altitude, floating down out of empty darkness to behold the glitter of red and green and yellow lights, flung out like a fabulous jeweled scarf. Phoenix. Next stop L.A. The usual warning glowed against the forecabin's door, cigarettes were stubbed out in the midget ash containers, the pretty hostess made her customary competent double check on seat belts.

Steve didn't have to climb across the tweed girl, she was in the aisle on landing. Nor did he try to jockey the big man for second place, the Albuquerque approach still stuck in his craw. He waited until the aisle was moving before joining the tail end of it. As he passed the crumpled soldier, the boy blinked sleep-grained eyes and closed them again in disinterest.

Outside, the desert heat of the day lingered in the stillness. The stars were bright and sharp as pins. The usual scattering of men and women who, at all suburban airports, watched the plane come in, were there, leaning against the wire fence, sizing up each passenger as if they'd never seen a stranger before. The passengers headed for the lunchroom or to stretch their legs in a stroll along the portal. Steve walked as far as the portal but the big man was too much in evidence there. His voice, if not his words, came reverberating along the walk. Steve walked back to the grass plot for his cigarette, standing in the half-shadow of a dusty tree, smelling the good, hot air.

On the field the big yellow oil-service trucks were diminished to miniature under the giant Connie wings. The soldier boy emerged from the plane; he was small as a toy, high in the open doorway. The green tweed girl came along the path from wherever she'd disappeared to. As she passed, her eyes met Steve's. Hers flicked away at once; she was discomfited that she'd turned her head to see who was standing there, more so that it had been he. Steve grinned. It was the first moment of relaxation he'd allowed himself in four days.

The twenty minutes were brief. The passengers began trailing early towards the gate, just as if they believed the plane would take off on the dot. They knew better. Steve dropped his cigarette stub to the grass and brought up the rear. He remained well to himself crossing the open field. He was hoisting himself up the uncomfortably steep steps of the ladder when he remembered that he hadn't seen the big man. Against his will—out of curiosity, not nerves—he checked over his shoulder. The man was only now striding through the gate, stopping just inside it to exchange words with the attendants. They were six-footers but the man topped them.

Steve continued up the ladder, ducked his head and reentered the plane. As he proceeded forward along the narrow aisle he checked the passengers automatically, unobtrusively. The hatchet face and three others had disembarked for good at Phoenix. There were three new ones, all women, teachers, smartly dressed, off to a special meeting on the Coast. They unfurled snatches of bright talk a little too loudly, excited in journey's beginning.

The big man didn't plunge down into his seat until just before the take-off. As he clipped his seat belt, he addressed his companion: "L.A.'s fogged in, Timothy." His voice was strong enough to carry through the plane. "It'll be Palmdale or Palm Springs." Whatever else he had to impart was lost in the rabbit rustle of the other passengers. And also because, as if realizing he'd created a commotion, or satisfied that he had, he was content to speak down.

The hostess tried to answer the bubble of questions with the panacea or the professional smile. "We don't know yet. It's possible we may be able to land at Los Angeles. Or Burbank." The pretense soothed some of the protestants. "I'll let you know as soon as the captain has word."

Steve didn't ask any questions. In late November you could expect fog on the Coast. He didn't like this disruption of schedule. He'd given himself a week, including flying time, to take care of the Davidian business. It was overestimation; with any luck at all, it wouldn't take three days. He wasn't superstitious, but a bad break at the start of a job was bad luck. Not that he was worried about missing Albion. Albie would be waiting at the airport whatever time Steve put in. But whatever plans had been made for a meeting tonight wouldn't come off.

The girl put away her book and removed her horn-rimmed glasses. She didn't like this either. Steve spoke to her. Not like a guy trying to get acquainted but like a disgruntled traveler. "Where's Palmdale? I know Palm Springs but where's Palmdale?"

She turned to him and he saw her eyes for the first time without the protective coating of glass. They were too big for her face. Just now they reflected the green of her suit; they were colored like a cat's eyes and were as unwavering.

"I don't know exactly." Her voice was without coloration. "North, I think. In the desert."

He waited a proper moment before asking offhand, "Your first trip out?" as if it were also his first.

"No. I live in California." She was disturbed but not at him. "I wonder what time we'll get in. If they'd told us about this in Phoenix—"

"They never tell the passengers anything," he replied. "They're worse grannies than medicos for keeping the populace ignorant." He eyed her. "You being met?"

She shook her head briefly to discourage questioning. He wasn't discouraged. He went right on talking, as if he were one of those guys who never caught on to a brush-off.

"I am. I was," he amended ruefully. "How long the guy'll wait, I don't know." Albion would wait until hell froze over. But it sounded more human this way.

She murmured vaguely, "We'll be so late . . . an imposition . . ." She ended the conversation there, snipping off her light beam, settling herself for sleep.

He didn't push it further. He too settled himself, although he had no intention of dulling his wits with sleep, or any particular need of it. He was a night man.

It wasn't too long before the hostess went forward. Now they'd have it. She returned almost at once, put on the top lights, and took her stand for a speech. As charming as if she were bringing good news. Not the information that they were landing at some God-forsaken hole where busses would be sent to carry the passengers to the International Airport. Everyone came awake and full of questions. Yes, their luggage would go along with them. Yes, there was a telephone in Palmdale and there'd be time to put in a call. It was the tweed girl who asked that one; someone was expecting her if not meeting her. The hostess parried, she was gentle and bright, and she got away as soon as possible, leaving the passengers friends in misfortune, not seatmates by accident.

The girl said, "She said telephone, singular." Her narrow shoulders gestured: And all of these people!

"I noticed she said there'd be time. How much time?"

The man behind them leaned over Steve's chair. He was all right, his wife was with him, they were returning from a district Kiwanis convention. "Don't worry about time. It takes hours to dig up those old crates they send out to Palmdale. Stuffing out of the seats, broken springs, no heat—I said the last time I'd stick to the Chief."

The ones who hadn't been through it before were more resigned. The three young teachers of Phoenix were rather titillated over the unusual. The big man across the aisle actually appeared pleased over the development.

The pilot put the ship down in Palmdale only a little later than it should have landed in L.A. There was no scarf of jewels to guide him, only endless open space, forlorn pylongs, and a barracks-like shack. The stars were as bright as in Arizona but the air was chill, sending everyone hurrying to the shack.

It shouldn't have surprised Steve to walk into hustle-bustle. Theirs wasn't the only ship set down at this isolated way station; all other lines had been closed out by fog as well. But somehow you didn't expect a desert barracks to be milling with people in the late night. Balancing the confusion was the apathy of those who had been waiting far too long. They huddled beneath their coats on the rackety wicker couches and scuffed chairs. A handful of luckier ones encircled a big iron stove borrowed from an old-fashioned steel engraving.

Most of Steve's plane headed for the wooden counter where two farm women were selling coffee and cold, thick sandwiches. A sparser line formed outside the telephone booth. His girl hadn't been first, someone was already in the booth. She was next, the big man behind her. They were talking in desultory fashion, in a way a man wouldn't miss a chance to talk to an attractive young girl. Not that she was particularly pretty, certainly not now, her face pale and troubled, but compared to the other females in the shack, she was a Vogue model. Steve's gabardine when new hadn't resembled the one draped across the shoulders of the big man.

Steve edged to the outskirts of the food counter. He wasn't hungry; however, the stimulus of coffee would help pass the time. And from this vantage point, he could spot who had cared enough to be first in the phone booth. He was vaguely surprised when the crumpled soldier emerged. Although it was logical; the boy had been in a position to be first off the plane. If he had taken advantage of the last minute of leave, as kids would, he'd need to put in a call quick. The soldier shoved his cap over his other ear and dug his hands into his pockets as he neared the counter. It gave him a more shabby look. The hands-in-pockets gesture evidently wasn't an idle one. He was veering away when Steve got his eye.

"Buy you a coffee, kid." He knew how to say it with just the right rough edge to take off any smarm of charity. He'd worn a uniform himself not enough years ago. "If we can get near enough to buy one."

The kid said, "I'll help push." His sudden grin was more young than his face. The smile went into his eyes and they too were young. It might have been that all he had needed was the transcontinental sleep.

There was an entering wedge behind the sandy man. As Steve moved, he jogged the briefcase under the man's arm, but it was the sandy man who apologized, "Sorry." He balanced two cups of coffee, one for the boss, out of the way. The soldier nailed the spot.

The farm woman's voice was harsh. "Coffee? Beef or ham?"

Steve said, "Two coffees. Beef or ham, soldier?"

"Beef, I guess."

The boy was thin and kids were always hungry. "One of each," Steve said. While they waited he heard the girl's voice.

"Could you get me a cup of coffee?" She was holding a quarter over his shoulder.

He didn't take the coin. "Sure," he said, and "Make it three," to the gaunt woman. He swiveled his head. "Did you get your call through?"

The girl said, "Yes." No more.

The soldier picked up the paper plate of sandwiches and one of the coffees. Steve paid and took up the other cups. "Now if we can find a place to park ourselves."

They were lucky on it. The busses for an earlier plane were coming in, hostesses were passing the word to their charges. The soldier was quick at snagging the couch with the broken springs. It wasn't comfortable but there was room for three. They put the girl between them and passed the sandwiches.

She said, "I'm not hungry."

"Eat it. Good for you." The boy was taking a big hunk in his mouth but he managed the young grin. Surprisingly she reacted, half-smiling back at him. It made her look human, not like a pale green schoolgirl in tweeds.

Steve handed his sandwich back to the soldier. The kid was near ready for another. From under his eyes, Steve was watching the big man, over there by the stove. The man was watching the three of them or one of the three. It wasn't possible to know which way it was. When he started suddenly in their direction, Steve returned his attention to his own group. "At this time of night I stick to coffee."

There was time for no more before they were towered over. The big fellow said, "I got through, Miss Talle. The car's on its way. May I offer you a lift to town?"

Steve was faintly surprised that the man knew her name, they hadn't appeared to know each other on the plane. And she was evidently chary of giving it, there'd been no introductions between the three of them collaborating on this sprung couch over their late supper.

The man explained to Steve and the soldier, "When I heard in Phoenix about weather conditions, I wired ahead to have a car sent out." He laughed, "I've ridden the bus from Palmdale before." The invitation was proffered easily, no pressure, "If you men would like to ride along—"

The soldier accepted without hesitation. "Sure. Thanks."

Steve wasn't so sure. He'd like to know how this guy could find out where they'd be landing before the hostess knew. Possibly Mr. Big had ordered a car to proceed to all possible points. Even while he hesitated, Steve was telling himself it couldn't be a trap. The man and the girl and the soldier couldn't all be together on this, to prevent Steve Wintress from reaching Davidian. To excuse his hesitation, he said, "I'd have to go to the airport anyway."

The man stepped on his words. "Any place you like." His smile was almost as professional as that of the air-line hostess. "I'm Haig Armour." He tossed it out as if he expected them to know the name.

Steve's eyes didn't waver. Haig Armour, attorney with the Justice Department. Haig Armour, former big noise of the F.B.I. Steve had heard enough about Haig Armour, but he'd never run into the man before. He didn't know if tonight was an open move or accidental. Mildly he returned, "My name is Wintress. Steve Wintress."

If Armour recognized the name, he didn't admit it.

The soldier said, "Private first class Reuben St. Clair. Call me Rube." His smile was comic relief.

Armour set down his briefcase and reached into the pocket of his handsome weatherproof. "How about a little heat for that coffee?" He pulled out a leather-encased flask. "Brandy." It was out of character that he didn't give the Napoleonic date.

The girl said, "No thanks," and the private refused, "Afraid it might put me to sleep."

It could have been drugged and the three working together. But it didn't smell like anything but the best brandy. It was what Steve needed. He said, "Thanks. I was just wishing I had a drink."

Armour's assistant was coming across from the doorway with quick little steps. Steve began to drink his coffee. The sandy man had a sandy voice. "The car is here, Haig."

"Fine." Armour shared his smile with the three. "You ready?"

"You bet." Pfc. St. Clair pushed up on his long legs. He carried his sandwich with him.

Steve went on drinking the coffee. They wouldn't leave without him.

Armour took the Talle girl's cup and helped her to her feet. "You tell the hostess we're off, Tim. We'll want our bags." He remembered. "Timothy Leonard, Miss Talle, Steve Wintress, Reuben St. Clair." The name Leonard wasn't familiar to Steve. "These kids are going to ride in with us."

Steve didn't qualify as a kid but maybe he looked it to Armour. Or maybe Armour was considering Steve's stature, not the lines in his face. He drained his cup before joining the parade led by Haig to the door. He'd taken it too fast, he felt a little giddy. And again he wondered if the lacing could have been tainted, if the oddly matched trio actually were linked. The first blast of night air helped him to clarity. And standing around in the cold while the reluctant attendant unearthed their bags from the jumble helped more. There was nothing out of character in the luggage; the girl had expensive matched stuff, excess weight; Armour's was as expensive and as heavy. Rube carried only a small khaki bag as shabby as his uniform; Timothy Leonard's suitcase was unobtrusive. Steve retrieved his worn valise.

It was Timothy who directed them to an oversized black limousine, bigger than a hearse. But it was Haig who arranged the seating, stowing the soldier up front by the shadowy driver, relegating Timothy to an anachronistic jump seat, and deftly spotting Steve in the rear between himself and the girl. It might be accidental, but Armour knew how to fence in a man.

2

STEVE FOUGHT SLEEP. IT WAS ESSENTIAL HE REACH THE AIRPORT AND not some destination Haig Armour might prefer. But the brandy had been heavy and taken too fast. He knew he'd slept when the boom of Armour's voice shook him into consciousness.

The big man was leaning towards the driver's shoulder. He'd pushed aside the glass panel separating the tonneau from the cab. "My God, Wilton, how can you see anything?"

The machine was creeping through gray fur. They were on some planet where there was no light, no shadow, no presence, nothing but the shell in which they were encased, and the amber beams of their fog lights bending into the engulfing fog. The driver undertoned something without taking his eyes from the windshield.

Reuben commented cheerfully over his shoulder, "You can't see nothing. Nothing at all."

After a moment Haig decided to leave it up to the driver. He shoved the dividing partition tight and settled back again into the upholstery. "He said we're at Sherman Oaks. How can he tell!" He passed his cigarette case. Steve alone accepted; the girl might have been asleep.

"I've got to go to the airport," Steve reminded him. He had no idea of its direction. He took a light. "But you can let me off at any taxi stand."

"Nonsense," Haig refused heartily. "On a night like this? Private St. Clair wants to go to the airport too." He leaned across Steve, raised his voice. "What's your destination, Miss Talle?"

She turned her head slowly. Her eyes were blurred with sleep. "Benedict Canyon. In Beverly Hills." The yellow-gloved hands pressed together.

Timothy Leonard said, "Haig and I are stopping at the Beverly Hills Hotel. The same neighborhood."

"You don't mind riding first to the airport?" Haig said. It wasn't a question; it was the way it was going to be.

Steve protested uselessly, "Rube and I could hop a cab along the way. It would save you the trip." He knew before he spoke that Haig Armour had made up his mind on this before they left Palmdale. It was almost as if he knew that Albion was waiting for Steve Wintress and that it was a meeting he intended to witness. Let him. He'd see two old friends say hello, no more than that. Steve gave up. Actually at two in the morning in this pea-souper, a cab might be hard to materialize.

As they crept through Sepulveda Canyon, without reason the fog thinned out into tattered veils. They could see the dark walls of the pass, the white guardrails, even glimpse white stars in the overhead sky. And with no more reason, as they emerged into Westwood at the opposite end of the canyon, the night reverted to another furry density. Again they crawled tortuously along the highway. But there was some evidence of life here, a neon-decorated, all-night garage, the occasional glisten of pale headlight. It was long to the airport; Haig Armour hadn't realized how far out of the way it was. He was silently restive, his face against his window. The Talle girl seemed to be sleeping again. Timothy slept. Up front Rube St. Clair was gabbing with the driver, but the glass partition withheld their words.

They reached the airport at last, turning off in pale fog by the large blinking green arrow, following the road to the in-turn, past the empty acres reserved for parking, up to the curb in front of their terminal. Armour swung out of the car first. It was courteous, and the man's long legs must need a stretch after this run. But Steve wasn't happy about it; he wasn't taking any nursemaid into the terminal with him. He didn't want more trouble. This had been as ill-met a night as he'd had in years, he couldn't take any more.

Reuben was on the walk; he began to make his manners while the driver was bringing Steve's valise and the soldier's khaki bag from the trunk.

"Don't mention it," Armour pushed aside the appreciation. "You boys find out if your friends are around. If not, come back and ride in with me. I'll wait."

Steve's fists tightened on the valise handle. But he managed to speak quietly, even pleasantly to the bastard. "Don't wait. We'll be all right from here on in. Thanks for the lift." He walked away fast, the soldier on his heels. They separated inside the door, without any word, each on his own errand.

The terminal was as crowded as the desert shack had been, with those dogged friends and relatives who wouldn't give up. The loudspeaker rasped endlessly, "Flight Nine arriving by bus from Palmdale. Pick up your baggage at the street entrance. Flight Fifty-nine arriving—"

Albion wasn't in the milling crowd, wasn't leaning on the ticket counters or on the newsstand. Steve began a slow pace past the chairs. Each one was occupied by a stranger. The phone booths were empty. He went into the men's room, this too was empty. It didn't add up. Albion would not have left the air terminal until Steve got there, no matter what the hour. Unless something had gone wrong earlier and Albie hadn't come at all. But that didn't add up either. There'd have been a substitute. Albie was thorough.

Steve covered the room again, as if he could have missed Albie on the first count. He wasn't there on the second either. While he was knuckling his brains, his conscious eye beheld the two doors leading to the court in the rear. He strode to the nearest, the one on the right, and pushed out into the fine fog. Albion must have ducked out here for some reason, possibly because he'd spotted something off color within. Something Steve couldn't be expected to recognize; he hadn't met the California boys.

There were no shapes in the fog, no one on the bench just outside the door, no one leaning over the fence looking out to the blurred landing field. Steve walked over to peer down the empty ramp. No one. Nothing. Turning back he saw what he had missed before. Across the court on a smaller bench, there was someone or something, a darker mass against the fogged dark. For a moment he was motionless, conscious only of sounds, his breath and the dripping of fog from the roof. Then he moved quickly, quietly. It was Albion, hunched there in his worn raincoat, a shapeless, colorless hat pulled over his eyebrows. He might have been asleep, but his knees were placed together too neatly, his hands crossed over them in peace. Steve didn't touch him. He tilted the man's hat brim with one careful finger, but he had known before that. He walked away, returning to the lighted, busy terminal by the far door.

No one seemed to notice his re-entrance. He lit a cigarette, steadying it with cold fingers. The immediate move was to get a cab into Hollywood. He was heading for the street exit when the soldier emerged from Men's. Reuben's face had grown old again from fatigue or disappointment. From both. He said, "Your friends not wait either?"

"Looks like they didn't," Steve admitted. He couldn't have been as long outside as it seemed. Unless the kid had been told to wait for him.

Reuben walked along towards the door. "You don't suppose that Armour guy'll still be hanging around?" It was a wishful query.

"No," Steve said. Although he wasn't sure of the soldier, he offered, "I'm getting a cab. You can ride along with me to Hollywood if it'll do you any good."

Reuben was appreciative. "I'm heading that way."

And they saw the big car, the rear door still wide, Haig Armour emerging from the tonneau. "No luck?" Armour's voice implied that he'd known there wouldn't be. "You two must have taken the place apart, nail by nail." He'd changed the seating, he had Timothy by the driver and he himself took the jump seat. The girl slept on her corner. She didn't stir when Reuben shoved beside her, making room for Steve. But if you touched her she wouldn't topple; she was breathing.

"And now?" Armour asked.

"We'll get off in Beverly Hills." Steve settled his valise under his heels.

"Where are you going?" There was a hint of impatience in the big voice and Steve wanted to answer it straight: *None of your God-damn business!* But he said, "Hollywood. We'll take a cab from Beverly Hills. I'm sure Miss Talle isn't up to any more side trips."

"Yes." Armour agreed too readily. "You can drop us and then Wilton will take you two wherever you want." He blocked Steve's protest. "It's a hired car."

Steve shut his mouth. Rube was already accepting in his lacka-daisical fashion, "Well, thanks, Mr. Armour. Someday I'll give you a lift."

Fatigue silenced all of them. The fog ebbed and flowed about the car through Westwood and into Beverly Hills. They turned away from the city on a broad avenue sentineled with giant palms, slender and tall as Watusis. The fronds were lost in the dark white mists overhead.

The driver held speed to a walk. The avenue was sparsely lit, the intersections lost in the fog. Again theirs seemed the only vehicle in motion, themselves the only living organisms in a vanished world. The Beverly Hills Hotel was a beacon, its yellow lights penetrating the gray. The car didn't hesitate at the hotel. For a moment anger seized Steve. And then he realized from the growing darkness that they were moving into Benedict Canyon. The climb was tortoise slow, the driver pulling under far-spaced and dim street lights to de-cipher the street signs.

The girl said, "I don't know where we are." It was the first thing she'd said since leaving the airport.

Haig Armour didn't sound too sure. "Wilton will find it. You know your aunt's place?"

"I can't see a thing." Her yellow-crocheted forefinger rubbed against the window as if she could make a hole in the density.

One estate was like another on the Benedict Canyon road, shrubs and trees, the mass of big houses fading into the white shadows. Wilton was out of the car, turning a flashlight on the country-style white mailbox, lettered in black. And he was again in the car, head-

ing further up the Canyon. It wasn't more than a long city block before he repeated the routine, this time returning to open the rear
door.

"This is it, Miss Talle." He didn't talk like a chauffeur, there was
a quiet authority in his voice.

Miss Talle said, "Good night." She didn't say thank you, possibly
she'd said it before, or was too sleepy to care. Armour helped her out
of the car, Wilton carried her expensive luggage through the gate.
She stumbled after the man. He could have driven closer to the
house; the iron gates of the drive were closed for the night but he
could have opened them. Steve wondered.

Haig Armour took the place she'd vacated. It shoved the soldier
closer to Steve, Armour was bulkier than the slip of a girl. Through a
yawn, he commented, "Her uncle is Eldon Moritz."

The name was nothing to Steve. Or to Reuben.

"She dances. Ballet."

It meant no more than that Haig Armour had asked her a few
questions while they'd waited at the airport.

Rube asked, "Is she in the movies?"

"She's been in a couple. Just background motion."

Steve asked, "What does her uncle do?" If the name meant something to Armour, it wouldn't hurt him to know.

"He's a director," Armour said.

Wilton's steps crunched on the gravel. He came out of the fog,
climbed under the wheel without a word. He somehow managed to
turn the car in the narrow lane and it crawled down the long winding hill again to the lighted oasis of the hotel. End of the run for
Haig Armour and Timothy Leonard. Armour tried once more. "You
boys want to put up here for the night? I can take care of you."

Steve spoke up before Reuben could get in an acceptance.
"Thanks, I've got to check into Hollywood."

If the private was disappointed, he didn't let on. "I guess I better
find my outfit before they think I'm lost. I'll go on in with Steve."

They repeated their thanks, watched Armour's confidence climb
the broad steps to the hotel porch, the silent Leonard at his heels. A
uniformed attendant appeared for the luggage. And Wilton was suddenly standing at the car door, looking in.

Steve said, "You can drop me at the Roosevelt." Reuben didn't
say anything.

The fog held, now faint, now furry, along Sunset and the Strip
into Hollywood, turning over La Brea to the boulevard. Both Steve

and Rube swung out at the tall lighted hotel. They had their bags in hand, there was no reason for the man to leave the wheel. Reuben said, "Thanks for the ride." Steve added. "Thanks." He gave a half salute. You wouldn't be expected to tip Armour's driver, and besides, he wasn't a driver.

Steve stood there on the walk until the car had pulled away, filing in his memory what he had seen of the man. Not a hired driver. Plain-clothes cop? Federal Bureau? Haig Armour wouldn't be in town on an unimportant assignment. No one could say with certainty that Armour had actually left the F.B.I. Certainly he'd been prosecuting Justice cases, he was a lawyer, wasn't he? Weren't they all who had joined in Armour's generation. But it could be a cover-up for more secret Bureau work.

Reuben was eyeing the big hotel dubiously. "You going to stay here?"

Steve didn't like the way he was sticking, yet it needn't mean anything. It could be the kid didn't know his way around town and didn't have much coin. "No. I'm heading for a flea-bag up the street. I didn't think His Worship had to know." It wouldn't hurt to offer. "You can bunk with me tonight."

Rube spoke quickly. "I'm not broke. I didn't want any more handouts from Mr. Armour. Next thing he'd be winning the war single-handed." He crimped the grin. "It's too late tonight to start looking for the guys I was supposed to meet—"

"I said you could bunk with me," Steve repeated. It was too brusque. He softened it. "I already won one war. I don't want any more medals."

The hotel he was heading for was past Highland, halfway between the Roosevelt and the Drake. An easy walk even with the valise to carry. There didn't seem to be any big black car cruising the empty street. Rube had another dubious eye when they came abreast the Balboa.

Steve reassured him. "It's a flea-bag. But Hollywood style." The lobby was small and fancy, glassed like a conservatory. It had enough red leather banquettes to set up a cocktail lounge. "A friend recommended it." Albion had said it was convenient.

The desk clerk asked no questions, only the rent in advance of registration. He was a blenched old man, his sparse hair dyed a ruddy brown. Steve paid, handed over his valise to the soldier. They key he put in his pocket; let the hop pick up a duplicate.

He said, "I got to make a phone call before I turn in." He walked past the phone booths out of the hotel.

3

HE REMAINED SLANTWISE ON THE PAVEMENT OUTSIDE UNTIL HE saw Reuben disappear behind the elevator doors. He headed south then to Selma street. He'd memorized the location from Albion's notes. Even this near to Hollywood Boulevard, there were yet relics of a gentler day, old frame houses of the era of front porches and wisteria vines. These patches too would go; but they weren't shabby yet, they were well-kept, lived-in homes.

The fog was lifting with the early dawn; it was past four by his watch. He peered for numbers; he was on the wrong side of the street but he did not cross until he had found the house he sought. It was not as kempt as its neighbors, its gray paint was thinned by time. There was an old wooden swing and an old wicker rocker on the porch. The vines were without leaf this near to December.

No lights showed within, no shadow stirred behind the old-fashioned stiff lace curtains masking the front window. Steve climbed the three wooden steps of the porch without sound. He stood silently before the front door, not wanting to start this. After a moment his finger touched, barely touched, the bell.

He waited, his hands dug into the pockets of his coat, his hat half covering his eyes. At this hour a faint bell might not awaken a household long asleep. But he waited, reluctant to ring again, and the door came open. He couldn't see the man inside. A deep voice was overlaid with old European accent and suspicion. "What is it that you want?"

He answered, "Mr. Oriole."

The door was pulled wider, evidently as an invitation to enter. Steve walked in. He was in a small gloomy hall, papered in mottled wine color, cramped with an oversized oak hall tree, a chest to match, and a two-shelf bookcase. By a side window there was a worn leather armchair, eternally holding the sag of a large man, and a scuffed oak table strewn with newspapers. Above on the wall was a telephone with a coin box. A staircase climbed behind the chair, carpeted in the same worn green as the hall, the same color as the limp brocade drapery separating this room from what would be a parlor on the left. The staircase turned at a landing, hiding the upper floor. Directly forward where the hall narrowed into a corridor, another limp curtain covered another room. The only light on was a dim bulb hanging in the corridor.

The man was as shabby as the room. Flabby flesh drooped on his large stooped frame, on his shapeless face. He was half bald, the lank hair over his ears and neck a dirty gray-brown; his small dark eyes were both wary and uncurious. He wore gray trousers, shapeless as elephant shanks, a wrinkled shirt without collar or tie, and old felt bedroom slippers over brown cotton socks. He probably hadn't been to bed, only snatched a laydown while waiting for Steve to report.

Steve questioned, "Mr. Oriole?"

"I am Mr. Oriole."

"Steve Wintress." He didn't take his hands out of his pockets.

Mr. Oriole began plaintively, "Where have you been? I have for hours been expecting you—"

Steve interrupted, "Trying to get here." He demanded roughly, "Where the hell is Albion?"

"He did not meet you?"

"He did not meet me," Steve parroted. He knew how to deal with stationmasters like Oriole. Jump them before they could start on you. "No one met me."

Mr. Oriole spoke with concern. "Mr. Albion was there. He telephoned to inform me the plane would be late."

"Maybe he got tired waiting."

"Not Mr. Albion," said Mr. Oriole.

Not Albie, never Albie. He took orders with a bulldog grip. Efficient, trustworthy Albion. Steve wondered which side had killed him. Not why, only who. He said, "I've got to see him. He has my plans."

"I will telephone to him," Mr. Oriole said. Not with confidence.

Steve sat down on the oak chest, pushed back his hat, lit a cigarette. He needed a prop. Mr. Oriole put a coin into the hall phone and dialed a number. The sustained ringing sounded faint and metallic in the quiet. Mr. Oriole waited a long time before he hung up. The coin clacked down the chute, he retrieved it and put it in his pocket before turning. "There is no response."

"Where does he live? I'll drop around there." This was the point to make quickly. Stationmasters didn't like giving out an address.

Mr. Oriole was no amateur to be stampeded. He pried into Steve's face. "You want a room?"

"I have a room. I want to see Albion."

"I will send him to you. Where is your room?"

"Balboa Hotel. If you haven't his address, I'll take his phone number." When the man was hesitant, Steve asked, "What's the matter? Don't you want me to see him?" That would throw a delayed scare into the flab when he read the afternoon papers. The news wouldn't make the a.m.'s.

Reluctantly Oriole divulged the number. He didn't like doing it; it was his business to get people together, not arrange for them to make contacts on their own. He eyed the scrap of paper on which Steve had written the information as if he would snatch it from his hands. Steve tucked it into an inner pocket. "Don't worry. I won't hand it to the F.B.I."

Oriole tried for a laugh but it wouldn't come.

"And don't call me at the hotel. I have a roommate."

At Oriole's startled grunt, Steve smiled insolently. "You don't know me, Mr. Oriole. Wintress is the name, Steve Wintress. They send for me when there's a special job to do. And I do it my way." He rubbed out his cigarette on the heel of his shoe, pitched the butt towards the table before he crossed to the door. "If you find Albie, tell him I'm in a hurry to get back to Berlin." He slammed the door after him, not caring now how many he woke in that musty house. He didn't like armchair slobs giving him directions.

The morning was pale as he walked back to Hollywood Boulevard. No one followed him. It was easy to be sure because as yet the day of the city hadn't begun, he was alone on the side street, near alone on the blocks he covered returning to the hotel. In the hotel he passed the desk without a nod, passed the maroon uniform of the Phillippine boy into the elevator. He had to look at his key to know the floor. "Fourth."

He used the key to enter his room. Reuben's breathing was even in sleep. Steve didn't need a light to undress; he dropped his clothes on the armchair, yanked the window drapes across the narrow gray windows to shut out the coming of daylight. At the clatter of the metal rings over the rod, the soldier raised his head. His voice was druggish. "Get your call made?"

Steve said, "Yeah. Don't wake me in the morning."

It would have been easy to thump the pillow over coming problems, but he didn't. He needed sleep; he would sleep. Whoever killed Albie wasn't going to run away, he'd be around to see how Steve was liking it. Because there was only one reason why a smart guy like Albion would have dropped dead at the International Airport last night. One reason only, to keep him from meeting with Stefan Winterich.

It was after eleven when Steve awoke, not a long enough sleep, but more than he could hope for again for the duration of this job. He glanced towards the opposite bed. Reuben was still embedded in blankets, his spiky brown hair rising like pins from the pin-cushion of the pillow. Steve propped to an elbow to regard the sky through the ragged line between the curtains. It showed gray.

His movement stirred Rube. The boy creased his eyes. "What time is it?"

"About eleven-twenty. Time to get on the job." He lifted the phone from the table between the beds.

Rube reached out for a cigarette. "You here on a job?" It was the first personal question he'd asked.

Steve said, "A little insurance investigation deal." He had the right credentials for it, too, in case anyone got too nosy. It was the kind of job that gave a man a legitimate excuse to poke around in varied neighborhoods. He'd memorized Oriole's coin-box number last night. He gave it to the switchboard, said "Call me," and added, "Send up some coffee and stuff. Wintress, four-ninety." He told Rube, "We'll have breakfast this morning on the boss." A man needed a bit of coddling now and again. He lit a cigarette himself and pushed the pillows behind his shoulders.

Reuben said, "I ought to get going and see if I can find those guys. One of them has an aunt lives in an apartment on North Cahuenga. We were going to bunk with her."

"You on leave?"

"Yeah. I'm being reassigned. I just got back from two years in Berlin."

Steve's face didn't say anything; his face was trained. Berlin. And the phone rang. He slurred into it, "Who's speaking?"

The voice said, "Mr. Oriole." It was the right voice.

"Wintress. What's the news?"

Oriole had had it. He begged, "You must come here at once."

"What for?"

"It is not something to speak over the telephone. Mr. Schmidt is waiting for you. You will come." It was half question, half command.

Steve wanted to laugh. Here the name was Schmidt. It wasn't so much the news putting the tremolo in Oriole, it was a man called

Schmidt. He said, "Soon as I get dressed and catch a bite of breakfast," and waited for the hysteria. He wasn't disappointed.

"You must not wait for these things!"

"I'd look pretty funny running around Hollywood without my pants. See you." He hung up, yawned a grimace. But he got out of bed. "I'll go ahead and shower. If breakfast shows up, don't wait for me."

"Sure," Rube said. He appeared young and disinterested lying there in the bed. And he'd just come back from Berlin. He said for reassignment.

Steve didn't waste time in the shower, but Rube was swallowing coffee when he emerged. The smell was good. "Pour me some, kid. I'll shave while I'm eating." He plugged in his razor. Rube carried the coffee and a plate of ham and eggs to the bureau. "Should think you'd be spending your leave with your folks."

"What for?"

"Usual thing, isn't it?"

"Uh-uh," Rube said. "My old lady's got a new boy friend. She didn't want me around cramping her style."

"She can't be so old," Steve commented. "Your pop?"

"He took a walk twelve years ago."

"Where'd you live if you lived there?"

"New York."

"I was born there." Yeah, he'd been a New York kid once himself. A long time ago. He detached the razor and began to put on his pants. They could stand a press. He had a couple of clean shirts and a neat tie with little pink birds on an elongated navy sky, a girl had sent it to him for Christmas. He wore the plain maroon one. The shine on his shoes was still good enough with a rub-up. "Look," he said, "no use carrying your kit around all day. Bring your pals back with you around five and I'll buy the dinner." Big-hearted Steve. But he'd feel better if he made certain that there were pals before the soldier moved out.

"Well, thanks." Reuben was in character this early.

Steve caught up his coat, put on his hat, ducked back in to grab his room key and stow it in his pocket. He kept it there when passing the desk. No sense in advertising your comings and goings to strangers. There was a new man on the desk, a tall, thin, younger one, with a face like a sea gull.

It was as gray as fog out. Steve covered the few blocks to Oriole's steadily but without undue speed. Let them wait. He pushed hard on the doorbell this morning. There'd been a flutter behind the starched lace when he climbed the steps.

Mr. Oriole's face was wobbly. He hadn't washed, hadn't changed his clothes. "Come in, Mr. Wintress, come in."

Deliberately Steve delayed. "What's up?"

The flabby hand pointed towards the parlor. The green hangings were pulled apart, just enough for a narrow man to pass through. "Come in. Mr. Schmidt is waiting."

There was always a Smith or a Schmidt or a Smithsky. This one was a precise middle-aged man, wearing a banker's blue suit and a conservative tie of blue on navy blue stripes. His black shoes were small and high-polished, his fingernails dull-polished. His rimless glasses had no expression.

Mr. Oriole said, "This is Steve Wintress, Mr. Schmidt."

Schmidt said, "I've heard much of you, Mr. Wintress." He shook hands like a man in a countinghouse. There was no warmth in his voice. It could have been a tape recording.

Steve inclined his head. The parlor was small and hadn't been redecorated since the house was built. It was golden oak and green plush, as crowded with furniture as the hall. A luxuriant fern sprayed green fronds from a table by the front window. Steve took the straight chair by the side window, leaving the plush one for Schmidt; the light for Schmidt's face, for Steve's back. He asked again, "What's up?"

Schmidt said, "Albion is dead." His hand tightened imperceptibly on the newspaper he was holding. Early edition of the p.m.'s.

Steve reached for it. Schmidt had to lean far out of his chair to pass over the paper. It was a trick Steve had learned too long ago to remember where. To make the other fellow subservient. The story was a small one near the foot of the front page. "The body of Frederick Grasse—" that had been Albion's name—"was found early this morning," and so on. Officialdom believed that Grasse, feeling unwell, stepped outside the terminal for fresh air. Heart attack."

Steve read it word for word. He handed back the paper, again letting Schmidt come out of the chair for it. He propelled the question, "Who killed him?"

Mr. Oriole twisted his dirty hands. Schmidt said, "You believe he was killed?" His voice was dry as a pod.

"I don't think he dropped dead so he couldn't meet me." Steve came out of the chair and began pacing the square of old carpet. It could make guys like Schmidt and guys like Oriole nervous. "It wasn't the Feds—"

Schmidt interrupted virulently. "The F.B.I.! Cossacks! Tools of the capitalist dictators—" He was primed to go on with the well-worn speech but Steve cut him off.

"Don't tell me. Write your congressman." He walked over to Schmidt and stood above him, making him lift up his glassy eyes. "It wasn't the Feds. They take us alive. They want talk, not dead men. Who killed Albie?"

Schmidt said rigidly, "We will find out."

"Okay. And while you're finding out, what do I do? Play the ponies?" He walked back to the gushing fern. "Albion was carrying the information I need for this job. I've got to have that dope."

"You will have it." Schmidt eyed Mr. Oriole.

"By tomorrow morning."

Oriole's mouth drooped. "It is impossible!" At the warning of Schmidt's face, he explained hurriedly, "Mr. Albion worked for long weeks. We do not know how many places he visited, how many persons with whom he spoke." The excuses were not being accepted. He swallowed hard. "It will be difficult."

Steve was brusque. It was either that or weep with the guy. "You think we're the only ones after the Davidian report? Who came in on my plane last night? Haig Armour."

"He is no longer with the F.B.I." Schmidt was full of knowledge. "He is here on another matter."

"Says who? What's big enough for him out here but Davidian? I've got to have that dope tomorrow."

Schmidt said thinly to Oriole, "Put everyone available on it."

Steve relented. "Make it noon. That gives you twenty-four hours." And that gave him twenty-four hours.

There were gaps which only Albie's knowledge could fill. Oriole and his research squad would never close all of them. Albion was too smart not to withhold some keys. Because in this racket you didn't know whom you could trust or for how long. But Steve was ahead of all of them; he'd been in on the Davidian business a lot longer than a couple of weeks. He'd been in at the very beginning, in Berlin. Which was nobody's business but his own, certainly no business of this puny West Coast outfit. In twenty-four hours he might not need Albion's material. Meanwhile, looking for it would keep the Schmidt crowd occupied.

He went back to the chair and gathered his coat; he hadn't removed his hat. "Noon," he repeated.

Schmidt came up on his small polished feet. "May I give you a lift?"

"I need exercise," he said ungraciously. He added to it, "I've got some thinking to do. If Mr. Oriole can't get me that material—"

"He will," Schmidt assured him, and "Oh yes, I will," Oriole quavered.

Steve completed his sentence, "—I'll have to do a bit of scratching around."

"You couldn't say that Mr. Schmidt appeared alarmed, but neither was he complacent. His minions didn't scratch around, you could bet; as they followed procedure. He pattered after Steve to the swinging draperies. "Is it true that you knew Davidian in Berlin?"

Steve gave him courteous attention. Even a neat little Continental half-bow.

"It is absolutely true," he said.

II

HE TOOK HIS TIME WALKING BACK TO HOLLYWOOD BOULEVARD. Not much of a boulevard, none of the elegance either of the old-trees variety or of glassy modern towers. The one big hotel and the one big department store were at opposite ends of the main stem; westward the boulevard dwindled into a residential section, eastward it moved on downtown. There were a couple of big movie houses like delusions of grandeur scattered along the way. But mostly the street was hometowny, an overgrown Main Street. It was probably why Hollywood Boulevard had become a lodestone. Any American, except perhaps a born New Yorker, would feel at home on it.

Large red trolleys clattered through the centerlane, small yellow busses stumbled against traffic. Vintage cars and an occasional better one crowded the curbs; endless little shops and movie houses and cafés backed up either side of the sidewalks. And endless men and women and kids sauntered on the treadmill pavement. The pace wasn't that of a city, it was California easy. The shop windows were decorated for Christmas shopping, heavy on the red and green and pocket-size cellophane trees dusted with stars. The street was decked out in the same spirit. Great green metallic trees grew from the sidewalks, giant tinsel stars and bells dangled overhead.

Steve hadn't been followed from Oriole's. He couldn't be sure that he wasn't picked up on Hollywood Boulevard. He was conspicuous in his hat and gabardine. The grayness of sky didn't matter to these people; they didn't wear hats, men or women, and the only coats were on older women. After this morning, Steve was certain that Schmidt would decide to put a dog at his heels. Schmidt didn't go in for unorthodoxy. It was possible that he might be deterred by orders to let Steve Wintress alone, but this depended on how strong New York had made them. You couldn't count on Smithsky not to promise one thing and perform the diametric opposite.

Steve knew where to start without Albion's findings. He alone knew where Davidian had first holed up in Los Angeles, he hoped the knowledge remained his alone. He had intended to bypass the seven-month-old trail, it had been Albion's job to bridge those months. But it was all he had now.

He accepted the off chance that a dog was already at his heels. Better to smell him out and elude him now rather than attempt it in the heavier traffic of downtown L.A. He walked towards his hotel leisurely. He timed it to double back and be the last man on board. Two stout women and a soiled youth in a school jacket had boarded ahead of him. They appeared harmless enough. At the next stop it was women and kids. He checked a half dozen stops and checked off these passengers at various points along the boulevard. Not one of those he'd noted was left on board when the car clattered through the tunnel into the subway terminal.

The ride had been an hour long, a typical ride to the downtown area of a city, the shops growing more shabby in neighborhoods left behind as the crocodile metropolis crawled westward. The only off-beat sights were the dirty white round of once-glittering Angelus Temple, and a small lagoon with swans rising out of the placid water.

It was after two when Steve came out of the terminal into the crowded downtown streets. This far from the ocean the overcast was thinned, the sky created an illusion of a watery sun. His coat was a burden. He knew the city well enough; he'd had plenty of leaves here in the old war, the one to end war. He walked the half block to Fifth, turned the corner and moved on up to the corner of Olive. The park called Pershing Square was boarded up, behind a wooden fence excavators had plowed up what once had been the refuge of old men and pigeons.

From caution out of experience, Steve didn't continue directly to Bunker Hill. He stopped first in a small drugstore across from the Biltmore Hotel and shut himself into a phone booth. He faked a call, waited what seemed long enough. No one had come into the store after him, no one was loitering outside when he left the booth and continued his climb up the hill. This had been an elegant part of town. What remained was beyond pride or even remembrance of the past. The dull smear of cement covered where once there had been flowering lawns and the benediction of trees.

Unlike its sister back streets of New York, this one was near to deserted. No housewives squabbled amiably as they rocked their baby carriages; no children ran under heels into the traffic. There was no traffic, not even a passing car. Nor was there curiosity evinced in a stranger, and he well knew a stranger was as recognizable in this isolated sort of community as on a village green. And as little welcomed. One thing was definite. He had not been trailed; he was alone on the block.

He found the number he was seeking, a big broad house, three fine stories of once-white frame, standing on a high-cut back terrace. There was a side porch where the family would have rocked on a summer's night, looking out upon the quiet hills beyond. When the house was young. A flight of run-over cement steps led to the top of the terrace, a cracked cement walk to the house. He climbed sagging wooden steps to the porch and crossed to the front door. No one appeared to challenge the intruder. The knob turned loosely under his hand and he entered the murky hall. There were defiantly closed doors on either side of a large center staircase. A pay phone against the wall reiterated a nervous jangle. He didn't linger below, but began to climb the footworn stairs. Somewhere a baby wailed, somewhere a radio sang about a lovesick girl, somewhere a man and woman quarreled in short ugly spats.

On the second floor he walked a length of more closed doors, noisome and silent, and continued on up the back staircase. Three F was on third, the poorest location, without light from front or rear. He rapped on the dirty wood. When there was no response, he rapped again more sharply. He heard the loud outthrust of a door from the floor below, a man yelling perdition at a shrilling woman. The man's heavy shoes clattered down the stairs. And Steve rapped a third time, hard, under cover of the confusion.

The door came open an ell. In the aperture there was a segment of an old face, wrinkled past recognition. Only the kerchief wound about the head gave indication that the face belonged to a woman. The eyes were black and small as black buttons. And malevolent. The mouth spat, "Nah."

Steve put his shoulder against the door before it could close. He didn't expect her to understand, but he said, "I am looking for a friend."

"Nah," she repeated.

She pushed at the door but he was stronger. "I know that he lived here."

She muttered an unintelligible stream of sound. And from within he heard a sharp command in what appeared the same tongue. It could have been Czech. The order must have been to admit him because her grudging hand opened the door. Not wide enough to walk through but he could sidle inside.

It was a rather large room, it might have been the nursery in those older, gentler days. But it was diminished by dirt and time, by the big brass bed, and the stove and rusted sink, the cretonne-covered wardrobe, the oversized round table and motley chairs. There was a narrow window against the far wall, in front of it in a teetering rocker an old man wheezed in his sleep.

These things Steve saw, but only in suspended memory. For there was only one thing he knew he was seeing, the girl who had spoken the command. She was sitting upright on the tumbled cot against the farther wall, her short dark hair tattered about her face. She was wrapped in a kimono of purple cotton with giant pink chrysanthemums blooming over it. Her bare feet curled under the purple hem. Her hair was sleepy but her eyes were as big as the old woman's were small, and were as black and hard. He had never dreamed of finding her here. The one person he would not seek; the one person he didn't ever want to lay eyes on again. It was Janni.

His voice was as hard as her eyes. Only by keeping it so did he dare speak. "What are you doing here?"

"Did you think I should be in Beverly Hills or maybe Bel Air?" She held the kimono tight across chrysanthemum breasts.

He was without an answer, afraid lest he cry out to her, more afraid lest he move towards her.

She demanded, "What is it you want?" She loosed one hand, pushed it through her hair in the old familiar gesture.

Because he didn't know what to say, he asked stupidly, "You were asleep?"

"I work nights."

At the sudden anger that flared into his face, she laughed out loud. "You think you will find me in the cinema? The new Marlene Dietrich perhaps?" She laughed again, that short brutal laugh. "Yes, I am with the cinema. At nights I sell tickets on Main Street. It is a fine job."

He too could be brutal, to hide his relief and his agony. He said, "I'm looking for Davidian."

The mockery went out of her. The old lady hardened in the background, the old man slept on. Janni said, "He is not here."

"Where is he?"

"I do not know."

"He was here."

She flamed, "Haven't you made enough trouble for him? For all of us? Get out and leave us alone."

He didn't move. "I'm looking for Davidian."

"You think we have hidden him?" Her voice burned. "Look under the bed. Look in the stove. Look in Grandfather's pants. Look! He is not here."

"I know he is not here," he said distinctly. "But I know he was here. Where did he go when he moved on?"

Her mouth was insolent. "If I knew I would not tell you. But I do not know. When he went away, I told him I must not know. Because of such as you."

"Her?" His shoulder gestured to the old woman.

"She knows nothing. Not even her name."

"If you see him, will you tell him I am looking for him?"

Her eyes hated with cold, bleak hate. "Why should I? To send him running again?"

He forced it on her, from across the room. "Will you tell him that?"

She shrugged and she tightened the cheap kimono about her. Beneath it there was nothing but her body, the curves and planes that came alive in a man's hands.

"Tell him that. Let him know. It's better for him to know."

She gave no response at all, only the width of her blank, black eyes. He didn't know what she would do. She would decide. He turned on his heel. The old woman had the door open for him. There was a curse on her blanched lips.

He wasn't noiseless leaving the house; he defied its ugliness. At the front door he paused briefly before stepping out into the city. If a tail had caught up with him, it wasn't visible. He went on down the hill to Pershing Square. He rode the trolley back to Hollywood, to his hotel. Blanking the memories from his mind, mocking at desire. A street girl; maybe she was selling movie tickets on Main Street and maybe she wasn't. Maybe she was singing the little song again, dancing the dance. She had been fifteen when they first met, five—six years ago. He'd been too old for her then; he was too much older now.

Reuben was stretched out on the bed, perusing the comic strips in the evening news. He said, "What do you think? We're asked to a cocktail party."

"Who?"

"Feather Talle. She'd called about a million times before I got in so I called her back. She was calling you but she asked me to come along."

Steve lay down on his own bed. "Forget it. Trolleys don't run to her ritzy dump. Or busses. And I'm too old to hitch."

"She's sending a car." Rube was slyly triumphant. "Haig Armour's car."

Steve frowned. He didn't get it unless two and two were actually four and she was one of Haig's little helpers.

Rube continued. "She said Haig said he'd be delighted to pick us up. He's invited too."

He would be. Haig and his damn car and damn driver.

"How the hell did she find me?"

"She said it was easy. She just started calling Hollywood hotels until she found this one."

"You go," Steve decided. "Say you couldn't find me."

"I couldn't do that. It was you she wanted."

It wouldn't hurt to go; wouldn't hurt to find out for sure what Haig Armour expected to get out of him. He yawned, "Okay, you win. But you take on whats-her-name."

"Feather," Rube admitted sadly.

"My God." He climbed off the bed. "I'll take on the cocktails. What about your pals? Find them?"

Reuben was embarrassed. "I found where they used to be. They've already shipped out." He went on quickly. "I'm getting out of here, don't worry about that, Steve. Only I'd sort of like to take in that cocktail party first."

Steve laughed. "I'm not trying to get rid of you." Maybe there'd been pals, maybe not; maybe Reuben St. Clair was a dog on his heels. It was better to have him underfoot than to have to spy out a stranger. If he was just a soldier with no place to go, he'd come in handy to keep Schmidt's boys out of the room. "You might as well stay on with me as long as you're parked here. We don't seem to get in each other's way."

"You mean it?" The boy was appealingly grateful. "It's a lot better kicks than being alone. I don't like to make out alone. I wouldn't want you to think I'm sponging. I was kind of rocky last night but I cashed a check today." He darted to the jangling phone, said happily, "I sure thank you," and into the phone, "Yeah, we'll be right down."

It was Wilton again. In lobby light he looked like any human being. Not much different from Steve, same build, about the same height, same average face. Same dead pan. He stated, "The car's around the corner," and let them follow him. Haig wasn't in it; Haig had gone on ahead to set the stage.

He put them in the back seat, took his place at the wheel. He drove out Selma, there were lights upstairs and down behind the lace curtains of Mr. Oriole's. It would be worth a penny to see Oriole's face if he beheld Steve Wintress in a Fed car.

Early dusk covered the Strip. Reuben wasn't talkative; he was sight-seeing out the window, getting his kicks out of the scrawled signature of Ciro's, the awning of the Mocambo. Peering into passing Cad convertibles for movie stars. The car followed the old bridle path on Sunset into Beverly. They didn't hesitate at the hotel, yeah, Haig had gone ahead. They rolled up the Canyon and through open gates tonight to the front steps of French Provincial grandeur. The grandeur was sustained. Feather wasn't at the door; a white-coated Philippine boy, twin to the Balboa's elevator operator, took their hats and whispered, "This way, please."

The hall wasn't so much, it only smelled of money with its icy candelabra and polished rosewood. The library, to which they were escorted, was something else. A vasty warm room of books in maple, of soft-patterned couches and deep chairs, of winter roses in silver bowls; a room of giant eucalyptus logs burning in a mammoth white brick fireplace. Haig Armour stood by the fire at the far end of the room, Feather jumped up out of the pillows on the elongated primrose couch. She was dwarfed by the enormity of the room and she looked childlike in the white satin shirt, the slender trousers of blue-black velvet. She'd discarded her horn-rims, her face lifted like a crystal flower out of the satin ruff at her throat.

"I'm so happy you could come," she recited, her pale hair swinging against her cheeks. She didn't say it happy.

Haig was as easy as she was rehearsed. "Hello, Steve. Hello, Reuben. You boys get rested up today?"

Steve said, "Hello," and turned his eyes on the low table with setups of the finest silver and glass.

Feather said, "Won't you help yourself? I'm not good at mixing."

Steve poured a good one of bourbon, the best bourbon. He added enough soda, gave place to Reuben, and made himself comfortable on the couch. Reuben and Haig carried their drinks over to the bookshelves as if they were interested in literature. His eyes followed them briefly, returned to the girl. He punched a cushion, his fist sinking into the down and leaving no imprint. "Sit down, lady," he directed her. As if he didn't know, he said, "And what do you do for a living?"

She curled in the corner. "Nothing yet. I want to be a dancer."

"Why not?"

"I mean a really good one. It takes so long, and then you're too old."

He tested the drink. Potent. "I used to know a dancer. She was a good one, too. In great demand, every night." You weren't permitted to mix business and liquor. It wasn't orthodox. He got away with it because he could do a dangerous piece of work better than anyone in the outfit. And unless he could do it his way, it wasn't done. They were afraid a guy would start talking if he drank, and on that, they were right. But it wasn't necessary to talk. He never talked unless it came in handy.

Reuben and Haig were still among the books. Steve moved a little closer to Feather, she in turn pushed herself further into the corner cushion. "What do you want to dance for? With this setup?"

"It isn't mine," she said defensively. "My aunt married it." Her fingers were white and rigid against the cushion, as if she would spring if he edged nearer. He wanted to try it just to see how far she could jump. Her question halted him. "Where did she dance?"

"In Berlin." He looked unseeing into the amber of his glass. His voice was hard. "You didn't ask me what she danced for. I'll tell you. She danced for nylons and a good lipstick—and a bed."

Feather sucked in her breath. He turned his head slowly, looked her over from the smooth crown of her petal head, down her thin body to her velvet toes. "You wouldn't, would you? You'd go without. But when you got hungry enough—"

She jumped then. Not because he had moved but because she had an excuse. "Elsabeth," she shrilled. "Come meet my friends." She almost ran the long length of the room to greet this Elsabeth, a slender woman with exquisite golden hair, an exquisite French-cut dress, discreet jewels, and a face that showed her years.

Haig and Reuben returned to the party. Feather said, "This is my aunt, Elsabeth Moritz." She made the introduction before tucking herself again into the couch corner. Steve was surprised that she returned to it.

Elsabeth was polite to Steve and Reuben. But she put herself beside Haig Armour, asked him for a drink. "What a day! I thought the committee would never come to a decision." She didn't identify the committee. She took the tall glass from Haig, the properly made drink, only half filled. "Thanks, so much." Her voice was nicely modulated, her smile had a friendly warmth, yet somehow both were artificial. If you washed away the top layer, you'd find something else; ten to one a hard-boiled kid in the line, bitching her way up the ladder to position and money. From Prospect Park to Benedict Canyon in twelve tough steps. Steve rather liked her.

"Eldon not here yet?" she asked Feather. "Poor dear. The shooting schedule on this new epic is simply gruesome. You know how Danton is." She was confidential about Danton in the rueful lift of eyebrows.

Haig said, "I'm a great admirer of your husband's work, Mrs. Moritz. I've wanted to meet him for a long time."

She accepted the compliment with a gracious inclination of her head. Haig carried on, mentioning details of one picture and another. Either he was an honest fan or he'd done a lot of research today. Steve didn't think Haig had that much time for movie-going.

Steve said to Feather, "Last movie I saw was Casablanca. It was good too."

She waited to see if it were a joke. When he didn't laugh, she asked, "Really?"

"Sure."

She'd evidently been briefed to take care of him because she kept her cat eyes on his face, just as if he were revealing something important. If she were expected to make friends with him, he'd make it easy for her. He'd get more from this awkward kid than from Haig Armour. The man's polish was the real stuff but it didn't affect the steel beneath.

"How about you and me and Rube having a bit of dinner later on?"

For a moment she didn't answer. Then she breathed, "I'm sorry. Haig's already asked me."

He wasn't surprised. "He's too old for you, baby. And I'd say Rube's a bit too young." He winked at her, let her think the bourbon was responsible. "Now I'm just about right." He reached out his hand to pat her velvet knee and watched her shrink back into the corner. He didn't know whether it was he who scared her or any man with ideas. "How about it?"

She said, "I can't." She wasn't sorry. "I've already accepted his invitation."

"In that case," Steve announced, "I'll have another drink." He went first to Reuben's chair. The soldier was odd man; he was sitting there quietly as if he were at home in the rich room. Steve put his hand on the khaki shoulder. "How you doing, fella?"

The grin was ready. "Looks kind of like you're taking on the drinks and the girl both."

Steve nodded portentously. "Just softening her up for you, kid." He was at the setups when Eldon Moritz appeared at the far archway.

Elsabeth lifted her voice, you had to lift your voice for it to carry that far. "You're frightfully late, dear. You'll have time for just one drink before we dress."

He said, "Oh God, what tonight?" He approached with quick, nervous steps.

"Come meet Feather's friends. Dinner with Marty before we go to the *premiére* of his latest."

Moritz was a neat man, almost dapper in his pin-striped suit and discreetly handsome Charvet cravat. He had no resemblance to an artist, rather he was the tired businessman, his dark hair receding to baldness on his long head, his mustache two pencil strokes, dark crayon under his eyes.

His wife introduced Haig and didn't remember the other names. Steve presented himself and gestured, "Reuben St. Clair." Eldon mixed himself a double rye as he acknowledged the introductions. He drank before asking Reuben, "Any relation to Stryker St. Clair?"

Rube wriggled. "My father, sir."

"Thought so. Family resemblance. We were at Princeton together." He joined his wife and Haig.

Steve re-estimated the kid fast. Not Sinclair, St. Clair; his old lady and her now boy friend would be stashed up on Park Avenue, not in some cold-water flat; Stryker St. Clair was a Dun and Bradstreet name, an old Blue Book name, a new café society name. It hadn't been orders to stick with Steve. Just a poor rich boy, a lonesome kid, looking for a friend, not a free ride. You could get too suspicious.

Steve swerved back to Feather. "Want to change your mind about tonight, baby?"

She'd been looking long at Haig but she jumped her attention to Steve as he spoke. She tried to turn on a little charm but she wasn't much good at it. "Why not tomorrow night?"

"I may not be around tomorrow night."

Her pale eyes studied him, looking for the joker in this.

He expanded, "I'm on a quick job."

Her lashes flickered. It could have been admiration; it could have been relief that he wouldn't be bothering her any longer. Reuben was taking it easy, maybe dreaming he was back home with the folks. Haig and Eldon were being technical about movies, Elsabeth was timing them. Steve leaned to Feather. He was confidential. "You ought to latch onto Rube while you've got a chance. Get yourself a dump like Auntie, swimming pools and all the fixings. You heard who your uncle said he was."

She was softly indignant. "What makes you think I want these things? Do you consider it fair that Eldon Mortiz can spend a hundred thousand dollars on this house while whole families are living in one room?"

"He works for it, doesn't he?"

"It isn't Eldon," she returned quickly. "He has a conscience. It's just the whole capitalist system where such things can happen." She bit her lip as if she'd spoken out of turn.

Steve didn't swallow bait. He undertoned, "I think I'll have another capitalistic bourbon while it's free to the peasants. How about you?"

"I don't drink." She was prim.

"Then you aren't a hundred-per-cent, red-blooded peasant. We take when the takings good from these rich bastards."

No one saw how weak he poured it. Elsabeth was demanding, "We must run, Eldon. Marty won't forgive us if we make him late for his own *premiére.*" Eldon didn't like leaving when the party was centered about his abilities, but he finished his glass. Elsabeth performed a gracious good-by all around, Eldon nodded distractedly to the unknowns and suggested to Haig, "Let's have lunch. I want to explain my message in that one." He followed his wife.

Feather smiled timidly at Haig. "I'd better change too." She skipped after the others, to report to them too?

Steve waited only until she was out of sight. "I don't get her. What's she scared of?"

"You." Haig had an amused eyebrow.

"Me?"

"She was quiet as a pond until you arrived." He was again at the bookshelves. "A real artist, Moritz." He pulled a book, riffled through it. "Did you read about the excitement at the airport last night?"

Reuben asked, "You mean the guy found dead of a heart attack?"

Heart attack, hell. Haig Armour knew better; he wouldn't be mentioning it if he didn't know more than what the news vendors were putting out.

"If either of you had wandered outside when you were looking for your friends, you'd have discovered him."

"Yeah." Steve elongated the word as in admiration of Armour's imagination. "Too bad we didn't." Despite precautions, had the law someway tied Steve up with Albion? Or was Haig fishing? Because Steve Wintress's name and its implications weren't unknown to him?

Haig replaced the book. It made a slight click returning to the shelf. Like a gun cocking. "The man was waiting for our plane." He said it pleasantly. But he was watching Steve.

Steve handed him one. "Was he waiting for you?"

Haig shook his head.

"Then how do you know about it?" He couldn't play it innocent like Rube, he wasn't the type. He had to settle for the wise-guy attitude of the half drunk.

"One of the attendants at the airport remembered his questions regarding our flight." Haig was extraordinarily careful with his cigarette ash. It made a soft gray capsule in a translucent jade tray. "The odd thing is that no one from the flight turned up to identify him."

This time Steve didn't hesitate. "You must have had a special interest in this guy the way you've been looking into him."

Haig didn't have to respond. Feather's appearance in the arch was sufficient diversion. She'd changed to a slender black dress and pulled up her hair in an effort for sophistication. It didn't amount to enough.

But Haig chose to answer. "I'm always interested in oddities." He dropped the subject there. "Why don't you fellows come along to dinner with us?"

"Now, we wouldn't want to move in," Reuben began.

"Why not?" Steve decided. The way a guy with too many quick ones could be expected to perform. "Why not? Why let Mr. Armour have all the fun?" He gulped the rest of his drink.

Haig asked, "You don't mind, Feather?"

She said, "Oh, no," but she wasn't quite sure. She did it pretty well. Just as if she and Haig hadn't planned the whole layout before Wilton delivered Steve and Reuben into their hands. As to what they wanted, Steve still wasn't too sure.

2

As host, Haig Armour took over even as he had the night before. There was no choice of cafe; the party arrived at Haig's hotel.
He swept them to a reserved table in the glossy dining room, allowed
them to inspect the mammoth menu and exquisite wine list while he
ordered. No one opposed. You didn't oppose a torrent.

He timed his grenade until they were lulled by luxury. "I understand you boys are from Berlin." He didn't bother to explain where
he'd picked up the information. "Did you happen to run across a
fellow there called Davidian?"

No one stopped eating.

Reuben shook his head. "Uh-uh." He dug into his oyster cocktail.

Steve made a play at trying to place the name. "Davidian? Don't
think I did. What his racket?"

Haig smiled. "You might say he's an artist."

You might say that. An engraver could be called an artist, that is,
if he were as artistic an engraver as Davidian. He could make money
you'd have a hard time telling from the real thing. The Germans
had known it; that explained why he didn't end up a handful of
bones or ash. The Russians had found out about him; they'd cleared
him with dispatch of any Nazi stain. The Americans had a file on his
talents. And another one on his activities.

"Friend of yours?"

"No," Haig answered with the same offhand smile. "But a friend
of mine went to Berlin to meet him."

Steve asked, "Was he worth it?"

"He wasn't there. He'd disappeared."

Somehow the word, simple enough in itself, assumed a sinister
quality, something foreign to the elegance of dinner in Beverly Hills.
Feather's hands were nervous at the celery dish. Reuben put away
his oyster fork. It was he who asked, "Disappeared?"

Haig studied the boy briefly. He nodded.

Steve wondered. Could it be Haig didn't know which one of the
two was looking for Davidian?

"From the American zone?" Rube probed.

"From the Eastern sector."

Steve narrowed his eyes on Haig. "How did your friend expect to find him if he was in the Russian sector? The Reds don't like Americans poking around in their business."

Reuben said, "That's a fact," and launched a couple of anecdotes about guys he'd known who had tried to wander over the boundary. He even brought up the old familiar friend of a friend who had vanished on a harmless foray. Haig listened courteously.

The girl turned her head to Steve with pallid indignation. "We wouldn't want them poking into our business either." It was evident that she'd been primed to get him popping off. Her earlier guff about capitalism was part of the same. He let Reuben answer her.

"But their guys don't disappear over on our side. We just bounce them back fast."

Haig lit a cigarette. "I'm trying to find Davidian." Was he angling for an informer? Did he hope that Steve would sell out to him; could it be he had heard that Steve worked for hire, not devotion to a cause? The waiters were a stylish drill team, removing plates, making order out of disorder before bringing the steaks.

Steve hooted. "In Beverly Hills?"

Haig lifted bold eyes. "Does that surprise you?" He knew it didn't. He might think Rube was playing a hand in this, but he knew Steve Wintress was in Los Angeles for only one purpose.

Steve asked innocently, "Why would a man like that turn up here?"

Haig shrugged. "Possibly to meet a very good friend of his. Janni Zerbec."

Somehow the glass in Steve's hand didn't splinter. All of them were eying him. If he didn't brazen it out, Haig would wonder out loud what was bothering him. He brazened, "Is Janni Zerbec here?"

"Yes, Tim saw her today." Haig was casual. "You know her?"

Janni wasn't one for idle talk, certainly not to the Gestapo. Yet she didn't know the shape of U.S. officialdom. It wasn't the ugly iron spikes or hunks of jagged stone she was conditioned to; it was clerks like Timothy or smooth operators like Haig Armour. She wouldn't know how dangerous they could be. Steve decided to play it dumb. If she'd mentioned his visit to Timothy, he would brand her a liar. Let Haig prove which one lied.

"Isn't she the girl who use to dance in those blackmarket cafés?" If only Feather couldn't add. If only she'd forgotten the earlier moment of his indulgence in remembering Janni. His question sounded genuinely curious; this Berlin pin-up of earlier G.I.'s shouldn't be linked with his personal bitterness over a dancer. He grimaced. "The joints out of bounds for us G.I.'s?"

Feather's wide eyes widened. "You mean she danced for G.I.'s and lived in the Eastern sector?"

"Maybe she couldn't read the signs," Rube said dryly.

Haig's eyes hadn't moved from Steve. "You were in Berlin with the Army of Occupation?"

"I was one of the first guys in."

Reuben's smile wrapped Steve up in a new blanket of friendship. The kid would have been in high school when Steve was rolling into Berlin. The old men had been sent home, the high school crowd had taken over. Same job, no modern improvements. There wasn't even a concept of peace any longer between wars. Nothing but stalemate between Armageddons.

Steve became garrulous in imitation of soldiers. "There were plenty of girls entertaining us conquering heroes. But only one Janni Zerbec. Everybody knew Janni."

"Off bounds," Haig commented.

Something in the way he said it made Steve ask what he didn't want to ask. "Did you?"

Haig had been waiting for this. He let his smile grow reminiscent, his dark eyes slumberous. "Yes, I knew her."

Steve managed to speak evenly. "You were over there, too, when the war ended?"

"I was there ahead of the lines."

And Haig could have lined her up before Steve found her. It wasn't true. Steve was sure it wasn't true. This lie was a part of Haig's master plan, only that; something labeled Operation Davidian, with Directive A: dissect Steve Wintress; Subdirective: try Stimulus Janni. And watch Steve Wintress bleed. It wasn't going to work. Haig couldn't hear his heart thudding: *Keep your fine manicured paws off Janni, keep your richness for the Feathers—keep away from Janni!* Haig could hear only the question he spoke aloud, "What the hell's she doing here?"

Haig said, "Perhaps Davidian will answer that."

Davidian shouldn't have made contact with her; he'd been warned to stay away from anyone out of his past. Steve asked bluntly, "Are you out here to ship them back to Berlin?"

Haig laughed, "They appear to be here legitimately." He stopped laughing. "Unless they move into the wrong crowd." The waiters were again tidying up the table. "Besides it's not my business. I'm in a different racket now, as you would put it. My doctor advised a quieter job."

Like hell. Somehow Steve managed a smile. "So you're looking for Davidian to ask him about his income tax."

Rube told the waiter, "I'll have chocolate layer cake with my ice cream."

"In a way." Haig continued smoothly, "You might say I'm interested in the amount of money he's made this year."

Did Haig honestly believe that Davidian was opening up his engraving business in Los Angeles? It was the kind of maneuvering the department had found successful before; it might be tough to apprehend a guy for murder or wife-beating or subversive activities, but you could move in fast on income tax irregularities. You could use the threat to bargain for the report.

Haig was asking, "Do you get out here often?"

"No." They couldn't pin on him the coincidence of Davidian and Janni being in these parts.

"I find it a particularly interesting community. It has a heterology of its own but it isn't as easy to be lost in it as it is in New York, for example, or Berlin or London. For a fairly simple reason. It doesn't have the ancient warrens of those tired old cities. It is difficult to find a hiding place in a meadow or on the plains. Or in the wide sprawling spaces of Los Angeles. There's too much daylight and not enough shadow."

Steve said sardonically, "Then you won't have much trouble in running down this Davidian."

"Not much." Haig was complacent. "This community has another aspect which is both peculiar and helpful. It is neighborly. Unlike New York, or Berlin or London, where there is, you might say, a psychotic revulsion against so much as recognizing a stranger, the good people here open their arms in welcome. Therefore, undue reticence creates conversation; it actually becomes suspect. And conversation ripples like a pebble in a pond, to the milkman and the breadman and the ice cream man, in the supermarket and the laundromat and the P.T.A. meeting. Whenever I see street after street of neat little while houses, or pink or green or yellow houses, I know that even the children playing on the walks will recognize the presence of a deviationist."

He had it all tagged so neatly. Yet Davidian had hidden out for months now. Successfully. Perhaps Davidian himself had perceived the pattern, perhaps he was hiding in the open. The danger in this solution was obvious; the kids on the block would be singing about the nice new man instead of the nasty new man. You couldn't win the way Haig had outlined it. And Haig could be right, he wouldn't often be wrong.

An urgency to get back to Janni rode Steve's nerves. She'd have to tell him where Davidian was; the F.B.I. had come too far. It wasn't safe for any of them now.

3

IT WASN'T EASY TO GET AWAY. HE DIDN'T DOUBT THIS HAD BEEN ONE OF the purposes of Haig's fancy dinner. To keep him from his job. He made his exit on a palpable excuse about business, insurance business, leaving the three of them at the table, still tied up with coffee and dessert and the check. He caught a cab discharging a couple outside the hotel, announced, "The Biltmore," loudly, in case Haig had a man hanging around. There was no cab waiting to follow and no car took out after him. It was a long ride, not as long as by trolley and bus, and not as time-consuming. But the expense account wouldn't stand many of these jaunts. He'd have to get hold of a car if he was going to track down Davidian in these wide open spaces. Moreover, a cab was too easy to follow.

He played the game in the Biltmore Hotel. The lobby was full of conversation, businessmen in responsible business suits. He couldn't spot a tracker. He went to the desk, asked for a guy who had vanished into Siberia a year back, not a name Haig could check quickly. From there he went to the house phone, put through a call to 819. No one was in earshot when he made it brief to the wrong number at the other end. A fancy flight of steps led to the elevator. He took them fast, caught an elevator waiting, before his call could be traced. He rode to five, a middle-aged couple got off ahead of him but they minded their own business, heading to a room, opening the door and closing it after them. After that he wasted no time in the rug-hushed corridor. He was quick to the fire stairs and he descended on foot. He left by the side door of the hotel.

There weren't too many people walking around the downtown streets at this hour until he reached Main. Its garish honky-tonks were going full blast. He sauntered along, despite the urgency pressing him. Plenty of movie houses cut their marquee lights and let the cashiers go home before midnight. By sauntering he didn't make noticeable his examination of the girls remaining on duty.

She hadn't been lying about her job. She was in the glass cage at one of the meanest of the dumps, leaning on her elbow looking at nothing. When she saw him, the half-smile was turned off. "What do you want?"

"I want to talk to you."

"I have nothing to say to you." She made sure he'd know she meant it by glancing over her shoulder for the bouncer. It was the first time Steve had taken notice of the man by the entrance door, a tall, thin punk with sideburns and greasy black curls. Probably considered himself baby's little protector because she let him walk home with her on nights when she hadn't anything better to do.

"I think you have. I've been with the F.B.I. tonight."

She doubted it.

"They were talking about you."

She asked harshly, "Why can't you leave me alone?" The punk was watchful, ready to step across the miniature lobby and make something of Steve.

"You know why."

She said, "I can't talk on the job."

"What time are you off?"

"Not until two."

"I'll be waiting."

Slim was advancing, one foot at a time, as if he found nothing very interesting in bouncing gents with ideas. Steve shambled off. He didn't want to hit the punk. It wasn't the poor guy's fault.

There were plenty of saloons on the street but he needed a place where he could keep an eye on her, a place where she'd know he was watching and that she couldn't pull a sneak. A decent little Italian restaurant was further up the street on the opposite pavement. It didn't have to hide its business behind curtains. Steve bought the morning paper at the corner and gave it a try. There weren't half a dozen people inside including the help. He took the front corner table; it didn't give him much of a view of her cage but it would do. He didn't want coffee and crullers but they would permit him to hang around. He'd have a long wait; it wasn't yet midnight.

Steve glimpsed the headlines in the paper, the four horsemen galloping there as usual, and as he glanced across the way again he almost upset his coffee. She was leaving the cage, the fellow was going to take her place. He waited to see which way she moved, watched her shrug a coat about her shoulders, watched the punk hand her her purse, his hand lingering stickily on hers.

When she cut across towards the restaurant, Steve relaxed. She wasn't trying to run out. He picked up his paper, kept at it even when she came into the place. He heard her speak, "Just coffee, Pepe." He didn't hear what else she said, she might have been asking Pepe to throw the bum out. Steve kept reading the paper. Until she came to the table, carrying her coffee cup. Until she sat down with him.

He didn't get out of his chair. It wasn't the custom on Main Street. He said, "You're off early tonight."

"I'll make it up tomorrow night." She gulped at the coffee just as if it were good, set the cup down and began fishing in her handbag. "Not that it matters to you."

"Have one of mine?" Steve handed over his cigarette pack.

"So you are paying for information now?"

He didn't answer, he lit her cigarette. She loosed her red coat, it was bargain basement but it was red, and she wore it with a flair. Her dress was a cheap shiny satin, too shiny. On her it had more style than Feather Talle would have dressed by Adrian.

"What story did you give that bum?"

"He is no bum. He is the assistant manager. I explained to him that you were my cousin and that you became ugly when you drank too much. I would have to get you home or there would be trouble."

"And he believed it."

"He could observe you had been drinking." She swallowed more of her coffee. "As could I."

"Not that much." He pushed his crullers to her, she'd eat anything. "Did you tell Davidian that I was looking for him?"

"I do not know where Davidian is."

He caught her wrist in pincer fingers. As if she were handling poisoned barbs, she moved them one by one. "You will not touch me."

"Sorry." He wasn't. He was in a churn of anger. "But you can stop lying. I'm not the only one who knows better."

"I do not lie."

He tried again. "You know how to get in touch with him."

"No." He was ready to slam her when she added through an airy swirl of smoke, "He knows how to get in touch with me."

He hopped on it too eagerly. "You've seen him."

"No."

"Janni!" She must realize that time couldn't wait on her tricks. "When will you see him?"

"When he so chooses."

Had they been alone, he might have rattled the truth out of her scornful mouth. They weren't alone. They were in a restaurant where she was Pepe's friend and Steve was her drunken cousin. Because she was pleased at infuriating him, he tried patience. "If you had to get to him in a hurry—"

"There is no way."

She lied. She was too clever to let Davidian escape her. She was as experienced as he, more experienced, in the sly twists of the underground. What Steve didn't get was why Davidian had delivered himself into her hands in the first place. The first contact could have been accidental, but why continue it? Davidian knew her record. It wasn't much different from his own; two guttersnipes out for what they could get. They'd never trusted each other, their only link had been Steve. And then all at once he did know. Davidian needed an address. Someone to pass on his pay to him.

He said, "The F.B.I. is after him."

She was unmoved. "For what reason? He does not work."

"One of their men came to see you today."

Pellets of rage flecked her words. "You set that goat on me!"

"Don't be a fool," he advised sharply. "The last thing I wanted was for them to know about you. Haig Armour sent him."

She spoke unfamiliar syllables. "Haig Armour." Her English wasn't proficient enough to take it other than phonetically. "Who is this?"

"One of your Berlin playmates." Anger was coming up into his throat again. "You couldn't forget Haig Armour. He is rich, important, a magnificent man."

"No, I could not forget this kind! It is because I have this rich, magnificent protector that I live in a hovel with the old ones and work at nights on lower Main Street." She thought about it. "I did not know him."

"He knew you were here," he pointed out. "He sent Timothy Leonard to talk to you. What did Leonard want to know?"

"Where is Davidian? What else would he want? To carry me to his rich—"

He cut in. "Did he mention me?"

"Perhaps he just mentions your name. I do not know this Steve Wintress, Stefan." Her eyes slitted. "What do you tell this man of me?"

"Nothing."

"Now it is you who are lying."

"Him, nothing. Haig Armour—"

Her temper was rising and his slow smile helped it. "What do you tell him?"

"Nothing he doesn't know. I've heard the name Janni Zerbec. Who hasn't? The babe of Berlin." His hand was above her wrist but he remembered not to touch her. "The dancer in all the best cafés."

She spat. "It was jealousy. I was superior to the café dancers. They were old and spavined. They were afraid to have me be seen. It was for this reason I must dance on the street and in private quarters—"

He asked, "Did you know Reuben St. Clair?"

"Who is this?"

"A G. I. He was in Berlin."

She said, "I do not remember. There were so many soldiers. German soldiers, American soldiers, English, French, Russian soldiers. I do not remember their faces or their names, only what they give to me."

"You've stopped lying," he said insolently. "What about Haig Armour?"

She glowered under her ragged dark bangs. "I have told you I do not known this Haig Armour." Again she gave the name phonetic quality. And he didn't know which one spoke true, she or Haig. She was peering past the window. "We have quarreled sufficiently. Now I can take you home. You will behave as if I take you against your wishes."

"Who'll believe that?" She couldn't meet his eyes. She hadn't forgotten, no matter how much she wanted to, no matter how much she wanted to believe she had. He put on a scowl as she walked him out of the place. The fellow who'd taken over her job could watch them depart.

They turned west at Third Street. She said, "Here you may leave me."

He countered, "I haven't the faintest intention of leaving you. I am here for information."

She flashed, "There is no information I can give you. Or your friends. Tell them that. Tell them to leave me alone. I know noth-ing. Nothing!"

"You know one thing, Janni. How to put me in touch with Davidian. Listen to me." He took her arm, holding it rigid until she ceased resisting. "He is expecting me. We planned this before he left Berlin. It is essential I see him before the others do." They walked together. "Just why are you holding out on me? Hasn't he told you he wants to see me?"

She said savagely, "Maybe he trusts you. I know better."

"What's your percentage?" He flung the insult. "You think you can make a better deal?"

She was trembling with anger. "I would not touch your deals. I wish only to be a good American." The anger subsided. "This is what he wishes also, only to be a good American."

He ignored the appeal. "Davidian looks out for Davidian."

"You do not know him now! He is no longer a man to be beaten, kicked—he is free! I will not turn him over to you to be trapped again in your dirty organization."

"Listen," he demanded. "This hasn't anything to do with any or-ganization. This is a private matter between Davidian and me." He stressed it. "No one else figures in it."

"You are working for the party."

"I work where I get paid." How much did he dare say? It wasn't safe to deposit information with anyone. Not on this kind of job. He couldn't trust her.

Her voice was a smooth, cold stone. "I do not understand this. That you can work for them, betray your own people. For money!"

"It's a good enough reason," he said callously. "You're the last one to point the finger. Let's leave my conscience out of it. And yours. All I want is for you to get word to Davidian that I'm here looking for him. That's all. Not next week or the day after tomorrow. Now. Let him decide if he'll see me. You can believe it or not but if I don't get to him fast, he's in for trouble."

"Where you are, there is always trouble," she stated.

He hadn't realized it but they were at the Fifth Street incline that led to Bunker Hill. Without warning she twisted her arm from his clutch. "Stay away from me. I have enough troubles." She began to run up the hill.

He could have followed her. But he didn't. He'd given her enough to think about. She might not recognize it as truth but he had told her true; he had to see Davidian alone before either side moved in.

4

ON THE LONG TROLLEY RUN BACK TO THE HOTEL, HE HAD TIME TO think about Davidian. No matter how much Janni wanted to believe that Davidian had changed, Steve knew better. He was using Janni.

The man could be yet hiding out in the battered old house where Janni lived. This Steve doubted. It would not have been safe for either of them. Wherever Davidian was, it must be a place where there was sufficient seclusion for him to work on his report. It would be a poor place, the old man's purse strings would be a poor place, the old man's purse strings wouldn't pry any wider than small change. But not too isolated, Davidian wasn't the recluse type; he'd be needing someone to smoke a cigarette with, to argue philosophy and politics and historical accidents with. He'd be needing a woman. Wherever he was, he'd make friends. Not caring that friends could be dangerous. For Davidian, danger was the norm.

There was some pattern of communication worked out between the two. They wouldn't risk letters. They would be wary of the telephone. Their good Americanization program would not as yet have erased the deep-rooted suspicion carried with them from Europe. They could meet accidentally, two strangers on a park bench, exchanging the hour; two strangers passing on the street. The solution was so obvious—the all-night movie. Where Janni could be found every night; where Davidian was only another shabby man buying a seat to rest his skinny bones. He could have been inside the grimy theater tonight while she led Steve away by his nose. He cursed her just above his breath. Goddamn little slut.

If he'd been in a position to offer her a wad of dollars, she'd have sold him a ticket and personally ushered him to a seat beside the man he sought. Haig had the wad; all he needed was to offer her enough to overcome her repugance at selling out to the police. Once he caught on to that, events would move fast enough Haig's way. The worst of it was that Steve didn't dare ask for extraordinary funds from the organization; he had to work cheap. While time closed in inexorably.

The trolley trundled past the hotel and Steve jabbed the bell. He swung off at the next stop, annoyed at overriding his destination; it meant he was off key and he couldn't afford that. It hadn't to do with the physical actuality of Janni; he was through with that. He could touch her wrist, her arm, without his blood remembering.

He walked back the two blocks. The lobby smoldered in its customary shadow, the nonexistent clerk posed behind the desk, the Philippine boy rode him silently to the fourth floor. He opened the door with his key, saw Reuben leaning against the bath door and then saw the upheaval of the room.

"What the hell?"

"Don't jump me. I just got in."

There'd been so little to disturb, he and Rube traveled light. But that little was upside down on the dirty rug. They hadn't taken his gun; it was a dull high light on the rug. Rube couldn't help spotting it but he didn't say a word.

"The lousy bastards." It wasn't his side, they would have searched the place unobtrusively twelve hours ago. Leaving no traces. Nor would the F.B.I. leave a mess. Not unless they chose to. This was Haig Armour's idea, more psychological unnerving. Steve tossed the gun into his valise. "Sorry." He began to pick up the rest of the stuff.

"You're up to your neck in something, aren't you?"

Steve shook his head. "Just a job. Run of the mill."

"It's tied up with Haig Armour."

"Believe me, kid, I never saw him before last night. Purely accidental."

"He said you'd gone to meet a girl."

"Wise guy." Stripped, he lay on the bed, finishing his nightcap cigarette.

"She got more on the ball than Feather?"

"Wouldn't take much for that."

"Feather's a funny girl. She acts scared." Rube cut the lamp but the neon glow from the cocktail bar across the street gave low-key visibility. He'd forgotten to pull the lank curtains across the windows. It was just as well, maybe the sun would wake them. If there was sun in the morning.

"Scared of men. Except for Uncle Haig. The protective type." Steve wondered out loud, "What did you do after I left?"

"We danced. But she had to get home early. She had a lesson or something in the morning, she said."

"Who took her home?"

"Well, I did. In Haig's car."

"And Haig's chauffeur." Steve added, "Who subsequently delivered you here."

"Right. He doesn't act much like a chauffer." Rube creaked to an elbow. "Haig's kind of a curious guy."

"About what?"

"You and me. Shacking up here. He kept trying to make out we'd known each other in Berlin. And this girl you two had been talking about."

Steve asked it. "You didn't run into this Janni Zerbec over there?"

"If I did, she didn't tell me her right name. The ones I met were all named Greta."

Steve wasn't going to be a curious guy. Any more than Rube was, not one word about the gun. He'd just go on wondering where Reuben fit or if he fit. At least he had the kid at hand, or vice versa as the case might be.

The room wasn't much brighter when he woke than when he'd slept. Another fog-bound morning. Winter in California. When he emerged from the shower, Reuben was stirring. "What time?"

Steve pushed his last clean shirt into his belt. "Almost eleven. I've got some business to attend to. Think you can keep out of trouble?"

Rube grinned. "I kind of thought I'd go down to the broadcasting studios today. Maybe I'll win us a washing machine."

Steve knotted his tie. "If you don't we better find us a laundry." He slipped into his jacket, took another look at the sky and grabbed his hat and coat. "See you later." He rode downstairs, picked up the morning papers at the corner newsstand, and made for the nearest lunch room. While he waited for his ham and eggs, he drank coffee and searched for mention of Albion. There wasn't any. Albie had moved out of the news as unassumingly as out of existence. No one was interested in him now but the F.B.I.

Steve left the papers with his tip and continued up the boulevard. The sun was beginning to clear away the overcast, pushing small tatters of blue through the dirty gray. He didn't need his topcoat after all. The giant green tin Christmas trees were picking up a glint, the shiny silver ornaments swinging above were turning to silver.

He was on Mr. Oriole's porch exactly at noon, pushing the bell while the hands on his watch met at the top of the dial. Mr. Oriole didn't open the door; it might have been his wife, might have been his mother. She was heavy-hipped with worn hands and shoulders. Her tongue said brokenly, "Come in." She pointed to the parlor. "In here."

No one was in the parlor. Steve didn't sit down. He looked out the side window at a straggle of pale little flowers against the neighboring fence.

Mr. Oriole had slept in the same clothes. He came in complaining feebly, "You're right on time." A thin sheaf of papers drooped from his pudgy fingers.

"I planned it that way." Steve held out his hand. "You have the information?"

"I have done the best I could. You did not give me much time."

"I don't have much time." Steve kept the hand extended. The sharp bell was a rasp across nerve ends. No wonder the woman had looked tired with that racket interrupting her days and nights.

Oriole said nervously, "That will be Mr. Schmidt."

"A conference." It wasn't unexpected.

Schmidt said only, "Good morning," yet somehow in the two words he conveyed distaste for Oriole's uncouth appearance and his displeasure that Steve was here first.

Steve answered the good morning briefly and turned on Oriole. "I told you I have no time to waste. Let's see what you've turned up." He forestalled Oriole's move to pass the papers to Schmidt by stepping up and taking them. He returned to the window, teetered on the edge of a straight-backed chair, his shoulder to the other men. He covered the sparse accounts rapidly; reread, pausing where there might be a clue, then slapped the sheaf on the edge of the fern table. The fronds trembled. Schmidt had to cross the room to retrieve the document.

"So this is all I get." Steve didn't hide disgust. "Davidian came to L.A. maybe seven or eight months ago and checked in at a Bunker Hill apartment house, boarding with a girl named Janni Zerbec and an old couple who might be her kin. By the time we got on to this, Davidian was gone. Vanished. Being thorough, Albion called at the apartment, a broken-down, one-room affair. He didn't see how they could take in a boarder," Steve grimaced. "Albion must have forgotten his Berlin experience. He found out nothing from the old couple, they don't speak English, only some obscurely Slav dialect. The girl spoke English but persisted in knowing nothing. She admitted Davidian had moved out, she had no idea where. Why did he move? Perhaps because he found a better place, perhaps because he no longer had the money to pay board to them. The girl was in no way cooperative in her responses. She insisted Davidian had been gone from there for six months."

Schmidt had retired to the couch. He was following the report by eyeglass as well as by ear. Steve got to his feet and began to pace the mottled carpet as he had yesterday. To focus attention on himself.

"Albion alerted certain trusted workers to check the obvious places. The missions were investigated, the Skid Row charity joints, the county jail. Davidian wouldn't be the first bum to take advantage of bed and board on the town. The investigators were hampered by having no firsthand knowledge of Davidian, no photograph, merely Albion's memory of a man he met maybe once or twice five years ago. The official description's vague enough, about forty years old, sallow complexion, dark eyes and hair, small hands and feet, height five feet four or five. It fits dozens. And easy enough to change that description in six months with good American food and California sun." He broke off sharply. "I wasn't sent here to walk the streets looking for a familiar face under a new disguise. I'm here to pick up the Davidian report. That's my job. To get the Davidian report."

"You knew he had disappeared," Schmidt said.

"Davidian was supposed to be located before I got here. Albion was closer than this or he wouldn't have alerted me to come. He wouldn't waste my time. Where's his report?" His hand was all-encompassing scorn of the papers Schmidt clenched. "Hack work. From hack workers. All of it ending in a big round zero. The girl used to walk through Pershing Square at noon. It could have been to feed the pigeons; it could have been that she was aware of a certain face in the line-up of derelicts loafing on the benches. Who knows? She never spoke to anyone, not while our hacks were around." He said unpleasantly, "So the Square's been chewed up, maybe I should burrow in the debris and see if Davidian's hiding under a hunk of dirt? Albion could have given me Davidian. Albion's dead."

"It is unfortunate."

He hated Schmidt's guts, the righteous son of a bitch. "Yeah, unfortunate."

Schmidt said stiffly, "I was referring to Albion's refusal to conform to the imperative of sharing his total information with our committee. It is unfortunate that he was of a secretive nature. He did not report fully to us."

Steve menaced, "Are you saying he reported to someone else?"

"We do not know," Schmidt said evenly. "We do know he was frequenting the offices of the F.B.I."

"No!" They couldn't believe that. Not even Schmidt could believe that Albion had been ratting to the F.B.I. If Schmidt had had Albion liquidated there was something more behind it, Schmidt's jealousy of a more important worker, or his rage at being unable to force Albion to rigid conformance. Schmidt would find out how unfortunate it was that Albion was gone. After Steve turned in his report to Berlin. "I don't believe it."

"It is authenticated."

A narrow cold man who couldn't see beyond the dogma on his eyeglasses. Or who used that dogma for his own opportunities. Steve said, "There's only one thing that interests me at this moment. Why didn't you get Albion's information before—he died. I'm back where he started weeks ago. With Davidian and a girl."

"You could talk with this girl." Maybe he knew that Steve had seen Janni, maybe not. Schmidt knew too much.

"I've talked with her," Steve admitted. "I got just as far as Albion did. Nothing."

Mr. Schmidt removed his rimless glasses and peered for a dust mote. "There are ways—"

This time Steve could turn the anger loose. "Where do you think you are? Germany? Russia? Or in the funny papers? This is the U.S. You don't go around smashing up women unless you want to pay for it. I don't." He stopped short and pointed a fist at Schmidt. "Just in case you get any more screwball ideas, let me tell you this girl was conditioned under both the Nazis and the occupation. You can liquidate her but you can't squeeze one drop of information out of her. Unless she wants to give it. She wouldn't be alive today if she were intimidatable."

"You know this girl?"

"Yes, I know her." He wasn't certain how much to reveal. Another glance at Schmidt's impassive face and he made the decision; Janni's safety might depend on his putting his personal mark on her. "And maybe I can find out a way to get her to talk, she is the one known link. I'm working on it." He pushed back his hat. "The only trouble is the F.B.I. is hot on her too."

"You had dinner with Haig Armour last night."

Steve made no attempt to reply until he glared through into the colorless eyes. "Yeah," he said softly. And then he shot the question, "Why don't you set your hot-shot spies on finding Davidian instead of checking me? You know," his smile was unpleasant, "I wouldn't be surprised if I turned up the Davidian report despite your help." He swerved to the silent Oriole. "I need a car."

Oriole's eyes faltered to the boss. "This can be arranged?"

"Never mind about arrangements," Steve told him. "I want a car. I'm not a fat capitalist who can hire cabs. If I have to hoof this town, I won't get any further or faster than your stooges."

"You have a car available?" Schmidt asked of Oriole. His distaste of Steve was in his white lips.

"There is my own car. It is not so good—"

"If it runs, it'll do," Steve said.

"This report?" Schmidt questioned. He lifted the papers.

"You know what to do with it." Steve let out a short laugh. "If you get something with a lead in it, let me know."

"Any help we can give you," Schmidt promised dully. "We have assured our friends in New York that we will cooperate with you to the extent of our faculties."

The bastard had checked with New York since the meeting last night. The thorough Mr. Schmidt. New York hadn't phoned him, such preliminaries had been fulfilled through Albion before Steve left for California.

Steve said, "You might try thinking up some answers on Albion's death. For instance, why the F.B.I. should be interested in a heart attack." It would corroborate Albie's treachery in Schmidt's books but it would also let the bastard know that it wasn't as easy to get rid of a man as he might have thought it would be. "They haven't tied him up with me yet but they're worrying it. If they should get too close, I'll want you to divert them."

Schmidt said, "I understand." It was the kind of routine he could carry out. Planning it would keep him busy for another twenty-four hours.

Steve said to Oriole, "Where's your car?"

"It is in my back yard. I will drive it out for you."

"Never mind that." He trod on Oriole's heels. He hadn't expected to get a look at the ground floor layout this early. Behind the portieres was what should have been the back parlor. Obviously Mr. Oriole used it not only for his private office but also as a lunch counter and for naps. A ragged quilt of faded rose and blue was lumped on a scabrous leather couch. The roll-top desk was littered with papers, the stale scraps of a bun, a cup with a scum of yellowed milk over cold dregs, and a plate smeared with what might have been cherry pie. The anachronism was the austerity of green steel filing cabinets. The room smelled unclean, the smell of Oriole. There was a telephone on the desk, a personal line, no coin box.

Mr. Oriole half apologized. "My wife, she has not cleaned in here today, it seems." It was automatic, a little joke he would make whenever anyone viewed his squalid quarters. He divided old-style sliding wooden doors at the right; Steve hadn't seen their like since he was a kid visiting a widowed aunt in upper Manhattan. The dining room was small and drab but neat. In the kitchen the tired woman was scrubbing a wooden sink drain. An electric icebox was the one touch of the twentieth century here.

Steve followed through to the back porch, a clutter of broken relics, a bird cage, a washboard, a child's wicker doll buggy. Mr. Oriole knew the path through the junk; for all his bulk he disturbed not one useless object. Latticework masked the porch from the neighbors. The four splintered steps down into the back yard were unmasked.

The yard was overgrown with weeds and dried grasses. The car stood in the open; it wasn't much, a plain black sedan of too old a vintage. Mr. Oriole took two keys, tied together with soiled twine, from his pocket. He said tenderly, "It runs pretty good. Most of the time."

"I'll take good care of it." Steve opened the car door.

Mr. Oriole was pressing over Steve's shoulder. "The lights are here." He pointed a dirty forefinger. "The starter is this one." It wasn't what Mr. Oriole wanted to say. It wasn't why the man's soiled breath was against Steve's neck nor why his back was hunched to hide Steve from anyone looking out the window. Nor was it that Steve might be unable to locate the windshield wiper. The words came fearfully in a whisper, "I could tell you something."

"Yes."

Mr. Oriole pointed to another button but he didn't label it. He was more afraid, having spoken this much.

Steve followed Oriole's lead, pantomiming an examination of the dashboard. He said impatiently, "For Christ sake, go on." He expected it to be about Albion, he went so far as to expect a hint that Schmidt had decreed the same end for Steve Wintress.

"This man came to my house asking for you."

"Which man?"

"The one you call Davidian."

This out of a clear sky. Steve didn't turn on him, he knew the risk Mr. Oriole was taking in confiding the information. "When?"

"It was—" He pondered, his breath heavy. "It was on Monday night."

"Why didn't you—"

"I did not know of you. Mr. Schmidt did not tell me until Wednesday that you were expected. He does not confide in me."

"You knew of Davidian."

"Yes," he admitted. "I did not recognize him. I had not been told of his appearance." He shrugged. "And if I had, there are so many men like him." He tried for a pathetic joke, patting his own big stomach. "He has not become rich and fat in this land of dollars."

He couldn't keep Oriole here too long, Schmidt would become suspicious. Steve slid over in the seat. "Get at the wheel. Start showing me how to start the car, as if it had tricks."

Oriole moved fast for a man of his weight.

"Now give it to me."

"It was early evening. He stood on the porch. I did not invite him in, I did not know him, how could I guess? He asked for you by name. Stefan Winterich. But I had not been told Stefan Winterich was coming to us." He wouldn't soon forget this grievance. "I thought perhaps he had the wrong house number. Or perhaps a trap. We must be so careful always of a police trap?"

"Sure," Steve agreed. "Was he on foot or wheels?"

"On foot." Oriole caused the car to give little huffing noises.

"Positive?"

"Of this I am certain." He would have stood peering from behind the lace curtains after the man. "There was no car on the street before he came or after he left. He was a poor man."

This put Davidian in a new location, Hollywood. A far cry from Skid Row. He could have ridden the trolley, the same as Steve. But how had he got on to Mr. Oriole's place unless he'd been sniffing around the Hollywood hangouts?

Mr. Oriole was insistent. "I did not guess, you understand this? How can a man be expected to guess that a stranger . . . I said nothing just now—" His small eyes turned to the house. "I am afraid Mr. Schmidt would not understand this. But he had not told me your name or that you were coming." He was sweating, his shirt smelled.

"Don't tell Schmidt," Steve advised. It was what Oriole wanted to hear. He'd made a mistake and mistakes were not allowed. He'd confessed to it, either because he was afraid he'd be found out or in a sincere effort to be of help. As to whom he should make confession, he'd had to choose between Steve and Schmidt. He'd chosen Steve. He would hope he was backing the right man, he couldn't know. Top men came and went fast in the organization. It would have been a hard decision for Oriole to make; Schmidt was his bread and butter. But Steve might be the marmalade; he was higher up, he must be to have been sent from Berlin to New York to Los Angeles. Unless this whole business was a trap dreamed up by Schmidt and Oriole to put Steve in a spot. You could never be sure of anything.

Steve knew what the answer would be before he asked. "He left no message, nowhere to look for him?"

"Nothing." Mr. Oriole was clambering out of the car. His chin quavered. "You understand why I said nothing?"

Steve said, "As long as you keep on saying nothing you're safe. If Davidian comes back, find out where he lives. If you have to follow him yourself."

"Oh yes. Yes, I will do that."

He slammed the door, stepped on the starter. "If Schmidt wants to know what took you so long, tell him I'm an idiot about machinery."

He backed and filled, got the car into the driveway, and noted the hand holding aside the lace curtains as he rolled past the side parlor window. Mr. Schmidt would not have overlooked the delay. Yet somehow Steve was certain that Mr. Oriole would cover well, that he was long accustomed to protecting his own interests.

III

Steve drove directly to Janni's. Near two o'clock. She should be just about getting up. She'd been in early last night. He knew no short cuts but he knew the direction of town. He had no trouble until he reached the downtown section. It was cut up into a maze, he went in and around tunnels, one-way streets, dead-end streets, long blocks without intersections, before he found the trick of reaching Bunker Hill. He'd have a hard time finding it again. The town was on a building spree; despite government controls, white concrete towers were rising above the scaly old tenements. Steve parked in front of Janni's apartment. He saw no forbidding signs.

The street was as empty of life as it had been previously. He climbed up the old steps to the creaking porch, entered the scabrous hallway and began his longer climb up to her room. There wasn't as much noise through the walls as yesterday, now it was rustles and whispers, but the smell of age and dust and bad cooking was unchanged.

She wouldn't be surprised that he had returned. She knew he didn't give up easily. The old woman's hostile face answered his decisive knock.

He pushed in. "I'm here to see Janni." He didn't care if she understood.

She let loose her unintelligible imprecations. She was probably telling him that Janni wasn't here. She wasn't. Her cot was made up, an old army blanket smoothed over it. The old man sat by the window making fine stitches on a white *glacé* glove. Not half enough light sifted in but he didn't need light. After centuries of glove-making, he would sew out of his unconscious. And dream of a proud and ancient day when he was glove-maker to dukes and queens. He was too old to understand the new order. He didn't raise his dim eyes from his work; an altercation between the old woman and a visitor was too usual, or he was stonedeaf.

Steve demanded, "Where is she?" He pointed to the cot. "Janni?" The old lady started off again but he shouted at her, "You can drop that stuff. You can talk the language enough to tell me."

Out of a sullen mouth she muttered, "She has gone out, fool."

"Where?"

"Her business she does not tell me."

Steve shouted at the old man. "Where did she go?" There was no response. Nothing but cranky fingers and a minute white stitch.

The woman laughed. But she would not speak again.

Steve gave up. "If you find her first, tell her I'm waiting for her." He didn't slam the door behind him out of respect for the ancient craftsman.

He let off steam clattering down the flights of steps, banging out on the porch. And he saw her. She was on the sidewalk coming towards the house, her arms wrapped around a large brown paper sack. She wasn't dressed for company, a yellow scarf imprinted with crimson cabbage roses was tied over her hair; she wore dark slacks and sweater, flat-heeled slippers. She didn't see him until she lifted her eyes before climbing the final flight of steps. He waited there at the top, leaning against the grimy white pillar.

She gave him no greeting. Not until she stood beside him did she speak. "What do you want now?"

"Where have you been?"

"It is perhaps your business?"

She would have walked by him but he stepped in her path. "Did you see Davidian?"

He followed the droop of her eyelids to the green fronds of carrots, the dirt-purple of beets, the dark loaf of bread.

"Oh yes," she said loftily, "I have been driving around in my Cadillac convertible calling upon all my gentlemen friends." She shifted the grocery sack in her arms.

He said, "Let me take it," automatically. She started to pass it into his hands and then with the suddenness of thunder, both were motionless, like children playing statues.

They stood too long, their eyes meeting, before she broke by him. "Go away. I don't want to see you again." She was in the house and the touch of her slippers on the staircase blurred back to his ears before he came alive. He walked on down the steps to the street, got in Mr. Oriole's old car and drove away.

It couldn't be that she had remembered with him, the same moment, the identical, unimportant moment. It had been dusk then and he had been framed in a doorway more shabby than the one on Bunker Hill. Behind him there had been a murky hallway and a staircase as steep and multiodored as the one she was climbing now. She had come through the blue evening carrying a sack in the same way, her arms wrapped about it in the same way, as if it were a baby she carried. It hadn't been a clean brown paper sack; it was dirty burlap, used over and again. That night she had come laughing and the laughter hadn't left her eyes when she saw him waiting for her. When he said, "Let me take it," she'd passed it over to him, whispering, "Oh, so many good things, Stefan," and she'd followed close on his heels, up, up, up the rotten staircase to the mean little room . . .

His fist clenched until it ached and he beat it on Oriole's steering wheel until pain cut away the ache. He kept his mind on driving then. He watched his speed and the side streets and the confusion of traffic signals. He couldn't afford to be picked up. Not without a driver's license. Not with his reasons for being in the city.

He reached Hollywood Boulevard and slowed further for its traffic. There were new signs from Vine Street north, "Temporary No Parking"; there were service trucks stringing lights overhead, among the bright tinsel decorations. On either side of the boulevard, men were roping off areas halfway to the trolley lines. Some kind of big doings must be on for tonight.

He made a right turn because it was easier than trying to make it on the left, circled a block and drove past his hotel to a parking lot in the rear. He'd be better off on foot for the next trip. There wasn't going to be any spare parking space on the side streets with the main stem blocked off.

He headed for Highland; he found the address of Albion's shop easily enough, not more than a half dozen doors around the corner from the boulevard. The layout was just what he'd expected. It was always the same, the Thomas Jefferson or the Thomas Paine bookshop; never any imagination. Never the Benedict Arnold or the Lenin.

This one looked the same as any and all, a small plateglass front window with books in formula display, popular books of the day in slick jackets, capitalistic books. No lousy propaganda items such as *I Escaped from a Soviet Concentration Camp* or *I Used to Be a Communist Spy*, but no lives of Little Father Stalin either. Good, honest, safe books for the window. Inside you could buy another kind.

Within, the place was neat and small and quiet. There weren't any customers, which could have been the reason the eyes of all three clerks converged on Steve when he entered. He'd seen them all before, in one city or another. A young fellow, tan, dark, intense, horn-rimmed, neat as the shop in his dark suit, his conservative tie; two young women, one blond, one brown-haired; one a little too plump, the other a little too thin; neither pretty, but neither homely; both horn-rimmed, both wearing sweaters and skirts. Both would be hopelessly in love with the young man but he'd have a girl who modeled or did bits on the television screen and who hankered after a director if she couldn't land a producer. She wouldn't give a damn about a brave new world except for herself. And the three would know all these items about each other, whether or not they'd admit such minor matters to be important. They didn't have to worry about frustrations because they had the great bulbous-breasted cause to rest their emotions on.

Steve didn't fool around with any table browsing. He moved back into the store. The young man came towards him. "May I help you?" His voice was almost as good as Haig Armour's, not as flamboyant but with the same upper-class modulations.

"I'm looking for Frederick Grasse."

The girls might have popped side glances at each other, their fingers may have tightened, but the young man was contained. "He isn't here. Is there anything I can do for you?"

"I'll wait." Maybe he could figure a way to get into the office if he hung around. And then he realized he wasn't first with the idea. There was someone coming out of the cubbyhole hidden back there in the gloom.

The three clerks relaxed just a little. You wouldn't know the young fellow needed to relax until he did. He said, "Mr. Grasse won't be in today." And Mr. Schmidt was with them. He hadn't expected Steve.

Steve said, "You're ahead of me." The clerks were surprised that he knew Mr. Schmidt.

"I wished to check personally," Schmidt said.

"Mind if I have a look?"

"Not at all." The reply was too prompt; there'd be nothing left for Steve in the cubbyhole. Schmidt pointed his hand at the young man.

"Llewellyn, this is Mr. Wintress from New York. A friend of Frederick's."

"Yes, sir." The young man was alert.

"Llewellyn Meadows," Mr. Schmidt identified him. "Assistant manager to Grasse." To the young fellow he said, "You will give Mr. Wintress your co-operation."

"Yes, sir." A well-trained assistant. If Schmidt had said, "You will bump off Frederick Grasse on Wednesday night," would Llewellyn have had no response but, "Yes, sir?" In his nice, polite voice?

Schmidt turned to the girls, making a frosty attempt at a smile. For some reason they brightened under it. "Miss Batts and Miss Zahner." Steve never did find out which was which. "Mr. Wintress." All of them went through how-do-dos as if this were a silver tea.

Steve said, "See you later," to dismiss Schmdit. But he had to idle over a book while either Miss Batts or Miss Zahner fluttered at the important man—"Your review of that new picture was simply devastating"—while the other one smirked assent.

Mr. Schmidt deprecated, "Thank you." But his shoulders were almost jaunty as he walked out of the store.

The blond shared her admiration. "There isn't anyone with Jo's touch, is there?"

"What kind of touch?"

She withdrew her comradeship. She was hurt if not suspicious. "He reviews motion pictures. He is the only honest reviewer in the city."

Steve didn't care where Schmidt peddled his propaganda or how. "Where's Grasse's office?"

Llewellyn said, "This way, Mr. Wintress."

Steve let him lead into the gloom. He kept his distance until Llewellyn had reached into the cubbyhole and pulled an over head light. It sprayed on a work-laden desk, old wooden filing cabinets, stacks of books and magazines and a morass of loose papers. Llewellyn flattened himself against the files to admit Steve. He wasn't needed but he lingered. He had something on his mind. "It was you he was meeting at the airport."

"Yes."

"He had the heart attack before you arrived?"

"Yes."

Llewellyn knew better than to ask why Steve had come inquiring for a dead man. You don't ask foolish questions if you are ambitious.

Steve asked, "Had he been sick?"

The youth was startled to a quick answer, "Oh, no!" and then he wasn't sure. "I mean, I don't know—"

"No heart attacks before?"

"Not that I know."

"Have the police been around?"

Llewellyn was cautious. "The police?"

"Asking questions?"

He showed his confusion. "Why should—" It caught up on him and he looked a little sick. He hadn't been told. But he understood. "No." And then he wondered if it were a true answer. There'd always be a few strange customers dropping in, actually interested in books. The police didn't necessarily wear uniforms. He went back to, "Not that I know."

"Don't tell them anything."

The gratuitous advice put Llewellyn back on his feet. The sneer on his nicely shaped mouth was a well-bred one. "Tell the police?" And then the sickness seeped back under his skin. He wanted to comment but he'd been conditioned to accept gospel, not question it. He faltered, "Mr. Grasse was a good man."

Steve said shortly, "He was a friend of mine." Because the anger came up in him when he thought of Albie dying alone, without cause, in the fog, he added, "Someone didn't want us to get together." He didn't give a damn if Llewellyn did pass on the thought to Mr. Schmidt.

He went to the desk and twitched a segment of the papers. It would take a team of men long hours to plow through this mess, longer to make a detailed report. There simply wasn't that much time. The top layer had been disturbed by Mr. Oriole's men, Schmidt had been second. He too must have known discouragement. If embedded in the junk there was a morsel leading to Davidian, the man must be found more quickly than the clue could be.

In the doorway, Llewellyn waited like a flunky. Steve posed a question, "Did he ever come here?"

"Who, sir?" Easier to lose your faith than your breeding.

"Mr. Grasse was to put me in touch with an old friend of mine from Berlin." Steve had no way of knowing how much Llewellyn had heard; the young fellow was as poker-faced as Schmidt. "I flew out from New York for that meeting." The clerk would recognize the importance of such a move; the New York office didn't fly specialists out every day.

"If this man came here, I know nothing of it. Mr. Grasse said nothing."

Albion would say nothing. And certainly Davidian could be expected to have more discretion than to walk boldly into a center. Yet he had called upon Mr. Oriole looking for Steve. The risk would appeal to his sly humor.

"Perhaps he came when Mr. Grasse was out. A small man, small hands and feet—" He went on describing the Davidian he had known and the Davidian who had appeared on Mr. Oriole's porch Monday night.

Uncertainty came to the young man's face. "I don't know. There was a customer—" He broke off. "You should talk to Pam." He walked quickly away.

Disregarding fire hazard, Steve lit a cigarette. He rested himself on the papers which covered the desk.

Pam was the dark-haired one. "It was the funniest thing—odd, I mean. This man came in one afternoon—"

"When?"

"When?" she echoed. "About two weeks ago, I think. Wasn't it about two weeks ago, Lyn? Mr. Grasse had gone to the bank, I remember."

Together, they figured. Two weeks stood, possibly a little more, a little less. Steve didn't care that close but he didn't interrupt. He'd asked the question. Two weeks was about right. Steve had still been in Berlin. Waiting for word from Albion.

Pam went on with her event. "He wasn't anyone you'd notice. Lyn and Portia were busy so I took him. We don't bother anyone who just comes in to browse," she explained, "but he didn't. You know, like you this afternoon, you were waiting to be asked and Lyn asked. And I asked him, this funny little man. You could hardly understand him, his accent I mean, and what he wanted was a book of Russian poetry, in Russian, you know, a very obscure book. We didn't even have it listed."

More of Davidian's humor; he'd invent author and title.

"He didn't look as if he could afford to buy a book," Pam continued sympathetically, "but he was very nice and polite. It's the system," she declaimed loyally, "that makes a man hunger for books and not have the money to buy them." With that off her chest, she proceeded. "As he started to leave, he said he wanted to give me something for my trouble and do you know what he gave me?"

Steve didn't have the slightest idea and said so. He wouldn't have been surprised if she'd said a map of the Kremlin. Hand-lettered and signed by Joseph Stalin.

"A Russian ruble!"

"Counterfeit." Steve smiled the word.

"How did you know?" Both pairs of horn-rims grew anxious.

He said, "It was a hunch." Davidian up to his old tricks, passing out his calling card. A Davidian ruble. Made by Europe's finest engraver; he'd tell you so himself. Steve was sorry he'd spoiled the girl's story. "Go on, then what?"

She wasn't as glib now. As if she were afraid he was still ahead of her. She spoke defensively, "Well, I'd never seen one before and it was a queer thing for a man to hand you, like a tip, just as if you were in Russia, only tipping is capitalistic and in Russia—"

"I know all about that. Get on with it."

"Well, I showed it to Lyn and Portia and we were all excited about it. Or interested," she defended. "When Mr. Grasse returned from the bank, naturally I showed it to him." She let her bright eyes blame Steve; this was the part he'd spoiled. "At first he was interested too, and then looked at it more closely and said it was counterfeit."

She could get back to normal now, it was again her story. "He got terribly excited, I mean for Mr. Grasse, because he was always quiet, you know, and wanted to know all about who gave it to me and had me describe the man. He even went out and looked in all the shops around here although I told him the man had been gone, oh, for at least forty-five minutes."

Steve didn't need to ask if Davidian had left any clue as to where he might be found. He hadn't. Through some listening post he'd learned that Albion was seeking him. This had been his thumb to the nose. And Albie had so recognized it; Albion had known that Davidian had waited until the coast was clear before leaving his card. But Albion had come closer than this before sending for Steve.

"The man didn't return?"

Llewellyn said, "We've watched very closely, sir. Mr. Grasse asked us."

"Going home and coming to work. And on the street. Mr. Grasse thought he must be living in Hollywood." Pam said passionately, "I'd know him anywhere. But I haven't seen him."

You won't, Steve said to himself. But this placed Davidian in Hollywood even more surely. His listening post was definitely here; not only had he learned of Oriole's station but also that Frederick

Grasse was Albion. It came to Steve, one small check that could be made. He asked, "How many bookshops have we?"

Llewellyn began the tally. "North Hollywood, Santa Monica, one on Jefferson Boulevard—"

Steve said, "Call them. See if this ruble-tipper has been around any of the other shops."

"Now?"

"Now." To the girl, Steve said, "I'd like to see the ruble."

"But I gave it to Mr. Grasse." He should have taken that for granted. "He said he'd give it back." She turned her eyes to the hopeless desk.

Steve ordered, "See if you can find it."

Llewellyn was efficient. He'd completed one call. "He hasn't been in North Hollywood."

"Shove your chair to one side," Steve said. "Pam is going through the desk papers." There could be a message on the bill, one for Steve alone to recognize. More Davidian tricks. "Or anything connected with the man," he told her. "See if Mr. Grasse made any notes." He had an errand of his own. "I'll be back in an hour. I'll tell your girl out front to hold the wheel steady."

The last thing he expected was the complication of Haig Armour out front. There was no way to pass unnoticed. Haig had the effrontery to put on a surprised act. "Why hello, Steve." He gave it the best fancy-meeting-you-here intonation.

Steve didn't play it big. "Interested in books now?"

"Why not? Nice little shop Grasse had."

He tried walking out on that but Haig stopped him.

"I've been looking for you."

"In bookstores?"

"I figured you'd turn up here." Nothing about having the place under surveillance. "Let's go have a drink."

He couldn't say he had a more important assignment. He didn't want Haig's men following. They'd know the Oriole address but he wouldn't lead them there. Schmidt was too suspicious a bastard and too quick on the trigger with his suspicions. Steve didn't intend to finish this job on a lonely beach with a bad heart.

He said ungraciously, "If you insist."

Haig was amused. "We can make it later if you're busy."

"One time's as good as another."

They walked out side by side. Steve couldn't manage a word of warning for the blond to pass on to the others.

Together they returned to the boulevard. "Any choice?" Haig inquired.

"That's a laugh."

There were plenty of corner saloons, disguised as jazz joints, yet somehow they shrank out of sight during the shopping day. It was by day a woman's street of hats and dresses and shoes and jewelry, of five-and-tens and movie matinees.

"How about Musso's?"

Haig had named the sole remaining dignity of the boulevard. The old English front with the leaded windows hadn't changed in twenty-five years. Nor had the somber quiet of the *décor* within. At this hour the place was uncluttered and unhurried. They walked past the empty booths to the old-fashioned taproom hidden in the rear.

Haig waited until they had their drinks before starting anything. But he didn't waste time on preliminary social stuff. He stated the fact, "I'm looking for Davidian. So are you."

Steve gave a quick laugh. "You're not going to suggest we pool information?"

"No, I'm not. But I'm going to warn you. You aren't going to get the Davidian report."

If Armour next boasted that he already had the report, Steve would bust him one. No matter what it led to. He was afraid to ask it straight. He made it a taunt. "What makes you think I'm not?"

Haig drank comfortably. "I'm here to see that you don't."

Steve said, "And you don't hold to let the best man win."

"No." Haig passed his cigarette case.

Steve refused, pulled out his own pack. He wished he were as sure of himself as Haig appeared to be.

Haig continued, "I always win."

"That's a pretty big admission. Maybe I could say the same."

"It wouldn't be true." He leaned a steady elbow on the table between them. "Would it?"

Steve didn't answer. Instead he asked, "You did come out here for this job? Not the phony line you gave out."

"That wasn't a phony. But I turned the case over to Timothy Leonard. Would you like to know why?" He was smiling, a dirty smile.

"Spring it."

"I knew you wouldn't be sent on anything minor."

Steve shook his head. "You're telling me it was accidental we took the same plane?"

Haig laughed a real one. "You'll be accusing me next of plotting the fog."

Steve stuck to the point. "Accidental?"

"And if I told you we had a tip a man was heading to the Coast to see another man? Nothing particularly interesting in it, your messengers go back and forth constantly. If the tip didn't furnish the name of either man? But suppose I told you that on the plane an astounding human cross-file named Timothy Leonard recognized Stefan Winterich, or Steve Wintress, if you prefer? And where Stefan Winterich makes a personal appearance, something is going to happen?" Haig refreshed his throat.

"What about Feather? She accidental too?"

Haig signaled the waiter. "Two more, please." He stubbed out his cigarette. "I'm afraid I don't know about her."

"You got acquainted damn fast."

It wasn't all in the open. Feather was to be withheld. Steve didn't care, she didn't worry him any. Maybe after all she wasn't a plant; maybe Haig thought she was on Steve's side. That would be one for the books, an innocent bystander and both sides thinking the other had her under orders.

"I don't get it." Steve tasted his fresh highball. This was quota. It wouldn't be funny if Haig pulled the old one of getting the opposition talkative.

As if his side line were mind-reading, Haig remarked, "I thought you fellows didn't drink."

Steve showed his teeth. "We're human too, you know. Some of us do, some don't."

Haig accepted it. "What don't you get?"

"Why you're giving me this pitch." He could play the open-faced hands too. "Why don't you lock me up? You guys can always think up reasons to get rid of your opposition."

Haig said flatly, "I need you. Would it surprise you to know that with all our sources of information, we didn't know until recently that Davidian was in this country?"

It didn't surprise him. "Noooo!" He drawled it sardonically. "The great F.B.I.?"

Haig's mouth tightened. "We've made up for lost time, I can assure you. But we haven't found him. You're going to do that. You were his friend. He believes you're still his friend, working this deal for him. He doesn't know that you're under orders. You know how to reach him."

Steve pretended amusement. "So I'm to lead you to him and fade out while you pick up the report without interference?"

Haig said evenly, "Frankly I don't give a damn whether you interfere or not. I wouldn't mind in the least getting rid of you for good. I don't even mind if Davidian is a casualty, he's lasted a long time for a spy. All I want is the report." A slight change came across his face. It made him look human. "And I don't want the girl hurt."

Steve waited until he could speak without giving anything away. "What girl?" He didn't want the answer.

"Janni. Janni Zerbec."

He'd half believed her denials of Haig. That was why it slugged him in the pit of the stomach. He had a hard time spitting out the words. "What about Janni?"

"I said it. I don't want her hurt."

Steve tried to fight the sickness that was spreading like poison through his veins. Haig had everything she wanted, power and position, style and brass, money. She hadn't wasted any time; she'd wrapped him up fast. In one meeting? In how many meetings? She hadn't changed any; she was what she'd always be. *Had she given Davidian to Haig?* Were they only waiting for Steve to catch up to the trap they'd staked for him, to catch two birds at once? He wouldn't let them pull it off; this was his baby, he'd set it up. He'd bring it off the way he'd planned it no matter how many angles Haig Armour played.

He heard Haig's voice, the timbre of it. "She doesn't want any part of your deal. Stay away from her."

"Leave her for you?" He couldn't laugh, he tried it.

"You think she'd rather have you?" It was a quiet challenge.

He couldn't see Haig's bold handsome face; it blurred before his eyes. "Okay. Take her. She's yours. I give her to you, no strings." The voice wasn't his own. "But after you've loaded her with minks and rubies and dollar bills and everything her bitching heart desires, remember what I'm telling you now. There's part of her you'll never have. And that part you'll want until you're too old to care, and even then you'll want it. That part belongs to me."

He didn't know how he got out of the booth, out of the restaurant. But he was on the street gulping the air, walking away fast and hard, not knowing or caring where. Somehow with his hat and coat on him. She'd lied, just as she always lied when it suited her dirty little schemes. Just as she was lying about not knowing how to get in touch with Davidian. He ought to go to her right now, slap her with the lie.

God! And what if she had lied? *What's Hecuba to me or I to Hecuba that I should weep for her?*

Nothing mattered except finding Davidian.

2

EARLY TWILIGHT SIFTED DOWN UPON THE SHINY CHRISTMAS CRYSTALS and stars and metallic trees. When his eyes and brain began to clear, Steve found he was almost to La Brea. The street was roped off this far up the boulevard. It was necessary to retrace to the corner in order to cross. The Roosevelt Hotel loomed; he rounded the corner and used the side entrance. Only one telephone booth was occupied, and it by a large-size man whose hefty fur-coated dame leaned against the half-opened door. Steve wondered if they were cooking up a story for his wife or her husband. One thing sure, they weren't Haig's hirelings; they'd been here first.

Steve took a booth, put in his coin and called his own room. He didn't expect Reuben to be around but there he was at the other end of the line. Did the kid sit around all afternoon just waiting for Steve to check in? Steve didn't ask; this time it was a break. "How about us dating a couple of gals and making a night of it?"

"Gee," Rube began, then his voice flopped. "Trouble is I don't know any girls in this man's town. Only Feather."

"Stick around," Steve told him. "I'll be there with my little black book." He hung up, put in another coin and dialed again. No one was leaning around the booths; the couple had gone off arm in arm, satisfied with their dime's worth. He answered Oriole's voice, "Wintress here. I'm coming around for some information."

"You will not be long?" Mr. Oriole sounded anxious. "I will wait for you, you understand, but it is that tonight is the Santa Claus parade—"

Santa Claus parade. It explained the streets, the baubles, the colored lights. Steve said, "I'll be there in about thirty minutes. Will that do?" He had to get Rube started first.

"You understand," Mr. Oriole protested too much, "It is not myself. It is that I have promised the children and my wife."

"Don't worry. You'll get to see Santy Claus. What I want won't take long." He left the hotel by the same side entrance. There was parade excitement in the air this early. Some particularly eager beavers were spreading their newspapers and blankets for front-row seats.

Reuben was finishing a shave. "What's the scoop?"

"You have Feather's phone number?" The Moritzes were unlisted.

"Yeah. Want me to call her?"

"I'll call. I want you to take the car and pick up my girl." My girl; that was a good one.

"You promoted a car?" Rube mopped his cheek.

"An old heap. But it's wheels. Janni lives downtown. In a dump but don't let that throw you, she's okay." He explained, "She doesn't have a phone."

Rube had rummaged a scrap of paper out of his coat. A Crestview number was pencil-printed on it. "Janni," he repeated. Well, he'd heard enough about her last night to be curious.

"I haven't time to pick her up, I have to see a man." He wrote her address on another scrap of paper. "Don't take no for an answer. Tell her we're going to have a front-row seat to see Santy Claus." Steve flung out his hands. "Why am I briefing you? That's the first thing they teach you army Joes, how to sweettalk the dolls. We'll meet at—" He'd go right back there, his head high. He'd have it out with her there. "—Musso's. It's across the street, up a block or so. The car's in the lot in back of the hotel." He dug up the parking stub.

Reuben was slicked up real pretty. And Steve wouldn't have time for a shave. The boy took the keys. "How're you going to get Feather if I've got the car?"

"Feather's going to join us, sweetheart. Run along. Remember, don't take no."

"I won't." Out came the slow grin.

Steve was asking for Crestview before the door closed. Feather might have ten other dates but he doubted it. She didn't react as if she were accustomed to the rush of fellows most girls of her age enjoyed. If she should have Haig Armour plans, Steve would have to convince her that a change was desirable. Someone had to take care of Rube while Steve worked on Janni. He sprawled on the bed while waiting for the Moritz houseman to get her to the phone.

Her soft hello came through.

"Feather? Steve. Look, Rube and I are lonesome." He didn't give her a chance to break in, just kept it moving fast. He had no time to waste on her. "How about meeting us for dinner and we'll take in this Santa Claus parade?"

She was hesitant. "I don't know. I'm not dressed."

At this hour was she still hoping Haig would call? Or did she have to clear through him? "We aren't fancy. Say about seven, Musso Frank's." He wouldn't mention how she was to get there. Let her figure that out. "Okay?"

He barely gave her a chance to say, "All right," before he hung up. He was out of the room at once. He'd have to move fast.

The widewalks were beginning to jostle. And there were cops all over the place. Steve ducked down the nearest side street and proceeded to Oriole's. The door was opened before he could ring. The parade must be important, Mr. Oriole had washed his face and was wearing a jacket over a clean shirt. He didn't invite Steve into the parlor.

He spoke hurriedly. "This information you wish—"

From the dining room came the quelled voices of youngsters. Steve wondered how many little Orioles were waiting there and if they all looked like Pop. "Where would I find friends in Hollywood? Our friends."

Mr. Oriole didn't believe it was this easy. He began with the bookstore and Steve suddenly remembered Llewellyn and Pam, the job he'd set them on. "Ring them for me."

"The store will be closed at this hour."

"Not until they hear from me."

Mr. Oriole's face drooped but he was obedient. While he put his coin into the slot and dialed, he continued the tally. A record shop, a small café, a magic store. His eyes rounded at an answer to his call. He passed the phone to Steve and stood on one foot then the other.

Steve questioned, "Llewellyn? What did you find?"

"None of the other shops have had our experience."

"What about the desk?"

"Nothing. Nor any notation."

Steve mumbled sounds.

"Is there anything further, sir?"

"Not tonight. Enjoy the parade."

He could hear the smiling condescension. "I'm not going to the parade, sir. I have a committee meeting."

"Enjoy the meet. And thanks for hanging around." He banged up the receiver.

Mr. Oriole continued as if there had been no interruption. "And there is, of course, the popcorn man."

Nothing but bad breaks, that pattern hadn't been disturbed. Albion had not thrown away that ruble; 100 to 1 he'd had it in his pocket when he went to the airport to meet Steve. "What about the popcorn man?"

For the moment Mr. Oriole forgot his anxieties. "He has a little cart with glass over and about it to keep the popcorn warm and clean. He pushes the cart himself and there is a lantern in it with such a nice yellow light. It is a real lantern that burns, not electric. And a little whistle, such a nice whistle." His smile was nostalgic. "Once I was the popcorn man." He added too quickly, "It is much better the work I do now and this big house."

Steve asked, "Where do I find him?"

"He walks the streets at night selling his popcorn. And meets many people." The small eyes were shrewd. "If his feet get tired, he sets down the wagon on any corner he chooses and the people come to him."

There wouldn't be a much safer way to deliver messages. It didn't sound like the efficient Schmidt; it would take someone before his time, someone with more imagination and romance to invent the popcorn man.

"He is easy to find because of his nice yellow lantern. And the little whistle."

"Yeah." Steve nodded thoughtfully. The dining room was becoming impatient. He hurried. "Where did Albion live?"

Mr. Oriole didn't withhold the address this time. "It is a rooming house."

"Friends?"

"No. Mr. Albion preferred not. It was safer, he believed." Oriole wasn't as sure as Schmidt that Albie was a traitor. He spoke as of a friend.

"Who took over his things?"

"Temporarily it is Llewellyn who is in charge of the store."

"I mean his personal stuff, his clothes, that kind of thing."

"I do not know this. You may ask Mr. Schmidt."

Steve said, "I will. Better get those kids off to the parade." He went to the door, opened it.

Mr. Oriole could smile again. "Always they enjoy the parade. There is Santa Claus—" The smile disappeared as if it were Cheshire. "You understand, they do not believe this superstition," he said carefully. "It is only—" He extricated himself. "It is Hopalong Cassidy and Roy Rogers they wish to see."

"Yeah, kids are all alike." He was sorry for the old boy. Trying to live up to Schmidt's standards and yet give his children a happy life.

He had time to visit the gathering places, or some of them, and still beat Feather to the restaurant. There were cops all along the boulevard by now, cops and family parties with innumerable children. The adolescents were even more numerous, they paraded on the sidewalks, boys and girls in jeans and bright wool shirts, shrilling cryptic messages to attract the others' attention. The spirit was holiday, Steve hadn't seen anything like it since he was a boy. The spirit was so good it was contagious. He didn't want to be on his gritty little errands, he wanted to be one of these people, just having fun.

A job was a job. He took the far address first. This wasn't one of the clean, shining record stores of the boulevard, it was no more than a hole in the wall, a front. It was open but not patronized. A young man was lolling on a folding wooden chair behind the cash register, reading the evening paper. He looked up at Steve. He didn't rise.

"Is this your place?" Steve didn't like the sullen face.

The fellow flickered an up-and-down glance. As if he'd sized Steve for a plain-clothes cop, he asked with open insolence, "Yeah. What about it?"

Steve gave him more rope. "I'm looking for a guy who's giving out phony rubles."

The smile jeered. "No kid?"

"Has he been in here?"

"Nope." He resumed the evening paper.

Steve let him have it, cold and ugly. "I'm from New York. Mr. Oriole sent me here."

The paper dropped. The fellow was on his feet, stammering something about not knowing.

Steve eyed him. "Now suppose you answer my question."

The slack mouth became voluble, sweat was breaking out on the unwashed face. But the answers added up to a negative. Small wonder. Davidian couldn't have any fun in this dump. Nor would he waste his handiwork on a lout.

Steve said coldly, "I shall recommend you to Mr. Schmidt." He walked out while whey-face was still stammering about being sorry. It took him a couple of blocks to get back to the crowd's good humor. He should have clouted that one across the mouth when it first opened. It was better to see that the guy was pitched to the lions along with Schmidt.

He had to pass Musso's to retrack to the magic store. The usual dinner crowd overflowed the small vestibule. Steve pushed through to the head waiter. He gave his name for a table for four, watched it written at the foot of an already long list. It would be at least thirty minutes before he came to the top of the list.

He ducked out, threading through the ever-increasing street crowd towards his second goal. It was a poor edition of the boulevard's better magic stores but it was busy tonight. Two middle-aged men, much like junior Orioles, were doing their best to take care of things. Steve waited while Tweedlededum sold false noses to five shrieking teen-age girls. The man was giggling as heartily as the girls. He wiped his eyes with a fat little finger as he turned to Steve. "And now, what can I do for you?" His accent wasn't as heavy as Oriole's.

Steve said, "For a gag, I need a ruble. Do you have any?"

If the man was uneasy, he covered up. "We do not have any real money. Only the phony, you know, stage money."

"I hear there's a fellow in Hollywood making phony rubles. He hasn't tried to sell any to you?"

"No." The man tapped his shiny head and thought some more about it. While he was wondering what Steve was truly after. "No, I have not heard about him." He glanced upward slyly. "I don't think this man, he's very smart. This is America, Mister. Rubles are not wanted here, not even bad ones." He wasn't going to be caught out by any undercover investigator. "Anything else I can do for you? A false nose, maybe?" He laughed as if he'd made a wonderful joke. He was still laughing when Steve went out.

There wasn't sufficient time remaining to check the café; it was past seven. He didn't mind keeping Feather waiting but he'd hate to be pushed down to the foot of the reservation list again. Feather was there, standing just inside the door, trying to peer through shoulders. Steve came behind her and touched her elbow. She swerved a little fearfully.

"Been waiting long?"

She said, "Oh," before she recognized him. She needed those glasses. "No, only a minute or two. It was terrible getting through traffic. And finding a place to park." She wasn't dressed up, just a blue knit and small hat to match, a cream-colored tweed jacket about her shoulders. She'd fluffed her hair a bit, she looked quite pretty.

He said, "Hold it while I check the reservation." He edged through the crowd. The list showed only two names on top of Steve's, plenty of others beneath it. He'd timed it just about right. He reported back to Feather. "Not much longer."

She gave him a quick smile. She would prove tonight that she wasn't afraid of him. "Where's Reuben?"

"Coming. Unless he's already here and holed up in the bar." He doubted it; there'd scarcely been time for a round trip to town, even without the delay of convincing Janni. "Do you want to shove through for a drink?"

She said no, with a glance at the solid ranks blocking them.

"Suits me." He eyed her. "You're looking very pretty."

She lowered her eyes. "Thank you." She didn't like personal attention, at least not from him.

"Seen Haig today?"

"No. Have you?"

"I had a drink with him here this afternoon. He might still be around."

She perked up on that.

"I suppose this big parade's old stuff to you."

"I haven't seen it in years. Not since I was in high school."

"You don't go for such mundane pleasures?"

She defended herself. "I haven't been here much. I've been studying in New York."

"That explains the hat. The New York touch."

She leveled a glance at him "You don't like me very well, do you?"

"Because I mention your hat?" He laughed. "Hollywood girls don't use them, I've noticed. Not often."

"You don't," she repeated.

He heard his name called as she spoke. "I'll break trail." By pure chance they rated a good semicircular booth midway in the narrow room. She slid in at the left, leaving room for him beside her. He didn't follow. He sat on the right where he could watch for Reuben. He told the waiter, "We'll have a drink while we wait. Feather?"

She said, "Just a sherry."

"Make mine a Manhattan." He didn't know why he'd gone fancy; devil-may-care to show Miss Prisms? He picked up the conversation. "Let's put it this way. I don't think you go for me. You're afraid. Why?"

"I'm not!" she denied with heat.

"Maybe it's this. You don't go for young men. Not that I'm so young, but Rube is. Most girls would think he was a pretty good shake, nice-looking kid, easy to be with, and if you're the kind who thinks seriously, the family's okay, your uncle said so. Instead of making time with him you play up to Haig Armour, who's old enough to be your father. Why? Because he's old enough to be safe? Or is it an uncle complex?"

She was furious. "I didn't play up to Haig any more than to anyone else. And if I did, you of all people—" Her lips pressed into a rigid line.

The waiter set down the drinks. He was old and splay-footed, the waiters here were all comfortably old. "You must order your dinners early if you do not want to go hungry to the parade." Paternalism was one of the attractions of Musso's. "At eight the lights will come on. It starts! But it will be eight-thirty," he confided, "before it gets to us. Even later."

"As soon as the others get here," Steve promised. The stem of a cherry curled over the rim of his squat glass. It was the night when Janni foraged the jar of cherries that he'd concocted the Manhattans. Maraschino cherries in the rubble of Berlin. He drank and he told Feather, "Forget it. If Haig's what you want, go after him. But you've got competition, Feather; you're pitted against the best there is."

She said thinly, "I don't want Haig. I don't want any man. I haven't time for any man. I have my work." She sounded like a fifth-grader reciting from memory.

And he couldn't tell her what a little fool she was. That work was a cold island on which to isolate yourself, while all the warm, beautiful realities surged by. Because Reuben and Janni were pushing past the barrier.

Janni wasn't expensive like Feather. Her raggedy hair was tumbled, her scarlet dress was cheap, and her coat red, the same red coat. She was lucky to have one coat. But she didn't need sleek grooming; she was the quickening of your heart and the racing of your blood. The throb of your loins. The anger for her which had strengthened him was no more.

Reuben could have let her go over to Steve. He wasn't stupid. He slid her into the booth and himself after her, shoving Feather over to Steve. Steve had sent Rube after her, he couldn't hate the kid for it. He'd known the risk. Rube was young and alive. Steve said factually, "Feather, this is Janni, and vice versa."

Rube said gaily, "Hello, Feather," not a kid out of it tonight. The guy with the best girl, sure of his prowess. "What are we drinking?"

"Make mine Manhattan," Janni said.

For a brief instant her eyes haunted Steve. Or maybe he was just hoping that the curve of a stem on his glass had stirred her memory too. The silly little phrases that returned to slice the heart in your breast. A jar of cherries that lasted a week or was it two? A jar of cherries and a mean attic room.

The drinks came to bridge the moment, to blot out days which were better forgotten. After the dinner order was given, no memories remained. There was no love or hatred, only a job to be done. Steve waited his turn. He waited until Reuben finished making a good yarn out of his adventures in finding Janni's place. Then Steve tossed it out, as if it, too, were the beginning of a funny story. "What do you think, Janni? Davidian's in Hollywood."

The shine left her face, her eyes became flat jet disks.

"You have found him?"

"I'm getting warm. He's been up to his old tricks." He confided to the others. "This is a guy we knew in Berlin. A counterfeiter."

Feather frowned. "Last night you said you did not know him. When Haig Armour asked."

Steve told her, "It wasn't any of Haig Armour's business."

Rube echoed, "A counterfeiter."

"Yeah. Slickest one you've ever seen. A real artist. He made the plates for the phony stuff the Nazis intended to plant on us. Fooled plenty of experts."

"A Nazi." Feather's voice crawled.

"And a Commie too," Steve continued cheerfully. "After the Russians took over, he went to work for them. Getting them ready for their conquests."

Feather's disbelief silenced her. Reuben came to the point. "How could a guy like that get into the United States? What's he doing here?"

"That's what I'd like to know." He was sardonic. "Me and the F.B.I."

Janni flared into the sudden silence, "They can't hurt him. He hasn't done anything wrong. I don't believe what you say!" She hadn't given him to Haig; she was protecting him from both sides.

Steve asked, "What did I say? Not that he is in trouble. There's no law against handing out phony bills that I know of, so long as it's rubles, not dollars. But with the F.B.I. after him, could be—" He let it lie there; maybe she'd change her mind, maybe she'd start considering that Steve wasn't as big a menace as government officials.

The dinners were being placed and you didn't spoil good food with controversy. Janni laid Davidian aside to sniff over her plate. Reuben didn't care about Davidian anyway, he was out for fun. But Feather continued to worry the story. "Maybe I could find out from Haig why—"

Steve cocked his head at her. "Eat your dinner." Janni was alerted and Steve added, "We'll talk it over later."

They finished the meal in spite of the increasing hubbub of excitement from the street outside. A steady exodus of diners warned of the parade's nearness. Steve waved a bill at the waiter. "Hold our table. We'll be back."

Janni ran ahead with Rube. She could lay trouble aside, you learned that in Berlin. Steve was left with Feather. She might not have been sniffing her patrician nose but she wasn't amused. They reached the street just as the myriad-colored bubbles overhead sprang to radiant light. The voice of the long boulevard answered with a multithroated cheer. The faint sound of a band from Vine Street, blocks below, was an obbligato to the shouting of children. Rube was jockeying Janni into a better position. Steve maneuvered a hole for Feather and himself. Not that she cared, but he liked parades.

The opening was quiet, with a Nativity scene and angel-robed carolers, reminder of the first Christmas before the plunge into holiday merriment. The good humor of marchers and onlookers alike struck Steve anew. This wasn't a European parade for the purpose of fluffing the ego of a dictator or to flaunt the bristle of military strength. It wasn't a New York parade, stage-managed by some junior Ziegfeld, precise as the Rockette's routines. This was small-town in a big town, kid bands, stream upon stream of kid bands with high-stepping girls twirling batons and twisting brief satin skirts; skinny boys in fancy uniforms blowing loud on their shining horns, beating loud on their drums. This was Western, with silver-decked palominos and cowboys in silver-studden chaps, with trick riders and proud horseflesh and the children yelling for more. It was drums and bugles pacing the quick step, dancers and clowns, and the glaring spots of the TV cameras. The glamour of Hollywood was minor, a number of glistening floats, candles on the icing of a cake. Overhead the little lights beamed red and yellow and green on the silver stars and the shiny Christmas trees, far overhead the true stars were pale in a deep cobalt sky. And Steve saw Davidian.

Only the face, the sharp ferret face wedged between a woman's fur collar and a man's elbow. Peering out eagerly at the show, directly across the street from where Steve was standing. He might as well have been across an ocean and a continent. Separating him from Steve was a solid phalanx of onlookers; beyond, children pressed from curb to ropes, the police patrolling their safety. In the center the river of prancing bands and horses and trundling floats continued its unending flow.

Steve muttered, "Back in a minute," to Feather, not caring if she heard. Janni and Reuben didn't. Steve walked as far as Highland before he was able to dart across to the south side of the boulevard. He retracked then, eeling through the onlookers. It was slow going at best, made slower by the search for one small man. The audience was constantly shifting for better position; there was no promise that Davidian would have remained where Steve had left him.

When he reached that section, he paced more slowly. There wasn't a chance of pushing through to where he could look into faces; he had to be content with unidentifiable back views. By patient moving with the crowd, he managed at last to catch sight of the fur collar. But no thin, shabby man pressed against it now; on either side were gabbling women.

It hadn't been an illusion, Davidian had been in this neighborhood. He was here now, lost somewhere in the mass, peering under some other shoulder. With agonizing slowness, Steve continued on, examining coats and shoes and the backs of heads. He walked all the way to Vine and waited out the combined bands of Orange County before he could cut over to the north side again. His eyes followed the montage of faces across the way as he headed back towards the restaurant. He saw fat and thin faces, dark and light faces, faces from Europe and Asia and Africa, all the American faces, Hollywood faces, but not Davidian's.

He'd forgotten Santa Claus until he saw his face too, the great jolly whiskered saint in his traditional red and white, riding on top of the finest float of all, crying his "Merry Christmas" through the amplifier, while Hollywood snow sifted a benediction over his head. The children and Santa Claus shouted joy to each other. Steve didn't join the chorus.

3

THE ONLOOKERS BROKE RANKS QUICKLY AFTER SANTA'S FLOAT PASSED, hurrying to reach their cars, to be first in the clog of traffic. Steve jostled his way through the confusion to Musso's. The three were again in the booth, the vacant place was beside Feather.

"What happened to you?" Rube wanted to know. "We've ordered dessert."

"I thought I saw a friend across the street."

Janni whispered, "Davidian."

"I saw him."

For a moment she was frightened and then she began to laugh. She knew him too well, she could read his failure. "But you could not find him in the crowd!" She slanted her eyes at Reuben and he began to laugh with her. Because he wasn't an innocent or because her laughter was infectious as a parade and ice cream and youth.

Reuben laughed. "Chocolate cream pie á la mode."

Feather's words slit thin and cold. "I'll find out about him from Haig." She actually put a hand on Steve's arm. As if she were sorry for him, as if she wanted to help him.

He covered the hand. He didn't tell her that Haig didn't know as much as he did. "Thanks, lady." Her flesh quivered under his touch.

The old waiter set the desserts. He beamed, "A good parade this year, a real good one. Better than last year." He said it annually. And meant it.

Reuben and Janni were savoring their pie and ice cream. There was no way to separate her from him. It was always tough to get an occupation army out once it was in. Rube said, "We're going dancing at the Palladium. Kenton's there."

"Janni has to work."

"She's taking tonight off." He grinned. "Why don't you and Feather come along?" Big-hearted Reuben.

Steve lied, "I'd like to." He apologized to Feather. "I have a business date."

"It's all right," she assured him defiantly. As if she were pleased that he wouldn't waste time on a dance hall; that he, like she, was dedicated to work.

They broke up in front of the restaurant. He watched Feather round the corner to her car. He watched Reuben and Janni disappear towards Vine. Over the deserted boulevard, the colored lights were darkened, the ropes and stanchions were removed, only the litter of torn newspapers remained as reminder of the brightness of parade time.

The Prague, his last address, was only a couple of blocks away. Steve left the boulevard and walked towards it slowly, as if he were tired, but it wasn't that which made his steps heavy. It was a small *café*, gimcracked with atmosphere, the usual red-checkered tablecloths, and candles dribbling down the sides of old wine bottles. A fat man with a greasy mustache played a sentimental violin and a taffy-haired lad, who needed a haircut, a balalaika. The music wasn't Prague, it was a musical comedy piece. *My darling . . . my darling . . .* the violin crooned. And the balalaika tinkled an answer, *My darling . . . my darling . . .* Cigarettes swirled a blue fog around the candle flames. Behind the cash register was a big busty woman in a flowered peasant-style dress; her hair was dyed the color of fresh brass. Steve didn't try for a table, he went directly to the woman.

"I'm looking for a guy."

She spoke pure New York. "You a cop?"

"Do I look like a cop?"

"Cops don't always look like cops."

"I'm not. That's why I'm looking for a guy. To tip him off."

"Maybe you think this is a bookie joint?"

"He isn't a bookie." He leaned an elbow on her counter. "He's a little guy, thin, dark, doesn't speak English too good. He's been going around passing counterfeit rubles."

She gulped, "Nuts."

"Yeah. Did he hand out any here?"

Words were beyond her.

"To the waiters? Would they mention it if he did?"

"Mention it?" Her tower of brass nodded precariously. "Rubles yet!"

He said, "Thanks," and he went out of the place. Davidian might have been in any and all of these blind alleys but with a different joke.

There remained Albion's boardinghouse. Eleven o'clock was too late to pay a call but he could walk by, if there were signs of activity he might inquire. He hadn't any other lead except to walk the streets looking for the popcorn man. His steps began to take on the rhythm of an old song, abridged to his own needs:

Oh, have you seen the popcorn man, the pop-
corn man, the popcorn man,
Oh, have you seen the popcorn man
who lives in Hollywood . . .

Albion had lived south of the boulevard. It was another of the relic sections of Hollywood, a half-dozen frame houses left behind when business moved in. The address he had been given was the tall house next to the corner. There were signs of life, plenty of them; the parlor lights were bright behind undrawn shades, the voices were loud and merry. In one of the foolish coincidences of the everyday, the radio was singing the same old song of the Prague duet, *My darling . . . my darling . . .*

He walked up to the open screen and he found the bell. The man who appeared smelled of beer. He was just a man, maybe a shoe clerk or an electrician or a cop off duty. He said, "Come on in. Party's not over yet." He didn't wait for Steve to explain himself as a stranger, he held open the screen and Steve followed him into the parlor.

There were several men who might have been the host's brothers, there were women to match, and there was a fat old woman billowing over the best chair. And there was the reason for the party, a teen-age girl who'd marched in the parade. She was still wearing her brief red satin skirt and her soiled, high white boots. Her satin top hat was on the table with the beer. The girl—she couldn't have been more than fourteen, all knobs and angles—was leaping in excited dance steps until Steve's entrance halted everything. Everything but the radio moaning its song of heartbreak.

He began, "I'm sorry to bother you."

The fat woman came out of the chair. Her face was flushed from the beer, one strand of her scant gray hair hung over her ear. "You are looking for a room?" She pushed at the strand but it fell again rakishly over the little fat ear.

He was sorry to bring remembrance of death into this celebration. But death had been here; it was not his doing. He said, "I wanted to ask about a man who used to live here, Frederick Grasse."

The silence was even more silent. These people had known him better than anyone had known him in his last months. They had lived with him.

The man who'd admitted Steve asked bluntly, "Are you from the police?"

He'd never been taken for a cop as often as tonight. "No," he said, "I'm the man he went to the airport to meet. My plane was late." And he asked, "The police have been here?"

"Been here!" The teen-ager wagged her frizzy hair. It was bleached almost white. "We've had tons of them! They keep coming!"

It must have been her mother who spoke petulantly, "Don't exaggerate, Melba." She had the same rabbit nose of the young girl and whining lines about her lips.

Steve said, "I suppose the police took all of his belongings."

The old lady was suspicious.

"I'm an insurance man from New York," Steve explained to her. "Mr. Grasse was making out a report for me."

Insurance was something she could understand. "You won't find it here," she told him. "They took everything."

"They tore the room apart," Melba exaggerated further. The soft song had died, some noisy cacaphony had replaced it making all of them shout. No one turned off the radio; they were accustomed to its competition. Melba rounded her eyes. "Do you think he was murdered?"

"Melba!" her mother complained. "Where do you get such ideas?"

"Well, the police don't tear a room apart when a man dies of heart failure, do they?" Having made her point, the little girl grabbed a cookie and crunched it between her crooked teeth.

"The kid's got imagination," her father said proudly. "And she's got a point," he told the roomful, gesturing with his beer bottle. "Do the police move in when a man dies natural? When Pa had his heart attack, did the police move in?"

They'd been over this time and again, making the same points, the same rebuttals. It was in their faces. The old woman was the only one not amused by the untoward excitement. She glared at them but she didn't say anything. When she looked at Steve there was a spit of fear behind her washed-out eyes.

Steve asked her, "I suppose you've rented the room?" It wouldn't do him any good to see it, the police would have taken anything he could want.

"I rented it the day after," she defied him. "Lucky. Very lucky."

The police had known from the beginning it wasn't heart; they'd autopsied and known; they'd torn up the room and left it for renting the next day.

He said, "Thank you," and turned to go. If they only knew how to tell him. They'd seen Albion daily while he was hunting down Davidian; they'd seen him while he fumbled for the trail, when he'd been cold and then warm, hot, when he'd reached sight of the goal. He tried again, "Did you see him when he left that night?" Had he known he'd been marked for the sacrifice? Had he believed he could be safe long enough to meet Steve? He must have believed that, he'd reached the airport.

The woman slapped at the irritating wisp of hair. "I saw him." She'd told it so often, it was by rote. "He came home from the bookstore about six-thirty and changed his clothes. I met him out there in the hall. I asked him if he was going out. Just making conversation. He told me he was meeting a friend at the International Airport. He said the plane might be late because it was already foggy but he had his key with him. I lock up at eleven."

Steve nodded. Albion had been alone, she'd mention it if there'd been a friend with him. She'd answered all these questions before. "Do you know what time it was when he left?"

"I don't watch the clock." She was tired of him, she wanted him to go away and leave them alone.

But he kept on. "Before dinner or after?"

The shirt-sleeved man, he must be a son, said, "Before I got home. Because I asked Grammaw, I asked, is Fred home? I'd brought some beer and I thought we could have a beer. I don't like drinking alone. Sometimes we'd have a beer together before supper. But he'd already gone."

"So you had it alone," the wife said sourly.

"So what's a beer? You think a beer makes an alkie out of a man?"

Steve said, "Thanks." No one seemed to notice. He went out into the night. The radio and the loud voices and the smell of beer followed him up the street.

Somewhere within this small section of the city's map, Davidian was waiting for him. Why couldn't Davidian have sighted him when he sighted Davidian? The man must know he was in town; why no message? He could answer that one. Because Davidian was under Steve's own orders; the contact must be made Winterich to Davidian, not the reverse. It was that extra measure of safety. But Davidian was too cute not to figure out a way to reach Steve without making contact. Unless he had and Janni was deliberately withholding it. Or unless Davidian had sold him out.

Oh, have you seen the popcorn man . . .

A man who knew those walking the streets of Hollywood. No bobble of a yellow lantern. No smell of hot popped corn. Janni and Rube were still dancing or they'd parked somewhere in the car Steve had promoted. The boulevard was deserted, the shop fronts dim, the office buildings empty shafts. Gusts of music rattled from the jazz bars. Steve turned in at the dull lobby of the hotel, started across its emptiness to the elevator.

But it wasn't empty. The man on the settle laid aside the morning edition which had been masking his face. He said, "I've been waiting for you." Just an ordinary guy, Steve's size, wearing a beaten brown hat and a trench coat as old as Steve's. It took a second look to recognize Wilton.

"What for?"

"There's some men who want to see you."

Steve started by him. "Bring them around. Ten cents a look."

Wilton halted him. Not violently. With no more than a disinterested finger upon the sleeve of his coat. "I'd come if I were you."

Steve took out his cigarette pack, lit one while he thought about it. "That's the way it is?"

"That's the way."

He hunched his coat. "Let's get it over with."

Tonight it wasn't the big hearse. Just a sedan, nothing shiny, nothing you'd notice.

Steve said, "I'll sit up front. I get lonesome."

Wilton gave a nod. You couldn't get much out of this guy.

"Don't you get tired running errands for the brass?"

"Don't you?"

It was a fair retort, both of them were working stiffs, neither called the shots.

"What does Armour want now? Didn't he get enough this afternoon?"

Wilton didn't bother to answer. He carried along on Sunset to the Doheny hill, on down to Santa Monica Boulevard. When the Beverly Hills city hall loomed a white and golden fairy-tale tower, Steve tightened. He could take questions, not a lockup. He relaxed when Wilton directed the car straight ahead, following Santa Monica across Wilshire, continuing on past dark woods. And on, until he drew up in front of an inconspicuous motel. It had some Spanish name on it.

"Haig's moved," Steve commented.

Wilton said nothing.

"You can run out of dough fast putting on a front." He didn't feel as flip as he sounded. He could crack Wilton one and take off. But it would necessitate getting out of town fast, and he couldn't leave town until the job was done.

Wilton stood beside him on the sidewalk. "Number ten's in the rear. It isn't Armour wants to see you."

Steve didn't move. He hadn't considered it this way. "Suppose I don't like this?"

"You don't have to like it. You'll save yourself trouble if you take it."

Their eyes met on even keel. Wilton was right, he knew he was right, and he knew Steve understood. There were plenty of ways to get a guy who didn't co-operate.

"Coming?"

Steve dug his hands in his pockets. "What do you think?"

Their steps were solid on the concrete walk leading to the rear right bungalow. Wilton rapped on the door. The man who opened it was a narrow dark young fellow in a blue suit. "Hello, Cal. Mr. Wintress?"

"Who else?" Steve returned insolently. The two men waited until he walked inside. But no lock turned behind him. He stood in a miniature living room. There was another guy on the couch against the further wall, heavier set, balding; his suit was gray. Not an elegant tailored job like Haig Armour's gray, just a suit like the blue one, or Steve's own.

The blue suit gestured, "Mr. Wintress, Hale."

Hale said, "Sit down, Mr. Wintress. You know Ferber and Wilton."

He didn't sit down. He didn't have to. Ferber returned to his straight chair backed up to the window. Wilton took another chair, swung it around to protect the door.

Hale said, "We're having a beer. Join us?" The beer cans were on the low table, moist beads stippled on them. A paper sack had crumpled to the floor. These were temporary quarters.

Wilton said, "You might as well sit down, Wintress. You'll be more comfortable. And you might as well have a beer. Or do you drink only with the brass?"

The three men were a triangle hemming him in. He lifted his shoulders, took the place they'd left for him, the one comfortable chair. He might as well take the beer as well. "Okay," he said. "Get started." There was probably a recorder under the couch or in the curtains. They wouldn't get anything on him.

"We're curious about Frederick Grasse's death," Hale began.

"You think I killed him? I got witnesses. Ask Wilton. Top brass ones."

"What makes you think he was killed?" Ferber had a college man's voice, smooth, educated.

They knew the answer. "The Feds don't get curious about heart failure."

Hale asked offhand, "Why was he rubbed out?"

"You know more than I do."

"No," Ferber denied in his quiet way. "We don't. We don't know why."

Steve pushed up in the chair. "For God's sake, you think I know why? After making a trip all the way from New York to see him?" They knew damn well he had nothing to do with Albie's death. Their informers would have reported how important it was for Steve to see Albion. "Why the hell don't you find the killer and ask him why? Why figure me in?"

"Because," Hale said, cracking another beer for himself, "you and Grasse were tied up with another man. A man who has disappeared."

Steve said, "I don't know anything about it. I came out here to see Grasse. He was dead before I arrived." They couldn't change his story.

"You knew he didn't die a natural death."

"For God's sake," Steve said wearily. "I guessed it. Haig Armour wouldn't be interested if he had."

Ferber put in, "What's happened to Davidian?"

Steve didn't answer.

"Grasse is dead. Davidian is missing. You're left. Top dog."

He didn't like it. Not even with the knowledge that they were only playing him, figuring he might spill something.

Wilton announced without interest, "Even Commies have their little spats."

He wanted to walk over and push his fist through Wilton's face. "So Grasse was a Communist? Do you have to ask a guy to take a loyalty oath before you call him a friend?"

Hale ignored that. He remarked, "You know what I think? I think there was a slip-up in plans. I think Davidian and Grasse were bumped off too soon. Before you got your hands on the report."

He lost his temper. "Davidian isn't dead!"

Wilton said offside, "He does know more than we do."

"He isn't dead." But the cold hand on his neck wouldn't lift. Like Haig, they were so damn sure of themselves. Davidian wasn't dead, not yet. Davidian was too experienced to be dead. He wouldn't let it happen until he turned over the report. And he wouldn't turn it over to anyone but Steve. He spoke quietly, in control of himself again, "I saw him tonight. At the parade."

They didn't believe him. They had a dossier on Stefan Winterich, a story of betrayal and death; they wouldn't believe anything he said.

"And he turned the report over to you?"

For the record Steve said flatly, "I didn't get to talk to Davidian. He got lost in the crowd. I don't know anything about a report." If Hale had checked with Armour, he'd know damn well that Steve knew about it. But it was different talking across a Musso table with Haig and talking to a hidden wire recorder. One which could, by a carefully arranged accident, fall into Schmidt's hands. Divide and destroy. Let Schmidt destroy Stefan Winterich; keep Haig Armour's manicured hands clean.

"Don't you?" Ferber let the legs of his teetering chair clack down hard on the linoleum floor. But his voice was still nicely modulated, Harvard grad. "You don't know that Davidian escaped from Berlin, the Eastern zone, that is, carrying in his head the war plans for Soviet expansion through Western Europe? You don't know about Davidian's photographic memory, considered as fabulous as his draftsmanship? You don't know that he managed to carry a few notes with him to bolster that memory? Or that heads fell like walnut shells in East Berlin when Davidian came up missing?"

"Maybe I heard something about it." It wouldn't have been possible to be in Berlin and not hear about it. And they'd know it. When it was discovered that it wasn't Davidian in the t. b. ward but just another scrawny guy who hardly resembled him, everyone in both zones heard plenty of Davidian.

"But you didn't hear that he was writing a report of what he learned while engaged in certain work for the Reds?"

Steve told the truth. Not that they could recognize it. "That didn't leak out." The clamp of censorship saw to that.

"You didn't come to L. A. to grab that report?"

"You mean he hasn't turned it over to his American pals?" Steve jeered.

"It's possible he doesn't mean to turn it over to us," Ferber said. "It might be he plans to sell it."

To the outfit with the biggest bank roll. They could believe this yarn. Davidian's reputation as a dirty little spy was well established.

"You can stop worrying," Steve scorned. "I'm broke."

"There's only one thing worries me," Hale stated. "Where's Davidian?"

Steve laughed.

"Something's funny?" Wilton demanded.

"Yeah." He laughed some more.

"Hand us a laugh."

"You've got it." He gave them the same needle he'd used on Haig, it always worked. They were so damn proud of their organization. "The great F.B.I. with all its terrific brains and stupendous resources can't find one little guy. And they think I can."

He let his glance pace over the three of them. "I'm a stranger here, remember?"

Ferber said quietly, "It might be easier for an old friend from Berlin to find him. A guy whom Davidian might believe to be his friend."

He didn't like Ferber. "That's the way you see it."

Hale rested his heavy hands on his knees. "There is something you'd better know, Wintress. If anything happens to Davidian, we're picking you up for murder."

Anger flooded him. "Like that!"

"Like that." Hale jabbed a hand towards the door. "Take him home, Wilton."

Steve was on his feet. "No wonder Haig Armour has such a big-shot reputation. He can railroad anyone who gets in his way." He hit all of them with his buckshot words. "You've been following me around. Okay. Just keep on. Stick closer to my tail. Because if anything happens to Davidian, I want witnesses that I didn't do it. Witnesses almost as good as I've got for Albion's murder." He started to the door. "I don't know how in hell you figure I'd want Albion out of the way—" In anger he'd used the wrong name, the private name. But there wasn't one of the three who didn't get it. "If I'm here for the reason you've dreamed up, God knows I'd be an idiot to get rid of the one guy I needed to find Davidian." Somehow he managed a degree of dignity. "Frederick Grasse was my friend."

Ferber said almost sadly, "In your decalogue, Wintress, a friend is a friend only as long as he conforms to orthodoxy. You have no friends."

Steve circled their faces; Hale was an old man, Ferber young, Wilton between; in detail each one was separate but each wore the same face. One that was steady, purposeful, and merciless. He wondered fleetly if there were real men behind the faces or if the organization chose only men with these faces. He'd wondered the same of his own organization. There was plenty he could say; plenty he'd like to tell them. Hale, the sledge hammer; Ferber, the knife; Wilton, the punch to the jaw. He held his tongue, walked past Wilton into the night air, damp and fresh from the Pacific, a few miles further west. In silence he proceeded on to the car, silence broken only by Wilton's steady heels behind him and the riff of cars passing on this quiet stretch of the boulevard.

He maintained the silence on the ride back to Hollywood. He had nothing to say to Wilton nor Wilton to him. Each was no more than a cog in his particular pattern. If they changed sides, they would be unchanged as men; if they were on the same side they would enjoy comradeship, not enmity, but neither man would be changed.

At Sunset and La Brea, Steve said, "Let me off anywhere along the line."

"Wherever you say."

"I don't want the F.B.I. delivering me to my hotel this time of night. There might be talk."

Wilton said no more, he stopped at the next corner. Walking was better. Streets were peaceful in the early morning hours. Steve passed Oriole's. He was too tired to report, much too tired to wait while Oriole routed Schmidt out of bed to listen to the night's developments.

The sift of street light through the window of his room showed the shape of Reuben in his twin bed. Rube said, "I'm not asleep. Put on the light."

"I don't need it."

Reuben said, "You must have made out. Coming in at this hour."

"I told you it was business." He didn't want to ask but the kid was waiting for it. "How did you make out?"

Rube stretched for a cigarette, the match made a small cone of light. "Pretty much of an all right." He wasn't fooling anyone. "That Janni's a swell kid, isn't she?"

"Yes." It stuck in Steve's throat.

"Swell dancer."

She ought to be. She'd danced her way out of the rubble, she who could dance even in rubble. A kid in a scramble of kids begging from the conquering heroes. A begger kid, with matted hair, dirty rags on the stink of her body. But she'd danced. Fire and joy blazing out of her black eyes. That and hate; he hadn't recognized the hate at that time. He'd been a dumb, good-natured American like Reuben. Fifteen years old and she didn't look more than twelve. He'd thought she was twelve when he tossed her a chocolate bar and a couple of cigarettes. Until she came to him, put her mark on him. Because she'd picked him to get her out of the muck.

"I want to explain something," Rube said solemnly. His skinny shoulders hunched against the headboard of the bed. "I wasn't trying to make out with your girl. But she said she wouldn't come unless it was with me. She said you wouldn't care." In the half-light he searched Steve's face for a clue. "I feel like a heel, Steve. You've been regular with me. But the way she said it—I can't explain exactly—but it didn't seem as if it was important. She made it kind of a part of the fun of the evening.

"I didn't care," Steve said. "Skip it."

"I'm not saying it right."

Steve laid his clothes neatly over the chair before he came to bed. "I understand, Rube. I know Janni. I know she can make things sound however she wants them to sound." Trivial, gay, terribly important, terribly sad. While her devil within mockingly observed the effect. "But she was telling you the truth. I didn't care if she was with you. It's not that beating me. It's the conference I've been in."

He'd made it right. Reuben's guilt faded out of his young voice. "I said I'd call her tomorrow."

"Okay."

"I told her I'd take her to some broadcasts."

"Sure." If Reuben kept her busy enough, Haig Armour couldn't be hounding her.

"She's been here almost a year and she's never been to a broadcast."

Reuben wanted to talk about her, it was that way when you were excited about someone. That way when you loved. A long time ago Steve had had to give up that small but sometimes essential luxury. It didn't matter to him any longer. But he wished to Christ that Rube would shut up about her.

IV

HE DROVE TO ORIOLE'S IN THE MORNING. NOT THAT IT WOULDN'T HAVE been simpler to walk the few blocks but he wanted to reassure the poor old guy that his shabby car was okay. He hadn't announced his intention to drop in. He hoped he could catch Mr. Oriole alone.

Mr. Oriole was chewing on a cinnamon bun when he answered Steve's ring. Crumbs were caught in the rough of his chin. A coffee-stained napkin dangled from his belt. He wasn't surprised to see Steve, but he apologized, "I am sorry." He was trying to hide the bun in his large soft hand. "I did not get to bed early. So a late breakfast."

Steve said, "Take your time."

"You would perhaps join me for a cup of coffee? And cake? My wife bakes excellent coffee cake."

Steve started to refuse. And then he didn't. Mr. Oriole was sensitive and Mr. Oriole was helpful. A man's feelings were worth more than a few minutes' privacy. Furthermore, the coffee Steve had gulped at a corner white-front hadn't been the last word in breakfast. He said, "I haven't had any good coffee cake since I left Berlin."

The woman was embarrassed but the two small boys, and they were replicas of Mr. Oriole, were only curious. Mr. Oriole said, "My wife, Ingeborg. She does not speak English much. And two of my sons, these are named Jim and Jack. The other children work on Saturday mornings. Very fine sons. Five of them."

No wonder the woman looked old with six men to do for. She rubbed her hand on her apron before extending it to take Steve's. It was a light hand with baking. Steve resented the intrusive doorbell, not only because he was afraid it spelled Schmidt. The smile left Oriole's fat cheeks as he plodded to answer. It might have been that Schmidt too had called for a private confab.

Steve didn't follow him. He beamed at Mrs. Oriole and stuffed away another wedge of cake. "You're okay," he murmured. "You've put me back on my feet."

She spoke gently, in her halting accent. "A man needs a woman to cook for him. You have no wife?"

"Not yet."

"Do not wait too long." Her eyes crinkled. "The best ones go first."

"I've found that out."

Mr. Oriole returned, undraping the napkin from his pants. "It is Mr. Schmidt," he said hopelessly. "He is waiting for us."

"Dandy." Steve finished his coffee. "Thanks, Mrs. Oriole."

She took his hand again. "You remember what I tell you."

"I'll remember." They exchanged a blessing.

Schmidt was stiff in the best chair, crease in his pants, starch in his collar, briefcase at his polished heels. He was in good humor. "Good morning, Mr. Wintress. You have news?"

"I have." Steve lit a cigarette. "The cops picked me up last night."

He'd smashed whatever dream Schmidt was harboring. Behind the lenses the eyes lost their luster. "For what reason?"

"They didn't give a reason. They asked questions."

"Concerning?"

"Concerning Albion's death."

"Why are they intervening in this? For what purpose do they meddle?" The thin nose was pinched with white anger.

"They don't go for executions. This is a free country."

"Yes." The word was a snake. But Schmidt didn't proceed into dialectics. He would know Steve could recite the speech as well as he.

Mr. Oriole ventured, "This is not a nice development."

"They want to mix me up in it."

Schmidt considered. He would be pleased to offer them Steve but he didn't dare. There were higher authorities protecting Stefan Winterich. "You were not here."

"That's what I keep telling them."

Schmidt said slowly, "I do not understand this."

"They made it clear. Albion and me—and Davidian." Schmidt lifted his panes of glass. "They can't find Davidian."

"Can you?" It was in the open now, Schmidt's resentment of an outsider being injected into his kempt affairs.

Steve faced Schmidt coldly. "That's why I'm here." He didn't elaborate. "I was warned that if anything happens to Davidian while

I'm in town, I'll be pulled in for his murder." An idea stirred in Schmidt but Steve quashed it. "I'm telling you to warn all of your eager beavers that if anyone lays a hand on Davidian while I'm in town, it will be not only the end of your job, Schmidt, but all the way down the line. Got that?" He waited for an answer.

It came under pressure. "I understand, Mr. Wintress."

Schmidt would be a threat from now until the end of one or the other of them. If for nothing but this humiliation before the subordinate Mr. Oriole.

"You do not expect them to reach Davidian before you do, Mr. Wintress?"

He'd been waiting for Schmidt to slash. "No, Mr. Schmidt, I don't. If they were on their toes, they would have had him before now. He's been leaving his calling card all over Hollywood." Oriole quivered but Steve wasn't giving him away. "Albion knew."

"He did not tell me!"

"He also knew the value of silence in some matters." Steve went on factually, "I'll get the Davidian report for you. I simply want to make sure in advance that none of your staff makes any more mistakes."

"You may be sure." There was open hostility behind the glinting eyeglasses. He quoted himself, "We wish only to co-operate, Mr. Wintress. We realize you are working against time with Haig Armour and his Gestapo after the same material." As far as Schmidt was concerned, Wintress would have to prove himself the miracle man. "May I suggest again that the girl could be made to talk? I understand there is a lover in the Soviet zone."

Schmidt was behind the times. "You refer to Janni Zerbec?"

"I do."

"I told you once I'd take care of her. That stands."

The lips were dangerously thin. "Very well, Mr. Wintress. I understand."

Steve accepted the insinuation. He didn't move until Schmidt dropped his eyes. "Good." He quit the parlor then, knowing Oriole would follow to the front door, to be certain he was out. He'd have that long. He let Oriole open the door for him but on the porch he turned back. Schmidt couldn't overhear even if he had his ears against the parlor drapes.

"I couldn't find the popcorn man."

"He went home early." Mr. Oriole was nervous. He had a session ahead with Schmidt. He didn't want Steve on his neck too. "Because of the parade, you understand. He sold out his popcorn early. But to-night he will be around. Perhaps on Ivar in time for the intermission?"

"I'll look for him." He swung away but was halted by Oriole's soft voice.

"The services are this afternoon for Mr. Albion. You will be there?"

"No one told me."

"Mr. Schmidt intended to mention it. He had so many things on his mind."

"Where?"

"In Santa Monica. At four o'clock." Mr. Oriole read off the name and address of a funeral parlor.

"Why Santa Monica?"

Mr. Oriole said, "His family lives there. It was his home." He was mildly surprised that Steve didn't know.

"You'll see me." Steve clattered down the wooden steps. Schmidt had deliberately withheld the information. It would have been hard for Steve to explain to either side why he had not been present. He would be present.

He drove the heap back to the hotel, left it in the back lot. Reuben was making like a crooner while he polished his shoes. He cocked an eye. "When did you join the early birds?"

"It wasn't for fun. What about Janni?"

"I'm taking it easy waiting for noon. There's a public phone at her place. She's going to be downstairs at noon for the call."

Steve lounged on the foot of Rube's bed. "I've got a suggestion. You don't have to like it or take it but here it is. Call her at noon but meantime I'll start on downtown. You tell her I'm on my way and to be ready. I'll bring her back to you and you two can do the studios while I go about my business. Then we can all meet for dinner."

"Okay," Rube said. What else could he say?

"I've got some things to talk over with Janni. Might as well do it while I'm taxiing her to you. Save time."

Rube was quiet. "She's not mixed up in this thing of yours, is she?"

Steve went at it carefully, "She's not mixed up in anything with me, Rube. And she doesn't intend to be. You don't have to worry about Janni." He continued, taking it slow, "But the man I'm here to see roomed at Janni's when he first came to L. A."

"The counterfeiter?"

"He's not in that business any more. Except as a gag. He never did it for profit, Rube, only for a favored position. You don't understand. You couldn't. Not the way you've lived. You don't know the provocations of Europe."

"Maybe not." Maybe yes, he'd been in Berlin. "He's a friend of Janni's?"

"Not particularly. She knew him." Through Davidian's friend. Stefan Winterich. "She'd help any refugee to get started in an alien land." Unconsciously his voice toughened. "She knows where Davidian is. She won't tell me."

"Why not?" The quiet, unanswerable question.

"I wish I knew." He repeated, "I wish to Christ I knew." He waited but there were no more questions. "See you soon."

The sky and the air were balmy, the way California should be. A picnic day. If the world and you were young. Neither would ever be again. Because the grime of Europe was embedded in your very bones, you couldn't forget reality in these endless streets of white houses, green handkerchief lawns, flowering vines in brilliant winter bloom. The decay of Janni's neighborhood was more closely attuned to this era of destruction. He drew up before the woeful house. Maybe the world would have been a better one if it had lived in eternal summer. Even this dump was gay with red blossoms climbing its scaling walls, redder flowers billowing about its tired porch.

He was early. He sat in the car until twenty past the noon hour, giving her time to get back to her room after the phone call. He didn't want to surprise her. He took it easy on the stairs. As he headed down the corridor on second, he had to step aside for a painted, angular blonde in a garish green dress. She was in a hurry but she slowed her teetering heels for his attention. Incongruously she twitched his mind to Feather.

He took the last flight and strode to Janni's door. There was the usual nothing on his first knock and he knocked again. He expected the old woman's evil eye at the door's opening but it was Janni herself standing there, barefoot, her purple and pink bathrobe about her, her face softened with sleep. When she recognized him, she said automatically, "Get out."

He pushed the swift-closing door and was inside the room. She was alone. "Why don't you call the police?" She wouldn't, not to protect him but out of fear of involving Davidian. He lifted her hand off the knob and banged the door shut. The impact trembled the walls.

She threatened, "Get out of here."

"Didn't Rube tell you I was coming?"

"Rube?" She pushed at her scalloped hair. And then she came suddenly awake. "What time is it?"

"It's past noon." Steve helped himself to a chair. "Get dressed. He was to tell you I was on the way to pick you up. I'm to deliver you to him."

She yanked open the door. "You will wait outside while I dress."

"I'll wait right here. It'll give us a chance to talk things over."

"There is nothing for us to talk over."

He settled himself, lit a cigarette. "Get dressed. You're keeping Rube waiting."

She glared but she banged shut the door. Again the walls shivered. She ignored him, walking to the stained sink beside the stove, splashing soap and water. He kept quiet until she was toweling herself.

"Have you seen Davidian yet?"

She walked back to the wardrobe, swept aside the limp cretonne curtain and eyed her few dresses.

"You're going to see him today. This is the day you give him his dough."

After a brief moment she removed the hate of her eyes and carried her clothes over to her bed. She dumped them there, turned her back on Steve, and began to dress.

He grinned, "I know plenty, sweetheart."

She said viciously, "Don't call me sweetheart."

"A colloquialism which slipped out. Pardon, Fräulein Zerbec. Where do you pay off?"

She perched on the edge of her cot to slide the sheer nylons over her exquisitely long legs. He'd given her her first nylons. The other kids had been happy with chocolate. She'd been as hungry as the others but she'd wanted nylons and a red lipstick.

"If you know so much, find out." She dropped the kimono, slipped the narrow black dress over her head.

"I'll find out if I have to stick to your tail every minute of this day and night." He made the words count. "I don't want to go that far."

She smoothed the dress over her breasts, down her small rounded hips. "You are a louse," she said serenely, but her eyes were jagged with anger.

"You've picked up a few colloquialisms yourself, sweetheart."

She began to brush her hair with fierce strokes.

"Haven't you learned by now that Davidian wants to see me? That I'm the only one who can peddle his report?"

Carefully she put down the brush. "Why do you go on with it?" She spoke quietly. "Do you honestly believe you can double-cross the party—and live?"

He didn't figure in her fears; it was Davidian alone. He said curtly, "Think it over. I'm meeting you and Rube for dinner."

"And your fancy blond?" Her moment of weakness was gone. She stood at the smeared mirror, coloring her mouth. "La di dah!"

"Maybe this will help you decide. The F.B.I. picked me up last night for a little talk. They've warned me if anything happens to Davidian, I'm the fall guy." He got to his feet. "Nothing's going to happen to Davidian while I'm in town."

She caught up her red coat, her cheap black purse. "You are leaving soon?"

"As soon as I've talked with him."

They shouldn't have looked into each others' eyes. Too long a moment. She said unsteadily, "We must not keep Reuben waiting longer."

There were no more words until they were just another man and woman in just another car trundling along the busy streets of the city. He had to reach back into memory for the words that raised her question.

"Where do you go?"

When the job was done? "Wherever I'm sent."

"Back to Berlin?"

"Why not? A job's a job."

"You have not changed." She spoke not with regret but stating a fact.

"Did you expect it?"

"No." There was no more than a faint shading of doubt. "You made your choice. And you are stubborn."

"Let's say logical. Sounds better."

"However you say it, you would not admit to being wrong."

His laugh jeered. "You say I'm wrong."

"Before I came to your country, I accepted that you could be right. That you were right when you believed you had picked the side of ultimate victory." She shook her head. "Now I know how wrong you are. And I do not understand how you can believe otherwise."

He said, "I don't get you, Janni. There's only one reason you wanted to come to the U.S. and that was to pick up some of those gold and silver chunks that pave the streets. And those refrigerators and swimming pools and big cars and fancy clothes and all the rest of it. What have you got? A slum almost as bad as you were raised in. Bargain-basement duds. Ten-cent perfume. A job that doesn't pay you enough to eat right, a job that only the hopeless would touch. That's your land of promise. Empty promise. You'd have done better to stay in Berlin."

"No," she said and she was so very sure of herself. "That is where I know you to be wrong. Not even if I could have those gold and silver things in Berlin would it be better there. What you hold in your hand does not matter. There is something more important. To be free."

"Free!" He snorted. "Free to live like dirt. That's good?"

"It is good, Stefan, to be free to live as I will. To go to a dance or to a church or to a movie, or to stay home; to read whatever I wish to read, to speak in any way I wish to speak, to think as I wish to think. Day or night to do what I choose, without fear." She was like a torrent. "No papers! It was many weeks before I lost my fear when walking home from work at night, very late, I would spy a policeman. I would begin to search for my papers." She illustrated, scrabbling into her purse, and then she smiled, happy as a child. "Until I learned to remember—no papers!"

He grimaced, "And you think it's right for the rich bitches to have Beverly Hills and you Skid Row?"

"I am free to move to Beverly Hills."

He denied it with a laugh. "There's a little capitalistic device known as the economic system. Boiled down it says that the guys at the top aren't going to let the guys at the bottom come up. They're free to keep you down below. And you're free to stay there."

"You know better." She wasn't angered. She was almost patient with him, she spelled it out primer-clear. "I am free to go to school. And the school is free. It is called adult education. When I am a stenographer I will not remain on Main Street. When I am a good stenographer I will move to Beverly Hills. If I want to move to Beverly Hills. If I do not, I will not have to move there." She studied him somberly. "You cannot understand, Stefan, because you were born to freedom. You do not know what it means always to be a serf, always to live in fear of the masters. I was born to the Nazis. When they were gone, there were new masters. There was no change, only a different name. It was worse than before possibly, for they were alien masters; they did not even speak the language of their serfs. You were born with freedom from fear. This I never knew for myself until I came to your so big and beautiful land. I had been told but I did not know how to believe it until I myself knew it to be true." Her lips tightened. "And I do not understand you and those like you who would destroy this freedom. For what? For your own ugly reasons."

"You wouldn't be blabbing about freedom if the cops were chasing you. If the F.B.I. was on your tail."

"The criminal must always be afraid, yes. And the traitor." The word curled from her tongue. "In my country it is not only the evil men who live in fear, it is everyone, the good and the honest and the innocent. Everyone who is not corrupted by the master race. Whatever name these masters call themselves."

The car was moving along Hollywood Boulevard and Reuben would be taking her away from him. She wasn't the girl Steve had known in the Berlin gutters. She was Janni but she was someone new.

She stated, "It is for this reason I will not deliver Davidian to you. I will not risk his freedom."

Steve didn't say anything. He left-turned and drove into the lot. In her stilt heels she came to his shoulder. Berlin street kids who were raised out of wartime garbage didn't rise up tall and serene as did California youngsters.

He steered her into the lobby. From the nearest banquette a shined-up Reuben jumped to greet them. "I was about to give you up." He beamed at Janni. "Hello."

"It is my fault. I oversleep. I apologize to you." She was soft now, a woman with woman tricks, not an adversary.

"Don't you apologize," he told her. "I was just afraid this guy had decided to keep you for himself."

"That is not possible."

You could take it any way you wanted; you could skip it. "I've got another date," Steve said. With a dead guy. "There's a little place on Cahuenga. The Prague. Meet you there about seven."

"Okay." Any dump was okay with Reuben. As long as he had Janni. He was already skipping her out of the lobby. If Janni's eyes had sharpened at the meeting place named, Steve couldn't tell. It could have been a trick of the light.

2

HE RECLAIMED THE CAR AND DROVE OUT SANTA MONICA BOULEVARD, shoddy save for its Beverly Hills beauty spot, to the city which named the highway. The house of dead men was the usual mansion, this one something out of Colonial Old Spain. The surrounding homes of the living shrank humbly away from its elegance. For the living, crusts; for the dead who couldn't taste it, icing cake. Steve walked up a gracious flower-bordered walk and into the marble foyer. He removed his hat on entering; it was that kind of atmopshere.

The office attendant was a corseted matron in black satin. Her blue-white hair was waved with wig precision, the rouge on her pink powdered face was too bright. The corpse wouldn't be painted any fancier.

Her unction didn't hide the coarseness of her voice. "May I be of assistance?"

"I'm looking for Frederic Grasse's family."

She tiptilted a watch brooch. "The funeral won't be for more than two hours, Mr.—"

"I know." He bottled his impatience. "It is the family I'm looking for. You have the address?"

The fishy eye she protruded at him turned him into a shyster. She had a good reason to be wary, this elegant dump wouldn't care for the police background of Albion's death.

He forced a sad, sweet smile. "I am an old friend of Frederick's. I just arrived in town from New York and learned—" He let his hands spread his regret like treacle. "I hoped I might be of some comfort to his mother. Fred and I were boys—" He kept slathering it on because she liked it that way. He even pulled out a handkerchief and honked his nose.

The dame was still dubious. "It isn't usual, Mr.—"

He side-stepped the name again. "Years ago—" A word or two was all needed, she supplied the remainder out of the echoes of experience. And it finally worked. She retreated into her small office while he waited in the doorway, snuffling into the handkerchief. She consulted a card file.

"Mrs. Grasse lives on Seventeenth Street." She recited the house number.

He repeated it as if it were a dirge. "I can't thank you enough." He recalled he was a stranger. "Is it far?"

She figured. "About twelve blocks." She tapped the card.

"I have been loaned a car."

That cheered her. He wasn't just a bum, he could borrow a car. "Just drive out Wilshire or Santa Monica. The house is south of Wilshire." Across the tracks, her nose inclined. Not too far across for this outfit to grab the business.

He restated the thanks and moved fast. Before her dubiety reheightened and she thought of calling the mortuary brass, or staking him out for a cop. There should have been a cop around. But they wouldn't expect any of Grasse's friends to show up this far ahead of the funeral.

On wheels it wasn't far to Seventeenth Street. The Grasse bungalow was yellow frame, midway in the block, indistinguishable from the other bungalows in the neighborhood. It wasn't shiny and it wasn't art but it was tidy. There were the usual red flowers clustering about the steps and against the house. Early-blooming poinsettias were tall against the windows.

Steve parked in the nearest space, up the street. The Grasses had other callers. Or the clan had gathered. He knew nothing of Albion's family, only that there was a mother. Albion was forever speaking of his old mother, with no apparent reason he would bring her into a zone of conversation, and, after a sentimental moment, permit her to leave. Conscience? Or was it only by holding fast to her hand that Albie had the courage to stand up to a hostile world?

Steve walked back to the house, up the walk and up the shallow steps to the door. So many walks and steps and doors in so many worlds. Behind the doors a home. For him never a home. A room in a flea-bag, a final resting place in a trash can in some alley. Alleys were the same all over the world, as were the little houses. He pushed the bell and heard the answering chimes.

The woman who appeared was tall and sparse, her black dress serviceable, not new for the funeral. She had a thin, sharp face, tearless behind her gold-rimmed eyeglasses, her hair was beginning to gray. She waited for Steve to speak.

"Mrs. Grasse?"

"I am Miss Grasse." She didn't ask him in. She held the door almost with defiance, certainly with rejection. This wasn't the usual mourning house open to all who came bearing the drooping leaves of sympathy.

He felt impelled to explain himself. Not to force entrance, but in exoneration. "My name is Steve Wintress. Your brother and I were friends."

Nothing softened in the lean woman. If anything she became more rigid.

He tried harder. "In Berlin. I hadn't seen him in five years. I was looking forward to it. When I arrived, I learned he was gone."

She didn't welcome him, but she said, "Come in." Out of curiosity concerning a part of her brother's past?

The hallway was small and sunny with a yellow plaid wallpaper. It was uncluttered; there was an unframed modern mirror, a three-legged mahogany table beneath it. On the table, in the exact center of a square of white linen, a silver vase with green branches was placed.

She led into the living room at the right, another small room and on any other day a pleasant one. The furniture was old but the flowered covers were clean, the wood polished, the mantelpiece unadorned. There were minor etchings on the walls, one of Washington Square with the Arch a slant at the right-hand corner, one of the fantasy skyline of Manhattan, one of a river and a young apple tree. Frederick's nostalgia for a more serene past?

Miss Grasse said, "Mama, this is Mr. Wintress. He says he knew Fred in Berlin."

Mrs. Grasse rose from a straight chair, a chair which didn't belong to the room. It was maple, decorated with some unidentifiable small white-paint flowers. Probably from a breakfast-room set. The mother was her daughter twenty, thirty years hence. As tall, as spare, more gray, more lines on the skin. But there were deeps in this face that would never be in the spinster's. Mrs. Grasse had borne life and death.

"You knew Fred?" There was German in her speech, a long time ago.

Steve took her hand and he felt shame. He hadn't come as a friend; he'd come to ask questions. Determined on answers.

With increasing disapproval, Miss Grasse said, "My sister, Mrs. Knott, and her husband, Mr. Knott."

These were plain people; the sister could have been older or younger, she was softer and more round but these qualities didn't allay the hostility in her. The husband had the tired look of a man who had worked hard and honest for long years and small reward. He, too, was hostile. The only warmth was in the dry hand of the older woman.

It was she who urged, "Sit down, Mr. Wintress," and she indicated the big flower-covered chair. The company chair. The brother-in-law left it and put himself between the two Grasse girls on the flowered couch. His white collar was especially white against the weathered red-brown of his neck, and his stiff Sunday shoes were heavy on his feet.

"We bury Frederick today," the mother said. There was no outward grief, whatever agony curled her heart because she buried her son was covered by her flat black bosom. Nor was her mourning dress new. "You were his friend?"

"Didn't he ever speak of me?" He and Albion had been friends, if ever he'd had a friend in the organization. Albie talked of Mama away from home; at home wouldn't he talk of his friend?

"Fred didn't live here," Miss Grasse stated. Her diction was coldly precise.

Her sister added to it. "He lived in a room in Hollywood."

"It was his business," the mother explained to Steve. Perhaps the stranger would believe this; the others would not. "He worked very hard at his business. He could not live so far from it." She wasn't a soft woman, she said it without emotion, "He was a good boy. He came to see me." She dared the others to doubt it.

Steve repeated, addressing her alone, "He spoke of me? Steve Wintress?" Because of the sisters he couldn't say, "Of Stefan Winterich?" Because their enmity was too near the surface.

"Fred didn't mention his friends to us," Miss Grasse said. "We didn't know his friends."

Mr. Knott made it clear. "We didn't want to know his friends."

They knew. They knew Fred's business and they were good citizens all. They despised. Only the mother. She knew; she would have been told, over and over; she would have been told with throttling anger, with acid spite. The disgrace of Fred. But he was the son she had borne and she was old and had wisdom. She could wash his sins with pity.

"He was too young to die," she said. Tired, gray Albion was too young to her. Was it because he was a man, small of stature, amid tall, stony women that he had compensated by taking a little unnatural power to himself? There was always a reason. For every one of them a reason.

The mother continued, "He did not tell me he was sick. I scolded him because he works too hard. He is thin and no good color in his cheeks, but I did not know he was sick. He would not worry me."

The other three exchanged eyes. They knew Fred hadn't died from sickness; they knew the police wouldn't question and re-question about a sickness. When Steve was gone they'd tell the mother again, barb it into her heart. While he was here, they couldn't. They were respectable, too respectable to mention the police before a stranger.

"He came to see you recently?"

"Every week he comes," she said proudly. "On Thursday. Every Thursday without fail. It is the night of Marguerite's bridge club." Two against Marguerite. "I give him a fine dinner. Dumpling stew. It is his favorite ever since he was a little boy. Dumplings." She put the passion out of her voice. She wouldn't make dumpling stew again. Marguerite would eat for health, whole wheat and fresh greens. "He ate too much. Because it was so good."

"He didn't mention I was coming to California?"

"He didn't bring his friends here," Miss Grasse stressed grimly. "He didn't talk about them. We didn't want to hear about them."

"I'd written him I was coming." He hung on as grimly. If only he could speak alone to Mama. "I hadn't seen him in five years. A reunion."

"It is good to see old friends," Mrs. Grasse sighed. "I do not remember if he spoke of you."

And the break came. There'd been so few, Steve deserved this small one. The bells chimed. Miss Grasse went to answer; it was safe, she left her sister and the husband on guard. No one spoke. The two on the couch waited tensely as if they feared the ring meant another of Frederick's friends or again the police. Mama Grasse didn't care; she mourned Absalom, her charity covered the why and how he had betrayed them.

There was crisscrossing of voices in the hall, young and old, female and male. Aunt Gertrude and Uncle Nicholas, Cousin Barbara and her husband, and Aunt Anna and Cousin Willie. The little room was overfilled with too many people and their words. But under cover of the confusion Steve could speak privately, in this moment when the Grasse sisters were trapped by the relatives.

He said to the mother, "He planned to meet me."

Her pale blue eyes flickered. "You are the one?"

He pushed ahead quickly. "Was there no message for me? You

have his things?" The police would return mementos to the next of kin. They had released Albion; they wouldn't retain the belongings.

"Yes." The hesitation was too long but the sisters continued to be cornered by weeping Aunt Gertrude. "There is no message, nothing." She saw his refusal to believe, because her eyes like Albion's could see. And because Steve called Frederick friend, among his own who had rejected him, because she grasped for one kindness to her boy who had died alone, unwanted, too soon, she said, "I will show you."

She put her heavy-veined hand briefly on his wrist. He started to follow her but Miss Grasse's voice whipped across the room. "Mama!"

The mother's voice was strong. She knew Marguerite wouldn't make a scene, not before the relatives. "I will show Frederick's friend the fine lace shawl he brought to me." Her bedroom was the first beyond the living room, a warm, rose-colored room. There were framed pictures on the wall, family pictures. Three little girls in stiff hats and high-buttoned black and white shoes, two little boys in sailor suits, unreal as cartoons. Steve wondered where the other children were now; he didn't ask. Children were born and they died. She had opened a long bureau drawer and from tissue paper lifted out a folded black lace shawl.

Steve remembered. "I was with him when he bought it. In Berlin." The first time he'd heard about Mama. He touched the delicacy of the fine lace. And he remembered the aged man who had sold it, the furrows in his pallid cheeks, his blackened teeth. He remembered how the old man had held it in his withered hands before he could let it go.

She unfolded it. "See? How big it is!" Her voice was powerful. "It was much too fine for me." As she spread it on her rosy satin bedspread, she was pulling open the small drawer of her bed table. Her voice went under her breath. "This is what came from his pockets." While Steve touched the keys, the license case, the half-roll of mints, she spoke up loud again. "He was a good boy. He was never in trouble. Never!"

And Steve's fingers closed on the ruble, folded so small to escape attention. Not to be thrown away, for Frederick had preserved it; not to be shown to the shame of the good sisters. Steve unfolded it, his back to the woman. She wasn't watching him, she watched the door.

"He could not give me so much as Marguerite, no. She with her fine position, a high school principal she is, for ten years now. He was not so successful."

No message save that Albion had carried it as message, the proof that Davidian was in the city.

Her voice lifted, "Ah, Gertrude! My shawl, you remember this fine lace Frederick brought to me from Berlin?"

Aunt Gertrude blocked the doorway. She mourned, "Always so good to you, your son."

Softly Steve closed the drawer. Miss Grasse's nose quivered behind her aunt's heaving shoulders.

The mother said, "His friend was with Frederick when he bought the shawl for me."

Miss Grasse didn't believe. She didn't know what Steve wanted here but she knew his coming wasn't honest. Her eyes was trained to spot excuses.

He said to Mrs. Grasse, "I must go. Thank you for your kindness."

She was a little fearful. As if, in his leaving, he was taking away another part of her son. She took his hand and pressed it. "Come again to see me. Thank you for coming today. Thank you."

Had Albie spoken of Davidian, perhaps a funny story to make her laugh, about a little man who made money and who was hidden in the open streets but no one could find him? No more questions. Miss Grasse was at his side until he was shown out the door. She remained on guard in the doorway until he was beyond the path and out on the sidewalk. Her silent mouth was repeating, "We don't want to know Frederick's friends."

3

ON THE CORNER OF FOURTEENTH STREET THERE WAS A SUPERDRUG-store and supermarket. On impulse, Steve swung into the parking lot. He took the drugstore, found a phone booth and called Feather's number.

The precise voice of the manservant wasn't certain that Miss Talle was available. Before investigating, he was insistent on the name of the person calling; he'd been trained to preserve the Eldon Moritz privacy. He was worth every cent of the three or four hundred a month he'd demand.

Feather came on the phone. She said, "I have only a moment. Haig is waiting for me."

"Have you found out anything?"

"Oh yes." She sounded pleased.

"When do I see you?"

She was hesitant. "I don't know whether I can get away."

He told her flatly, "If you have a date for cocktails with me, you can get away." Either she was without any experience or she didn't want to get away.

She hesitated further. "Y-yes."

"I'll meet you at five. Wherever you say."

She didn't say anything but she was there, he could hear her faint breath. She might be consulting Haig.

"Well?"

"Could you make it at six? It may be difficult."

"Six. But I can't stay long. I have a dinner date." Tonight he wasn't going to drag her along. "Where?"

"The Beverly Hills."

"I thought the point was to shake that guy?"

"Oh yes, he's stopping there," she remembered vaguely.

She was the dumbest girl he'd ever met; no one could be that dumb. "Well, where?"

"The Beverly Wilshire?"

She wouldn't know any dumps, only chromium-plated *bistros*. There wouldn't be any dumps in Beverly Hills. He'd buy her one drink. "Don't be late," he said and hung up. That one would be wasted money. But he couldn't miss any bets. She just might not be Haig's girl.

When he left the booth he realized he hadn't eaten since breakfast. There was time for a sandwich. He sat down on an upholstered stool at the soda fountain, ordered a cheese and coffee. The sandwich came fresh, wrapped in wax paper. He ordered another, and, lured by a shiny brown-and-cream illustration hanging on the mirror, topped it off with a chocolate soda. He hadn't had a chocolate soda in years and it was good. It was like being home.

And then it was time to put in an appearance at the farewell to Albion. Not for Albie's sake but because both sides would speculate over his absence. In their respective myopias they wouldn't consider he might stay away in protest against furthering the ancient ugliness of gathering about an empty rotting shell, a custom perpetuated out of superstition and greed. Albion was gone, a part of infinity. He might even be a part of blessed infinity, he'd made mistakes but the Divinity wasn't the party. You could err; you could, if you had to, hug grievous error, and be forgiven. God could forgive Albion his mistakes, God and Albie's mother.

There were plenty of cars around the funeral home. He was late, the macabre festivities hadn't begun but within there was a sizable audience. Not mixed. Schmidt and Oriole and Frederick's friends were on one side; on the other were relatives and the family friends. On the outskirts was the law. He recognized Hale's jaw line and Ferber's shoulders. Wilton was further offside where he could check each entrance. Were they hoping Davidian might show? Steve didn't join any group; he took a doorman's position on the opposite side from Wilton. He'd only gone into his folding chair when the immediate family appeared and the man who must be the minister. Mrs. Grasse hadn't veiled her face, her shoulders were straight and her chin; she wouldn't weep. Not for an audience.

The minister spoke briefly, without spirit, he might have been rented with the hall. He was safer with the words of the Lord; his voice strengthened as he read from his book:

> *Have mercy upon me, O Lord; for I am weak:*
> *O Lord, heal me; for my bones are vexed.*
> *My soul is also sore vexed:*
> *but thou, O Lord, how long?*

He was too young to have known Frederick Grasse; had the Lord guided him to this Psalm? Or was it the mother?

> *Depart from me, all ye workers of iniquity*
> *for the Lord hath heard the voice of my weeping.*

There were hushed steps of more late-comers. Two heads turned, Steve's and Wilton's. There was no need, Haig Armour and Feather didn't hide in the rear. They moved down the short aisle until they were directly behind the family party. Feather couldn't have known she was coming to visit the dead; she was dressed for cocktails in a cap of violets, a spray of them at the collar of her blue suit.

> *Let all mine enemies be ashamed and sore vexed:*
> *let them return and be ashamed suddenly,*

the minister intoned as he closed the book. He didn't try a eulogy, merely a brief prayer for a man who had been and was no more. The murmur of *Amen* came feebly from both sides. No one wept.

It was over and Haig Armour was moving up to the family. Anger spurted into Steve. Armour couldn't be permitted to invade the mother's privacy at this time. Part of the anger could have been his own shame but Steve moved rapidly. And vainly. Feather stood in his way, cat-eyed, smelling of violets. "I want to tell you—"

In that moment, Haig reached Mrs. Grasse. Steve set Feather aside. "Hold it." He didn't bother to see how she took it; he reached Haig.

And he heard the rich voice, properly subdued. "May I express my sympathy, Mrs. Grasse? I knew your son a good many years ago. I had hoped to see him while I was in town."

Steve wasn't needed. The watchdog sisters had closed in and the impresarios of this affair. Mrs. Grasse had only the same words, "He was a good son," and she was conducted away.

Haig turned and looked into Steve's face. If he was chagrined over the brush-off it didn't show. Steve said sardonically, "You were an old friend of Fred Grasse?"

"Hello, Steve. Maybe I knew him."

The mourners were filing out. Schmidt was interested. And Wilton. Neither came forward.

Steve said angrily, "She's decent. Call off your hounds."

"I can't hurt her. Nothing can hurt her further." Haig's jaw was squared. "She might like to know that there are some who aren't willing to condone murder."

He hadn't seen Haig angry before. Maybe it was the presence of the assassins, the hypocrites, mouthing amens. Steve demanded, "And you think you'll find a killer by heckling her? She doesn't know his friends or his enemies. Miss Grasse doesn't allow them in the house."

"You've been there."

"Yes. Unlike you, I was an old friend of Frederick's. Like you I hadn't seen him for a long time. And hoped to see him while I was here."

Haig said, "Maybe you did see him."

"Meaning what?"

"There was time enough. While you were looking for your unknown pal at the airport. Time for more than a few words."

Haig's boys hadn't accused last night. Haig hadn't outright before. It rocked Steve but he hung on. "He was dead when I was on the plane. With you."

Haig said nothing.

"You know damn well he was dead before I got there." They weren't going to saddle this murder on him, no matter how much Haig would like it that way. "The police know. They released the body, they know when he died."

Haig quoted, "The tolerance of the body to certain alkaloids is different in different men. They can't be certain whether Grasse got his before he went to the airport or later."

The attendants were working around the edges of the auditorium, cleaning up for the next show. They wished the two men would carry their argument outside. Feather had drifted to the door, as if she didn't want to hear what they were saying.

Steve's fists ached from their clench. "You'll have a hard time hiring witnesses who can put us together. I came here to do business with Frederick, not to kill him. I can prove that."

"Not on the witness stand," Haig said smoothly. "You wouldn't dare go on the witness stand and reveal your business with Grasse."

That was it. Rage ate at him, knowing they could do this to him, knowing he couldn't make testament of the truth of the matter between him and Albion. Even if they couldn't prove their case, and they couldn't without perjury, they could tie him up long enough to make him worthless on the job. Haig had many ways to win his victory.

Steve whispered, "You bastard."

Haig said, "Don't worry. I don't believe the police will bother you for a few days yet." He moved with the taunt, towards the girl.

Steve waited until they'd gone. When he came out of the place, the pitifully small cortege was driving slowly away. Haig and Feather were advancing to a Cadillac roadster. Ferber and Wilton idled by a plain black sedan as if concluding desultory conversion. Schmidt and Oriole duplicated the performance by another sedan. Steve knew what they were all waiting for. The number-one pigeon. He had no choice. He moved down the walk and joined Mr. Schmidt and Mr. Oriole. It couldn't be news to Ferber and Wilton that he belonged in that category. They'd had his friends tagged before now.

Schmidt asked, "What had Armour to say to you?"

He didn't have to answer. It was none of Schmidt's goddam business and it wouldn't hurt to tell him so plainly. Nor would it hurt to speak up. "He wanted me to understand that this doesn't close the file on Albion."

"So?"

"He's still trying to put it on me. He's capable of having me picked up for questioning. To keep me from reaching Davidian. If that happens, you're going to have a hard time explaining to New York why I wasn't given proper protection."

Schmidt didn't move an eyelash.

"If that happens," Steve pounded it, "you're going to get me out of it fast. If you have to turn yourself in as the killer."

Schmidt inclined his head. The smile on his lips wasn't nice. It was Mr. Oriole whom Steve had frightened. He would have to pick the victim, arrange for proof. Even if he had to turn himself in. Schmidt wouldn't be touched. He was the brainy kind, safe until Steve could undermine him at headquarters. Unless something happened to Steve. His insolence was icy. "Don't worry, Mr. Wintress. We will take care of you."

Steve propelled the question. "Who did kill Albion?"

It didn't disturb Mr. Schmidt. "We are working on that, Mr. Wintress."

Steve didn't shove in the man's face. He simply walked on to the car and drove away. Neither Armour nor Schmidt was worth his blowing his top. He wasn't here to fight big shots. He was here to get the Davidian report.

He should have insisted that Davidian pick a safer locale. But the little guy had seen too many American movies or heard too many tales of eternal palm trees and orange juice. Or was it that Janni was here? Davidian wasn't a man you could drive; Steve had had to have his co-operation. And what was the difference? There were outfits working in every city, Des Moines or San Francisco or New Orleans, name any of them. There was activity in even the small towns.

You couldn't outrun danger, not when you were in the business that Albion and Davidian and Steve were in.

He remained on Wilshire into Beverly, parked the old crate a block away and walked back to the hotel. There was nothing cozy about this lobby: it was as big and glittering as a movie set. Feather wouldn't be early. Time for a phone call.

The phone rang on and on in an empty room. Reuben and Janni would find out he was late when he didn't show up on time for dinner. They wouldn't care how late he was. The call hadn't been to find out if she'd gone to the room with the soldier. It didn't matter to Steve if she had.

He left the booth and found the cocktail lounge. It was crowded and noisy, high-class noise, Beverly Hills brand. He had a straight one standing at the bar and returned to the lobby. She wasn't very late. She was still dressed up like a cocktail-hour girl but she didn't play her part. She stood timidly by the revolving door, looking out myopically into the lobby. Steve went to her.

She fumbled, "I tried to be on time. But Haig insisted I have a drink with him before I dropped him at his hotel. I thought it was better. He was angry."

He guided her elbow back towards the fancy bar. The head waiter found them a sliver of space; it didn't take him long to bring a sherry and a weak highball.

Steve asked her, "What has he got to be angry about?"

"This man. The funeral—" She didn't want to continue. "He was murdered. Haig thinks you—" Her eyes scuttled away from him. "You didn't. You were on the plane. But—"

He said sourly, "They couldn't pin it on me but they could hold me too long. What about Davidian?"

She wasn't listening. "Is Haig really F.B.I.? He says he isn't. He says he's a lawyer with the Department of Justice. But Eldon says—"

Steve told her, "He's been an important Federal man for years. What did you find out about Davidian?"

She admitted, "Not very much."

"Haig won't talk?"

"I don't believe he knows. He seemed to be trying to pump me as much as I was pumping him." She seemed embarrassed. "As if he thought you might have confided in me."

If that was a come-on, he ignored it. "He doesn't know where Davidian is?"

"I don't think so. Only that he's in touch with this girl—Janni." She breathed hard against his shoulder. "I know I haven't found out much for you. I'll do better tonight." She was too eager, as if she had to convince him that she was on his side, not Haig's. "We're going to have dinner with him at the hotel. Eldon and Elsabeth and me. And Eldon is going to help me. Eldon's very good at things like that."

Steve said, "My God, did you have to rake in your whole family?"

"Was it wrong?" Her lip fell. "I wouldn't have only I thought—" Her shoulders hunched tremulously. "I mean I thought because Eldon knows everybody, he might know—"

"He couldn't possibly know the man I'm after," Steve said. "Davidian's not a movie star."

She caught his wrist. "I'll find out something tonight. I promise you."

"I'll give you a ring." He put a bill on the table.

"After dinner. I'll go home right after dinner." She didn't want him to go; she was fine-strung as a race horse. Her mouth was opening to spill a further delaying action. For what purpose, he didn't know.

He got to his feet. "I'll ring you after dinner." He swerved away. He was threading through the tables, almost to the door, when he noted Eldon Moritz sitting alone, almost directly opposite to where Feather was now alone.

It wasn't the first time he'd wondered what cooked with Eldon Moritz. But it was the first time that it bothered him sufficiently to wish that he weren't already too late for his appointment at the Prague. He'd have liked to join the man for a few presumptuous questions.

It could be that Eldon was only keeping an avuncular eye on his wife's niece and her odd companion. It could be but it wasn't. Not the way Eldon was casting a calculative eye on the girl. Not the way Feather reacted to men old enough to be her uncle. It didn't necessarily have to be a thing between the two. And it was this riding Steve as he steered Oriole's old boat over to Hollywood. There was the matter of Haig's interest in Eldon Moritz, they'd gone chummy fast for a couple of professed strangers. You could never know who was undercover these days, it added to the hazards of what once had been a comparatively simple occupation. One item stood out with clarity, with Feather sandwiched between Haig and Eldon, she was as trustworthy as an adder.

4

THE SMALL PARKING LOT ATTACHED TO THE PRAGUE WASN'T VERY POPular on a Saturday night. A few cars stood forlorn in the angular shadows. A slovenly boy ambled out of a wooden kiosk to take thirty-five cents from Steve in exchange for a yellow ticket.

After the lonely lot, the café was pleasant. The mustached man and towhead boy were making sounds of music. Through the candlelight Steve spotted Janni and Reuben against the wall. He headed for them, ignoring the beckoning eye of the brass-haired woman at the cash register.

"Sorry to be so late."

Reuben and Janni were already eating something Hungarian and their salad greens were strong with garlic.

"We did not expect you," Janni said complacently. She'd cleaned up somewhere—in his room?—she looked scrubbed.

"I said I'd be here." He told the waiter, "Bring me the same." He put his elbows on the table. "When I say I'll be somewhere, I'm there."

"Ha," she mouthed. She was looking for trouble.

And he wasn't in any shape to take it. "What does that mean?"

She slanted her black eyes. "It means, Ha Ha Ha."

"Skip it," Rube murmured.

"Why should I skip it? After those many times when I have waited on the corner, and waited, and waited, for the very dependable Herr Winterich. Ha Ha."

Why this? For God's sake why? She'd kept the past out of it so far, brutally so. Why drag it in tonight? Was she striking out of fear, fear that his delay meant he'd caught up with Davidian? So he'd kept her waiting sometimes, so he'd had to cut appointments without warning, it was over and done with. She'd known he wasn't a free agent.

She shoveled in another mouthful. "And so," she explained to Rube noisily, "when I make an appointment with Herr Winterich, no longer do I expect him. Maybe he will come, maybe not. Who knows?" She licked a bit of gravy off her finger. She didn't say, *Who cares?* It was implicit.

Reuben tried to quiet the waters. "How was your day, Steve?"

"Just dandy." The waiter set a bowl of potato soup in front of him. "I went to a funeral."

She stopped eating.

"The guy at the airport."

"Was your friend?"

"Yeah." He didn't explain why he'd denied him heretofore. To Janni he said, "You remember Frederick Grasse." They'd had him to supper, he'd furnished the schnapps.

She remembered too well. "Albion. He brought you a pair of shoes. American shoes. He is dead? How?" She cut the word like a whip.

"Heart failure."

Over his shoulder the brassy woman called, "Ah," as if she'd been searching for Steve. "I have news for you."

He didn't tip her off to silence. He preferred Janni to hear the news, whatever it was. "Yeah?"

"But it is Bona who should tell you. I asked questions." She waved imperiously to one of the waiters. It wasn't the one attending their table but it could have been. They were all of a type.

"Bona," she said, "this is the man who asked, you know."

Bona twitched his mustache. "It is like this," he began. The other waiter moved in, snatched away Steve's soup dish and replaced it with the goulash. Bona glared his comrade away.

"Wanda was asking about the ruble." Wanda was the woman nodding her glittering pompadour.

"Where did you get it?"

"This I am telling you." Bona wasn't going to have his moment sucked away by undue haste. "I am in the kitchen waiting for the order to be served and the talk turns to Russia. Quite naturally, you understand. There is at the time a dishwasher, a starved dog who works cheap, you understand, because he can eat his fill."

Janni began mopping her plate vigorously with a lump of bread.

"But this man says he is in possession of rubles. This I do not believe. He dries his hands and his arms and he proves it to me." Bona took from his hip pocket a wallet. From it, with care, he extracted the slip of paper. "This one he presents to me."

He allowed Steve to handle it.

"When did he work here?" Steve passed the bill to Janni, let her see for herself. Bona tried to figure without success. Wanda thought it was maybe a month ago. She wasn't sure. She didn't keep records on cheap dishwashers.

"You don't know where he lived?"

They didn't.

"His name?"

"Jake. Just Jake."

The ruble came back to the waiter. He was folding it when Steve said, "It's a phony."

"How?" The man's face fell apart.

"Counterfeit."

Bona didn't believe. He examined it on one side and the other and then he put it away as if he suspected Steve of pulling a fast one. Steve said, "Thanks for the information," to the disappearing apron.

"You're sure?" Wanda frowned.

"I'm sure. Makes them himself."

She didn't follow the waiter, she trailed back to her own corner.

Steve began to stow away his goulash.

"So?" Janni was furious. "He works as a dishwasher to get enough to eat."

"Maybe. Maybe for some other purpose."

"He works as a dishwasher," Janni said heatedly. "He is working, not making money."

"Who said different?" Steve finished his plate.

Janni dropped her anger while the waiter brought the dessert. But before he was out of earshot, she returned to the fray. "Why do you make trouble for him? Asking questions of these people? Getting all of them to spy on him?"

Steve said, "I wouldn't have to if you'd tell me where he is."

"I have told you—"

"It doesn't matter any more," he cut in. "Feather's getting the dope for me." He gave meaning to the lie by a look at his watch. "Remind me to call her after dinner."

Janni disbelieved but she couldn't deny. She thought she alone knew the way to Davidian yet she couldn't be sure. Because Steve knew her so well, he could be amused by the act she began to put on. A light raillery against Feather as an opener, followed by a mockery of Steve for being led along the garden path by a simple girl who didn't know enough to open her umbrella in the rain. For the main show, a biting scorn of Steve, who could slump so low from an established reputation as a huntsman to be forced to depend on misinformation from a stupid animal like Feather. She threw in the implication that it must be Steve's declining powers as a male which could make him interested in such a milk-and-water specimen as Feather.

As always, Steve let her perform. When she broke off to suck the last of the chocolate from her spoon, he tried a point of his own. Janni knew more of local conditions than he. "So she's young, untried, an amateur, I'll grant you. But her uncle is Eldon Moritz."

It was a good try. Janni stopped pretending. It appeared that this was news to her. Unpleasant news. She asked indifferently, "Who is Eldon Moritz?"

She knew who he was all right. She'd recognized the name without delay. But Steve gave her the full answer.

"He's a movie big shot, lives in a comfortable twenty-nine-room cottage up Benedict Canyon, complete with swimming pool, butler, unlisted telephone, everything you've seen in his movies. That's where I'm heading for tonight. To get my information in an easy chair with a good highball, not in some crummy hall room with a gun in one hand and a dollar bill in the other."

She said viciously, "You don't know what you are doing. You are a fool. But you have always been a fool." She was making words, nothing but words. Because she had no way to stop him from going to Feather. And she was afraid of Feather. She spat, "You trust any *halunke*."

"No," he said deliberately. "I learned better than that. A long time ago."

Reuben wasn't enjoying this. He was trying to act as if he weren't there but he couldn't go on endlessly drinking out of an empty coffee cup.

Steve dropped Janni. He said to Rube cheerfully, "How about ordering a brandy and another round of coffee. I've got to make that call."

He had to pass the counter to get to the phone. The woman called to him, "Mr. Winterich." He hadn't given her his name. "You understand I had no idea this dishwasher was important." They were all so fearful of making a mistake, even an inadvertent one. "I am in the kitchen so little, I don't even know who is hired."

He told her, "It isn't important. It could have been but it isn't."

Some of the worry lines went out of her powdered face. "If I'd had an idea—"

"Sure, sure," he assured her. Tell it to Schmidt or Oriole. He wasn't interested. He shut himself in the booth and called Feather. She'd reached home; she said she was alone, the others had gone to a movie. Her voice sounded farther away than Hollywood to Beverly. But he gathered she had something to tell him. Something she called important. He couldn't miss any bets. "I'll be there within the hour."

The woman was still chewing on her worry. She halted him as he left the booth. "You don't think—"

He stopped to invent. "The guy who taught me this business advised me not to think. Leave that to the number ones, he used to say. That's the rule I follow." It would give her something else to ponder. It might keep her from confessing her error.

The hot coffee was poured. A cheap brandy stood in liqueur glasses at each of the three places. Janni's glowering anxiety tightened her dark brows. Steve sat down and tasted the brandy before speaking. She'd never ask. It was good to keep her waiting; because he wanted to hurt her and because he couldn't; because he could only strike with these petty twigs.

He said finally to Rube, "I'm sorry I can't give you kids the car. But I'll need it to get to Benedict Canyon. I'll probably be late. Think you can amuse yourself?"

Her violence burst out. She shoved her chair from the table, shouted, "I can amuse myself without your mangy car. I am going to work."

Rube tried to protest but she had no words for him. She lingered only long enough to down the brandy. You learned in the gutters not to waste food or drink. And she was gone, her red coat a streaming danger signal behind her.

Rube was on his feet, not believing this.

Steve said, "Let her go."

"But—"

"She gets that way. Temper."

Rube sat down. Not accepting Steve's dictum. Resenting it. Resenting Steve. He couldn't hold it back for long. "What the hell's the matter with you tonight? There was nothing wrong with Janni until you sat down here and started needling. No wonder she got mad. Every time you opened your mouth, you socked her."

He didn't want to scrap with Rube. And he certainly didn't want, as if he were a spoiled child, to say that she'd started it. Even more he didn't want the soldier getting serious over Janni. He maintained a calm objectivity. Or tried for it. "You forget, I've known that piece a fairly long time. She's not the gay, charming kid she's giving you a picture of. Believe me, she isn't."

"So you can sock her because she's come up from the gutter?"

"Up from the gutter to Skid Row."

Rube's fists knotted.

"Okay," Steve said quickly. "That's not why. I don't care whether she's Skid Row or Bel Air. That has nothing to do with what she is. There's plenty of her kind both places. It's what she's doing to Davidian that burns me up."

"Protecting him?" She'd been at Rube and he'd listened.

"Protecting him? Yeah. From the only guy that can help him, the only friend he's got."

"You?"

"Me."

"You and God and Stalin."

"You're talking like Janni." It wasn't Rube's fault. Janni could take any of them, make pretzels out of them. "Who the hell does she think she is, making Davidian's decision?"

"If he wants to see you, why doesn't he? He's all over Hollywood, washing dishes, watching Santa Claus." Rube's voice was deadly. "Being careful he's two jumps ahead of you."

Steve downed his coffee. He couldn't give Reuben the whole picture. He was upset about having it like this but there was nothing more he could do or say now. "Sorry. Maybe you're right." He pulled out his wallet, replaced it when Reuben said with austere determination, "This is mine."

And Reuben could be right. Davidian did know that Stefan Winterich was in town; even if Janni had withheld the information, he couldn't help knowing, his ear was against too many of the right keyholes. Steve couldn't be sure of Davidian, you couldn't be sure of any man whose life had been a lie for twenty years. Or more. Davidian might have been born a moral contortionist.

How could a man ever be sure of any other man? This was the age of treachery, the age when the lie was made dogma, when evasion was a sanctified virtue and ignorance a sacrament. It was the age of words but the words no longer had meaning, they had been subverted into the gibberish of the new jungle. There was no more honor; how could Davidian be an honorable man? Loyalty was only a banner to be dragged through the slime; how could Davidian be loyal? In the time of Davidian, there were no verities. No, Steve could trust Davidian no more than he could trust his beloved or his friend. Such trust was archaic, there was no longer a place for such reactionary weakness.

The night was milder than it had been earlier. Steve tossed his coat on the seat beside him and spurred out of the lot. In the small light of the kiosk the slovenly boy continued to pore over his comic book. He didn't look up to find out if the man and the car belonged together.

Steve drove too fast out Sunset to Benedict Canyon. The canyon road lay in darkness and shadow, the road lamps were far apart, the moon and stars too distant for color. The Moritz gate was open and he pulled up to the front of the house. He left his hat with his coat in the car. He touched the discreet white button which caused chimes to sound within the palace. The house was dark save for the faint illumination of the hall. This could be Haig's trap; he would not be surprised. But he'd had to find out.

Feather herself opened the door. When she saw it was he, she said, "Oh, Steve."

The hopes he'd had out of hopelessness that she could deliver the goods, began falling. She couldn't help him if she wanted to, she couldn't even speak a definite hello. But he was here and he went inside. To hear what she had to offer.

She said, "I'm in the library," and she led him towards the far room.

"Did you have any trouble treaking away from your party?"

"No. I said I must go home and rehearse. It's true. I'm auditioning next week for a show." She'd made it true. She'd cleared a space for work and she was wearing ballet slippers. Her hair was tied up with a black cord. It bobbed like a horse's cropped tail.

The French windows were open to the gardens at the back. There'd be a blue pool, under moonlight now; bright striped umbrellas and chaise longues for sun. Janni would have lived in peace and beauty here; this girl somehow seemed cramped in a confine of her own making, afraid to lay her hand on any of the richness. Was a dancer so single-minded? Idly he wondered if she could dance, if perhaps she would come alive in motion and music. He would never find out.

She went to the phonograph and stilled the music. He recognized the bluebird motif from the *Sleeping Beauty*. She gestured to the same low table. "Have a drink?"

"Not now." And he took his same place on the couch, waited for her to press against the same down-cushioned corner. She was fluttery, over being alone with him, over the trap? He said, "You've got something?"

She didn't understand, she curled her hand over to the table where her horn-rimmed glasses were laid.

"On Davidian?"

She said, "Yes." She was more contained with the horn-rims on.

"Well?"

Color flushed into her cheeks as she began. She was stalling for time. "He worked in Berlin, the Eastern zone. Very secret work. No one knows why he wanted to leave or how he managed it." Her hair bobbed nervously. "But he did leave and he's in Los Angeles. Naturally the F.B.I. wants to find him because they hope he'll inform to them about Soviet plans. And the Soviets must find him first because they can't be sure that he won't be made to talk. They can't trust him anyway because of the way he took leave from Berlin." She said anxiously, "No one understands why he's been hiding out from you. You were his friend." She interrupted herself, "You know all this, don't you?"

"Yes," he said. "But I don't know where he is. Did you find out?"

The word broke sharp from the open French windows behind them. "No!"

It wasn't this interruption which Feather was expecting. She turned as quickly, as startled as Steve. Janni was in the room; she came rapidly around the couch to Feather. "You must not tell him. Davidian escaped, he is free. You must not betray him to them."

Feather turned uncertain eyes on Steve.

Janni demanded her attention. "Tell him nothing! He is a Coco."

Bewilderment masked Feather.

Janni cried, "Don't you understand? He is a Communist." She said it plain, cold and plain, "A Communist agent."

Again Feather turned her eyes on Steve. No longer were they uncertain behind the lenses. She came to her feet; she was smaller than Janni because she was without heels, otherwise they would have been equal to each other. At this moment in both, the dark and the fair, was a steely force.

Feather said, "Did you think I didn't know?" And she smiled, a terrible, idiot-proud smile. "I too am a Communist."

Janni was silent. Only her eyes moved, from Feather's pale glistening face to Steve on the couch. Her black bitter eyes admitting her defeat.

Steve covered with a cigarette. He needed a moment for adjustment, while Feather was giving Janni the old pitch about the honor and the glory of the cause. He'd known she was dedicated but he'd thought it was to ballet slippers, not to this work. Feather had been on his side all along, she'd been hanging around Haig Armour for his side, not the reverse.

He let out the smoke slowly as he rose from the couch. His side had placed her on the plane in Kansas City. To watch Haig? Who wasn't even on the case then? Wearily he knew better, it was the same old dog on dog; someone to keep an eye on Steve, an operator so new and so dumb that Steve wouldn't be suspicious of her hanging around him. They'd been right; he hadn't suspected her.

She'd stopped her speech-making and turned to him. "What can we do with her?" He'd never noticed before how small and sharp were her teeth.

He said to Janni, "Get out of here."

Feather sucked in her breath. "No." She clutched his arm, shook it. "You can't let her go. She knows too much."

He set her aside. "Go on," he repeated to Janni.

It was as if she couldn't move, as if the look between them held her frozen. Until Feather thrust forward, pushing a glass to Janni. "Before you go, have a drink."

Steve cut it viciously away from her hand. It fell to the floor but it didn't break. The liquid smeared over the rug like blood.

Feather cried sharply, "Why did you do that?" Her mouth was ugly.

He struck her across the ugliness with such force the back of his hand burned. She stood swaying. Her hair was shaken loose from the cord, it dangled against her cheek. He said, "I'm running this show." He spoke again to Janni. "Get out." Her dark eyes were wide and empty. He shouted it, "I said, get out!"

It shocked her to her senses. She turned and fled to the windows. Without expression he watched her until she was engulfed by the night.

Feather was whimpering in disbelief, "You're letting her go."

He could hear Janni's faint running footsteps. Only when there was no longer sound did he return his attention to Feather. There was a red welt swelling over her mouth. He said to her, "Pick up that glass."

She shivered.

He repeated roughly, "Pick up that glass."

Without looking at him, she bent her knees until she was crouched on the rug. Slowly she picked it up. Her mouth was making little animal sounds. She remained there, crouching, holding it in her hand.

"Put it back on the table."

As slowly she came to her feet. When she had set it down, she stood by the table immobile. He walked over to her and laid his hand on her thin shoulder. It trembled uncontrollably beneath his touch and his anger surged. He spun her about and shoved her towards the couch. She fell back on the cushions, looking up at him. The pupils of her eyes, magnified by her glasses, were distended blackly across the pale irises. The look was of fear but she was excited by her fear.

Later his disgust would rise. For now there was nothing but the anger. "Keep out of my business."

She shook her head, the pale hair slapping vacantly against her cheeks.

He repeated it, making it clear. "Keep out of my business. When I'm on a job, I do it my way. And no punk is allowed to interfere. Didn't they tell you that when they put you on me?"

Her bruised mouth hung half open; her eyes didn't move away from his face.

"I asked you a question."

She had trouble speaking. "He said . . . I'd learn . . . a lot . . ."

"From me? Or about me? I hope you've learned. Just keep out of my way from here on in. I've got a job to do and I don't need you dragging my heels."

She was trying to say something and he waited. She managed to whisper, "You let her go."

As he moved towards the couch she cringed back into the cushions. He kept walking until he was standing above her. "Listen, simple. If ever you do get to where you're running a show, remember this. Don't ever pull an assassination on your own parlor rug. There's nothing harder to get rid of than a body."

He walked out on her with that, still on the hard treads of his anger.

V

HE WENT BY THE PATH THAT JANNI HAD TAKEN. NO ONE TRIED TO STOP him from leaving. He saw no one as he passed through the quiet gardens, walked around the house and slammed into his car. He got away fast. He was beginning to feel a little sick. If he hadn't been there, Janni would not have escaped. But Feather hadn't had the death cup at hand for Janni: she hadn't expected Janni, only him. Feather hadn't thought that up on her own, she'd been following higher orders. Someone on his side who didn't want him around. Or had become too suspicious.

He'd known it when he struck down the glass, not because he'd been afraid Janni would drink from her enemy's hand, but out of his fury. He'd delayed after only to give Janni a good head start. Let her get away safe. While he handled the trouble. He'd expected trouble but it hadn't materialized out of the twenty-eight other rooms of the Moritz château. That didn't mean it wasn't waiting to catch up with him.

Raising his eyes to his rearview mirror, he caught the shadow there. His voice was a threat. "Come on. Who is it?"

"You are being followed. But carefully."

He knew Janni's accent. He asked, "What are you doing in my car?" He could take any danger alone, but not with her along.

She flared back at him. "I am hitching. How did you expect me to get back to the city?"

"The way you got up the canyon."

"This is the way."

Hidden on the floor in the rear, yes. He'd been careless, he hadn't thought of looking.

"Yes, you are followed."

He too had been watching the mirror. "Yes." The shadow of the lightless car was evident. He was still a couple of turns ahead, no more.

"If you will pull in at the next estate—"

"Don't tell me my business."

She tossed out a laugh. "Who taught you?"

She didn't expect an answer. He said, "Keep your head down. If it's the girl, we're all right. She's a dummy. There could have been others staked out. She was too quick with that drink."

"She was jealous." Again the laugh mocked.

He cut his lights before he swung without warning into the drive, silencing the motor. As he ducked out of vision, he undertoned, "She doesn't give a damn for you or me. She's a fanatic."

He hoped this mansion was far enough from the drive and fast enough in sleep not to investigate a stray car. They were silent as the approaching car neared. It sped by. Steve counted a slow twenty before starting his motor again.

Janni said, "It was the girl. She was alone. Unless someone was hiding with her."

On her way to report failure of the mission. "You took a chance."

"She did not see me," she scorned. "I am experienced."

He let it go, backing without lights.

She told him, "Go in the other direction."

"I know what I'm doing." He was curt but she only laughed again. Nearer now. She was a shadow behind his shoulder. He ordered, "Stay down."

"I am joining you." She was over the seat as light as blown thistle, not touching him in the transition.

"It is better," she said complacently. "She is looking for a man not for a man and his girl." His eyes slanted briefly to her but she was lighting a cigarette. She took one breath of it and passed it into his fingers.

He said, "Thanks." He didn't think about her mouth touching it.

She lit one for herself, pushed into the corner and was quiet. Not until they were beyond homes into the silent darkness of the canyon, did he pull off the road.

She cried out, "Why do you stop?" Her eyes pried into the darkness.

He reassured her, "We're safe," and said bluntly, "I want to talk to you."

This time he lit the cigarettes, passed one to her. She shivered a little but he didn't notice. She didn't say thanks.

He didn't know what to say, he'd said it all. He couldn't knock the information he needed out of her. She couldn't be cajoled or threatened or tricked. She was too experienced; she'd been tempered in Berlin for too long and too often. For some reason of her own, she would protect Davidian, even to the extent of walking into danger herself.

The cigarettes made a thin fog between them. She said, "You should not have struck her."

"She needed it." He said, "Don't waste any tears on her. She wanted to kill you."

"I know," she said simply. "But it was dangerous to strike her." She turned in the seat to see his face. "Her uncle is a most important man. To the party."

He hadn't known it. He didn't tell her. He boasted, "So am I."

"He is more important. He is Mr. Moneybags. They need him more than they need you."

She always knew so much more than he. "Who told you?"

"Everyone knows."

"Then what made you come barging out to Feather with your big news about me? Did you think it would surprise her?"

"I could not believe she was one of you," she said. "So stupid. You admit she is stupid."

"Sure. Stupid. And dangerous." He went back to the question. Because he must know. "Who told you about Moritz?"

"It is easy to learn these things. There are some of us who keep our eyes and ears open. Some who have escaped once from the terror and who do not wish to be forced to run again. It is wisdom to keep informed."

Davidian had told her, Davidian, who hung around picking up information in the right spots.

Her eyes glittered in the dark. "When you tell them of me, tell them they will never find all of those who watch them. They may erase me, but I am nothing. They may kill Davidian—but when one of us dies, there are many more who take our place."

"I'm not going to tell them about you."

"Why not?" Contempt sat lightly on her lips. "They will be proud of you that you have discovered a new plot. The watchers and the listeners. Perhaps they will decorate you with two red bloody stars, one for Davidian, one for—"

He put rough hands on her arms. Between his teeth he told her, "I'm not trying to kill Davidian. I'm trying to help him. How can I make you believe me?"

He shouldn't have touched her. He shouldn't have been with her here in the isolation of the night, his fingers biting into the flesh beneath her red coat, their eyes locked in hate one for the other. Her lips moved but she said nothing. From him without volition came one word, one desolate cry, "Janni!"

And he was holding her to him, so desperately, so close that they were one shadow. "My darling . . . my darling. . . ." He whispered it, trying to bring her more close to him, his hands under her coat, after this eternity of time warming themselves again on the fire of her body. Blindly he found her mouth. And he held her, so that the fibers of his suit would be imprint on her flesh, holding in her the deepest wells of the earth and the sharpest ecstasy of the stars. When he drew away it was so little, only that he might look into the wonder of her face.

She smiled up at him. "Stefan." Her hand touched his cheek gently. She was not gentle. "Stefan. I have been alone."

He said, "I love you." He hadn't said the words for so long that they were as a strange language. They were good, the old words, the simple words. They were honest. He was not ashamed to say them over, "I love you, Janni."

"We can be together now." Her voice was rich as the fruits of the earth. "As you promised we would be."

He couldn't lie to her. Not even to quiet his own agony.

She stirred in his arms to see his face. As if she didn't know what would be there. She cried out, "We can be together now? Stefan, Stefan—"

He whispered again, "My darling . . . my darling . . ."

"Stefan." She hid her face against his arm. She wasn't made of weakness, after a moment she raised her head. "Take me with you, Stefan. Wherever you go, take me. I can always get a job. I can sell tickets in cheap movies anywhere in the world. No one will know I am with you. I'll keep out of sight, I will never let them know."

It was the time to bargain. To ask for Davidian in exchange for a promise of their happiness. A promise he couldn't keep. He kissed her and knew the flame of her hope. When he put her away, he again lighted cigarettes for both of them. He said, "If I can get this job ticked off—"

She moved in the curve of his arm.

His eyes held on the dark road ahead. "I'm due a vacation. Maybe we could get a car and just take off. See the country. I'd like to show you the country." He went on just as if she were an innocent who could believe his words. "Texas and New York and Missouri and Cape Cod."

"As once you promised we would." She could make believe too. "And we'll choose the one we like the most and find there a little house—"

"And live on clams or hominy grits or fried chicken—" The dreams a man dreams. He broke off and his voice was like cinders. "Where's Davidian?"

She regarded the glowing tip of her cigarette for a long, long time. She said, "He's waiting for me at the Main Street movie."

He didn't release his breath. He took another pull at his cigarette, it was burned almost to his fingers but he held on to it. He had to hold on to something. "Alone, Janni. I'll have to see him alone. You can't be there."

She didn't say anything. She was crying. Janni didn't cry.

He pitched his cigarette out of the window, took hers from her mouth and threw it away. "Janni—" She came to him but there was no longer hope in her, only the same desperation of passion that had eaten away his heart. He memorized her with his hands and his mouth as if he would never again be permitted to touch her. "Janni. Tomorrow—"

She cried, "Tonight! Take me home with you."

"I can't." It was the final bitterness. "I couldn't anyway. Reuben—"

She was defeated. "And I am not alone. The old ones are always there."

"Tomorrow night. I'll fix it up some way, baby. I'll be through the job. I'll come for you early, you can say your aunt is sick—"

She put her hand across her eyes. But she wasn't crying any longer. "You'll come, Stefan?"

He said from his deepest heart, "I promise you. There isn't anyone or anything that will keep me away tomorrow night." He'd make sure of it. He'd lay the plans so carefully that nothing could take away this one night for them. They deserved one small scrap of life.

She lifted her head. "Take me downtown now, Stefan. I'm late but Joe understands. He believes Reuben is my sweetheart, leaving for overseas duty. Tomorrow night I will wait for you."

"I'll come," he repeated quietly.

There were no other cars that followed the lonely road to Mulholland, dropped down again into the city. He drove in silence; she remained apart, she might be sleeping but she wasn't asleep.

When they reached Spring Street, she said, "Don't drive to the theater. It's better I go alone."

"Yes." He pulled up to the curb.

She looked into his eyes. But all she said was, "Davidian will be safe?"

"I promise you."

"Give me time to get there. Do not know me when you buy a ticket. You will find him inside. He always sits on the left. He does not sleep, he likes movies."

She was gone with no more words. He idled the motor until she had turned the corner on Main. He waited a little longer before following. Main Street was tinny-bright. Loudspeakers squalled music from open doors; there were boys in sailor suits and soldier suits just as if it were war days, girls in paintbox dresses edging in on them. Honky-tonk bars were open-armed. Laughter was hysterical. He drove past the gaudy nightmare, past pawnshop row, past her theater and into the block of the missions. He turned on Second at the dark Cathedral corner. At the end of the block he found a space, parked and locked the car. You didn't take chances in a neighborhood like this one.

She was enclosed in the glass booth. Even the old bums who bought tickets would know she was beautiful; they wouldn't know why she was more beautiful tonight. She had a magazine on her knees, it was open but she wasn't reading it, not tonight. She glanced up when his shadow fell on her.

His bones ached to splinter the glass, to consign to hell the Davidian report, the oaths and the loyalties, the dangers and the rewards. There was nothing that mattered, nothing but his need for her. He said, "One," and put down his coin. Her hand didn't touch the ticket, a machine shoved it at him. Her eyes went down to her magazine at once, there was no betrayal but the quick rise and fall of the silk covering her breasts.

The punk at the door didn't know him. He accepted the stub and let Steve pass into the ill-smelling box. There was no usher. Steve stood at the rear until his eyes could adjust to the dark. The screen was noisy, mounted cowboys were clattering bullets into a mountain pass. When he could distinguish the seats, he started slowly down the left aisle. The theater wasn't half full; it was early, not yet midnight. There were some kids clustered together but the derelicts sat apart from each other, suspicious of their own kind. He recognized the shape of a head, or hoped he did, halfway down the left aisle, the aisle seat left vacant for a friend. No one close enough to overhear a word spoken under the tongue. Steve slid into the empty seat. He didn't turn his head to make sure.

"It took you long enough to come," the mutter insinuated.

"I have a car."

"Where is it?"

"East of Main on Second. End of the block." He was ready to lift out of his seat.

But Davidian murmured, "I must see the end of the picture. The end is very exciting. He rides the villain over the edge of the parapet."

"You've seen it once?"

"I have seen it since nine o'clock." The titter was soundless.

"For Christ's sake."

"It is very exciting."

The house lights didn't come up at the finish. This was a bedchamber for men who hadn't the price of a bed.

"You go first. I follow."

Steve obeyed. Not certain Davidian would show up. Even now he didn't trust Davidian. Especially now, because being with the man was to be reminded of the silverfish elusiveness. He couldn't be certain Davidian wouldn't stay for the third or fourth showing. Very exciting.

Steve didn't look at Janni as he left the theater. It was better not to see her. He was unlocking the car door when Davidian materialized beneath his shoulder. Steve hadn't heard him approach.

"Not much of a car," Davidian commented.

"It beats walking."

"You are too easy satisfied. Give me a cigarette. I have just run out."

"Did you ever buy a pack?"

Davidian chuckled agreeably. "Thank you." He took four, deliberately, tucked them into his shirt pocket. A fifth he put between his lips. "A match, if you please."

Steve handed him a used folder.

"It is like old times, Stefan," Davidian mused.

"You've missed me?" He asked it, "You have the report finished?"

"Did I not promise you?"

It was going to be all right, he could relax. "Where do we go?"

"We do not go together, Stefan. Have you forgotten so soon what you have learned? Or do you believe there is no danger in Holly-wood?"

"I'm not quite the fool you've been."

Davidian offered his amused cough. "You have been hearing of me?"

"Why do you take such chances?"

"Stefan, Stefan," Davidian choked. "There was no risk. Davidian knew what he was doing." Always he'd had the colossal conceit of the great of the earth, this half-starved puny man in the broken shoes, the shabby coat, the bare head with its thin covering of hair. "The chance I do not take is to drive to my house with Stefan Win-terich. This risk is too great."

"You mean I'm poison?"

Davidian puffed on the cigarette. "You do not know?"

"Maybe I do," Steve said savagely. "Well, how do we do it?"

Davidian considered. Quite as if he hadn't thought it out carefully in advance. "You will let me out." He considered it more thought-fully. "It is Saturday night, yes. At the Palladium, a palace of the dance on Sunset Boulevard near Gower, I will leave the car. I will mingle with the departing dancers and those leaving the broadcast studios."

"We meet where?"

Davidian whispered the street. "The brown house. Once it was a brown house. A modest house. To suit a modest man."

"Who gets there first?"

"It matters not." He'd smoked the cigarette to its burning ash. He flipped it regretfully out of the window. "You will have the key." He palmed it from his pocket, a ten-cent key, the kind that opened a dozen doors. "If I am not there yet, you will visit with Stella. I leave it to you what you tell her. One thing only, no one must see you come." He wasn't mocking now.

"You think I'm still walking around because I take chances?"

"No, Stefan. You do not take chances. You are a careful man." There was only the faintest flavor of contempt.

"Who's Stella?"

"A very fine woman. She tries to fatten me. For her sake, I venture to believe." He sighed noisily. "Poor Stella. I am unworthy of her."

"Is she safe?"

"But Stefan, how can you ask? She knows nothing! When I leave she knows no more."

Steve understood. "That's how you've hidden. Kept moving."

"An Arab in the night."

"Yes. Without folding your tent." Before neighbors could grow too neighborly. Before they became curious.

Davidian wheezed, "How can one, when there is no tent to fold?"

The sky lights of Hollywood were moving closer to the windshield. Davidian said, "You will drive a little more carefully and the red light will stop you at Gower."

Davidian had the car door open before the wheels were motionless. Steve didn't turn his head. There might have been no one beside him in the car. Fleetingly he wondered if he would catch up with Davidian again.

2

WHEN THE LIGHT CHANGED, STEVE DROVE ON TO VINE, FOLLOWED IT to Hollywood Boulevard and headed west. He was uneasy passing Davidian's street. It was an empty street, only two houses on it, an unused street, the business offices shuttered, not even the inevitable Hollywood parking lot to give it light and movement. There was no reason for anyone to walk into the mouth of that street at night except to visit one of the two houses. And he had to go there unseen. Again he cursed Davidian, it must have been deliberate; only someone seeking to make danger would have insinuated himself into one of those houses.

He drove on up the boulevard to Highland, followed it to an all-night filling station. He left the car for gas while he went into the office and rang Oriole. The anxious voice said, "Where have you been? I have tried to reach you."

Steve snapped, "Where do you think I've been? Working. I'm coming around. In about thirty minutes. It's important."

"You have found—?" There was hope.

"I've got plenty to report. Thirty minutes." He hung up. With Steve expected in thirty minutes, none of them would be currycombing the streets for him.

He paid the attendant and drove on. Mr. Oriole would be getting Mr. Schmidt out of bed. Unless they were all there now, the careful Schmidt, an hysterical Feather, and a rich irate uncle. They'd forgive if he brought them the Davidian report. He wondered if Elsabeth was in it too. But certainly, her diamonds would have an extra glitter because of the secrets she shared of a great day coming, secrets her lunch and tea and cocktail ladies didn't dream. Aunt Elsabeth would think her diamonds were to be safe.

He circled in and around before parking the car on Franklin, north of the boulevard. Not too far from his destination, but far enough so that if anyone should spot the heap, they'd have a hard time knowing which way he had headed.

He walked unhurriedly to Davidian's. At the mouth of the street he cut the corner boldly. Davidian might not be so foolish after all. You could be sure if you were alone here. He faded into the alley before approaching the houses, noting the courtyard behind them, the back door of the once-brown house, the flat roof obtruding from the second story, an easy drop into the yard. He waited, listening, but no footsteps crept after him. He was swift moving to the house; he opened the door with Davidian's key and closed it fast.

He was in a narrow unlighted hallway. He stood there not moving, his hand on the doorknob behind him, unsure as he must be always with the slippery Davidian. Wondering if the enemy had offered better terms, if this were the ultimate trap. And then there was a scratch on sand and a firefly glimmer of light. He looked up to it, saw the shape of Davidian at the head of the stairway. The glimmer disappeared and Steve climbed the stairs in its memory, followed the darker shadow in the dark another flight. The stairs ended at a door, a door which opened on well-oiled hinges. When it was closed, Davidian struck another match.

"The attic room," he said sardonically. With the match spurt he found a low lamp, turned it on. No light could show to the street below. The windows were curtained in black.

The ceiling was low, the walls bare, the floor unpainted. There was a broken cot; an upholstered chair, its cotton molting from the arms and side; a crippled dining table and discarded chairs. Davidian was a collector. There were orange crates, corrugated boxes, the quite good lamp. Steve sat on one of the chairs.

"You like it, Stefan?" Davidian showed his discolored teeth. "I knew you would feel at home here." He rooted into a box and brought forth a bottle of red wine. "This too for your homesickness." From an orange crate he took two unmatched glasses. "I am sorry there is no woman, but a man is not permitted everything." He overfilled the tumblers, bent and sipped from the best one. "Not bad, this California vintage. I am becoming a good American even to my palate."

"Besides it's easier to find a bottle on an unguarded shelf."

There had been no other way to keep alive in the world of Davidian. It was not dishonesty, it was survival. When all else had been stripped from man, one law alone remained, to survive.

Davidian said cheerfully, "You are insulting." He settled in the musty armchair, as if it were a throne. "Ah, it is like old times, Stefan." He reached for his glass. "A cigarette, if you please."

"There are four in your pocket," Steve reminded him.

Davidian refrained from smoking. Biding his time until absent-mindedly he could reach for one when Steve brought out his pack. As he knew Steve would. And as Steve knew, it was an old gamble between them. Like old times but no rustle of Janni behind the door, cutting the bread and cheese, her happy heart singing an accompaniment to the men's words. Tonight the pain of her had eased, for separation was temporary; there must be a means whereby they could run away together tomorrow night, if only for brief respite. He had the car, a few hours and they could be over the border into Mexico. They could be married in Mexico. He was turning soft thinking marriage, that came from a trip home, away from the ugly realities of Berlin.

Yet, sipping the sweet wine—Davidian's taste was appalling—he did not outthrust the idea with violence as he had in the past, knowing it to be treachery to Janni to take her as wife. He was growing too old for the life he had chosen at the finish of the second war for power. He could be valuable at a desk; the sands of his luck had run out so often, it was time to stop while there was yet time. The end for an agent was always the same unless he could stop, refuse the one more job. With a wife and children, they'd have to let him quit.

Davidian's room was not the place for solemn decision, not with those sly, lizard eyes probing the shadows of your face. He was here on a job. But he was loath to get to it, because with the job done there would be no reason to delay longer with wine and a cigarette and an old, if not trusted, friend. He took out his cigarettes, almost a fresh pack, put one between his lips and absently set the pack in the center of the table. Perhaps favoring himself the slightest bit. Let Davidian reach.

He could enjoy a little more time. He had protected himself for at least an hour. "How long did it take you to find this place? How long did you watch it, day after day, for a vacancy, becoming more and more avid for its danger?"

Davidian smiled. "You make it tedious. It was not this way. First there was Stella. I became acquainted with Stella."

"Yes, that way." Steve sighed into the wine. One way or the other with Davidian. A trick or a woman. And he enjoyed success with women somehow, this verminous, feline rodent. Steve asked, "Why did you insist on Hollywood? Was it because Janni had come here?"

Davidian choked. "Stefan, Stefan. Must it always be Janni for you? Are there no other women?"

"Was it?" Steve demanded.

"Yes." He stopped coughing. It was the first honest word he'd spoken. "What man would not choose Hollywood when he had been forced to listen to you and Janni describe it in the rich colors of a Gaugin? You remember? When you were endeavoring to convince Janni she must leave you? Before the danger should become the fact of her being shot by one side or the other because she is generous and sells to both?" Davidian cleared his throat delicately. "She was a stubborn girl. It was difficult for me to convince her that it was you who planned to inform on her." He drank wine. "As you paid me to do. Because you are soft about Janni, because you wish her to be safe." He argued; "Where else would I choose to come when you endeavor to convince me—"

Steve interrupted, "It was because of Janni."

The true Davidian emerged briefly again. The cold dangerous man who dwelt beneath the cap and bells. "Yes, because of Janni. Because you would no longer be around—" He shrank from Steve's face. Then he said simply, "Because only Janni I can trust."

And this could be true. Steve said, "You were not to communicate."

Davidian observed his dirty nails. "But I communicated with Janni."

"Who are the old ones?"

"I found them for Janni. For her protection." The teeth flashed. "She is so desirable, is Janni—" He helped himself openly to a cigarette.

"You didn't trust her too far. She couldn't reach you. You moved too often and without advance notice." She'd told him the truth. "You trusted her only for your own convenience. An address."

"For her cut she is happy to play postmaster."

Steve glowered.

"But certainly. For money she is always happy. Ten per cent." He flung his hands petulantly. "You send me so little."

"It was the best I could do."

"And of this I must pay ten per cent to Janni. After your fine promises, behold me! The attic! The shoes!" He extended them.

"You'll get it all now."

Davidian was eager. "The house? The little car? Money?"

"All of it."

"And my papers. A citizen."

"That takes more time. But you'll get it. In exchange for the report."

Davidian's eyes lidded. "There is something I do not comprehend, Stefan."

"Yes?" Now came trouble.

"The report. Why is it I must run in two directions? Neither the F.B.I. nor the C.P. must know of the report. Why must it be given privately to Stefan Winterich?"

Steve said coldly, "I like a cut myself."

Davidian flicked up greedy eyes.

Steve laughed in his face. "If you think you can make a better deal alone, go on, make it. Would you like to know, my friend, what will happen if you try? The F.B.I. will take your report and dump you back in Berlin. Or the C.P. will take your report and exterminate you, to make sure you do not write another one. In either case—" He cut his forefinger across his throat.

"I am satisfied," Davidian said quickly. "You will give me all you promised?"

"Have I ever lied to you?"

"No. Oh no," Davidian assured him. He drained his glass. Moisture stood on his lip. He eyed the empty bottle. "We need a little more, I think. If you could spare a dollar, Stella may be awake—"

Steve rooted in his pocket, counted a dollar in change. Davidian's fingers closed over the silver. He started to the door, shook his head thoughtfully and returned to the orange crate. "Ah yes! A bottle escaped my eye." The silver jangled in his pocket.

While Davidian's finger twined around the cork, Steve said, "You knew I was in town. Janni told you. And you saw me at the parade."

The lips tittered. "Yes."

"Why did you keep me waiting?"

Davidian drew the cork with dignity. "You insisted you would come to me when it was safe. I wished it to be safe." He poured for himself alone.

Steve took the bottle from him. "You're a Goddamned liar." But he knew why. The man's malice wasn't a trifling thing. Only by making fools of those on top of him had Davidian managed to cling to a shred of dignity. "You do have the report?"

Davidian squirmed into his easy chair. "Must I repeat myself?" His ink-stained fingers warmed themselves on the tumbler. "Not so much a liar, my dear Stefan. It will surprise me if you complete this job in good health." He toasted Steve silently. "I am your friend. I tell you this because I am your friend. I planned to welcome you when you arrived but the plane was too late."

"Albion?"

"Is dead," Davidian said complacently. "You believed he was your friend. You did not know he had become suspicious. Too suspicious. Poor Albion."

Steve shook his clanging head.

"Did you believe he visited the F.B.I. as an informer? Did you not know he was looking for information about you?" He repeated, "Poor Albion, he wished so badly to lay his hands on the report. How surprised he was the night I permitted him to catch up with me! And how happy. Because now he could get the report for his good friend Stefan. For no other reason, to be sure, but to surprise you at the airport by having it in his hands. He was even willing that I too should meet you at the airport, when I was reluctant to permit him to carry the papers." The lips drew back over the pointed teeth. "So trusting, our good friend Albion. He believed I too was trusting."

"If I'd been on time—"

"How simple it would have been. None of this hocuspocus. Albion and you and I. Old friends meeting. He did not know he would become sleepy. You were too late. I could not remain after Albion—"

Steve said huskily, "Skip it."

"We are friends?"

"Yes." He'd have done it himself, have been forced to do it to eliminate the threat. There were no friends; there was only the imperative: Survive! The wine was making Steve sick. "Where's the report?"

"You have a purchaser?"

"I've told you often enough, yes. Hand it over."

"I am a careful man." Davidian sighed. "But who knows when I am not careful enough? It would not be safe here where I live with my wine and my books."

Steve spat the words. "Where is it?"

"It is safe." He mouthed slyly, "Tomorrow—"

Steve was out of the chair. "Why waste my time tonight?"

"It is a waste of time to drink wine and talk of the old days with a friend?"

Steve spoke one cold warning. "I can't sell it until I get my hands on it."

"I will bring it to you tomorrow." He smiled piously. "Not too early. First I must play the organ at Dr. Ormigon's church. You did not know I am a musician?"

Hidden in the organ. Or under the altarpiece. Or in the preacher's Bible. Yes, the report was safe.

"How will you get it to me?"

Davidian patronized. "That will be my problem. Yours will be to arrange the quick sale. You notice I trust you, I ask for no receipt." No receipt; only a knife in the guts, a noose for a collar, Albion wine for betrayal. "You will be careful leaving here. It is well you carry something, just in case." He went to his dirty cot, lifted the mattress. "My books. You did not know I am a poet?" He selected a small volume. The binding was of rotting leather, the pages were penwritten with cramped letters. "You will not be able to read these, I regret, they are in Rumanian." He put it in Steve's hands. "It is well to carry a bone to toss to the wolves."

"It's safe to toss this?"

"Perfectly safe. It is not my best poetry." The lips twisted. "But should you be discovered leaving, you have been visiting Stella. She will agree."

Steve nodded. He slipped the volume into his jacket pocket. His topcoat would cover the additional bulk.

Davidian said suddenly, "Be careful the popcorn man does not see you depart. I do not wish to leave Stella yet." His smile was mocking. "He watches this house often, a suspicious man, but I am too clever for him." He hesitated, and then continued, "He and Albion were good friends. Possibly Albion confided in him? I would not wish any harm to come to you until after the sale is complete, you understand."

Davidian held open the door until Steve had descended to the sleeping second floor. From there on Steve walked in darkness. It was safer in the dark. He did not need to go outside to spot the little yellow lantern. It was reflected in the window glass of the front door.

He retreated to the rear of the house. He knew the password should he be challenged: Stella. He slid the bolt on the kitchen door and was outside. A silent bolt, a silent door; Davidian was a handy man about the house. Steve was as silent on the kitchen's shallow steps. Protecting himself against the wall of the house, he edged to the corner, to where he could glimpse the street. The popcorn cart blocked the mouth of the alley. Again he retreated, brushing the wall, until he reached the back steps. There was no way out except across the empty courtyard. The house masked it from the street but when he ducked out into the shadows at the far end of the alley, he was observed. He heard the piping little whistle and the rattle of wheels. Without appearing to pick up speed, he lengthened his stride.

Hollywood had gone to bed, the streets were deserted as those of a lost city. The cops were never around when you needed them. He didn't want cops, he must go it alone. It was no more than a half-block to Hollywood Boulevard but he stuck to the alleyways. He'd have a chance to elude the popcorn man in their murk, none at all on the lighted boulevard. At this hour it, too, was a desolate road.

The bobbing yellow lantern, the faint whistle followed inexorably. Steve didn't run, only a frightened man took to his heels. He wasn't afraid but he couldn't afford to answer questions tonight. Because he wasn't hampered by a pushcart, he was able to outstrip the popcorn man. He cut over to the boulevard just below his hotel. And knew he'd been tricked, the yellow lantern waited on the corner. There was no way out of it but to brass. He walked steadily to the danger.

The man beside the cart wasn't anyone, he was motley, he'd fade into a crowd. Unless you'd had experience you wouldn't recognize in his face the marks of the beast. He said, just passing the time, "Out kinda late, Mister. Popcorn?" His voice was scratchy, as if phlegm were lodged in his throat.

Steve shook his head and kept on walking.

"I been waiting for you."

He stopped. "What for?"

"You been wanting to see me."

"I don't now."

"You stayed pretty long in the brown house."

"Yeah?"

"I missed you when you come out." He took hold of the handles of the cart, preparatory to turning it. "Guess you got plenty to say to Mr. Oriole."

Steve said quietly, "I'm not going to Oriole's."

"They been waiting a long time."

"Tough."

"They sent me to fetch you. I kinda guessed you might be at Stella's house." The grimace wasn't pretty.

Steve demanded, "Do you know who I am?"

"Stefan Winterich." It didn't mean a thing to him, a man Oriole wanted fetched, no more.

"Go back to Oriole's," Steve said. "Ask the boss, the big boss, to let you have a look at the directions on Stefan Winterich's job."

Uncertainty began to trouble the man's face.

"Ask him for the Berlin directive. If you can read, take a look at the signature." He smiled at the sudden fear glazing the porcine eyes. "And present my compliments to Mr. Oriole and his guests. Tell them I miscalculated slightly. I'll meet them tomorrow night, instead, early, say ten o'clock." The business wouldn't take long once it was set up. Janni went on the Main Street job at ten; he'd pick her up within an hour of that.

Steve's tongue whipped. "If anyone doesn't like it, tell him to read that directive." He walked away then, across the street to his hotel.

The old man with the dyed hair was behind the desk. Steve said, "Don't put any calls through until noon. Just in case you forget, I'm leaving the phone off the hook."

The lights were on in his room, Reuben's bags were packed, the kid was lying on the bed in full uniform. He was wide awake. "I thought you'd never get here." His smile was hesitant.

Steve said, "You're not leaving?" He'd almost forgotten the words between them, it seemed months ago.

"I have to be in San Francisco tomorrow. My orders were waiting for me when I got back to the hotel. I'd been expecting them."

"You can't leave at this hour." Steve flung his hat and coat at the chair.

"I figured on getting out at midnight." The smile flickered. "But I couldn't walk out without seeing you, not after—" He talked fast, embarrassed. "My old man always said two guys can't carry one dame. It just doesn't work. I'm sorry, Steve."

Steve tried not to sound too tired. "Don't apologize. I should have kept my mouth shut."

"I've been trying to call Janni. To say good-by."

"She's all right," Steve told him. "I found her."

Reuben must have been able to see it was all right. He said, "You'll tell her I tried."

"I sure will."

He chewed the end of a match. "She thinks a lot of you, Steve. She's afraid of this business you're mixed up in."

Steve lay on his bed. The book was a stone slab in his pocket. "Did she tell you about Berlin?"

Rube didn't answer. He wondered how much she had told the boy. Of a guy who deserted the American Army after beating up a snivel-nosed major who accused him of operating on the black market? Of a guy who joined up with the Cocos in the Eastern zone? Or only of love in the rubble.

Steve said, "She needn't worry. I know what I'm doing. Didn't she tell you I was the smartest operator in the business?"

Rube's face was torn apart. He was very young.

Steve said, "I thought you were here on a job. To watch me. I still don't know." And because he didn't know, he had to force things, instead of shaking hands and saying, *I'll see you, kid.* "What was your job in Berlin? Why were you sent home just when I was?"

Reuben said dully, "My outfit's being transferred to the Pacific. We got a week's furlough. There wasn't any reason to hang around New York. My old lady's shacked up with a new boy friend. I told you that. My old man's too busy for me. All the other guys went home. I wanted to have a little fun." He didn't look at Steve. "I don't know what you're trying to tell me. I don't want to know. I'm nothing but a private, first class. If I thought you were—" He looked at Steve then, out of slaty blue eyes. "You've been swell to me. You didn't have to take me on. I don't want to know about your job. Janni's still in love with you."

Steve let out his breath slowly. "Whatever anybody tells you, Reuben, this is God's truth. I'm here only for one reason, to take care of a friend of mine. Davidian." In a way it was God's truth.

"That's good enough for me." It wasn't but the boy wouldn't start brooding again until he was alone. He wondered if Steve had found Davidian but he didn't ask. It was better not to ask questions.

Steve said, "You'd better get some sleep. You'll be falling over your own feet before you get to San Francisco. The bus is hell."

"The bus is out," Rube said. "I'll have to fly now to make it." He stretched out on the bed again. "I'll catch another nap. I had one while I was waiting for you. Until your laundry came."

e raised up cautiously. "My laundry?"

the chair." A flat brown-paper parcel. "A shirt they forgot.
guy said he thought you might be needing it for Sunday."

teve was steady-voiced. "Who brought it? When?"

Just before you got in. A hell of a time to be delivering the laun-
iry." Reuben laughed. "I think the little guy had been out on the
town. With a bottle of vino."

Two bottles. Steve opened the bundle just as if it weren't important. As if it contained only a shirt. That was what it was, a shirt. A
silk shirt, the white yellowed by time, not a very clean shirt. Covered
every inch with what appeared to be a scroll pattern in black, but
was infinitely small letters inscribed by an engraver's fine hand.

Safe delivery. It wasn't often that Steve loved his fellow man but
for this single moment he loved Davidian. Steve, not the book of
poems, was the bone flung to delay the wolves while Davidian completed safe delivery. It would be the devil's own job to unravel the
letters, possibly coded, probably in the little man's own Rumanian
tongue. There were trained men for such work. It wasn't Steve's
worry.

And how else could Davidian have protected the report but by
wearing it on his back when he fled from cave to cave? Where else
was it safer than in a nest of dirty laundry when Davidian was trotting about the streets of Hollywood playing his little jokes?

Steve crumpled the paper and string into the waste basket. He
opened his suitcase to put this shirt in with his clean ones, and felt
something in the pocket. He drew out a fresh-minted ruble. He
began to laugh, he couldn't help it. The mark of authenticity,
Davidian's calling card.

Reuben said, "Something's funny?"

Steve shook his head. "Delivering laundry at two A.M. I was wondering what his boss would say!"

Reuben laughed with him. In his attic Davidian would be coughing until he choked with mirth.

3

You couldn't tell time by the windows. But his watch read
four when Steve rolled off the bed. Reuben was quick. "You can't
sleep either?"

"No use wasting any more time. I'm going to shower and change."

Rube put on the light. "I never can sleep when I'm hungry. Wonder if there's an all-night stand hereabouts."

Steve was stripping off his clothes. "I could do with a cup of coffee myself." He stopped midway to the bathroom. "Look, Rube, you want to do something for me?"

There was scarcely a hesitation. "Sure, Steve."

"I had to leave the car last night. If you'd pick it up." He dug out the key. "It's on Franklin, around Wilcox. If you'll bring it around, I can run you out to the airport."

"You don't need to—" Rube began.

Steve's slow smile stopped the protest. "You're doing me the favor, kid. I'll even throw in a big breakfast." He locked the door after Rube. He didn't waste any time in the shower; he was dressed again when the soldier returned.

Rube said, "I parked it by the side door. Plenty of room this time of the day." He took up his khaki bag.

Steve buttoned his topcoat over the book. They stopped at the desk. Steve said, "I'm not checking out. Just the soldier." He left the room key. Nothing upstairs for anyone to find.

He didn't care particularly if anyone followed, taking Rube to the airport was legitimate. He could get clear later. But there weren't any signs of activity. No one got up this early in Hollywood.

The morning turned a pale gray as the car traveled through the sleeping streets. Steve swung over to Olympic at Fairfax. "We ought to find a place to eat somewhere along the way. Don't know that the airport café would be open at this hour. You're not in a rush, are you?"

"If you're not, I'm not. I'll probably have to wait around for a seat on a flight."

Rube picked the place. It looked good and they were far enough from Hollywood not to worry about being interrupted. If they'd been going to run into interference it would have developed before now, or it would wait until after he'd dropped the soldier.

They sat at the counter, ordered big—orange juice, oatmeal, ham and eggs, stack of wheats, coffee. Steve knew he couldn't touch half of it, not at this hour and with his stomach nerves like guitarstrings. But Rube could eat double. It was his good-by party.

There was a phone box hung on the wall the same as at Oriole's. He didn't have to have a booth. "I am going to make a call." He could dial the exchange he needed from this location. He held on while the line rang. The counterman was busy at the grill. Rube was watching the sizzle of the ham.

The voice came on the other end. "Hello."

"Hello. Mack in?" It didn't matter what he said. As long as the other party made the right answers.

"What number do you want?"

His mouth bit into the mouthpiece. "W-5." He drew back, "Yeah, I'll hold on."

The answers were right now. He was memorizing instructions. "Okay, I'll call later."

He returned to the counter. Reuben asked no questions. He was eating. The counterman was reading the Sunday funnies.

Continuing on west they passed early churchgoers. At this hour there was no heavy traffic on Sepulveda, they were at the airport too soon. Steve didn't waste a quarter on the robber barons who guarded the endless acres fenced in for parking. He drew the car to the curb in front of the terminal.

Reuben said, "Thanks for everything, Steve." His handclasp was warm and strong. But things weren't the same. "Good luck."

"Thanks, kid." He wanted to say a lot more. But all he said was, "Maybe we'll run into each other again someday. If the big shots ever figure out that peace can pay bigger than war."

Rube grinned. "I hope we don't have to wait that long." From the curb, he said, "Tell Janni good-by."

The tall thin uniform, young and crumpled, walked away to the terminal. Steve drove off. Death in a ditch, death in a gutter, what difference? The fruits of war. Maybe Rube was a lucky one, maybe he'd come back with medals and the same easy grin, maybe he'd have a little house someday like any little house and a nice girl and a couple of kids. He could dream for Rube too.

Before heading over to the beach road, Steve took his gun from his pocket and locked it in the glove compartment. He didn't want its weight on him all day. He made sure that there was no one following him on the beach road north. At this hour you could tell. The surf was tossing restlessly, the water was dull as the sky. He parked where he'd been told, above the canyon on the road to Malibu. He slid down the shallow incline to a strip of sand. The sun was watery, the air had not warned up yet. But he stripped to the waist, made a pile of his clothes, lay on the sand. If there were California nuts who sunned without sun, he was okay. He was following orders.

He wasn't there long before the surf fisherman showed up. The fisherman wasn't cold; he was padded in a sheep-skin jacket and heavy whipcords, a peaked cap and wading boots. Steve waited a little longer before he spoke up. "Any luck?"

The fisherman turned his face, it was round and bland, his eyeglasses were rounder. His shaggy white eyebrows joggled. "Not yet." He dropped his worn basket into the sand beside Steve. "You like fishing, son?"

"Haven't the patience. Is there a lookout?"

"Yes. Have to get up early to be a good fisherman." He babbled on like some Izaak Walton.

Neither man was conscious of the basket while Steve transferred the folded yellow shirt covered with its minute scrollwork. "There's a book too which might be useful. Might not." Another sleight of hand and it lay on the shirt. "He called it something to toss to the wolves. You can't trust him."

"Never could."

"You can pick him up at Dr. Ormigon's church this morning. He plays the organ for services. Maybe."

"Maybe not." The fisherman took off his cap to protect his pipe from the offshore breeze. He was bald as a seal.

"I'll be at Oriole's tonight at ten."

"Rather early."

"I've got a date after," Steve grinned. "I'll have friends there."

"Don't worry about that." The old fellow had got the pipe glowing. It looked like a stove.

Steve began to button on his shirt. He was goose-pimples. "Think maybe I could manage a little vacation?"

"I can't answer that one."

"Where's the report for me?"

"You'll find it on the floor of your car. Take good care of it today."

"Don't worry." Steve was standing now, buttoning his coat to the chin. A quart of hot coffee might thaw him. And a quart of brandy.

"You'd be smart to get lost today."

"Yeah." He pulled his hat over his forehead. "He killed Albion. He says."

"Albion caught up with him?"

"He says with both of us."

"He's always been a liar. But it could be. Albion was clever."

"Yes." He waved a hand. "Good fishing, Pop."

"Takes patience." He cast his line into the surf.

The car was where he'd left it. Undisturbed. On the floor was the other report. He heeled it under the seat with the sludge and crumbs and chewing-gum papers. No one would look for it there. There wasn't any sign of a lookout, just cars from the south driving towards the north, cars from the north driving to the south. The sun was clear, it was going to turn into a blue day. A day to take your girl to the beach, later on build a fire of driftwood, later still watch the stars come out, one times a million stars. Tomorrow. He and Janni would follow the coast of Baja tomorrow. It would be warmer and bluer and there'd be a million times a million stars to cover them.

Get lost. Pull into a motel, get some of that lost sleep before nightfall. Pass time easy. Keep away from Haig Armour. Run like hell from Schmidt's boys.

He couldn't take it easy. Not until he'd seen Haig. He drove back into Beverly Hills, up the bowered driveway of the swank hotel, parked the old crate. It looked worse than ever among the Cadillacs and palm trees.

He asked at the discreet desk for Haig Armour. The clerk couldn't have been more courteous had Steve belonged knee-deep in carpet. He checked and then recalled cheerfully that Mr. Armour was at the pool.

It was warm around the pool. There were some pretty, bronze starlets sunning in beach chairs, some dark and virile athletes showing off on the high board. The rhythmic thud of a tennis ball on the adjoining courts was counterpoint to the splash of the shining water Haig was resplendent in bathing trunks. He left the cluster of sun bathers when he saw Steve. "Were you looking for me?"

"Surprised?"

Haig drew a bright canvas chair up to one of the white-painted tables. He gestured Steve to another. "I am rather," he admitted.

The sun was too hot in this protected area. "Why? Feather turn me in?" Steve shed his topcoat. "But you know more about me than she could tell you."

"She says you attacked her."

"Does she? You know more about her than I ever will." Steve put his fist on the table. "Maybe she'll move over to your side now.

That's all these kids are looking for, something to believe in, something to work for, and a little excitement thrown in. Why can't you get them on your side?"

"Feather's not the ordinary kid."

"No, not exactly. Maybe she isn't worth worrying about. But most of them are."

Haig said tiredly, "We try. Maybe not hard enough." A white-coated boy shadowed the table. Haig asked, "Too early for a drink?"

"Not a beer."

"Two." He waited until the shadow faded. He was casual. "I heard you'd blown town."

"Without the report?" Steve smiled. "Reuben left. I told the hotel I'd be back. Your spies must be suspicious bastards."

"They lost you after you left the airport. Have you found Davidian?"

Strange how you could be having the chills one hour, sweating it out the next. The beer was just right. "I'm still looking." He asked it. "What was Albie after at F.B.I. headquarters?"

Haig said, "You don't know?"

"I don't."

Haig studied him. "He might have been trying to make a deal. He might have been using that as a false face to find out if you'd made deal. Who killed him?"

"I did. Radar." It was hard to say what he'd come to say. "One thing I want you to know. Janni's an innocent bystander."

Haig didn't say anything.

"That's all she's been in this whole business. She's not mixed up in it in any way."

Haig went on listening.

"Just because we knew each other a long time ago, don't get the idea she's on my side. She's here clean. She wants to be a good American. That may sound corny to you, but that's all she wants. She's working for that."

"It may sound corny to you," Haig said. "Not to me."

"Give her a chance. Leave her alone."

"Maybe I can help her."

Steve stilled the brutal pound of his heart. Sure, Haig could help her. She'd be valuable to Haig's outfit, she knew the ropes. Haig could help her in too many ways. You couldn't call a man a bastard when you were asking a favor. If tonight brought the ultimate danger, Janni would have someone to look out for her. Nothing was going to happen, not on an easy job like this.

"I just wanted you to know," Steve said.

He walked away. He could get lost now.

4

HE SPENT THE AFTERNOON ON THE PUBLIC BEACH AT SANTA MONICA. Beach kids all around him for safety. The report wrapped in his coat made a nice pillow. He might have caught a little nap, the rocking surf was soothing as a cradle.

He ate a good dinner in the canyon just off the beach. The next couple of hours he eliminated in a double-feature movie on Wilshire. When it was time to start for Hollywood, he took it easy.

There'd be a getaway car, he didn't have to park too near Mr. Oriole's. The old house looked quiet enough when he rolled by. But there were lights on behind the lace curtains and the shades were drawn. They were waiting for him.

He found a spot on a side street headed towards Sunset, left the car there. He walked back to Selma. The report was under his arm, the gun in the right-hand pocket of his jacket. He didn't like to pack a gun but sometimes it was needed. When you were too rushed for a knife. He kept his fingers crossed that nothing had altered the schedule. He climbed the porch steps, hit the bell.

Mr. Oriole was a little cross. "So you are here."

"Who were you expecting?"

The door widened. "After last night, we did not know what to expect."

Steve walked in. "What are you grousing about?" His voice was louder than it should be, to make sure it was heard in the next room. No sense going through the routine twice. "I was out working. You were sitting around on your fat behind."

Mr. Oriole's lip pouted but he only said, "In here," and parted the portieres.

The Eldon Mortizes weren't there or their lovely niece, they were too elegant for dirty business. But Schmidt was there, and Llewellyn, the bookshop fellow, already promoted to Albion's position? A burly six-footer who could drive piles with his bare fist was by the side window. His companion was the popcorn man. Steve

wasn't surprised at the aggregation; this was it. The hatchet squad
and the executives. First they'd have the report, then they'd hold
court. Maybe Albion had passed on his suspicions. Maybe it was
only Schmidt's jealousy. Easy enough to send black-bordered regrets
to New York, accident in line of duty; better yet the outright
lie that Stefan Winterich was a traitor. Even a suspected traitor
didn't rate an investigation, much less a tear.

Steve took an arrogant stand, in line with the back-parlor exit.
"Quite a gathering," he commented.

Schmidt was cold. But he couldn't quite disguise the crackle of excitement as his eyeglasses glinted towards the manuscript under
Steve's arm. "You have the Davidian report?"

"Certainly I have it. You don't think I'd be here wasting time if I
didn't."

Schmidt's fingers trembled.

"The question is," Steve said insolently, "can you take care of it
reaching New York safely?"

"You may depend on that." Schmidt's voice was almost eager.

Steve didn't pass it over yet. "I wasn't asked to bring it back. My
part of the job ends right here."

"That is my understanding."

"Just so it's clear," Steve said. He walked over to Schmidt's chair.
"It's your baby now." He let it drop to Schmidt's lap.

The neat fingers clutched it. The eyeglasses lifted after a moment.
"You took care of Davidian?"

"What do you mean?"

From behind him he could feel the creak of the brute and the ca-
tarrhal breathing of the popcorn man. Mr. Oriole twined his plump
hands together. Only Llewellyn, made in the Schmidt image, was
unperturbed.

Schmidt almost screamed it. "You allowed him to escape?"

"He's around. All I did was get him drunk enough to talk. And
take his God-damned report away from him."

Schmidt said thickly, "The F.B.I. will find him."

"They haven't."

"He can write another report." Schmidt was the type to worry.
"He's a traitor. He can't be let go."

"I follow orders," Steve said. "That way I stay out of trouble. My
orders didn't say anything about Davidian. Only to get the report."
He moved as if he were about to leave. "I got the report. Okay?"

The scream was rising. "We don't know where he is."

Steve smiled. He swiveled his head to give all of them a good look at the smile. But he was getting nervy. It was time something should be happening. "You want me to bring him in?" The contempt for Schmidt's organization was as open as if he'd spit on them.

Schmidt was saved an answer. It began to happen. Steps on the porch, the doorbell. Mr. Oriole didn't believe it. He moved uncertainly in the direction of the disturbance. There was silence awaiting his return. It happened fast then. Schmidt clenching the report as Oriole returned with a big man; it was Hale. Ferber had come in the back way. There'd be others on the doors; a friend out back.

Hale said, "Federal Bureau of Investigation. Mr. Schmidt?"

Schmidt knew his rights. "I do not understand."

"We've got a few questions to ask you. And you, Mr. Oriole. And your Berlin friend, Steve Wintress, or Stefan Winterich."

Schmidt sputtered, "This is an outrage! You invade a private home—"

"We've got a warrant," Hale said patiently.

Ferber said, "I'll take those papers."

Schmidt hadn't known Ferber was behind him. He wasn't going to give up the report easy. They were both hanging onto the phony report. Steve dived as he announced, "I'm not taking this rap." Ferber was too busy to grab a gun. Oriole was in Hale's way. Steve dived for the back parlor, cracked out the window. He heard Hale's shout, Ferber's reassurance, "He can't get away." And a rumble, that would be Hale, "Where do you boys think you're going?" The goons wouldn't get to duck out.

And he was in the blackout of the back yard, cutting swiftly for the fence. A heavy hand on his shoulder halted him. "Come on."

He mouthed, "W-5," but the hold wasn't released. It couldn't be there'd be a mess-up now. There was no time for a confab, he had to get clear and fast.

He tried to wrest away but the clamp held on his shoulder. He didn't want to use the gun but it looked as if he'd have to. He was struggling for his pocket when the guy undertoned in his ear, "Come on, you fool! Why do you think the engine's running?"

He heard the purr of it then; recognized the shape of a car in the driveway headed towards the street. He let the fellow drag him along.

"Get in. Lie on the floor, pull the robe over you until we're out."

As Steve ducked into the rear, he caught a quick glimpse of the man. Wilton. He burrowed under the robe. Wilton was at the wheel and had the car rolling.

Steve told him, "I've got a car around the corner in the next block. Drop me there."

Wilton said, "You're driving this one."

A shapeless hat, an old raincoat. A man who was as much like him as his own brother. He should have caught on before. There were always earmarks of a man on a special assignment. He felt the swerve of the car out of the drive. They were picking up speed.

And then the implication of the words slashed through. He yanked the cover off his face. "I've got a bag and a hotel bill."

"They'll be handled."

He tried again, raising his voice enough for the weight of it to carry through. "I've got to make a stop."

"No stops."

"Look here, Wilton. It's safe. No one's looking for me tonight. The little Cocos won't move until Schmidt gives the word. And Schmidt's going to be too busy tonight to worry about me." It wouldn't take a minute. "The F.B.I. will know you've got me under wraps." Wilton could keep the car gunned while he picked her up.

"Orders, Steve."

Desperation tore the words from him. "I've got to, Wilton!"

She was there waiting for him, the pulse in her throat beating. He'd told her he'd come, that this time he wouldn't let anything keep him from coming.

"Sorry, Steve." Wilton meant it; he'd know; he was in the cage himself. "I've got to put you aboard a fishing smack at San Pedro before midnight. We're cutting it fine."

It wouldn't take a minute. Just while he told her it couldn't be tonight. The road from Hollywood to San Pedro wasn't by way of Main Street. *Some other time, baby.* It wouldn't take that long to look on her face once more.

"I signed you on two days ago. You'll find the duds I wore back on the seat. Once we get loose on Sepulveda you can change."

She'd wait for him until he didn't come. And then she'd walk home alone, hurting; hurting like hell tonight; tomorrow, hating.

"Your name is Dick Wilton. You'll get your new orders in LaPaz."

The punk in the sharp suit and the curly sideburns would want to take her home. She wouldn't let him tonight. At least tonight she'd walk alone.

"I drive the car over the border and ditch it. Your coat and hat will be in it and enough identification. You're getting away to Mexico." He made it clear. "We won't use you in this country again until it's safe." Until never. "Can't take any chances. You're worth too much to us, Steve."

The car was on a straightaway now, moving fast. Faster, further away from her waiting there. Her breasts rising and falling like proud music under the stars; her eyes watching every passer-by, eyes brighter than the brightest stars. Tomorrow they would be stones. If he could stop thinking about her . . . "How did the F.B.I. get into this?"

"We asked them in." There was relief in Wilton's voice. Steve was taking it. "We needed them. The C.I.C. hasn't any power in civvie matters. They get some men they've been watching; we get the report. Pop ought to be setting the real one down in Washington by now. No one will ever know the one you gave Schmidt was a phony. It'll be returned to us unread. Too bad, we coded a beaut. You can start changing, Steve. But keep down."

Don't take any chances. We need you. We need the bloody heart out of your body.

"How much does Haig know?"

"About you? Nothing. He knows our outfit loaned me to the F.B.I. to take Stefan Winterich. Unless he starts figuring. He's smart."

Smart enough to know that Steve was telling him that Janni might need help? Beyond the line of duty? Yeah, smart enough. Smart enough not to mention Steve, to let her forget, to take over.

"Conceited bastard."

"You're wrong. He's a straight shooter. He played it that way because of your reputation for arrogance, to beat you at your own game."

"He hates my guts."

"He hates the guts of anyone who's venal enough—or ignorant enough—to sell out to the Kremlin."

So he was a decent guy. So she'd be better off with him than she could ever have been with Stefan Winterich. Don't think about her. "What about Davidian?"

"He's safe."

"There isn't a safe place left," Steve said. "Nowhere in our world."

"That's why we're in this business," Wilton said.

Yes, that was why. The agents and the special agents of the Counter Intelligence Corps. Trained in—he could quote it word and letter—". . . the art of catching spies, also the science of denying the enemy the information he must have . . ." The expendables.

Eating danger and hanging onto the hope that men of good will would someday realize the old, old dream of peace. Until then there was the job, a dirty job, because war was dirty. You didn't need a proclamation calling it war; without peace, war was. Steve was a good agent, he could stoop to any dishonor without conscience, steal from a blind begger, bribe a saint, lie to the beloved's face, murder without trace or tear. A monotone along the dusty alley of death.

Wilton said, "We think we can keep him safe. He's going to work for us."

"You can't trust him."

"We know. We've had others like him. But it's surprising how a man can change when he has plenty to eat and a decent place to live and a doctor to take care of the sore spots. When he's treated like a man. You can cure hate."

Steve had squirmed into the rough pants, the work shirt, the leather jacket. The suit he'd worn, this cloth her hands had touched, would disappear with Steve Wintress. And Davidian. She'd believe that he had hounded Davidian into another rotten exile.

"They'll catch up with him, Wilton." That hurt too. "They can't afford to let him go."

"Don't be so sure. We know a few tricks ourselves. He'll have you to dinner when you get back."

When you get back. If you get back. There's an end to everything, there's an end to this game. If only he could have told her. Who do you think held the gun at that guard's spine while Davidian scurried across the barrier? Who fixed it so that you could get away to the refuge of this last, very best hope of all men, this land still of the free and the brave? If only he could have touched her.

"You say something, Steve?"

"Nothing."

Some other time baby. Another year. Another eternity. *My darling . . . my darling . . .*